THE COMPLETE ROADTRIP Z

LILITH SAINTCROW

Print ISBN: 9780999201329

THE COMPLETE ROADTRIP Z

For Maddy and Nicky,
who would survive.

In an emergency, y'all don't rise to the occasion; y'all sink to the level of your trainin'.

—Archilochus, by way of my Navy grandfather

SEASON ONE: COTTON CROSSING

[1]

SAY HELLO

THAT BRIGHT LATE-AUTUMN DAY, LEE QUARTINE GOT IN HIS BIG
red-and-white Chevy with every intention of talking to her.

He took a minute before he cranked the engine to stretch out his
fingers against the steering wheel, to settle his lean ass in the seat just
right, and to look at the freshly washed walls of his yellow manufactured. The pressure washer was a good deal, even if he'd had to outfit
it with new nozzles and clean out the tubing, not to mention tune up
the innards a bit. People were goddamn wasteful, but at least the
pressure washer hadn't been dump-dandruff. Just a chunk of metal
and hose sitting patient as a turtle on the side of Route 12 with a
cardboard FREE sign attached. Looking a bit lonely, to tell the truth.

Getting the last junked hulk out of the meadow was going to be a
bitch, but he had the flatbed trailer and could probably ask Bobby
Dorff to come by and lend a little muscle. If Coop's Wreckers
wouldn't take the old blue Ford shell to go with the other heaps Big Q
had left his loving grandson, there was always the quarry. He might
even have some fun out there after he dropped off the junked frame,
take along a .22 and plink in one of the dry scars left by digging for
this, that, and the other.

Yessir, the old place was looking pretty good. The dead-grass rectangles where the other rusting cars had crouched—*one day Imma fix em up*, Lee's granddaddy had mumbled on the porch once or twice, clasping his cuppa joe or a jolt of rye—would fix themselves next spring. Nonna, if she happened to hear, would sniff, the sound that meant *then get your ass to it*. Poppa Quartine always pretended not to hear, because picking a fight with Nonna was bound to get a man six things he didn't want and a half-dozen more he didn't like either.

Through Lee's half-open window, the trees whispered. All the shameless ones were pretty much naked for the season, bare branches thrusting into deceptively rich golden sunshine. Indian summer-sun, but the shadows held little sparkles of frost. The staid and starchy trees, the ones that kept their high collars and long sleeves even in summer, always looked sideways-smug at empty, shivering branches until snow laid a coat over all, great and small. The ruts were going to be frozen stiff soon; Lee thought it was damn likely there would be some ice before the snows moved in.

But not yet. Today the sky was a deep, aching blue, Lee had the keys in the ignition and the paper Landy's bag sitting on the passenger side of the bench seat. The books inside weren't due until next week.

He'd shined his boots, even. Combed his sandy hair carefully, and gave himself a once-over in the bathroom mirror. A sly devil with blue eyes had winked back at him.

Right on time, his stomach tensed up.

"It's just fine," he told his windshield. "All you gotta do is say *hello ma'am*. Just walk right on up and say it. Natural like." Just like he said hello to Maye at the drugstore, just like he said *evenin' Percy* to Sheriff Blotzer every time their paths crossed. It wasn't any different than the girl at the bank when he took his paycheck in on Friday, not trusting that direct-deposit bullshit.

A check was paper. A check was *real*. Not as real as cash totted up when the whistle blew, but times had moved on. At least he put his money in a bank, unlike Poppa Q.

That big old bastard had never trusted what he couldn't shoot. It was a wonder Nonna had married him, but she had and he died thinking she shat rainbows and pissed sunshine, which was pretty goddamn near the truth. Certainly she was the most patient woman put on earth; her patience muscle got a workout each and every day keeping Big Daryl Q on the straight and dry.

Lee was stalling, and he knew it. He twisted the key, and the engine caught. Running along like clockwork, that beast. He'd checked the chains yesterday, too, in between the pressure washer and considering the meadow in front of the pretty yellow manufactured, clean and snug and ready for winter. His arms ached a little, but the grim snarl of barbwire in his stomach was worse.

"Just got to say hello," he told himself again, but it didn't sound so good this time. He popped the brake, dropped it into gear, cut the wheel, and got going.

THE DRIVE WAS SO FAMILIAR HE COULD'VE DONE IT BLINDFOLDED —well, *maybe*, and if there was no drunken asshole on Slatter Curve— but today it was also pretty, and anticipation boomed under his ribs, high on the left side of his chest. An ironed chambray shirt, sleeves folded up just so, his daddy's prized leather vest worn so often it conformed to Lee as well as it ever had to the old man, his best jeans, and well-shone boots. Even a dab of that Vetiver stuff a blue-vested girl at the WalMart halfway between Lewiston and Cotton Crossing said was the best-smelling for her money. If she thought he was strange for asking, well, he didn't have to go back for the pharmacy, he could get anything else he needed in the medical way at the drugstore in the Corner. The VA was on the other side of Lewiston, too, if he took sick.

Yeah, he was as ready as he could be. Except that barb wire in his stomach, rolling up like yarn caught on a kitten's paws.

His mouth turning to a thin line and his hands tensing on the wheel, Lee drove on.

[2]

OPTIMISM

GINNY MILLS OVERSLEPT, WHICH MEANT NO TIME FOR A leisurely cup of tea. A hurried shower, a wriggle into the skirt she liked least, a quick wrap-and-pin of her dark, braided hair around her head, and jamming her fingers in the car door when she half-tripped on the cracked pavement of the duplex's driveway was what she got instead. It was distinctly irreligious of her to swear so viciously on a Sunday, and no doubt plenty of the people in the county she served would look askance—if they knew what *askance* meant—but thankfully, none were in the vicinity to hear her. Her neighbors, the McCoys, were already at their small Baptist church halfway to Hatchie Ground, since Amy McCoy ran the Sunday school there. They had invited her a total of eight times since she moved in, but she had an excuse for each and every one.

Where do you church was a constant question around here, and her standard answer was *in Lewiston*. It was the county seat, stuffed to the brim with both taverns and holy rolling places; if someone pressed for details she could pretend to be distracted and escape.

She doubted anyone around here knew what shabbat was, anyway.

It was her day to work at the Cotton Crossing mini-branch, by far her least favorite location. If it wasn't the teenagers making out in the stacks or damaging the books, it was the idiots who expected her to hand-hold through their internet surfing, or the dry-box busybodies glowering in judgment of everyone else had the misfortune to be in their vicinity. There were a few quiet old men who sat down with the newspapers, by far the most inoffensive patrons, and some of the housewives had reading tastes that were actually pretty respectable.

There was one in particular—a pale-to-transparency woman so skinny her cheekbones were past model-shapely and into frankly alarming—who was slowly but surely working her way through Dickens. That particular patron warmed Ginny's heart and broke it at the same time, seeing the shadows of black eyes and split lips on her with some frequency. A librarian couldn't do a damn thing about that, except forgive any overdue fines that came that particular client's way.

You could tell a lot about people by what they ordered in a small-town diner. Ginny's sample of the Corner's oddities was limited to the literate, and it often occurred to her, with a great deal of grim amusement, that such a self-limiting data set was unusable for any serious academic.

The good thing about Sundays was the ten-minute commute. She made it to the Crossing branch at her usual time, her stomach growling from lack of breakfast and her mood taking several turns for the worse when she saw the strip of parking lot—shared with the closed-down Elks Lodge and the laundromat on one side and the tottering-but-not-quite-dead Just In Tyme Antiques, which limped along by fleecing summer tourists, on the other—was, as usual on Sundays, full of broken glass. Nothing to do in the Crossing but break bottles and tip cows, after all.

The glass meant street parking, and there was a line at Motton's Coffee, so there wasn't even the prospect of a substandard bagel.

At least there was no snotty nose pressed agains the branch's plate-glass door. The papers were on time, and she raced through setting them out, getting everything turned on, and muttering imprecations at the dank chill. The heat was old and cranky; it would be noon before it warmed up in here, and she'd only have a couple hours of decent temperature before she closed up early.

At least there were a few English Breakfast teabags left in the breakroom, and a forgotten box of stale granola bars in the very back of a cupboard. Sundays were half-days, and she was lucky to have a job at all. Library science majors were the forgotten of the academic tribes, like Moses, barred from the Promised Land. You didn't go into this field for the money, that was for damn sure.

And she'd thought a season or two of small town life would be *romantic*.

The coffeemaker spat out sour, mineral-smelling water, which would ruin the flavor of the tea. It didn't matter. Soon she'd have blessed caffeine, and she stood little chance of being mugged on her way to her car at night, even in Lewiston. Her coworkers were reasonable enough, the volunteers were by and large genuinely helpful, and after she closed the doors here at two o'clock she could go home and spend the afternoon with some chardonnay and Netflix.

"That's right," she told herself, making sure the *Times* was set just where old Elmore Creary would look for it, on his favorite table in front of his favorite chair—of course, it was the creaky one, and several times she had wished vengefully for it to splinter and dump him on his wide, sexist keister. "Optimism. You'll hear from them soon."

And that put a smile on her face, even while her tongue dug at bits of ancient granola stuck between the teeth her sainted parents had paid for a decade of braces on in addition to college so she could waste herself in a tiny town miles and miles away. Never mind that it was temporary, which her mother gamely mentioned almost every time Gin picked up the phone. Never mind that she was sneakingly grateful for the distance, especially when it came to things like the *grandchildren* question.

Her sister was answering that one quite nicely.

"Optimism," Gin repeated. Because last night, she'd pressed *send* on eight separate applications, and several years of hard work and self-denial were going to pay off. Seniority, even in a county system like this, counted as Experience, and that was the only thing lacking from her resumé. She'd be back in New York or Boston soon, handling fragile and precious texts in the land of decent takeout, high crime, and smog dyeing the snow gray instead of white on the pines cupping the Crossing and frowning at Lewiston.

She even had time to run another round of hot water, and that meant two cups of tea and a much improved temper by the time blonde-bobbed Philly Lou, her Sunday helper and cheerleader for the Crossing Guards football team, burst in with a breathless excuse for being late and one eye constantly on her ubiquitous, pink-jack-eted smartphone.

Which reminded Gin she'd left her own goddamn phone at home.

Some days you just couldn't win.

"I don't understand." Madge Harmon blinked blearily at the glowing screen. "I thought *you* had the password."

Ginny took a firmer hold on her temper than she had ever believed possible. The blue-haired biddy probably remembered the days of scrubbing with washboards, which had no doubt lingered in this benighted stretch of the country. "No, Mrs Harmon. The password is *your* special code for when you want to sign into your email."

"Oh, Charlie took care of that." She adjusted the reading glasses on her snub nose. Once, Mrs Harmon had probably been a fresh-faced dairymaid-looking lass, and her round cheeks had probably been extremely attractive. Now, though, with her blue eyes sunken and her cheeks quivering a little, she looked like a perpetually startled Ewok. "And it just always opens up on *my* computer. He said, and I'll never forget it, *we'll use our most favorite word.*"

"Great." Ginny moved the cursor to the password box. She had the strong suspicion she didn't want to know what that favorite word was. "You just type it in there, and it'll let you look at your email."

"Oh, good. I want the pictures my daughter sent me. She's in Canada, you know."

I know. You've told me eight times. The urge to pinch the bridge of her nose was rising. "Okay. Well, you can send her an email from here."

Mrs Harmon peered at the screen. "But what about the password?"

"Just type it in." Ginny shifted her weight; her back wasn't aching yet, but it was only a matter of time.

"But..." A faint hint of color rose on Mrs Harmon's cheeks. "I don't know how to spell...oh, dear."

"Spell what?" Thank God she'd stepped into her favorite shoes this morning. They were heels, yes, but they were reasonably comfortable, and as soon as she got home it would be yoga pants and the biggest, comfiest socks she could find. *Hold that thought,* she told herself grimly. *Just another hour and a half.*

"But it's our password!" Mrs Harmon looked scandalized. "I can't tell *you.* Can't you use yours?"

Ginny suppressed a small, granola-scented burp. "You mean, to get into your email? No, my password only works for mine."

"Well, that's a damnfool way to do it. Librarians should have—" Mrs Harmon began to mutter, and Ginny straightened as she heard a cough from the circulation desk.

It was him again, one of the Sunday regulars. An extremely unlikely savior, but she'd take what she could get. "I'm sorry, Mrs Harmon. I really wish I could help. Maybe you could check your email at home?"

"But I want the pictures now, to take to the bingo with me." The old lady sucked on the front of her dentures, a quick habitual slurp. "I want Betty to see them."

Ginny decided against telling Mrs Harmon the public computers couldn't access the branch's office printer, and the pay-as-you-go copier was far too ancient to speak wireless either. Maybe the old lady thought the pictures would flutter out of the screen in a nice paper packet. "Try to remember how to spell your password. I'm sorry, there's someone at the desk." She patted the old lady's soft, talcum-scented, padded shoulder before she walked away, though.

Hip-checking the ancient, swinging half-door that led behind the checkout was so habitual she barely noticed it. "Hi there." Her smile was wide and unfeigned, mostly because you had to have a sense of the absurd to work this kind of job. Philly Lou, all the way over in the children's section, cracked her bubblegum, and a shiver of irritation went up Ginny's spine. "You're back early. Worked your way through everything?"

The man—she'd dubbed him Military Felon, because his sandy-darkish hair was too short for the leather biker vest with the too-faded-to-be-deciphered patches on the back, but the tattoo peeping out from under his left sleeve looked faint and blue like jailhouse work—nodded. He was built rangy, and had a pair of dark, piercing eyes. He carried a black baseball cap just as ancient as his vest. On Sundays he came in, spent about fifteen minutes in the quite considerable Westerns section on sagging pasteboard shelves, standing under a John Wayne movie poster, and brought an armful of them to the checkout. He didn't seem to understand how the book drop worked, so Gin checked his former week's bounty in for him. Each time he brought them back in the same creased but still serviceable paper bag from the tiny Crossing grocery store—Landy's, where you could buy a sticky container of cinnamon Red Hots that had probably been on the shelf since the first Bush administration. You could also get milk in glass bottles, and bring them back for the deposit.

Small town living, indeed.

"What did you choose this time?" She began the process—turn the book over, run the barcode under the scanner, check title and author to make sure. At least this county library system had decent inventory infrastructure. One of her former classmates was working out in Wyoming, in a tiny place where they still stamped paper card-stock with due dates. Progress had brushed the edge of *this* particular armpit of America. "Zane Grey. Good choice. And some of the series. They're really popular." *Hotspur*, one of the paperbacks screamed, in lurid red font. A seventies version of a half-naked saloon floozy was hanging onto a guy who looked like he'd stepped off the old *Bonanza* show they used to have in reruns when Gin was a kid. Romances for men, really, although you couldn't call them that.

Military Felon didn't say a word. Just looked at her. The set, steady expression on his face turned what might have been a kind of sullen attractiveness into something downright forbidding. Was he thinking she was judging his reading material? Of course, this guy never did say anything. Just stood there while she checked his books, then touched the brim of whatever hat he was wearing and hurried away. Maybe he thought he'd get cooties from talking to an out-of-towner.

She finished the stack. He took each one as she slid it across the counter, and packed it into the bag. She glanced at his pile of returns. *Huh.*

For a second she thought of telling him he'd checked out *The Lone Star Ranger* this time, too. Then she decided to leave well enough alone. "Well, there you are. Due back in three weeks, but I'll probably see you before then. Have a lovely afternoon, Mr Quartine." She took her best guess at pronouncing it, as usual, and as usual, got nothing in return. Not even a correction. He just reached up as if to touch his hat-brim, getting sandy hair instead because he'd taken off his cap like a good Boy Scout. Then he turned sharp as a pin, the "Military" half of her private name for him winning, and headed for the door at a long-legged, limber clip.

Ginny clicked to the other screen and began checking the returns in. Philly Lou popped her gum again, and Ginny shook her head, her hands moving automatically and her internal countdown to quitting time clicking forward step by step.

[3]

NUMBER HASN'T CHANGED

"I'm an idiot," Lee muttered. "Pure-d grade-A idiot." His tongue had just stuck itself to the roof of his mouth, while he stood there like a dumbfuck watching her beautiful wrists move, her dark-green, almost black nail polish slightly chipped, her big dark eyes open and welcoming. No wedding ring, but that didn't mean much nowadays. The braid wrapped around her head wasn't quite loose, but a few stray strands of buckwheat-honey hair were coming free, and it suited her. No earrings today, though. Usually she wore small, pretty gold hoops and a thread-thin gold bracelet or two. He would bet they were all real metal, too. She was *class*.

And today she'd even *talked* to him. Said his name—well, it would be right there on the computer screen, wouldn't it, and she'd pronounced it wrong. Today she was in a knee-length herringbone skirt he hadn't seen before and a black sweater, one with a scoop neck that showed her collarbones. Even *those* were pretty, for God's sake.

He'd never noticed how many of the goddamn songs on the radio were wailing about some broken heart or another. Finally, he switched to AM, but that was full of windbags, pulpit-pounders, and the weatherman talking about snow chances. Any fool with a nose could tell there wasn't any yet, though there was a bit of iron on the breeze if you sniffed deep. Lee spun the ancient radio dial some more, the craving for a cigarette rising under his skin. He hadn't smoked since he was twenty, but damn if he didn't want to go back to it now. A shot or two of something hard wouldn't go amiss, either.

Have a lovely afternoon, Mr Quartine. She pronounced it a different way each time, like she was searching for the right one, and he couldn't even correct her.

He finally found a news station; a soothing female voice—not as pretty as the library girl's, but all right—purring along in that educated way.

She talked that way. Each word distinct, none of them rubbing against each other. Poppa Q would have called that *Yankee,* and mocked it. *Talk like they's spittin' the words, boy. You don't ever trust that.*

According to the news, there was another war in the Middle East. Lee's shoulders hunched slightly, his chin dropping. That part of the world was a blood fountain, and every goddamn politician wanted to keep it that way. Another weather report, *nice mild fall weather,* the man said. Back to the female voice, while Lee waited for the turn onto the highway. Something about a big old protest in DC, and last of all, a reminder to get your flu shot. *The Center for Disease Control recommends yearly shots for the elderly, the very young, and those with compromised immune systems. This year's flu season is expected to be the worst in recent history—*

Well, wasn't that just peachy. Something about it nagged at him, but he was too busy to chase it down because the little sedan in front of him had slammed on its brakes. Which meant Lee had to as well, and thankfully he had new pads on the truck because it was a mite heavier than those fiberglass imports. A screech of peeling rubber behind him, and he hoped he wasn't about to get into a smash-up on a Sunday afternoon to top everything off.

The hold-up was a dead porcupine. The poor thing wasn't even bloating yet—not enough heat, and its gut was split open. You wouldn't even want it for meat, though it might do in a pinch. People remembered the lean times around here—at least, the older ones did, and Poppa Q had imparted a deep and abiding respect for the old 'uns in his little grandson.

Lee exhaled, hard, shaking away all sorts of uncomfortable thoughts. Sooner or later he'd get up the nerve to say something to her. He just had to work himself to it the right way.

He was coming up on Cherry Hill Road when it occurred to him that sometimes she went across to Mayburn's Diner after she locked up the Cotton Crossing library. Not that he'd been sitting in his car watching like some kind of preee-vert, as Poppa would call it. He'd just *happened* to notice her crossing the street two weeks ago, while he propped a book on the steering wheel and tried to fool himself into thinking he was reading a Louie Lammer something or another about a man who got dropped into Russia and had to walk out, or some such foolishness. If a man wanted to sit in his truck and read it was his own damn business, right?

He decided against hooking the right on Cherry Hill and going back into town. Next week he'd plan it so that he went in the library around closing time, and maybe, just maybe, she'd lock up and head across the street. It might be easier to talk to her in the diner, a simple *hello there*. Maybe even offer her a cup of coffee, though the swill they had in there was likely to push a big-city girl's nose into the air sooner than saying *turn off the paved road*. Motton's was where the good coffee was, or so they said.

The radio kept going. Something about a riot in New York, now? He grimaced a little, reached over, and flicked the knob. It died with a squawk and he drove the rest of the way in silence, his lips moving every once in a while as he tried out different sentences.

Hello there.

Well, hello.

It's the library gal!

Nothing sounded right, but he could keep trying. If there was one thing he was good at, it was practice.

. . .

THE LITTLE RED LIGHT ON HIS ANCIENT MESSAGE MACHINE WAS
blinking. Plenty of people had those cell phones, but something about
them just rubbed Lee the wrong way. When he was out, he was *out*,
and if someone wanted him, they could wait until he was good and
ready to answer. Besides, he'd heard they could be tracked, and he
wouldn't put it past the government to use the little electronic boxes
just like tagging a deer. People wandered around staring at the things,
they also *drove* staring at them. It was enough to make him want to
mount something heavy-duty on his truck and hire a gunner.

Now wouldn't *that* be satisfying. No doubt he'd find quite a few
takers for the job.

Two messages. One, a recording about carpet cleaning. The other
was...well. A cigarette-roughened rasp, the snap of command hiding
under an easy almost-drawl, and the sense that the speaker was
sitting bolt-upright on something mildly uncomfortable.

Colonel Grandon also sounded tired, for once. "Lee? Pick up if
you're there, son." A pause. "Number hasn't changed. Give me a
jingle, will you?"

Lee stood next to the pink Formica kitchen counter his grandmother had set numberless bowls of bread dough to rise, and for a
moment he wasn't in the familiar manufactured, the holes worn in
the carpet from many vacuumings and the thin wood of the cabinets
glowing with finger-oil and Murphy's soap. He was standing on
concrete instead, a hot wind pulling at aluminum siding, flies buzzing
on deadmeat and—

"Nosir." Lee's own voice startled him, hard and crisp. He almost
jumped out of his own damn skin. "That ain't in the paperwork. Ain't
calling you back."

His mouth was dry, his heart going a mile a minute. Why the
fuck was the man calling him? It couldn't be anything good. He
wouldn't pick up the phone just to shoot the shit, would old Colonel
Strap-Yo'-Balls-On Grandon. No, there were only two reasons he'd

bother and they both boiled down to him wanting something out of one Lee Quartine.

It was almost a relief to have something other than his own dumb ass to think about, though. Lee stood stock-still for a few minutes, breathing deep and sweating, hearing the wind pick up as the sun headed downslope towards its nightly rest. Days were getting shorter.

One good thing about not getting a damn cellphone, he could say his number'd changed. Or that the message-tape had malfunctioned somehow. Maybe Grandon would find someone else to bother.

Yeah, and maybe you'll talk to that girl at the library after all.

When he could move again, he headed for the fridge. There was an emergency six-pack tucked on the bottom shelf, behind the pickle jar, and he suspected he needed at least half of it.

[4]

FLU SHOT

ABE JACKSON, FIFTY-TWO AND GREYING, SETTLED IN A FAMILIAR, creaking chair with his chest tight and his palms suspiciously damp. The smoked glass wall separating his office from the rest of the floor, a drawback masquerading as a perk, was a blind eye watching him, especially at this hour. Down in the basement the boards were up, frantic motion hurry-scurrying with damage control and strike vectors. Several hot zones had been pushed rudely down the priority list. Putting out fires was an Umbrella specialty; when he'd been young and juicy at this job he'd actually enjoyed it.

FBI. CIA. NSA. DHS. Alphabet soup, and then there was the Umbrella, the uncle nobody in the family wanted to talk about. Recruiters even managed to make it sound glamorous, until you realized it was a glorified janitorial detail. Scrubbing and shoveling shit all day long and most of the night, too, especially when you had an active Situation.

The files were scattered across his desk. CLASSIFIED. EYES ONLY.

And, worst of all, PROJECT STEVE. Chowder to cashews, laid

out on paper, someone's bright idea picked up in a fucking commit-tee. The science was great, but instead of truth, justice, and Captain Fucking America, there were four major cities on lockdown, the media getting restless, and the military suddenly crying in their soup because the civilian testing to build a better soldier was going to eat the entire damn country for lunch and probably everything on the continent for dinner before looking around for dessert.

He had to put the papers away, button his collar, straighten his tie, and go back to the basement soon. Leadership was important in a crisis, and his was the ass in the fire now, whether he liked it or not.

New York. Chicago. San Diego. Houston. Whose idea had it been to deploy *there*? Probably a halfhearted attempt at masking. When dealing with biological agents, though...

The idiots. The goddamn *idiots*.

He flipped through the lab trials. Color pictures of lacerations, taken a few days apart, showing healing with incredible speed. Reports on oxygen uptake, metabolism profiles, stress tests—you could just see the pencilheads creaming their shorts.

Small-scale testing on enlisted subjects returned results inter-esting enough that civilian testing was floated as an option, just like with the Penobscot retrovirals. They figured, well, the "flu vaccine" delivery had worked before, might as well do it again, the infrastructure was in place.

Except someone, somewhere, had fucked up. Or good old Ma Nature had decided the bastards tinkering with her double-helix art needed a finger-singe or two.

Abe pinched the bridge of his long, narrow nose. Nothing in this pile of paper would offer him a solution. Nobody downstairs knew how bad it was. He'd briefed the two upstream heads who were cleared to take this to the President, who was probably still in shock. That motherfucker was an *idealist*, and would probably have a stroke if the future dimensions of Abe's inevitable course of action was, through some clerical error or fucking miracle, revealed.

He dropped one of his big-knuckled, manicured hands to his left. The drawer whispered open, and the bottle of Wild Turkey glowed mellow amber, right next to a small black case with both numeric and thumb locks. A long, longing look at the case, his grainy, bruise-circled eyes blinking quickly, and he shook his heavy head. Not yet.

There was also a sleek black rectangle snugged into the side of the drawer. He pressed the power button, it scanned his fingerprint, and his monitor blinked back into life.

"Only one way to love your country," he muttered, hardly aware of speaking.

His cell rattled and buzzed, buried under a two-page inform sheet on recombinant vaccine method and the heftier background checks on the science team behind Steve's trials. He snatched the phone, glanced at the screen. It was Sienna, and he accepted the call with a swiftly quashed sinking sensation in his gut. "Hey, honey."

"Good evening, Abe." His sunny-tempered wife thought that was hilarious. "I'm about to go to bed."

"Tease." It was getting goddamn hard to compartmentalize. It had been ever since the first reports from the Queens clinic had come in. Spending so long looking at possibilities and seeing the patterns play out got you into the habit, and after a while, you couldn't shut it off. "I'll be home soon, sweetheart. Just got to put in one more appearance at a meeting."

"The man who never sleeps." That small tinge of jealousy. Oh, Sienna Jackson was proud of her husband in the hush-hush industry, and for a while it had seemed a delightful game. Abe was lucky to have snagged her instead of some goddamn college-fed feminist who would want to stick a nose in where it didn't belong, and he knew it.

"Getting older, though." Aged about twenty years in the last week, it felt like. "When's retirement again?" Another one of their private jokes.

"You tell me." The sound of sheets moving as she shifted. "When you get home, just whisper it in my ear."

"That's a deal, sweetheart. Love you."

"I love you too." Surprised. He rarely said it first.

Abe hung up, closed his eyes, and tried not to think about what he was going to have to do. Really, it was simple, and the quicker he did it...

The cat was well and truly out of the bag, despite all the roadblocks, travel restrictions, media blackouts, and no-cell zones at his disposal. There were at least two confirmed exposures flown out of Newark in the past week, one for London and the second for Missouri. At eighty percent communicability, the spread rate was pretty goddamn geometric. Christ knew how many unconfirmed exposures made it out of LAX or Houston. Still, it was his duty to make sure.

And Abe Jackson would be damned if he'd let the rest of the world pick America's bones.

He tapped his codes on the sleek ergonomic keyboard and straightened the avalanche of papers while he waited for the channel to clear. The papers would go in the safe, though there was really no point. Also shelved would be the question of whether he was wrong. If the infection burned itself out inside the US, the borders would have to be closed hard to keep it from re-entry. If it burned itself out overseas...

He'd run the numbers so many times they were luminous behind his eyelids every time he blinked. Four out of five of the initial infected in Queens had infected others, rubbing against crowds, talking to neighbors, buying coffee. Carrying around a cloud, like Pigpen in the old Peanuts cartoons.

Except Pigpen's cloud was visible, and harmless enough.

His monitor woke again as the channel clicked to clear. Abe typed.

CODE RED GAMMA SCEN 4 (4). You always repeated the scenario number, to cut down on error.

The cursor blinked. It asked for verification, and he typed in the string.

The agents were prepped, and had been waiting for go-time all week. Once he sent the word, the ball would roll, and any sad sack running in front of it would be crushed. Nondescript, thoroughly trained travelers would fly out through other airports, carrying the nasal sprays camouflaged as OTC allergy meds. Their destinations were chosen for maximum spread efficiency, and once they arrived they would use the sprays at carefully chosen public places, then... circulate. The 72 hour incubation period was optimal but not guaranteed, and they would spend as much time as possible in proximity to civilians.

Patriots, one and all, even though they had no idea what would happen once they snorted the goddamn sprays. If one or two of them suspected, or was immune by some freak chance, the others would overlap. The percentages were high enough.

SCENARIO 4 (4) ACTIVATION COMMENCE.

It asked if he was sure. He typed POSITIVE COMMENCE and the keycode, again.

The cursor blinked. The machines thought about it for a few seconds. Abe's palms were not merely damp, now. They were flat-out *dripping*, and there was an obstruction in his throat. He loved America, and he loved his wife, and now his job shoveling shit had turned into making sure nobody would spit on the corpse of the former...and that the latter would never see the world crumble from under them.

It asked again if he was really, really, *really* sure, no takebacks and no second chances. Once he did this, he would have to go downstairs and watch the boards until Hank Johnston came on deck for the next twelve-hour shift. Poor Hank was probably chewing Tums by the dozen now instead of getting some sleep. He was a faithful subordinate who had no idea things were already fuckered beyond repair.

Abe Jackson, the most clandestine motherfucker in the Umbrella, confirmed. He exhaled, hard.

He pressed the return key.

Five minutes later the papers were locked in his safe; Abe stood, straightening his tie, and glanced around his office. At home there was the gun safe, and black-haired Sienna sleeping peacefully in their married bed. She wouldn't wake up when he crept into the bedroom, or when the world stopped spinning. It was the last labor of love he would perform before blowing his own brains out.

He couldn't wait.

[5]

A NORMAL MONDAY

Satisfaction, Ginny often thought, was crossing things off a to-do-list, even a purely internal one. Yoga pants, check. Big thick comfy socks, check. Finally getting her hair out of braids: check-ity-check-check.

There was her phone, right on her nightstand, still plugged in. And lo, what to her wondering eyes should appear but four separate messages from her mother, in varying states of concern. Ginny traipsed downstairs to the kitchen and plugged her electric kettle in, splashed enough filtered water for a decent cuppa, and thumbed through her texts as well. Sally Urtins had a birthday coming up, the main branch was putting together a "celebration" for her. They wanted everyone to contribute to pizza. Ginny rolled her eyes, scrolling through everyone's responses to *that* suggestion. Nobody was brave enough to say *hell no*. Even Sally herself probably didn't want the folderol, but Bobbie Evrard—the branch head—loved any excuse to squeeze cash out of her employees for "events" that mostly served to feed her need to swan around and commit atrocious acts of small talk upon unwilling subordinates.

Briefly, Gin contemplated calling in sick on Thursday. She

headed for the kitchen. Opened the refrigerator, viewed its contents critically, sighed and closed it when the kettle chirruped at her. The first thing she was going to do when she moved back to real civilization was order decent takeout every day for a *week*. Each meal from a different continent, and she'd eat every single one with chopsticks to boot.

Her phone began to buzz, and the Beastie Boys began to scream about how you had to fight for your right. Another sigh welled up, but she hit the "talk" icon and plastered a smile on her face to make sure her tone would be just right. "Hi, Mom. I forgot my phone at home, and I work on Sundays."

"There you are!" Mom sounded *distinctly* un-chill. "Have you seen the news?"

How would I? "I just got home. What the hell?"

"Something's happened. In New York." Breathless movement—Mom was probably carrying the cordless into the kitchen, cupping the mouthpiece secretively.

The bottom dropped out of Ginny's stomach. "Are you guys okay?"

"We're upstate, with Flo. She's turning into a pumpkin, oy! And glowing, too."

In other words, when are YOU going to make us a grandchild, Virginia? They didn't even care that Bill had run off with that secretary, because Flo was about to squeeze a pup through and there would be a hefty chunk of alimony by the time Dad's lawyers finished with the sap who had married the favorite daughter. "I'll bet." *Did you just call to try to make me feel guilty?*

Well, to be honest, the guilt would happen pretty naturally. Yesterday's Saturday was Shabbat, but Ginny worked all day. And her parents loved her, there was no question about that.

"But it's the city, Virgie." Her mother's voice hit the high sharp pitch of gossipy excitement. "They closed all the bridges yesterday, can you *imagine?* We were lucky to get out, but if Flo goes into labor we won't be able to use Dr Schneider—"

We. As if anyone but Flo would need medical attention. Of course, Mom would probably act like she did. Ginny gathered the rest of her patience for the day and hoped it would be enough. "They closed what bridge?" *Did you call to give me a traffic report?*

"All of them! Haven't you seen the *news*?"

"I don't have cable, Mom." *Or a television. And I've been at work, remember?* Librarian was an honorable vocation, but a Mills girl was supposed to marry well. So far, Ginny was 0-2. "Why did they close all the...Jesus. *All* of them?"

"*All.* Staten's closed, anything past Brooklyn—you can't get there, unless you swim. Jersey's full of National Guard. The bridges are shut down, nobody's flying into JFK *or* Albany." Disaster was almost as good as gossip. "Or out."

"I heard there were demonstrations or something." Driving home, she'd only listened to half a news report before flipping the dial to find something that wasn't country, Bible-thumping, or more country.

There wasn't much.

"Virgie." Almost hyperventilating. Now Mom would be waving one hand, her sterling-silver charm bracelet jingling unless she was in pearls today. "No demonstration. Something's going on. They have helicopters. There's National Guard in *Manhattan*, of all places, although it probably will do more good a little north. But, listen, honey."

"Hm?" Her tea was almost done. Ginny swirled the bag—cinnamon tea, no caffeine because it was past 3pm and she didn't want to be up half the night. What could be happening that they'd close all the bridges, for God's sake?

Her mother had already moved on. "When are you coming to visit next? You'll have to take a train, since Albany is closed. But we can get you a ticket."

There it was. Drop everything and run across several states to play fetch and carry for Mom's vapors. "Is Flo there, Mom?" Listening to her sister complain would get her off the hook for a while.

"She's sleeping." Mom *tch-tch*'d, almost a tongue-click but not quite. "I just thought it would be such a nice surprise for her, and since we're already in Saratoga there's plenty of room."

"I'll see if I can get some time off work." There. That was graceful, and noncommittal.

"Maybe I should call your boss—"

Oh, hell no. "That would be unprofessional, Mother. Is Dad there?"

"He's at the golf course. It's Sunday." A faint sniff. "And in this weather."

I'm sure he's in the clubhouse with a Scotch. Ginny made another noncommittal noise. It was nice and sunny here, but Saratoga was probably seeing some winter already. So, Mom was uneasy, and wanted someone around to unload her anxiety on. It couldn't be Flo, since she was the holy one right now, and Dad had prudently taken himself out of range. "You must be worried, with everything going on."

"Me? Oh, it's in God's hands." But that pulled the cork from the dam, and for the next half hour it was a cavalcade of *what-ifs, and-sos,* and *but I told them, I saids.* Ginny's tea cooled, she opened her laptop on the kitchen counter and started looking at the news. Something about protests against a pharmaceutical company and some unrelated traffic jams was all she could find. It wasn't like Mom to be hyperbolic about *that.* Closing all the bridges wasn't on any of the news sites.

Weird.

Mom was getting older, and with Flo unquestionably the star of the current drama, she would be wanting *someone's* undivided attention. The retirement of a queen bee was a protracted affair, and Mom was still not reconciled to it. So Ginny made all the right noises, listened, soothed, and hung up an hour later with burning eyes and a crick in her back from leaning on the counter, as well as a hypoglycemic headache and a growling stomach.

"There," she told her phone. "My weekly duty, done."

Just one more reason to get a hotel room when she went to see the eventual spawning. Flo might even be glad to see her. Eventually. Once the fuss died down.

After all, it was Ginny who'd caught Bill and the secretary *in flagrante delicto*. And true to form, she was the one Flo blamed. *You just never want me to be happy*, her older sister had screamed at her that long-ago night. *You never! You never!*

It was usual. Flo knew she could yell at Ginny all she wanted, and her sister would still be there. At least, that's what Ginny wanted to think about the whole thing. It was a sign of a strong sororal relationship.

Yeah. Maybe avoiding the birth would be a good thing?

Ginny sighed and went looking for a box of cereal, hoping the milk in the fridge was still good.

Monday morning dawned clear and crisp, Indian summer hanging on with teeth and toenails. Ginny shuffled out to her patio—a rectangle of pebbled concrete, looking over a weedy back yard she paid Stevie Prince from the duplex at the mouth of the cul-de-sac a few dollars or so to mow when it got ragged in summer. The McCoys had a sprinkler, but Ginny didn't bother. All her potted plants were trimmed or brought in for the winter; there was no cheerful row of geraniums with leaves as big as her hand, no flashes of red peeking out of the terra-cotta strawberry jar with its open cups on its sides. Her hanging tomato planter was a mass of yellowing foliage she would have to clean out. They didn't bother to compost in this part of the world; she couldn't bring herself to start a heap here and possibly argue with the McCoys over what they would no doubt consider a garbage pile visible through the four-foot chainlink fence.

She wrapped her fingers securely around her mug and yawned, enjoying the slanted, still-warm sunshine. At least this part of the country had reasonable rent, and she'd lucked into the duplex. It was a daily drive to Lewiston, but the crime rate was low, the roof was secure, the heat pump worked just fine, and though she sometimes heard faint bumps from next door when the kids were really rambunctious she didn't hear them breathing all the time the way she would in a city apartment. The air was better, too, unless you went down to the river where the lone textile mill was still operating. Probably at a loss, to be a tax break for whatever company had bought and closed all the others. It was an article of faith out here in Cotton Crossing that the mills had been stolen by jobs in China, but they were fiercely anti-union here, too.

Which didn't make a lot of sense, but what in small-town America did? It was the hometown of "working against your own interests," that was for damn sure.

Monday morning had become her new favorite thing. Everyone else was at work, and she had a quiet neighborhood, almost all her own. Taking the half-Sundays, with Monday and Tuesday off, meant she had more than a weekend, plus the extra pay from working when nobody else wanted to was extremely welcome. All things considered, she was a lucky duck.

She took another sip, finding her tea had cooled to that perfect temperature—hot enough to warm all the way down, but not scalding. The only blot on a marvelous sunny autumn morning crisp enough to need her bathrobe and slippers as well as yoga pants and a pajama top was a steady thopping noise.

No, several steady thoppings, in different areas. Helicopters. Ginny frowned, shading her eyes; her tea caressed the air above it with thin steam-tendrils. Maybe the base near Lewiston was doing maneuvers?

She watched the metal birds swoop and circle. There were at least three she could see, but the noise said more were about, rising and falling in waves. Why on earth did they need so many?

Taxpayer money wasted like a mofo, right there. She sighed. Any red-blooded American librarian took a dim view of the military-industrial complex. Although, to be charitable, maybe the helicopters were all for firefighting in the summer? The forests here weren't old-growth, but any wood would burn.

Her phone spoke up, vibrating against the countertop inside. The Beastie Boys, again. Putting that ringtone on had saved her sanity. It wasn't that she didn't love them, it really wasn't.

It was just that sometimes, every once in a while, she was tired of being a disappointment.

Later, she would wonder why she didn't turn around and run for the phone. But this was a normal Monday, and her mother was calling early. Maybe the baby had started to drop, or something. By the time Ginny got inside, it had kicked over to voicemail. She scooped up her phone and weighed it in her free hand. Finally, she closed the patio door, sighed, and called her mother back.

There was no answer. Just the muffled sound of helicopters from outside.

[6]

TRAINED FOR THIS

IT WAS CHEAPER TO SHOP IN LEWISTON, BUT THE GAS TO GET there cost more and Lee never liked wasting time in transit, either. So it was Landy's for milk, turning in his washed bottles for the deposit because pennies didn't grow on trees, and thank God the store was grandfathered out of compliance with the dry laws. Driving over the county line just for a six-pack wasn't worth it.

There were few things about the Crossing Lee liked more than having some convenient beer. He didn't usually come into Landy's on Tuesdays, because it was Military Day, and he hated showing his ID to get a discount. Everyone knew he'd been in the Army, and everyone knew he didn't like to talk about it, which was blood in the damn water.

He stood on ancient black-and-white linoleum in front of the cold case, looking at his options—when a man didn't drink often, he could get a bit choosey—and knowing he was going to probably get some of the fancy beer in brown bottles. A shadow fell across the case, and the bottom of his stomach dropped and surged at once, a wave over the side of a wallowing rowboat.

It was the library girl, and he was seeing her in jeans for the first time. A pale pinkish top showed under her black North Face jacket, and her hair was pulled messily back. Free of the professional shell of a skirt and blazer, she was even prettier, if such a thing was possible. Her hiking boots were only borderline functional, but she was a city girl, and probably didn't know that.

She caught the quick movement of his head and glanced up at him. "Hello there." The smile lighting her face was made brighter by the dark rings under those dark eyes. She looked like she hadn't had much sleep, and her milk-fair complexion was the type to show it.

She was actually *talking to him.* In *public.* Instead of being trapped behind the library desk where she had to make nice with every customer. Were they called customers at the library? He didn't know.

And, Lord have mercy, she continued. "How are the Westerns treating you?" Her shoulders turned toward him, as if she really wanted to know. Those big dark eyes, interested and bright.

"Uh," he managed. "Uh, fine." This close he could see the gold hoops back in her ears, and her necklace was one of those invisible chains with a small crystal nestling a bit below the notch between her collarbones. Maybe it was even a real diamond. "Hi."

"Hi." Her smile widened. Those teeth, the kind you saw in toothpaste commercials. "I don't want to trouble you if you'd prefer not to talk, but maybe you could help me?"

Does she need to know what type of beer to buy? He floundered for a moment, and his mouth opened. Had he brushed his own teeth this morning? He damn well couldn't remember. "Sure. Anything." His cheeks were hot. Too hot. Was he *blushing?*

Fluorescents buzzed overhead, and the cooler breathed a slightly sour chill over both of them. She shifted her weight—without the heels she wore at the library, she was a little shorter, and stood differently. "How *do* you pronounce your last name? I keep thinking I'm saying it wrong."

"Oh. Quartine. Rhymes with *brain.*" His mouth kept going. Was he mumbling? He couldn't tell. He also had the severe, overpowering urge to check if his fly was zipped. "Surprised you asked, ma'am."

"I just wanted to pronounce it correctly. Since you're a regular." She held one of the ancient wire baskets for those who didn't want to push one of the anemic carts around, and there were a lot of leafy green in it. Tomatoes, too. A glass quart of milk. Maybe she was one of those nuts-and-berries city girls—but no, there was a wrapped package from the meat counter in there, too.

"Yeah." That about finished up everything in Lee's head. She was *talking to him*. He hadn't felt this way since Marcie Fluegels had hit him with the dodgeball in fifth grade, right in the nuts. Breathless, flushed all over, and completely goddamn incoherent.

The library girl kept examining him, expectant. He wasn't throwing the conversational ball back, maybe. But what else was there to say? He racked his brains. Usually he was good under fire, he knew what to do next. He should have trained for this, but even his wildest dreams hadn't included her starting up the talking.

Well, his wildest dreams had involved other things, if he was absolutely honest, but...

"You lookin for beer?" he managed, pointing at the case. *Oh dear God and Sonny Jesus, did I just say that?*

"Some decent white wine, actually, but I think I'm going to have to go with a hard lemonade or two." Her smile faltered for a moment, came back. Was his expression normal? He sure the fuck hoped so. She leaned over to grab a four-pack of that hard lemonade stuff—well, girly drinks for girls, that was all right. "Thanks, Mr Quartine." Pronouncing it carefully. "I'm glad I could ask you."

"Me too," he managed.

"See you Sunday." Now the sunshine was back. She flat-out *beamed* at him, turned on her toes, and was gone down the back of the store, disappearing into the aisle that held cereal and other dry breakfast stuff.

Lee's jaw worked for a second. His heart, trying to decide whether to sink or fly, settled on turning over and pounding as if he was back in basic training, running before he learned to pace himself. He realized his palms were sweating, and *also* realized he was going to have to talk to her again. On Sunday.

That meant four and a half days for him to practice, and to find something to talk *about*.

He stood stock-still for another few minutes, trying to think of what he'd come into Landy's to get. He even considered picking up some of that hard lemonade, but the cashiers today were Cindy and Holy Hannah Hruber, and both of those chatterboxes liked to air their gums out about everyone's purchases. Lee Quartine buying froufrou girly drinks would start the chins wagging with a vengeance.

A man needed beer, and that was that. Especially when he had no idea how in the hell he'd just gotten so lucky.

"...SOMETHIN IN THE WOODS," HOLY HANNAH SAID, HER DRAWN-on, perpetually surprised eyebrows settled comfortably in their usual high curve. "That's what Donny said." Her screaming-red bouffant, lacquered in place, bobbed as she nodded, her blue plastic earrings swaying. "Found a deer all mangled up."

Round old Madge Harmon shook her head, tut-tutting. "Poachers?" she ventured, timidly, thumbing through a fan of coupons as Hannah tapped at her register.

"Not unless them poachers got a wood chipper to run it through." Cindy Hruber's hands, long pink nails clicking, sorted efficiently through Lee's purchases, swiping them across the laser reader. "Hello there, Little Lee."

"Morning." Lee selected a Payday bar from the candy rack and added it. *Little* Lee until the day he died, because his daddy was Lee Senior and his grandaddy was Big Q. Christ only knew what they'd call Lee's kids, if he ever had any. "How's Al?"

"Oh, gettin along." Blonde-frosted, wide-hipped Cindy wasn't interested in detailing her brother's adventures in the Bledermark Home up in Lewiston, for once. Normally, anyone who happened into Landy's on a Tuesday morning could expect a chowder-to-cashews of the eldest Hruber sibling's current medical woes. It was a damn miracle the man hadn't shuffled off the mortal coil yet, but if there was a simple way to do things, a Hruber would find the exact opposite, for no other reason than it was there. Just like accepted wisdom held that you couldn't have the Plembees and the Schoenfelds at the same barbeque if you wanted to avoid fisticuffs, the Quartines were quiet but went crazy if a wrong was done them, and the Carters would tell a lie just for the hell of it, except for Big Elbert Carter, who would only grunt. "You come across anything strange out in your neck, Lee?"

"Other than the whirlybirds, no." *You'd have to be blind not to see them Apaches roaming around. Maneuvers, maybe, except why would Grandon call me?* It was a puzzle, and one he didn't like the look of. Might be time to get his ditty bag out again and make sure everything was in its proper place.

Just in case.

"Charlie said maneuvers." Mrs Harmon craned her neck to look up at Lee, blinking owlish. She was a Tappersen before she married into the Harmons, and they were all nervous. "What do you think?"

"Been a while since they took Apaches out of mothballs, ma'am." It was probably the most that had come out of his mouth in Landy's ever, and Cindy blinked her heavily gooped lashes twice, surprised.

Holy Hannah craned her neck to get a good look at him. "Well-now," she said. "We was just talking about the critters torn up in the woods."

Lee grunted, an interrogative sound, which was all the priming *that* pump needed. Turned out Donnie Casabroac had been in the diner this morning, with pictures on his phone from his last hunting trip. Something had torn up a deer *"like one of them UFOs,"* he'd said, and while the general consensus was that it was foolish to believe in lights in the sky unless you were one of them druggies, the pictures were, in the considered opinion of the Rayburn's Diner Morning Brain Trust, damn funny. Donnie was too dumb to pull a fast one, as people said with varying levels of approbation or pity, and the morning crew at the Rayburn's counter had a great deal of collective shootin' knowledge. All in all, it was the sort of topic that could keep everyone in town exercised for a good long while.

Cattle mutilations, Lee remembered. That was what Donnie was talking about. Huh. There was weird and god*damn* weird in the world, and you saw a lot of it when your job was to shoot and be shot at. It wasn't a big step from slicing up cows to slicing up deer, and Donnie might be stupid but he knew the difference between a big cat or bear kill and something else. You didn't have to be a scholar to figure that out.

"The Lord will tell in time," Holy Hannah finished, portentously. "You want these beers in a paper sack, Lee?"

"Yes ma'am." The heat on his face had gone down. Maybe he didn't look like a mouth-breathing fool, maybe they hadn't noticed him talking to the library girl. Maybe he should go over to the diner and listen to some of the fellas chewing the fat over it.

And maybe monkeys might fly out your ass, Lee. He needed to get his beer home. Roll the window down so the chill breeze could scour his cheeks, which were heating up again. They couldn't damn well decide if his thermostat was broken or not.

"Charlie told me there were riots in San Francisco too." Mrs Harmon's very round face was puckered with worry. "The news is full of them."

Charlie Harmon was a Fox News-watching good ol' boy who swore the gummint was out to steal everyone's money and turn 'em into queers. Lee touched his hatbrim to Holy Hannah, took his two crinkly paper bags, and tried not to scan the parking lot to see if the library girl was still there.

It didn't matter, anyway, because she wasn't. There was, however, a black Crown Vic with shaded windows, parked at the far end of the lot, and that made Lee Quartine's nape tingle.

He decided to drive the long way home.

LOOK HER BEST, THANK JESUS

"I don't understand," Shirley Bassari repeated, pinching the bridge of her nose. The brightly lit pharmacy shelves around her, ranked with bottles and boxes, were as familiar as her own underwear drawer, and about as interesting at the moment. "They want us to *what?*" She didn't mean to say it loud enough to drown out the canned country music piped into every corner of the blue-and-yellow Hatchie Ground Bargain Zone. But for God's sake, this was ridiculous.

Lewis Engstrom, the head of the pharmacy department, ran one liver-spotted hand over his balding head. His anemic combover stayed where it was, plastered down by a generous palmful of Krew Comb. Or maybe even Crisco. His lab coat was a little dingy around the hem, too. Divorce had not been kind to him, but probably a damn sight kinder than his ex *wanted* it to be. "Box up all the flu vaccine we just got and send'er back."

"But..." Her headache was about to get a lot worse, Shirley sensed. Her own white coat was bleached *and* ironed, because she took her medical duties seriously. "Well, okay. What's left of it."

"How much we got?"

A *real* pharmacist would know, she thought. "Got shipment last Monday." Shirley was just a tech, but they were congenitally under-staffed; she was pretty certain she could have done Lewis's job almost as good as he did. He fondly referred to the techs as "my girls," but any idiot could figure out it wasn't really a *compliment*. Especially not when you were, like Shirley, nearly forty blessed years old and built, in her late mama's pungent phrase, like the brick shithouse's girlfriend. "No shipment yesterday, though. We only got about a couple dozen doses left. Everyone's been coming in for them." And no wonder, with all the television and radio telling people to get their flu shots. Midge, the little Korean girl, was the one who handled that, and last week had kept her busy. "Midge was getting tired of sticking them, bless her heart."

"Company should pay for employees to get 'em." Lewis said, for the fifth time since the higher-ups had told them to push the flu vaccine.

"Might stop half of us being out sick." There was a tickle in Shirley's own throat, though that could be all the bullshit a girl had to swallow to hold down a job and feed her kids. Her hands moved deftly, capping a bottle of generic sertraline pills. The brassy tint to her blonde curls hardened every time she went to Prunella's Beauty Corner, but she was determined to keep the dye job. Even though she was washed up and too fat, she could still look her best, thank Jesus.

"Now who's sick?" Lewis folded his arms, just standing there watching her work. He could have taken a hand, but didn't. Just stood there leaning against the counter, an aggressive little beer belly straining at his lab coat. His name tag was askew, too. He wasn't even checking the mirrors to see if anyone was waiting in line.

Shirley's headache mounted yet another notch, shaping up to be a real corker. Her nose was itching, a sure sign she was coming down with something. "Brenda called in sick this morning, remember? It's Midge's day off."

"Well, maybe I should call her in." He looked happy at the thought. Men, worse than hound dogs. Midge was trim and cute, if you liked Asian girls. Some men thought they were docile, but Shirley thought privately that tiny firecrackers could take a finger off as well as big ones.

She made a noncommittal noise and ignored a flicker of motion in the mirror. She was *busy*, dammit, and if Lewis wasn't gonna help with the six scripts she had lined up, he could damn well deal with whatever shuffling dumbass came up to the counter.

"Go ahead and box them up when you're done with that," he said, finally. Whoever was at the counter cleared their throat—sounded like they had a wet one. Now that she thought about it, the entire store was full of croup and sniffles, customers as well as employees. At least she wasn't working in grocery. Here, she had the counter to keep customers from getting all cozy and breathing on her.

"All right." Shirley hunched her softening shoulders and moved to the next prescription. Typical. Lewis wouldn't take care of it himself. He took his sweet time bellying up to the customer, and began listening to some incoherent babble about cough syrup.

Shirley coughed, twice, turning her head so she didn't get any on the supplies in front of her. Her neck was uncomfortably damp.

It was gonna be a long shift.

[8]

SHE'S GOT PEOPLE

"Ginny?" The connection crackled, then firmed up. "Hello?"

Of course it wasn't her mother, it was Bobbie Evrard, calling on Ginny's day off. Which could bode no good. "I'm running errands," Ginny part-lied, rustling the grocery sacks as she bent over her Toyota's open trunk. A chilly breeze flooded her garage through the open door, and a dog was barking lazily out by the road. "What can I do for you, Bobbie?" *Don't ask me to come in today. Don't you dare.*

"I'm so glad I got hold of you! Listen, there's a community meeting at the Crossing branch tomorrow, and Annie can't make it. Do you think you could work that evening? It's time and a half."

Huh. Ginny straightened, staring sightlessly at the back of her garage with its neat pasteboard cabinets. Half of them were empty. "What happened to Annie? Is she okay?"

"Her mom's in the hospital." The boss sighed, a deep and familiar sound. "Kidney trouble. It's looking bad, and I want to give Annie all the rest I can. Half the county's out sick with one thing or another."

Well, even though Bobbie loved to swan around and micromanage, she *also* took care of her people. Ginny heaved an internal sigh as well, made sure she was smiling before she spoke again. "I can do it, absolutely. I'm going to have to leave my regular branch early though. Say, at 3pm? That will give me enough time to get there and set up."

"Say no more, I'm changing the schedule now." Relief tuned Bobbie's voice a half-octave higher. "You're an absolute lifesaver."

Yeah, right. Ginny reached for another bag, rustled it aggressively. "Tell Annie I hope her mom gets better."

"Sure thing. Thanks, Ginny. You're amazing."

Well, that was nice to hear. Ginny hung up and straightened, turning to gaze at the cul-de-sac. The kids were at school, her neighbors were at work, and it was quiet except for the hum of traffic in the distance, the soughing of a breeze that was a little too chilly to be comfortable, and a helicopter somewhere. The dog had stopped.

She checked her phone again. Nothing. Just the call from her mother yesterday morning, the one with no voicemail attached. Ginny had left a voicemail last night, and another *this* morning. Was Mom mad over something? No, if she was, Dad would have picked up; if Flo had gone into labor, Dad would be the one on the line, too, because Mom would be fussing over her favorite daughter. Besides, Ginny hadn't given her mother anything to be even slightly annoyed at.

Not like *that* ever mattered. Ginny tucked her phone back into her pocket, settled her purse on her shoulder, and got to work. She carried her groceries in, and used the putting-away time to dial her parents again. This time, the voicemail didn't pick up. It just rang, and rang.

Ginny frowned, standing in front of her open refrigerator, and tried again, goosebumps spilling down her back.

And again, it just rang.

Weird.

It wasn't just weird. It was downright worrisome. She probably wouldn't be able to sleep tonight, either. At least, not well.

She closed the fridge, and decided she'd look up train tickets online after dinner. Just in case.

. . .

SHE TRIED CALLING FOUR MORE TIMES. DINNER WAS A SALAD with roasted chickpeas; she picked at it while she stared at her phone or tried to focus on her laptop, where Netflix was serving up a romantic comedy about a time-traveling New York prince, or something. Halfway through, her doorbell rang, and she heaved a sigh worthy of Bobbie. Probably a missionary or something, but she hauled herself wearily up. It was already dark, and she flicked the porch light on. "Who is it?"

Some of the people here just opened up without even asking. Most of the doors didn't even have peepholes, for crying out loud. Small-town crime rates, but still. Better safe than sorry.

"It's Harry, from next door." Harry McCoy was a cheerful, round, pot-bellied good ol' boy, a machinist. He wore a worried frown, and Ginny's heart sank. Was it the plumbing, or had one of their kids gotten sick? Amy was a nurse, but—

"Hey. We wasn't sure you was home." He almost chewed on his mustache, sucking his upper lip quickly into his mouth. "So quiet, you know."

Is that a bad thing? She suppressed a burp from the tahini dressing—chickpeas and tahini were natural co-conspirators. "I try to be. What's up?"

"You got people in New York, right? We was watching, and Amy said, my God, but Miz Mills has fambly in New York—"

Her stomach dropped and her heart began to pound. "What?"

"You watching the news?" His small dark eyes were honest and bright with concern, catching the gold of the porch light.

"I don't have a TV," she managed. Her lips felt funny—a little numb, as if she'd bolted a couple shots of vodka. "I mean, just my laptop, I watch Netflix. I—"

"You want to see this, I think." His nose was full, and he sniffed deeply, a wet sound.

"Oh. Okay." Her voice didn't want to work quite right. "Let me get my phone." She didn't even grab a jacket. Her heart had lodged just behind the top of her sternum, and was pounding away. He waited, stolid and patient, on the front step, and preceded her like a battleship towing a tug.

The McCoy's, the layout a mirror image of her own half of the duplex, couldn't be more different that her nest. The heat was blasting, for one thing. Crowded with heavy, scuffed furniture and full of the thick smell of meat roasting, it was also loud. The television—a fifty-inch flatscreen for showing every pore on a televangelist's nose—was attached to the wall, with a cable box crouching on a battered, scratched DVD hutch below. The screen was full of an announcer's face—an older man, his jowls heavy with responsibility and the enunciation of a true anchorman. The makeup along his nose was running under the heat from the lights, and the inset over his shoulder was full of weird flashes.

"Oh, good. Honey, don't you have people in New York? I was just saying—" Amy, rosacea in her cheeks blooming in the tropical heat, almost tripped over a pile of laundry their eldest, Harry Jr, had been corralled into attempting to fold. "I sent him over, I was just saying, I *know* she's got people in New York!"

Ginny stared at the television. A map unfolded on the other side of the anchor, now. It was the *state* of New York, not the city, and there were red blossoms all over it. No, pulsing red circles, growing and shrinking.

"Settle *down!*" Amy yelled into the kitchen, where their younger boy, Bart, was screaming that he didn't want to do the dishes. "Harry, for God's sake, either whup that boy or stuff a sock in his mouth, it's his goddamn turn! Honey, come over, sit down, I *know* you ain't got no television over there."

"I watch Netflix," Ginny mumbled. There was something scrolling at the bottom of the screen—numbers, and names. Names she knew.

Albany. Syracuse. Hartford. Saratoga Springs. Utica. Stamford.

"The military has us locked out," a reporter said in another inset, pressing one hand against her ear while something burned behind her. It looked like a department store, going up in flames. "Nothing is certain yet, all we know is that the chaos has spread to Scranton. There's activity on the streets and—"

The camera jolted wildly, and something...happened. Confusion, a dark shape leaping on the blonde reporter's back. A scream and a jolt of static, and the announcer had gone pale under his makeup. "We, ah...we seem to have lost contact with our correspondent near Scranton. I repeat, the city of New York, which has been quarantined since Sunday afternoon, has apparently suffered some kind of terrorist attack, and the surrounding areas are suffering some kind of...we just don't know. Details are sketchy. The Department of Homeland Security has released a statement—"

"*Mooooom!*" Bart appeared in the living room doorway, a sodden dishtowel hanging from his fist. "Why can't *I* watch teevee?" He was thirteen, his springy hair bowl-cut and his face a galaxy of acne. The poor kid looked like he was put together wrong, his big hands and small feet not matching, his chest sunken but his legs thick. In a little while every bit of him would catch up, probably when he hit steroids for high school football—the only rival for religion in places like this.

"—terrorist attack," the announcer repeated. "In addition, more attacks have been reported in San Francisco, Houston, and Seattle."

The sound cut out for a moment. The ensuing silence was broken by Harry McCoy. "Oh my good Lord," he said. "Terrorists."

Amy pressed her fingertips to her mouth, hard. Bart dropped the towel, and Harry Jr let out a soft, shocked "God*damn*," neither of his parents took him to task for.

Ginny found her own hands knotted together. "But..." Breathless, and her heart pounding so fast. *But New York.* "It's the whole...a whole *state*."

None of them heard her, because it was only her lips that moved. She didn't even hear herself, because a rushing had filled her head.

[9]

HARD TO FIND

The privacy-tinted Crown Vic vanished as soon as he hit the highway, but that didn't mean much. So Lee swung out toward Lewiston, taking his time, annoyed at using the extra gas but needing to do some thinking.

Unfortunately, the thing he was thinking most about wasn't someone behind privacy glass following him. It was the library girl, and the shadows under her eyes. Looked like she wasn't sleeping. Why would that be? He didn't hear that she was sweet on anyone, but then again, librarians weren't a high-value topic in the Crossing. Not like hunting, or strange things in the woods. He would've had more luck hearing all about her before he enlisted, back when the Crossing was smaller and everyone's business was everyone else's.

Of course, then it would have been all over town that Little Lee was head-turned by an outsider. Whole lotta outsiders in town nowadays. The world had grown a little smaller, and Lewiston had gotten bigger, sending its tentacles in every direction.

His Chevy hummed along. He swung out on Dory's Loop, climbing halfway up Pearson Mountain—really, just a hill with pretensions, but a wide one. Which meant he could take the old logging road higher up and drop to approach his place from the opposite direction, something he did randomly at least a few times a month. You didn't want to wear *too* deep a rut, that was a good way to get ambushed. The wind rushed by his window, the milk in his Landy's bags occasionally clinking against a beer bottle. It would be warmish by the time he got home, goddammit, and he kept thinking about those circles under her eyes. Those jeans—it was indecent, how good a woman looked in Levi's. Or maybe just that particular woman. It couldn't be that hard, working at a library, right? So that left something else bothering her. Family trouble? He didn't know.

It irked him. He wanted to know, couldn't suss out a way to find out short of asking her, and that was no kind of option. He'd barely even said hello.

She'd been the one to talk to *him*. Maybe he hadn't done too badly, though. She noticed the books he was taking. What did that mean? Anything? Well, a librarian probably noticed *everyone*'s books. Did they notice and *remember* them, though?

Nothing in his driveway. He cut the engine, his window cracked a bit, and listened. Dusk had already filled the hollers, and it was clear enough to freeze tonight. A frost-on-the-punkin night, Nonna Quartine would have called it. Nothing out of the ordinary in the trees. Birds and critters bedding down or waking up, all the fine hairs on Lee settling where they should be. Of course, maybe he was all tied in a knot over her actually speaking to him, and missing something critical.

Or he was being ridiculous. They wouldn't send out a squad to drag him in to talk to Grandon. This was *America*, for God's sake. Or at least, it used to be.

Well, that was an unpleasant way for his thoughts to be tending. He took his time getting out, getting the groceries situated. No, they wouldn't send a squad to drag him somewheres. But the light in his living room was on, and he hadn't left it that way when he started out.

Someone was in his freshly painted manufactured home. And Lee Quartine, dammit, had a good idea who it was.

He at least had the politeness not to be sitting down when Lee came through the door. Instead, the graying middle-aged man stood at ease at the back window, staring out at the strip Lee cleared religiously even if he didn't want to take the ancient, wheezing riding mower to it. Clearing your firing lines was just good housekeeping.

Best not to let anything sneak up on you.

Grandon was in civvies, but his high-and-tight pretty much shouted *armed forces, thank you and goodnight.* He had a broad, set face, acne scars on cheeks and chin, and small piercing blue eyes that more than one person had called piggish. His gray suit was creased in all the right places, and it was probably even tailored. When you had to deal with the suits, it was a good idea to have one, and Grandon was, Lee supposed, the best you could hope for. At least he stopped shit from flowing downhill, as much as was possible. There was some shit even Nonna Quartine's beloved Sonny Jesus couldn't halt in its tracks. Grandon's broad back was almost square—he'd put on some weight, probably from the drinking. Or just from paper-pushing and club sandwiches.

Lee headed for the kitchen. He didn't even pretend to be surprised. He also didn't offer Grandon a beer. Even if the door was unlocked because he lived out past the limits, he didn't like the idea of someone just walking in. Especially if that someone was a man he never wanted to see again this side of the Last Judgment.

When Lee had his groceries situated and the bag folded up proper, he stepped back in the living room. The Colonel had turned around, and settled at ease again with his back to the window, almost as if Lee was the ranking officer expecting a report.

"Hello, Lee." He looked much older. Great pouches of flesh sagged under his eyes and off his jawline. The bits under his eyes were so dark they looked bruised, and Lee shut away the thought of the library girl. It wouldn't do him any good here.

He'd made the old man speak first. When you didn't particularly mind silence, you had an advantage over all kinds of folks. "Sir." Brief and neutral.

"I apologize for just stopping by." A rich, fruity baritone. "You're a hard man to visit."

Not so hard, if you *found me. The VA's got me on file, too.* Lee leaned against the doorway from the short hall into the kitchen. The urge to straighten up and snap a salute died under the knowledge that he was no longer part of the command chain. Nope, he was out, honorably and fully out, and staying that way. He wouldn't say a word about the killing floors and the dead men's eyes, open wide and reproachful, the hoods and the blood. Holding his mouth shut was a promise he'd made, and he was going to keep it.

But not for this man. There was a difference between keeping a promise and keeping it *to* someone, and it had taken Lee some hard thinking to find that gap.

"Lee, son..."

Lee shook his head. *Nope.*

"We need your help."

Oh, do you, now? Lee examined the man's face. Yeah, it looked like the Colonel hadn't been sleeping. Was it another "small war" somewhere the sand swallowed blood and the heat laid a man flat before noon? Maybe somewhere deep in a steam-hot hell they called a "jungle" when what they meant was "something we want is in here"? Or was it just pulling a trigger, somewhere, on some poor shit-bird some faceless suit in some nameless department had decided was a threat?

"Jesus Christ, son." Grandon's faint frown was a thunderclap of irritation. "Haven't you been watching the news? We've got a situation here, and I don't have anyone else to send with the—"

Lee turned around again. He headed back into the kitchen, opened one of the cabinets, and got down one of his grandmother's glasses. She called them carnival glass, for the oilslick sheen on their cold, hard surfaces. He filled it from the faucet—the well water around here was good for whatever ailed you—and drank.

When he came back out, Grandon was near the door. There was a manila envelope on the ancient split-bottom coffee table, and a package wrapped in brown paper, too big to be a cut of meat.

"Watch the news, Lee." Grandon delivered this over his shoulder. "Then call me. Number's still good. Until it reaches this part of the country, that is."

Huh? But Lee didn't bite at that, either. He also didn't care if Grandon was hoofing it back to the road in his suit, or if someone was coming along to collect him. It wouldn't be like the old man to leave a bomb on the coffee table.

Not a physical one, anyway. And why would he call him *Lee* instead of, say, Lieutenant? Or even just *Quart*, for God's sake?

He was probably figuring on Lee being curious. But there was a great advantage in knowing when to stuff curiosity in a hole and nail a lid over it. While it might be all right to be curious about a certain honey-haired big city miss, it wasn't healthy to be wonder about the cryptic comments of a man who, while he didn't pull a trigger himself, was adept at getting enlisted schmucks to pull them over and over.

The phone rang, and Lee almost, almost flinched. It was only Horace Slipot, though, telling him something about a community meeting at the library, and damn if Quartine shouldn't be there because there was a lot of talk, and Horace wanted Lee's opinion.

Horace, more than likely, wanted to *tell* Lee what his opinion should be, but he'd been Lee Senior's friend and one of the few men of that age Big Q respected, and this was also Horace's way of saying he wanted a ride to the meeting because it would be dark driving home. Lee agreed, mostly because he was—useless to deny it—a little rattled.

After he told Horace to settle himself and that he'd be driving, he scooped up the folder and the package, thought about it for a second, and carried them both to the broom closet, where he put them on the high shelf next to neatly stacked paper boxes of ammunition. And Lee further decided not to turn his ancient but still usable tee-vee on.

Maybe it was time to crack one of the books he'd got from the library, instead.

[10]

HAM'S HUNTING

HIS GIVEN NAME WAS SAMUEL, BUT FOR SOME REASON, everyone called the oldest Plotzee boy "Ham." Stories ranged from it being the only way his sister Libby could say his name to it being his favorite meat, but he never told one way or the other. He was generally held to be the quietest of the Plotzees, almost as quiet as one of the Quartines, and a little "touched." His two younger brothers were both married, but Ham never showed much interest in girls, even in high school. Nor did he follow any acceptable sport.

He would have been suspected of queerdom if not for the one thing he *did* love: hunting. When you could get him to talk, Ham Plotzee could tell you the latest in compound-bow research—even though he used a rifle, and only a rifle thank you—and deer urine, how to eat snow to turn your breath invisible in winter, the time he found a stone in a doe's guts. Doc Grampton called it a bee-zo-ar, but Ham just called it the lucky rock, and kept it in the pocket of his hunting jacket. He could tell you about deer blinds and gutting, the splash and slither of hot intestines, making your own bullets. Pressed to articulate just *why* he liked hunting, he'd look at you with his close-set, muddy eyes like you were asking him why the earth was round or the sun burned, or why he lived in that trailer on the back end of the old Plotzee property. It just *was*.

Right now he stood, slightly pigeon-toed, his big soft shoulders slumped and his thick cheeks bristling with day-old stubble he scratched with thick fingers while he stared at the ground, his lips a little pursed. A tuneless noise, not quite a whistle, slid between them.

Leaf mould and damp dirt, moss and rotting wood. Something heavy on the forefoot and fast had smudged through here, and the tracks were so bizarre he shifted from foot to foot too while he studied them. He knew these woods, almost like the back of his hand. Other men went to the bar, or watched the tee-vee. Ham plodded out into the wilderness, sometimes even without his gun, just a K-bar and a canteen. He could not articulate the deep satisfaction it gave him, the burning secret knowledge that out here away from town he was close to a god.

Not *the* God, the Lord God his gramma always talked about. Ham only went to church every other week, which was the bare minimum if he didn't want gramma and his ma both climbing the side of his head. Sundays were good days to be hunting, because everyone else was in church except atheists.

Ham was pretty sure atheists were also libruls who wouldn't know what to do with a rifle if you paid 'em. Donnie Casabroac had been spouting off about something in the woods, and some of them at the diner believed he was onto something. Ham, of course, thought Donnie C was fulla shit, but these tracks were...strange. For a bare second the idea that someone was playing a big ol' joke on the Crossing bubbled to the top of his brain, but he was in one of his Special Places in the woods, hard to get to unless you knew exactly *how*, and who would go to that trouble?

So Ham kept his rifle ready, and moved through the shaken-naked trees, uphill. The tracks were cutting across and up, almost like a dog's, but no dog would move sideways like this. No pawprints, just those smears. After a little while, he crouched carefully, a twig breaking under his right foot—sloppy, he told himself, he knew better, but the marks were just so *interesting*. He couldn't for the life of him figger out...

Aha. He put his free hand down, holding the rifle well clear. Touched the edge of one of the smears with the pinkie side, and imagined scraping down and sideways. *That* was the movement. The thing was going fast, and its back legs were bigger than its front, so it went cockeyed. Which intrigued him all the more, because—

A low, hissing, rumbling growl brought him upright-kneeling in a hurry, scanning the trunks and trash-brush around him. Undergrowth pressed thick through shortleaf pines. Downhill and east there would be hickories and scrub oak; there had been some clearcutting around here in the long-ago. He lifted the rifle, cautiously, finger well clear of the trigger and all his hairs standing up. His mouth filled with the sweet taste of danger, and anyone from town might have had a hard time recognizing Ham Plotzee, because he looked downright *radiant*. His eyes cleared up, blazing hazel-gold, and his face was no longer stolid and sullen but alive and flushed, a small childlike smile pulling back his thick lips and letting little corncob teeth peep out.

His ears all but twitched, his breathing turning slow and soft, heart galloping with the excitement that was better than anything— holding a girl's hand, drinking the whiskey that made his head hurt and his hands all dumb, even the approval on Plotzee Senior's face when Ham came home with good venison or raccoon fur.

The bushes to his right shook. Ham tracked smoothly, bracing the rifle, his knee digging into wet earth, grinding in mud and pine needles. There was no glare of orange in the thicket, and it was a *big* critter, the branches whipping back and forth. Ham slid his finger over the trigger, every thorn, every autumn-ravaged leaf, every stick standing out in sharp clear detail as the best part of hunting filled him from top to toe with singing joy.

It boiled out of the thicket, and to Ham's credit, his shot took it in the throat—well, mostly because the realization *oh shit it's a person* skewed his aim. He only had time for that horrified thought before it was on him, a haggard flopping scarecrow of what had once been a heavyset older woman, her clothing in rags except for a blue polyester apron, her strawlike red-dyed hair now slimed to her skull with wet mud. Her teeth worried at the coat-cloth over his shoulder as Ham fell over backward, and he batted ineffectually at her while she nuzzled, her cheek worming in a parody of tenderness, until those working, clacking jaws found his throat.

[11]

MIXED NUTS

THE WORLD WAS A RIDICULOUS MOVIE PLAYING ON A SCREEN IN front of her, and Ginny moved through it with the utter calm of desperation.

No call from her mother, or from her father, *or* from Florence. Ginny called several times a day, every number she could think of. Mrs Hurtzinger down the street from her parents' house. Flo's soon-to-be-ex-husband. The Caprasans, whose daughter Selina had been Ginny's best friend in high school. Selina herself was no longer friendly—college had taken care of that—but as far as her parents were concerned, Ginny was the Good One. She'd even dug in a box that hadn't been opened since she moved, resurrecting her old college address book. Back before smartphones and Google, it had been reli-giously updated. A Mills girl did not forget birthdays, anniversaries, or who had insulted whom at the last family or country club get-together and needed to be separated like toddlers.

Did you hear? Everyone in the Crossing, or at work, asked her. *You have people in New York, right?* Or the old famous standby, *are you okay?*

No. She was not okay. No airplane tickets, because the airports were shut down. Buses and trains both a no-go. She could drive, but the National Guard had roadblocks up. The internet was ablaze with news, dire prognostications, grainy pictures of the roadblocks and the straight-faced young men nervously guarding them. *Armed* young men, cradling ugly guns Ginny didn't know the names of.

She kept dialing, it kept ringing. Every break from work, every stoplight, every—

"Fruit punch?" She smiled, her cheeks aching. The community meeting was well underway, Ginny was what library employees called the Refreshments Gnome, and it was probably for the best. All she had to do was smile and keep the Hydrox cookies and cheapass punch flowing. Anything else, Christie could handle.

Funny, how Ginny had dreaded the thought of the next call from her mother. Funny, how she sometimes looked at the ringing phone and her stomach would fall with a sickening thump. Or a text from Flo would land, full of passive-aggressive sweetness, and she would grit her teeth.

But now...It was a gated community, she kept telling herself. It was *safe*, that was why they had moved out of the apartment in the city. They were just sitting tight and waiting for it to blow over. Nothing happened in that neighborhood full of retirees, unless you counted heart attacks and broken hips.

Great, Ginny. Real great. "Here you go," she said, with a bright smile, and handed Mrs Harmon a cup of punch.

The round-faced old woman merely nodded distractedly, dabbed at her nose with a ragged Kleenex, and wandered away. Mrs Harmon looked more like an Ewok than ever, especially with her thinning grey hair not neatly curled but sticking up anyhow. Was she having trouble getting through to her daughter in Alaska?

Ginny tipped her head back, looking at the ancient bar-fluorescents. Standing on a ladder to change those bad boys out was no fun at all.

Sure, Ginny. Think about the lights.

Someone cleared his throat, officiously. She brought her chin back down. Sol Beauford, the mayor of Cotton Crossing, was at the podium Ginny and Christine Clare, the weekday librarian at this branch, had yanked out of storage in the back just in time. Why this wasn't at the Grange, Ginny had no clue, and Christie had muttered several times during setup that she didn't know either and clearly it was some sort of comment on *something*.

Christie had family in Cincinnati. Presumably she had no trouble getting through to *them*.

"You're a lifesaver." As if the thought had summoned her, Christie appeared at Ginny's elbow.

"Not really," Ginny mumbled, as the mayor tapped at the arthritic microphone, producing a squeal of feedback. "Is he running for re-election?"

Christie's fair blonde face crumpled with glee. She was homely in that attractive way only strawberry-blondes could manage, lacking only a dirndl and a couple of braids to turn her into one of the von Trapp children. Her ankles were a bit swollen, though, and she moved like it hurt, especially after setting up all the chairs. Ginny's own back was none too happy about wrestling *those* motherfuckers out. "You'd think, right? Everyone's nervous. I think they think terrorists are coming after the Crossing personally."

Every town in America probably feels that way. Ginny rubbed at her left wrist, where a clattering metal chair had bitten her earlier. "Kind of funny they haven't made any demands, though."

"Some people just want to watch the world burn." Christie put both fists to her lumbar region and leaned back, sighing. The mayor was bloviating on about how this was a national emergency, and the Crossing had a duty that he knew it would fulfill.

A ghost of amusement touched Ginny's lips. "You saw that movie too?"

The door opened for a latecomer, letting in a burst of smoke-tinted autumn air. It was an old man, his red suspenders holding up a pair of britches probably born the same year Ginny was, and a wisp of white hair on his egg-dome head. He shuffled proudly, however, and his escort was familiar. It was Military Felon, Mr Quartine-rhymes-with-brain, and he held the old man's arm very gently indeed.

"Would you look at that." Christie blinked her big baby blues. The freckles on her nose had run together, like she'd been baked with sprinkles. "Never thought I'd see *him* in a library."

Ginny quit rubbing her wrist. It was going to bruise, there was nothing she could do now. "Huh?"

"Lee Q. He's hardcore townie." Christie's nose actually *wrinkled*, like she smelled something bad. "Redneck serial killer of the week, right there."

"He comes in every Sunday for Westerns." Ginny looked down at the punch bowl. It was holding up tolerably well, it seemed. She didn't even remember refilling it. "Should I be worried?"

"Westerns?" Christie laughed, cupping it behind a hand so she didn't disturb Beauford's speechifying. "Holy cow, really?"

"By the yard." Ginny's mouth twitched. She couldn't help but smile, Christie looked so horrified and amused all at once.

"...our great nation. Now, Sheriff Blotzer and Chief Randall have a couple words to say to y'all." The mayor smiled pacifically, his oiled-black hair swept back from a ferocious widow's peak and his maroon tie just a little too tight. His nose was reddened, too, and he rescued a precisely folded red handkerchief from his inside jacket pocket. "Thank you, thank you."

Polite applause echoed; Christie headed for the checkout counter. She was probably going to search for the old bottle of powdery aspirin or the slightly less ancient ibuprofen. It looked like her back hurt like hell. Mr Quartine got his elderly companion settled, looked around, and aimed for the refreshments table.

Ginny kept the smile plastered to her face. "Punch?" she said brightly, when he came into range.

"Just one." Without a hat, his dark hair flopped a little onto his forehead. He kept it so short at the back and sides she'd suspected a buzzcut, but the top was a little long. "Horace says he's thirsty."

Horace? "Is that your dad?" Her hands moved without any real direction on her part, dipping the ladle and filling the paper cup neatly.

"No ma'am." He looked a little bemused at the notion. "He knew him, though." Mr Quartine watched her hands, and Ginny glanced down to see if she'd spilled any.

She hadn't. He was just staring. Why? The bruise wasn't showing already. "Oh. I'm sorry."

That got an immediate reaction. "No need. What I meant to say was, he was a friend of my daddy. I'm driving him, because he don't see so well at night."

This is the most I've ever heard you talk. "That's nice of you." Her throat felt funny. Blocked, a little. Her father didn't see well at night either. He didn't drive past sundown. At least, not comfortably. Something hot was in her eyes. She handed him the paper cup, carefully, and his fingers brushed hers. "You want to take him some cookies? There's mixed nuts, too."

"Plenty of those."

She looked up in time to see one of his eyebrows arch a bit. She caught the joke, and probably would have laughed if the rock in her throat hadn't swelled. *God, please, let them be all right. I'm sorry, just let them be all right.* "There certainly are," she managed.

Mr Quartine examined her for a long moment.

Her nose was full. It was just like Christie to head off and leave Ginny here to deal with this.

"You all right?" He sounded honestly concerned. His eyes were a lot lighter than she'd thought at first, and she was only seeing it because he leaned a little over the table to get a good close-up. Just like peering at a bug on a windshield.

"Fine." *Mom. Dad. Flo. They have to be all right. They're fine, the phone lines are just messed up.* "Thank you. Sure you don't want a cookie?"

"No ma'am." He looked like he wanted to say more, but ended up turning sharply—he almost spilled the punch—and stalking away. That leather vest of his was really old; the stitching was fraying in a couple places. One of the patches on the back looked familiar, but she had to look away toward the front door, taking a deep breath and willing the tears to go away.

By the time Christie came back, Sheriff Blotzer had sneezed twice and was talking about the need for calm and no foolishness. Ginny headed for the back to start the prep for putting everything away and sniffled into a napkin, trying to cry quietly.

[12]

GET YOU HOME

Lee got Horace settled in the truck. "A damnfool," the old man muttered darkly, patting at his breast pocket to make sure his tiny notebook and mini-pencil were still where they should be. "Percy always was too big for his britches."

"So I do believe," Lee muttered in return. If there was a bigger waste of time on a Wednesday night, he wasn't sure he'd ever encountered it. The big news wasn't the curfew, though that was the thing they spent the most time on. Mentioning that there would be checkpoints on the highway and some of the main roads had been glossed over so smoothly most of the Crossing's residents—or at least, those who had the time and inclination to come to one of these shindigs—hadn't even quailed, being more worried about the goddamn curfew.

Terrorist attacks. Was that what Grandon had been on about? Whatever had happened was miles from here, though, and they had to have resources onsite for dealing with it. This was *America*, for God's sake. Sea to shining sea, and who in their right mind would decide the Crossing—or even Lewiston—was a good target?

Horace had wanted to stand around bitching with old Skip Grainger, too, and the two old men had settled near the front door of the library while the two girls finished cleaning up. Lee wanted to hurry them, but old Skip, leaning on his cane, couldn't be moved with anything less than a tractor.

Besides, the two old tortoises twining necks meant Lee got to help stack the chairs for the library girl. *Ginny.* That's what the other one called her. A nice name. He hadn't heard it before, and now keeping his ears open had paid off. Besides, those chairs were heavy sumbitches. Wrestling them around was no job for a pair of ladies.

With the front of the library locked up, the girls said their good-byes. He guessed the Toyota was her car, and he was right. He slammed Horace's door, his throat doing some funny things.

Ginny had her phone out, and lifted it to her ear. She stood there for a little bit, watching as the blonde headed for a maroon Volvo with bald tires. Finally, dropping her phone into her black purse—looked like a map satchel, really—the library girl walked with her braided head down, a blue knitted scarf wrapped around her pretty neck, visibly shivering. Her skirt was blue, too, and her calves worked smoothly, bare to the wind. She halted, looking at her car, and her shoulders sagged.

Those circles under her eyes were darker, and she'd disappeared once or twice during the meeting, coming back with a slightly reddened nose and damp, matted eyelashes. Lee kept his ears peeled, but nobody said anything about *her.* Just about the goddamn curfew.

Wait a second. Take a closer look.

Ginny tipped her head back; the other woman—the blonde with the softly moving hips and gentle, pacific smile—had already started her car and dropped it into gear. Wasting no time getting out of Dodge. Lee's Chevy was the only other vehicle left in the lot, and the Ginny's Toyota sagged near the back right end a little more than it should.

Horace was rolling down his window. "What is it?"

"Looks like she's got a flat." Lee glanced over the parking lot again, checking his ground. The streetlights looked cold, the circles of glow around their bases pulled tight. The wind had veered around from the northeast, and it smelled not only of ice but of snow, too. Maybe the weather-monkeys had been right.

The night was clear, but it wouldn't stay that way. The blonde girl's Volvo vanished, taking a hard right onto Thrush Street.

"The library gal? Oh, shit." Horace reached for the door handle. "You got a jack in this thing?"

"Course I do." Lee took another few seconds to think the situation over. Yeah, she had a flat. She stood there, looking up at the sky like she was asking God why he was so damn mean, and her shoulders trembled under her wool peacoat. Shivering, or something else? "You stay here, Horace. No need for you to get frostbite."

The old man was determined to rescue a damsel or two more in his life, though. "The hell I will. Think she's got a spare?"

"Hope so." Lee tapped the door. "I mean it, stay in there. I ain't having you come down with pneumonia." With that, he set off across the lot, glad he'd worn his old boots. They gripped just right, and he didn't have to worry about the glass. Ginny didn't look down until he got within ten feet, and her sudden, flinching movement made him stop dead.

"Looks like you've got a flat." The words came out smoothly; looked like third time was the charm talking to her. "You got yourself a spare?"

"I..." Her nose was red. There was a glitter on her cheek—a tear-track? Maybe. Good Lord, was she crying over a flat tire? Nah, there had to be something else. "Oh. It's you." She sounded surprised, and those big dark eyes were swimming. "I...I think I have Triple A, I just..." Honey curls worked free, falling down into her face, and part of that shaking was the cold. She was out here bare-legged, despite the peacoat. "I should call, or..."

"Come on." He held out a hand. "You got a spare in there?"

"I...I think so." She blinked, and yes, those were tears. Blinked back, her mouth firming and her chin lifting a little, like a good little soldier.

Lee's fingers itched to be doing something useful, and that funny tight sensation in his chest might have made him think he was having a problem with the old ticker if it hadn't been usual from every other time he saw her. "Well, let's take a look. That your key?"

She did have a spare, it turned out. Looked like it hadn't been touched since the Toyota came off the factory line, but it was better than a flat. He started his truck, introduced her to Horace, put her in the driver's seat with the heater on, and took his jack, his iron, and his flashlight from the shovel box in the truck bed.

It felt good to be doing something right again, even if he skinned his knuckles twice working the jack to where it needed to be.

THE SECOND TIME SHE GOT OUT OF THE TRUCK, HE HAD JUST sworn a lug nut loose—the third one, and the toughest sumbitch he'd wrestled in a while—and was sweating a little despite the wind picking up. It was so cold he couldn't get even a breath of her perfume when she appeared at his side.

"Can I help?" She bent down to peer at his progress. "Hold the flashlight, anything?"

He craned to look over his shoulder, his breath a cloud shredded by the moving chill. "You can get back on in the truck so you don't freeze to death, ma'am."

"It's *Ginny*." A tremor of a smile. "Not ma'am."

He unfolded from his crouch, glad to rest his legs for a few seconds, and offered his right hand. "Pleasure, Ginny. I'm Lee."

"Oh. Yes." She gave a soft shake, and now he was worrying that he'd greased up her fingers. "Short for Virginia."

"Mine's just short."

Her tentative smile eased up and widened. It was getting easier to talk to her, and he wanted that smile to stay, but it was damn cold out here.

"I just...I should help." She crossed her arms, cupping her elbows, hugging herself. Against the cold, or against him? "I have Triple A, I could at least call someone out to—"

"Take 'em an hour to get here, or more. Be on your way before then. Just go back to the truck, keep Horace company, he ain't talked to a pretty girl since the Bush administration."

"The first, or the second?" Her teeth began to chatter halfway through the last word, and Lee scratched at his cheek, smearing a bit of greasy dirt on his stubble. "Seriously, let me do *something*."

It was damn nice of her to offer, but this was Lee's job, and he intended to finish it. "Get on back in the truck, Miss Virginia." His ears perked, and he half-turned, looking across the lot. "I'll have this all done up in a jiff."

The laundromat at the end of the strip, on the other side of the FOR RENT signs in the old Elks Lodge windows, was shuttered, dark and squat. Between it and Thrush Avenue there was a strip of waste green, scrub bush that had lost its green unless it was thorny enough to draw blood. Lee's eyes narrowed. His night vision was pretty good, and he could swear something was moving in there. Too big to be a possum, and it was too early in the winter for the deer to be desperate enough to traipse through the Crossing. The bushes rustled, and the back of Lee's neck prickled.

She sounded amused instead of nervous, now. "I think that's the first time in my life someone's called me Miss Virginia."

Might not be the last. "Proud to be the first." He did *not* like the idea of something in the bushes, no matter what it was. "Listen, get on in the truck and warm up. Horace gets confused sometimes, and I don't want him thinking about drivin."

"Yes sir." There was that ghost of a smile again. He froze where he was, his attention split between the way the expression made her even more impossibly beautiful and the sense that something was in those bushes, probably watching them. "Mr Quartine?"

It's a fair ways away. Just keep an eye on it. It bothered him, though. "You can call me Lee."

She nodded. Her teeth kept chattering, and she inhaled sharply. "Thank you, Mr Lee." All in one breath, so the words didn't get chopped up.

Just Lee. He didn't say it. At least she didn't call him *Little Lee.* He might die of embarrassment. As it was, he scratched again at his cheek and nodded. "Go on now, get warmed up."

He watched her walk back to his truck, purring along nice and sweet. Horace was probably already asleep in the passenger side. When she got in and slammed the door, whatever was in the bushes rustled and rattled...and took off, vanishing behind the laundromat.

Lee bent back to his work, only slightly slowed by a persistent unease. He kept checking over his shoulder the whole time, but whatever had been in the bushes didn't come back.

When he was done, he paced back to his truck. Horace wasn't asleep, his mouth was moving a mile a minute; Lee rapped on his window twice with his unskinned knuckles.

"—tell you, look at that. Good with his hands, that's Little Lee." Horace grinned pacifically.

Oh, for Chrissake. "I put the flat in your trunk, ma'am. That spare won't go above thirty mile'n hour, though."

"It's all right, I live on Sixteenth." She peered past Horace's large nose, her earrings glittering in the glow from the dash, and he had no time to wonder what stories the old man had been filling her with.

"Hm." He nodded, and hoped his face was shut tight as one of her library books. "Well, let's see if'n it'll start up." Welcome warmth poured through the open window onto Lee's hand, and she immediately opened the door on the other side. All told, it hadn't taken more than a half-hour. She'd still be waiting for a tow truck, shivering in her car.

The Toyota started just fine; she sagged in the driver's seat with a sigh of relief. Her radio was on, giving out a tinkling set of notes from the classical station in Lewiston. She snapped it off, and started rustling in her black purse. "So...what do I owe you, Mr Lee?"

"Not a damn thing." He winced inwardly. "Sorry. I mean, nothin at all." Maybe she didn't know how damn insulting that was. At least he was talking without stuttering. Small mercies. "Listen, we'll folla you home. Make sure that spare holds up."

"Um." She bit her lower lip, darted a glance at the truck, and he could have kicked himself sideways. Now she probably thought he was a creeper, and God knew he wouldn't mind finding out where she hung her hat. "I...I mean, that's not necessary. It's just a couple miles."

Of course, she'd said Sixteenth, and he could just look for her car. Which certainly made him *feel* like a creeper, because he could easily talk himself into it. You got into the habit of figuring out things like that, and it didn't go away. "Horace'll give me hell, pardon my language, if we don't make sure you get home all right, ma'am."

The small smile had changed, turned into an uncomfortable, placatory expression. "I could call when I—"

"I don't have no cell." Short, clipped little words.

"Wow." Her eyebrows went up. "Really? That's...wow."

Yeah, I'm just a backwoods idiot. "But I'll give you my number, and if you want, you can leave a message on my machine." He tried not to think about turning around and driving back to the Crossing if the spare went out on her.

"You have an answering machine? That's amazing." She pulled her legs in, settling herself on the seat, and he tried not to look at her knees. Her skirt had ridden up, and it was distracting. "Like, with a tape and everything?"

"Ayup." *Still works, no reason to get rid of it.* His hands throbbed, from the cold and the effort.

She tilted her head back and regarded him. He was trying not to loom over her slightness, and his scraped hand throbbed in time to his heartbeat. "You can follow me home," she said, softly. "I'm just not used to, you know, strangers being helpful."

"They don't do that in the big city?"

"Not in New York, no." She sobered instantly, her expression slamming shut just like a door.

"That where you're from?"

"Um-hmm." A quick nod. "I have...my family's back there.

Anyway, yes, thank you. Maybe I can get you and Mr Horace some coffee or something?"

He sensed it was merely a polite offer, and shook his head. "No ma'am. Giving him coffee after 8pm means he'll be up all night, and guess who he'll blame for that." He reached for the brim of his hat, realized he wasn't wearing one. Maybe that was why it was so damn cold, even though the inside of his chest had turned to hot milk. "Let's get you home."

[13]

DO ANY GOOD

Dr Harry Vardalam, recently divorced and nursing an ulcer his now-ex wife had of *course* suspected before he did, hunched over the printouts, rubbing at his burning eyes and pushing his steel-rimmed glasses up. His graying mane—thank God he wasn't losing his hair—was wildly mussed. Sometimes he thought it made him look a little dashing, like Feynman. The tensor lamp over the table focused a raw white circle of brilliance, but the rest of the lab was dark. The centrifuges and other machinery were motionless. There was no point in sequencing or investigating further, you couldn't stuff the monster back in the coffin.

Pandora wasn't applicable, Harry thought sourly, because that bitch was entirely innocent.

Oh, there was plausible deniability—taking the step to experiment on the general population had been greenlit at the highest possible levels, and it was a millions-to-one chance that anything could have gone wrong, so on, so forth. But when the right hand didn't know what the left was doing, when everyone was firewalled from everyone else, things slipped through those smooth, curving walls. It didn't matter, at this point, whether someone had been asleep at the switch and let a live batch through, or if there had been a jiggle in combining it with the dead flu. Viruses were good at surviving, good at changing shape, and good at spreading themselves. Little packets delivered straight into cells, hijacking the body's processes to expand. This particular strain had been chosen for its recuperative powers. Controlled, it could grant better functioning, higher sensory acuity, higher oxygen uptake, all things that would help build a better soldier.

That was probably the first mistake. Mutation was a fact of life, testing with the dead strain only a stepping-stone. *Watch out for that first step,* they used to say in the cartoons. *It's a lulu.*

Had it resurrected? Mixed with live flu somehow, even though it wasn't supposed to? Had someone decided it could go in *any* vaccine, not just the dead one?

"What can you tell me?" Hank Johnston said, from the other side of the table. He was a bland man with a bland, shadowed face, and at first Harry thought he was chewing tobacco until the other man pulled a container of wintergreen Tums out of his open briefcase.

Harry pulled a rolling chair up. He kept stumbling over the question, trying to fit the pattern together inside his aching head. "New York, San Diego, Chicago." Two of the three biggest cities in the US, and you could make a case that anything that went into San Diego would spread down into Tijuana and up to LA in short order. From there, well.

"And Houston," Johnston added.

A short, burping laugh escaped the foul taste in Harry's mouth. "Houston? What the fuck?"

"Don't ask." Another man might have said it offhand, but Johnston didn't have an *offhand.* Not during this visit.

Tissue samples from some of the first casualties were intriguing, until Harry stepped back and considered the effects on the whole organism. That was the trouble with defense work. The larger lines got hazy, your focus got laser-intense, and before you knew it, you had people coughing up a live strain subtly different than the safe one, the one that behaved. "Okay. With the metrics you've given me, we're looking at...well, you want the bad news first, or the bad news?"

Johnston's shadowed expression didn't change. Or at least, what Harry could see of it didn't. "Don't fuck around, Vardalam. You're not my only stop tonight."

"All right, all right. Look, with what you've given me, all I can say it, you'd better hope it burns itself out. Or that there's a cure being mass-produced in some DOD basement."

"What about overseas?"

"If sixty percent of them managed to reach the target populations listed, it's worldwide." And then, if America had the cure, the military-industrial complex would have its biggest payoff yet. If, that was, anyone was around to actually *pay* them once this finished. "You boys sure know how to spread the pain."

"Wasn't my decision." Did Johnston sound irritated?

He damn well *should*, Harry thought. The flu. The goddamn *flu* vaccine. "I can't tell if—"

He was interrupted by Johnston's coughing. One, two, three deep-chested, dry sounds.

Harry leapt back, the chair falling over and barking his calf a good one. "Jesus *Christ!*"

"It's bronchitis," Johnston said, dryly. "Had it for months. Not running a fever." His hands were busy inside the briefcase, stowing the Tums.

The tensor lamp wiggled, a wobbling searchlight. Harry rubbed at his forehead, sheepishly. "Yeah. Okay. Not that it'd do any good, with the way this thing spreads." His gaze strayed back to the print-outs. "It's fascinating."

"Yeah." Johnston closed the briefcase, but didn't lock it. There was something in his hands, a dull metal gleam. "I'm sorry about this, Doctor."

Harry Vardalam's heart lodged in his throat. "What are you—"

"Housecleaning." Hank Johnston squeezed the trigger. A dark hole appeared in the center of the virologist's forehead, and he staggered back, clattering over his discarded chair and falling gracelessly. The body was a sack of potatoes, and the sudden brassy stink of death rustled through the lab. "Not that it'll do any good."

Johnston coughed again, this time rackingly. The tensor lamp's glow didn't show the great clear beads of sweat on his forehead. The loose ends he could reach were tidied away. If there was a cure, it was outside his bailiwick. The Umbrella, even in what could be termed its death throes, was thorough, and its apostles concerned only with their duties.

Moments later, the lab, like the entire building, was empty.

[14]

RING AGAIN

ICE CAME IN THAT NIGHT, THE SKY TURNED TO BEATEN IRON. Winter arrived all at once, and whatever weeds had luxuriated in leftover summer curling up and yellowing under the assault. Martin's Motors had a cloudy front window and a Hawaiian calendar behind the front register, posters about worker safety and taking care of your car from the seventies plastered over every inch of space, a wheezing coffeemaker giving out a tang of burned Folger's, and a bell on the old, piss-yellow counter.

Ginny waited for a few minutes at the counter. The place smelled like dry snot and engine grease as well as cooked instant coffee, but this was where Mr Quartine had told her to bring the car. *Don't go to Shellack's, he'll gouge you. Go to Tip & Thurgood's—it says Martin's on the window—and tell Billy Tipton there Lee Quartine sent you.*

She probably should have taken the car to Les Schwab in Lewiston, but that would mean freeway driving, and Lee—she couldn't call him Military Felon now, it would be uncharitable—was right, the spare wasn't rated for anything over a crawl.

The door to the garage itself was open, and an unholy racket poured into this shed passing for an office. A radio was blaring some country song about a goodbye town, and she wrinkled her nose a little. Why did all the goddamn recording artists affect a drawl when they were from Schenectady?

Finally, she tapped the bell, and the tiny ding made no impression on the general hubbub. But about half the hubbub stopped on a dime, and a squat fireplug of a man in blue overalls with *TIPTON* stitched on his breast pocket appeared in the door, working at his grimy hands with a red lint-free shop rag. He had muttonchops and stiff, bristly black hair, and only needed a cigar chomped in his teeth plus an Italian accent to be from Brooklyn.

"Y'hallo," he half-yelled, the word turning to taffy in his mouth. "What can we do you for?"

"Hi." She tried a smile. At least she'd passed out as soon as her head hit the pillow last night, waking up with her uncharged phone clutched in a sweating fist and the wind keening at the edges of the duplex. "I, uh, have some tire trouble. Lee Quartine said to—"

"Little Lee? Hang on." He yelled back over his shoulder. *"LEE YOU SUMBITCH, GET ON OVER HERE."*

Ginny winced. The racket diminished by a third, and the man turned back.

"Sorry about that. Gotta yell, or they don't hear you." He grinned, showing very white teeth. "You from out of town?"

Well, she'd heard *that* in a million different ways, in every business in this shitty little burg. "I work at the library."

His muttonchops were truly extraordinary. "The what now?"

You've probably never been inside one. "The library."

"Oh, yeah. I read off'n my Kindle nowadays." He nodded sagely, and a familiar face appeared over his blue-clad shoulder. "Lee, you know this gal?"

Lee Quartine ducked his head a bit, reaching as if to touch a hatbrim when his gaze met hers. "She got a tire needs fixin, Tip. Still in your trunk, Miss Virginia?"

Huh? It took her a second to figure out what he was saying through the music, and she finally nodded. "It is. Right where you left it."

That made the short squat guy's eyebrows climb up the top of his forehead, two hairy beetles arching surprised backs. Lee just nodded. "Keys?"

She still had them in her hand, and before she thought about it she looped them at him, a nice accurate throw. His hand shot over the short man's shoulder, and he caught them, including her Hello Kitty keychain. Kitty was in a red devil costume, her tiny un-hands holding a small plastic pitchfork that had broken off during its stay in her various bags.

"Holy sh—" The short guy ducked too late. "Gol*durn*it, *warn* a man!"

The corners of Lee's hazel-ish eyes crinkled, and he outright *grinned* at her. It made him look a lot younger, and she couldn't help smiling back. He wasn't nearly as old as she thought. "Keep on your toes, Tip." Lee clapped Tipton's meaty shoulder, and vanished with her car keys.

That made the short man examine Ginny from head to *her* toes, and she shifted her weight from one foot to the other, wishing she hadn't worn heels. But she had to head off to work if she got out of here in anything resembling time. Bobbi Evrard had told her to take the day off to get her car fixed, but if she went home after this she would just prowl her house, calling everyone she could think of in New York and getting no answer but unable to help herself from dialing again, again, and again.

The thought made the bottom drop out of her stomach.

"Sorry," she offered, awkwardly. "I'm a little...it's been a rough week."

"Yeah, tell me about it." He shook his head. "Everyone's jumpy round here, thinking one of those towel-heads gonna shoot 'em at any minute. Buncha fools, you ask me." He waved the rag at her, apparently forgetting she was an out-of-towner, or maybe just assuming she shared his racist little thoughts on the matter. Although she could at least agree heartily that this part of the US was full of fools. "Have some coffee while you wait, ma'am. We'll get you right fixed up, shouldn't take long."

"Thank you." She was already digging for her phone. Surprisingly, this place had free wifi, and at least it was warm though the door to the garage was wide open. She settled in the single anemic orange plastic chair, foregoing the offer of boiled coffee, and dialed her parents again, plugging her other ear to shut out the noise.

She listened to it ring, again.

And again.

[15]

PRICE TAG HIDDEN

"She ain't from around here." Billy Tipton was interested as all get out, as Lee found the culprit wedged in the tire. It wasn't glass, it was a damn bolt, probably dropped off someone's truck and driven over, neat as you please. It was an easy patch, though. "What you doin at the library, Little Lee?"

"Community meetin. Old man Slipot needed a driver." He tried to make sure his face was shut tight, again. At least he was dirty, it wouldn't show if he blushed.

Or so he hoped.

"Mighty kind of you." Tip had a busted fuel pump to deal with, and Lolly Harlowe's Cadillac was having unspecified trouble again. Lady Lolly wouldn't drive anything else, since the Caddy had belonged to that Confederate sumbitch she'd married way back at the turn of last century or before. Between Lee and Tip, they'd kept the old thing running well past its Biblically-appointed threescore and ten, so to speak. "She's pretty. For a Yankee."

"Hadn't noticed," Lee lied. "Hey, Juju!"

Jujube Thurgood swore violently, metal clattered, and he glared at Lee from under a station wagon hauled in that morning. "What you want?"

"Throw me a tire plug, willya?"

"Get it your own damnself." But Juju stamped for a pile of parts, his close-cropped, wooly head bobbing. He'd gotten that limp in Iraq, and when Tipton came back and took over his daddy's business, Juju came with him. Tip called him "my brother" and fixed anyone who said—or even *implied*—shit about it with a steely glare that shut them up right quick. You didn't want to test a Tipton's temper, and Billy was a Major on his mother's side, too.

The people who didn't like being glared at went to Shellack's, though they knew Harvey Shellack Jr was a cheat. Lee figured that was one way to suss out who was worth a damn and who wasn't in the Crossing.

"So, you been goin around fixin Yankee girls' tires, there, Lee?" Tipton had the bit in his strong, even teeth, and was fixing to run with it.

Lee contented himself with a grunt, checking the reamer and giving the edges of the hole a grinding. Not too wide, or the plug wouldn't fit. He'd been expecting the top of a beer bottle or something like that, tearing and gouging. He was also surprised she'd listened to him about coming here.

"Me, I don't fancy me no curly-haired city girls." Tipton propped a hip against the Camaro stupid Billy Nodlesse had bought. The thing leaked oil like a sieve, but he kept pouring his paychecks from stocking at Landy's into it.

"We all know who *you* fancy," Juju weighed in, stamping up with a plug and a frozen-shut jar of cement for it. "She brought her Nova in here just last week, and you gave her a discount."

Discount was more like "free." Lee almost winced. He wouldn't want to be the one yanking Tip's tail about *that*. Juju was probably the only one who could get away with it.

Still, he couldn't help himself. "You know she's still married, right?" *And Andy Bowe has a shotgun he ain't afraid to use.* Tip had been sweet on Lila Bowe since high school, when she'd been Lila Anderson on the cheerleading squad. Andy married her quick, before anyone knew how true the Bowe mean streak ran.

"Everyone knows." Tip's broad face reddened, and he kneed the Camaro's side, viciously. "Everyone knows what he does to her, too." This was old news, but at least it got them off the subject of curly-haired Yankee girls. It would take a goddamn miracle for Lila to leave Andy. Especially with the kids.

You couldn't run with rugrats clutching at your legs. Nonna Q said once that some women got to be like dogs if you beat 'em enough, too—got to thinking they couldn't even crawl away, and just hunkered down waiting for the hurricane to pass. Poppa Q had remarked that a woman who let a man beat her was a fool, and Nonna had refused to cook for him for a whole week. It only took two cans of cold beans he had to shovel himself for him to say he was sorry, but she didn't forgive him for five days after that.

It was the sort of thing that stuck with a kid. Especially when she slammed a rolling pin on the table when your grandaddy sat down to eat his favorite fried chicken and hissed *I didn't cook this for you, Emanuel Quartine.*

Juju just shook his finely modeled head, as if Tip was too stupid to be believed but he wasn't going to push the issue. "You got that fuel pump pulled out yet?"

"Shit." Tip stamped away, and Lee glanced up. He could just see her through the window to the back of the counter—the chair was placed so you could keep an eye on whoever sat in the office. She had her phone to her ear, but her mouth wasn't moving. She was just...listening.

Family in New York. Well, the news out of there wasn't good, from what Lee heard on the radio in the Chevy this morning. It was a long way from the Big Apple to the Crossing, that was for damn sure.

When he stepped into the office again, she was sitting like a schoolgirl, her ankles crossed neatly, staring down at her phone as if willing it to ring. He cleared his throat, and when she looked up, those big dark eyes were full of something lost. You could see right into the back of someone when they looked like that. She blinked, though, and had her walls back up. Today there was no sun to bring the honey out in her hair.

He wasn't used to *wanting* to talk. It was a damn uncomfortable sensation, like a boil in the middle of your throat, pushing any damn-fool thing out to relieve the pressure. "Any news from your folks?"

She shook her head, hurriedly rising; the braids wrapped around her head barely keeping the curl confined. Looked like they wanted to work free with a vengeance today. He wondered what her shampoo smelled like, and decided *that* thought wasn't good for him. Too damn distracting.

"Not yet." She stepped to the counter with the nervous quickness of a doe, her heels making soft feminine sounds. "What do I owe you?"

"Don't you worry none." He tried to sound reassuring. Outside the office door, Juju cussed at something and Tipton answered him. It was Tip's day to pick the music, and his iPod plugged into the CD player was full of nothing but country. It was irksome, but not as much as Juju's opera. *Just listen,* Juju would say. *That's Kathleen Battle, you asshole.* "Phones are probably just corked up."

"It just rings and rings." She rested her purse on the counter, digging in it. "And the news...I just don't even."

She didn't say what she just didn't even, just pulled out a slim calfskin wallet-and-checkbook number. It looked fancy. She flipped it open, and Lee could have kicked himself. "No charge, Miss Virginia."

That earned him a startled, wary look. "But—"

"Just a hole in the tire. Weren't no trouble to fix. Here's your keys." He handed them over, and wished she didn't look so...well, so goddamn chary. But a pretty girl was probably used to all sorts of presents that had a price tag hidden under the wrapping. "You just call us if'n you have more trouble."

"I can't just not pay you. I mean, I appreciate the gesture, but—"

How about I buy you a cup of coffee, and you tell me all about your folks? That wasn't something he could say, though. Patience was the best policy right now. At least he could make a few words come out, if he wasn't looking directly into those eyes of hers. Inspiration struck. "Wellnow, there is something."

"What?" Her shoulders tensed up, just a bit.

"Well, Tip in there got his Kindle, and he reads all sorts. I never did like reading in school, but it ain't so bad now. Trouble is, I don't know where to start." *I am lying my ass off.* "Maybe you could do me a list of things a man can work through that ain't *War and Peace?*"

"You know about *War and Peace.*" A smile dawned far back behind her eyes, and spread over her face like sunrise over the mountain. Lee damn near lost his breath. "That's a good sign. I'd be happy to."

"I'd be obliged," he lied again. And he *did* lose his breath, because that smile was bright enough to turn a man inside out.

Shit. Now he was gonna *have* to start reading.

[16]

THIRD REFORMED FISH FRY

The Third Reformed annual Fall Fish Fry was usually a roaring success. This year was no different, though a bad cold was running through the entire congregation and those heathens who just came for some of Bill Porter's fish stew. He had some sort of fancy French name for it, but served with cornbread it was good enough nobody cared. Bill never did give out the whole recipe for it, and those who sought to compare versions he parted grudgingly with over the years often came to grief. The weather was fine, mild sunshine but a chill wind, just damp and cold enough to make the long firepit for the baked taters and charred fresh-caught a comfort. Smoke and the smell of good things filled the air, and perhaps that was why there was so much coughing and sniffling going around.

Margie from the diner was there, with trays and trays of her famous jalapeño cornbread cooked in the church's capacious kitchen, along with Hannah Dee's braided rolls and pots of Samantha Harlowe's—Lolly's granddaughter, and just as stubborn as any of that line—baked beans. Harvey and LaWanda Shellack and their entire brood were there, managing the parking and just generally being officious; Pastor Denbrooke more than once had to shake his head when one of his flock came to him looking worried. *No*, he kept saying, *I talked to the sheriff, there's no parking tickets this year either.*

The Bowes showed up but left early, as did the McCannocks and the Pooles, but that was no surprise since the Pooles were all but feuding with the Crearys and everyone knew *they* would be late. The only Creary who ever arrived near time for anything was old Elmore, because his mother was a Packer and the Packers were even *born* early. Old El being on time was splitting the difference, so to speak.

The fry was supposed to be dry, being church and all, but this was ridge-runner country. So of course Harvey Shellack brought beer and the Francklins, who wouldn't be outdone by anyone, had their usual big jar full of lemons and ice. A couple fifths of vodka were added in the parking lot, the entire thing wrapped in a towel, and the whole Francklin tribe—at least, anyone who was tall enough—walked around "shaking the baby" until the towel froze to the glass. And as usual, every year, some of the kids got their hands on the lemons after they were fished out, and the Francklins looked down their noses at the Shellacks who just snuck in *beer*, and cheap beer at that.

At least this year nobody fell in the fire, and the barbecue grills brought by every family ended up scrubbed clean as a whistle for once. Maria Porter was heard to say she couldn't remember a better Fall Fry, which was amazing since she generally found fault with anything her beloved home church *First* Baptist did not host.

Perhaps one or two people might have been forgiven for thinking that it had gone well because the heathen crowd usually drawn by free food was awful thin, and some familiar faces were missing. It was the first time in a long time Lolly Harlowe hadn't shown up with her beloved Cadillac, even though Samantha said the boys at Tipton's had fixed it up just fine, drawing a sour look from any Shellacks around to hear. Polly Denbrooke's apple pies were missed, since she was laid up with the bad cold that was doing the rounds; the Clooneys and the Beaujolaises were missing too, and half the

Howisons. But all in all, everyone agreed, wiping runny noses or feeling the foreheads of flush-cheeked children who had probably been at the Francklin's lemons, it was a success.

It was also, though none of them knew it, the very last.

AN HOUR LEFT

Sunday. A full week since she'd talked to her mother. *Still* no answer, and she couldn't raise anyone else. The internet, for once, was no goddamn help at all. All her emails to Flo—or anyone else on the East Coast—fell into a dark well. No reply, not even a bounce.

It was, Ginny had decided last night, time for desperate measures. She already had a call *and* an email in to Bobbie, explaining the situation and apologizing in advance for the scheduling difficulties that would no doubt result. Just sitting around was no longer an option, even if all the news outlets said not to travel towards the affected areas.

If there were no trains, no planes, and no buses she was left with automobile. She was already packed; all she had to do was stop at home after closing up the Cotton Crossing branch and pick up her suitcases, stuff what she could from her fridge into the cooler, and *go*. She'd already made up her mind to avoid the checkpoints on the freeway towards Lewiston after sitting in her car for a good hour at one Thursday evening, and again on Friday. There was no subway to use, and now she understood Californian road rage better than she ever had living in New York.

Which added up to her taking the most current road atlas the Crossing branch had up to the desk, since she couldn't call up a map on the checkout terminal *or* stare at her phone and try to figure out alternate routes while she was supposed to be serving patrons. There *had* to be a way to avoid the roadblocks, and while she was at it, she'd have to think about the intervening states too. She had GPS and could pick up an atlas on the way, but a little pre-research never did anyone harm.

Now that she was planning and making mental lists, everything seemed a little brighter, even if the library was full this morning. No few patrons were congregated at the reading tables, buzzing over the latest news. Whatever it was, Ginny barely cared. Come three o'clock, she would be on the road. She didn't even care that blonde, pink-phoned Philly Lou hadn't seen fit to show up.

Ginny traced a gray line with her finger. Logging road? It looked like it went over the county line, and if it did—

"Takin a vacation?" Lee Quartine stepped back from the counter, visibly realizing he'd startled her. Today he wore a shearling jacket over that same leather vest and pressed chambray shirt, and it made his shoulders absurdly bigger. "Sorry, Miss Virginia."

Ginny pressed her right hand to her chest, exhaling. "Jesus." It came out on a whisper, almost a squeak. "Wow. I didn't even hear you."

"Didn't mean to spook ya." Today it wasn't a baseball hat; a battered cowboy hat with a broad leather band dangled from one work-roughened hand. He really looked better without a hat, but maybe it was camouflage. Or like the ugly, boxlike brown sweater she'd worn all through sixth grade, a comfort item. He also held the same paper Landy's bag as usual. His hands were clean for a mechanic's, a faint redness around his nails. Looked like he'd scrubbed until he broke the skin.

Lee glanced over his shoulder at the reading tables, and the crowd. "You all right?"

Very few people were using the computers today. It was the first time she'd seen *them* empty on a Sunday. Some of her regular readers were missing, too. Elmore Creary hadn't come in, even though she'd laid the paper out for him, and as Ginny blinked, trying to slow her racing pulse, her unease sharpened to a keen edge against her already-frayed nerves. "Yeah, I'm just..." She flipped the atlas closed. "Just making some plans. I can't get through to my parents. It's been a week."

That made him tip his chin down and examine her. His eyes were pretty piercing when they lightened up; she hadn't noticed how he *looked* at things before. Maybe he'd just had to watch her for a while before he figured she was worth talking to. Insular, like the rest of this town.

Now that she'd said it out loud, the words kept spilling free. "All the flights east are cancelled. Same thing with trains, and the buses don't go any closer than Ohio and are full anyway." *I'm doing the nervous talking thing.* "It's just so...*weird*."

"Huh." He absorbed this, swinging his hat once, twice, shooing an invisible fly. "Yeah, had to go the back way into Lewiston yesterday."

"There's a back way?" That sounded promising.

A brief nod, dark hair falling over his forehead. "Ayuh. Need a bit of jacked-up, though. Rip the bottom right out of your Toyota."

Well, shit. "Great."

He took a long look at her, his jaw set, and finally nodded slightly, like she'd made a good point. "Might be best to stay where you're at."

"I can't." She said it as if she'd just realized as much, and maybe she had. "My parents are older, and my sister's pregnant. She's about to hatch any day now. I just...I need to be with them."

"Kin is kin." He obviously wanted to say more, but stopped and glanced over his shoulder again.

She was probably keeping him from canoodling with his fellow townies. "Oh, hey. Can you wait here for a second? I have something for you."

He nodded, that short quick decided motion, and she headed for the employee room. She'd even found a camouflage gift bag and some matching tissue paper, and that was part of why she'd been caught in the crush coming back from Lewiston on Friday.

When she returned, he hadn't moved, other than to set the Landy's bag on the counter. He was watching the reading tables, a faint line between his eyebrows.

She pushed the camo bag across the counter. "Here."

"What in the he—I mean, what's that?" Lee tilted his head a little more, and his look of bafflement was so honest she was hard put not to laugh.

"It's for you. I stopped at the Schaply's in Lewiston. Some reading material to get you started."

He poked at the tissue paper as if he expected it to bite him. "Huh. Do I open it now?"

"Sure, if you want. Your list's in there, too." It was the only time she felt actually *good* about something in a whole week, especially because his disbelief turned to a slow, easy smile that did good things for both his eyes and his mouth. Ginny rested her elbows on the counter, bending to relieve the ache in her lower back. One day she was going to wear comfortable shoes to work, but that day was far off. "I divided it into threes. You'll see."

"Huh. Zane Gray." He fished out the new paperback edition of *The Lone Star Ranger*. "He a classic?"

"You've checked out that one twice, I thought I'd get you one of your own. There's some Jack London in there, too. I think you'd like him. Plus there's Hemingway, but don't be scared. You'll like him too."

"Wellnow." He turned *The Lone Star Ranger* over in his hands. Shadows of engine grease worked in on his knuckles, looked like he'd about rubbed himself raw to get it off. "I checked it out twice?"

"Uh-huh." She watched him rustle the paper, looking at the other books. "Thank you for fixing my tire."

"If I'd known you was fixin to drive I'd've changed the oil, too."

Well, wasn't that chivalrous of him. "I got it changed a month ago, it's fine."

He found the card. It was just a simple blank one, with kittens on the front—everyone liked kittens, even country boys, right? A Mills girl always did her thank-you cards correctly. "Look at that." He stared at the inside as if it was written in code, and finally closed it, tucking it into his vest. Looked like he had a secret pocket there. "That's real nice, Miss Virginia."

"Thank you, Mr Lee." She straightened, and pulled the Landy's bag closer. "I'll check these in for you."

"Do I take the whole bag?" He rustled the tissue paper again. "It's a nice one. You could reuse it."

"Well, it's yours now. You can carry your ammo in it." Christ knew the people around here loved their guns.

"Prolly too heavy." He straightened, too, carefully sliding the card's envelope into the gift bag. "Guess I got my readin material for the week."

"I guess you do." *I probably won't be back to hear how you liked it.* She had finished emptying the Landy's sack, and folded it up carefully for him. "Good luck, Mr Quartine."

He nodded, reached up as if to touch his hatbrim, remembered he didn't have his hat on when he almost hit himself with the book in his hand, turned around, and marched out, leaving the Landy's bag. But he carried the gifts close, like a schoolboy with an assignment he didn't want to let the rain get at.

Ginny's good feeling couldn't last, but it was nice while it stayed. It was one o'clock. She had an hour left before she could close up.

[18]

HE TALKS STRAIGHT

Well, damn. Lee realized he was wearing a big stupid grin just before he walked into the Mayburn Dinette, and pulled the corners of his mouth down to their accustomed places or where he thought those might be. So she was looking at heading out to try to reach her parents? Examining a map with a serious, abstracted air, he'd startled her but good. She was back to the gold hoops in her ears and the thin gold bracelets, and her hair was twisted up in a fancy knot at the back of her head.

The gift bag was heavy paper painted to look like old-style jungle camo, and the note on the card was simple. *Thank you so much,* signed *Ginny.* Even her handwriting was pretty. And *new* books. Fresh, with their spines uncracked and their pages still crisp white. *You checked that one out twice.*

Was it the kind of thing all librarians noticed, or had she...oh, *hell.* He hadn't even asked her when she was fixing on leaving. He'd taken a peek at the fluids in her Toyota when he'd fixed the tire, topping off the windshield wiper tank, but if she was going east it would need—

"Well, Little Lee." Margie, her hair as red as Clairol could make it and her long-nosed face like an old statue's, sang out his name soon as he stepped inside. "Been a while, honey. Want some coffee?"

He nodded, heading for the booth in the far back. The church crowd was just finishing up, and he could put his back to the wall and think about things. He had to clean the table off himself, both Margie and Steph had their hands full. He didn't mind, it got him what he wanted, which was something to do with his hands while he mulled over things.

"Hey Lee," redheaded Rooster called from the kitchen. "Want your usual?"

Lee tipped a nod his direction too, squinting a bit. Today the cook's T-shirt was white, and that was a good sign. It was when Rooster got mournful you had to watch out for him.

Everything in the Dinette was familiar—the red-checked vinyl tablecloths, the orange vinyl of the booths, the one crooked barstool on the end nobody sat on because it was where old Pop Fisk had his last coronary and hit the floor kicking. Fisk was a big man; one of his boots jackhammered the base of the stool, and that was that. There was the ancient pay phone in the hall to the restrooms, the glow of the scrubbed black-and-white linoleum, and the hiss of something hitting the grill. The Sunday rush left the place full of the ghost of bacon, toasted bread, all sorts of potato products, coffee, and the humid exhalation of a crowd bringing all its heat and noise inside because outside was too damn cold. It was gonna snow; the only mystery was why it had just threatened instead of dumping the season's first frosting.

At least Margie and Steph were too busy to bother him for a bit. So he could settle and look at the books. The card was in his breast pocket, and it felt...warm. Like a secret campfire, banked and hidden in a dell.

When Ginny bent over, resting on the counter, her scoop neck had loosened a little, and made it hard to think. He'd barely noticed all the old-timers gabbing near the library tables—everyone who was dissatisfied with the mayor and the checkpoints on the highway would naturally congregate there, especially since the Elks Lodge used to be right next door. There was the Grange, of course, but it was on the outskirts of town, not right here convenient. Besides, YoYo Howison had the keys, and old YoYo was a cranky bastard who didn't take to change in his routine well.

The Jack London books looked a little thin. They were both about dogs. The Zane Gray...he hadn't even cracked the ones he'd brought home, preferring that Louie Lammer guy. The Hemingway —the name sounded familiar, but he couldn't quite place it. *Farewell to Arms*. Huh.

"Hullo, Mr Quartine." Stephanie Meacham, with her daddy's blue eyes and her mother's wispy changecolor hair, halted breathless at his table. Her pink apron had a smear of ketchup right at waist-level, her hair was sliding out of its ponytail, and she looked flushed and lathered as a runaway horse. "Got your coffee right here. You want orange juice?"

"No thank you. How's your folks, Steph?"

"Oh, Daddy's fine. Mama's upset over the news. Everyone's talking about it."

All over town, jaws were working. "Yeah."

"Wow." Steph set down a thick white china mug, and if his nose was still good, they'd made a fresh pot of coffee instead of giving him the cooked leftovers. Margie was all right. "You readin Hemingway? We read him in school."

"Didya?" He slid the gift bag off towards the ketchup and the salt and pepper shakers, standing to attention like good soldiers. "He any good?"

"Real good, I think. He talks straight. Not like Shakespeare. I hate that shi—I mean, I don't like him." She pinkened afresh, and hurried away. The cash register near the front door began its usual clinking and dinging, and the bell on the door jangled as people filtered out. Rooster was listening to something in the kitchen— sounded like a news report. It took a while for the crowd to clear.

By the time Margie brought his ham and eggs—over easy, white toast with no butter, the ham cut thick and a pot of gravy for dippin'—he had already read the first few bits. It wasn't bad. The words were short, and he understood them. They were laid out nice and simple. He'd never been assigned *this* to read in school. It might have kept him interested. He'd known soldiers like the one in love with the nurse, and wondered what the nurse saw in the man.

Margie slid his plate easily along the table. "Never figured you for a scholar, Little Lee."

"Hi, Margie." His choice of reading material was going to be all over the Crossing by dinnertime, unless she had something more interesting to pass along. "How's you?"

"Oh, running my ass off. Nobody going out to Lewiston anymore if they can help it, means they come back in here and to the Tasty Freez." She rested her broad, capable hands on her ample hips, her big red hand-beaded earrings swaying. "Even the delivery trucks have a hard time gettin through. I swear, Lee, whole world's gone crazy."

"So I keep hearin."

"It's terrorists." Her voice dropped, low and confidential, and her blue gaze was unsettled and sharply intelligent. No moss grew on that girl, they all said. "They ain't lettin anyone go east of Lewiston. Stoppin cars right on the road, especially out near base. I hear some of those roadblocks got soldiers with rifles, Lee."

"I ain't seen any yet." He weighed up the likeliness of it. "That's serious, if they got 'em out where anyone can see." Grandon's visit was taking on a different tone, now. Still, some stubborn part of Lee didn't want to open the damn envelope the old man had left, or that package. If old Hold Yo' Balls Grandon was expecting Lee to jump into shit headfirst again and get drowned, he had another think coming.

"Don't I know it. Percy and Blotzer are both takin' orders from some colonel." Both of Margie's sons had gone into the Army. Both had been sent to Afghanistan, too. One had come home in a box, the other was on his second tour of duty. "I don't like this, Lee. What if it's the UN? They gonna come take *our* guns away and burn our flags too."

I think they'd have to vote on that shit first, Marge. "Wellnow, that would be quite a feat."

She agreed with a wry half-smile and a toss of her bright-red head. "Half the people at First Baptist didn't show up for church today. And then there's that crazy talk about things in the woods. You hear about that?"

"Some." He wanted to go back to the book, but Margie wouldn't let him until she'd unloaded her cargo. So Lee ate a few slow bites, not tasting a single bit of it, and nodded and made the right noises until the bell over the door jangled again and Mark Kasprak stepped in, thin and nervous, his Adam's-apple bobbing and his indigo parka big enough for two of him.

"Margie?" Kasprak was so pale he looked damn near transparent, his straight thick dishwater hair a bird's nest. "You, uh, you might wanna close up." He took a deep breath, hectic color high on his thin cheeks. "There's something in the road."

[19]

STAY WITH ME

It didn't take long to load the car and make sure her plants were all watered. The sky was still a dark-gray pan and the wind getting ready to cut everything in its path when Ginny pulled out of her driveway. She turned the heat up, glad she'd stopped to change into jeans and her hiking boots. A few feathers touched the windshield—tiny snowflakes, dashed away as she drove back into downtown Cotton Crossing. She didn't have to go towards Lewiston, she could head north for a bit and *then* try working east.

She hadn't heard back from Bobbie, but that seemed a small consideration now she was packed up and ready. She'd stop at Landy's just before they closed. The place had no decent cheese, but it had about fifty different types of pop—and quite a few energy drinks. She could drive all night if she had to, then make decisions in a hotel closer to her goal.

Motton's Coffee was still open, and the diner, too. A little caffeine pregaming was probably a good idea. The best thing about being a confirmed tea drinker was that coffee wired you *right* up when you occasionally partook.

Sunset dyed the west bloody behind the low end of the mountains, a furnace that made the moaning wind even colder. Ginny turned left off Main and pulled into one of the angled spots on Third, the Toyota's nose whispering into kissing distance of an old discolored brick wall. On its other side was Happy Cow Feed Store and Dry Goods, and you could still see a mural on the brick proclaiming as much. Faded, pitted, and worn, it had obviously been painted in the fifties. Postwar boom had come tardily to the Crossing and left early; the reverberations could still be seen if you knew how to look.

You could find history in the oddest places, she thought, bracing herself for the cold. It wasn't that bad while she was between the buildings—Third was really a glorified alley, when all was said and done—but the instant she stepped out onto Main she got a faceful of small icy snowflakes, stinging her cheeks. Motton's was across the street, and maybe, just *maybe*, she could get there and score a decent espresso before they were really for-truly closed.

There was a strange popping, zinging noise. Ginny swung around, staring up Main Street, and at first the shapes she saw didn't make any sense.

Something was in the road, straddling the anemic yellow line on cracked pavement brushed by long tails and feathers of hard small snow-pellets whisked along by the wind. At first she thought it was a dog, because it crouched, then it swelled upwards and she saw it was human-shape. There was another zinging noise, snatched away by the wind, and a chunk of the paving near the thing threw itself into the air.

What the hell? Her mouth fell open a little, and she stared, trying to figure out what on earth was happening.

Another shadow darted from the mouth of Fifth Street, which ran at a slight angle because of the slope of downtown. More pops, zings, and now she heard faint yelling. Headlights bloomed behind a wispy veil of dry snow, coming over the crest of Cotton Hill.

Something jangled behind her, but she didn't move. What the hell *was* that thing? The shadow was moving at a ground-eating lope, and even though it was human-shaped, nothing human moved like that. It was *wrong,* and more chunks of pavement began to evaporate, jumping like popcorn.

Wait a second. Those are...that's guns. Someone's shooting at those things.

What were they? She squinted, trying to see clearly through the haze of tiny whirling white. A third creature showed up, scuttling out from Fifth Street on the right, and someone was calling her name.

"Ginny!" He grabbed her, and she let out a hurt little cry, because he had an arm over her chest, picking her clean off her feet and dragging her backward. "Goddammit, woman, they're shootin! Come on!"

The headlights glared from a Jeep, dabbed and splashed all shades of military green, its engine suddenly revving to shred the wind's low moaning. One of the things had turned, its head making a queer quick fluid movement as if it was sniffing, and it surged upward right before flashes poured from the throat of a gun mounted high up on the Jeep's back end. Ginny, transfixed, watched as the exploding chunks of pavement stitched busily up Main Street and caught the sniffing thing. It twisted and jerked like a wet sheet on a clothesline in a storm, and now she heard yelling and the deep barking of a helicopter's blades. There were men in uniform in the Jeep, one of them working the gun that was making all the popcorn, and Lee Quartine, his shearling jacket flapping, dragged her bodily through the diner door and spun, flinging them both to the ground.

Ginny's head hit something hard and she yelped again; someone else was saying *ohmyGod oh my God they're shooting,* a woman was yelling *get the fuck down, you idjit!*

She lay on sticky linoleum, staring at a line of barstool posts bolted to the floor, their flared bases marching away down the long counter. A trickle of gummy heat slid down her forehead; she began to thrash because someone was on *top* of her, he had her pinned and nothing made sense, there was a rushing in her head and—

"Calm *down!*" he yelled, practically in her ear, his breath brushing her cheek. "I ain't gonna hurt you, just calm *down!*"

She froze. Her heart thundered so hard it threatened to push her right out of consciousness. The noise in her head made it hard to think. He was heavy, and the chaos was now large and furious. Glass shivered into breaking, the windows chewed by the yells and the hideous *chuggachuggachugga* of the gun. The man atop her tensed, curling over like he wanted to shove them both into the linoleum, and Ginny Mills began to scream.

IT SEEMED TO STOP ALL AT ONCE, BUT MAYBE THAT WAS ONLY because she ran out of breath for screaming and could only make soft, choked sounds. Or maybe it was because Lee Quartine rolled off her and gained his knees with an easy, reflexive movement, hunkering low and peering out the diner's shattered glass front. Cold poured over her—of course, the windows were broken. It all happened so *fast*. Someone was heaving, deep retching sounds. Someone else was sobbing, and for a moment she thought it was her sister. Flo cried like that when she was a kid, messily and completely, making little shaking, sucking noises on the inhale.

Ginny's breath came in huge shudders. She blinked, swallowed, and tried to *think*.

"Lee?" A woman's voice, from the other side of the counter. "Lee, is it safe?"

"Hang on." He moved forward, duckwalking, his boots grinding on broken glass. It was *everywhere*, the whole front of the diner was shattered except for the knee-high brick wall that had held the window up. The bell on the door made a soft tinkling as the wind keened, bringing in the reek of exhaust and fresh air as well as a funny coppery smell. "Just everyone stay where you are." His back looked very broad under the shearling, its hem brushing the floor behind him.

The gunfire was retreating down Main. Ginny looked to her left, to her right. Her hair was probably full of crap now, the floor was *filthy.* She rolled carefully onto her side, pushing herself up. *The car. I have to get back to my car.*

"Stay down, Miss Virginia." Lee didn't even look back. Could he hear her moving? "Just stay where you are."

Oh, hell no. "My car." Her throat was so dry, the words were a frog-croak. "I have to get back to my car."

"It ain't gonna go bad, and you don't want to be out there right now." Lee shifted easily in his crouch, peering over the window-brim. "Kasprak?"

"Yessir?" A young male voice behind her. Ginny flinched, her head whipping to the side to see a skinny teenage boy who had taken shelter in a booth midway down the diner. He had a shock of dark hair, big muddy-dark eyes, and looked about as scared as Ginny felt right now.

"How many of them critters did you see?"

The kid's Adam's-apple bobbed. His hair might have started out with an emo-fringe across his forehead, but it was a bristling tangle now, ratted up by wind, motion, and sheer terror. "Just one, and the Army guys."

"How many Army? Walkin, not ridin." Lee sounded very calm. He kept peering through the now nonexistent window, let out a sharp breath. Ginny pulled her knees up, hoping she wasn't sitting on broken glass, her right hand braced on the only piece of floor around her that wasn't full of sharp edges, dust, and other crap. Shards of a thick white ceramic plate lay under the counter; she stared, trying to figure out how they got there. Something sticky dripped in her eyes; she seemed to be moving through mud, lifting her free hand to rub at her forehead. Had someone spilled something on her? Coffee? Syrup?

"Two-three?" The boy's throat moved as he swallowed. "On foot. Looked like they was tracking the...the critter. The thing. Lee, I could swear to God that thing was..."

"What?" Short and even. How could he sound so...so *unruffled?*

The kid shook his head, ducking back into the booth for cover as a spatter of popping sounds drifted on the wind. He looked like he was peering over a bannister on Christmas morning. "It's crazy."

"Well, spit it out." Lee shuffled back, still duckwalking, and half-turned on the ball of one booted foot, looking down at Ginny. The color drained from his close-shaven cheeks.

"I could *swear* it was wearing old man Sandleford's coat. That blue one. With fur." His parka was so huge, he was almost lost in it. The boy hunched, his fingers braced on the booth-back, trying to make himself smaller.

Ginny could relate. *Okay. First step, standing up. Then get to the car. Go home.*

Everything around her went away with a whoosh, receding in a gray haze. She sagged, and Lee caught her shoulders, his fingers sinking in. "...shock," she heard him say, from very far away. Motion all around her, and someone brushing at the sticky mess on her forehead.

"Ginny. *Ginny.*" Someone saying her name. "Ginny, honey, you stay with me now. You just stay with me."

I don't want to, she thought, syrup-slow. *I want to go home.* Going upstairs to her bedroom, closing the door, and getting into bed sounded like the best option, given the situation, and to do that she needed to get to her car. Once she got home, she could *think,* and...

Hands on her. Her arm lifted, someone holding her waist. Ginny tried to help, staring numbly downward, struggling to think.

Later, all she could remember of the next twenty minutes were vague flashes. Her own voice, answering persistent questions, someone holding something to her mouth. Liquid scorched as it went down her throat—it was coffee, strong and sweet, and she would be awake for driving if she could just get to her car.

The only other thing she remembered was Lee Quartine's voice, slow and patient but with a snap of command.

You stay with me, Ginny. You just stay with me.

[20]

NO SECONDARIES

HE GOT EVERY CIVILIAN INTO THE KITCHEN WITH A MINIMUM
of fuss, all but carrying Ginny. Little Steph Meacham'd caught a
chunk of glass through the top of her arm, but the ancient first-aid
kit was still good. Mark Kasprak got a pressure bandage on her
while Rooster hit the gas shutoff valves for the grills and turned the
deep fryer and everything else off. Margie gathered up everyone's
coats, it was getting cold as fuck in here with the windows gone, and
Lee lifted Ginny's hair, checking the shallow slice along her
forehead.

Bright blood streaked Ginny's chalky face, and she shivered,
clutching at her purse. "My car," she whispered. "I want to go home."

"I know," he told her, grimly. Shock was dangerous—he wiped at
the blood with a wad of paper napkins, then grabbed a fresh pad of
them and clamped them on. Head wounds were messy, but this one
was superficial. He checked her pupils—dilated so far her irises were
thin rings, like the gold bracelets she wore. "We'll figure it out. Just
stay with me, Ginny."

"I want to go *home*," she repeated. She wasn't shivering, and that
was a bad sign.

"I know, darlin." The shakes were a damn natural response, though, all things considered. "Just you stay with me now."

"Who's that?" Margie appeared, hunching nervously and glancing over the order-up counter. Her earrings swung, clacking like little beaded bones, and though she was calm, her cheeks were dead flour-white too.

"I know her. That's Miz Mills, from the library," Kasprak volunteered. "That too tight, Steph?" He bit his lower lip, anxiously, and now Lee knew his reason for coming by the diner late on a Sunday. He was probably looking to walk Steph home, braving even Bull Meacham's temper. Which bespoke a certain strength of character, or just dumb calf-love. Mark was only nineteen, and Steph was what, two years younger?

Lee couldn't ever remember being that young.

"I...I think it's fine." Steph gulped. Her fine, changecolor hair had darkened, full of dust like Ginny's. "What the hell *was* that?" She rubbed her palms on her ketchup-spotted apron, a little harder than necessary.

"Army, looked like." Lee didn't want to say more, but he had to. "Huntin down whatever was in the road." *Someone's gonna get chewed out for this.* Firing on a civilian street? Who was dumb enough to do *that*? The thought that maybe the situation was suddenly bad enough to require it was uncomfortable, to say the least. "All right. Everyone get your coat on, and Rooster, you want to peek and see if the coffeepot got hit? Need some strong and sweet for all'a'us."

"Yessir." Rooster Clane had been in the Navy a while back, and he was steady despite his habit of going on a tear every Friday out at the roadhouse near Elm Creek. He was a short, banty little man, with a ruff of thinning red hair and a round Irish face full of broken blood vessels and a many-times-broken nose. For all that, there were very few men in town Lee would feel relieved to have in a Situation, and he was one of them.

"Lord, I'm glad you're here." Margie, blinking heavily, shrugged into her long, puffy, violently pink coat. She'd never get shot during hunting season wearing *that.* "What the hell is goin on, Lee? What was out there?"

"Is it the terrorists?" Steph Meacham's voice broke on the last syllable. Mark glanced at Lee, his eyes round.

Time to steady the troops. "I don't know *what* it was, and if'n it's terrorists the Army's on them now." Easy to say it it with confidence he didn't feel. There was a squidgy sensation deep in his gut, one that usually only showed up when things were about to go sideways worse than they already were; how he hated that feeling. "We'll have a little coffee, make sure the ruckus has died down, then Rooster'll take you home, Margie. Kasprak, tell me you or Steph drove here."

"Yes, sir." The boy nodded. Give him something to focus on, and he was just fine. Grateful for it, even. "Just bought me a pickup last week." Unconscious pride swelled his shoulders a bit, and Steph looked up at him, her baby blues widening.

Looked like the calf-love went both ways.

"Then you'll drive little Stephanie there home and make sure she gets in her front door all right." It was a damn good thing he didn't have to load the kids in his truck along with Ginny. "Where you parked?"

The boy eased himself down to sit with his back against the freezer door, as close to Steph as he could get. "Right on Third."

That got Ginny's attention. Her chin came up a little. "Third Street," she said, softly. Even her lips were pale. "I...I parked there."

You ain't drivin, darlin. "All right. Now listen, Mark, you want to swing out on Third, turn west, and go down a bit before you cross over to get to the Meacham's. The Army might stop you, but if they do, just say yessir and nosir and tell them you're takin her home."

"The Army?" Margie was still staring at the wreckage. "Imma sue them for this. Ruined my front window, and now there's bullets in my seats."

Good luck with that. "Yeah, you do that after you get home,

Marge." Lee restrained the urge to run a hand through his hair. Might be broken glass caught in it, and where was his hat? It didn't matter.

Rooster appeared with the sloshing coffeepot and a few cups that had survived, trapped by broad capable fingers through their handles. His cook's apron was filthy with the remains of the Sunday rush, and now full of dust, too. Funny thing, how every time a building got shot, the air was full of grainy shit.

"You was in the service too, Lee. What you think of this?" Rooster had also swiped a handful of sugar packets, and crouched to tear them open and dump them in the coffee while Margie gave the cups a going-over with another wad of napkins to clean them out.

"Don't know what to think, yet." Lee almost winced. Ginny's gaze had sharpened, her pupils shrinking a bit. He didn't like how pale she was. "Ginny? You hurt anywhere?" He'd already asked her that four times, and she seemed fine, but the blood drying on her face gave him a funny feeling. Unsteady, like the shimmer over gasoline. Added to the squidgy in his gut, it was an unwelcome distraction just when he needed to be doing his thinking cold.

She reached up dreamily to touch his hand, holding the napkins to her forehead. Her fingers came away tacky-wet with blood and gritty with dirt, and she blinked at them. "Oh. No."

Distant gunfire popped outside. No secondary troops coming in to look for casualties. That meant he needed to get all of them out of here, because it was still a hot zone.

"Hold this." He took Ginny's hand back, not liking the way she was staring at the blood. Pressed her palm firmly to the napkins. "All right? You hold that. Pour out that coffee, Rooster, and everyone take a swig. Then we gotta move."

It had finally decided to snow. Outside the diner's back door was the alley parallel to Cherry Lane, and it was a straight shot down to Third. Lee checked it, sniffed the wind, and heard more gunfire, moving mostly eastward. *Clear enough*, he decided, and hustled them out. Rooster and Margie hurried up the alley for Rooster's big-ass black Ford parked behind the Clapton County Credit Union, and Ginny, under Lee's arm, had largely lost that disturbing glassy-eyed look. Still, he kept hold of her, and Steph Meacham rushed Mark along since the boy was trying to look everywhere at once.

Instead of small, hard spatters, the snow had turned into thick fat goosedown, the wind slacking just a little and the sudden slight warming only serving to underscore how cold it would get later when the howler truly arrived. It would muffle shots, but also cover movements. The package stuffed inside his shearling was bulky and uncomfortable, full of sharp edges, but he managed.

Kasprak's new truck was a small yellow Chevy, and as soon as they reached it Ginny began pulling away. Lee had to clamp his arm down to keep her still while he cautioned Mark again. "You be careful, you hear me? And give my best to your pa."

"Yessir." Mark closed a pale, shivering Steph in the cab. "Thanks."

Lee nodded, and Ginny finished shaking his arm away. Her Toyota crouched a few steps to windward, snow melting on its hood. He hadn't thought to ask what she'd been doing on the street—coming into Mayburn's for Sunday dinner? Who knew? The thing was, she was probably still shocky, and driving wasn't a good idea. "Miss Virginia. *Ginny*."

Mark wasted no time starting his truck. Lee lengthened his stride —she was moving along right quick. "Ginny, now slow down. You ain't thinking so straight right now—"

"I want to go *home*." Some color had returned to her cheeks, and her chin set.

"I understand that. But—" He searched for something that would distract her. "You ain't in no shape to be driving."

"I'm *fine*. I just want to go home." Traces of dried blood clung to her pretty face, and her hair was well and truly tangled, the braids across her head coming loose. Curls sprang free, catching snowflakes, crowning her with winter. She'd started shivering too, just like little Steph, and Lee hoped Bull Meacham wouldn't see red when Kasprak drove up with his wounded daughter.

That wasn't his problem right now. His problem was digging her soft little hand in her coat pocket, fishing out her keys, and halting, swaying a little. She stared up Third Street, past her car, and Lee's skin shrank all over him. Was there another critter up there?

Don't think about that. Just get her somewheres safe. "I know you want to go home, but I'd 'preciate a ride to my truck, ma'am." He kept moving, nice and easy so he didn't spook her. "Hand me them keys, and we'll get you home, I promise."

She turned then, sharply, honey-dark curls swinging, and looked up at him. Thin threads of paper from the napkins clung to the slice just under her hairline. Looked like she would bruise around it, too, her skin was so fine. It about knocked the breath out of him, because she was so close he could *feel* the heat from her even through her coat and his. Her bottom lip trembled just a bit, and Lee's hands itched fiercely. He had to get her out of here, he could still hear firing around east.

The pop-pings of thrown bullets had stopped moving away. Which side of Sixteenth did she live on? He finally remembered, but it took longer than he liked. Getting distracted was bad for him.

Bad for them both.

"You promise?" Looking at him like she'd never seen him before.

"I do, darlin." He'd promise just about anything to get her under cover right about now. "Give me those keys."

Thoughts moved behind her dark eyes. She was coming back, thank God. They had to move, but if he pushed her, she might decide he was up to no good, and that would make things unmanageable. "You...okay. Wait. Where did *you* park?"

"Just off'n Sixth. Hopin they didn't shoot my truck."

A quick, nervous shake of her head, like a surprised horse. "Jesus Christ. This is insane."

"Yeah, well, whole lot of that goin on." He should check over her shoulder, look at Fifth and Main for shadows, anything approaching. He couldn't take his eyes off her, though. Her nose reddening, the fans of her dark lashes, a stippling of dried blood on her cheek. Her lips. Her mouth was downright sinful, pursed a little like that.

"Okay." Her shoulders went back and her chin lifted a little. He'd seen that before, her little movement, bracing herself. "Get in."

"Darlin, you ain't in no condition to drive."

"It's *my* car," she replied, and took a step back, toward the Toyota. Another. If she slipped, he'd have to lunge to catch her. "I'll manage. Come on."

[21]

A WHOLE LOT LESS, AND A WHOLE LOT MORE

GINNY TURNED THE KEY, THE ENGINE CAUGHT JUST AS USUAL, and a hot splotch of relief opened behind her breastbone. "Oh, thank God."

"Amen." Lee was all but doubled up in the passenger seat, his long rangy frame too big for an import. "Best to go down the alley to get to Sixth. Real slow."

"Yeah." Now that she was in her own car, the last half-hour began to feel distant. Dreamlike. Her hands shook a little, but that was okay. Everything was okay now.

No, it's not. They shot at me. In broad daylight. On the street.

"Sure you don't want me to drive?" He sounded worried.

Well, that was reasonable, she told herself. This was a worrying situation indeed. "I'm *fine*." If she kept repeating it, she might eventually believe.

Backing out, turning the wipers on because the snow was thickening, flipping the headlights on. Dropping the car into drive. All things her body knew how to do. The great thing about it was once you learned, you just thought about where you wanted the car to go, and you didn't have to...

You didn't have to think about glass shattering, or pavement popping like popcorn, or someone laying on top of her. Or the noise as the world went screeching off course, a vast shattering overwhelming racket filling your skull.

"Here's Sixth. Hang on a minute." Lee leaned forward. He smelled like coffee, fresh air, and some edge of clean soap and male she couldn't quite place. He looked both ways, though there was nothing but snow beginning to accumulate at the edges of the streets. Seen from here, Cotton Crossing looked normal, and the feeling of being in a nightmare returned, closing iron bands around her lungs. This was unreal. Even the past week had to be some kind of practical joke. An illusion. Something. "All right. My truck's right there. You live on the west side of Sixteenth, right?"

"What?" Other than the engine running and the wipers' steady heartbeat, it was so *quiet* in here. The thought of turning on the radio scraped against her nerves. Her scalp itched, and Lee's profile was straight and severe as he studied the street.

"What's your house number?" He stared out the windshield like the snow, or the general situation, was a puzzle he wanted to solve.

You should know. You followed me home. "801. 801B, it's a duplex."

"All right." He exhaled, sharply. "Let me out here. You turn left and go on down until you hit Poplar by the Kramer house with all the whirlygigs in the yard, then turn up. It'll zag a bit, but it'll get you home without goin through whatever's happenin eastward. Imma bring my truck and folla." His drawl had thickened, if that were possible. "You just go slow, and you keep your doors locked. You see anything strange, you just keep going. You hear me?"

Bossing me around is not going to help. But he had a point, avoiding Main Street was a very good idea. She hadn't known Poplar went all the way through, but now she did. "All right."

He gave her a long critical look, that piercing gaze uncomfortably chill now that his eyes had lightened past hazel, almost into yellow.

What did you say to a man who had dragged you into a diner and thrown himself over you? Nothing seemed even remotely applicable.

"Lee?" His name sounded strange. They pronounced it more towards the back of their mouths, almost like *lay*. The others in the diner had obeyed him without question, like these sorts of things were ho-hum small town living.

"Yeah?" That grim set to his mouth told her he expected another problem to solve.

"You saved my life." *I would have just stood there. Why? I don't know, but I would have.* "Thank you."

He ducked his head a little. Where was his hat? His hair was full of grit, and snowflakes turning to crystal droplets as they melted. "I, uh. Well. Welcome. You're welcome."

It was entirely inadequate, really, to just give a polite two words to a guy who had dragged you to safety. What *did* you say?

She didn't have a chance to figure it out, because he opened the door and was gone into the snow, head up, scanning Sixth Street. He moved oddly, and after a moment she realized he was looking for cover along the front of the ancient dry-cleaner's and a small storefront that had stood empty for as long as she'd been in the Crossing.

He was less felon and more military. A whole lot less of one, and a whole lot more of the other, it seemed.

She watched until she saw his red-and-white truck begin to back out of its parking space. It was running, he had his headlights on, he was going to be fine.

Ginny took a deep, shaking breath, hit her turn signal, and turned left. He'd told her to go slowly, and it was snowing, but she just wanted to be *home*. He was right, Poplar did go all the way through, and as soon as she saw her duplex she let out a grateful half-sob.

That was when the worst thought of the day hit her right in the stomach and spread a loose, sickening heat all through her.

Oh, God. Did this happen to my parents, too?

[22]

OLD MIZ CLAMPETT

"LET ME OFF AT THE CORNER." STEPH HUGGED HER BACKPACK, heavy with homework she wouldn't sit in a booth at the diner and finish, now. Her hair was full of stuff and she couldn't stop shivering, even though Mark had the yellow truck's heater on full blast. The sidewalk crept by, snow whirling in thickening curtains.

Mark frowned at the road, his bony hands capable on the wheel. "Lee said—"

"Daddy'll have a cow if he sees me riding with a boy." No matter *what* Mr Quartine said. Although if *he* was there, Daddy would probably listen before he started yelling. Little Lee just had that way about him, people said.

"I could talk to him." Mark's hair stood up wildly, and anyone who looked at them might think they'd been Making Out instead of... oh, she didn't want to think about that. It made her head hurt. Maybe some Army boys were joyriding, the way Daddy said he'd done when he was young, knocking mailboxes over.

Except diner windows weren't mailboxes, and bullets weren't baseball bats. Steph rubbed at her hairline, grimacing at the gritty stuff in her hair. "He'll take one look at me and thinks something happened."

Mark was sweet, not like those other boys. "Well, something *did* happen, we got—"

"Yeah, but not the something Daddy'll think." She shook her head, deciding to wait on picking her scalp clean. A shower sounded mighty good. "Nah, just let me off at the corner. He'll call the diner to check up anyway, and then Mama will call Margie at home and they'll listen to *her*."

Mark slanted her a single worried, dark-eyed glance, his cheeks burning. Probably just red from the cold. "It just...I wish I could talk to your dad."

"It wouldn't help. Believe me." Her shivers eased a bit once the truck warmed up, and she watched Third Street go by out the window. Mark carefully went west, and everything was fine until he hit the brakes. That snapped her chin forward, and she saw the...the *thing* lollop across the road in the whirling snow.

It was a *woman*. It looked like Bessie Clampett, who had the trick of making paper-thin gingersnaps and painted plates that the old ladies bought each other for birthdays and anniversaries. But Mrs Clampett would *never* be out in a snowstorm in only a thin print dress, her fish-white, varicose-raddled legs pumping and her pale-pink undies showing as she scrambled on all fours, her head bobbing funnily. Her reddish wig was askew, and as Steph goggled, almost unable to comprehend what she was witnessing, the short cap of fake auburn curls flew free, bobby pins skittering away. Mrs Clampett's bare feet stamped on the pavement, and she bolted into the greenbelt next to the closed-up Chevron station.

Steph darted a glance at Mark. "You saw that, right?" Squeaky, and breathless.

"I, uh." Mark swallowed hard, the funny bump every boy started to get in their throat bobbing up and down. "It, uh, looked like old Miz Clampett."

Something hot and rancid was in Steph's throat, and it wasn't the coffee Mr Quartine had insisted everyone drink. She swallowed, her stomach flipflopping uneasily, and the thought that Mark might not like her as much if she horked all over his new truck was the only thing that kept her from doing it.

"Steph?" Mark shook his head, violently, as if trying to dislodge what he'd seen. "Am I crazy?"

"No," she whispered. "Her wig is still there."

The glossy fake-red pile lay inside out on the sidewalk, snowflakes catching in its nylon cap.

"Jesus." Mark sounded choked. "Jesus *Christ*."

At school Steph would have made a face at the taking of the Lord's name in vain, because it's what her mother did in public, though Mama could lay down a string of swears more blistering than even Daddy's full-throated cascade when he skinned his knuckles on something. Once, when she was younger, Steph had set out to ask her mother why one set of swears was okay but the other was BLAS-PHEMY—you could hear the capital letters every time Mama said it —but she lost her nerve halfway down the stairs.

Her hands ached, probably because they clutched at each other with hysterical strength. "Uh, Mark?"

"Yeah?"

"Maybe you *can* drive me all the way home."

"Yeah." He nodded, and checked to make sure the truck was in gear, though he hadn't moved the shifter. "Yeah, I think I should."

[23]

UPTOWN

Nice little duplex, painted brown, snug and trim. Yard mowed, still green in spots from the just-fled false summer. The left half of the duplex had a maroon minivan crouching in the open garage and a child's plastic playhouse on their lawn; Ginny had a doohickey to open the garage door for her half. The Toyota pulled into that neat, bare little cube with cupboards along the back and stopped, brake lights flashing a bit before she cut the engine.

He'd had a chance to peek in her backseat. She had a cooler in there, a nice blue plastic cube. You could store a a week's worth of campin' food in something that size, so she might have been on her way out of town.

The thought of her driving into trouble like they'd just had without someone around to keep her head down just about turned him cold, despite his truck blasting heat from the vents. Something was going on in Cotton Crossing, and despite doing his best to ignore everything outside his small piece of stompin' ground, Lee had heard enough to know that it was happening elsewhere, too. A whole lot of elsewhere, which meant interesting times ahead.

The Toyota's brake lights went off, but she didn't get out of her car. Lee cut the truck's engine and got it settled. He spent a few moments looking down at the small rectangular metal box peeking out from under the seat. It was attached to the seat mounts with a steel cable, and stayed there, rain or shine. Every two weeks he took its cargo out, checked and cleaned it.

Question was, could he—or *should* he—take it inside? Mostly, toting it was more bother than it was worth. Some bastards with teensy balls had to have one with them even in the goddamn john to make a point, but Lee figured if he wasn't in a war zone or fixin' to kill, why, he shouldn't carry.

Unfortunately, his combat sense was tingling. *They was out on the street in broad daylight, with a merry little popper on a Jeep. Not a Humvee, but pretty effective. Mobile and nasty, with infantry coming along the sides. Pigeon shoot, dammit, but no secondary troops to check for casualties. What the hell?*

Ginny wasn't likely to take kindly to him bringing a piece inside. She was a city girl, and probably what Poppa Q would have called a damn librul, defending every amendment except the Second.

You're assumin' she'll invite you in, Lee.

The thing was, he didn't want to leave her alone. Maybe he should just...get her settled, and see how she was?

Hell. He was more worried about *her* than he was about why Main Street had just been shot to shit. Or why Grandon had shown up at his house. Lee sighed, took Ginny's package from under his coat, and laid it on the seat. The fancy gift bag was torn and crumpled, and a dull, pointless anger struggled to surface under the grip he had on himself. Every time you got something nice, the world decided to step on it.

At least the books were all right, though gravy had splattered the cover of the Hemingway. Lee sighed, stacked the books neatly, and reached for his door.

Ginny still hadn't gotten out of her car. She was just sitting there, her garage a cave with boxes stacked all along the far side—looked like she hadn't even unpacked all the way—and not a toolchest or a rack in sight. Lee tapped on her window, and she flinched. But that got her moving.

She got out of the Toyota like her bones were creaking. Probably were, too, he hadn't helped by landing on top of her. But *damn* it, she'd just been standing in the street. Frozen like a rabbit. That was usual for civilians—you sank to the level of your training in a crisis, and normal folk didn't have much call to hit the floor when there was incoming.

Lee waited for her to say something, thumbs stuck in his belt. Out of the wind, it wasn't bad, but the snow had begun in earnest, skipping along on a brisk breeze that rose sharpish when it got its legs under it. It was gonna drift up anywhere there was a wind-shadow. Occasionally he glanced down the cul-de-sac towards Sixteenth and found himself tensing. This kind of weather put blinders on. You wouldn't see someone until they were too close to avoid, especially after a few hours.

Finally, Ginny moved again, half-climbing back in the car to get her red purse. "Why don't you go inside?" A soft, flat question, too calm.

"You ain't invited me." He looked for a way to close the garage door. "Should close this up, Miss Virginia."

"Just press the button, it's right there." She straightened, caught him looking out at the cul-de-sac, and whirled, one of her braids slipping loose and falling over her ear. She stared at the snow and the street like she expected to see the Second Coming, and Lee realized he'd spooked her.

"It's all right." He tried to sound soothing. "Ain't nothin out there."

That earned him a mistrustful, hopeful little glance. "Are you sure?"

"Yeah." *Sure enough.* Something bothered him, though. "Just lookin. Don't like being surprised."

A brittle, jagged little laugh escaped her. "Oh, yeah. That would be a bad thing. That would just finish today off *perfectly*."

Snow slid into the garage, fingering along the floor with a dry hissing whisper. Lee decided, turned sharply, and two long strides got him to the door leading inside, with a rickety wooden step braced under it. He pressed the rectangular red button wired to the wall to the left of the door, and after about eight seconds of clatter he was alone with Ginny, the wind suddenly a comforting whistle because it was *outside*. A whole lot of things were better on the outside of your walls.

"Okay." She hitched her purse strap a little higher and reached for her fallen braid, pushing at it with her fingertips. "You can go on in. I have to...I think I should bring the cooler in."

"I'll do that. You go get warmed up."

In the end, she popped the trunk and brought in her suitcase, a pretty black number with wheels and a handle so you didn't break your back lugging it. Lee toted the cooler, and kept trying to figure out why he was so uneasy.

He should have been downright overjoyed at being invited into her house. Instead, he knew he was missing something, and he didn't like that feeling. Not one bit.

GOD DAMN, BUT SHE WAS UPTOWN.

It was a big place for a single girl—two bedrooms and a master bath upstairs, a living room bigger than his own, downstairs half-bathroom, a neat kitchen all scrubbed and shiny with new appliances, dining room attached, a glass door out onto a patio. It looked like a showroom, all the furniture matching and the bookshelves arranged with little knick-knacks. There wasn't a doily in sight, just books, more books, a pale cream couch—surely you couldn't sit on the thing, was it just for show? And plants in pots, on the south-facing windowsills or clustered underneath, taking advantage of every scrap of light. Upstairs was smaller, so the living room had a skylight, and the peculiar cold infinite glow of snow filled the room. It was a little chilly, because she'd turned the heat down before she left but hadn't opened the cupboards so the pipes wouldn't freeze. Damn good thing she'd come back.

What got to him most were the books. She worked around them all day, and it looked like she came home to more of the same. Even her knick-knacks were quality—an elephant carved out of some shiny stone, a small wooden statue of a fat man with his eyes closed, probably praying, a little bell that looked like sterling silver, a blue glass apple on a high shelf between two thick books on European history. The pictures hung up were actual *art*, too, copies of paintings he wouldn't be able to name but she probably could rattle off all sorts of trivia about.

Christ. He knew she was class, but this was...

The half-bath downstairs was just sink and commode, sharing space with a small but new stacked washer and dryer set, but it was full of peach towels and washcloths, small decorative soaps in a glass dish, sparkling-clean mirror, and a framed picture of an old-timey sailing ship. It was enough to make a man feel like a lout for pissing. Regardless, his back teeth were floating, and he at least knew to use the liquid hand soap instead of the pretty little rosettes of scented froufrou. Even that liquid was scented with peach.

Jesus.

The mirror showed him a stubbled idiot with dusty hair standing up every which way, hatless and in a scuffed jacket full of crap from the diner floor. Cheeks raw from the cold and his hands still grimy no matter how much GoJo he used, his jeans well past news and fraying at the hems, and his old Army kickers. He was a sad goddamn sight, and he was likely to knock something over or sit on it wrong and break it if he stayed here.

Water ran upstairs. The heat pump kicked into life. The best thing to do was probably to go out her front door, crunch through the rising snow, get in his truck, and get out while he could.

He stood in the middle of her living room—she'd even left the curtains wide open, for God's sake. His truck sat patiently in the driveway, the snow still melting on the hood and windows but coming down thicker and eventually winning. He could make it home all right, even without chains, if he left in the next hour.

Lee rubbed at his eyes. He was nervy as shit, and that was not good. He kept thinking he saw things moving in the flying snow, like the things the Army boys had been shooting down.

Human size. Human shape. But movin' wrong.

There was one thing she didn't have. A tee-vee. Just those book-shelves, and he couldn't turn *them* to a news channel and start piecing things together. He watched the light fade out the window by degrees, squinting every time the snow eddied or whirled, and saw nothing but figments of his own imagination.

Lee's hands turned into fists. Hell of a goddamn day, he was still keyed up from being shot at again, and he needed something to *do*.

Unfortunately, he couldn't think of a goddamn course of action that held any promise of satisfaction whatsoever. So he stood there, squeezing his bitten nails into his palms, and pretended he was on sentry.

Might as well.

[24]

IS IT USUAL?

It wasn't until she was halfway down the stairs, comfortable in a sweatshirt and yoga pants, that Ginny realized she'd been a complete asshole. He stood, arms akimbo, staring out the front window, and he hadn't even taken his coat off. His shoulders were taut, and even though he was rangy he still had a good deal of muscle packed on him.

She should know, he'd dragged her bodily into the diner and then landed on her. To keep her from getting...shot.

With her hair clean and the rest of her still stinging-warm from the brief shower, she felt a million times better, which just made it even ruder for her to abandon a guest. Had he been standing there the whole time? "Jesus," she said. "I'm sorry. That was really rude of me."

He turned just his head, a catlike motion, chin to shoulder. "Whatnow?"

"Do you want to get cleaned up?" It was a relief to have something to organize. "You can take a shower upstairs. I don't have anything clean that'll fit you, but I can go next door and borrow something from Harry. If, you know, you need it." She took a deep breath.

His hair was full of dust, and hers hadn't had any broken glass in it that she could feel. But he'd been on top of her when the windows got shot, so he was probably covered in the stuff. "I'm not sure you want to go driving in this, especially with...Jesus. I should—are you hungry? I can make something." What did she have? Not a lot, it was the end of her work week, her shopping day wasn't until Tuesday, but she could come up with something. Ginny shook her head a little, trying to clear it. As long as she was thinking about cleaning him up and getting them both fed, she wouldn't have to think about... anything else. The things in the road. The popping, the roaring, bullets plowing into everything. The entire world had veered off-course and was in the ditch, wheels spinning and engine belching smoke.

The rest of Lee turned to match his head, easily. "I could eat a bit."

"Yeah, you were at the diner." Now she even felt bad for being in her big comfy socks.

"Was gonna do some readin, had me some dinner." He nodded again, probably forgetting he wasn't wearing a hat. Of course, they took them off when they came inside. Pretty much all the older men did, and most of the younger. "Little late, but I'm glad I did."

"Me too." She couldn't think of anything else to say, and he was looking at her strangely. Those eyes of his were still lighter than usual, and under the mess of dark hair on his forehead they peered out fiercely, intent on her face. His stubble had shown up, too, dark like his hair but faintly gold at the tips.

It was the first time she'd had a man in this house, other than the plumber during the event with the McCoy's upstairs bathroom last year. Lee stood, just staring at her, and the awkward sense that he expected her to say something put a rock in her throat. He was probably as uncomfortable as she was, stranded in a virtual stranger's living room.

All right. Let's get going. "I'm going to go next door and ask Harry for some clean clothes for you. You can go upstairs and use the shower, there are towels in the—"

"I'll come along." Lee's shoulders relaxed even further. Maybe she was doing something right. "Man might like to know where his clothes are goin. I ain't too bad, though, just my coat."

"Oh. Okay. Let me get some shoes." Why was he looking at her like that?

As soon as she stepped out the front door, her hair turned to an icy weight. *Ugh.* She hissed in a freezing breath through her teeth, taking the concrete steps one at a time. It was a short walk to next door, but she stopped halfway there—Lee had moved out into her front yard, slipping his coat off his shoulders. He shook it, gently at first, then gave it a couple of good cracks. Snow whirled and puffed, and Ginny shivered.

She continued shuffling towards the McCoys' front door, stepping carefully in her unlaced Nikes. They were the only shoes big enough for these socks, and she was probably going to have wet feet by the time she got back inside.

Lee arrived, and draped the shearling across her shoulders. "Here."

Oh, for God's sake. She pressed their doorbell. The coat was, needless to say, a welcome warmth. But that meant he was standing there in a chambray shirt and his leather vest, and if *she* was already shivering, he was going to get frostbite. "You need it more than I do."

"You gonna catch cold with your hair like that." His jaw had set, his eyebrows drawn together, and he looked close to furious.

What the hell is he mad at me for? "I'm a grownup, Mr Quartine. A few minutes won't—"

THUD. The door shuddered, wood splintering, and Ginny almost went over backward.

Lee caught her elbow, steadying her. "Sonofa—"

"*Jesus!*" she yelped at the same time, which would have been funny, but whatever was behind the door hit it again.

POW. More splinters popped out around the doorknob—the

deadbolt was locked, and tearing free as whatever was behind the door started scratching and scrabbling.

Lee pulled her back, and they both almost fell off the stairs. She caught her balance before he did, and hauled on his arm to keep him upright in turn, her Nikes slipping on fresh snow and the shearling almost falling free too. He kept backing up; they ended up standing in the McCoys' front yard, Lee pushing between her and the duplex. "That normal?"

"What?" She couldn't get a breath in, so it came out squeaky. Snow blew in her face, stinging slightly before it melted.

Lee regarded the door like it was a rattlesnake. "I mean, they got a bear in there as a pet, or is that how they get salesmen off their front porch? Is it *usual*?"

"N-no." Snowflakes clung to her eyelashes, she blinked them away. "Jesus. Their garage." The McCoy's garage door was wide-open, the maroon minivan crouching next to the ATVs they some-times fired up in the summer, the kiddie pool they put out on hot days, and other ephemera you accumulated when you had kids and a paycheck.

"I knew somethin was off," he muttered. "That ain't normal neither, I take it."

"No." *Jesus Christ*. Her brain seized up for a second, trying to figure out the right word for this situation. There wasn't a single one that seemed to apply.

"All right." He eyed the front door, which shuddered again. Whatever was inside wanted to get out, bigtime. "I want you to go on in your house, while I see what's in there."

"Like hell." She tried to slide his coat off her shoulders, but he grabbed the front, holding it closed. "They're my neighbors." *A raccoon, maybe? Yeah, sure. A super-sized one hopped up on steroids.*

Lee grimaced slightly, yanking the coat even tighter around her. "Yeah, and whatever's in there might be whatever they was shootin at down in the street, you think about that? I ain't havin you hurt."

Bang. A long vertical splinter popped out of the door. Maybe

Harry was in there doing some home renovation? Just a relaxing time with a sledgehammer on a Sunday evening.

The things on the street. She'd been trying *not* to think about them and the way they moved, their jerky, unnatural speed.

"Now go on inside," Lee Quartine said. He seemed to think she would, because he let go of her and set off for the open garage door to their left. Going inside was a good idea, a flat-out *great* one, and Ginny wavered between retreating to her own house and following, clutching his huge but undeniably warm coat around her shoulders.

Afterwards, she would think of that small vacillation and writhe with embarrassment. There was nothing as humiliating as finding out how much of a coward you really were.

In the end, the decision was made for her, because the door disintegrated as it was hit again. A blur of wild, snarling motion crammed itself into the new hole, one hand—it *had* to be a hand, nothing else was shaped like that—gripping empty air and spattering dark fluid onto the steps.

Hot terror boiling in her chest, Ginny bolted after Lee.

[25]

FIXED TO HIT CONCRETE

GINNY RAN INTO HIS BACK, AND THE NEXT FEW SECONDS WERE confused as hell. A flash of annoyance—she should have done what he *told* her, did she think he just flapped his gums for fun?—died when Lee heard the snarling, and he shoved her past him and into the garage, moving back in a quick light shuffle and wondering what the hell was making that noise. It didn't sound like any animal he'd ever—

It galloped out into the front yard, kicking up bits of snow. Human-shaped, all right, but again, moving *wrong*. Looked like a heavyset man, in a Sunday best suit but no tie. Clots and splashes of dried blood poured from his foaming mouth, giving him a bib of gore. His balding head glowed in the dusk, and Lee's shoulder hit one of the minivan's side mirrors with a *thunk*.

He swallowed a curse, and the man-thing paused, crouching, his head tilted just like an inquisitive dog's. Ginny's breath rasped behind him. "Oh God oh God," she whispered, and probably didn't even know she was saying it. Lee's shoulder burned with pain, but he didn't have time for that, because the man-thing turned its head back and forth, a quick, intelligent shake, and began to lope forward on all fours. Right for the garage, and Lee.

And Ginny.

Well, shit. No firewood in here, which meant no axe he could see. There was a toolchest though, up against the house, with a narrow space in front of it for standing. Lee stepped back, hoping to herd Ginny that direction. "Back up," he snapped. "Back *up.*"

Well, she did. She headed right for the door into the house and kept going. Lee grabbed the front passenger side door of the minivan and wrenched it open just in time. The thing, rising on its hindfeet now that it had a good head of steam, ran into metal and glass, and *it* was making that snarling noise. Yellowish foam splattered from its chewing, working mouth.

Ginny let out a sharp, terrified cry. Lee snapped a glance back and saw, hanging on the pegboard right next to the door, something that would do.

The thing ran into the minivan door again. Lee snatched the claw hammer from the pegboard and snapped another glance at Ginny, who had run into the jerry-built wooden stair in front of the door to the house, wide-eyed and paper pale. Her hair, wet and full of curls, was a river down her back, and she was lost inside his shearling, clutching at the coat with her soft slim hands.

Even scared to death, she was beautiful.

He gave the minivan door a kick, just to get the thing's attention. It kept working forward, but the door had hit the side of the garage and stuck fast in drywall, and all the thing's frantic motion just dug it in deeper. It lunged, its face smacking the rolled-up window with a wet splorch.

"Harry," Ginny said breathlessly, behind him. "Oh my God, *Harry.*"

So this was the neighbor. Looked like he was having a hell of a day too. Drugs, maybe? Shit. Was *that* what the Army boys were chasing down? Lee decided it didn't matter. He also decided this asshole didn't look like he was going to settle down and be reasonable. That left the option Lee liked least, but was, ironically enough, best at.

"Hey." He pitched it louder than Ginny's horrified repetition of the man's name. "Yeah, you, you ugly sumbitch. Look at you."

It could have backed off and gone around the minivan. Instead, the thing froze, and its eyes—strangely filmed, turning gray and mooshy inside the sockets—rolled, blinking. It turned its head again, like a cat trying to pin down a mouse skritching. Ten to one it was the doorbell that had set it off. Anything else inside the neighbor-house was likely to be unpleasant. How many kids were in there?

Worry about that in a bit. For right now, watch this thing, cause it looks like it's thinkin.

"Yeah," Lee said. "I'm talkin to you, asshole."

Whatever he was expecting, it wasn't what the thing did. It dropped, barking its elbow against the side of the van with a hollow sound, and shimmied forward on its belly, its hands out and curved into claws, snake-quick, grabbing for Lee's feet.

He kicked it, just hard enough to stun, then dropped to one knee and brought the hammer down, hard and fast.

Ginny cried out again, miserably. Bone crunched, blood spattered, and gray matter squirted. Lee hit it again, because those arms were still going. The hammer smacked right behind the thing's ear, shattering bone, and the third time, he fixed to hit concrete floor, going all the way through.

It stopped moving. He gave it another tap, just to make sure, and stopped, his sides heaving. His shoulder seized up, and he hoped he hadn't pulled anything. He waited, but the twitching in its arms was just the nerves figuring out they were dead-for-real. *Jesus Christ.* Despite the cold, sweat gathered in his armpits. *What the fuck?*

"Harry," Ginny whispered behind him. "It's...my God, it's *Harry.*"

Lee fought the urge to drop the hammer. You couldn't let go of a weapon until all hostiles were accounted for. He did scrabble backward, crab-walking like a kid, until his back met Ginny's knees. She was alive, he was alive, and the damn thing laying under the minivan's door, illuminated faintly by the dome light, kept twitching. He licked his dry, burning lips, tasting salt sweat and dust. "You know him?" Of course she did, but giving her something to focus on was called for.

"I...that's my *neighbor.*"

"Was," Lee correctly dryly. "*Was* your neighbor. He on the drugs?"

"What?" She was having a little trouble with this. What civilian wouldn't?

Thought I was done with killin'. Lee forced himself to breathe a little slower, and a little slower again. *Dear God and sonny Jesus, I thought I was done.* "Drugs, darlin. Is he on the drugs?"

"I...I don't...he's *married.*" At least she wasn't screaming. She sagged against the door to the house, and he sagged against her to keep her still.

"Wellnow, I never did hear that stopped anyone." He cleared his throat, felt the flinch that rippled through her. "You hurt?" Her knees pressed into his back, but he didn't mind.

A long pause. "N-no. I don't think so. Are you?"

Nice of her to ask. "Bumped my arm a bit. Think it's fine." *Bet it'll stiffen up by tomorrow, though. Get moving, Lee. Figure out the next step.* He could smell the thing now; it was ripe. Death had a brassy odor all its own, but this was rot and a foul sewage exhalation. Probably the sphincters giving way. Life's ending was more often than not soaked in shit.

"Harry," she repeated. "Oh, my God. He's married. Kids."

Fuck. Lee nodded, though, slow and easy. The right side of his neck threatened to seize up. "All right." *Go over your options, Lee.*

"Police." She got there quicker than he did. "We have to c-call the police."

"Pretty sure they gonna have other things on their mind, darlin." *Shit. That just slipped out.* Well, he was in it now, he might as well keep going.

"But we *have* to." She sounded very sure. You sank to the level of your training indeed, and what was every good little girl trained to do? Call the cops.

Who knew, Percy Blotzer or his deputy might even have some good advice for once. "Okay. I'll take you back'n your place, you lock the doors and call 'em."

"But..." She struggled with this for a moment, her knees trembling. "You're leaving?"

What? "Hell no. Gonna check to see anyone livin' in there." *Shit. Just cussed in front of her.* "Sorry."

"Sorry?" She began to move. "For...Jesus Christ, for *what?*"

"It ain't right to cuss in front of a lady."

"Oh, my God." She was *definitely* moving now. Her knees pushed businesslike at his shoulders, and he exhaled a bit.

Time to get up, and get this sorted, Lee.

SHE WOULDN'T GO BACK TO HER HOUSE. "ALL I HAVE IS MY cell. *They* have a land line. They're my *neighbors.*" It was hard to tell which carried more weight for her. The minivan's other side was clear, but she also refused to go out the open garage door. She just shook her head, her wet hair swinging. It was longer than he'd thought, that heavy fall, and he could have smelled her shampoo if she'd let him get close enough.

Oh, Jesus Christ. Lee took a hard grasp on his patience. It was probably best to keep her where he could see her, at least for his own peace of mind. "How many in there, then?"

"Four." She shook her head again, faster this time, as if whipping away water or a bad thought. He had her backed against the toolchest, since that way she didn't have to see the corpse on the floor. "No. That's Harry. So there's only Amy, and the kids. Three."

"Here." He reached for his coat, pausing when she flinched, and held the shoulders so she could slip her arms in. "Ma and two little 'uns?"

"They're...teenagers. Not little." Her pulse beat a frantic tattoo in her throat, and her pupils were dilating again. With the sun gone down and the wind up, it was getting colder. He needed to plug in the engine block heater on his truck.

Ginny's hands worked against each other, fingers knotting together and loosening only to clench up again. She was going to break them if she kept that up. At least she was *in* his coat, now, not just clutching at it to keep it straight.

He could have taken her hands and calmed her down, but he probably had blood on him, and he still had the hammer. It was tacky-wet now, not dripping. "All right. It laid out like your place in there?" He *also* could have zipped and buttoned the shearling, but smearing crap from the hammer on it wasn't a good idea.

"Mirror image." Her jaw quivered, whether from her teeth wanting to chatter or from shock he couldn't tell. Two bright crimson quarter-drops stood out on her cheeks. "Yes. Exactly."

"All right." He pretended to think it over, watching her face. The thin slice near her hairline had clotted up nicely, but she was so pale the bruise around it glared. She was all right, though, and moving fine. "Now you listen. You *stay behind me*. I tell you to freeze, you freeze. I tell you to get down, you hit the floor. You understand me?"

A quick nod. Her gaze skittered away, across the minivan's side. She could probably imagine what was on the other side, and it bothered him. She shouldn't have to see that shit.

"What did I just say?" *Get her mind off that.*

"Stay b-behind you. Get down when you tell me. Freeze." Another quick nod, tendrils of her hair drying out and springing up into curl, falling in her face. She was holding up damn well. A good little soldier.

"Fine." It *wasn't* fine, he'd prefer her in her house all nice and safe while he cleared this, but unless he was going to pick up and carry her, that wasn't gonna happen, and whatever was in this side of the duplex wasn't getting any fresher.

It was then he saw the crowbar, half-shoved under some boxes. *Oh now, that looks useful.* He tossed the hammer on the toolchest with a clatter, and she flinched again. He was already past her, working the length of metal out from under a box of *The 700 Club* VHS tapes. Looked like someone liked their Pat Robertson. That also snagged on something he'd heard earlier. "Huh. Where they church, you know?"

"What?" Now she was staring at the hammer, and he shouldn't have left it there. Too late now.

"Your neighbors." Slow and easy. "Where do they church?"

"I don't know." Very softly. "Oh. No, I do. A Baptist one, near Hatchie Ground. They kept inviting me, though." Her voice caught. "I never did."

Half the folk at First Baptist didn't show up today, Margie had said. First was on the road to Lewiston, not west toward Hatchie. That could have led Lee down some interesting mental paths, but he couldn't start straying at the moment. He hefted the crowbar experimentally, and pushed past Ginny again, bumping into her to get her eyes off that goddamn hammer. "Well, next week, if you want, I'll take you wherever you go. Come on now."

[26]

FIRST AID

It was a good thing she hadn't eaten anything.

The smell was monstrous. The kitchen was a shambles, the phone ripped off the wall, cupboards open and broken dishes scattered higgledy-piggledy. The attached dining room was curiously untouched, the china hutch against its wall squat and polished-gleaming just as usual.

The living room looked like something had exploded, flatscreen TV starred with breakage and laundry flung everywhere, the big brown couch and Harry's recliner torn to smithereens. Stuffing floated lazily on drafts from the heating vents, which were still going full-bore. The heat was whistling out the busted front door, and when Lee passed the thermostat in the hall between kitchen and living room he turned it all the way down. The heat pump clicked, probably grateful for the respite.

This had to be a dream. She followed Lee's broad back through the house, the patches on his leather vest shifting as muscle moved underneath them. When the heat pump wound down it was silent except for the wind mouthing the corners of the house, rattling the front door.

And the *smell*. It was awful, deeper than spoiled meat or rotten eggs or a rancid bar bathroom from her college days, it was flat-out horrible, and deep instinctive revulsion turned her stomach into a knotted, writhing mass.

Lee paused at the bottom of the stairs, shaking his stiffened hair out of his eyes. He pointed at the half-wall between the entryway and the living room with his left hand, the crowbar raised in his right. "You wanna stay right there, Ginny. Next to the door."

"Okay." The urge to add *Mother may I?* trembled on the tip of her tongue, but she bit down against it. "Lee..."

"Hm?" All his attention was up the stairs, and with his face set and intent, he was almost handsome. "You just stay right there. Anything other'n me comes down these stairs, you get on out the door and into your house, you hear me?"

I hear you. The floating unreality of the situation hit her again. Nightmare. Hallucination, maybe? It would have to be a *group* hallucination, and she tried to think if she'd read about them. A fine time to wish she'd gone for a psych degree, or hadn't washed out of med school just before graduation. Her father had been so disappointed; she was supposed to be a doctor. Nothing else would do for Isaac Mills's firstborn. Flo was the miracle baby, after they told Mom she'd never get pregnant again. By then, though, the mantle of responsibility had been conferred, and there was no taking that shit back.

I should have left earlier. I should have left right when Mom hung up. I should have known.

Lee edged up the stairs, his back to the wall. One at a time, moving smoothly each step. He looked a lot different than the diffident, silent man who had checked out Westerns for six months. Never a word that whole time, until she'd seen him in Landy's. Maybe people thought librarians, like teachers, were hung up in a closet when the day's work was done; they weren't actual *people*, just services? So maybe he had to see her outside the library before she was all right to talk to?

This man was intent and almost graceful, moving like he knew exactly what he was doing. The same way he'd set about changing her flat tire, or getting everyone in the diner ready to move.

And here she was, her teeth clenched so tightly they groaned a little, her entire body twitching. Jumping, like bits of pavement popcorning under bullets.

I just wanted some coffee. And some snacks. Her hands gripped each other, tighter. Tighter.

Lee spent a little while at the head of the stairs, looking around. The stairwell light wasn't on, but there were stripes of golden electric glow from the bedrooms. A gout of fresh, snow-laden air gushed through the hole in the door, and she inhaled gratefully.

It made the smell worse when she stepped away, though. "Lee?" Her whisper tiptoed up after him. All of a sudden, she didn't want him to go around the corner and out of sight.

"It's all right," he said, but he didn't move. Cat-quiet, cat-still, he stood braced between two stairs, studying the upper level intently.

She put her foot on the first step. *Nothing about this is even remotely all right.* Her tongue crept out, wet her dry, chapped lips.

Lee's shoulders set, a heavy invisible weight settling on them. "Two kids, right? Boys?"

"Yes." The banister was splintered halfway up. If she'd been home, she might have heard all this. Or had it happened while she was at work? She might have come home, cleaned up, hurried through packing, and all the time, dead bodies behind a thin partition of drywall and lumber and...

Oh, God.

She barely realized she was creeping up the stairs. There was a huge splotch of something dark on the right—the wall, shared with hers. The splotch gleamed, still wet, and the thought that she'd climbed up and down her own stairs while this...this...

"Ginny." Slow and calm. "I don't think you wanna see this."

You're right. I probably don't. She kept climbing. They were just like her stairs. The carpet was more worn, because they'd lived here for years. How many times had she heard the boys galloping up and down and rolled her eyes?

Well, they weren't galloping anymore. She was able to see through the railing along the hall leading to the master bedroom. Her gorge rose, but she managed not to spew. She just gagged a little, a soft choked sound—

—echoed by another, a quiet hissing noise.

A tortured, indrawn breath.

AMY McCOY LAY IN THE SHATTERED REMAINS OF THE MASTER bedroom door, her back and buttocks a mess of blood and deep gouges. Pressed against the wall, Bart and Harry Junior lay tangled together, but Ginny could barely tell which was which, since their heads were...God. The soft sound was coming from Amy, her ribs twitching as they rose and fell at strange intervals—first long, then short, then short again, then long, random little breath-flutters.

"Oh my God," Ginny whispered. "Is she..."

"Hold up." Lee pushed her back against the shut-tight bathroom door. "This ain't right. Just hang on a second."

"But she's alive! We have to..." She searched for the words. "First aid! We have to *help* her."

Lee's arm turned into a steel bar; he pushed her back again. "Ginny. There ain't no first aid for that."

"But she's moving, she's..." The words died in Ginny's throat.

Amy's breathing quickened. Short little puffs, a train going uphill. A creaking sound, a long gassy exhale, and the stench intensified. Shudders raced through the battered, bloody body. It wasn't like a body on television, even in one of those "gritty" crime shows.

"Ginny." Lee planted his left foot carefully, next to Bart's limp, outstretched hand. At least, she thought it was Bart's, it wore a red shirt she thought she'd seen him in once or twice. "You need to go back down those stairs. Now."

"What are you going to do?" It was a stupid question, she could see his entire body tensing, the crowbar lifting. "Lee, you can't, she's still *alive*—"

Amy McCoy's head lifted from the floor, its eyes wide and gray-filmed. Her jaw worked, her cheeks splotched and flecked with blood, and foam bubbled at the corners of her lips. There was a cracking, a creaking, and her arms reached forward, fingers curving down to dig into the carpet. The pressure made a soft, wet sound, soaked-in blood bubbling up, and Amy's head wove from side to side, loosely and eerily, as she pulled herself forward.

Snap. Snap. Her jaws worked, her teeth clapping together hard. She coughed, spat blood and foam, and that same thick animal growl that had burst out of Harry rose from her chest.

Her legs...her legs were *gone*. Her thighs tapered to ragged, bloody points flecked with splintered bone, as if they'd been stuck in a giant electric pencil sharpener. The light in the bedroom was on, and it was pitiless, illuminating strings of gnawed muscle and nerve trailing behind Amy McCoy as she scrabbled down the carpeting towards Ginny and Lee.

Lee didn't hesitate. He stepped close, but not *too* close, and brought the crowbar down.

[27]

AN OPERATION

BILLY TIPTON HAD TAKEN THE 4X4 AT JUJU'S INSISTENCE, AND it was parked around the corner from the ramshackle trailer. He told himself this wasn't a foolish idea, it was just checking on her what with the strange news and all. He could play with the rugrats a bit, too—little Andy Jr and Samantha who had Lila's eyes. They were good kids, and Lila swore Andy didn't touch them. *Just me,* she would say, sadly, hugging herself, cupping her sharp elbows in her soft palms. Wistful like that, you could see the girl she'd been; she didn't smile anymore like she used to in high school. Which was a good thing, the high voltage had nearly killed him then, and it might if she ever did again.

The snow was coming on hard, and he couldn't stay for long. The paper Landy's bag in his left hand was heavy; last time he'd ended up in Lewiston he'd blown a twenty on a bunch of gimcrack toys from a novelty shop. The kids would like that. As long as he kept it light and easy and about the kids, Lila wouldn't say *you shouldn't.*

He could beat Andy Bowe into the ground, he supposed. The Bowes were thick with the Blotzers, and Percy the sheriff was already a problem, what with his feelings about Juju. Who had never done a damn thing to the man, it baffled understanding. So much about the world did, really. You could make everything simple, but everyone clung to complicating things.

Tip knocked at the trailer's door again, heard stealthy movement on the other side. Would she keep it closed up, because Andy was home soon? *I ain't scared of him*, Tip kept telling her. The goddamn asshole might even straighten up if he thought Tip was going to give him a fist or two. The only thing some jackasses understood was force, and Tip was ready to give a little bit. Just not in front of Lila, for God's sake. The last thing he needed was her getting afraid of *him* too.

The porch vibrated a little underfoot, unsteadily. Andy Bowe was no fixit man. If he'd just stay off the sauce, he might turn out to be something, and sometimes Billy wasn't sure if he wanted that *or* if he wanted the asshole to wreck himself in a car accident and solve the whole damn problem of—

The door unlocked, swung open a few degrees. Lila Bowe, glassy-eyed and flushed, looked out. Her hair hung limp and lank, still golden as it had been in high school, and her eyes were just as blue, though bloodshot now. "Billy?" she whispered, and his heart lodged right up in his throat while his fists ached.

A bruise spread over the right half of her face. A fresh one, and deep, her eye was swelling shut. She coughed, a little, and blinked at him.

Tip leaned forward. She tried to hold the door, but he was a lot heavier, and the snow was a good excuse for him to want to get inside. He was in before you could say boo; the kitchen was a damp dark cave. It wasn't much warmer than it was outside, and he set the bag on a counter tacky with ketchup stains. "Good Lord, it's cold out there." Bright and normal, like he hadn't seen the bruise, like his hands weren't aching to become fists.

"You shouldn't..." Lila shut the door and leaned against it. The entire place was silent as the grave. Painfully thin, wrapped in a couple layers, she shivered and clutched at fabric high up on her chest, over her heart like it pained her. "My God, Billy, he'll kill you too."

It took him a second to catch up. Billy turned, his Army boots grinding in something gritty on the kitchen floor, and stared at her.

Lila clutched at her left arm, a sloppy, clumsy wad of gauze with a maroon rosette in its center glaring against the torn sleeve of her yellow sweater. Her leggings—flowered blue ones he'd seen before—were dirty, which was unlike her, and sagging at the knees, dark with some unidentifiable liquid. Her tennis shoes were filthy with gravel, and her socks were mismatched—one red, one yellow as her sweater, again unlike her. The trailer was full of cold fresh air, and now he saw why—the sliding glass door in the living room, heading out to the unfinished deck, looked like a bomb had hit it.

And it was quiet. Too quiet, because by now the kids should be chattering at him and calling him *UncleBillywillyouplease* and jumping up and down, and too loud at the same time because the wind moaned through the shattered door.

Lila's cheeks were ruby, even the bruised one, and her stare too glassy. Her swelling eye glared at him, and Billy Tipton planted his feet, reaching for his hat to take it off now that he was inside. "Where are the kids, Lila?"

She shuddered, her hair moving solidly, ratty and unkempt. She was normally so neat and clean, and did her best to keep the trailer scrubbed. "Got sick. So did *he*." She shivered a little. "All sick, and... they're with *him* now, Billy. It's better that way."

He frankly stared. This wasn't like her, not at all. *I'd die before I let him touch the kids*, she swore each time. *It's all I got left, Tip.*

He was about to ask her again where the kids had gone, but her gaze sharpened for a single, terrible instant. Then, she threw her head back and screamed, a long piercing cry not unlike a cheerleader at a big game but with a raw undertone of loss and grinding, her throat swelling. Her knees gave, and he lunged to catch her before she went down all the way. She convulsed, her hands flying wildly, and clipped him a good one on the shoulder, hysterical strength her scrawny arms shouldn't have had.

Billy bent over her, trying to keep the seizure, or whatever it was, from cracking her head against the floor. Little birdlike bones, and it was the closest he'd ever gotten to her. Through the dirt and the smell of violet-thick sickness, there was the scent of her shampoo—Prell, though he didn't know it—and his entire body surged with the thought that he was gonna get her to the hospital, that he was gonna be the hero he'd always known she needed but didn't see. A lifetime of waiting, of thinking of her in the middle of Afghanistan and later, in Iraq with the dust and the heat and the little *pops* that were the snipers, if you heard it they didn't get you, but he was already *got*.

He'd been got ever since junior high and an afternoon in the park, sitting on the grass and watching Lila and her popular bubblegum friends laugh and loll, tinged with the gold of rightness. Her short Cotton Crossing High cheerleader's skirt, her smooth tanned legs, and the kindness in her china-blue eyes.

That was what he was thinking about when she made a strange, grind-rattling noise in her chest, and her teeth sank into the space between his neck and shoulder, her nose nuzzled in tight and unerring where his button-down was loose and his jacket unzipped.

Billy let out a short bark of pain, his hands biting and slipping. She was burning up, writhing in his arms, and he toppled over her, hot copper spurting as she worried at his flesh like a terrier. Trained instinct took over, because she rippled and bucked against the floor, and there was a sickening *crack* as she strained against his hold. He was trying to pin her, but his knee sank deep in her belly and her teeth slipped free as she bawled, a low inhuman noise.

"*Lila,*" he screamed, his knee slipping and his left hand clamping shut around her thin biceps, getting her arm overhead. "*Lila stop it, it's me it's Billy stop it!*"

The floor heaved, and she just wouldn't quit. They rolled, a confusion of arms and legs on a filthy floor, knocking aside two empty pizza boxes and a half-full two liter of Shasta orange pop, and her teeth champed as she tried to get them near his throat. The horrible sound grated up from her chest, and her hair was vines of sickness, stiff and matted.

Red unconsciousness descended. It was the goddamn war all over again, only they didn't call it war. They called it an *operation*, like cutting out a cancer, but it spread and spread, and there was no end to the blood.

Another crack, like a good dry seasoned piece of firewood on the block, the axe brought down cleanly.

Billy Tipton, blood soaking into the shoulder of his coat, lay on the dirty floor and cradled Lila Bowe's slack, head-lolling body.

The wind picked up, and snow blew into the trailer.

[28]

PAST POLITE

Hot water beat against Lee's back, slid down long-healed scars, worked at the bruise beginning on the back of his right shoulder. It felt good, and he would have liked it to last.

I was done with killin, goddammit.

He could have stayed there until the water ran cold, but he was worried about Ginny.

The towels she'd used were still damp. Her shower, her towels, he was brushing against things that had touched *her*. He scrubbed all over himself, trying not to be distracted by *that* particular thought. Instead, he had to figure out a whole list of other things, first among them how he was going to deal with the pile of shit that had just landed on both of them and showed every indication of getting deeper by the minute.

At least his skivvies and undershirt were still clean. His jeans weren't too bad. He'd closed up the house next door as best he could, for no other reason than the dead air inside would help insulate her half of the duplex. While he was at it, he'd went knocking on doors. The two other duplexes in her cul-de-sac were closed up tight, no porch lights on, no sign of movement inside. The curtains and blinds were open, but Lee didn't want to go peering in their windows. It was a good way to get shot, or if there were more of those...*things*, glass wouldn't hold them back for long.

So he'd simply trudged back through the falling snow and shook his head when Ginny asked if anyone, *anyone* was home. *If they are, they ain't answerin,* he told her, and the immediate leap of fear in her dark eyes socked him right in the gut.

She didn't have an extension cord long enough. He had a water-proof one in the truck, neatly coiled, so his engine block heater was doing its job, the cord slid under her garage door. He'd checked all her windows and doors, pulled the curtains, and left her in the bright kitchen, hugging herself and staring at the pictures held to the fridge with blown-glass magnets—an elderly couple, the man with a stubborn curl to his salt-and-pepper hair and the woman with wide dark eyes that matched Ginny's, both hovering protectively over a young woman with a sleek chestnut mane and the same sweet curved shape to her mouth as Ginny.

Family. Her kin.

Lee threaded his belt through the holster, laced himself back into his boots, checked the Beretta M-9 and slid it home. Ran his fingers back through his wet hair, too long for the military, and worked his shoulder a little bit. Just a helluva bruise, he hadn't pulled anything. Should have iced it. Too late now, just gonna have to deal. Story of his life.

Ginny was right where he'd left her, in the kitchen. Only now, she was at the stove, stirring a pot of something. She had a frying pan out, too, and the good smell of butter and bread under heat rode the warm air.

"I can't get through." She didn't turn around. Her hair was drying, a cloud of curls she probably cursed at every time it tangled. It made a man's fingers itch, really, seeing it down like that.

"Say what?" He checked the hallway. Her front door was locked tight, everything in here was just fine. All the trouble was outside, but his nerves weren't quite convinced.

"I keep calling 911, but I can't get through." Her cell phone lay on the counter, a sleek black rectangle with a shiny raspberry-colored case. It looked expensive and finished to a high gloss, just like her. "Just a busy signal."

"Prolly a lot goin on out there." He kept moving, impelled. Her shoulders hunched; she looked much smaller than usual. Or maybe it was that she was in sock feet instead of heels, the grey sweatshirt proclaiming YALE across her narrow back. It was too big for her, man-sized, and she kept pushing the sleeves up as she stared down into the frying pan.

His mouth was watering, but whether it was from missing his lunch or the fact that he was so close to her, he couldn't tell. He wanted to ask whose sweatshirt it was, decided not to.

Two sandwiches. Golden-brown, perfect crusts. Looked like she made a mean grilled cheese. The pot to her left held a thick red—tomato soup. She sniffed. Wiped at her face with her free hand. "It's not ringing anymore."

"What?" Close enough to feel her heat. Close enough to smell her hair. Her shampoo smelled like oranges, but it was different on her than it was in the bottle.

"My parents. I've tried calling everyone I ever knew. Even Bobbie."

Bobby? Was it his shirt? "Who's he?"

"She. My boss." The last word broke halfway too, and she flicked off the burner with a quick, vicious motion.

Oh. Now he felt like an idiot, but the hot sharp poke in his guts was a spur to a maddened horse. "She live in town?"

"Lewiston." She sniffled again. "Get a bowl, will you?" She pointed at a cabinet. "Or two, I guess. Though I don't feel much like eating."

"All right." He didn't want to move away. What he *wanted* to do was take the last step and put his arms around her, and tell her *it's all right, it's gonna be all right.*

That was most likely a lie. He didn't like the way his thoughts on the situation were tending. Sure, her neighbor could have had a drug-fueled psychotic break and caused all that damage, but the wife upstairs with her legs missing should *not* have been able to belly forward like that. And the things on the street, moving just the same as the man next door, with jerky, uncanny speed...

Not to mention Grandon's visit, the roadblocks, the news from both East and West coasts. If it was terrorists, they were doing a damn fine job of it. And he'd been just sitting on his ass. Not that there was anything a single man could do when the entire world decided to go tits-up.

What *could* he do? Just wait for everything to right itself or settle into the new shit same as the old, waiting for the end the way he'd been waiting all his life.

There were funny green flecks in the cheese. "It's Havarti," she told him. "With dill." A fancy cheese, for a fancy girl from New York. He didn't even know what he was doing here.

Oh, yes you do, Lee. You know exactly what you're doin.

So he set his jaw and tried it, while she picked at hers and the wind howled outside.

It actually wasn't half bad.

THE NEXT MORNING DAWNED SOFTLY, FILTERED THROUGH falling snow. It hadn't frozen, it was just dumping about a foot and a half of sound-killing flakes onto Cotton Crossing. Lee woke up in what Ginny called her spare bedroom, his shoulder a bar of pain and his head full of bad noise. It took a few seconds, staring at the white popcorn ceiling, to figure out where the hell he was and whether he had to be ready for patrol. Sprawled on a folded-down futon, above sheets that smelled of brand name fabric softener, breathing in the smell of a room kept closed up for long periods of time, he heard dim sounds filtering from downstairs.

Voices.

That brought him upright, curling up to sitting, thrusting his legs from beneath the single blanket he'd used on top of the comforter because he'd slept with his boots on. Grabbing his shirt and his belt, he considered leaving the gun behind for a moment, but then the sounds downstairs rose in pitch. Whoever he was, he sounded angry.

Oh, hell no.

He was halfway down the stairs and moving fast before he realized it wasn't an argument.

Ginny sat on the couch, her knees pulled up and her hair curling wildly in every direction. She stared at her coffee table, where a sleek silver laptop stood open, its screen full of looping, whirling colors. She clutched a big, wide red mug of something that looked hot, steam lifting from it, and tilted her head, listening to what sounded like a radio broadcast. No sweatshirt. Instead she was in a thin blue cotton tank top, her shoulders bare and pale.

Oh, man. The cloth clung to her, and Lee just about lost whatever sense he'd woken up with. His mouth, full of sleep, went dry, and if all of him wasn't standing to attention some parts certainly were.

"And it just kept *coming*, man," someone was saying. A young male voice with a California accent, pitched high with excitement or frustration.

"The CDC mentioned the foaming at the mouth," the announcer broke in, a rich fruity tone used to being listened to, enunciating the end of every word clear as day. "Have you seen anything like that?"

"Oh yeah." The kid on the line swallowed audibly. "Don't let them bite you, man. The fast ones, they're pretty nasty. You gotta hit 'em in the head to keep 'em down." A thin thread of static ran through the words.

"That's what we've heard." The announcer's tenor held a slight edge of hoarseness. Sounded like he'd been talking a while. "Thanks, Brian. Stay alive out there." A short pause. "For those of you just joining us, this is Keith Stapleton on livecast, taking calls from everyone who can get through. We have a full-scale national emergency here, folks. We have multiple reports of people going crazy, maybe from some sort of sickness, maybe from a bioweapon. It's spreading like wildfire. The President addressed the nation this morning at eight AM Eastern time, and the CDC has given out a list of do's and don'ts. *Do* stay calm, stay in your homes if you can, and watch for sudden high fevers over 103. Do *not* go out seeking contact with the infected—don't try taking selfies with them, okay? If you're bitten by an infected, disinfect the wound as thoroughly as you can and seek medical attention." A long, tense pause. "I'm gonna go ahead and say this now, folks: be careful out there. Lots of you are talking about seeing the military doing some really scary stuff. Now, the President says our brave soldiers are putting themselves at risk in a national emergency, but we've heard a lot—and I do mean a *lot*—of really messed-up stuff in the last few hours that tells me maybe, just maybe, they're shooting first and looking for bites or foamy mouths later."

Shooting first and looking for bites later. Yeah, that sounds famil-iar. Lee's stomach had dropped and was now tying itself in knots. This was bad.

Another thread of buzzing static. The announcer coughed and took a drink of something. You could hear him swallow. "All right, let's hear from another caller! Hello, you're on Stapleton's Nexus!"

"Keith! Long time listener, first time caller—"

Lee took another step into the living room, and the motion caught Ginny's attention. She started, violently, and the liquid in her big mug sloshed. She winced as whatever it was splashed her hand, hurried to set it down on the coffee table and push the laptop closed. "Ouch. Hi." Bounced to her feet—in more ways than one, he had to force himself to watch her face instead, pale and set with a tremulous, hopeful smile. "Did you sleep all right? I'll make breakfast. I've just been listening. This guy, he livecasts all the time, he's in Penn-sylvania."

"Oh." Lee nodded. He needed coffee to jump-start his brain into making some kind of sense of all this. He *also* needed to get plannin'. "Is that good?"

"He says there are people going north. That means if I get *there*, I can probably get up to my parents."

Oh, Lord. Yes, he definitely needed coffee before he could handle this. "I ain't sure that's a good idea," he began, carefully.

Her chin lifted, her mouth setting itself stubbornly, just the way it had yesterday. Good Lord, even in the morning she was pretty as springtime. "I don't care if it's a good idea or not. I have to get there. I *have* to."

"Well, all right then." He was pretty much doomed as soon as he said it, and knew as much. "We'll take the truck. Long as we stop at my place on the way out."

He hadn't meant to say it so baldly, or maybe he had. In any case, it brought Ginny up short. She looked down at the red cup-bowl she'd been drinking from, settled in a ring of moisture on her coffee table. The quick motion—a retreat, gathering herself—actually pinched him high up under his left ribs.

"Ah." All the uncertainty in the world, packed into one polite, drawn out little syllable.

Well, no wonder. He was just a backwoods dumbass. Just fine for changing her tire, but not a *guest* or anything. Not what Nonna Q would have called "a prospect", of minerals or of...anything else.

"It's nice of you," Ginny continued diplomatically. "But don't you have people here you want to, you know, check on?" She picked up the cup, carefully. A woman used to deflecting, gently and with a smile, like all pretty ones learned to do.

"Tipton and Juju." Lee made the words nice and even. "Prolly old man Slipot too. But all my kin are dead, Miz Mills." The last to go had been Lee Senior, dead of a stroke over in Colville Correctional while Lee himself was in Syria.

Lee barely remembered reading the official letter, folding it up and putting it in his breast pocket. Out in the field, you functioned better if you knew you were already a corpse too, and the dead were numb.

"Why would you want to go with me? Or were you just being

polite? I mean, I think we've moved past polite." Her eyes were wide and worried, but at least she was looking at him now. Perplexed, all her weight on one leg and her hip stuck out a little, cupping that big mug in her soft, finely made hands, the dark greeny-black nail polish chipped a little. Only enough to underscore how pretty even her fingertips were.

Yeah, I beat in a man's head yesterday, polite's gone with the wind, like Nonna used to say.

Oh, *hell*. His mouth opened, and as usual, he knew he was going to say the wrong thing. "Not polite." It had been so much simpler when he just didn't talk, even if he kicked himself up one side and down the other each time he kept his mouth shut. "I ain't gonna have anything happen to you."

Her quiet matched the silence of the snow outside. She regarded him, several expressions he couldn't decipher moving across her face, and months of holdin' his peace bubbled inside him.

"I just ain't gonna have *anything* happen to you," he repeated, finally. "And you know why, you're a smart girl."

There. It was out in the open. It was a goddamn relief.

[29]

LADY TO THE END

Trying to sleep hadn't worked. Tossing and turning in her bed, hearing over and over the thumping, meaty sounds of skulls shattering and that horrible, groaning growl, seeing Lee Quartine's face terribly blank and set. Or seeing, vivid in the darkness, the stumps of Amy McCoy's legs working against bloody carpet. *She musta barricaded herself in there with the kids,* Lee had said. *And he came right on through. They tried to protect their mama.*

God.

Yeah, sleeping wasn't an option. So she'd gotten up and began calling again. Her parents' number didn't even ring. Flo's cell didn't, either, just clicked into dead air before the call cut off with a trio of beeps. She'd tried all her coworkers, too, getting voicemails for the ones in Lewiston or Hatchie Ground, trying to decide whether or not to leave a message.

Hi, it's Ginny, it's the middle of the night, and I was wondering if any of you had to kill your neighbors?

She'd thought about going out to knock on doors, but her bravery didn't extend *that* far, especially at midnight. So she'd started digging on the internet, a bunch of sites down and others taking forever to load. Around 5am a little notification that the Nexus was on popped up. She'd clicked on it, and the familiar livecast she'd listened to since moving from New York made a burst of relief spread in her chest, so hot and aching she thought for a moment she was having a heart attack. She'd burst into tears, and had longing thoughts of kissing the laptop screen.

And now this. For a moment she couldn't quite figure it out, but then the way he was looking at her—half stubborn, a quarter flat-out afraid, and a quarter soft and intent—made a weird sort of sense. Ginny had seen that look on men before, but never so...openly. And never directed at *her*. Even Alec hadn't looked at her that way, and he'd been long-term.

Or so she'd thought. Until that party. Between the Jagerbombs and the chanting of frat boys, she'd found out just exactly what he thought of her, and the only good part of that memory was how she'd been sober enough to push away grasping hands and leave.

"Oh." She tried not to sound anything other than baffled, and ended up breathless. The intensity of his gaze, especially with his eyes lightening into hazel, was disturbing. Well, a whole *lot* about this was disturbing. "I, uh. Wow."

"You don't have to do nothin bout it." Lee's dark hair, its chestnut highlights mussed into softness, fell over his forehead, and he glared from under it, as if daring her to argue. "I'm just tellin you, I ain't having you hurt. You wanna go, we'll go."

What if I'd prefer to solo this road trip? But that wasn't a good idea, was it?

Not if there were people wandering around foaming at the mouth and biting. Not if there were a bunch of guys shooting anything that moved. Not if there were roadblocks and probably looters and all sorts of chaos.

So she examined him, blinking her grainy eyes and feeling the effects of the four cups of English Breakfast she'd already taken down in her slightly trembling fingers. She thought he'd just warmed up to her in front of the liquor at Landy's, but maybe not. How far she could trust him? A Nice Guy often thought you owed him something, and if he was one of *those*, she was better off getting rid of him politely but thoroughly now, before anything else happened.

Really, though, if he'd wanted to...you know, *do* anything to her, he'd had chances. Like last night.

He knew how to change a tire, too. Then there was the fact of him beating Harry McCoy's head in with a hammer. What kind of person could do something like that?

Not me. Not ever. She wasn't sure if she should think that or not. People were capable of...well, all sorts of things.

And he was so *calm* afterward, not even pale. Just...set, as if he was doing a slightly disagreeable but necessary chore. Cleaning the gutters. Taking out the trash. Plus, you'd have to be blind to miss the gun on his belt. Rifles and pistols were as common as candy, trampolines, or flatscreen televisions out here. She knew that...but still.

Okay, one thing at a time. Her quiet, beautiful living room was no longer soothing. "You mean you were coming into the library for half a year and never spoke to me because you..." Her word-finder was having some serious trouble. What the hell was coming *next*, for God's sake?

"Couldn't get up the nerve." He shrugged, an easy movement. He was built deceptively lean, you could miss the wiry, rangy strength in his hands or the breadth of his shoulders. It took a lot of force to break a skull. Not to mention grab an adult female and pull her through a diner door.

"Okay." She lifted her tea, decided it was still too hot to drink. Lowered it. "So...look. About yesterday." Those *sounds* kept coming back, haunting her. Meaty, bone-splintering thudding, the crackles of spongy bone shattering.

He didn't look away. His boots were on, and tied neatly. Had he slept in them? "I was in the Army, Miss Virginia."

"Yeah, I guess that would explain it." The world kept slipping away from underneath her, coming back with an internal jolt. Sooner or later she wouldn't be able to catch up when it moved, and what would happen then? This was just so...*bizarre*. "And you saved my life." *Twice, even.* "I mean, again."

Why did he nod, looking almost pained? Without a hat and his leather vest, he was entirely different. There was no library counter between them, nothing but empty air. It was stupid to worry about what he'd do if he had her alone in a car in the middle of nowhere. They were effectively stranded right now. Not only that, but everyone inside the diner had obeyed him implicitly. He was respected, in his own quiet way, and maybe that meant he wasn't half bad?

Maybe. It wasn't a lot to hang your estimation of someone on, and people had facades. Ginny had her own, and she was beginning to think it might crack under the pressure.

"Yes ma'am." Looking not at her but *through* her. A thousand-yard stare she'd only seen in magazines, or history books. Weary soldiers, staring into a camera's eyes.

It was that look, more than anything else, that convinced her. She waited, but he said nothing else. *Okay. Right. Fine. Good. All right. What the hell do I do now?* "Breakfast," she said, finally, with more certainty than she actually felt. "Are you hungry?"

"I could eat." He just kept *looking* at her that way. "Better do it soon, though. No telling when the power'll go out."

Well, isn't that a great thought. He was right, though.

She had the depressing idea that maybe he had a habit of being that way.

THE ROADS, UNPLOWED, WERE CARPETS OF SOFT WHITE. THE truck handled them all right, chains on the tires biting and Ginny flinching at every slight bump, sure they were going to career into a ditch. The bigger roads had markers at regular intervals, but he kept away from those streets, looping a wandering course working north through the fringes of town and eventually running parallel to the highway on a patchwork collection of country lanes. The houses drew back from the road, their silhouettes changing, and the the ditches got deeper. It should have been a beautiful drive, but the overall effect was...creepifying.

For one thing, almost none of the houses had lights on. Sure, it was afternoon, but still. Not a porch light, not a single golden window. No tire tracks, except for a looping, crazy set of them on Peacock Road that went straight off the pavement and over a sharp drop. Lee glanced at them and shook his head; the question of stopping to look for survivors died on her lips.

There was only one FM station coming in clearly, the smaller Christian rock one in Lewiston. In between solemn hymns, the disc jockey—his voice scraping, painfully hoarse—was reading from the book of Revelations, and it only took two sessions of *that* before Lee switched it to AM and began hunting.

...recorded message from the National Weather Service. A hazardous conditions warning is now in effect for the following counties...

That was all. Over and over.

"What did that fella on your computer say?" Lee finally asked, working the truck gingerly through a left-hand turn onto Marbury Road. He hadn't driven them into a ditch yet, but she couldn't relax.

Ginny, staring out the window, shook her head, slowly. At least her hair was braided and securely wrapped. "Just what I told you." A monotone. "That it's spreading. People get a fever, they don't know how. Once the fever gets over a hundred and three, they start foaming at the mouth and getting...violent. Then there's...everyone who called in, the ones that had seen it, said crazy things about dead people. The same thing—foaming and attacking, but *after* they're dead. Some of them said it started in major cities. Nobody knows what..." Her throat was dry. It was too bright, even though the cloud cover was thick and gray, promising more snow. "None of it makes sense, from an epidemiological—"

"The what now?" He didn't sound disdainful, only curious.

"The study of epidemics. That's what this is. But it's so *fast*. It doesn't present like anything else."

"Pre-zent?"

"You don't normally get that kind of response with a fever." Her hands held each other, tighter and tighter, her fingers all but creaking. "It uses up the body's reserves too fast. 103's just on the edge of cooking the brain. More chance of febrile seizure, but that's rare in adults."

"Huh." He considered the white wasteland outside the windshield. "How you know all this?"

"Med school." She could, she supposed, just say she looked it up on the internet. It would have been easier, but like all good ideas, it arrived a few seconds too late.

"You a doctor?"

"No, I'm a librarian." *I washed out.* It hurt, but only for a moment, a swift glancing pain she was used to by now. It was better to gloss over those wasted years. She was a spinster according to her mother's stuck-in-the-fifties life calendar, working low on the totem pole in the back end of nowhere. A flat-out failure, even though she'd gotten her master's in library science in record time. Flo had done better, according to her parents. And MBA and marrying a rich man plus giving them a grandchild was acceptable in ways Ginny would never be.

"Well." He considered this, feathering the accelerator. "Smart enough to be one."

"I just don't apply myself." The words tasted bitter. She forced her hands to unclench. "I'm lazy, you know."

"Don't look like it from here."

"Yeah, well." Her fingers tapped at her right knee, her most comfortable jeans with the small hole there, just right for tracing when she wanted to think. Now she studied his profile, deciding that if they ended up in a ditch there was nothing she could do about it. There was a certain de-stressing that followed that particular realization. "It could be that people go so deeply comatose others *think* they're dead. Except one or two of the people calling in were medical professionals, they seemed pretty sure. And febrile seizures just aren't common in adults, *and* there's no list of symptoms other than the fever. And irritability."

"Yeah, they seemed pretty goddamn irritable." He took his foot off the gas and the truck slowed, coasting. He rarely touched the brake, and the slow creeping speed was maddening. The houses had pulled together on either side now, they were back in town. "Sorry."

Huh? "For what?"

"Ain't right to cuss in front of a lady."

"You think ladies don't say *fuck?*" *Or maybe I'm not a lady. God knows Mom despaired of me ever being quiet enough to qualify.*

One corner of Lee's mouth crept up slightly, hovered there. "That's up to you, darlin. Way I was raised, a man don't use that language in front of 'em."

How chivalrous. An unwilling smile teased at Ginny's own lips. She tried to banish it. "Am I still a lady if I swear?"

"You'll be a lady to the end of your days, Miss Virginia, far as I'm concerned." They rolled down a slight incline, Lee studying the road with that intent expression, as if he could see right through the snow-pack to the pavement underneath.

Well, isn't that a relief. "Great." She tried not to sound sarcastic. And probably failed.

For some reason that made his slight smile broader. It crinkled the corners of his eyes, tilting his lips ever so slightly. His hands on the wheel were sure and deft. And scraped-up, probably from broken glass.

So much blood on the carpet, and splatters of bone and gray matter. How communicable was this sickness? And what if he started getting feverish? What if she did?

Ginny looked away again, out the window. Sometimes her brain just worked too goddamn well.

[30]

KEEP HIM COMPANY

Tip and Thurgood's house was two blocks from their business, a small square blue tract number with carefully painted white trim, frosted just like a wedding cake. There were tire tracks heading into the garage, blurred but neatly lining up with Juju's half. So someone had been up and around yesterday during the snowfall. "You gonna stay here?"

He could have guessed she didn't want to.

"No way." That same quick, nervous shake of her head as she undid her seatbelt. Wrapping her hair up in braids all the way around looked heavy, and it made her neck that much more slender and graceful. He'd never seen another woman do it up like that. Maybe she didn't need a hat that way. "What if something's in there?"

"Then you're safer out here." And she wouldn't have to see him do...anything he might have to, if Billy or Juju had come down with the irritables and a foaming fever.

Behind her, the window was full of eerie gray stormlight. His nose said the snow wouldn't begin again for a few hours, but he wanted to be home before then. It was a damn good thing he could navigate with his eyes closed round the Crossing. Concentrating on keeping the truck on the road was hard when he was also keeping an eye out for motion in the ditches or between the houses. And her, sitting on the other end of the bench seat, tapping at her knee or just breathing, was enough to distract the fuck out of him.

"Do you really think that?" She was already reaching for the door, a thin gold bracelet glimmering under the cuff of her jacket. In her own car, she could press a button and the lock flipped open, just like that. His wasn't nearly so nice. "Or is your wife likely to be home?"

Oh, crap. "This ain't my house. It's Tip and Juju's."

"Who?" Her fingers played with the door release, running nervously along the silvery bar. *Damn* distracting, to see her touching things that way.

"You met them." *Guess it didn't stick.* "Martin's. The garage."

It only took her a moment or two. "Oh, yeah. Your boss."

It shouldn't have stung him, but it did, hard and sharp right in the throat. "He ain't my boss."

"You work for him, right?" A transparent look of bafflement, her shoulders up a little and her chin dipping forward. Did she mean Tip or Juju?

Her coat was fine for a ski lodge or going around town, but not for any serious traipsing. Those hiking boots, too. He'd have to find some real ones, small enough for her feet.

Lee shelved that on the to-do list. No use in crowding his head just yet. "Three days a week." *They need the help, and I need somethin to do. About to get busy with other things, though. Goddammit.*

"Oh. Okay." She pulled the catch, there was a burst of cold snow-fresh air, and she slid lithely out of the truck without even checking the mirror.

Son of a bitch. He bit back the words, untangling himself from his own belt and yanking the keys from the ignition. "Hey. Hey!"

She was halfway to Tip and Juju's blue-painted door, and turned to look over her shoulder with a hesitant smile. A blush from the cold on those creamy cheeks, her wide dark eyes fringed with dark lashes, the honey in her hair showing up even through the gray light, the unconscious grace, all set against a snow-caked house and the thin, dangerous slice of the front door, just a little open.

Just slightly ajar.

It wasn't just cold out here. It was flat-out *freezing*, because the black ice was all through him, fingernails to bone. He sprinted, almost slipping on the snow crust before his weight sank through and his Army kickers dug hard, looking for pavement underneath. He grabbed her arm, yanking her back, and her feet almost slid out from under her. "Jesus, woman! You *want* to get killed?"

Her soft, half-swallowed cry of alarm fell into the deep well of a winter afternoon, and he was uncomfortably conscious of how *quiet* it was. There was no hum of traffic, and the snow on Tipton's street only held only two sets of tracks—his truck, and Juju's 4x4. Unless someone else had pulled into their garage, which wasn't likely, but with the way things were going, he wanted to be *sure*.

"Ouch!" She regained her balance, shedding his grasp with a quick, violent shake. "What's *wrong* with you?" Four hard, bullet-quick little words, but they lost all their punch halfway through, because the door moved.

Juju Thurgood, his cream-colored sweater and jeans spattered with drying blood, staggered out onto the porch in his sock feet, dark eyes ringed with white and close-cropped wooly hair stiff with sweat. His mouth worked a little, and he probably never knew how close he came to being ventilated, because Lee's hand dropped to his side with blurring speed, arrested only by Ginny blundering back into him and Juju's wild, high-pitched, barely coherent cry.

"*BIIIIIIIIILLLYYYYYYYYY!*" he howled, and dropped to his knees. The entire porch shuddered, and the wind began to rise.

"He came home all beat up," Juju repeated, hoarse and hollow, shivering even though Ginny draped the threadbare red plaid throw from the manky brown couch over his broad shoulders. "Told me he didn't wanna talk about it."

Lee, his arms folded, cleared his throat. The living room wasn't that bad, but the smell, all to familiar by now, was drifting down from upstairs. Juju had laid Billy Tipton on his bed, crossing the man's hands on his chest. A bib of dried foam poured down Tip's front, and even though his black-haired head was crushed on one side, he looked curiously peaceful. Billy's muttonchops bristled, the foam stiff among black strands.

"You think Andy had somethin to do with that?" The way things were tending, Lee'd be relieved if he only had to deal with Andy Bowe. Who was, all things considered, a coward, like any man who'd hit a woman.

"I dunno," Juju husked. The way he hunched down, he looked almost as small as Ginny, who bit her lip and put her arm awkwardly around him. "He said she bit him, that was all. *She bit me, she bit me.*" He shuddered like a spent racehorse, his blunt-nailed, bloody hands working at each other. "Then he..." His head dipped further, and Ginny's arm tightened.

She didn't seem to care that Juju was all spattered with stink and blood. She sat right up against him on the couch, glancing nervously at Lee with a line between her eyebrows and that small worrying at her bottom lip. He wanted to tell her to turn loose, it was dangerous to get close to someone that might get it into his head to start foaming and twitching, but he couldn't see a way to do it quiet-like.

"He fell on down like he been hit." Juju shook his head, violently, his shoulder bumping Ginny's chest. "I put him to bed. Woke up a little later an' he was screamin. Then he started...growlin. And foamin at the mouth like the rabies."

"God," Ginny whispered, and outright hugged Juju. Soft arms, looking to console.

Lee braced himself. "He bite you?"

"What?" Juju blinked, peering up at him. "Bite me? Lee, for Godsake, I kilt him."

"You din't have much choice, if he was comin for you." Lee kept his arms folded, though his hand itched for the gun, just in case. "It ain't just him, Juju. Whole lotta crazy people foamin and bitin out there."

"I tried to call the 911." Juju shuddered again. "Line was busy. Figgered I'd get through and head out before...before the police come."

Wise of him, considering Sheriff Blotzer and whatever deputy he'd sold a badge to that week wouldn't be big respecters of civil rights, so to speak. Lee's sigh, heavy as Nonna Quartine's had been once in a while when her husband had done something she considered foolish, surprised him. "They got other things to worry about, Juju. You did right."

"I kilt him," the man said again, and dropped his head into his bruised, battered hands.

"Did he bite you?" Lee didn't like pushing the question. He liked the thought of what he'd have to do if Juju said *yes* even less. Ginny, her teeth driving harder into her lower lip, looked at Lee, and the comprehension in her clear dark eyes hit uncomfortably close.

"What? Naw." But Juju's chin jerked up a little. He was no dummy. "Jesus, Lee. You sayin that..."

"That's what the *news* is saying." Ginny squeezed his shoulders again. "It seems to be transmitted through bites. Which is kind of weird, because where did it *start*, then, and that's a really inefficient way to spread. It can't just be through—" She caught herself, looked down at her knees. "It's not your fault, Mr Thurgood. You did what you had to."

Juju shook his head, and maybe Lee would have tried to reassure him some more, but the overhead fixture flickered. Juju flinched, and Ginny made a soft soothing noise.

Well, goddammitall. "You better get cleaned up 'fore the power goes out. You can follow us in the four-by." Shit if he didn't just want to leave the man here, but...well, how would that look to Ginny? It should bother Lee to even consider leaving Juju with Tip's body upstairs and God knew what crawling the streets.

Or it did bother him, but not as much as would be decent. That was what working in the sand and blood did, whittled at a man's decency. If you had only the regular dose to begin with, or God forbid a skimpy one, it whittled down to just about nothin'.

Juju nodded, but made no attempt to move. "He just fell down. Goddammit, Lee, what the blue *fuck*'s goin on?" He darted a look at Ginny, as if just noticing her presence. "Sorry, ma'am." The wind rose outside, a low moaning scrape against the tract house's corners.

"You guys." A slight, pained smile got Ginny's teeth out of her lower lip. "I guess it's that Southern gentleman thing. Let's get you cleaned up, all right?"

"Huh?" Juju, bemused, let her gently bully him to his sock feet. Man wasn't even wearing shoes. There was even dried blood in his wooly hair, and a spatter of yellow foam-crust on his cheek. That was goddamn uncomfortable to look at.

"He apologizes for cussing in front of me, too." She tipped her heavy-braided head at Lee, and steadied Juju as he rose, creakily.

"That's 'cause he's been sweet on you for—"

Oh, hell *no*. "Juju, get cleaned up and get some shoes on." Lee didn't quite bark it, but he was close. Getting everyone moving before the true shape of the problem sank in was the best way to work this situation. "Ginny, why don't you go on in the kitchen and fix him up some coffee? He likes it with sugar, boy's got a sweet tooth. Imma make sure everything's closed up good."

"But...Tip..." Juju shuddered, and Ginny tightened the plaid throw across his broad shoulders.

"We can't do anything for him now," she said, practically enough. "Go take a shower and get some fresh clothes. Lee's right. You should come with us."

"Where y'all goin?" Some sense had come back into Juju's gaze.

It was on the tip of his tongue to say it didn't goddamn matter, but Ginny was pale, Juju was shaky, and responsibility settled on

Lee's shoulders with an old, familiar galling. You never escaped it, once it wore its groove. "My place, but first we got to check on Horace. Get movin."

"It doesn't make sense," Ginny repeated. "If it's transmitted through the bites...it's just so *inefficient*. It couldn't spread that fast."

Lee kept the truck from drifting. Behind them, the 4x4's headlights stayed steady. Juju knew what he was doing, and driving might keep his mind off Billy Tipton's body. The four-by had a winch too, which would help if disaster hit, and when they picked up Horace the old man could sit back there and talk Juju's ear off. Better than Horace sitting in *here*, cozying up to Ginny and calling him Little Lee.

"The bites have to be secondary," she decided. "God, I wish I could just check WebMD."

"What's that?" Damn, but she was smart. Lee was beginning to feel distinctly slow-going.

"A site hypochondriacs use to scare themselves, mostly. But I could cross-reference the symptoms and..." Her chatter trailed off, and when he dared to take his eyes off the road, she was too goddamn pale, her mouth set and her eyes shining brim-full.

He had to look where they were going, or they'd run right into a ditch and that would be embarrassing as shit. "Hey." He couldn't take a hand off the wheel either, that was a sure way to invite something bad to happen. "Oh, hey now, darlin. It's all right."

She made a short, broken little sound, and Lee's foot itched to come down on the brake. He could stop the truck and say something, maybe, but what?

"It's *not* all right," she managed, a little thickly. "It's not ever going to be all right. People are *dead*."

People die every day. That didn't seem a helpful thing to say, so he searched for something else. And came up empty, of course.

Loose Rock Road split off here; he found it by touch, feathering the accelerator a bit. The chains gripped. Tomorrow, driving was going to be worse. Finally, he excavated something from the soup his brain felt like whenever he got a good lungful of that slight sweet perfume she wore. "We're still kickin. I intend to keep it that way."

Horace's turn was coming up. They crept forward, and Juju was still steady on their tail, hanging back enough not to crowd. Lee drifted the truck into a sharp right, waiting for the little catch in the back that would tell him he was past the danger point. He was still waiting to feel that catch with her, and something told him it might be a long while before he did.

"I'm glad," she said, finally, very quietly. "I don't...I mean, I'd probably have...I don't know. If not for you."

It would have warmed him clear through if it hadn't been the last thing he needed her thinking about right now. "Aw." That was all he could manage, since the truck began to slide. He turned into it, realizing he was sweating under his shirt. God *damn*. The entire world had gone topsy. He had his hands full, and she said nothing else.

Maybe there was nothing *to* say.

He'd rarely been so glad to see Horace's mailbox—a miniature, handmade red barn on a leaning post—or to feel the dip in the road that warned you to turn *now*, dammit, because the other side of the old man's driveway was crumbling. The snow was a pristine blanket, broken by the hillocks of Horace's chainsaw mushrooms grouped in combinations across his front yard. There was no use in living on a few acres if a man didn't decorate, old Slipot believed, and some tourists even stopped to buy the damn things. They always wanted to buy the animals, too, but the old man wouldn't sell those.

They were to keep him company.

"What is *that*?" Ginny pointed.

"Bear," Lee answered out of the side of his mouth, as the truck shuddered over washboard under snow. Slippery-slithering, they made it to the turnaround, and it was powerfully tempting to cut the engine, not bother with setting the brake, go straight into the old man's kitchen, and open the cabinet where he kept some Wild Turkey.

"A bear?" Puzzled, Ginny leaned forward, gazing through the snow.

"Chainsaw bear." His hands were only shaking a little. Christ, but this was exhausting.

"Chainsaw bear," she repeated, dubiously. "Oh, of course." And again, she popped the lock and was out of the truck before he could say boo.

"Don't—" he began, but she was already out. *What was that?*

The sound drew nearer, a frantic barking. It should have been welcome, except Horace would *never* let Ol' Bastard out for long in this weather, and it wasn't the dog's high-pitched greeting noise. Instead, it was a half-crazed sound of distress, and Ginny was walking right into it.

A bluetick coonhound burst around the corner of Horace's trailer, eyes wide and white-ringed, snow flying and the noise reaching a higher pitch. Ol' Bastard flat-out *bayed* as if he was about to tree some poor beast, and galloped for the intruders on his slice of the earth's pie.

Lee's fingers had turned to wet sausages. He fumbled with his seatbelt and struggled out of the truck as Juju bumped to a stop behind him. Lee almost lost his footing, breaking through a crust of ice that boded no good, and Ginny's sharp cry yanked him around the front of his truck, slipping and scrambling.

"Oh, aren't you adorable!" She crouched, stray curls worked free of her braided hair and falling in her face, and Ol' Bastard skidded to a stop, his yodeling yip-yawing into a hound's characteristic tell-you-all-about-it. "You *are*, you're beautiful! Look at you! Where's your human, little fellow? Where's your person? Did they leave you outside? That's not very nice, is it?" Babytalking, a soothing stream of words, she reached out cautiously, and the bluetick slobbered over her fingers and threw himself at her for pats and pets, still yapping a mile a minute. "Oh, you're *soaked*, you poor thing! Who's left you outside, huh? Who's done that?"

Lee stopped short. He heard Juju climb out of the four-by and crunch up behind him, and the urge to rub his eyes as if he was dreaming was damn near overpowering.

"Well shit," Juju said quietly. "I never thought I'd see someone that dog wouldn't try to eat."

"Me either." But that wasn't what was disturbing him. "Where's Horace?"

Juju, solemn, eyed the front of Slipot's house. "I was just wonderin that."

"Lee?" Ginny craned her neck while Ol' Bastard threw himself down in the snow and almost begged for a bellyrub. "He's hungry, and he's wet all over. Who would leave a dog out like this?"

"That's the trouble," Lee said. "Horace never would."

They found the power off and the back door half-open. Old Man Slipot was nowhere in sight.

[31]

WOLF

Horace Slipot never knew the world had ended, because
of a squirrel.

It was a mangy one, probably diseased, or so he thought when he
saw it hopping through falling snow near dusk, its wiry bottlebrush
tail mottled with lost fur and its sides scabbed. Still, it leaped
between fat falling flakes, pausing at the apex of every jump like it
had some special dispensation from ordinary gravity. They looked
light as feathers, but Horace wasn't fooled—those little fuckers were
muscle-packed and *mean*. You got close enough and you could see
their claws, meant for digging into bark and keeping the tiny bastards
from falling to their doom.

Sometimes he even thought about putting one of them in a
stump, but the time wasn't right yet. You had to know the animal
before you could carve it. The chainsaw didn't forgive halfass
measures, and though Horace would never have articulated it in
quite such a way, he *understood*, and that was good enough.

He would have laughed himself into a fit if anyone called him an
artist, but he was one all the same.

Ol' Bastard, his nose at Horace's knee just like usual, could tell something had caught his owner's attention. The hound made a little throaty sound, weirdly modulated at the end. They were talkative beasts, and truth be told, ever since Wanda had passed on, he liked hearing the dog's narration of his day. From the state of his breakfast bowl to his hankering after a long walk full of smells, Ol Bastard was determined to tell Horace every last thing that was what.

Just like Wanda used to.

"Well, boy," Horace said heavily, "it looks like there's a little fellow out back."

Ol' Bastard—Wanda had named him Kenneth, but Horace thought that was a damn fruity name for a dog—knew that tone in his master's voice, and wagged his hind end so hard it threatened to come off. His fringed tail whapped back and forth, and he crooned his *oh yes yes let's go outside* song with gusto. During Wanda's last illness, Ol' Bastard had been all but inconsolable, only quieting down when Horace brought his wife home for her final days. They'd tried to talk him out of it, all those young doctors and starched nurses, but ol' Doc Willoughby had come down on Horace's side of things, and that helped. Wanda had settled into their marriage bed with a sigh, and had not left it until she was cold.

And oh, hadn't the dog howled when she came home! He'd leapt on the bed as soon as she was settled, and curled into her side, staring into her wan, parchment-paper face adoringly. *Oh, Kenny,* she'd told him. *You'll have to look after Horace when I'm gone.*

"Don't say that," Horace murmured, the past bending over into the present in Chinese fan-folds. He set his half-full coffee cup on the counter and stared, unseeing, out the kitchen window. "You just don't say that, honey. You gonna shake this off."

Sometimes he wished he hadn't insisted on that. Maybe it would have been easier if he hadn't been so determined to see her pull through. Not on him, because there was no easy way when your wife's cancer roared through her body and ate everything in the cupboards before gnawing at the walls and foundation to boot. But... on her. Horace would have liked it to be a little easier on Wanda, and sometimes at night he thought about it long and hard while Ol' Bastard snored at the foot of his empty twin bed, stuck in the spare bedroom they'd never had a child for.

He didn't sleep in the bigger bedroom anymore. It just felt wrong.

Horace rubbed absently at his aching left shoulder as he headed for the back door. Ol' Bastard pranced behind him, his singing modulating into the *oh yes I'm gonna go outside* song. The dog almost managed to get his head between Horace's worn-out knees in his haste to worm his way out into the snow, but as soon as he stepped onto rickety stairs outside the back of the doublewide, he actually paused and looked back at Horace, his mild dark eyes wide with astonishment.

Each damn time, the dog acted like he'd never seen snow before.

"Well, go on," Horace said, glancing toward the sparse treeline. The squirrel was still there, sitting up straight and tall on top of a chunk of maple Horace was intending to turn into some company. He didn't know what was sleeping inside the wood yet. When he did he'd fire up the chainsaw and set about hacking it loose.

But Ol' Bastard stopped, every line of him quivering. He almost vibrated in place, craning his loose, flexible doggy neck so he could stare up at Horace.

"What, you afraid of it?" Horace stumped down the steps, not realizing he was still in his house slippers until he was a few strides away from the tiny porch he'd built so Wanda could drink her coffee and look at the back yard in the summer. Her garden boxes were full of weeds now, he didn't have the heart to yank or cut them down. Some of the company—the stag lifting its mouth to the sky, the second bear he'd ever carved—were set in the boxes. She'd grown vegetables, he grew dumb statues. "Oh, *hell*." His socks were going to get wet, but he was out here now, and while he was he could take a look at that chunk of maple.

Might as well see if it felt like talking yet.

Ol' Bastard, his indecision vanished, rocketed off the porch for the squirrel. Thin spatters of snow sprayed, the dog skidded, and

Horace began to laugh. He couldn't help it—Ol' Bastard looked so *surprised*, and the squirrel bolted for the treeline. Ol' Bastard gallumphed after it, his ears flopping madly, and there was definitely something wrong with the squirrel. It was too slow, and if the damn dog caught it, he'd probably chow down before Horace could make him drop the corpse.

Harold sped up, stepping high and wishing he hadn't opened the door. He made it to the huge chunk of maple and wheezed, leaning against it. His stomach was unhappy, and his left shoulder now hurt like a motherfuck. "God *damn* it, come back!" he yelled, but Ol' Bastard was closing in for the kill.

At least it was swift. The old man sagged against the maple trunk, his eyes rolling back. The double shock of sudden cold and activity squeezed at his chest with a bony fist, and his last thought was *it's a wolf of course it's a wolf* before the world narrowed to a pinprick.

The squirrel reached a trashwood sapling and clawed desperately up the trunk. Ol' Bastard leapt, pranced, and howled in fury until it occurred to him his master wasn't offering encouragement *or* displeasure. When that thought worked its way through his agile canine brain, he trotted back for the house, calling out to help the poor benighted human—he grasped, dimly, that they did not smell a fraction of the glory of the world that poured in through his own nose —find him.

His master, curled around the bottom of a large chunk of dead tree Ol' Bastard had already marked several times as his own, was already dusted heavily with quick-falling snow.

[32]

SECOND TO A BOTTLE

"Rick, for God's sake." Margie Mayburn put her hands on her hips. "Nothin's gonna happen to me."

"Pardon me if I think different, Margie." Rooster Clane leaned against the door, all five-foot-five of him, and glared at her. The broken veins on his nose glared too, and it might have been funny, except Margie liked her privacy. He was allowed to come over when *she* said, and stay when *she* said, and if he made a fuss about leaving, there was always provoking him until he flew out the door.

So far, though, provoking wasn't working.

"You'll be more comfortable drinkin at home," she sallied, wishing she could take her earrings out and shimmy into her sweatpants. There was some ice cream in the fridge, and Christ if the power was going to stay on, she figured she might as well eat the pistachio while the gettin' was good, so to speak. There wasn't anything on the news that told her anything otherwise would be a good idea.

"Ain't drinkin while we're under fire." Rooster shook his head, the bristle at the back of his skull scraping her kitchen door, along the pretty beveled glass panes on the top half.

She had her own little house on Mulberry Street, a tidy frame number, and if sometimes the mortgage took her down to pennies because the diner was in the red that month too, well, that was *her* business. Ever since she'd moved back to Cotton Crossing, she kept a line between *her* business and the whole parade of *town* business that came trompsing through the diner door.

Rooster had his own place over the Happy Cow feedstore, a tiny space with a cot, a commode, a hotplate, and not much else. He said he didn't need more, the Navy taught him to live small, and she was pretty sure that wasn't *all* it taught him. There was cooking, of course, but that could've been picked up anywhere.

When he'd shown up that afternoon, blue tattoos all over his arms and his cocky stride shouting *temper problem*, she hadn't been impressed. But the man could cook, and she'd been able to get rid of Sal Shellack, who had always been a troublemaker and stole freight to boot. Sal was over in Colville Correctional, and she wondered how the prisons were keeping things going. They had to have gennies, right? And overseas, her boy, her little Eddie...

Best to just leave that be. Her boys were gone, and the emptiness inside her when she dared to think about either of them was too big to bear up under.

Margie was a big believer in bearing up. You did your duty, by God, and you kept your mouth shut. Being married to Harvey had taught her that much, at least, and getting prepared to divorce him had taught her other things. If he hadn't gone drunk as a skunk off that bridge, she might have shot him instead and been closed up in a jail herself, and where would her boys be then?

Don't jine the Army, she'd told them. *That's what did for your Daddy.* Neither of them listened.

Men never did, and Rooster was looking to fix that principle in solid stone yet again.

Margie took a hold on her temper. "I have my .45, and I have my deadbolts, and I have my tee-vee, Clane. And *you* need to get home and tend to your own knittin." She put her right hand down on the kitchen counter next to the stove. "You have your dinner packed, so you go on now. It ain't your night."

"Margie, for God's sake, there are *things* out there. You saw 'em, the Army's shootin em, there's riots and—"

"Exactly, but there ain't no riots in the Crossing, and the Army ain't gonna come down my street, so you just get along, now." She patted the tile—it was bright pink, and Lord she loved it. Harvey would have hated her kitchen, but praise be, he had never seen it. It was a far cry from the shitty little apartment in Chi-town he'd drank them both into. In fact, the kitchen was the exact shade of pink that a certain bathroom in a certain Chinese restaurant in Chicago, and wild horses wouldn't drag out of her that she had it because it was exactly the same shade as her private parts, too.

Nobody needed to know *that*, and any who could guess kept their mouth shut.

For a moment, she wondered if she would have liked Rooster better if he didn't go on his tears. A woman could only stand being second to a bottle for so long, and God knew Margie was more patient than most, but still. Most nights nothing happened, they just watched the tee-vee and made bad comments about the characters. There was one particular show with a mother and a daughter, both wisecracking rich kids, and they both liked how the talkin went so fast most couldn't catch it.

But then, there would be the moment at the end, when she'd have to make the decision: let him stay or not? And he never made any fuss one way or the other.

"Margie." He scooted himself even further against her back door. Coming in the front was for company, he said, but she knew it was because there were fences and he could at least make an attempt to keep everyone out of her business. That was to be appreciated in a man. "I know this feelin. It's a bad one. I'll sleep on the couch, but I ain't leavin."

"For Chrissake." If she picked up something and heaved it at him, he'd probably duck. He'd be a nigh-on perfect man, would Rick Clane, if he didn't *drink*. "What do you think is gonna happen?"

"I don't know. What I do know is this ain't right, and if'n somethin happens I'd rather be here than above the Happy fuckin Cow, Margie. I drink so much as a drop, you throw me out inta the snow, I won't make a peep."

"Oh, *Lord*." She threw her hands up. "*I promise*, right? *I promise I won't touch a drop, I won't hurtcha Margie*, I heard all that before. I feel damn sorry for you, Rooster, but a man drinks once, he'll do it again, and when he does there's his fists. I ain't got nothin but the cookin wine here, anyway. Unless you gonna drink my Listerine."

He stared at her for a few moments, his pupils dilating, and the pit of Margie's stomach turned into a red-hot dollop of melted metal. If you kept pushing, sooner or later every man would get the knuckles ready, and he was no exception.

Except Rooster Clane's hands were loose and slack at his sides. He just *looked* at her, and for a brief moment, Margie Mayburn, her maiden name thank you very much, thought maybe it was a shame she couldn't let him stay. Not ever again, not after this. He thought he had to take care of her, which would have been fine, but a man who touched the bottle was not a man Margie wanted around permanent-like. They were all right for a casual thing, a friendship, because women at forty were at the high end of their hormones, she heard, and besides, he was funny. He laughed at the same things she did, and sometimes threw popcorn at the tee-vee when the daughter on that show made a Horrible Decision, like she always did.

But he always picked up the popcorn afterward, too.

"Margie..." Breathless, like all his air was gone. Like Margie had punched him.

Then he straightened. His face slammed shut, and the Rooster-for-Richard Clane she knew—the man who sometimes had night-mares and always closed the door softly in the morning on his way out to open up the diner if it was his shift—retreated behind another man, the one he was in public. It was like seeing a city couple go out the door and knowing they'd only left a fifty-cent tip.

Finally, he got his wind back. "You ent gotta feel sorry for me," he said, and fumbled for the doorknob.

She could have stopped him then. *Rooster, I didn't mean it.* Or something similar, soft and apologetic. All part of the dance.

Instead, Margie-for-Margaret watched him get the door open. Watched him step outside, slowly, the back of his head a knob atop a stiff, accusing bar of hurt. He closed it gently this time, too, and the metallic smell of snow and a deep freeze coming filled her pink kitchen, the heart of the safe, empty little space where she could eat pistachio ice cream and wait for the power to go out and things to get truly shitty, the way they always did.

From outside, muffled by the storm, came a series of deep, racking coughs, fading as Rooster exited her back yard. He would drive home in the damn snow, and that would teach him, wouldn't it?

"Shit," Margie said. Her forehead was uncomfortably damp, and her own throat tickled as well. If she came down with a cold, that would just be what she deserved.

She shuffled across the pink linoleum, deliberately taking her time in case there was a knock and a shamefaced *I can't go, it's too cold,* and when she finally threw the deadbolt the little sound went straight through her.

[33]

ARGUE WITH GRIEF

Horace's backyard was a wasteland of white humps and hillocks, with only Ol Bastard's tracks showing how the dog had run hither and yon, wearing a circle around a couple stumps. Lee stood on the back porch, his breath pluming in the cold, and thought about things.

Inside, Juju and Ginny were getting the dog fed and dried off. Had Horace wandered off into the woods, foaming at the mouth and moving with that quick, eerie speed? Was it worth trying to track him? The house was cold with the power off and the day was more than half gone; how long ago had the old man stepped outside?

None of the roads were plowed. The radio was full of shit that didn't make sense, and according to Ginny the internet was too. This particular brand of not-making-sense was way worse than the usual serving of inconsequential babble. The world had slid off its axis and was heading for a deep-ass hole. He had to make a few decisions now about where he wanted to land.

How widespread was this thing? The man on Ginny's computer was up Pennsylvania way, and that was a bit of a walk. Was it moving west?

Riots in San Diego, they said. Huh.

Well, he'd get Ginny up to his house, where he was fairly sure any foam-mouthed sonofabitch showing up could be dealt with proper. There was the genny and the stove, too, so they wouldn't freeze. He and Juju could chop enough wood for the winter, if it came to that. There would be ways of getting food, between hunting and sliding into town to look for canned, dry, toilet paper, and the like.

The only problem with that plan was Ginny's insistence on gettin' to her folks. There was also the thought that this might not be a temporary bump in the road. But that was ridiculous, right? In the cities, they had the infrastructure to deal with outbreaks. They *had* to. The Crossing was a little pissant town, so no wonder it got the short end of the stick...but if this terrorism, or sickness, or Act of God, whatever it was, reached all the way into the damn backwoods, what would it do to people crowded together in concrete anthills? Biting was an inefficient way of spreading something, sure—like rabies—but what if there was another way?

Shit. It was just after noon, the sun would only go down from here; there was another load of snow on the way if the clouds were any indication, not to mention the flat metallic taste of the air. If Horace was running around in the woods, there was nothing more to be done for the old man.

Lee eased the back door open and edged inside. Ol' Bastard was crooning vigorously, and it sounded like Ginny was talking back. Hounds were vocal creatures, and Ol' Bastard was talkative even for them. Living with Horace, maybe he had to be.

"...was in the Army," Juju was saying. "Tip and me, too."

"So you're friends." Her tone changed. "Who's a good boy?" Ol Bastard replied with a modulated, happy little yowl. "Get you dried off...there. Yeah, he seems pretty...well-respected."

"Well, he's quiet, is Little Lee. Call him that on account of his daddy being Lee Senior and his grandaddy what raised him being Big Q for Quartine. They're all quiet, Tipton says. *Said.*" There was a rattle—Ol' Bastard's food bowls, being packed up. Lee stood in the utility room, closed his eyes, and shut the door softly.

A few moments of silence. Even Ol' Bastard didn't make a sound.

"I'm so sorry," Ginny said, softly. "You must've loved him very much."

"He was my brother, ma'am." Juju cleared his throat. "Saved my ass in Afghanistan—sorry, ma'am. Well, we was always lookin out for each other."

"Was that where you knew Lee?"

"Oh, naw, not with us. He was in—"

Oh, hell no. He grabbed the door, wrenched it open, slammed it and shot the lock. Serve him right for eavesdropping, Nonna would say. You never learned anything good that way. "Juju." It was back in his throat, the burr-snap of the Army, and he had to swallow twice. "We got everythin?"

When he stepped into the kitchen, nobody looked guilty. Why should they, just makin' conversation? Ol' Bastard, in fact, looked about as satisfied as a hound could without someone rubbing his belly; he was on the orange Formica counter, his snout buried in one of his metal bowls, happily crunching on kibble.

Old man Slipot would have a fit.

Juju gave him a thumb's up. "Any sign of Horace?"

Lee shook his head. The old man was a lost cause, and Lee had the living in front of him to deal with. "Let's go."

"Lee?" Ginny slid the bowl away from the dog, who made a chagrined sound but was too well-mannered to protest more when a human moved the food. "What's his name? Juju won't tell me."

Oh, shit. He tried to remember what Mrs Slipot had called the dog. Ever since she died, Horace called him *ol' bastard,* and that stuck. You didn't argue with grief, and a man could call his dog whatever he liked. But it wasn't something he could say to *her.*

Lee could not, for the life of him, remember the dog's original name. Instead, his brain latched on to a nasty little kid from his elementary school days at Ridgeline under the benevolent, myopic gaze of Miss Prudence on the playground. The kid had freckles running together like they'd been baked on, all over his thick cheeks, and the spots on Ol' Bastard's sides reminded him of that.

He hadn't thought of that kid in years. What was his goddamn name?

"Trav," he said, finally. *That's right. Travis McKinnock. His people moved away after the mill closed.* Why the blue *fuck* was he thinkin about that kid? He needed to get home, and have a little peace and quiet and some hard thinkin that wasn't his brain just doing the rabbit-chase.

"Is that short for something?" Her color was back, and she rubbed behind the dog's ears. He gazed at her adoringly, and another hot, almost unidentifiable feeling smacked Lee right in the gut. Shit, he probably looked at Ginny that way his ownself. He was an idiot.

But a useful one, maybe. Now he had both her and Juju to look after, and the damn dog as well.

"Traveller," he decided. *Since that may be what we're doing.*

"I never knew that," Juju piped up. "That's what the missus called him?"

Lee nodded. It would take too much time to explain, and the dog might as well have one name as another. "You got his chow?"

"What about a leash? A collar?" Ginny framed the bluetick's face with her hands. "A handsome boy needs a handsome collar, yes he does."

The dog waggled all over and licked her nose. Lee, his neck tight as load-bearing cables, decided he would, after all, snatch the Wild Turkey from Horace's cabinet on their way out.

The old man, wherever he was, didn't need it anymore.

[34]

UNDER THE SHADE

Percy Blotzer was in a bad way.

The sheriff of tiny Cotton Crossing, reporting to Lewiston because it was the Haggard County seat, was a large man. He reeled drunkenly from side to side, a shoulder hitting first one wall along the stairs, then the other. The fever had him, and it was a dilly. He wasn't quite sure why he was here, except for the fact that things had gone all to hell and this was where he belonged, not in the house where Manda...

Oh, but Christ, he couldn't think about Manda. Home from the hoity-toity college, snappin' off the ends of her words just like a damn Yankee, but still sittin' next to her pa in church. *Daddy, I have something to tell you.* The picture on her phone. *We'll get married after college.* Her wide-open smile, with the gap between her front teeth closed up good now. He could remember her at eight, with one of those teeth gone and her hair like two hanks of honey yarn. Best thing to come out of that marriage, for God's sake, and she was marrying...

"Oh no you ain't," Percy said, and tripped. He went down hard on the last three stairs, falling into damp, rancid darkness. Lights were out, he had to yodel up the stairs to one of the deputies. "No you ain't, no ma'am."

You can't stop me, Daddy. Manda, with her wide blue eyes, and the boy staring out of the phone had smooth caramel skin and a wide nose.

"Didn't raise you to marry no—"

That's racist, Daddy. Please stop. And the way she looked at him, her nose a little up just like her mother's. God damn but he hated that, the way Cindy stuck her face up and looked at him like he was some sort of lower creature. She'd remarried a lawyer, down Tallahassee way, and that caused some talk in town. Oh, Percy knew the jokes made at his expense, and sometimes he grinned his big ol' aw-shucks grin at them while somethin' deep in the back of his brain ticked each one in a column.

A Blotzer would get his own, come the end of the day.

"You get on out of here!" he yelled, thrashing on the floor, and the fever was cold but he couldn't shiver, sweat pouring off him hot and rank, and why was he even here?

Left the house. Slammed the door and out into the snow, yelling at Mandy. "You get on outa here! You marry that boy you don't come back, you hear me? *You hear me, Manda Jane?*"

Big blue eyes fulla tears, the way they were that day in the courtroom, when Judge Vickers asked her who she wanted to stay with, her ma or pa. Sometimes Percy thought it wasn't right to make a kid choose like that. But that was later. At the time all he felt was hot justification when Manda said *My daddy.*

Of course, Cindy wasn't even in the courtroom. *God I gotta get out of this one-horse town, why did I ever marry you, we were supposed to get out of here, Percy!*

It was just that he was under the weather. That cold going around. That was why he'd grabbed his gun, drew a bead on Manda Jane's little red Toyota that he'd scrimped and gouged for so she could go off to college in style. The realization of just what he was doing hit him all at once in his icy driveway.

Pointin' his service revolver at Manda, for God's sake. At his own flesh and blood, his own little girl.

Sheriff Blotzer found himself upright, weaving terribly as he tacked across the dark concrete-floored hall. Nobody in the cells down here, middle of the week and everyone indoors. Power was out. Why was the power out? His phone hadn't rung since yesterday, and now he realized, dimly, that it wasn't normal. His cellphone—paid for by the county, because by God, he kept the law around here, and everyone knew their place when Percy Blotzer was in uniform, yessir —had been on the fritz too. Maybe he should ask them Army boys. Why couldn't Manda have liked one of *those* boys?

Daddy, you look a little under the shade, Manda had said when she arrived, hugging him. *You been eating? Taking care of yourself?* Fixing him dinner, and after that, sitting him down on the couch with a serious expression. *Daddy, I have something to tell you...*

If he drew his service revolver now, he knew what he'd find. Manda's car had zigzagged, but he was sure...

There would be a bullet missing. He'd broken the law. He'd shot at his own daughter, his little girl. His head throbbed, fit to burst. He was sick. And he had broken the law.

Percy Blotzer's brain, hovering on the edge of 103.9 degrees Fahrenheit, began to cook.

[35]

FAMILIAR IN THE PAST

LEE'S LITTLE YELLOW HOUSE LOOKED LIKE A FAIRYTALE, ALONE in a wide, bright white meadow dwarfed by wooded, snowy hills, the trees hooded and secretive as cloud cover thickened again. A muffled shape on one side of the driveway looked like an old truck, but it was hard to tell under the cold white blanket. There was a long low corrugated building to the right, and that was what he aimed the truck for, bumping out of what felt like ruts. The house itself was a trim, snug manufactured, freshly repainted and obviously cared for. Maybe he even had a garden. You could probably grow plenty out here. Tomatoes, it got hot enough in the summer. All sorts of things. Maybe even weed, who knew?

Ginny was just grateful for the prospect of a bathroom, and to get the dog's head off her lap. Traveller had passed out as soon as the car began to move, snoring unconcernedly, and while she didn't begrudge him the rest—the poor thing probably hadn't slept much last night, if the state they found him in was any indication—she didn't really like the suspicious warmth under his jowls.

Eventually, she'd shifted his head enough to be sure, and...yeah. He'd *drooled* on her.

Every once in a while, Lee took a hand off the wheel and patted the sleeping dog's hindquarters, gently. He didn't look away from the snow in front of them while he did so, it was a simple, reflexive movement. That was, Ginny thought, just what she'd come to expect from him.

When he cut the engine, the dog twitched, and the ticking of cooling metal was very loud in the sudden quiet. Juju's black four-by-four bumped up on her side, a nice neat parking job. It was kind of funny, the way cars huddled together just like people, even when there was plenty of space. The corrugated building looked like a barn, and she thought of horses—or a cow? Maybe he milked his own?

She searched for something applicable. "It's beautiful." Ginny patted Traveller's head, smoothing marbled fur. "*Whose woods these are I think I know.*"

"Huh?" Lee stretched his hands out, probably aching from clutching the wheel. "About twenty acre, from my grandfather. He done him some business in his time."

"Oh." She absorbed this. "No, I mean, it's a poem. Robert Frost."

"He any good?" Lee's eyes were bloodshot. No wonder, squinting into the snow-glare all day.

"Sometimes." She shifted on her side of the bench seat. "You're a good driver."

"Thank you, Miss Virginia." A small movement, like he wanted to tip his hat. Where had it gone?

"You lost your hat." Was it that she didn't want to get out of the truck this time? Clinging to the familiar, even if it had only become familiar in the past few hours?

"Yeah. The diner." Lee leaned back against the seat, and it was the first time all day she'd seen him relax.

The 4x4's door slammed, and the dog pricked his ears. He was awake now, one eye half-open, watchful. She'd always wanted a dog, but certainly no animal would ever dare step foot in her mother's house, not even a cat. A cat would have been nice, maybe. "You look better without one." She reached for the door, and Traveller scrambled upright, his tail whipping frantically.

A few desultory flakes of snow whirled down. Juju was already at the sliding door to the shed, or barn, or whatever it was, obviously familiar with Lee's place. Was this the actual house, and the yellow one something else? She peered curiously inside the corrugated building, finding a bunch of equipment, neatly hung tools, tool chests, and a couple worktables. Traveller, *sans* leash and collar—because, Juju said, a good hound would stay with you, really—roamed inside to sniff everything, despite Ginny's cry of caution.

"He'll be okay." Juju opened a metal cabinet to show extension cords neatly coiled. "Lee, Imma plug both these bastards in, aight?"

"Power could be out. But might as well." Lee slammed the truck door. "Genny's just for the house. We can move 'em later, if we gotta. I don't smell no ice comin."

Juju nodded. "Me neither."

She might as well have been invisible, even to the dog. Ginny hugged herself, her red leather purse bumping her hip. Her cooler was in the back of the truck, and her suitcase was probably damp from flying snow. It was a hell of a time to wish she was still at home —but no. Alone, in her house, knowing what was next door, having to go up and down the stairs and imagining the large wet splotch on the wall on the other side...*no*. She stared across the snowy meadow, and a shiver that had nothing to do with the temperature grabbed her from shoulders to heels.

She wanted to keep going, heading for her parents. The trouble with pausing was that all of a sudden your brain got full of the fact that something awful had happened, eating every other thought and replaying terrible things, like the *pockpockpock* of bullets all around you, or the groaning, growling sound Amy and Hank both made, or the heavy clicking of teeth snapping together, or Tipton's body lying on a bed, his hands crossed on his chest and his head horribly misshapen—

"Ginny?" Lee was right next to her. His hand fell back to his side —had he meant to touch her shoulder? "Didn't mean to startle you."

She had to swallow twice to get her pounding heart out of her throat. She'd just been staring into the distance, thinking about dreadful things. Was it a coping mechanism? If it was, it sucked. "Christ. I'm sorry. What can I do to help?"

"Go on inside." He pointed at the yellow house. "Ain't locked."

Good Lord, they didn't lock their doors out here? Of course, what would break in? A wild moose? Did moose come this far south? Ginny couldn't remember. "My suitcase—"

"I'll get it."

She set her shoulders and lifted her chin. "No, I'll carry it in. And...the dog. We can't leave him outside."

"No ma'am. Been a while since I had a dog in the house." The corners of his eyes fanned with crinkles, but his mouth was a straight line. "All right then."

It was an unexpected relief. She nodded, briskly, and got moving.

As long as there was something to do, she wouldn't have to consider what might have happened to Mom and Dad. And Flo, who might even have gone into labor.

Oh, God.

[36]

SON

His place still had power, go figure. The temperature dropped sharply as night fell, but the wood stove did its work well, and dinner was a far sight better than anything Lee ever cooked for himself. Juju leapt to help clear the table—Ginny had sat where Tipton usually did when he was over for coffee, and the other man's eyes had teared up—so that meant Lee got up too, and Ginny left them with the KP. Which was all right, but Nonna would have shooed them both out, not trusting them with dishes. Of course, Nonna would have double-scrubbed every plate Juju touched, too, being Mississippi gentry. Her great-great had fought with Stonewall Jackson; Big Q's had signed on with Frémont, finished with Sherman, and maybe even done some jayhawking on the side.

His grandparents didn't talk about the war but once or twice Lee could remember, and both times ended with frosty silence on Nonna's part. For his own part, Lee followed Poppa Q. And the Army tended to cure a man of bigotry, if he let it.

Lee had the idea Ginny, being a Yankee and a city girl, might not have gained *all* Nonna's approval, but that was a minor consideration. He didn't realize what she was up to until Traveller, his dinner bolted and his throat full of yodels, made his going-outside sound and the front door opened. "Shitfire," he muttered. "You go on out and watch, Juju."

"Huh?" But Thurgood was no slouch in the brains department, so a hot second later the man's brown eyes widened and he stiffened. "Oh, man. You think they out here, too?"

"Been talk about things in the woods for a week now." Lee plunged his hands into soap bubbles and hot water, wincing a little. "Better safe than oh, fuck."

"Amen to that." Juju strode for the dining room, halted, and turned back. "Lee?"

"Ayuh?" *Get on out there and make sure she don't get no harm.* But he set his jaw. That would be damn impolite.

"Tipton allus said you were good folk." He cleared his throat, and stumped away.

That meant something, and Lee stared into the soap bubbles, his neck tensing up again, as the front door closed again. *Good folk.* Well, that was easy when you had a steady job or a little put by, or a monthly from the Army. It was a damn sight harder when you were hungry. Or afraid.

Fearful people did fearful things, and if the three of them had survived so far, there were bound to be others. Those others might be dangerous as rattlers, especially if they were scared enough to shit peach pits. How far did this thing spread? Canada? Mexico?

Now he was getting ahead of himself. All during dinner, he'd been conscious of Grandon's package in the coat closet, full of God-knew-what. Lee couldn't decide if it would be better if the damn thing had no connection to the current bitch of a situation, or worse.

Lee hunched his shoulders, and set to scrubbing the skillet Ginny had made fried rice in. Damn tasty, and nothing he would have ever thought to cook. She kept the conversation going on light things, asking Juju about where he was from, what music he liked—and the two of them went back and forth about opera like Nonna Quartine and one of her henfriends about the daily soaps. Juju was damn beside himself that someone else knew who that Kathleen Battle woman was.

Lee caught himself listening for Traveller's noise, filtering in faintly from the front. The house was quiet, but not in the way it had been while it was just him. It felt...good, he decided, to have the kind of calm almost-silence that meant people, his people, were close. Comforting.

Even if he couldn't stop wondering what was in that damn package, and how it was likely to fuck up everything even more.

He settled Ginny in the master bedroom, and Juju in the guest room—the sheets on the bed probably still smelling of the rose sachet Nonna used. Nonna's antique Singer and the old cherry wardrobe would watch Juju sleep, and Ginny...well. It was damn distracting, thinking of her in Lee's own bed. *No, it's fine,* she said, when he offered to change the sheets. *The power might go out with them still in the washer.*

Practical. He wouldn't have thought of it.

Are you sure? Juju asked.

You're company, dammit, Lee told him. *I want the couch, in case somethin happens. But you can spell me for a watch or two out here, if you're so damn determined.*

Traveller, of course, kept his nose right at Ginny's heels, and the damn dog was probably going to end up on Lee's bed. Christ.

He waited a long time, sitting in his recliner and watching the front window full of snowlight. On his lap, the envelope and the package were slight, negligible weight. Lee Quartine had a jelly glass with two fingers of Wild Turkey in it and a whole lot to think about. The night light over the kitchen stove was on, and if it blinked off, he'd know the power was out.

That would give him an entirely new set of problems, and he hadn't finished chawing at the ones he had.

Inside the envelope was a whole clutch of papers, but the one he spent the longest on was addressed to him in a fine, flowing copper-plate script. Grandon had gone to school somewhere cursive was a must. Nonna's writing had looked like that, but Poppa's, not to mention Lee Senior's and Lee's own, was chickenscratches at best.

Ginny's writing was just as beautiful as the rest of her.

Son, Grandon's letter began, and Lee had stopped there for a few moments, looking out the front window, his hand aching to curl into a fist and crumple whatever this was. The wood stove could handle some paper just as well as it handled everything else.

But the files were full of medical jargon, at least from what he could tell. And with people falling over frothing at the mouth, well, it didn't take a genius to tell they were connected. Grandon had been up to his armpits in this, whatever it was.

When the urge to put his fist through something, anything, had receded, Lee read the rest of the letter.

SON,

I KNOW YOU WON'T LIKE ME CALLING YOU THAT. BUT I HAVE TO TELL YOU, LEE, YOU'RE THE CLOSEST THING TO A SON I EVER HAD. I'M SORRY IT WENT BAD FOR YOU. YOU CAN'T KNOW HOW SORRY.

I EXPECT YOU PUT THIS IN A CORNER AND FORGOT ABOUT IT, FIGURING I'D BE WRITING TO TELL YOU TO DO SOMETHING. IF YOU DIDN'T, I'LL BE SURPRISED. THE PAPERS SHOULD BE PRETTY SELF-EXPLANATORY. THE PACKAGE HAS TO GET TO GEORGIA. ATLANTA, TO BE PRECISE. THE CDC HAS FACILITIES THERE. IF WHAT I THINK HAS HAPPENED...BUT THAT'S BESIDE THE POINT. IT'S GOT TO GET DOWN THERE, SON. ANYONE ELSE I GIVE IT TO MIGHT GET COUN-TERMANDED. MAYBE THAT MIGHT EVEN MAKE YOU DO IT.

CONSIDER IT A LAST REQUEST, BECAUSE I'M PRETTY SURE BY THE TIME YOU GET AROUND TO READING THIS I'LL BE CASHIERED WITH A NINER OR SOMETHING WORSE. REMEMBER YOUR VERY LAST TOUR? THE VACCINE TOP-UPS YOU GOT WHEN YOU CAME BACK? THEY'LL BE INTERESTED IN THAT DOWN IN ATLANTA TOO.

I'VE BEEN IN THE FIGHT LONG ENOUGH TO KNOW WHAT'S

GOING TO HAPPEN WHEN THIS THING BREAKS LOOSE. I WISH TO GOD I DIDN'T.

I MEAN IT, LEE. YOU'RE THE SON I WANTED. I SHOULDN'T HAVE DONE WHAT I DID. I CAN PRAY THAT GOD FORGIVES ME, BUT WHAT I AM REALLY HOPING FOR IS THAT YOU WILL.

It was signed *Harry.* Not Colonel Grandon, not with a simple scrawled *G* like he used to. The stationary said *Major General Harold E. Grandon.* Old boy had got himself a promotion.

Lee sat there in the dark. He took a sip of Wild Turkey and let the burn go all the way down.

The package was a soft case, and inside, nestled in little niches cut from foam, were three vicious-looking syringes. Standard Army issue, capped and full of a vile-yellow liquid. KEEP IN COOL DARK PLACE, the sticker on the outside said, and BIOHAZARD.

Of course he remembered the "vaccines." Never had them coming *back* from a tour before, but he hadn't made a fuss. You learned not to. And now that he thought about it, most of his unit had come down with flu something awful just after Columbia. That was the "very last", and he'd all but begged Grandon not to send him in. *I'm tired of killin,* he'd told him. *You won't like what you get, you send me in there.*

Afghanistan was bad. Iraq was worse. Then there were the *other* places. None of his unit had ended up quite...sane? Was that the word? Topper ate a chunk of lead, I-Dog went with drain cleaner, Summers and Blow got the cancer—only maybe it hadn't been, whatever they injected...had they died foaming at the mouth? Jesus Christ. Then there was Hall, called Hallelujah for his habit of praying before a jump, and Peanut, both just...disappearing. Peanut had a wife; she said he'd just got up from the dinner table one evening, kissed her cheek, said *it isn't your fault, Helen,* and walked out the front door in his slippers.

She hadn't seen him since.

All the things Lee'd moved back to the Crossing to escape swirled around inside his head now, old bad gas in a mineshaft. He lifted the glass again, but it stopped halfway to his lips.

Lee leaned forward, the chair smoothly rocking with him. Good thing he hadn't put his feet up. He eased upright, the papers and package falling from his lap with soft sounds, and took a few long swinging steps, ending up in front of the window.

His front yard glowed with snow, strange winter half-light. Lee squinted, restrained the urge to rub at his eyes. His long driveway, the double set of tire tracks pressed into it, the covered mound of the old truck up on its blocks...and the treeline on the far side of the bumpy dirt road. Something flickered there.

Deer. Gotta be a deer.

Except deer didn't move like that, all jerk-twitchy. It lolloped out of the trees and into the road, and it wasn't alone. Two more, one ponderously fat with what had to be a hunter's orange vest flapping around its capacious, stained gut, the other small.

Child-sized. And wearing a bright-orange cap, if Lee's eyes didn't miss.

Lee realized he still had the glass halfway to his mouth. He lifted it the rest of the way, and knocked back the entire cargo in one shot.

They melted back into the trees, but not before the one in front dared to dart across the street and lower its face to the tire tracks. Its head bobbled, and Lee could swear he almost heard the thing *sniff*.

"Hell no," he whispered, unaware of speaking. "Oh, *hell* no."

He stood, staring at the treeline, rolling the jelly glass in his sweating hands, for a long time. Until he heard Juju begin to stir in the room that Lee, as a boy, had slept in. Slowly, as if in a nightmare, he shuffled across the room and gathered up the papers and the syringe-bearing softpac.

Better, he thought, to put those out of sight.

$$[\ 37\ ]$$

HARD MONEY

Juju Thurgood never thought he'd have trouble sleeping after the Army. You learned to drop off wherever you were, and if you didn't, exhaustion took care of that for you. And here, in a warm enough bedroom, in a real bed, he should have been out as soon as he made up his mind to be.

But nothing in the service had prepared him for this. He kept hearing the awful ratchet-growl sound, Billy's eyes gone blank and weird and film-grey, the fever splattering them both with sweat and the rank yellowish foam...God.

Juju turned over. The sheets were cool and slick, and smelled of roses. Lee's house felt different now, too. He'd never stayed the night here before; the killing quiet of snow outside couldn't cover up the ticks and tocks of the structure settling for the night, or the sense of other breathing presences. It was like when Tip was home, downstairs drinking on the couch or with the tee-vee on low.

Best not to think about it.

Except who would be able to ignore what he'd done? To the end of his days he'd feel his best friend, his *brother's* head cave in under the blows from the ugly-as-fuck lamp in Tip's bedroom, the one with the heavy glass base he bought at an Atlanta flea market on furlough one drunken afternoon.

I swear, Tip had said, *in a hell of dust and noise and blood, if'n we get home, Juju, you and me gonna go into business together.*

For a cracker to keep a promise like that, and then get his head beat in...it wasn't right. None of this was right.

Of course God was a cracker himself, of that there was no doubt. Nothing else would explain the goddamn world. It was just like the big old asshole in the sky to bring Tipton and Juju both safe through two tours apiece with no worse effect than the scar on Tipton's thigh, some hearing loss, and real juicy nightmares, then turn around and make one man beat the other's skull in.

Maybe Juju should've let Tip bite him.

She bit me, Billy moaned. *Lila, Lila...she bit me.* More he wouldn't say, already shivering and feverish. Juju had considered calling the 911, but couldn't get through. Maybe if he'd been a medic, or something else, he could have...what? Tied Tip up? Administered something other than a beatdown?

Tipton's hands at his throat, squeezing. *Billy don't...Billy don't...Tip...*

There was an animal inside every goddamn man no matter his color, and that animal wanted to live. Juju turned over again, roughly, his hair scraping the pillow. Checked his watch. Maybe he'd dozed off, maybe not. He didn't *feel* rested. Christ, he could have told Tipton that woman would bring him trouble, but how did you tell a man that when he had his mind fixed?

Juju suspected he'd never feel rested again.

Lee was all right, but Tip was his *buddy.* Ever since Mosul, when they'd shambled together out of the smoking, screaming cauldron, a rough pressure bandage on Billy's right leg and Juju's entire body one slow grumbling song of pulled muscles, there was no other word to describe it. In the foxhole together, and out the Devil's asshole. And Lee, goddamn Lee with his stripes and his cold gaze, too quiet for any real friendship but a steady commander all the same.

Well, lookit what the cat drug in, Lee had said, grabbing Juju's other arm, ducking under it to help support him. *You boys are a mite late.*

Fuck...you... Juju had replied, between deep painful breaths. *Sir.*

The laughter. He'd never laughed so much as he had with Billy. For a white boy, he was pretty fucking funny. And half the garage was Juju's, on paper and legal. He'd taken it himself over to Lewiston to a black lawyer, and of course you could never relax completely in dealings like that but he'd paid hard money to hear what he already knew: Billy Tipton's word was good.

To hell with it. Juju sat up, rubbed at his head. Slid his feet out from underneath the sheets, made the bed on autopilot. Bounce a quarter off that motherfucker. The wardrobe in the corner watched him, the sewing machine gilded in a fall of snow-night glow from the window.

Company, Lee called him. What Juju really wanted was to hear Tip stamp his feet and bellow, *Juju, you home?*

Even when he knew, he liked to ask. Or he wanted to make sure he wouldn't get shot by a nervous sentry. Habits did that to you, burrowed in all over like ticks and refused to leave. Silence was for enemies, for the knife and the hand over the mouth.

George Unwin Thurgood, nicknamed Juju by his blessed mama, exhaled hard as his chest seized up. Her bent over, wheezing a little, and waited for it to pass. God wasn't just a cracker. He was a monster.

Not because he'd taken Tipton, but because he'd left Juju alive.

[38]

UTILITARIAN ARGUMENT

GINNY WISHED SHE COULD FOLD HER ARMS. AS IT WAS, SHE drew herself up, full height, and fixed Lee Quartine with the glare that usually worked on people who got carried away at the computers on a quiet library afternoon. "How about you back up and try that again?"

Juju had already excused himself to take Traveller outside, even though she'd just brought the dog back *in*. It didn't take a genius to figure out he wanted to get away from this conversation. Her hair was probably sticking up every which way, and she usually had trouble sleeping in unfamiliar beds. Last night, though, she'd zonked out as soon as her head touched the pillow. Even if it smelled like someone else. Which wasn't...bad, precisely, but now she was uncomfortably aware that she'd been in a guy's bed. On unwashed sheets.

It felt too...personal.

Lee stood in his kitchen, the window over the sink glowing with directionless, snowy light, and took a gulp from a mug with a faded, much-washed Army logo stenciled on the front. His bloodshot eyes were back to dark hazel, and his cheeks were freshly shaven. "We'll go looking around town. You stay here."

"Repeating yourself is not an explanation." She tried for a reasonable tone, found it. Her own mug—thank God she'd packed decent teabags—was big enough, but it had a stenciled NRA logo, of all things. It warmed her hands quite nicely. His collection of dishes was was just what you'd expect, even if there was Wedgwood in the china cabinet in the dining room. Every house she'd visited here had one of those hutches, usually stuffed with dusty Depression glass and mismatched teacups with "gold rims."

That, of course, led her to her neighbor Amy's pride and joy, a teapot painted with overblown tea-roses and its cracked, delicate, matching cups. At least Amy's hutch in the dining room had been left unscathed, even if everything else had been smashed.

The thought made her stomach curl up around the pancakes she'd cooked this morning, and she leaned against the silverware drawer, its ancient brass handle digging into her hip. The pain was welcome, it steadied her.

Lee's hair was messy too, and there were dark circles under those bloodshot eyes. It didn't look like he'd done a lot of sleeping last night. "Truck might not be the best, once I don't know the roads. Juju and me'll go looking for what we can find, and supplies too. Might as well stay where it's warm."

That part was reasonable enough, but she wasn't going to be distracted. "Where exactly are you going to find supplies?"

"Wherever we do, might be some of those foam-mouthin bas—uh, I mean, folks, around. Juju knows how to shoot."

So they were both going to go out armed. That was troubling enough, but he really hadn't answered her. "Are you going to steal a car? Is that what you're saying?"

"Ain't sure it's stealin, at this point."

Well, that was a utilitarian argument if she'd ever heard one. "All right. And you intend to shoot someone?" She leaned a little harder into the silverware drawer, its pressure reminding her to keep her temper.

"If it looks like they gonna bite me or Juju."

Again, reasonable enough, but not *quite* what she was asking, and he probably knew it. Ginny, unfazed, was not about to let this go. "Are you going to shoot someone and take their car?"

"Don't see no need for that."

Well, it was good to know carjacking wasn't his plan. "And you want me to stay here." *Little woman waiting in the cave while Big Grok goes out to hunt, is that it?* Irritation bit briefly at her throat, she kept her tone level. Of course they assumed she'd do the cooking, and that was fine, but this was something else again.

"You ever gone hunting?" He took another gulp of coffee and winced. It was undoubtedly too hot. He probably needed the caffeine, though.

"No." *Not unless you count cadging free drinks in college.* "I just think we should stick together. What if something, you know, *happens?*"

"You're better off here, with the genny and wood stove, and the truck. And Ol—I mean, Traveller. You can get out to your folks in the spring, if this thing don't blow over by then."

"Blow over." *It goes all the way up to Pennsylvania, for fucksake.* How far west did it go? Hadn't she heard something about San Diego?

The past few days were receding like a nightmare, but not nearly quickly enough. There was no waking up from this. There was no *blowing over,* she thought. And spring was...God, that was *months.* Ginny's toes curled inside her thickest pair of wool socks.

He took another gulp of coffee. This time he didn't wince at the scorching. "You worried we ain't gonna come back?" Did he actually look slightly pleased at the notion?

Oh, for God's sake. "That would be a reasonable thing to be worried about, wouldn't you say?"

"Sure. I'd also say you can see if my phone'll work for your folks, and see if you can get a signal on the tee-vee. See how far this thing's spread. If a 'mergency broadcast shows up, be nice if someone was here to get it."

Ginny didn't point out that they could all just turn the fucking radio on in whatever car they ended up in. "Fine." She blew across the top of her mug. His phone was a landline, and he was right—she could start dialing, see if she could raise someone, *anyone*. Maybe he even had cable out here in the sticks. Christ knew these people loved their cable tee-vee.

"And you can look around and think about what we need for travelin. Juju and me, well, we run light. But you might, you know. Need things."

Christ, like tampons? Or yoghurt? "Okay." A funny, fluttering feeling in the pit of her stomach would not stop. She ignored it, and decided now was the time to set the tone for all their future interactions, so help her God. "So we've established you have good reasons for asking me to stay here, right. What about the other bit? The *don't leave the house* bit?"

"I, uh." Lee all but winced. "I may have said that wrong." He didn't quite look ashamed of himself, but it was close. His shoulders went down a little and his chin dipped, like a teen boy called on in a poetry workshop.

You think? "Yeah. You might have."

"Listen." He set his mug down on a pinkish Formica counter losing its color around the edges. "I ain't exactly easy in my mind about leavin you here alone. So I'm askin you, please, to be careful when you take Traveller out."

"Much better." She set her own mug down, just as carefully, and folded her arms like she'd been wanting to do all along. Sometimes the little things helped. "You don't have any neighbors, Lee. So unless there's starving bears with a yen for Manhattan girls in the trees, there's something else. Right?"

"Uh." A number of expressions crossed his face, settling somewhere between chagrin and unwilling admiration. He pushed at his hair with one hand, settling the longish bits on top. "Well. They was talk about things in the woods, Miss Virginia." His accent had thickened, and maybe it was deliberate. Maybe it wasn't.

"But you're okay with Juju taking Traveller out, right?" Oh, logic. A woman's best friend.

Lee shifted, uncomfortably. "It's daylight, and he knows how to handle himself."

As if she didn't. Well, to be absolutely honest, "handling" herself had not been high on her list of Life Skills. He was right. "Well. I'll be sure to exercise all appropriate caution. When are you leaving?"

"Huh?" His slow, sleepy blink might have bamboozled someone else into thinking he was confused, but not her. Oh, no. Ginny thought she had a pretty good handle on Mr Lee Quartine, smarter than he liked anyone to know and used to letting his drawl and his good-ol'-boy aw-shucks do the work for him.

Her arms tightened, her fingers digging in. "It's a simple question. When are you leaving?"

"Uh, well. Soon as we can, I reckon."

"All right. Go on, then." She restrained herself from saying *shoo* by sheer force of will.

Now he looked downright chagrined, head a little down and his bloodshot gaze half-wary. "I didn't mean—"

"Oh, I know what you *meant*, Mr Quartine," she informed him. "But I'm not in the Army, and you don't bark orders at me. Are we clear on that?"

"Yes ma'am," he mumbled, and exited hastily. She got a good whiff of him as he did—male, a faint tang of leather, a little bit of citrus, and a faint fading note of alcohol. Maybe *that* was the circles under his eyes.

Right now, she was only a little irritated that he hadn't shared.

[39]

PINK BEDSPREAD

Pink bedspread, pink curtains, a big mirrored closet. The bedroom even *smelled* like a girl, a powdery pretty odor with an undertone of apples. A wicker hamper near the door held laundry, and the mirrored closet was half open, showing part of the room and soft blue reflected snowglow.

Wild horses wouldn't drag it out of him, but Mark Kasprak sometimes had dreams about sleeping next to Steph Meacham. Not like this, though, with both of them huddled fully clothed under all the blankets in the house, and Steph making those soft agonizing sounds when the nightmares started.

He didn't blame her. This was some nightmare shit, and he was almost glad he hadn't been to his own trailer yet. Maybe his dad was worried, maybe not, but Mark had some ideas about the deep, racking cough his dad had been complaining about. The same damn cough Mr and Mrs Meacham had, to hear Steph tell it, and maybe the same fever too.

Steph's dad. Now *there* was a nightmare, one he hadn't been asleep for. Mark moved a little, restlessly, trying to shake it out of his head. Steph whimpered in her sleep, and he wished he could comfort her. There probably wasn't any damn comfort, really. Not for this.

Here he was, next to a girl who made his insides turn over and all of him sweat whenever he saw her at school, and he couldn't even get a hard-on. Maybe it was the cold, but Mark didn't think so.

Bull Meacham had run right out of the house and at the truck, his jaw working and his big broad hairy chest naked to the wind. Barefoot, in striped pajama bottoms, he'd thrown himself on the hood, and Steph had started to scream. The only reason Mark didn't scream too was because the truck slid sideways as he jerked the wheel, flinging Steph's father off. The old man hit pavement with a cracking sound, and that hadn't been the worst.

Oh no. Not by a long shot.

The worst was Mrs Meacham inside the house, in her housecoat and slippers, her eyes gone all grey and funny and her throat swelling as she made that awful, horrible growling. She hadn't been able to get too loud because something, or *someone*, maybe even Mr Meacham, had chewed most of her throat right out.

It was no use. He wasn't gonna be able to sleep, but it was too cold to get up and walk around. Steph flat-out refused to leave the house yet, even though they'd had to barricade the front door with furniture to stop Mrs Meacham—or whatever it was—breaking back inside. With the power out, it was a cave. Was his truck gonna freeze? He should have plugged in the engine block warmer. Dad had told him to make sure he got one, if he was gonna spend his money on a piece of crap car.

It wasn't a *car*, it was a truck, even if it was yellow. It was *freedom*. And there was no fucking power, so the engine heater was dead anyway.

And he'd run over Steph Meacham's father with his truck. The old man got caught on the undercarriage, and dragged up into the front yard. Throwing the truck into reverse hadn't helped, just dragged him into the driveway, the tires making weird sounds and Steph making an inarticulate sound that rhymed with *Noooooo...*

Mark jerked awake. His arm, under Steph's head, tensed, and she woke up with a squeak and clutched at him. "What is it? What?"

"Nothin." Mark cleared his throat. Here he was in a girl's bedroom. Pink bedspread, under all the damn blankets. He was sweating, for God's sake, and he didn't even remember falling asleep. "Bad dream."

"Me too," Steph whispered.

She wasn't even angry, or at least, she wouldn't let him leave. Maybe it was what they'd had to do to her mama, or the 911 not working, or any of this fucked-up situation. And how fucked-up was it that Mark was glad he could stay here? It was better than home at the trailer, that was for damn sure. And his dad, drunk more likely than not. Yelling at him about the truck when the old man spent all his monthly on rotgut, for God's sake? Mark didn't feel bad at *all* about leaving his daddy alone, and that was a sure sign he was a sinner, like his grandmother would say.

But Lord, he did feel awful about Steph's mama. Getting into the house and finding her had been bad enough, and to hear Steph scream *Mama no Mama no Mama no please* while the lady tried to get her teeth on them both...Mark hadn't even really thought about it. He'd just *done*, like hittin' a woman—someone's *mama*, for Godsake— was an action just waiting under his skin to be let out.

Was he really like his daddy? *Blood tells*, everyone said. He wondered if Steph would move, so he could pull his arm free. It was already numb.

"Mark?" Steph, whispering again, her breath hot against his shoulder. He was sweating, goddammit, and probably reeked. In a girl's bed for the first time in his life, and he couldn't even *smell* right.

"What?" He used his free hand to yank the pillow down a little more. Had he been snoring? That would just put the icing on the cake, right?

"I'm glad you're here." Like it was a secret.

"Me too." He didn't realize it was the truth until he said it. "I'm sorry about all this, Steph."

She shifted a little, cuddling closer. "You think he was gonna hurt me?"

"Maybe." He didn't even pretend he couldn't guess what she was thinking. "Stands to reason. I know *she* was." *Great. Remind her that you killed her mama.*

Or you tried to. Her mama ain't dead. Mrs Meacham was out there in the storm with a hole in her throat, making that awful grinding noise with her teeth.

"But my mama..." She sniffled a little. "What's goin on?"

It was the same conversation they'd had all evening. At least there was food in the house. Sandwiches and milk were just fine by him, even if he had peanut-butter breath now. "Well." He searched for something to say that didn't sound crazy. "I, uh. You're gonna think I'm nuts."

"I'm thinking *I'm* nuts."

So he said the word out loud. It sounded ridiculous, and for a few seconds he was afraid she was gonna start laughing at him, that the whole thing was a hallucination or it was some sort of hidden camera thing and it was gonna be all over the internet and the assholes at school weren't just gonna laugh at him because he was poor and his shoes were worn out and his mama had run off with some insurance salesman but because he was *stupid*, too, and—

"Yeah," Steph said. "That's what I was thinking too." She snuggled closer again, and everything inside Mark loosened. Warmed up. His arm didn't feel quite so numb anymore, either. She even repeated it, too. Like she couldn't quite believe what she was hearing. "Zombies. Mark?"

"Huh?"

"Your arm okay?"

Hell, he couldn't tell if it was still attached. But something else had decided to start working, right in his pants, and if he moved at all she might figure that out. Her leg was over his knees, and oh, dear Lord, what was he gonna do now?

"Fine," he whispered. "Just fine."

A short while later, while both teenagers slept clinging to each other like shipwreck survivors, dawn rose pink and gold. Around Meacham house, long dragging tracks circled, filling up with snow.

[40]

GOIN' ON TOUCHY-FEELS

"You look like you been hit on the head." Juju squinted at the white-blanketed road, his hands sure and deft on the wheel, and feathered the accelerator. Chains bit deep, and the feeling of them digging in was comforting.

Comfort was hard to find this morning. "Do I now." It was nice not to be driving. But it meant Lee had little to do except watch the mirrors, the buried road, and think about how he'd put his feet wrong with Ginny all morning. If it wasn't her taking exception to them leaving her with the dishes it was her raised eyebrow when he told her to stay inside.

"You really like her." Juju was enjoying this. He all but grinned at the windshield, his bomber jacket zipped up all the way and two thick sweaters under it. His gloves lay on the seat between them, with Lee's own.

Oh, for cryin in the mud. "She's a nice lady." A ghost of her perfume and shampoo clung to Lee's shaken-clean shearling, or maybe he just imagined it.

"No, I mean, you *really* like her."

Lee restrained the urge to cuss. "Yeah, well, it ain't gonna do me much good if I do, now is it?"

"Why you say that?" Juju glanced at him, perplexed. "She likes you too."

How can you tell? But there would be no end of teasin' if he asked. Lee's discomfort mounted another notch. "Juju, watch the damn road."

"Can't see it. Goin on touchy-feels." But the younger man sobered, his full lips turning down. "What the hell is goin on, Lee?"

"Wish I knew." And wasn't that the damn truth. Except Lee had a few ideas, each more uncomfortable than the last.

Juju shook his head a little. With his hair smashed flat under a hunter-orange ski cap and his nose a little raw from the cold, he looked like a teenager. "Sounds like the Pocalypse to me. End Times. My mama would say so."

It was the first time Lee could remember Juju saying anything about his family. Lee rested his hands on his knees, not looking at the scrapes or scars across his knuckles. There was still engine grime under his nails, you couldn't scrub that shit out. Not like Ginny, clean and perfect. She even made his bed neatly when she got up, though he hadn't bothered once he left the Army and Nonna passed on. It felt like a rebellion at the time, but now it just seemed...sloppy.

Embarrassing. Even Juju made *his* bed, nice and tight-cornered like he was back in basic.

"Would it still be the end times if someone did it?" Lee turned the sentence around in his head, wiggled his toes a little inside his Army kickers. It was nice to have decent socks. "I mean, one of us. Insteada God."

"You mean, like the guvmint?" Juju chewed over the thought, then nodded. "I guess. God might as well do it that way."

Which was uncomfortably close to Lee's own thinking. "Guess it don't matter." Snowglare lit the inside of the four-by; there was no dust on the dash. Everything was neat and shipshape as Juju's own tidy self.

Juju drifted the four-by into a curve, careful and cautious. "Well, prayin might help."

Never knew you were one for that, soldier. "Goin beggin don't suit me, Juju."

"Me neither. We ain't really lookin for a car, are we."

"Oh, we'll take one if we find it." Lee supposed he should feel bad about telling Ginny what was technically a lie, but the last thing he wanted was her *worrying*. She seemed to be a right champion at it.

"I reckon we're lookin for ammo." Juju sucked his lower lip in, made a soft thoughtful sound. "And maybe other things."

"You'd be right."

Juju absorbed this. He was the cautious half of the Martin's Garage duo. When he spoke again, it was soft, meditative. "You think Tip's in hell? Because..."

"Nah." *He had enough of that in the service, and so did you.* "I'm thinkin it's more like the Rapture. Got taken because he was a good 'un."

"Well, then you'd be gone too."

Now that was downright polite of Juju to say. Lee contented himself with a simple, "Huh." Neither a confirmation nor a denial. "More like *you* would."

"Shit." Juju drew the word out, managing to convey shy thanks and discomfort at the same time. "I got me another question."

I'll bet you're just fulla them this morning. God knows I am. "Shoot." Lee's mouth twitched, realizing that was probably the wrong way to say *go ahead* at this point.

"Well now." Juju eased off the accelerator as the road sloped down. "You think Imma catch what Tip had? That why you asked if he bit me, I figger."

"If you ain't got it by now..." Lee let the sentence trail off.

"I been thinkin. Seems like people been talkin about a flu goin around, lately. Old lady Harlowe got sick, Patty Dupree at the Lightning tole Tipton half her church was out sick too. I heard a lot of coughin last week."

Lee shifted uncomfortably. "Winter comin in. People stayin inside and breathin on each other."

"But half a church out with the sniffles fore'nit snowed?"

Margie at the diner had said something similar. "I dunno—*shit!*" Lee didn't mean to yell, but the shadow darting from the ditch was too scuttle-quick, and both his feet dug into the floor like he was the one driving, hitting clutch and brake at the same time.

Juju was a little ahead of him, downshifting even though the four-by was an automatic, and *not* stamping on the brake or twisting the wheel. The four-by slowed, its black hood gleaming with melted snow, and the darting thing skidded to a stop, its head upflung and its gray-filmed eyes rolling. Foam spattered hot and rank from its working jaws, and vein-maps of livid crimson threaded from the corners of its lips.

It wore Pat Cambell's duct-taped boots, his orange hunting over-jacket with the fringes of duct tape hanging from each sleeve, and it had Pat's shock of rusty hair. His Campbells were Irish to the east, distinct from the German ones who lived west of the Crossing. *And ne'er the twain shall meet*, Nonna once said, working at bread dough with her capable hands. Pretty, like Ginny's, even when she got old and so thin a hard wind could knock her over. *Don't you never put the Campbells at the same table, less'n you want some trouble.*

"Easy there," Juju said. "Jesus Christ, he ain't movin." The four-by drifted forward, its tires sinking through the crust, chains gripping hard. "Lee? He *ain't movin.*"

"Keep goin." The sweat was all over him now, and his legs refused to relax. He was trying to stand up in his seat, and it wasn't working. The seatbelt gripped his hips, dug into his right shoulder. "See if he does."

"What if I hit him?" Juju sounded steady enough, but his knuckles stood up on the steering wheel and the whites of his eyes had swelled.

"It don't matter." Lee realized it didn't a split second after the words left him. "If he don't move you just bump him."

The thing wearing Pat Campbell's skin made a queer little movement with its head, for all the world like a dog trying to figure out which direction a sound was coming from. Its jaw kept working, and as the four-by crept closer, moving at an idle now, its filmed eyes rolled and its tooth-champing increased.

"Jesus," Juju whispered. "He ain't gonna move."

"Don't let that worry you." Lee searched for something else to say. "He always was an asshole."

A shaky exhale, half laugh and half whistling anxiety, shook out of Juju's throat. He still didn't touch the brake, which showed he was thinking. "Drives a Dodge. A half-ton, right? Big-ass truck."

"Never changes the damn oil in it." Lee thought it unlikely Irish Pat would ever drive again, but thinking about the truck was probably better for Juju's nerves than anything else, at this point. The thing's filmed, sightless gaze was downright creepifying, as well as its air-chewing. *Everything* about this was creepy as fuck, but at least they were in a car. Relatively safe, unless the thing decided to go through the windshield. But no, it just stood there, its head moving snakelike and its arms hanging loose, disjointed. "Huh."

"What?"

"I don't think it can see."

The bumper kissed the thing's middle. It hissed, staggering away and dropping to all fours. It lolloped in the same direction it'd come from, the fringe on its jacket fluttering merrily. Right before it dropped into the roadside ditch, it halted and looked over its shoulder, teeth bared, yellowish foam spattering its cheeks. A boneless shiver went through it crown to heels, and Lee was sure the creature was making that dry growling noise. It was a good thing they couldn't hear it over the engine and through the windows. "Jesus," he breathed. His legs finally unlocked, and he was absurdly glad he was sitting down. His knees, once they unlocked, felt a bit mushy.

"Yeah." Juju sounded just as shaky. "The goddamn Pocalypse, Lee. I'm tellin you."

Lee Quartine did not disagree.

[41]

BAD DODGEBALL

DISHES DRIP-DRYING, THE BEDS CHECKED AND LITTLE THINGS put away, and a blessed, very hot shower—he had good water pressure out here, at least—didn't take very long. Dialing everyone she could think of from Lee's landline didn't either. There was still a tone when she picked the handset up, but even the local numbers didn't ring. There was just a long silence after she punched series of numbers in, then three oddly spaced beeps and a return of said tone.

Trying to raise anyone over the state line just got her dead air, and dialing 911, after she reasoned the current events might not qualify as the dictionary definition of *emergency* but were still severe enough to warrant tying up the phone lines, just got a busy signal.

So she roamed the living room, Traveller pacing behind her and making small whuffling noises as he nosed at the worn but religious vacuumed carpet.

The single bookshelf in the house was child-sized, but it held an interesting assortment. Two Bibles, one of them an antique leatherbound monster that had a family tree on blank, creamy pages in the front, entries going back to 1802. Quartine used to be Quartaigne, no wonder he pronounced it like he did. The extra letters disappeared around 1860. It was pretty amazing to hold the book and think about other hands on it, to see the changes in the copperplate script. There were birth and death dates. Lee's father had an entry, his name and birthdate written in a fine flowing style but his death filled in with blue ink and a decidedly modern set of cramped numbers.

Seeing that gave her an uncomfortable feeling of prying, so she reluctantly closed and re-shelved the Bible. The other one was a red leather modern King James, mass-produced and not nearly old enough to be intriguing. There was a *Pilgrim's Progress* and a *Dr Gunn's Family Medicine*, the first downright antebellum and the other giving her a few moments of teasing on-the-tip-of-the-brain trouble until she remembered her Mark Twain.

"Oh, wow," she breathed, but the other shelves called, as well. Cookbooks—Fannie Farmer, and the familiar Better Homes & Gardens' red plaid. *Band of Brothers*, and another couple of books on World War II. There was one old battered plant identification manual, a copy of *Preserving It Right*, some Chilton's auto manuals. There was half a shelf of bird identification guides. Did he like birds, or was it someone else?

She couldn't decide between the first edition Fannie Farmer or the Dr Gunn's. Then she spotted a fresh, brand-new road atlas, and all other considerations became secondary.

The dog's nose was at her ankles the entire time, and when she settled on the ancient, sagging brown plaid couch, he gave her a look of such pitiable sadness she couldn't help but laugh, a thin little sound in the snowbound quiet. The fridge hummed and the fan atop the wood stove made a low thrumming, and she'd been inside long enough that the house no longer smelled foreign. The entire place was like Lee himself—worn down but clean, everything in its proper place, and stuck about twenty years ago.

Not that she was complaining. Ginny patted the cushion next to her. The dog almost levitated, and the next few minutes were full of his cold, wet nose in her face and his little crooning noises. She'd had no idea a dog could *talk*, but this one certainly did his best.

First, she opened it to the central map of the entire United States. Her finger tapped down, everywhere she'd heard mentioned on the podcast.

New York. San Diego, San Francisco. Seattle. Denver. Houston. New Orleans. Major cities. Starting at the coasts and working their way in, maybe? Who knew? The urge to piece things together and make wild guesses was well-nigh irresistible, but it wouldn't get her to her parents any quicker. More than once she caught herself tensing to get up and grab her laptop, before she reminded herself Lee had no wireless and probably not even a dialup connection. There wasn't even a modem jack on her laptop, either. Take away the internet, and even a librarian would have some trouble. Contrary to popular belief, they tended to be early adopters of new technology, instead of starchy old greyhairs lacking any sense of humor.

The most wickedly funny people she'd ever met were in Information Services, really. It was like coming home. She winced, tapping near where Lewiston should be on the map. It didn't rate a blip on the big spread.

So whatever it was had reached the Crossing as well as several large cities. That didn't bode well. *Nothing* about this boded well, up to and including Lee Quartine looking at her the way he did. It wasn't that she was ungrateful, it was just...

Ginny shook her head. Traveller began to snore, his snout wedged under the atlas on her lap. None of this got her any closer to her parents and to Flo. Were they holed up in the sprawling ranch house behind its low brick wall? Hopefully the gated community had shut down and someone could be sent for groceries. It was ridiculous to think *all* the infrastructure had broken down, right? There were at least two retired doctors in the neighborhood, so if Flo hatched...

She reached for her phone, again, despite knowing there was precious little cell service out here, but her hand stopped halfway. Her parents were okay. So was Flo. She had to believe that. They were probably worried sick about her, because even though she was a disappointment, she was still a Mills.

And they loved her. She *knew* they did, just like she knew she loved *them*. Aggravation didn't mean there wasn't affection.

"Fuck," she said, softly, a long aggrieved slide of a word with a short sharp consonant at the end, chopping it off. Lee had probably taken the truck keys with him. Maybe that was a good thing, because Ginny was seriously considering throwing her suitcases and cooler in and taking off.

All it took was a disaster to make her contemplate auto theft. So much for the survival of ethics in extreme circumstances. Of course, the situation could get a *lot* more extreme, couldn't it.

"You don't have any imagination, do you." She lifted the atlas a little, peering down at the sleeping dog. "Must be nice." *I think I have too much.* And God only knew what had happened to the nice old man who had sat in Lee's truck and chatted at her that chilly flat-tire night. At the time she'd wished he would be quiet for at least five minutes so she could think, but now she was grateful he hadn't...and a little ashamed of herself.

She wondered about her library patrons, too. And her coworkers. Oddly enough, it was Mrs Harmon she was thinking about, the old biddy who had only a foggy idea how email worked. Was she shambling around her house with a foaming mouth and parts of her gnawed off? What about her husband, and their very favorite word?

Oh, crap. Ginny set the atlas aside and covered her face with her hands. Her shoulders shook. She was *extremely* glad there was nobody but Traveller, fast asleep and cuddled up next to her, to see her cry.

TRAVELLER SQUEEZED THROUGH THE DOOR AS SOON AS IT WAS even remotely possible to do so, and careened off Lee's porch in a series of bounds. He stopped, two or three leaps away, and looked over his shoulder at her, his mild brown eyes wide, as if he suspected

Ginny was playing some sort of prank on him. As if he'd never seen snow before—she couldn't help but laugh again, a guilty sound half caught behind a cupped hand.

For all the snow, it wasn't that cold. Her breath made a cloud in the crispness, and the trees stood out in stark detail, each bough lined and limned. The air seemed clearer, and paradoxically thicker, full of pine and ice and freshness, a bouquet like a good white wine with an apple undertone. There were probably fewer combustion engines working to dirty it up. Either that, or it was that Rocky Mountain High bullshit, though the mountains around here weren't nearly as big.

Her mother liked John Denver. *Oh, what a voice, even if he is one of those long-haired boys!* Her father, of course, would sniff. If it wasn't Perlman playing, he didn't think much of it. Flo liked hip-hop.

Were they okay? Had the baby been born? Boy or girl? If it was a boy, Mom and Dad would be over the moon. A grandson. Flo would be the favorite forever, world without end, amen. A girl would be petted and spoiled, the first grandchild after all. Bar or bat, Mom would start planning the mitzvah either way. It was never too early to worry, in her book.

It was a relief to find her grainy eyes simply wouldn't produce more tears. Ginny waded in Traveller's wake, her boots turning soggy. They were supposed to be weatherproof, dammit, but tiny chilly fingers touched her toes.

Traveller yipped and bayed, working in circles around her, his tail held high and going fast enough to blur. She turned left to head for the barn—there had to be a snow shovel in there, and it occurred to her it would be a good idea to clear a path. Physical activity was good for you, right? It lowered stress hormones, and by God she was probably swimming with them. It was something she could *do* instead of sitting inside with the atlas and working herself into what her mother would definitely call a mishegoss.

The small door was unlocked, and she stepped into cold, sawdust and oil smelling dimness. Once her eyes adapted, she found everything was ruthlessly neat, just like inside the house. It really wasn't that surprising. Lee Quartine seemed a very *precise* sort of person. There were canvas-covered shapes—drill press, bandsaw, other machines. A tractor and a trailer, the concrete under them swept clean, right in front of the larger garage door, which had an opener with a single yellow eye. There were tool chests and pegboards, everything hung neatly and logically. A cherry-red riding mower. Well, with all that open space out there, mowing by hand could take hours.

A long, heavy wooden work table held a pile of what she thought was a mess before she realized it was a microwave, taken apart. Was he trying to fix it, or just curious about how it worked? This guy could fix a flat tire, drive in snow, and he knew what to do when someone was shooting all the way down Main Street.

Still waters ran deep.

She found a red snow shovel, head supported by two exactly-level nails, and wasn't surprised it was a heavy-duty metal one. Getting the thing down was a workout; she almost dropped it on the tractor and swore under her breath. As if someone, anyone, was around to hear.

If something happened to the guys while they were out getting another vehicle, or whatever it was they were really after, she'd have to take the dog, Lee's truck, and the atlas. The gun cabinet in Lee's bedroom, tall and glass-fronted, probably had something in it she could use.

The thought of pointing a gun at one of those...at, God, something like Amy McCoy, or her husband...Jesus. And what about other survivors like her? Basic logic said some of them might be unpleasant people, and even if they weren't, they were likely to be just as frightened and disoriented as *she* was.

That was how accidents—bad ones—happened. Were the hospitals overwhelmed, or full of fevered, mouth-foaming people and...

She decided not to think about that just at the moment, slipping through the barn's small door out into bright snowglare. Traveller's cries had taken on a peculiar stridency, and she blinked furiously, waiting for her eyes to adapt.

When they did, she lost every bit of air in her lungs. It just whooshed out, like she'd been punched, or taken a bad dodgeball in the stomach.

Traveller stuck his hind end in the air, his front half down, and barked. It was the classic *hey-come-play-with-me* you saw dogs do all the time.

The problem was, he was less than six feet from a slumped orange shape. A man in an orange hunting vest. A *big* man, too, with a generous pot belly and a bullet head, the type the good ol' boys around here kept shaved high and tight even if there was no military in their background. The new arrival stood, his jaws working idly, his eyes—oh, God, his *eyes* were film-scabbed over, cloudy-blind. His hands—no gloves, even in the cold—worked, clenching and releasing just like his jaw, but not together or alternately. They were just a *little* unsynchronized, and it was that tiny wrongness that threatened to empty Ginny of her breakfast.

Traveller barked again, wriggling his back end, and his voice turned insistent, demanding. Either he was saying *play with me* or he wasn't sure if this was a threat.

Ginny could have told him, if she spoke dog. Because the lower half of the man's face was spattered and smeared, not only with foam but with torn strips of something like hamburger and clotting, smeared blood. The man's knees bent, and through the soup her brain had become, one thought slipped through sharp and bright as a knife.

They're so fast. Oh God, he's going to eat the dog.

"Traveller!" she shrieked. "Run away! Run *away!*"

The dog cocked a single floppy ear at her, but the man jerked like she'd hit him. His head made a weird craning motion, muscles in his neck and shoulders working in ways they weren't supposed to, and it occurred to her that he might not be able to see, but he *heard* just fine.

"Traveller!" she called, again. *Get its attention. Get it away from the dog.* "You stupid dog, stop that! Run away!"

Trav barked again, wriggling, the end of each yip going up questioningly. The man wavered, shifting back and forth on his big feet. One of his boots was missing, and part of the sock on that foot had been torn away. The flesh was bluish, the toenails black against snow. Frostbite. Gangrene would set in soon. Why didn't he have both his shoes?

"No." She took another couple steps, gripping the snow shovel. "No, you don't. You leave the dog alone. You *leave him alone!*"

Before she finished yelling, the sick man jerked forward, with impossible, spooky speed. His hands, big, raw, and already starred with spots of frostbite, turned into claws. Traveller yipped and danced away, throwing up a fan of snow, and Ginny hitched the shovel over her head and bolted forward, her boots slip-sliding, the soft dense white dragging at her ankles, halfway up her shins. "*Noooo!*" she howled, hoping she was loud enough to distract the thing.

Sure enough, she was. It dropped to all fours and streaked for her, half-crippled hands slapping down, its body turning sideways as the legs worked more efficiently than the arms. Snow flew, and Ginny suddenly realized she had no goddamn idea what to do next.

Traveller, dimly grasping this turn of events was not optimal, skidded to a stop and half-turned to take a look. His tail stilled, pointing straight up, and his wonderful nose was no doubt untangling a sudden drift of chemical terror.

Ginny slipped, her left leg going out from under her. She regained her balance with a lurching leap her childhood ballet teacher might have congratulated, and the *thing* was right in front of her. This close she could see the collapsing of the eyeballs, the gray filminess wrinkling slightly over the sclera, and the chunks of...God, it *had* to be meat the thing was chewing on, two deep scratches breaking from the corners of its mouth as the jaw worked, and worked, and it tried to get ever larger mouthfuls of air, snow, anything. It was splitting its own cheeks to cram more into what locals would call its pie-hole.

She swung the snow shovel down *hard*, still yelling. Not words but a high piercing scream of effort, falling dead against the snow-carpet. The world slid sideways at impact, the metal shovel-head cracking partly against the thing's shoulder, one curved edge shearing through thin facial tissue and grating on weirdly spongy skullbone.

A hollow gonging noise filled their little bubble of snowy quiet, and the thing made a rusty, irritated growl. A human throat shouldn't have been able to produce that sound, and the sheer unreality of what she saw pushed Ginny back two slippery, heaving steps.

The thing hunched on all fours, shaking its head. Foam spattered, and crumbs of wet, half-chewed gristle flopped between its nicotine-stained teeth. Its throat was a ragged mess, a suppurating hole gaping on the left side. It should have been bleeding out in buckets with that kind of wound, but instead, it oozed a weird darkish fluid.

Ohshit what do I do now where's the dog oh god ohgod what next—

The rusty, hissing, growling noise thrummed in its chest. Its gray, spiderwebbed eyes rolled. Ginny staggered back, her breath high and hard and fast, puffing out in white clouds. She had to get the dog in the house...but these things, they could break through a door, right? She'd *seen* one do it.

It twitched toward her; Ginny screamed and brought the shovel down again. This time the curved blade hit square-on. A wet melon sound of breakage splattered fluid, brainmatter like gray oatmeal, and ivory chips on the trampled snow. Something was wrong with the blood, it wasn't bright red. It was almost maroon, and thicker than it should be.

That particular observation only occurred to her later, because she was already lifting the snow shovel again. Traveller, suddenly very sure this was not a delightful game of walkies or chase, approached in stiff-legged dashes, and when he arrived, he began to growl, an impossibly deep sound for a dog his size. It said *I mean business*, and the thing's caved-in head twitched as it slumped.

Ginny shrieked and brought the shovel down again, so hard she bit her tongue when the impact jolted her arms. And again, because the body toppled sideways, and Traveller's growl turned even deeper. The thing's pudgy arms and legs spasmed, the orange vest scratching at yellowed grass beneath the snow.

"OhGod," someone was saying, between deep sobbing breaths. "OhGod, oh God, ohGod." Ginny realized *she* was saying it, in a breathy, unsteady whisper, tasting blood from her bitten tongue.

The...the man, the *sick* man, the *patient* kept twitching, arms and legs jerking randomly. His jeans were wet to the thigh, and the ruins of a camo hunting jacket under the orange vest were stiff and filthy. Traveller darted for a flailing, flopping hand, and Ginny hissed a *No* that made the ruined mass of the head jerk. It was still trying to *hear* her. Its hand grabbed a fistful of snow, the arm bent, and it tried to jam the snow where its mouth should be. Instead, there was just an open hole with broken teeth, that strange discolored blood, and string-flaps of muscle working to open and close, open and close.

Traveller darted in again. If he got a mouthful of that—

"No!" Ginny lost the battle with her stomach. She leaned sideways; steaming, tea-colored and pancake-scented vomit burst free. It stung her nose and made her eyes water, and if not for Traveller's sharp bark of warning she might not have looked down to see the thing fish-flopping in the snow, trying to work its way nearer to her.

A sick man. A patient.

She'd assaulted a *patient*.

Oh, God, no. She snapped glance at the trees on the far side of the road. The long expanse of white that was Lee's front yard, broken only by a humped shape that was probably a busted car up on blocks, was probably safe enough. But those trees...anything could be in there. Hiding. Watching.

Traveller sniffed a few times. His lip lifted, and he growled again. Thankfully, he didn't seem too interested in biting it now. Instead, he edged for the steaming splotch of Ginny's puke. She stood, unsteadily, trying to *think*. There was probably a way out of this situation. She could probably come up with one. If she could just get in some air that wasn't full of the smell of this thing, the burning of stomach juice in her nose and throat, the high rushing sound in her ears.

The thing on the ground kept making that dry, awful noise. Just like Harry, and Amy. *Boys tried to protect their mama*, Lee's voice, quiet and sure, floated inside her head.

If she ran for the house, and got Traveller inside, she would have to watch out the front room as this thing...what? Would it fish-flop after them, or would it just lie there and twitch?

The shovel's curved head dripped thin brackish fluid onto the churned snow. Traveller looked at her, ears perked, head slightly tilted, as if he expected her to figure this out posthaste. She was the human, after all.

Ginny raised the shovel again. Brought it down. *Crunch.*

And again. *Crunch.*

Finally, the thing stopped moving. Her arms ached, a savage, dull trembling. She let go of the shovel, now stuck in...in the *thing*, and backed up a few paces, staring at the thing's shattered head. It reminded her of anatomy class. Pictures of trauma, only there was nothing sterile or surgical about this. Her stomach cramped again, but there was nothing to throw up. Her tongue hurt, too.

The dog whined, softly. At least there was something that would shut him up.

"Come on, Traveller." She didn't know if he would. She'd just *killed* someone.

Or—and this was the terrifying thing—had he already been clinically dead?

Amazingly, the dog didn't run away howling. He trotted behind her while she tried to look everywhere at once, edging for the house. The barn door was wide open and the snow shovel stood up in the corpse, right in the middle of the driveway, but the further she got from the...the body, the less she could even *contemplate* going back to clean up, close the door, put the shovel away.

No. *A big old serving of NOPE,* as Flo would say.

Ginny made it to the house. Shut and locked Lee Quartine's front door, and sagged against it while Traveller, apparently forgetting his new human had just murdered someone with a snow shovel, nosed at her wet jeans and began to yip-croon and talk to her again.

ICE IN ITS BELLY

"I dunno." Juju's jaw was set as he climbed sideways up the concrete steps, covering their six. "This *really* don't seem like a good idea, Lee."

Neither of them had drawn yet, though in Lee's case it was a damn close thing. "You can wait in the car." Lee examined the swinging glass doors. They were probably locked. He tugged at one, it opened smoothly. Go figure.

This heavy brick building had held the police station since the thirties, and the cells in the basement were movie-worthy concrete boxes with iron-bar fronts. Percy's wife Cindy used to cook for the prisoners, but after the divorce they were dependent on whatever the Tasty Freez had leftover at the end of a day. Margie had, once or twice, offered to cook for "the jail," but Percy's inherent cheapness—the Blotzers would never pay full price if they could steal, the saying went—offended her business sensibilities.

Lee wondered how Margie and Rooster had made out. The little Navy man was tough and it was an article of town faith that no moss grew on Margie herself, but neither of them were spring chickens.

Inside, worn blue-flecked linoleum older than either of them glowed dully, and the high narrow desk for the duty sergeant—most likely Grant Howison, since his nose was always so far up Percy's ass it was a wonder he could breathe—sat empty. Papers scattered on the floor, and that was a bad sign. Someone had been in here when the world went haywire, and had left in such a hurry they hadn't bothered to lock up.

Or hadn't left at all.

"We're clear." Juju exhaled sharply. A cheap brass bell on the door chimed morbidly as it closed. "They'll shoot me sittin in my car out there, if they can. Shoot me if they see me in here."

"Ain't nobody in here." Still, he didn't blame the man. Blotzer wouldn't even drink his coffee black.

"And what if it ain't a somebody but one of them things?" Juju followed him into the dampish, chilly cave of the station, automatically covering.

"Well, I don't think any of the critters know how to work a gun." It was damn good to work with someone who knew what the hell he was doing. Meant Lee could forget about his six and concentrate on what was in front of him. "Although...you might get your chance to beat the shit out of Sheriff Percy."

The prospect was enough to cheer both of them up. Juju's small sound of amusement bounced off the dusty ceiling tiles. "Now *there's* an idea. Huh."

"What?" Lee lifted his MagLite. A few moments later, Juju's clicked on as well, and the white flashlight beams played over linoleum, scattered paper, a sheet of rippled glass held in a door with *Cotton Crossing Police Dept* written in a curve, gold leaf glinting. Through that door and back was dispatch, upstairs was Percy's office and "evidence rooms." Downstairs were the cells, and the shower. He could almost hear his grandfather's voice, on one of the old man's regular visits to shoot the shit with Pat Huntington, whose heart attack had brought an end to the old style of policing in the Crossing.

"Power's out on Main, and on the west side, but not out at your place." Juju sounded thoughtful.

"Blown transformers, maybe." He didn't know if the station had a genny, and given Blotzer's penny-pinching ways, it probably didn't.

"Or the Army cut lines. You saw 'em in the street, shootin crazy."

"Could be."

Juju paused. "Gonna pick yourself up Percy's cruiser?" When he was satisfied nothing was behind them he moved again, which meant Lee could.

"We'll take another four-by if we find it, maybe. Mostly I want ammo. And a good rifle or two." *Grenades would be mighty welcome, too.* "Some of that SWAT gear. Maybe go near the base, see if we can get our hands on somethin there."

Juju considered this. "Bad idea."

"How you figger?"

"Survivors gonna be thinking the same thing. If'n there's a CO there, we could both be dragged into yessir-nosir, all passes canceled."

Wellnow, there was something he hadn't thought of. And then what would happen to Ginny, all alone? She'd find the spare keys for his truck, of that he was sure. Say she ran across a roadblock and protested at something or another? Depending on how widespread this thing was—and he did *not* like his suspicions in that quarter—she could get in a hell of a lot of trouble once she crossed the county line.

Or before.

"You're right." *I shoulda thought of that.* "It'd be nice to get some real firepower, though."

"Could turn your truck into a technical. Goodbye traffic jams."

"That'll keep the back end down, too." Lee was about to remark further on the advisability of maybe putting a winch on the front end of the pickup when a low, chilling growl drifted through the darkened doorway in front of stairs.

Going down. To the cells.

"Shit," Juju breathed.

Lee agreed heartily. "Don't suppose we could just leave it there." His hand dropped to his gun, and he heard the soft sliding motion of Juju drawing, too.

"Have it come up the stairs behind us." A tight, unhappy whisper. "Sure."

Stepping into the wet blackness of the stairwell was unpleasant enough. Going down, his heart settling into a high fast gallop and every hair on him standing straight up, was doubly so. Christ, he hated this sort of thing. It wasn't any comfort that he was all right at it, really. Why couldn't he have been good at something else? Music, maybe. Trick-riding horses. Sewing. Now wouldn't that be a sight, him hunched over Nonna's old Singer.

Wooden, linoleum-covered steps turned to stained bare concrete for the last half-dozen, and the floor was concrete as well. The walls drew away, and there was a heavy splorching sound as the thing in one of the cells heaved itself against the bars, beginning to make that dry, rasping noise too. Thin blades of flashlight glow played over the empty tiled shower-cubicle on the left, cut across two cells at the other end of the narrow high-ceilinged space, and splashed up the longer row of cells to the right. The officer's desk to their immediate right had been smashed all to fuck, and there was a tangled, hideous shape caught in its splinters. A badge gleamed, but it was impossible to tell which of the Crossing's fine officers of the law was there. The head was a mess; the body had already bloated in the relative warmth of an insulated basement. When it burst, there was going to be an even worse stench.

The thing making that low, nasty noise crouched in front of the second cell on the right. Another sharp glitter was a set of handcuffs, one half clipped to the door and the other to its meaty wrist. The only reason it was still trapped was because of the size of said wrist.

It had already gnawed mostly through, the way a coyote will eat its own paw off to escape a trap. It was big, slump-shouldered, and in a familiar blue uniform. It had Percy Blotzer's aggressive high-and-tight, but half its face was gone and its mouth was cracking as the corners as it chewed at its own arm, its feet in their spit-shined and muck-spattered shoes leaving black heelmarks on the smooth concrete floor as they worked.

"Oh, *fuck*," Lee heard himself say.

The thing's filmed eyes rolled. Lee lifted his gun, the morning's coffee boiling high up behind his breastbone.

"Godsake." Juju, almost breathless with revulsion. "Oh, Lord have mercy."

The shot deafened both of them, muzzleflash painting the walls with brief white and Lee's flashlight beam bucking wildly.

THICKENING CLOUDS TURNED IRON-COLORED; THERE WAS A howler coming in. It was likely to have some ice in its belly, too, and Lee decided it was better to get home before daylight failed completely. Juju was silent, his mouth pulled tight and his hands gripping the wheel. They'd made a good haul—bulletproof vests, plenty of ammo and various other assorted bits from the police station, canned and dry food from the deserted Landy's, a bigger bag of Purina and some of the fruit and root veggies that hadn't spoiled, all the first-aid they could lay their hands on. They didn't see a soul the entire time except the thing in the station basement, and that was probably best.

Still, there were prints and other marks in the snow. Not so many tire tracks, but a fair amount of foot traffic. Some of the marks were strange, long sideways drags, and Lee was busy thinking this over while Juju took the turn into his driveway. He'd just about figured out that it was someone on all fours, pushing themselves sideways, when Juju hit the brakes despite the snow and the four-by began to slide a bit.

"Lee?" Juju corrected almost immediately, the chained tires biting again. "Aw, *shit*."

Lee's head jerked up. There was something in his driveway. A flash of crimson, and his heart lodged in his throat with a jump that jolted his entire body. For a second he thought the red blotch was blood, but it was his old snow shovel, its handle sticking up at an angle because the blade was buried in a mess of something hunter-orange. A human-sized mess, and for a moment the entire world turned gray before adrenaline hit his palate with its familiar, padded metal hammer.

"*Lee for God's sake,*" Juju yelled, but he'd already hit his seatbelt, the little dealie that retracted nylon and buckle whirring. Not only that, but he'd grabbed the door handle and the cold outside hit cheeks, hands, and all through him. He was goddamn lucky he didn't break his fool legs, bailing out of a moving vehicle, even if it was creeping at barely a walk.

Big gut. Hunter's orange vest. Crushed head—the snow shovel had been applied several times. There was a mess of footsteps, small soles with a distinctive tread pattern, light on the heel, and dog paws. The four-by's engine purred as Juju aimed it for parking, obviously deciding Lee wasn't in his right mind at the moment, and Lee's gaze snagged on the open barn door.

Oh, Christ. Had she been driven in there to look for a weapon? Where were the other two critters he'd seen last night? One of them had been small. Child-size. Ginny was decent, she'd hesitate when it came time to bash a kid-sized head in. Hesitation was exactly what you couldn't afford, dealing with these things. They were *fast.*

So she'd let Traveler out, or maybe seen the small critter and thought it was a kid in trouble?

"Lee?" Juju cut the four-by's engine, hanging out the driver's door. He was a good sort, ready to back a man up. "Lee, the barn—"

"On it," Lee barked, and headed that way with long strides. The failing iron-colored light meant it would be a black cave full of shrouded shapes; was the power still on? His house windows were blank, too, no golden electric glow.

Somehow, he had his gun drawn. Juju slammed the four-by's door, and at least the other man was thinking—he had his MagLite, the beam weak in dying daylight but pretty damn useful inside. The motion-sensor floodlight above the big barn door ticked on, and while that was comforting—it meant he could flip the switch inside the barn

—it also wasn't, because goddammit, there was no light on inside his house.

Ginny. Where was she? Was she in the barn, chewed to flinders? Was he going to have to put a round in her pretty head, just to make sure she didn't sit up and start making that awful dry growling noise?

Juju flicked the lights on, glancing nervously at Lee as if he expected some kind of reprimand. Nothing hiding in there, everything where it should be except for the empty space where the snow shovel should hang.

Sonny Jesus, Lee kept thinking. *Sonny Jesus, I am a sinner, and I know it, but please, Nonna will tell you I mean well. Please let her be all right. Please.*

"Nothin' in here," Juju said, softly. "Lee?"

"No sign of the dog, either." That didn't mean much. Traveller could be in the woods, following his damn nose like the hound he was. "House's all dark."

"Maybe she..." Juju shook his head. He was chalky under his blue knit cap, mouth drawn tight and shoulders tense. "Christ."

The sound pulled both of them around in a tight circle. For a moment, Lee couldn't understand what he was hearing.

Then he realized it was barking and yodeling, a bluetick hound's welcome-home cry, and his heart pounded in his ears so hard he thought he might pass out in here right next to the trailer. Juju got to the door first, because Lee froze, gun down in ready and the cold in his bones retreating under a scalding wash of irrational relief and fresh fear. Just because the dog was here didn't mean she was all right, or even still...

Still *alive*.

Lee made it to the door, creaky-stiff like an old man, and habitually flicked the lights off as he stepped out. It hit him down low, right in the belly, and his shoulder hit one side of the doorframe because he flat-out staggered.

Now his porch light was on, and Ginny stood at the top of the wooden steps in her fancy hiking coat, deadly pale, hugging herself.

Traveller was already leaping at Juju's knees, telling all about whatever had happened while they were gone, but Lee could not have cared less. Her hair was mussed, a single braid down the back pulled loose, curls framing her face, and the look she wore about stopped his heart and made it try to break out of his ribs at the same time. He'd seen that stare before, on soldiers after combat and civilians after the bombing. A thousand-yard faraway, the *person* inside a body retreated to some far mental corner and only a watchful, shock-stunned animal part of them left to look out on the physical.

It was wrong. She shouldn't look that way. Of all the people in the world, *she* shouldn't look like the survivor of a three-day carpet blitz.

Lee wanted to run across the yard, snow be damned, and grab her. Shake her. Find out if she was all right. If she'd been bit. What had *happened*, for Chrissake. Instead, he just stood there like an idiot, because his legs wouldn't work. It was Juju who got there first, and began to get the first halting words out of her.

Lee, his heart thundering in his ears and wrists and ankles, was left to lock up the barn, unload the food and gear, and get Traveller herded inside. The dog showed little interest in the big slumping body, and a few flakes of snow were already on their way down. By morning it might well be covered. Lee left the snow shovel there, too, even though prying it out of a frozen corpse in the morning was going to be a job.

All the time, all he could think was *thank you.*

Thank you, God. Thank you, Sonny Jesus. Don't deserve this, will never deserve this, thank you.

He was not going to let her out of his sight again.

[43]

DIMESTORE-NOVEL COWBOY

Ginny stared at her plate. Spaghetti in red sauce, and they'd brought back a bunch of frozen, dry, and canned stuff, too. The meatballs were pretty decent. Even if the sauce made her stomach a little unsteady. "No," she said, quietly.

"New York's a ways away." Juju was persistent. "Maybe until we know what the hell, it's better to stay here. Or just go to Lewiston and look around."

"You can." There. That was diplomatic, right? He certainly could, if he wanted.

Lee hadn't said a word since stalking across his front yard and halting at the foot of his porch steps, looking up at her with his jaw set and a blush coming up his throat to stain his cheeks. He just stood there, staring, and she decided he was upset because she'd gone and gotten into trouble while taking Traveller out anyway, despite all his cautions. Maybe he was even upset about the snow shovel, too, who could tell? It was left to Juju to ask her what happened, and to awkwardly try to reassure her.

Which was a nice gesture, it really was, but Ginny was past being reassured. Under the sturdy rosewood table, Traveller nosed at her ankles, probably hoping she'd drop something for him. *He* seemed just dandy with recent events, and for the first time she found herself wishing she was a dog. It must be nice, not to worry about a damn thing.

"I'm just sayin." Juju lifted a forkful of spaghetti. "Leastways here you're safe, Miss Ginny."

"*Safe* is kind of a strong word." The water in her glass trembled a little as the table shifted slightly. Probably because her foot nudged one of the wooden legs as she pushed her chair back a little. The thought of just getting up, taking her plate into the kitchen, then going and repacking what little she'd pulled out of her smaller suitcase, was powerfully attractive. Except she couldn't imagine what might happen once she got to Lee's front door. What was she going to do, walk back to the duplex? Lug her suitcases to the freeway? Demand Lee's truck keys? Well, if he handed them over, what would she do? Take his atlas, too, and drive off into the night?

Yeah. That was a practical, level-headed plan. Sure it was.

Juju glanced at Lee, who said nothing, just twirled a healthy bit of spaghetti onto his own fork. He must be downright furious, but wouldn't *say* anything. She'd heard of the quiet type before, but this was ridiculous.

Well, he hadn't said a damn thing to her for six whole months, so she knew he could keep his mouth shut for an extended period. Had he even *read* the books he'd checked out? He must have. Maybe he was channeling a dimestore-novel cowboy.

"I'm going to my family," Ginny informed them both, her spine straightening, refusing to touch the carved back of the antique, wax-rubbed split-bottom chair. "If you don't want to come with me, that's fine. I would ask that you take me back to my house, so I can get my own car."

Juju cast another imploring glance at Lee, who still—big surprise—said nothing. He just put his fork down, his eyes still piercing-light, and reached for his own glass of water. They'd brought back beer, but at least neither of them were drinking.

That did it. Ginny pushed her chair back further and stood up. Her spaghetti was virtually untouched, and now the noodles looked like bloody, writhing things. Traveller peeked from under the table, wet nose twitching and his ears perked high and hard. The spots along his sides danced as his tail blurred side to side, and he was happy to follow her into the kitchen and stick his entire face into her plate. The meatballs were probably manna, for him. She patted his back while he ate, despite reading once that you shouldn't touch a dog when they had food in front of them. He didn't seem to mind—in fact, he stopped chewing long enough to wriggle under her hand, obviously enjoying it.

There was a soft sound from the table, shoe hitting shin. "*Say something,*" Juju hissed.

"What you want me to say?" Lee whispered back. So he'd talk to Juju, but not to *her*.

Fine. Ginny swallowed, hard. Her eyes prickled. Good God, how could she have any tears left?

"It's a long way," Juju pointed out, fierce and low. "You ain't serious."

"She got folks there, Juju." Quiet, and steady.

"Lee—"

"She's goin. That means I am."

Ginny smoothed Traveller's back. The dog put his face down again and made a low moaning noise of happiness.

"Damnfool," Juju said, very quietly. Lee didn't reply.

Ginny didn't know whether to laugh or scream. Why, in the name of God, did she have to leave the room before he'd open his mouth? Did they think she couldn't hear them? All the same, something in her chest eased. She slid down to sit instead of kneeling. Lee's kitchen floor was very clean, the worn linoleum scrubbed and no dust in the corners. Apparently he knew how to handle a mop, as well as everything else.

Traveller licked at her plate, then stuck his snout in the water bowl and lapped, noisily. Ginny rested her back against a cabinet and closed her eyes. It didn't help, she could still see the...the thing, the infected patient, and feel the jolts in her arms when she brought the snow shovel down again and again.

The dog finished slurping and stepped in her lap, his wet muzzle heading for her face. She rubbed behind his ears, and the thought that he'd need to go out again filled her with unsteady nausea. God. The world had gone mad. Maybe it *was* better to wait here, see what happened.

No. She couldn't think like that. Her parents, Flo...they needed her, and she had to do everything she could to get to them. It was just that simple.

Movement. Someone walked into the kitchen and put his plate in the sink; the light coming through her eyelids changed. They were lucky the power hadn't gone out here, even with the snow. Traveller was goddamn lucky they'd found him, she was lucky she'd gone looking for a snow shovel, and lucky Lee hadn't left her in the street to be shot. *Too* lucky. Sooner or later, she wouldn't be.

When she opened her eyes, Lee crouched in front of her, his hands loose and easy draped over his knees. He'd stubbled up, and his eyes were even more bloodshot than this morning.

He looked tired.

They regarded each other for a long moment, Traveller deciding that if *two* humans were here, they both needed to be petting him, and doing his best to inform them. She had to keep pushing his spaghetti-stained muzzle out of her face.

Lee's throat moved as he swallowed. "We're leavin tomorrow." He was hoarse.

Well, hallelujah and pass the butter, as the McCoys used to say. Ginny absorbed the news. "You didn't find a car, I guess."

He shrugged, a small movement that could have meant *yes*, or *no*, or *don't worry about it*, or *don't ask*. A very ambiguous thing, a shrug. "I ain't havin you hurt, Ginny."

What did *that* have to do with anything? "You're angry."

He shook his head. He really did look better without a hat, and if he'd let his hair grow out a little more, that would be even nicer. "Just goddamn glad I got a metal shovel, not one of them plastics."

Well, that was a nice thing to say. It really was. "Me too." There was something in her throat. At least it wasn't tears. "I'm sorry I didn't put it away."

He rocked back a little on his heels, his hands tensing, halfway to fists before they relaxed. "I'd'a worried if you did, darlin." For a moment it looked like he would say more, but in the end he just straightened and offered his hand. His skin was warm, rough in places, and he pulled her to her feet without any apparent effort. Traveller, desolate at being abandoned, decided to turn back to her licked-clean plate in hopes of finding some stray tomato or meatball molecule to comfort him.

Lee didn't let go until she looked up at him. He studied her intently, and this close she saw a fine white scar along his jawline, and where he'd nicked himself shaving that morning on his throat. It was disconcerting to feel someone else's body heat. It made you conscious of your hair all messed up, any stray flecks of red sauce on your lips, that you hadn't brushed your teeth since beating someone to death in the front yard.

Yeah. Especially that last part.

"You did right," Lee finally said. "Don't you worry, Miss Virginia."

Ginny nodded. It was hard to think. The noise threatened to come back, a rushing inside her head. "Okay," she whispered, and pulled her hand away.

She escaped to the bathroom while they took Traveller out, Juju asking something in a low anxious tone and Lee simply making a low noncommittal noise. Her face was flame-hot, she splashed cold water from the ancient tap and closed her eyes, hanging onto the scalloped sink for dear life.

So they were leaving tomorrow.

Good.

COAST TO COAST

ANOTHER LOAD OF SNOW HAD COME THROUGH, THEN CRUST-froze as the clouds cleared overnight and the temperature plummeted. Lee didn't like the idea of driving on a slick sheet of ice, but Ginny was up early making coffee and breakfast, and her nervous, transparent cheerfulness was a kick to the gut. Juju took his coffee cup into the living room and stood near the front window, studying the weather with a troubled expression; Lee joined him while bacon sizzled and eggs pop-fried. Traveller's nose was right at Ginny's calves again, the dog gazing adoringly at her when he wasn't begging for manna to be dropped.

"Still got power," Juju remarked, after a moderate gulp of thick black brew.

"Ayuh." Lee studied the rippling liquid in his own cup. "Juju..."

"Oh, don't even ask." Irritably.

"Be more comfortable to stay here." *Less dangerous*, is what he wanted to say, but that would be like waving a red flag in front of a bull.

"Until it ain't." Juju's boots were on, and laced. The scar on the back of his left hand gleamed, skin pulled shiny-tight over an old wound. "You need a six, my man."

"Wouldn't say no." With that, it was settled. Weighing having another person along to be responsible for against the fact that it was a damn good thing to have someone who knew what he was about in the mix if they ran across more of those *things* was enough to make a man's head hurt. The cold, rational part of him was coming down firmly on the *Ginny's safer with both of us*, but of course, that part of him wanted to lock the doors and talk her out of this cross-country foolishness, too.

He just couldn't figure out *how*.

Ginny fidgeted all through breakfast, leaping up every few minutes to pour more coffee, or get the salt, or fetch more butter. Her hair, braided neatly and crossed over the top of her head, glowed under the electric light, and Lee slowed down, eating with deliberation. He was no nearer a good decision than he had been last night, and that was saying something. At least he'd been tired enough to sleep as soon as he stretched out on the couch. Juju hadn't shaken him awake, either, figuring they would both be losing rest standing guard soon as they were moving.

Juju brought Traveller back in from the snow, the hound yip-yodeling with excitement and heading straight back for the kitchen. Ginny began clinking and scrubbing in a hurry, and Lee found himself in the living room.

The tee-vee was nothing but snow on two of the channels, a test pattern on the third, but when he flipped to the final one—the public channel, coming through clear as a bell when there wasn't atmospheric haze—he had to stop and stare for a moment, trying to make sense of what he was seeing.

"—Steve Penny, for PBS." A balding, sweating man in a rumpled plaid sports coat cleared his throat. The bags under his eyes would have to be checked as luggage if he flew anywhere, and Lee wondered if there were still planes in the air before it sank in that someone was indeed alive out there. Tee-vee meant organization, and he breathed out a profane, wondering term as Juju swung around behind him, ears perking at the sound of an unfamiliar voice. "This is the KOZK, the Ozarks Public Television, uh, station. Our phone lines are still up, and we're still taking your calls. We have a list of cities under martial law, which we'll go through at the top of the hour. For now, though, let's just repeat what we know."

Steve Penny's unshaven cheeks gleamed. He shifted uncomfortably in his chair. "If you're just joining us, please listen: the plague is widespread. It is coast to coast; we have unsubstantiated reports from outside the US. It starts like the flu, but with an extremely high fever. Once the fever and the convulsions start, *leave the sufferer*. I can't emphasize that strongly enough, folks. Once that starts there is no cure, no recovery, and the sick person becomes dangerous as a rattler." He stared into the camera, his eyes dead, gleaming holes. "They *bite*, folks. If you're watching, you probably know this as well as I do."

"Holy shit," Juju whispered. "Coast to coast?"

Ginny appeared, her hands dripping soapsuds. She stared at the tee-vee, her eyes round, and her lips moved a little, like she was trying to ask a question. The naked hope shining on her face hurt to see, and Lee fought the urge to turn the damn squawk-box off.

The living room was silent for a long few moments. Lee thought maybe the sound had failed, but there was a crackle as the man shuffled papers in front of him.

"Keep going," the man muttered. "Not much...friends, we don't have much time left. Trevor, you'll keep rollin for a bit?"

"Ayuh," someone said behind the camera. "I will, Steve."

"Good man." Steve blinked several times. "Good man...folks, I'm having trouble focusing, we've been broadcasting nonstop for...well, quite a while. We don't know how long we'll have power. The Army has stopped demanding civilian news outlets go dark. If we're still rolling after the list at the top of the hour—"

Static bloomed over the picture.

"No," Ginny whispered. "No, please..." Like she was begging

them to stay on the squawk-box, maybe with a personal message or something.

The picture came back, as if it heard her. "—like we don't have that kind of time, there's something going on with the relays. Be careful out there, and beware of armed bands roving around, Army or otherwise. And I'm just gonna repeat this: the plague is coast to coast, possibly worldwide, and do *not* try to help the sufferers once the convulsions start. It seems to be transmitted largely *but not entirely* through bites, and we have no..." Another burst of static.

"God A'mighty," Juju breathed.

The tee-vee died, its large glassy eye going blank, and a vast quiet descended. It was like one of those snow-globes, where you shook it and the world inside was full of whirling, but as soon as you set it down and forgot about it, everything settled. Lee had never liked them, mostly because of the crazy thought that *he* wouldn't appreciate it if his house was picked up and given a good shake. When he was a kid, he almost broke out in the sweats thinking about it.

Traveller whined softly. The humming, breathing sense of electricity living in the walls, ready to jump when you flipped a switch, was gone.

The power was out.

[45]

ONCE OR TWICE

It was kind of like a college roadtrip, really. Except if it really was, she'd be driving, because she'd been the Responsible One in their dorm. She'd only escaped being RA by the skin of her teeth, but her plan of maybe attending a couple parties had foundered on the fact that she really didn't even *like* drinking and ended up as the designated driver everywhere anyway. It was a new thing, not being behind the wheel, able to watch out the window as the scenery changed in tiny fractions. There was little to see except snow, and if she tried she could probably pretend the houses were just snugly closed up instead of probably empty, or full of twitch-jerking, growling things.

Walking past the shrouded corpse of the—

The patient. The infected.

—the *attacker* from yesterday had been...difficult, even though Lee had put a tarp, weighted down with bricks, over the whole mess. The snow shovel, firmly frozen into the mass, stuck its red-painted handle up, and looking at it made her queasy.

It was little comfort that it was behind her, possibly for good, now. She stroked Traveller's shoulder, rubbed behind his ears, and looked out her window as Lee drove, sometimes whistling a little through his teeth, a wandering melody of concentration. Every once in a while he broke off and tried the radio again.

Juju's 4x4 crept ahead of them, breaking through the crusted top of the snow and digging deep, chains tossing spatters and chunks of white when he hit the accelerator a little. After about a half-hour, Traveller settled with a sigh against her leg, nestling his head on her thigh and dozing. Every time the red-and-white truck bumped, his eyelids twitched, and she almost envied him. It must be nice to be a dog, and have no mental horsepower to drive a worry machine.

Then again, if they hadn't come along, he'd still be out in the snow. No, maybe he would have come in from the cold eventually. Dogs were smart, and the house's back door had been open. Would he have survived?

Oh, God. Now she was thinking about all the pets locked inside, all the way across the US. Would they start to chew on human bodies? Would the smartest eventually figure out how to get outside? It would be too late for a lot of them. Goldfish, hamsters, all those... rats might be all right, but cats...

"God," she muttered, rubbing at her other knee.

"Hm?" Lee's face didn't change, but something else did. A subtle shift, maybe in his shoulders, saying he was listening. Maybe it was just that he was so quiet she was forced to look for other cues.

Either way, at least he'd responded. It was an unexpected relief, but all of a sudden she wondered if sharing her morbid little thoughts was worth it. "Nothing. Just...thinking about all this."

"Betcha can't stop, huh." His eyes had paled, and squinting against the snowy light made the corners of them crinkle. His throat was oddly vulnerable, clean-shaven and with a worn flannel button-down fastened almost all the way to the top. He wore that same leather vest with its threadbare patches, and over it his shearling. All in all, he looked competent. Prepared. Even the backs of his hands looked ready.

"I wish I could." She patted Traveller's head. "Like this beast."

"But it just keeps goin inside your skull. I know." He nodded. "Chewin at yourself, my Nonna used to call it."

"Apt." A farmhouse set far back from the road, smothered under all the white, glittered painfully. She couldn't tell if one of its windows had a golden glow of electric light, and found her shoulders had tensed up. Traveller opened a mild brown eye, peering up at her, and snort-bubbled a little, blowing his lips out.

"I guess that's what *he* thinks." Amused, Lee patted the dog's hindquarters. "Must be nice, bein a hound."

"That's kind of what I was thinking." The truck shimmied a little, but dug in again and eased forward. It helped that it was downhill, but she worried about sliding. "Maybe after lunch, I'll take a turn at driving?"

"Maybe. By then we should be at the highway."

Now she had something else to worry about. Did he mean the freeway to Lewiston? "I thought there was a back way over the county line?"

"Not in this weather. Figger the bigger the road, the better."

"What about the...the checkpoints?" That was the single biggest problem she could think of, right off the bat.

"Worry about those when we see 'em."

Well, that was probably for the best. "So...where exactly are we going to stop tonight?"

"Lewiston, most likely."

"Okay." She thought it over, watching the snow rise and fall outside the window. When she closed her eyes, the glare remained, rods and cones too exhausted to stop sending information. Her sunglasses were in her purse, but if she moved Traveller might move too, and the drool-stain on her jeans get larger. "More food, and better roads. But also more...people."

"Maybe." His tone didn't alter. She couldn't tell if his expression had. It was kind of soothing, to just close her eyes and not think about the snow underneath, or the sweating man on the television screen saying *coast-to-coast*.

The truck bumped up on something under the snow and her eyelids popped open. "People and those...things."

"Don't you worry about that none."

"Why not?" A jagged laugh threatened to escape her; she swallowed it. "I'm thinking I *should* be worried, Lee."

"When we see 'em, *that's* the time to worry, Miss Virginia." He was just the same. *Phlegmatic*, that was a good word, but too heavy for his leanness. "And I tole you, I ain't havin you hurt."

"That's very nice of you." She sounded prim even to herself. *But that's also what bothers me.*

"You don't have to do anything about it," he continued, leaning forward slightly to feel around in the small necessaries-holder under the radio. "I tole you that before, but maybe you didn't cotton. I ain't gonna push." He finally fished out a pair of gold-rimmed aviator sunglasses, and offered them across the bench seat.

Nice of him. "No thanks, I have my own. Did you ever come into the library before I started working there?"

"Once or twice."

That wasn't what she was really asking, but maybe he didn't want to get into it now, while they were sliding around an ice-choked road at the end of the world.

Juju's brake lights came on, and he rolled to a stop. A crackling noise almost jolted Ginny out of her skin, but it was just the walkie-talkie Lee had produced from somewhere that morning right before they got in their vehicles.

"Lee?" Juju's voice came through surprisingly crisp.

"I read ya, Juju."

"You'd, uh, better come take a look at this."

[46]
GOOD AT THIS

Mark Kasprak and Steph Meacham, trudging along the shoulder, were both bundled up against the cold and wide-eyed as cartoon rabbits. "Oh Lord, are we ever glad to see you," the boy began, and the girl saw Ginny and let out a high sharp sob of relief. She let go of Mark and staggered for the only other female, who barely had time to get her feet planted before she was clutched like driftwood in a whirlpool and Steph began to tear up.

Lee's neck itched. Standing on the side of the road with two engines going and Steph bubbling with both tears and whatever had happened to them since the diner was too damn exposed. "Miss Virginia?" He pointed at the truck. "She looks half froze."

An arched, very pretty eyebrow told him Ginny was on the knife-edge of taking some offense, but she began drawing Steph for the truck, saying those soft low things women did when they were soothing. Lee examined Kasprak, almost lost inside his frost-tinged parka. "Where's your truck, son?"

"At...at the Meacham's. It ain't drivable." Mark's throat worked convulsively as he swallowed, an audible click, dry as a bone.

"Why not?" Juju, catching Lee's unease, scanned the far side of

Apple Valley Road. Seen like that—squinting, in three-quarters profile, Juju reminded Lee of Iraq, except it was snow rather than dry rocks. A desert all the same, and just as dangerous now.

"Well, for one thing, left the headlights on. For another, it's got most of Mr Meacham tangled up in the undercarriage." Kasprak, dead pale except for the tip of his reddened nose, was almost too cold to shiver. "Told Steph we should get out of town, but she ain't one for liberatin a vehicle, so to speak."

"So you were gonna...what, walk to Lewiston?" Juju shook his head, the ends of his green wool scarf bobbing. "Oh, man."

Lee thought it over. "Your daddy's place is out this way. Right?"

"Yeah. We went there." Mark's shoulders hunched. He looked even younger, now. Terror did that—it aged you, or turned you into a baby. Still, both he and little Steph were alive and neither of them had cracked, so there was that. The kid had some grit to him.

"And?" Lee prompted.

"He...Sir, you're gonna think I'm crazy, but..."

Only as crazy as the rest of us, son. "You get bit? You or Steph?"

That got a reaction. "What? No. Shit, no."

Lee pressed a little further. "What about Bull Meacham?"

"He...he tried to...God." Mark's lip quivered. He was putting up a good front, but he was, after all, only a kid. His breath plumed, short puffing clouds. Was he even shaving yet? "He tried to kill us both, I...we called the 911, but nobody—"

Lee raised a hand, and the kid shut up so fast he almost lost his tongue-tip between his teeth. It might've been kind of amusing, if he was in the mood to laugh at anything. "Yeah. I know. So, *neither* of you got bit?"

"Nosir." Mark shook his head, vigorously.

"What about fever? Coughin?"

"Nosir." Mark studied him closely. "So you know about the zombies."

"That what you're callin em?" Lee decided it wasn't a bad term, tried to think logically about what came next. The kids were dead-weight, but... "We're headed out of town, Kasprak."

"Can..." the kid blinked, hunched his shoulders. "Can we come with you? Lee? I mean Mr Quartine, can we go—"

"You don't even know where we goin, kid." Juju's gaze met Lee's.

He knew the question Juju was asking, because it was probably plain as day on his own face.

"I don't care." Mark stamped his feet, not childishly, but to keep the blood flowing. Sun-glare had blushed his young cheeks raw, and he didn't look like he'd been getting much sleep. "Always wanted to get out of this shithole town anyway, pardon my French. Now it's got zombies."

"Whole continent's gone under," Juju told him.

Mark's muddy eyes got big, and he rocked back on his heels.

Lee half-turned, looking at the truck. Traveller was probably having a fine old time in there, with two pretty girls cooing over him. Looked like the dog was licking Steph's face, and the girl's mouth was going a mile a minute.

Food. Clothes. Ammo. More people to worry about, take care of.

Ginny slipped out of the truck, slamming the door. She picked her way over to them, graceful in her expensive, all-but-useless boots. "Lee?" Big, worried dark eyes, curls doing their mightiest to strain free of her braids. "I think..." She glanced at Mark. "Her parents are gone. And yours, too, Mark? It's Mark, right?" Calm and quiet, and she laid a gloved hand on his elbow. "You look cold. Go get in the truck, we'll figure this out."

Are you serious? Juju's gaze asked. He knew as well as Lee did that this was *not* optimal.

But...shit. She pushed Mark for the truck. "Go on, now."

The boy went gladly, probably relieved a full-fledged adult had given him a task. When he opened the passenger door again, Traveller's excited yips boiled out. The dog, too. Jesus Christ, it was a three-ring circus here.

"A dog. Two kids." Juju didn't add, *and a civilian*, but he didn't need to. "Lee..."

"We can't just leave them here." Ginny sounded very sure. "Lee?"

What the fuck were they asking him for? The weight settled on his shoulders again, cutting a little deeper this time. They were looking at him because he was good at this, he'd been good at it all his life, and that was that, as Nonna would say.

"No," he said, finally. "Reckon we can't. Who you want in the four-by, Juju?"

"Aw, hell. Give me Kasprak, at least he won't *cry* at me." Juju sighed. "We gonna have to look for more food."

"I don't think there'll be a shortage for a while," Ginny pointed out. Her shoulders had gone down, and the relief shining in her dark eyes was enough to make a man feel faint and ten feet tall at once. "Unless the looting was really bad. But if it spread as quickly as the guy on the television—"

Lee's neck was itching. "Get on in the truck, Miss Virginia. You get on in yours, Juju, and I'll bring Kasprak up to you. I don't like standin out here."

It was faintly gratifying that neither of them argued. And also— useless to deny it—gratifying when he got back into the truck to find Ginny had scooted into the middle seat, Traveller wedged between her and Steph and damn pleased to be so. It almost made up for the distraction, the new worry of more mouths to feed, and the way Steph Meacham kept rattling on about her mama.

Lee dropped his truck into drive, and shook his head a fraction.

They were, he suspected, in for a hell of a trip.

...to be continued

SEASON TWO: IN THE RUINS

[1]

LIFE LESSON

THIS PARTICULAR BEST WESTERN THREE MILES FROM Lewiston was dark and empty, but an employee door tucked in a northern corner was easy enough to jimmy open. At least, it seemed easy when Lee and Juju did it, and Ginny Mills couldn't decide if they seemed altogether too practiced at the maneuver or if they were just handy enough it wasn't a problem. *Built to keep the honest people out*, Lee remarked, and Juju's grin in response made him look years younger. From inside, they could manually open the sliding glass doors in the front.

Fire codes were probably a thing of the past, too, now that the world had ended. *Coast to coast*, the man on the news had said. The illness raged like a wildfire—fever, flu, convulsions, coma, and the horrid grinding growling while the infected chewed everything they could. Everything, but most especially, anything living.

The hotel foyer was eerily tidy, a curved check-in desk standing empty and dark. The only sign of something not right, aside from the lack of electricity, was a vase of wilted lilies under a large logo made of cheap pasteboard and glass. Steph Meacham held onto Ginny's arm so tightly she was going to leave a bruise or two, but Ginny didn't have the heart to shake free. Instead, she studied the large, shadow-filled space. No bar, no attached restaurant, just an expanse of blue and orange carpet left over from the seventies and an alcove with the blank steel faces of two elevators, useless without power.

Had they failed with someone inside? Or in the cities, in the skyscrapers...Had it happened all at once? Or by degrees? How long had it taken for the world to fall apart? Had Cotton Crossing been bumbling along like Ginny herself in the duplex, chaos and blood spattering on the other side of thin drywall as her neighbors died?

"Rooms on the second floor at least." Juju Thurgood rubbed at the back of his left hand, where a shiny burn scar gleamed against brown skin. His blue knit cap had a cheerful pompom on top, bobbing as he glanced around, the same quick scan Lee used to gauge likely danger. His breath showed, a thin cloud, even though it was much warmer in here without the wind. "Safer. And we'd best take 'em together."

"Ayuh." Lee Quartine, lean and dark-eyed in a fatigue jacket over a tan sweater, ran stiff fingers through his sandy hair and glanced incuriously at the small bell on the counter. A mass-produced sign sat next to it, hard red plastic with white engraving. *Please ring for service.*

Nobody was going to be ringing for service for a while, Ginny thought. Traveller trotted away to investigate this new cave the humans had decided to shelter in. The bluetick coonhound's tail worked furiously, his nose to the carpet, untangling a smorgasbord of aromas. Doggie heaven.

It was the little things that disturbed her. No lights in house windows. Stores with their doors ajar, or their windows broken and snow spilled across goods pulled almost-free, left midway. When rural peeled away and suburban pressed close it wasn't so bad, but several strip malls clustering the highway showed signs of looting. No other cars in sight, though there were tracks on the rimed, salt-treated roads. The wreckage of a few abandoned checkpoints had been clear of at least one lane each time, but there was no guarantee that would keep happening along the way. They'd have to start driving on the shoulder or median soon, which gave Ginny all sorts of heebie-jeebies. If she'd been in her Toyota, she wouldn't have made it even this far.

Cotton Crossing had slept while the rest of the country broke apart. *Coast to coast*, the sweating man on the public broadcast station said before the signal cut out; somehow it was this empty hotel foyer that made it seem...well, not just possible, but like a done deal.

Her back ached from jolting in the truck all day. Ginny studied the clunky chairs, not truly meant for lounging. Polite fictions, a pretense that a hotel wasn't tiny boxes stacked on top of each other. Apartments, hotels, office buildings—clusters of boxes, all of them. Even her duplex was, individual rooms fitted together. Domestic Legos.

"—Miss Virginia?" Lee's voice broke across her thoughts, and he was looking at her, stubble softening the hard line of his jaw. He looked a lot better without his usual baseball cap, and with his buzzcut growing out. "What do you think?"

"Hm?" Her scalp itched. Were there magazines on the tiny tables between the uncomfortable, overstuffed, and probably board-hard chairs? Would there be magazines ever again, at least in her lifetime, if this thing was not just American but worldwide? *We have reports from other countries, too.* "Sorry, what?"

If her inattention bothered him, he didn't show it. "You want a room with Steph, there, or on your own?"

God, she wanted to channel Garbo, and be *alone*. But the blue-eyed girl clutched a little tighter at Ginny's arm with gloved fingers, and her babble in Lee's red and white truck, mile after mile of it, had burned itself into Ginny's brain.

*My daddy...he was makin this sound, and he ran right out at the truck. Half his face gone. And my mama, my mama...*Sobbing little breaths, the girl trying to process the damn-near-unprocessable.

"I think we girls should pair up," Ginny said, after a long pause. Steph relaxed, her grasp loosening a little and her thin fine hair wildly mussed. "I may even have some nail polish in my luggage; we'll have a slumber party." *We'll skip the face masks and the giggling about boys, though.*

Lee's gaze, piercing even in the cold semi-darkness, warmed. He gave a short, sharp nod, and ridiculously enough, the small bit of approval eased the knot behind Ginny's breastbone. "Aight." Stretching the words *all right* over a few syllables and dropping everything in its middle, like everyone did around here. "Mark, you stay near the door there. Keep Trav with you, and you keep yo' eyes peeled. Juju, you wanna come with me to see about a genny or such?" Getting Juju's nod, he turned back to Ginny and Steph. "You want to find us good rooms? Near the stairs, I'm thinkin. End of a hall."

Ginny nodded. "What if—" *What if there are more of them?*

Of course, Lee got there ahead of her. "Run away. Run down here and start screamin, that'll bring us in a hurry."

"Amen to that," Mark Kasprak, his dark eyes smudged with sleeplessness, muttered.

It was on the tip of Ginny's tongue to ask if maybe, just maybe, she should be armed, but the thought of a gun made her unsteady and queasy at once. Maybe something like a baseball bat? She thought it over, decided Steph was nervous enough to bludgeon Ginny herself if things got scrambled and more of the infected showed up, and that running was probably, all things considered, the best strategy. "That makes sense," she said, dully. It was taking her too long to plod from one thought to the next. "Oh. First we should check, though."

"For what?" Juju shifted from foot to foot, probably eager to find a bathroom. Maybe the pipes weren't frozen here? Now *that* was an encouraging thought.

Ginny patted at Steph's grasp on her arm, trying to comfort the teenager and probably failing miserably. "To see if this place has updated. If it's changed to keycards, the doors might not work, except from inside the rooms."

"They's on batteries," Steph piped up, her blue gaze brightening.

Thin tendrils of her hair—somewhere between blonde and brown, shifting colors as the light hit it—stuck to her forehead. "If it's keycards. When we went to Florida there was a red light on our door and they told Daddy it was the low battery light."

"I didn't know that." Ginny's face unfroze. What kind of expression had she been wearing? A normal one, she hoped; now she was smiling. The pleasure of learning something new, though muted, was still considerable. A sharpish smell of disuse had already filled the entire foyer. "Never mind, then. We'll figure it out; go ahead."

Mark whistled for the dog and headed for the square of grey winterlight falling through the door. Beyond the glass, Lee's red-and-white Chevy and Juju's black 4x4 stood patient and snow-caked on painted stripes, under the roof meant to keep Mrs Whoever and her bags from Pokomo from getting rained on. Juju and Lee, both with heavy black flashlights—now *those* looked useful, they could club the chewing, shuffling things with little trouble—headed off to find a service door. Ginny, her fingers nervous and slick, found the latch securing the little swinging piece of pasteboard that said *here is official space*, just like the one at the library's checkout counter.

God. She would never see Lewiston's Fifth Street library building again, or the Cotton Crossing branch she worked on Sundays. Never sit through another acquisitions meeting, or sip hot tea in the break room with Annie Collins, or hear her boss Bobbie's rolling Appalachian accent. Never going to street-park on Sundays because Cotton Crossing kids, bored and full of mischief, had filled the library lot with broken glass the night before. Never going to lay out the papers for Elmore Creary or wish vengefully for his squeaky chair to dump him, or patiently explain how to use the internet to a woman old enough to be her mother.

How was Mom doing? And Dad? Flo, and...the baby? The due date was...Good Lord, Ginny didn't even know what *day* it was. Without her phone or laptop, keeping calendar track wasn't so easy. Would survivors eventually be reduced to stone henges and counting on their fingers?

"Miz Mills?" Steph, anxious, still clutching at her arm. "You okay?"

Keep it together, Ginny. She took a deep breath, settling her shoulders, and a blinked furiously a few times to get her eyes to focus. Behind the hotel desk, everything looked different, the working side instead of the customer-service façade. "I am," she lied. "Help me find another flashlight back here, sweetie, and we'll look at the floor plan."

Steph's wan, sharply pretty face creased, but at least she wasn't as wild-eyed now. Ginny could see a shadow of what the girl would look like when she finished growing, high cheekbones and soft lips. "The floor plan?"

"Research is always better than going in blind." Ginny wasn't just soothing the teenager, but herself. It was easier to be steady when you had someone else to balance first. "Life lesson."

"Lots of that goin around these days," Steph said, and after a few shocked moments, their laughter—thin, unsteady, but very welcome—made the dark a little less clammy, and a whole lot more bearable.

[2]

NOT ENOUGH POP

".22 won't stop 'em." Juju shook his head, the pompom on his hat bouncing, while he played the flashlight beam over a gigantic bank of washing machines. The dryers on the other side, each door slightly ajar, were compound eyes peering at these interlopers. "Not enough pop, even with hollow ammo."

Lee Quartine made a noise of assent. He wasn't sure what kind of gun Kasprak could handle, but Juju had a point. Everyone played with .22s, even Steph could likely use one. Ginny, though...maybe not, being a city girl and all. Still, she'd been the one thinking to ask what she and Steph should do if they ran across one of the things. The critters.

Kasprak called them zombies. It was as good a word as any, but Lee didn't like it. He liked none of this. He had a couple other thoughts rolling around inside his head, but they weren't ready for outside yet. There was one he'd been waiting to broach when he got Juju alone, though. "Guns might not be the best idea."

"Huh?" Juju's boots squeaked a little. Out where the guests would be, it was all carpeted. Back here, there was no use for luxury, and the floor was bare concrete, worn to a glossy shine. "Aha, look at that."

"Hallelujah." A door labeled ELECTRICAL gave onto a small room full of circuit breakers and dust. "Them things, their eyes are caved in. They hear just fine, though." Lee examined the wall of breakers. "Guns might bring 'em home for supper."

Juju gave it a few moments of thoughtful silence. "Baseball bat?" He also examined the breakers. Tip had generally been for going in hot to overwhelm problems before they started; Juju favored the take-a-look-first approach.

Which suited Lee right down to the ground. "Got to work on my game anyway." Their boots no longer left damp prints, but he stepped carefully anyway.

You never could tell.

A half-snort of a laugh. Juju touched one breaker, another, getting them all clear in his head. "Didn't know you played."

"Don't. Could stand to start, though." Lee made up his mind to gamble on a couple switches, once Juju gave the all-clear. "We may be lucky. Looks like a couple of the mains flipped."

"Might be juice if we flip 'em back. Not alla them." Juju pointed, the sleeve of his bomber jacket creaking. A double-layer of sweaters underneath it blurred his outline, but he'd never look fat. "Just that one, and...that one, there. Yeah. That oughta do it."

Generally, if you wanted to know about the chassis or the propulsion, you asked Tip; if you wanted to know about the wiring, you asked Juju. Lee was just a general hand; he liked taking things apart, seeing their innards, and putting them back together. There was a deep, itch-scratching satisfaction to making anything work again. "Let's find out."

Two heavy clicks later a subliminal hum ran through the building. A low orange glow peeked under the door, and when Juju swept the heavy metal rectangle open, emergency lights made Lee's eyes sting a little. You adapted right quick to darkness.

Humans could adapt to just about anything. Just like cockroaches.

"Pass the butter," Juju muttered, sweeping his hat off and jamming it in a pocket.

"And give me the goddamn beans," Lee replied, reflexively. "No tellin how long it'll last. What else we got here, Mister Wizard?"

"Gimme a second." Juju eyed the boards. It was damn uncanny, the knack he had for electricals. He was a good teacher when he took a mind to share his expertise, but you couldn't catch genius the way you could cold. "And I'll show you some goddamn *magic*."

No restaurant, but the room-service kitchen was still stocked and functional. Steph brightened at this, and took to ordering Mark Kasprak around with aplomb, shooing the grown-ups away. "We can do this," she said firmly. "Imma teach Mark about a deep fryer."

"I know how to open a can of beans," the shag-haired boy muttered, but he was looking a lot better now. Some color was back in his cheeks, and Lee was thinking it was a good thing Steph was sleeping in Ginny's room. Young'uns bounced back from terror damn quick, and if hormones weren't the most powerful force ever invented, they were at least in the top five. Juju decided he'd see if the showers were warm yet and hustled off to find out before chow, taking Traveller with him. The dog wanted to stay with Ginny, but he was too well-trained to complain.

Much.

Ginny set off down the long, many-times-repainted service hall outside the kitchen as if she had someplace to be, head down and shoulders up, those pretty but useless boots of hers quiet as snowfall.

Lee had to stretch his stride to catch up. "Where you headed?"

She stopped dead, pitching forward sharply like her legs had decided on it without informing the rest of her. A few buckwheat-honey curls, worked loose of the two heavy braids wrapped around her head, bounced as she did. "The foyer." Pronounced in that fancy way of hers. *Foy-eh.* "I thought..."

He waited, but she didn't say what she thought. She simply stood, face-forward, set and pale, her dark eyes slightly red-rimmed. Come to think of it, she hadn't said much at all, beyond please-and-thank-you, with the notable exceptions of soothing Steph and wondering what the fuck to do if they found critters wandering around upstairs. There were shadows under her pretty dark eyes, too, and that blank stare was one he plain didn't like.

Not on her, at least. She shouldn't have to look that way.

"Ginny?" He tried again. "Virginia?" There was a clatter from the kitchen, and Steph's bright young laughter escaped through the swinging door.

It would have been easier if she was crying. Instead, Ginny stared, dry-eyed, her jaw working a little bit. Grinding her teeth? Or maybe trying to keep something shoved down.

He couldn't think of anything else to do, so Lee cupped a hand over her shoulder. Her coat wasn't thick enough to keep her warm, not with the way she was shivering. It was a subtle movement, a thin hummingbird tremor, invisible until you got close.

Real close.

"Ginny." He searched for the right tone. Soft, but firm. "Sweetheart?" It just slipped out. Not like he hadn't already made himself plain, but still. There was always that moment you broke cover, even when there wasn't likely to be any shootin, that made a man nervous.

Got her attention, though. She focused on him, big dark eyes swimming through the thousand-yard stare to focus. "How long?" She blinked, and came back home. "What I mean is, did you ever come into the library when I wasn't working there?"

It probably wasn't what she *really* wanted to ask, but he answered anyway. "Some." *When I needed me a Chilton's. Or to suss out a diagram.*

"When did you..." Maybe she didn't even know what she wanted to ask. He didn't have a clue why she was asking him now, but if it got that dull, fixed expression off her pretty face, he would give whatever answer she wanted to hear.

"Saw you at Landy's. Kept my ears open and heard you were in town on Sundays. Decided I could do more readin." It sounded simple, and in the beginning, it had been. *Just once*, he'd told himself the first time. Then, when he was in the library, he felt like a fool and couldn't very well walk out empty-handed, now could he? After that first time, there were always the books to take back, punctual, every week.

It had taken him a month or two to begin reading any of them, because he felt damn ridiculous just ferrying them around.

"Oh." Ginny nodded, slowly, as if he'd said something profound. "I wondered."

Probably wasn't all she was wondering. "I ain't a stalker, Miss Virginia." Well, maybe he *was*, a little. But he had good intentions, right? All the way down to hell, Nonna would have said. Lord, but he wished Nonna was on hand to give him a few pointers. Of course, she'd just tell him he was being a fool, which was nothing Lee Quartine didn't already know.

"No." Ginny's dark gaze sharpened even more. "I believe you."

Good. Slow and steady was called for here. "I told you, I ain't gonna push, neither. You don't have to do a damn thing about it. I just let you know so you could...know." Well, didn't that sound ridiculous, too. He was all but dressing up in clown-shoes and a funny hat.

Amazingly, she smiled. Just like sunrise, lighting first in her eyes, then dimpling her cheeks and pulling up the corners of her mouth. Her lips looked glossy with ChapStick. Was that what girls used nowadays? Hers was probably some expensive brand. "I *do* know. I'm grateful for it, too. I'd probably be dead by now, if you hadn't been there."

He didn't want her thinking like that. "You're a smart girl, Ginny. You'd've done fine."

She shook her head. "I keep reaching for my phone, and being reminded there's no service, and in a little while I probably won't be able to charge the damn thing, either. There go most of my smarts. Everyone offloaded them into phones and pads, and now? They're about as useful as bricks, except for whatever I downloaded."

Well, if that was a problem, he could fix it. "They got solar chargers. Any outdoors store'll have 'em."

"You planning on breaking into one or two?" Ginny relaxed a little, then a little more.

Lee realized she was teasing him, gently, and had to swallow twice before his voice would work. "If the occasion calls for it." Looking at her braids made him think of seeing her hair down, the curl to it and its rippling length. *That* wasn't an image guaranteed to keep him focused. "Not sure it's breakin in anymore, though."

"Yeah." She leaned into his hand. "Coast to coast, the television said. While we were having community meetings and drinking punch, the whole world was falling apart." The words bounced off painted concrete walls, fell flat.

"Then we spit and balin-wire it back up. Easy enough." In reality, it was never *easy*, but he wanted her to relax. Badly. "We're alive right now. I aim to keep it that way."

"That's good." She nodded again, thoughtfully. Her thin gold hoop earrings glittered. "That's really good. But listen, Lee. What happens when one of us gets sick? Juju? Me? Or, God forbid, *you* start running a high fever? What happens then?"

Just because she'd been quiet didn't mean she wasn't chewing over the absolute worst that could happen. Lee was thinking she excelled at it. "If it ain't happened by now it ain't likely to." When she stiffened a little, he knew it was the wrong answer. "If it does—"

"When," she corrected. At least she wasn't leaning away from him.

"*If* it does, I'll do what needs doin, and if it's me, Juju will. You can trust him." That was a rare damn thing in the world, and he hoped she knew what he was trying to express.

Maybe she did, but it didn't stop the worry train. Looked like it was an express. "Great. What if it's me?"

He weighed the advisability of telling her about Grandon in his living room before all this started, about the paperwork and the syringes in their little foam-filled hardcase. Or telling her he had a good idea what was in them, and that her parents were most likely gone already, unless they were damn tough, damn smart, and damn lucky too. There was no way to say anything that wouldn't bring up even more questions, and the last thing she needed right now was another helping of uncertainty.

Everything would go a lot easier if Miss Virginia Mills just learned she could trust *him*, too. "Nothin's gonna happen to you," he managed. There was something in his throat. Felt like a rock coated with peanut butter, and Lee realized he was hungry. "I promise."

"That's really nice, but you can't promise that, Lee."

Oh, yes I can. And if you come down with the creaking fever, I'll send Juju on with the kids and... He stopped right there, not willing to follow the thought all the way down.

It went quietly. He suspected it would come back, while he stood watch or tried to sleep, to keep him company.

"Yes, I can," he said, and pulled at her shoulder, gently. She was reluctant, and he knew he was pushing it, but he got his arms around her, and it was exactly as he'd imagined, only better. Small and soft, and the smell of her shampoo on clean, dark, braided hair. He could curl up around her like a shell on a turtle's back, or a snail's hard, protective home. Make himself a wall, shut his eyes, and anything that came would go through him first. Ginny relaxed, abruptly, her cheek against the chest of his shearling. He wished it was unbuttoned, and the flannel underneath. That would be right comfortable. "You got to quit worryin like that, Ginny. I need you to help run herd on the kids, and you can't do that if you're wastin yourself on dry frettin. All right? You leave the rest of it to me, you hear?" Mostly, people settled right down when they had a clear-cut job in front of them, and she was already a dab hand at calming Steph down.

It was over too soon. Mark let out a sharp bark of surprise, Steph laughed, and Ginny, reminded of their presence, pulled away. He wanted to keep hold of her, but *that* wasn't the right thing to do. And maybe because he didn't, because he let her go, she tipped her chin back and examined his face, not quite as far away as she would be if she didn't like him at least a little. Right inside the invisible line that edged a man's personal space. And one thing was for sure, Lee was going to need a *cold* shower, sometime soon. Jesus.

"Okay." A small, pale little word. "We're a team now, right? All of us."

"Includin you, darlin."

For some reason, that brought up another smile, the corners of her eyes crinkling and dimples beginning on her soft cheeks. Lee stood, helpless, and let it wash over him.

"Thank you, Lee." And with that, she was on her way down the hallway again, moving with a bounce that hadn't been in her step before. Like the weight had lifted, like she believed him. Like he'd made it better, and for once hadn't put his foot so far down his own throat he was chewin on kneecaps.

Lee exhaled, a long, drawn-out sound that wasn't quite a whistle or a word.

Yeah. Definitely a cold shower. Goddamn.

[3]

WONDER OF THE WORLD

"They had some lettuce left over." Steph plonked down
what she hoped was a respectable-looking salad in front of Miz Mills,
and studied the older woman's expression with wide, anxious eyes.
The tomatoes were mealy because of the cold, and the iceberg was
practically blanched, and the only thing she could think of was to put
olives and grated cheese on for color plus a couple cut-up apples she'd
brought from home. She knew enough to rub lemon juice on apple
slices so they wouldn't get brown, at least. "Used what I had, so..."

"Perfect!" The lady librarian smiled, and it looked genuine. Of
course, everything on her looked that way—solid wood instead of
plastic, real silver instead of the cheap bright junk you got from the
spinner at the drugstore with nasty old Maye Cooper watching you
like a hawk to make sure you didn't take off with it. "It's so nicely
arranged. You have an eye for this, Steph."

Steph's cheeks turned hot, and not from the grill. "Thank you,
ma'am. Now, there's fried chicken and fries and cheeseburgers too."
She didn't dare glance at Mark, who was nursing a bad burn on the
pad of his left thumb. "We got orange juice, apple juice—the pop ain't
workin, but—"

"Now look at that." Mr Thurgood grinned as he finished settling his belt, his damp hair curling up tighter and tighter and his teeth startlingly white compared to his dusky cheeks. "Steph, you could run your own diner, put Mayburn's to shame."

"That's right good, Steph," Mr Quartine chimed in. He'd just been outside, and his face was raw and a little flushed. Both he and Mr Thurgood were carrying open, as Daddy would have said, pistols at their belts. It was comforting, like a police officer at an elementary school crosswalk, watching over little ducklings. "Tuck in now, don't say grace."

The cheeseburgers were a little overdone, and the fries a little soggy, but it was hot food so nobody complained. Mark hopped around refilling everyone's glasses so Steph didn't have to, mostly because he'd already eaten most of the first batch of fries. She'd burned the first batch of patties, but nobody noticed the smell—or if they did, they didn't mention it. Miz Mills even asked for a helping of fries, with lots of ketchup, which was surprising. You wouldn't think someone so, well, *city,* would like plain old ketchup. Steph even showed Miz Mills the patting-trick to getting a glass bottle of Heinz to pour out with no fuss, and the smile she got in return made her heart blow up like a balloon.

Traveller was more than happy with the burnt patties and some of his dry kibble, and made a game out of hunting dropped fries. His tail blurred, whacking shins with painful vigor. Balancing their plates on the short counter for employees to rest covered trays on was crowded and scrambled, but all the same...it was good. For the first time since leaving the diner after it got all shot-up, Steph felt warm.

And...yes, maybe safe was the word. Or at least, *safer.*

Mr Thurgood swallowed three cheeseburgers almost whole before he slowed down, Mr Quartine went through the fried chicken like it was goin out of style, and Miz Mills got up to help Steph make another batch of burgers. It was almost like being in the kitchen with her mama, except there was no yell of *close the fridge door* or good-natured hip-bumping. Neat, dainty, and smart, Miz Mills figured out the grill and got to work, flipping the meat pucks with an authority that seemed kind of, well...

Well, *adult*. She was a librarian, yeah, which was just like a teacher, but she looked so young it was hard to remember. Especially when she pushed a few curls back, her braids all thick and pretty and the escaped hair looking planned instead of messy, and grinned at Steph. "This takes me back." A little sweat gleamed on her pale throat, her cheeks brightening from the heat. "I did a summer working for the college cafeteria, a long time ago."

College. That magical word, the thing Mama and Daddy were saving up for. Things had been tight a few years ago, and there had been fights over Steph's college fund. *Bull, we're gonna lose the* house, *for God's sweet sake*, her mother had yelled, but Bull Meacham was immovable when he set his chin on something. *We'll find a way. Our girl is goin to college, Mama, and that's that.*

A shiver ran through Steph, heels to scalp. Mama wasn't gonna be yelling anymore. Neither was Daddy. She'd managed to go for a little while without thinking about the horrible, rattling, growling sounds they made, and how Mama had tried to get her teeth in Steph's arm and then her neck, the sound the skillet from the morning's eggs made when Mark swung it at Mama's head...

"Steph? Plate." Miz Mills elbowed her, but gently, a polite movement. "Here. Take this to the table."

It was a very mother-y thing to say. Did Miz Mills have kids? Steph didn't know. Teachers and librarians were just kind of *there*; she used to think they hung them up in a closet over the summer, and only dusted off the year's necessary ones when September came around. She even had nightmares about it when she was younger— racks of teachers hung in the broom closet or boiler room at Cotton Crossing Elementary-and-Middle. Upside down, like vampires.

Well, there were zombies now, so why not? All those books and movies had been onto something. Maybe she should get herself a cross necklace. Like Mama's prize gold one, on its real fourteen-carrot chain. Why they named it after a root vegetable was beyond Steph, but she knew it meant *real* gold, not a fake that would leave green on your skin.

"Steph." Miz Mills pushed her, gently. The grill sizzled, sending up heat-shimmers. The lady librarian flushed prettily and her gold earrings twinkled; it didn't take much to see Lee Quartine was head-over-heels for her. It was just the way he looked at her, giving Steph a funny stomach-feeling when she caught him at it. There was something about a guy looking that way, really. Something special.

Did Mark ever watch her like that? She took a good look at him, while she walked the plate of cheeseburgers to the counter.

Mark had pushed his hands back through his dark hair to make it stand up, and he chewed slow and thoughtful as Mr Thurgood leaned forward, making a point. "—bigger kick than what you're used to. So you got to make sure you got it tight against your shoulder, son. You got that?"

"Yessir." Mark's nose was a wonder of the world, Mama would have said. He was scrawny, but his shoulders were wide, and he didn't laugh all goony, like a lot of the other guys at school did. No, Mark was serious, you could tell from the line between his eyebrows and the way he looked at things. Quietly, kind of like Mr Quartine.

Steph's daddy respected the Quartines. *Don't say much, but they ain't fools*, was the prevailing sentiment. Even Margie at the diner liked Lee, and she had no use for most, even town customers. *Little Lee's good folk*, she said.

But it was Mark who had gone rounds with Carter Shellack after school once, when Carter went around telling everyone Steph was a hoor just because she'd had two beers at that one party while his parents were out of town and laughed at him when he tried to kiss her. Sober Steph might have let him put his tongue in her mouth to be polite, but tipsy Steph found goggle-eyed Carty the most pathetic thing in the world.

Mark, much to everyone's surprise, hadn't folded the first time the youngest Shellack boy hit him. Instead, he'd grinned, bright red blood dripping from his beaky nose, and proceeded to beat Carty into the dirt.

He don't even hit as hard as my daddy, Mark had said about the whole thing, and only that. Nothing else. But after that, the whispers stopped, and she could walk through the halls without getting tripped, or whispered about, or laughed at much.

"More burgers," she said, leaning in on Mark's free side. He turned crimson, like he generally did when she got close, and she liked that.

It was Mark with the frying pan from the Sunday morning eggs who beat her mama away, bashing her out the door and barking at Steph to get something to block it, *quick!* And Mark who curled around her in her bedroom but didn't try any roaming hands or funny stuff, just held her while she shook and cried like a little girl. It probably hadn't even occurred to him to leave her behind. No, as far as Mark Kasprak was concerned, they were in this mess together, and that was another thing to like about him. Steph was under no illusion that any of the girls she called friends at school would do the same, or God forbid any of the boys she knew.

"Thanks, Steph." Mr Quartine reached for a burger, tendons prominent on the back of his hand. He'd taken off his fatigue jacket, and his tan sweater clung to a pair of broad shoulders. It was funny, she'd never really noticed how big he was, he was so quiet. "Hey, there any pickles?"

"I'll look." She should have thought of that. *Lord, what a ninny*, Mama would say.

Mama had tried to *bite* her. Rip her girl's throat out. Mama had...

"That jar, right there." Miz Mills pointed with a spatula. "Maybe you can help me, Steph?"

"Oh, sure." Her throat was full, and the words sounded funny, like she was underwater. "Yeah. Just...just a second."

Miz Mills halted, looking at her. Wide dark eyes, her pretty nose, and that thread-thin gold chain at her throat, holding one of those teensy crystal-things. Swarovskis, they were called. Or maybe it was gosh-for-real *diamond*. She was just so *city*. Probably knew the name of every fancy mustard, too. "I'll get the pickles. You mind flipping these?"

Steph searched for any indication that the librarian lady was angry, or even irritated, at having to tell a stupid teenager what to do. None seemed apparent.

When Miz Mills came back, Steph was busy mashing the patties with the back of the spatula.

"Maybe you can help me," the librarian said again. Steph sneaked a glance at her, and Miz Mills was smiling, her perfect teeth peeping out. It was enough to make you swear to floss even if you hated to. "I'm hopeless at fried chicken, you know. I stole a bite or two of yours, and it's really good. You think you could teach me your secrets?"

"Yeah." Steph wiped at her nose with the back of her hand. Miz Mills didn't seem to notice she was leaking. "I can do that." Her shoulders came down, all at once, and when the librarian put an arm around her, Steph leaned in.

Miz Mills's warmth, so different from the glare of heat off the wide metal bed of the grill, made the big, scary, topsy-turvy world shrink back to a manageable size.

[4]

AIN'T A WORD THAT APPLIES

Five AM rolled around, the hotel bed was warm enough and certainly comfortable, but nothing—not even counting back from five hundred and slowing her breathing down—worked. Even the subliminal hum of electricity throughout the hotel failed to soothe her. Ginny pushed the covers back and sat up, peering at the alarm clock. At least Lee had a sturdy wristwatch to set it by, and hadn't told her it was useless when she asked him for the time. Nobody had said, *we're not even going to be here tomorrow, why bother?*

They just probably *thought* it.

At least she'd been able to plug her phone in. It wasn't *quite* a useless brick with a full charge. Now she was wishing she'd downloaded more useful apps instead of a a digital cat game and Scrabble.

Steph, breathing deeply, lay on her side. Her eyelashes were dark fans, and with her sharp face relaxed she looked even younger. The girl had been close to tears a few times, but each time she squared her shoulders and soldiered on, almost pathetically grateful when Ginny distracted her or complimented her steadiness. Funny how comforting someone else pushed your own uncertainty and fear into the background.

Ginny sighed, picked up her phone, and squinted at it. It had the right time.

And, would you look at that, two bars for service. When she tilted the phone, though, they both vanished. Came back for a brief second, vanished again.

"My God," Ginny whispered, then clapped her hand over her mouth when Steph, wrapped in a burrito of covers, shifted and sighed. She scrambled for slippers, and shrugged into her coat over her pyjamas. A fancy word for a camisole and torn-up sweatpants, but it was what she had. She didn't like the idea of sleeping in boxers *here*, God only knew what was on the sheets.

She eased out into the hall, blinking against the light and freeing her sleeping-braid from the coat collar with an impatient yank. The whole hotel was glowing like a Christmas tree. Maybe other survivors would see, and their little group would wake up to other people in the foyer or the rooms? Ginny couldn't figure out if that was a comforting idea, or a terrifying one.

What about the shuffling things? Mark called them zombies. It wasn't a bad name—it was, in fact, extremely apt—but using it gave her a weird upside-down feeling. Zombies belonged in movies, and yes, in books. Safe between hardback or mass-market covers, contained behind the glass of a glowing screen. Not out here, where people bled and sweated and...

And died. Like her neighbors.

What about her parents? And Flo? Hopefully they'd all retreated to the house and locked the doors. Were they worrying about her right now?

Maybe not. After all, I'm not the favorite. She quashed that thought in a hurry. Of course her parents loved her. It wasn't anyone's fault that they loved Flo more. It was just the way the world ordered itself. Being an adult meant learning to live with those sorts of things, and not letting them turn you bitter.

Still working on that one, I guess.

Padding around a deserted hotel at night was spooky. She'd never noticed before how many blind spots there were, how *quiet* a building got when there weren't people around. It wasn't quite silence, but a haze full of stealthy sliding unsounds, and each time she approached a corner, a vivid vision of something shambling and rotting on the other side, jaws working and its chest vibrating right before making that deep grinding sound...well, it wasn't pleasant.

She almost jumped out of her skin when an icemaker behind her clattered, and had to lean against a wall of pink-striped paper, resting her hand on her chest and feeling her heart gallop inside its bone cathedral.

When she made it to the foyer, it was a relief to see lean brown-skinned Juju in an uncomfortable-looking chair, his booted feet resting on another, a gun in his lap and a People magazine open in front of his nose. Traveller snored, stretched out beside him, his ears twitching and paws moving a little. Chasing smells even in his sleep.

The idea that Juju was looking at the last edition of People, ever, was *not* even remotely amusing. They kept hitting her, those little things, and she was having some trouble absorbing the punches, so to speak.

"Well hello, Miss Ginny." He peered over the top edge of the magazine, wrinkles fanning from the corners of his quiet, velvety eyes. Traveller's dreaming-noises stopped, and the hound cocked an ear. "Good thing you made some noise, and I ain't jumpy."

"Very good thing." She hesitated in the arched hallway entrance, peered at her phone again. The service bars had vanished outright. Maybe she should just go back upstairs? But that was hardly polite. "And it's just Ginny, Mr Thurgood. Care for some company?"

"Well, I got me a hot read here." He grinned, the corners of his eyes crinkling further. "But I s'pose I can make some time for a lady like yo'self."

"You're a gentleman." Her own smile felt a little creaky, but it cheered her up. She settled in another uncomfortable foyer chair, kitty-corner from his, hunching her shoulders and burrowing her hands into pockets, and realized he'd chosen his spot so he could keep the front door in sight. "You're also on watch, huh."

"Ayuh." He nodded, rubbing at his jawline with a fingertip. Traveller wagged his tail once, twice, thumping on the thin carpet, and went back to sleep. "Lee's shift is in an hour or two. I could wake him up early."

She shook her head, her loose braid slithering across the back of her coat. "Why? Let him sleep."

"I'm sure he'd rather talk to you." Juju settled himself in the chair like it was the most comfortable furniture in the world, his well-worn fatigue pants belted low. "Boy's got himself a crush."

"Oh?" What was she supposed to say? Good Lord. A change of subject was probably safest. "Have you seen anything? Out the door?"

"Not yet." His good humor evaporated, and he dropped the magazine into his lap. There was a shiny burn scar on the back of his left hand; he rubbed at it with his right fingers, a quick habitual smoothing. "That what you worried over?"

Ginny hunched inside her coat. Her camisole's stretchy lace scraped across her decollatage, but she couldn't very well go digging to scratch it right now. "I'm worried about everything." *That's just high on the list.*

"Shouldn't do that. Give ya wrinkles."

Did he not notice she was, in her mother's deadly polite parlance, already on the shelf? "Yeah, well, I'm already there."

That seemed to finish up all the conversation either of them had the stamina for. Juju watched the glass doors, electric light playing over their vehicles, parked close. Two ribbons—one orange, one yellow—snaked across the floor and under the doors, attaching to the engine warmers on both the truck and the 4x4. They thought of everything, and she was just along for the ride.

"I feel useless," Ginny said, finally, staring at the 4x4's gleaming black hood. It felt like a secret, whispered when you didn't have to look at your conversational partner. Road trips and tourist attractions were where those sorts of things got told, where you didn't have to see someone else's expressions as they absorbed, judged, reacted.

Juju nodded, setting his jaw either stubbornly or thoughtfully. It was hard to tell. He'd taken his hat off, and his short, crinkled hair was luxuriating in the freedom. "Me too."

"At least you can shoot." *And fix things.*

"That didn't do Tip any good."

Ah. Ginny's heart hurt, a swift hot pinch. She remembered Mr Tipton—short and broad, with ferocious black muttonchops and an easy smile. He'd seemed a nice enough guy, in all of the five minutes she'd interacted with him. "You did what you had to, Mr Thurgood."

"Lee keeps sayin that." He shook his head, glaring at the front door as if he expected one of the infected to shamble past. "Don't make a damn bit of difference."

"It does. You just can't see it right now." God, what a lame thing to say. The psych classes she'd taken in premed didn't cover this at *all.* "It's a normal feeling."

"Normal." He tossed the magazine, glossy pages fluttering, onto a tiny round table bolted to the floor. "Yeah. This the Pocalypse, ma'am, and *normal* ain't a word that applies."

"You might be right." She shivered. "I mean, I'm not religious, but you just might be right about it being...that. Even if it is, there's no shame in defending yourself."

He gazed at his boot-toes now, staring like he had X-ray vision to count his toenails with. "You ain't religious?"

"No. I mean, we did bat mitzvahs for me and my sister, but we weren't, you know, observant or anything."

A brief, puzzled glance swiveled his chin in her direction. There was a small divot in the bridge of his nose, broken once a long time ago. "Meatzvah?"

"Bat mitzvah." Her smile no longer felt foreign. "Jewish."

Juju shifted a little. Those fatigue pants looked very comfortable. Pockets galore, and camouflage. Just the thing for the end of the world. "You're Jewish?"

"My mom is. So I am by default, I guess. But it was never a big thing." She watched the glass doors, the side of Lee's battered truck. He had everything in the back, for God's sake. And if she focused on that, she wouldn't have to look at Juju and see if he was going to say...anything.

You never could tell how people would react.

When he did speak, though, it was just soft and thoughtful. "Well, y'all got anything in your book that explains this?"

"Not really." She relaxed a little, then a little more. "Most of it is *well, they tried to kill us, some of us survived, let's eat!* Pretty much every one of our holidays boils down to that."

"Huh." He shifted, propping his Army boots more securely. Steel-toed, and dry now, their caps rubbed with polish. "Sounds like somethin my grandmammy would say."

"Are *you* religious?" It felt funny to ask. The only thing less polite would be mentioning someone's income, or taking notice of an embarrassing bodily noise.

"Mammy Liz dragged me to church every blessed Sunday until I went into the Army. After that, only time I ever prayed was when they was shootin at us." He sighed, and some of the tense hurtful alertness in him drained away. "Sort of concentrates a man's mind."

"I'll bet."

This time, the quiet holding them both was almost companionable. Ginny's eyelids grew heavy. She pulled her legs up, bracing her heels on the seat, hugging her knees. It was warmer that way. "Do you think anyone will see the lights?" she finally asked, softly. Almost whispering, a little girl up past her bedtime.

"Maybe. But not them things." Sounded like Juju didn't like calling them *zombies* either.

That was just fine by her. Her heels slipped on the edge of the seat, and she hugged her legs harder. Maybe the shivers would stop if she curled up tighter. "No?"

"They got bad eyes." He rubbed at the burn scar again. "But they hear just fine."

"Oh. Yes." It made sense. "That's right. The one in the driveway, it...yeah." It hadn't *looked* at her, its eyes grey-filmed and caving in. There was *definitely* nothing wrong with its ears, though. She'd yelled to get it away from Traveller.

She glanced down at the dog. Sprawled on his side, his speckled coat gleaming and his eyes blissfully sealed, the very picture of relaxation.

"Lee was about beside himself when we got there." Juju sighed, and now rubbed at the bridge of his nose. Did talking help him stay awake? "He's good folk, Miz Ginny."

"So are you," she murmured. "I'm really glad you're here, Mr Thurgood."

"Aw, well. It's Juju, ma'am, and thank you."

She suspected he wasn't *quite* glad to be here, but was too polite to say so. "You're very welcome. Should I make you some coffee?" Ginny *also* had a hazy idea Juju's feelings for Tip might have been... well, not exactly brotherly, but that wasn't something you could ask in this part of the US. Not like New York.

God, how she wanted to be home. Even Mom's vapors and Flo's hormone-fueled passive-aggressiveness paled in the face of all this.

"Nah," Juju said. "Ain't got but an hour or two left."

Go figure, she couldn't sleep up in a nice comfortable bed, but she dozed there, in the foyer of an almost-dead hotel, while a man with a gun eventually picked up maybe the last People Magazine ever and continued reading. When she woke up, he was still in the same position, feet propped and ankles crossed, apparently absorbed. He said nothing as she shuffled away towards her room, Traveller padding behind her and lobbying hard to jump up on the bed. When she let him, he snuggled up close and began to snore.

Maybe that was why she was gone as soon as her head hit the pillow, too.

[5]

I LIKE MY COCKTAILS

THE EASTSIDE AVENUE LEWISTON BEST WESTERN WAS EMPTY because the head manager Kenny Schmitt—despite what any of his employees would tell you just for the asking—was, at heart, *not* an asshole. Sure, he *looked* like one, from the smooth brown skull under his fuzz-curly combover to his brown polyester suit jackets and too-long maroon ties. He even *acted* like one, from his pissy three-strikes-you're-out policy to his habit of cutting hours if someone "got fresh" with him. His visible disdain for smokers sealed the deal, according to the housekeeping staff, who, like soldiers, might not suck on chimney stacks but would raise hell if their "cigarette" breaks weren't sched-uled in.

But no, way down deep the Schmitt-Stirrer—so they called him—was in fact *not* an asshole. Just a man committed to a goddamn fran-chise hotel since it was the one thing he had left after alcoholism and old age stole the only person he'd ever loved. With three-quarters of the staff out sick, the news getting worse hourly, and the military roaming the streets shooting at people they didn't like the look of, he spent hours on the static-filled, barely working phone telling everyone scheduled and *not* sick to stay home, that it wasn't worth risking their lives to get here, that he would take care of it, that they would still get paid at least half-time because this, in his humble opinion, fell under "natural disaster."

It wasn't quite "Act of God," he joked, over and over again, but it was close.

Kenny personally turned away travelers stupid enough to still be out roaming even with the weather and the checkpoints. Once everyone who had talked themselves into a room the previous night was also turned out, with much regret and protestations of concern for safety, Schmitt locked the door and shut even the emergency power off. Just like he would for a flood, or even a major tornado freakout like the big storms of '78.

He was a firm believer that if the buck stopped with him, why, he'd better be ready to make a decision and carry it out himself. You could even call Kenny Schmitt, when it got down to it, right decent.

At the moment, though, he was wishing he'd stayed at the Best Western. Because his quiet neighborhood full of small tract homes—all built on the same five floorplans—was full of crapheaded sniffers with half-eaten faces hanging flop-open, and he was running out of ammunition.

In retrospect, shooting from the master bedroom window was perhaps not his smartest decision. With several belts of Gordon's Gin —his late mother's favorite—tightening around his judgment and his hotel lying dark and shuttered halfway across town, though, he was, as his dear old Mama would say, at loose ends.

He'd bought the Smith & Wesson .38 after the cirrhosis took Mama Schmitt. It sat in its locked box in his closet through the long bleak winter the estate dragged through probate, a secret blued-iron friend he would turn to when everything was all said and done. The shock had been just how much she'd saved, scrimping and scrabbling for years. *For my boy*, her will read, and the only reason it dragged was because the government wanted its share. As if her taxes weren't enough, she hadn't even gotten old enough for Social Security. Then there was the insurance company, scenting cash like blood in the water. He would have gladly given the lawyers the entire estate just to make sure the insurance didn't get a got-damn penny.

In the end, it had only taken about half. What was left was still a good chunk. His employees would have been surprised that Ol' Schmittster, with his busted-springs Chevy and his polyester off-the-rack, didn't *need* to work, he just understood the value of a dollar too much to spend what his mama had so slowly, painfully accumulated. When the estate was all settled, he sometimes went to his closet and stood looking at the gunbox for as much as a half-hour at a time. Standing there, swaying slightly, usually in his yellowing undershirt with a hard little potbelly pooched out and his lower lip protruding, his mother would have recognized the pudgy, wistful child he'd been in a man's face.

Each time, though, he shut the door and shuffled away in his threadbare slippers. Until today.

The gin went down smoothly. He didn't really like the bite of tonic water as his mother had. *That quinine keeps me young*, she would joke, even while she turned yellow when her liver shut down and begged him to bring her just a sip, just a taste. *You know I like my cocktails, Ken.*

He drew a bead on one of the shufflers. Looked like Patsy Beaucannon from down the street, the hag who ran the Neighborhood Association and was always on people about dragging their trashcans in toot-sweet. Sometimes she tried to waylay neighbors by the mailboxes, but most put their heads down and hurried away when they saw her pink curlers on the horizon.

Those curlers hung off her skull on thin grey strings now. She moved barefoot in aimless shuffling circles, her cream-colored house-dress fluttering in the sleet-melting breeze. More crapheads gathered, lurching and bobbing in irregular loops. If you watched long enough you might be able to find a pattern to their wandering.

One thing was for sure, Patsy's jaws were still working. They all chewed, every single one of the crapheads. Their mouths cracked at the edges, and all afternoon he'd watched as stronger turned on weaker, stumbling ones, blundering close to tear at chunks of flesh.

Even the weak ones were quick when attacked, though.

When the level of gin in the bottle—liberated from a burning Piggly Wiggly's liquor aisle the day he closed his hotel up safe and sound for the duration—reached the halfway mark, he got the box out of the closet, loaded the gun with fumbling fingers, and opened the master bedroom window—Mama's room, still, because he slept in the small one. It just didn't seem right, otherwise.

It took him two tries to get the screen loose, and he set it prissily aside before taking aim.

At first they didn't seem to know they were being shot at. The gunshots fell flat into the curtains of sleet, and the herd milled around in smaller circles. Kenny couldn't seem to aim straight, but he kept reloading, sighting Peggy's pink curlers.

When the crapheads finally figured out they were under attack, they shuffled together in a mass, like wildebeests bunching up on a National Geographic show. It struck Schmitty as funny, and he took another potshot. This time the gun bucked wildly, and he swore, casting a half-guilty look over his shoulder when he realized the words had bounced out the open window.

Mama would have called that *strong language.*

He aimed again, carefully, sticking his tongue out a little. The fuzzy-sharp smell of gin, like potatoes in a dark corner for too long, rose in shimmering veils. It was a good aroma, a happy one, full of his mother's loose warmth when she'd had "a few cocktails." She was never a mean or loud drunk. Just happy, slow, and soft even when she had a hangover.

His next shot was a beauty, one of those fabulous happenings that follows around the god who looks after drunks and small children. Peggy Beaucannon's craphead evaporated, chunks flying in every direction, pink curlers bouncing.

"*Woooo!*" Kenny yelled, braced against the windowsill. "*TAKE THEM CANS TO THE STREET, BITCH!*"

That may have been a mistake. The gun squeezed out of his plump, sweating hand, landing with a clatter on the ice-rimed front walk. He realized, dimly, that he was lucky he hadn't shot *himself* with the damn thing, and a great pointless rage swelled up inside him.

"MOTHERFUCKERS!" he bellowed out the window.

They were dead, and walking the fuck around. The idea of driving out to Haggard County Cemetery and seeing if *everyone* had decided to come up, his Mama among them, was powerfully attractive one moment, and just as powerfully repellent the next. Kenny wavered in the window, only hazily aware of the crapheads finally noticing his existence.

The gin ignited, filling his skull with the kind of drunk that hits when you slide off your barstool for the first time and move, tacking unsteadily for the bathroom. Except Kenny Schmitt didn't know about that.

It was, you see, the first time he'd ever touched booze. When he lost his balance and toppled out the open bay window over his front walk, the sound of him hitting pavement was lost under the soft, persistent shuffling of bare or indifferently shod feet as the crapheads circled. The caving-in of his skull and subsequent hematoma would have killed him if exposure didn't, but neither had time.

The creatures, now quick and savage, scented blood.

[6]

RIGHT AS RAIN

LEE TOUCHED THE BRAKES, SOFTLY. HIS CHEVY COASTED TO A stop in front of Bateley's Sporting Goods, the shop's long glass front reflecting ugly grey melt. He didn't like the way the sky looked, a flat nasty iron pan. At least it was warmer, the winter's inaugural snowfall turning to slush and drips running off building corners. When it froze again, things were gonna get dicey. Maybe they had some time before the howlers came down from the north.

Best not to borrow trouble. He had his eyes peeled for any hitching, darting movement, but so far, they hadn't seen any of the critters again. Traveller was left safely in Ginny and Steph's room, with a big bowl of water and mournful eyes. The kids were under strict orders not to go anywhere outside the hotel alone; Juju had them in the fourby and was looking for yet more supplies. Lee himself was on the hunt for ammo.

Lots of ammo.

"I *thought* I remembered a Bately's here." Ginny sounded pleased enough for both of them. She was bright as a new penny this morning, and that eased something inside Lee he hadn't even known was wound clock-tight. "And *there's* the bookstore. That's where I got your present."

Oh. Tucked on the other end of the strip mall, past a closed-up gun store and an empty unit with soaped windows, was a storefront with a hand-painted sign: SCHAPLY'S BOOKS, dabbed in cheerful white and yellow by a shaky hand. "Well, we can go on in there, if you need to." At least she wasn't asking him if he'd read any. There hadn't been much time, what with recent events.

"I should get a fresh journal." It was the first time she'd seemed downright *excited.* She clasped her gloved hands together, and those dark eyes were all but shining. "For history. And...God, what does one read in the middle of the Apocalypse?"

He hadn't thought about it that way. Lee set the parking brake. "Huh?"

"I was up last night talking to Juju." She bounced a little on the seat, her hood flopping and those gold ear-hoops sparkling even though the day was a grey haze.

Were you, now. Juju hadn't mentioned it, but they were on a first-name basis this morning. Which was a vote of confidence from Thurgood; he didn't hand out his Christian name to just anyone. Spatters of melt touched the windshield as the wind freshened.

Lee made a noise of assent, just to let her know he heard, and put the truck in park, scanning the parking lot again. There were a few cars, mounded under slumping snow, and that bothered him. None were close enough to this end of the mall to be an immediate concern, but his hackles were up. He touched the keys in the ignition, his forehead wrinkling hard. He had some decisions to make about about gasoline, too. So far, he and Juju could find the overflow valves with little trouble, but how long until whoever survived had guzzled up all remaining go-juice? "Read some of that Hemingway last night on watch."

"Did you?" A sunny smile and sparkling eyes, all focused on him. She tugged at her pretty but useless grey gloves, settling them. She even looked graceful doing that, like Nonna in her Sunday best, fixing her veil and smoothing material down the backs of her hands and wrists. "What do you think of it?"

Lord, how was she so interested in what he thought of imaginary people? He cut the engine. "Don't know why that girl puts up with him." All the same, it was good. He said things direct, that Hemingway, and at the same time, there were things you could guess at. He didn't drag you to the pond and try to put your nose in, he showed you the water and let you figure it out.

"Well, that's love. Especially in fiction." She reached for the door handle, stopped herself, and her smile faltered a little. "Is something wrong? You've got that look."

Lee's forehead was a little tight, but his face didn't feel strange at all. Just usual. "What look?"

"Like something isn't right." Turning serious now, her mouth drawing down and her dark eyes turning grave.

Shit. He didn't want her worrying. "Just lookin at the parkin lot, that's all. Ain't seen any of them critters."

"Maybe they died off?" She didn't reach for the door again, and that was a relief. "That kind of fever, and the activity we saw from them...that's pretty metabolically expensive."

It made sense that they needed extra fuel, Lee decided. "Well, if they're eatin each other, maybe they've got enough in the tank." He didn't like that line of thought, or where it led. "Just let me look around a minute, get my bearings."

"Okay." She settled, and it was official: he could smell her shampoo. They had hot water for now, and girls liked being clean. Lee could also catch a breath of perfume, whatever it was she wore. He couldn't quite pin it down, except it reminded him of summer grass cut the day before, warm and forgiving and just a little bit spicy.

He considered Bateley's doors. Breaking the glass was the easiest way to get in, but was it the *best*? He hadn't slept much last night, and it was showing. Fatigue was a killer. "Ain't no help for it," he murmured. "Gonna have to break some glass."

"Well, yeah. Unless it's open." She leaned forward a little, peering through the windshield. "How many places do you think are just open, and why? Someone goes into work sick, falls down and convulses, then..."

"Then someone calls the ambulance, and it don't come on time?" Christ. He could *see* it playing out, all over the Crossing and here, too. Gas stations, mom and pops, liquor stores, Laundromats. When you scratched from paycheck to paycheck, going to work sick was a necessary. "If it's open, that means there're prolly more critters. So let's go easy, Miss Virginia."

"Critters." Her profile, thoughtful and sweet, sent a bolt of something hot and nameless through him. Even in this light, she looked impossibly *finished*. Each seam tucked away, each curl arranged, each inch of her buffed or glossed. "That's a good word. Better than the other one."

Zombies. Mark and Steph had made up their minds to call 'em that, and Lee thought the kids were having an easier time dealing with current events than the adults. After all, there were all the movies, and being young meant you didn't have a whole lot of mole-hills to compare life's mountains to.

He was busy looking at Ginny instead of the parking lot. Lee tore his attention away, gave the melting snow, lamp-posts, and moth-eaten shrubbery at the edges another going-over, scanned the sides of the building. Half brick, half concrete, probably real nice when it was built. Then the money ran out, and a slow slide downhill came along.

Lee studied Bately's door again, the faded lightbox sign with its old-fashioned lettering. *Bateley's HUNTING FISHING FOOT-BALL Sporting Goods.* "Huh."

Ginny followed his gaze, leaning forward a little. "What?" Another tantalizing thread of her perfume reached him. It really did smell like cut grass in summer, the day after you ran the mower and everything was dry and sweet.

"The open sign." It was flipped. So there might have been someone in there, after all.

"That's not good, is it." Ginny's breath caught midway through the sentence.

"Depends." His heart sped up a little. "You stay behind me, you hear?"

"Yes sir." It even sounded like she meant it.

THE SWINGING GLASS DOOR WAS UNLOCKED, AND BATELEY'S WAS a damp cave full of plastic and the monstrous hulking shapes of exercise equipment. It reminded Lee of a high school locker room; it lacked the edge of fermented sweat and adult male frustration an Army shuckdown would have. No, this was all new equipment and high-flying dreams, kids aching to be the next superstar and parents determined to live out their own unfulfilled coulda-wouldas through their cubs.

Ginny stayed carefully behind him, and it took longer than he liked to scan the aisles and get a good idea of where everything was. It was goddamn *dark*, even with soft grey snowlight coming through the decorated front windows. Someone with a fair hand had painted snowflakes and harvest cornucopias all over the glass, along with percentages off brands and equipment in big bold letters. He'd never before thought about how that stuff got slapped on a window, and now Lee found himself wondering if that painter would ever dab a brush again.

Nothing *looked* off, but all his fine hairs were bristling.

"Do you really need a gun for this?" Ginny whispered.

Did she really want him to answer that? She'd be right glad he had one if a critter showed up. "You ever been in here?" She'd be able to tell if things were rearranged or missing.

"God, no." She sounded horrified at the thought, peering around his shoulder, warm and close and thankfully safe. "What is *that*?"

He glanced at a lump of mangy taupe fur. "Looks like a deer." An eight-pointer, with dark, wounded glass eyes. Someone was proud enough to stuff it, but they probably hadn't eaten the meat. All for show, and that was a damn shame.

"But it's..." Was she lost for words? Still whispering, like a little girl in church. Maybe trying to be polite.

"Stuffed." Hadn't she ever seen taxidermy before? "Look, they got a cougar too. Big bastar—uh, a big fellow." The cat's peepers were yellow glass, and glittered balefully. It was posed in a crouch no feline would ever consent to, on a big plastic lump supposed to represent a rock.

"Corpses on display," she muttered. "Fabulous."

He was about to make a smartass reply—funny, how standing in the door of a dark sporting goods store with a gun in his hand meant he could talk to her without feeling the shakes—when all his interiors turned cold and iron-sharp. The metal taste of adrenaline hit the very back of his tongue and every angle, every edge in the entire store stood out in crisp relief as his pupils swelled.

The critter erupted from behind glassed-in cases holding two cash registers and signs proclaiming *You Broke It You Bought It* and *Unattended Children Will Be Sold As Slaves*, a hideous grinding growl filling its flayed chest. It was haggard and juicy, dripping a foul fatty grease while its jaws worked with a queer rusty sound, like the tendons were seized up. Looked like a male, from the narrow hips and broader shoulders, and zipped onto its heaving ribs was a red polyester vest with a plastic nametag proclaiming *FRED* over the news that *It's Better at Bateley's!* Strings of dark oily hair plastered its rancid-gleaming scalp, and it held its arms out stiffly, shuffling and blundering between round racks of camo vests and pants. Looked like military surplus there, a piece of good luck; Lee brought the gun up smoothly.

"Plug yo' ears, Miss Virginia." He wanted the critter focused on him, and it didn't disappoint—its head made that queer sideways listening movement right before the shot and muzzle flash. Ginny's cry of surprise was lost in the noise, and if there were any others around, that would get their attention.

"—*Christ!*" Ginny finished, and Lee banished a smile, scanning for any movement in the dim interior. She crowded even closer, and that was pleasant but it might mess with his aim.

So he finished breathing out, nice and steady, and dropped his weight a little to keep both of them balanced. "Ginny." Calm and focused, that was the ticket. If there were more, the noise would bring 'em out, and he'd deal with them one at a time. "You hear me?"

"I'm practically deaf," she whispered, shakily. "Yes, I hear you."

"Turn around. Put your back up against mine and watch that parking lot, okay?"

"Oh, God." But she obeyed, and her small slight pressure caused a few more interesting reactions to cascade all the way to the bottom of his spine. Not to mention in front.

Deep breaths. Just keep breathing. Tunnel vision wanted to close down, he scanned again, shaking the ringing out of his ears and *listening.* No grinding sounds. No blundering noises like something in a back room was disturbed and was floundering. "How's it look out there?"

"N-nothing moving." She probably wasn't aware she was still trying to back into him. "That I can see, I mean."

"All right. We'll just wait a second." Staying near the door wasn't good tactics, but in this case, he figured it was best. The thing had fallen into a rack of vests and lay there, chewed fingers twitching as nerves figured out they were really, truly, unplugged. He had to loosen his knees—her lower center of gravity meant she could do a good job of backing right through him. "Just to see if that got anyone's attention."

"What was it?" Each word ragged, quick, but soft. Sounded like she was having trouble getting enough air in. "Was it one of *them?*"

"Was." Lee considered the corpse. "Looks like he came into work on the wrong day."

"Oh, God." She surprised him again, taking an audible deep breath. "Is it...is it dead?"

"Should be. Half its head's gone." He expected another expression of disgust, but she stayed quiet. "Don't you worry, Ginny. Everything is right as rain."

"If this is right, I'd hate to see wrong."

Since she wasn't watching, he could let himself smile, a tight thin curve of lips. It wasn't a nice expression, and he'd worn it out in the field more than once. Tip used to call it his chewin' grin, because when it came out, someone was gonna get bit. "Nothin out there?"

"Nothing I can see." She shuddered, a tiny, wounded shake, but she quit trying to back into him. Which was a shame, really. She was soft in all the right places.

"All right. Come on in." The urge to look everywhere at once was overpowering, and familiar. Training overrode it, kept him ticking off quadrants, his eyes adapted to the gloom and his pulse beginning to smooth out. "But you stay with me, you hear?"

"I heard you the first time, Lee." Her sweet, prim, prickly politeness. "I'm not stupid."

No, indeed you are not. "I know." It was damn cheerful to hear her get a little irritated, he decided. "I'm repeatin it to steady my nerves."

"Oh. All right." That eased her up a bit. Wind her up and wind her down, both sides were just as fun to watch. "Carry on, then."

Which was exactly what they used to say in the Army. Lee filed it under coincidences to think about later and took another good look at the darkened store. "Looks like we're lucky. Lots of ammo here."

"Great." She didn't have to work to sound heavily underimpressed. Just like Nonna, when she was too polite to tell his granddaddy he was full of something smelling like a bull's rear end. Which wasn't often, really—by the time Lee was old enough to understand sarcasm, Nonna had decided she wasn't going to hold back much when Big Q was a fool. "You know, I wonder..."

"What?" He decided keeping her talking would keep her calm, too. If another critter showed up, he'd rethink the tactic. Fast.

Ginny cleared her throat, and when she spoke again, it was in something approaching a normal tone. "I wonder if they have a cricket bat."

Huh? "A whatnow?" He decided things were calm enough, and took a smooth, gliding step forward.

She didn't crowd him, but she did back up hurriedly, almost tripping over the threshold. "A cricket bat. You know, for playing cricket."

What the hell? Was she cracking up? "I know what a cricket is, but I ain't never played one." Was it a fancy word for a fiddle? Why would she be thinking of music, for God's sake?

"It's a British game." Much steadier now, she bumped into him, a butterfly touch. "Sorry. I just wondered. It seems like it would be useful if one of those...those *things* got close."

"Okay. Well, we'll look in the sportin half once I eyeball the ammo. You ever shot a gun before?"

"No. Of course not."

Three little words—*of course not,* like he was silly to even ask. "Well." He straightened a little, decided it was clear enough, and eased his piece back into the holster. They would have flashlights in here, not to mention batteries, and his old MagLite was due for an upgrade. "I figure now's a good time to get started. We'll find you one."

$$[\ 7\ ]$$

SO WERE THE LIVING

It was warming rapidly, even in the shadows of concrete city towers. If it froze again, they were looking at some disgusting times on the road. The supermarket—it was a fancy-dancy one, big, brick, and new with a parking lot full of the trimmed ghosts of ornamental bushes in concrete holders—was dead and dark as everything else. Juju stopped for a moment to scan the lot, and realized both the goddamn teenagers had fallen behind, holding hands like it was prom night or some such foolishness, their heads close together as they ambled.

Juju considered counting to ten, but his nape itched at being out of cover for any longer than necessary. "Lee said to stay together and keep alert." It was like herding cats, only cats had the God-given sense to keep their heads out of nooses. "You can't be stoppin to play grabby-face with each other."

"We *wasn't*," Steph bridled, but Mark Kasprak at least had the grace to look ashamed.

"He's right," the boy said, untangling himself from Steph's hand and casting a guilty glance at the slush-choked parking lot. His dark hair, combed down, was no longer a bird's nest, and the shadow of acne in the crease between his lower lip and chin was an angry red.

Juju restrained the urge to roll his eyes. Next time he was goin' off with Miss Ginny, who at least had *some* damn sense. He peered through the darkened windows, cupping his hand to block out thin grey winterlight. "Thank you, son. Now. Steph, you can shoot a .22, but I ain't sure that's enough to stop one of those things."

"I ain't sure neither," Mark weighed in gravely, the hood of his parka flopping a bit as he shivered. "Mr Meacham was still goin even after the truck hit him."

"Don't..." Steph, halfway between scandalized and breathless, hugged herself. At least her lips weren't blue, like they'd been yesterday. Her arms tensed, and she swallowed hard. "And Mama," she continued, determined not to be outdone. "She was still goin', even though Mark..."

"Don't think about that, Steph." Kasprak, awkward, tried to reclaim her hand, but Steph, her baby-fine changecolor hair piled atop her young head in a red scrunchie, shied away.

"I got to, now." Her shoulder almost hit the plate glass supermarket window, and Juju suppressed a sigh. Goddamn kids. Steph had good boots, but Mark's were busted-down puffy-top numbers that looked at least a size too small. Lee had taken the kids' sizes with him to the sporting goods store Ginny said she remembered, but if Juju saw anything reasonable along the way, he'd liberate it for the cause.

He decided to keep them in the here-and-now instead of thinking about home. "Your daddy ever let you use a shotgun, Miss Steph?"

"Nosir." Her cheeks and nose both reddened, she continued to hug herself. "He did let me shoot off his .45, though. Had a kick."

".45's good. That'll stop one of those bas—I mean, one of them critters." Lord, he was about to swear a blue streak right in front of the children. Things were indeed in a fix, as his grandma used to say. "Might find one somewheres, after we finish here. Now, listen. You *stay close* until we know it's clear. Don't go runnin off to find a bathroom, y'hear?"

"Yessir," they chorused. "Mr Thurgood," Steph added, for good measure.

At least they were *good* kids. Juju suppressed another sigh, scratched at his forehead under the blue pompom hat Tip always said made him look like a goddamn Canadian, and tried the door. Locked, of course, so he limbered up the crowbar and worked its business end into the slight gap, back-and-forthing it. It was a fine time to wish he'd done real breaking and entering in his younger days. He could have busted the damn thing with little trouble, but making a shit-ton of noise was not the best way to go about this.

Especially since the critters worked off sonar. Wasn't that a kick in the pants.

"Are we really supposed to..." Kasprak swallowed the back end of that question when Juju glanced at him. The teenager hunched his shoulders, miserably. Boy was gonna be tall and lanky, a string bean like Lee instead of a fireplug like Tip.

Juju winced. As long as he kept thinking of the next thing, and the next, he wouldn't have to dwell on the sound a skull made when it crushed under a lamp, or a grinding noise from the chest of his best friend. "Well, unless'n we wanna starve to death, we ain't got no choice," he said, for the third time that morning. *All the same, if they police shows up, y'all can stay and talk to them, but I ain't gonna.*

He decided not to say *that* out loud, and worked the door a little further. It gave with a squeak, a ping, and a rattle, lost in the vast amphitheater of outside-sound. Wind, dripping water, bird-twitters. Juju realized he was damn spooked, and it took him a second to figure out why.

No traffic noise. Nothing but air moving, the faint noises of animals getting ready for a winter-bed-down, snow melting, and the two kids breathing right next to him. Well, at least they'd hear the goddamn foaming, grinding critters when they started growlin'.

Wasn't that a pleasant thought.

"Never been in one of these before," Steph breathed, rubbing her pink-gloved hands together to warm them or with glee. "Look at that."

The floor was concrete, but dyed a weird smooth russet. The checkout counters looked brand new, each with a skirting of varnished wood, and the signs in the aisles all matched. It was the kind of place where slick-haired housewives brought their own bags, standing dark and deserted—it didn't smell too bad, though any grocery was gonna get rank after a while. Juju edged inside, his sidearm pointed down just in case, and strained his ears.

"Fancy." Mark Kasprak laughed, a bona-fide teenage-boy sarcastic snort, and Steph giggled. The two of them mugging for each other was enough to give a man the old acid burps.

He decided it was safe enough for the moment, and holstered up. "All right, seems clear enough. Miss Steph, you be lookin for things you and Miss Ginny might need, girl-like, and first aid supplies. Kasprak, you're on canned goods and dry, things that'll keep a long while. I'm gonna sweep what's left and look for necessaries."

"Yessir," Kasprak said.

That covered everything he could think of, except the most important thing. "And make a little noise, but not a lot, so I know where you are."

"Yessir." Steph, this time, her hands clasped like a schoolgirl's in pink camo gloves. Well, it was truth in advertising. Both of them were too goddamn young for this.

Mark's hands were bare, and raw with the cold. Juju added that to the list. "And if you see one of them things—"

"Sing out once and run," they chorused, good bright-eyed little students.

"That's right." Juju didn't like sending them off, but he *also* didn't want to be in here all damn day. "Get yo' lights out." They produced their flashlights, and switched them on without needing to be told. "Good. Take a basket and bring everything up here for us to pack it, y'hear? And be *careful*."

"Yessir." Kasprak scrubbed at his nose, already red and full from the sound. Steph set off, playing her flashlight beam over the aisle signs. The boy watched her, and Juju wondered if he knew what was written all over his young face. Something between hunger and bafflement, with a good helping of want thrown in to spike it with napalm.

Lord, to be that young again.

As usual, when shit went sideways, it didn't stop to take a breath first.

Juju made a circuit of the outside of the store, half to get the layout and half out of curiosity. He'd always wondered what it looked like when one of these was closed up, and now he knew. The produce section was bare except for potatoes and the like; when those turned to rot it would get root-cellar fragrant. The bakery was empty too, its wire shelves turned into sad hungry teeth. The meat counter's glass hutch was bare and clean, chilly white. The place was locked up tight, so it was likely to be clear. All the perishables were no doubt in coolers behind the swinging employee doors, and with the cold even tomatoes would probably keep for a while.

That was what he was thinking when he heard a low, nasty noise, a burr caught in a grinder.

Shit. He cleared leather, the flashlight's beam swinging wild, and Jesus but it was too damn dark. Instinct fought with training; training won, driving him into a crouch that saved him as the thing blurred growling from behind the gleaming, empty meat counter.

It was a heavyset man in a short-sleeved white button-down, now torn along the hem and bibbed down the front with a dark, spreading, gleaming stain. His suspenders and tie were both red, and his khakis had once had a sharp crease in front. Sensible brown loafers and a nametag finished the picture of a manager, maybe the last one to lock up or the first one in on a chill winter morning even though he wasn't feeling too good. A close-set pair of grey-filmed eyes rolled behind horn-rimmed Coke-bottle glasses somehow still attached to the crit-ter's head. The mouth worked, teeth snapping, and Juju's hand came up nice and smooth, the gun barking almost on its own. Muzzle flash painted the scene, lightning at the same time as the thunder.

Shit shit shit. Juju duckwalked sideways as the thing fell, its head steaming. Brain and bone splattered, and the thought that some of it might get *on* him brought up the oatmeal and coffee he'd had for breakfast, pressing hot acid against the back of his throat. It always happened like that; Juju Thurgood's stomach, despite a lifetime of practice digesting the unpalatable, was nervous when the killin' was over.

Every goddamn time. I hate puking. His back hit an endcap full of wine; glass chimed, bottles rubbing together. None of them fell, thank God and all the saints. Sweat prickled all over him. *Shit. The kids. Where are the kids?*

"Steph?" Mark Kasprak, his voice breaking, from somewhere in the store's middle. "*Steph!*"

"I'm right here." Irritable. "Where's Mr Thurgood?"

God damn you both, shut the fuck up. He cleared his throat. The corpse on the floor twitched a little. The critter's glasses had flown free, and the uninjured half of of the corpse-face stared reproachfully at Juju when the flashlight beam touched it.

"Stay where you is," he rasped, then repeated it a little louder. "Kids, just *stay where you is.*"

"Yessir," Steph squeaked. She sounded scared to death. Which meant she had *some* sense after all. Wonders never ceased.

He was gonna have to check where the goddamn critter—oh, hell, might as well call it a zombie like the kids did—had come from, just to be sure. Behind the fucking meat counter. In the dark.

The corpse's nametag said *Jim.* Right below, in heavy type: *STORE MANAGER—LET ME HELP YOU!* The cracker mother-fucker wasn't gonna be helping anyone anymore.

A flicker of motion to his right, and afterward, Juju didn't know why he hadn't squeezed the trigger. Maybe he'd heard a rustle of cloth, maybe it was the boy's flashlight beam, or maybe he'd just frozen. Whatever it was, he almost filled Mark Kasprak's narrow chest with 9mm bullets, and the goddamn idiot, standing there with his mouth fish-open and his hair springing back up in unruly spikes, stared.

"Sonofa*bitch!*" Juju hissed. "I told you to *stay put!*"

The kid just gaped. Juju decided his legs would work if he told them to, and swayed upright.

"Is it dead?" Mark whispered. His dark eyes were big as saucers, and Juju was very, very glad the kid didn't have a piece on him. Soldiers with that expression were just as liable to shoot their buddies as the enemy. Once a man started lookin like a deer, you took his weapons away and got him behind the lines right quick for a hot meal and something to loosen up the spring in his chest.

"Pretty sure." A thin trickle of sweat slid down Juju's spine. Jesus *Christ.* Even his bowels felt loose, and that hadn't happened in a long, long while. "I coulda shot you, boy. You gotta be careful."

Something flickered in Kasprak's pupils for a second. He swallowed, twice, Adam's-apple moving, and nodded. "Don't call me *boy,*" he said, flatly. "What we gonna do now?"

You's goddamn lucky I didn't callya shit for brains. Juju swallowed it, though. A lifetime of keeping what he thought of stupid white boys behind his teeth was a hard habit to break, even if he wanted to. Bottling that shit up kept you alive, though, like *yessir* and *nosir* and going on leave with a pale buddy each time, just in case.

Just-in-fucking-case.

Here it was the end of the world, and he still had to watch what he said. Especially since Frank Kasprak was a bigot with a mean streak. Would've joined the triple K if he could stay sober enough to attend meetins, was Juju's private estimation of the man, and probably taught his tadpole plenty. Apples falling next to trees, it was a goddamn tragedy.

The world was full of fucking tragedies, even after the Pocalypse.

Juju exhaled a sharp, bile-scented breath. "Imma check that back-room, make sure there ain't no more of 'em."

Kasprak eyed him. "Okay." A single, colorless word. "Want help?"

Nah. I don't think having a jumpy-ass kid behind me is a good idea. "Go stay with Miss Steph. One of you watches, t'other one shops."

"Aight." But the kid just stood there. "You sure you don't want some help, sir?"

So it was "sir" now. That, Juju decided, was a good thing. *Thank God I didn't shoot you, kid.* "I'll be all right. You just keep with Miss Steph and sing out if another one shows up, you hear?"

"Yessir." Mark turned around and shuffled past a display of corn chips, vanishing into the dimness.

Juju sagged on his feet. His hands jittered like they heard music, and his mouth was full of sour dry heat now. Yeah, the zombified assholes were dangerous.

So, James Unwin Thurgood decided, were the living.

GOODBYE TO OLD FRIENDS

THE BELL OVER THE DOOR JINGLED ITS USUAL MERRY CHIME; Ginny could have cried with relief at the sane, familiar sound. Even though the entire place was damp and chilly, even though the only light was through the front windows, it still smelled of paper and dust and the faint vanilla tinge that said *books*.

And books meant *safe*.

Schaply's New and Used was tiny, because the people around here liked their tee-vees more than the effort of reading. It was a wonder the place stayed open at all. The owner Paul, a cranky heavyset man with an ancient NRA baseball cap and John Wayne-sized suspenders, was nevertheless very gentle when you placed your purchases on the counter. You learned to take your change from said counter because he would not hand it to you, no sir, and you also learned to have your library card—not your ID—out if you had to write a check. He wouldn't take one from someone who didn't have a library card, and forget using your debit or credit cards. *Nosir*, he'd repeat, balefully, or *no ma'am, I don't hold with that credit foolishness*.

On the other hand, his stock was always interesting, and you could order just about anything through him at a discount. His nephew was a computer whiz, and liked the challenge of tracking down cheap books for his crotchety old uncle. She'd only caught glimpses of the kid—gangly in flannel shirts and jeans, black hair pasted down over his forehead and a pair of black cat's-eye glasses, bent over a laptop balanced precariously on Paul's paper-piled desk— but he seemed like a nice one. She suspected the store was what they called a "boondoggle" in this part of the country, gently going to seed, or maybe Paul had some savings and a pension he used to keep it running. You could invent all sorts of stories about a stocky liver-spotted man who ran a bookstore and whose coffee cup invariably carried a strong alcoholic tinge.

There was a Barnes & Noble on the other side of Lewiston, but she'd always preferred to come here. A shorter drive, easier to get back on the freeway, and patronizing a local business, right? Only now she was hoping they wouldn't find grizzled, ill-tempered Paul and his red suspenders, gone zombified and chewing on empty air. Or his nephew, quick and skinny and rotting.

It was silent, the welcoming silence of worlds resting behind covers, waiting patiently to be opened, profligate with their magic once you parted their pages. Ginny took three or four steps in, closed her eyes, and inhaled the beautiful, wonderful smell of refuge. When she turned to check on Lee, he was peering at the top of the doorway, digging in his back pocket. He produced a serious-looking multi-tool, and a few moments later was unscrewing the metal piece holding the bell.

"What on earth are you *doing?*" She shouldn't have shocked, really. After shooting one of those...things...in the sporting goods store, she was surprised at *this?*

"Rather not let those critters know where we are, if we can help it." He looked over his shoulder, his capable hands working away. It was mildly surprising how tall he was; at this angle, with the grey light falling through the dusty glass door, she could catch a glimpse of the tall, almost-gawky teenager he must have been. Had he been quiet then, too, or the class clown? Sometimes people changed. "Won't take but a minute."

Well, since he'd already popped the door open with a crowbar, she supposed she couldn't cavil. Was there anything he *didn't* have in the back of his truck, anything he didn't know how to do? The world had turned upside down, and all of a sudden people who were capable with things other than keyboards and screens were the ones who stood a better chance of surviving.

Or had they always been? Being poor, or even just redneck, looked like good training for the end of the world.

She tried to imagine being in New York while the sickness spread. It wasn't pleasant. So many people jammed together, living on top, underneath, cheek-by-jowl…the illness must have raced through like a wildfire. Was this what the Native Americans felt when smallpox arrived, and the whites with their guns on its heels?

What was that old line? We have seen the enemy, and he is us.

God. The immensity of the disaster hovered just out of sight, waiting to pounce on you the instant you relaxed.

"Miss Ginny?" Lee was *right* next to her.

Ginny jumped, halting an undignified *eek*; it turned into a painful hiccup-bubble. "*Jesus!*"

"Sorry." Lee's hand dropped back to his side. His hair, finger-combed and free of a hat, had loosened up considerably. The dark strands had chestnut highlights and the little bit of relaxation made him almost handsome. "Didn't mean to scare you."

"It's…" She swallowed the air bubble, or at least tried to, and coughed. *Heaven help me, I'm going to choke on my own spit. Great.* "No, it's okay. I just…I'm…"

"Tryin to catch up, right?" He nodded, spacing the words out. "Soldiers do that, too."

"Oh?" She waved her right hand slightly, like a fan. *I've got the vapors. Vapor-locked.* It struck her as funny, but if she started laughing now she'd look like an idiot. Or crazy.

"Ayuh." He didn't move, probably thinking she'd jump again if he did. There was something almost comforting in feeling someone that close, if you knew them. If not for their coats, she'd catch the edge of his body heat. Maybe she already was, because her cheeks suddenly turned into stove burners. "When they come back from a hot patch."

Is that what you call it? "Oh." There didn't seem to be much else to say, and he just *stood* there. Patiently. Waiting.

Well, it was her idea to come in here, so she set her shoulders and raised her flashlight. He and Juju both carried big black metal ones, heavy enough to club someone with; the hotel's emergency flashlights were plastic and much less sturdy. The haul from the sporting goods store included a few more of the big heavy lights—MAGLITE, the outside of the packages screamed—and pretty much all the batteries you could ever want.

The uncomfortable thought that maybe, just maybe, no more batteries would roll off the conveyor belts anytime soon stopped her in her tracks again. "God."

"Hm?" Lee made a mild inquiring noise, standing right where she'd left him.

Ginny had never noticed the nylon carpeting in here, blue with tiny brown and orange flecks. Industrial. The machines to make it were no doubt dark and motionless now. "I keep thinking about all the things that won't happen anymore. If this thing is worldwide, if it's..."

"Yeah, that'll give you the shakes for sure." Lee's flashlight beam rose, played over the Books of the Month display. That made Ginny feel a little faint, too. The machines for printing and binding. The editors. And God knew how many writers, gone. So many stories lying stillborn, so many historians and essayists and memoirists with things to say, silent as Rachel Carson's pesticide spring.

The problem wasn't that it was inconceivable, she decided. It was that she, trained by a lifetime of fiction, education, and imagination, could conceive all too goddamn vividly.

Inconceivable. What a term. *You keep using that word.* A joke from an old movie ran through her head. *I do not think it means, what you think it means.*

Ginny set her shoulders again, took a deep breath. Her braids were still damp from this morning's shower, and her head was cold. It looked like Paul had changed the display since she'd been in—had it really only been a few days ago? Now the books were about cold-frame gardening and weather disasters, and doorstopper classics— Moby Dick, collected Poe, a mound of Dickens—with a small hand-written label. *Good for keeping warm on a winter night!* Whether Paul Schaply had meant you could read them or light them was an open question.

Get moving, Ginny. She took another look at the store layout. "Okay. First things first. Journal. Maybe even two or three, just to be sure."

"Journal?" Lee hooked his thumbs in his jacket pocket and studied the store interior as well.

She headed for the spinner of blank Moleskines near the counter. Good enough for the Beats, good enough for the fall of human civi-lization. "Well, we're living through something historical. People are going to want to know what happened. And...I want to make lists."

"What kinda lists?" He glanced back at the door, like he expected one of those *things* to come barreling through. Or maybe he wanted to get out of here. Did books make him uncomfortable? Funny, she couldn't recall a week when he *hadn't* been at the Cotton Crossing library, not since she'd started working at that branch. He was one of the regulars, she'd assumed he'd *always* been coming in.

Would she have noticed otherwise? It was an uncomfortable thought. "Things I want to remember, or that I want *other* people to remember. Information plus culture is civilization. I mean, that's an oversimplification, but..." Here she was, jabbering on. "Anyway. Jour-nal. Then Foxfire books, and—"

"The whatnow?" Half-turning, he peered out at the parking lot again. Slush darkened his boots and the frayed hems of his jeans.

"They're books about...well, country living. How to do things.

Like how to butcher your own meat, how to build things, how to survive. We'll need plant identification manuals too. First aid and survival stuff—"

That brought his head back around. "You went to med school, right?"

"Yeah, but what if I'm the one who needs help? Or something happens but I'm somewhere else? Or something happens I'm not familiar with?" She shook her head, much more comfortable now that she had the beginnings of a clear-cut list. "And you may know how to do all the outdoorsy things, but *I* don't, and if something happens to you—"

"Ain't nothin gonna happen to me."

Typical male. He probably resisted going to the doctor, too, just like Dad. "But if something *does*. I can't just depend on you." The thought of Dad's beak-nosed, serenely set face pinched under her left ribs.

Hard.

"Guess not."

Maybe Lee didn't mean it sarcastically, but Ginny swung round and looked at him. His face was shadowed, turned away, but she could pick him out anywhere just by the *way* he stood. Deceptively easy, completely straight, shoulders a little back, not quite shouting *military* but saying it all the same. Quietly, as usual.

Still, he looked unhappy, and Ginny's conscience pinched a little. "If you don't like it in here, you can wait in the truck."

That earned her a sideways glance, his dark eyes piercing. "Huh?" A faint line had begun between his eyebrows, his attention lighting on her like a hawk on a sunny perch.

"You look uncomfortable." At least she could be certain he wouldn't take offense.

"Just watchin."

"For those...things?" She stacked three lined notebooks on the counter, thought about it, added another. No new pens, just the check-signing ones in an oversized coffee mug, but she could find plenty of writing implements at the hotel, and there were two in her purse.

"Or anything else," Lee said. "Weather comin in, too."

"Yeah, it looks awful out there." She could only hope they wouldn't get stuck in Lewiston, of all places. If she had to spend the entire winter here, she would chew her own arms off.

Now wasn't *that* a cheerful thought.

THE PROBLEM WITH BOOK-SHOPPING AFTER THE APOCALYPSE was that she kept thinking of more she wanted to take, to *preserve*. Sure, there was Shakespeare, but should she even bother with a Bible? Great poetry in some bits, allusions to it throughout the Western canon, but did it *really* need to survive, with all the trouble it caused? That went for pretty much any holy book except for Buddhist sutras, maybe.

God, she'd picked the wrong year to stop meditating.

Should she maybe look for some Neruda or Toni Morrison instead? Not that Schaply's would have Neruda. All the Seamus Heaney in the world, because he was a Dead White Man, but no Neruda. No Akhmatova either. There was one lone Sylvia Plath among the manly men of Paul-approved verse, and she decided *that* needed to be saved.

Lee's flashlight beam hit the sign overhead. "Poetry?"

Ginny suppressed a sigh. "Just saying goodbye to old friends." She took the slim copy of *Ariel* from its place. Let him think what he wanted. He was probably aching to get the fuck out of here and back to the hotel. Sometimes non-readers got nervous in bookstores. Ginny never understood *that*. Books didn't judge. They met you wherever you were, they deepened and changed as you did, but they didn't suddenly turn on you.

They were, in short, much better than people.

She was in luck—there was a box set of the first three Foxfire books, used but in grand condition. A couple used Army manuals she decided might be useful, and among the slim pickings on the botany shelf she found a reasonably good, if decade-old, regional plant ID manual. "Sweet success," she muttered, and went looking for anything medical. Paul organized according to a weird logic that only made sense if one squinted and guessed, and she felt only a slight twinge at going behind the counter to look for what she knew had to be there. Every bookstore owner had a stash of titles they wouldn't put out on display, and Paul's were interesting. Looked like he was into blacksmithing, and there was a How Things Work she nabbed as well as an almost-new Merck manual.

Was Paul still alive? At home? Worried about his store? She felt bad for just coming in and *taking*. Sports equipment and ammunition was one thing, but these were *books*. She cast around, lighting on an ancient printer, and rescued a piece of blank paper. The check-writing pens rattled in a van Gogh coffee mug on the counter; she selected a green one and wondered what the proper salutation was. *Dear Paul* was too informal, *Dear Sir* a little cold. She pushed a fingertip under her left-hand braid, rubbing at a pinpoint ache she suspected would turn into a headache later.

"What are you doin?" Lee, on the customer side of the counter, looked perplexed. He eyed her stack of picks like it was about to bite him, too.

"Leaving a note." Ginny decided she wouldn't date it, because she'd have to dig her phone out to remember said date. "So he knows who took his books."

Lee's expression hovered somewhere between mystified and amused. "I don't think it matters, darlin."

"This is a *bookstore*." *I sound downright scandalized.* She decided on *Dear Sir*, professional even if cold, and listed what she'd taken.

Maybe she was being an idiot, because a smile pulled the corners of Lee's mouth up. "All right, then. We about done?"

"Almost." *I'm sorry to have taken them, but they'll be put to good use, and when I come back I'll pay you.* She paused before signing her name, decided it was probably better not to. *Sincerely, A Loyal Customer.* "There. Let me just bag these."

"You do that." Lee tensed, and when she looked up he was gazing out the windows at the parking lot. He had a nice profile, when his mouth relaxed. Unfortunately, his lips turned into a thin, worried line. "I'll bring the truck up. You stay here, all right?"

Please. Please is a good word to use. She swallowed a hot burst of irritation. "Fine."

"I mean it. Inside, Miss Ginny. Will you?"

"Of course—oh." Her skin shrank two sizes, goosebumps going down her back, and her throat constricted. "Is it—oh, God, are they out there?" She hurried to bag the books, grateful Paul was more of a paper than a plastic person, and Lee reached over the counter, catching her wrist. Warm fingers, he'd taken his green woolen Army gloves off.

Ginny froze.

"No ma'am." He looked down at her, his eyebrows drawing together. "It's all right. Nothin out there but bad weather. Just bein careful."

"Oh. Okay." Her throat had closed up, her heart jolting up against the obstruction. And here she thought she was doing so well.

He didn't let go. "It's all right," he repeated, as if she'd disagreed.

Nothing about this is even remotely all right. Still, it was kind of comforting. "Okay." She tugged against his grip. "I'll, um, just get these bagged."

"Ginny." Why was he *looking* at her like that? "When it's time to worry, I'll tell you, aight?"

"Sure." *How very patronizing of you.* "Thanks. That's very kind."

It was probably the wrong thing to say, because he dropped her wrist and did a smart about-face, heading for the door with long swinging strides, his shoulders set and broad under his shearling jacket.

And Ginny wondered why on *earth* she was blushing.

[9]

A GOOD HYPOTHESIS

THEY MADE IT BACK TO THE HOTEL BEFORE AN UGLY SLEET began to lash the roads, which was good news as far as Lee was concerned. Ginny huddled on her side of the bench seat, three paper bags of books arranged and rearranged around her with careful solicitude at least twice during the ride. He'd scared her, right before they left the cold dark cave of the bookstore. Course, he'd scared her with shooting the goddamn critter in the *other* store, too. There was just no way around that particular hill, it was a downright terror-making situation.

Still, he'd thought she'd be...what, reassured? Especially when he told her to be. Nothin' yet he couldn't handle.

Juju and the kids were back, but the black man had the set look of a disagreeable patrol stamped all over his sculpted face. He stood in the foyer amid a pile of grocery-store loot, all neatly arranged in paper instead of plastic. "Bagged a motha in the grocery store. Fucker was tryin to get into the meat cooler."

"I got one at the Bateley's." Lee set down a box of clothing. Traveller, yip-yodeling his happiness at the return of his pack, wove around his knees. "So, they'll take dead meat if they can get it. Good to know."

"He sure wasn't lookin to chew on some celery." Juju rubbed at the back of his left hand and the old burn scar, straightening to stretch his legs. "Listen, Lee, next time don't send me out with the kids. Not half a brain cell between 'em. Boy almost got his guts fulla nine-mil, comin up on me blindside."

"Shit." Lee scratched at his neck. The hotel lobby was brightly lit; outside the canopy past the front door sleet came down in hissing curtains. "Aight, I'll put him straight. Thinking maybe we shouldn't none of us split up for a while."

"Well, you can send me out with Miss Ginny." Juju's grin was a shadow of its former self, but nice to see anyway. He scrubbed at his hair, a familiar motion, washing away worry and settling into being back from the zone. "She got brains, that girl."

Did she ever. "Plenty of 'em."

The rest of the grimness around Juju's eyes and mouth fled. "She likes you."

Oh, for God's sake. Maybe she did, maybe she didn't, he couldn't really tell. Lee poked at the box of clothing, and decided the subject needed changing. "I got baseball bats. Helmets, too." If they had to tangle with the critters, probably best to cover up. Bulletproof vests were good, but they didn't armor all the places someone could *chew.*

"Baseball bats?" Juju sucked in his cheeks, squatting to look through the box. "Shit, put some lead in those motherfuckers and we can have ourselves a good time."

"Amen to that. Keep the dog in, willya?" Lee headed back outside to find Ginny up in the bed of the truck, handing down the bats to Steph. Mark Kasprak, who should have been scanning for trouble, was instead leaning on the tailgate, probably cracking jokes because Steph laughed, tossing her thin fluttering ponytail in its red scrunchie. Ginny straightened, glancing out into the parking lot as the sleet's sibilant mouthing intensified. Some of her curls had come loose, and from this angle she was a nervous doe, head upflung in a wintry field.

Anyone drawing a bead would find her an easy target.

"Kasprak," Lee barked. His chest hurt, a pinch high on the left side. "What in hell you doin, son?"

The kid jumped like a jackrabbit, and Lee was hard put not to smile. "Nothin, Mr Quartine, sir, I just—"

"Nothin ain't what you out here for. Go on around the front of the truck and keep a lookout."

"There ain't nothin out there, sir." Kasprak set his chin and scowled. Apparently Juju's run-in with the meat-locker critter hadn't made much of a dent. For a second Lee wanted to run the kid ragged like he was in basic, but the fact that Ginny was watching took some of the savor out of the idea.

"I'm keeping an eye." Ginny, kind and soft. She glanced back at Lee, and her expression plainly said, *they're young, what are you going to do?*

Even a kid could get someone killed when there were hostiles roaming around. "Kasprak." Lee fixed him with a steady look. "You want to get yourself bit? Or Steph? Or Miz Mills there?"

"Nosir." The chin went back in, but the scowl remained.

Good Lord, Lee would have had the sense slapped into him if he'd ever looked like that, probably by his sainted Nonna herself. "You think you got some special critter radar gonna tell you where they is without lookin?"

"Nosir." Mark was beginning to get it. The ugly flush along his thin neck shouted as much. His shoulders trembled—probably, given his daddy's temper, he wasn't sure if Lee was gonna start yelling or cuff him one.

Frank Kasprak had always been a bully, and a useless one to boot. "All right then." Lee nodded, like Mark had redeemed himself a bit. "You just keep that in mind, and keep a watch out for our girls, y'hear?"

"Oh, for God's sake," Ginny muttered. "Lee—"

"Yessir." Mark did an about-face and headed for the other side of the truck.

Lee shooed Steph away with her armful of baseball bats and eyeballed what was left. Not much, just the ammo. He should hop up in there and give Ginny a hand, the cartons were heavy.

"They're just kids." Ginny bent her knees, sinking into a crouch far more gracefully than any man could manage. Maybe it was in the hips, the way a woman could do that and look catlike instead of squatting-toad. "Also, was that *our girls* bit really necessary?" She blew a stray curl out of her face, a quick, annoyed little huff.

Yes ma'am it was. He contented himself with a nod.

"Are you sure?" Ginny didn't move, examining him. "Well, I suppose you are, or you wouldn't have said it."

He hadn't noticed how thick her eyelashes were, a fringe around quiet dark eyes. Looked like she wasn't sleeping well, too, from the shadows underneath them.

Well, nobody these days was gonna be sleeping well. Up to and including old soldiers like him. Still...it would be nice to see some of that ease up. See her maybe relax a little. He was an idiot for thinking he could offer anything comforting at this point, but he could try. "We're all right, Ginny. I aim to keep it that way, that's all."

Maybe he'd hit on something reasonable after all, because a small, lonely curve of a smile brought the corners of her lips up. "I know. You're doing a good job, too."

That was nice to hear, and that pain high under his left ribs came back. Another pinch. Maybe his ticker was getting clotted up? Maybe he shouldn't have had gravy every time he went into Mayburn's Diner.

Ginny glanced over her shoulder again as the sleet-hiss intensified, hunching further, her small smile vanishing into fresh solemnity. "Steph was telling me there was one at the grocery store."

Of course she'd worry about that, too. "Juju said the same."

"Why aren't there any here?" She bit her lower lip, small white teeth sinking in. Just looking for more of the weight of the world to strap onto her back. It was enough to make a man wonder about her family, seeing the attempt.

"Not a lot of food?" He made it a question. Easier that way, instead of saying, *ain't sure and just glad it's working out that way.*

She rocked back on her heels. Her pretty boots were already showing strain under hard use; he'd picked out better ones in her size at Bateley's. She'd just accepted the big brown shoebox and packed it away with the rest of the stuff. Not even a murmur.

And right now, she didn't start screaming, or even look shocked. Just sat on her heels for a moment, blowing out a soft breath between her teeth. *Hisssss,* said the sleet, and *thump* went Lee's heart again, because she set her shoulders and her chin, and nodded. "That's a good hypothesis." Her voice dropped, she made another little movement like she wanted to look over her shoulder. Checking on Kasprak, he realized. She was so quiet, so contained, you could overlook how much worry she carried on those slim shoulders. "And a scary one," she continued, softly. "I don't think the kids have thought this through yet. Juju probably has, though."

Lee shrugged. There wasn't anything to say.

"I think we'd probably better turn the lights off tonight." Her gloves, cloud-grey and pretty instead of warm, curled up as the fingers inside them tensed. "Because if we're all lit up, that could mean food to those things. Or it could mean something else to other survivors."

And here he thought she'd need convincing, or an explanation for the decision he'd made in the truck on the way back. "That's a good idea."

"I'm just full of them. I can't stop." She rose, a dancerlike unfolding. Why did God design women to *move* that way? It wasn't fair. "Like what happens when we run out of canned food."

Jesus, woman, don't borrow trouble. "There's a lot of it out there," he began, hedging the words carefully.

"Sir?" Mark called, soft, nervous. "Mr Quartine, sir?"

Oh, god damn it. "What?" Maybe he said it a little sharper than he meant to.

"We should, uh, maybe go inside?" The boy's voice cracked. "I think they've found us."

LOSING COUNT

"It's so bizarre," Miz Mills breathed; she had taken off her coat and her dove-grey sweater's sleeves swallowed her hands; its hem reached almost to her knees. Traveller leaned against her leg, gazing adoringly at her chin. "Look at that."

Steph wanted to say she would rather not, thank you very much. She shivered, but forced herself to look out the window, because if Miz Mills could do it, so could she. Her own red wool sweater, a gift from her grandma three years ago, was stretched and full of holes, shapeless. Next to Miz Mills, she felt like a popped balloon.

A small, very scared popped balloon.

The zombies moved in irregular ovals through the parking lot. Mr Quartaine on Miz Mills's other side said nothing, just watched, a line between his eyebrows and his arms crossed over his chest. His familiar leather vest was damp, his fleecy coat open halfway. Sleet smacked the glass, melting, ran down in ripples.

"We could shoot from the roof." Mr Thurgood's face had turned little chalky under all its melanin. He was still all zipped up. Maybe it helped him feel better. God knew Steph was wishing she hadn't taken her own jacket off. She was cold all the way through, even though they still had heat.

"And let them know we're here?" Miz Mills shuddered. "Thank God you brought the dog up. He'd've gone crazy barking."

The zombies weren't pressing against the glass doors downstairs anymore. Mr Quartine had herded the teens and Miz Mills inside, carrying two boxes of ammo like they weighed nothing and whispering for Juju to kill the lights. The stairway doors were barricaded now, and they gathered in the room Steph and Ginny had slept in last night, looking over the parking lot. The shuffling dead people now ignored the truck and Mr Thurgood's 4x4; several had circled the vehicles while Ginny and Steph, holding hands like a pair of schoolkids, stood behind the hotel desk and watched.

The chewed-up, shambling things that had once been people also bumped against the glass door with small soft sounds, and Mark had let out a funny whooshing breath.

Easy, Mr Thurgood had whispered, his hand to the gun at his side. *Just move nice and slow. Let's go up.*

"*Do* they know we're here?" Mr Thurgood's elbow touched Mark's. "Kasprak?"

"I...they weren't hurryin." Mark was sheet-white, except for two round patches of hectic red high on his cheeks. He was zipped all the way up, too, the mangy fake fur around his pulled-up hood mixing with his bangs. "Just wanderin across the road. Wouldn't've seen em with the rain and all, except that one in the red hat."

The Red Hat zombie was a potbelly man in a dark parka with a flopping, torn-open parka hood spilling onto his broad shoulders. Steph shuddered again, *hard,* and Ginny put an arm around her shoulders. When the librarian spoke, it was with the businesslike calm of a teacher. "It's good that you did. I wonder if they're going to stay there, or if..."

"You think they might move on?" *Why are we all whispering?* Steph leaned into Miz Ginny's warmth. It wasn't her mama's, but it was still powerfully comforting.

"Well, they could be moving like a herd, looking for…looking for food." Miz Ginny's arm tightened. Her thumb moved a little, stroking Steph's arm. "That would make sense."

Steph was suddenly, irrationally glad she'd made her hotel bed this morning. It wouldn't be decent for the menfolk to see her sheets. Ginny's bed was made too, but her suitcase was open on top of it. Everything packed neatly, in its proper place. And all new, too. Nothing ripped, or torn, or patched. She was probably used to traveling, and knew all about who to tip and when, even in big cities.

Miz Mills had such a pretty voice, despite the flat Yankee twang. "They could decide there's nothing here, and move on," she continued. "They didn't see us, I don't think, but maybe they can smell us? Sense us?"

"Their hearin's good." Mr Thurgood spread his pink-palmed hand against the glass, fingertips touching gently. Faint condensation ringed his skin, living heat meeting cold slickness. Steph wondered what glass was made out of—Miz Mills probably knew. "Damn dog'll bring them right inside if he starts talkin when someone takes him out."

Mr Quartine still said nothing, just watched. His chin tilted down a little, and he studied the zombies milling in front of the hotel like they were a kind of puzzle, one he was sussing out. Steph wished he'd pipe up, because then she'd know what to do, even if it was just sitting tight and pretending they weren't trapped in here.

"We've got a little while before that's an issue." Practical, and soft, Ginny rubbed at Steph's shoulder, and Steph had the funny idea that maybe she wasn't so much comforting someone else as trying to convince herself. "There's a whole other side to the hotel, I can take him out there."

The line between Mr Quartine's eyebrows deepened. Standing like that, with the dark shadow of stubble on his cheeks, he reminded Steph a little bit of her own daddy. Except Bull Meacham was never this silent. Not in a million years.

Not even while he *slept*. Her daddy's snores could knock a house down.

Well, he's quiet now. Except for the growling. That was a bad thought, and Steph did her best to shove it away. She wanted to bury her face in Miz Mills's shoulder, even if the woman wasn't her mama.

"There's so many of them." Mark leaned forward. He hugged himself, his chapped hands swallowed by his coat sleeves. His parka was holding up nicely, even if his boots were leaking. "I keep losing count."

"Lee?" Mr Thurgood prompted, reaching for his collar. He opened his coat with his free hand, finally, and his sweater was cheerful black and yellow stripes. Like a bumblebee. It didn't match his hat or the rest of him, but it was nice to see the color.

Mr Quartine shook his head a little, a *don't bother me* motion. A scream rose in Steph's throat, gurgled on the fries she'd had for breakfast, and died away. Maybe potato starch hadn't been a wise choice, but what else was there? She suddenly longed for cereal—Rice Krispies, which she hadn't had since she was in grade school, cracklepopping their happy little song. With nice cold milk.

Milk was all gonna sour soon if it wasn't already, unless it was those fancy cartons of rice, almond, soy you could get at the Lewiston WalMarts. Were there cows going unsqueezed out there? Trapped in big barns? What about pigs waiting for their next meal? Or...or even pets? Dogs like Traveller, or cats?

Once you thought one uncomfortable thing, a bunch of others just showed up in a cascade. You couldn't help yourself. "I don't like this," Steph heard herself say, in a high, nervous little voice. "I don't like it, I *don't like it*."

"I know," Miz Ginny soothed, and stepped back, which meant Steph had to. Traveller almost fell over when they moved, he was leaning on the librarian's leg so hard. "Come on away from the window, sweetie. I, uh, think we can leave it alone for a while."

"Lee?" Mr Thurgood persisted, peeling his fingertips away from the window. "We should all sleep together tonight. Barricade the door."

All of us? Why, that ain't decent. A mad, inappropriate, completely irresistible desire to giggle shook Steph's shoulders. The trembling, nasty thought she might begin to scream floated across her brain, retreated, and came back, circling like a buzzard over the highway on a summer day. Just looking for some tasty roadkill.

Miz Ginny edged backward, drawing her along. "Come on. We should go sort through the groceries you brought."

"Uh...maybe..." That would mean going outside the room, and Steph was in no particular hurry to do *that*. Traveller followed, his nose all but glued to Ginny's calves.

Mr Quartine finally stirred. "Kasprak. You want keep watch here for a half-hour? Juju and me'll check the doors again, make sure they can't get in. Find a good OP."

"OP?" Miz Ginny looked over her shoulder.

"Observation post," Mark supplied, absently, his hands falling to his sides. "Yeah. I can do that." He stared into the parking lot, his fingers twitching. Still trying to count them. Like sheep, when you were trying to sleep. One-one-thousand, two-one-thousand, on and on.

"Good man." Mr Thurgood clapped Mark on his skinny shoulder. "What we gonna do about the dog, Lee?"

That brought Miz Ginny around in a tight, small circle, her comforting touch sliding away. Stray curls, working free of her thick dark braids, bounced. "What do you mean, *do* about the dog?"

"I mean, he'll bring the whole damn crowd of them down on us." Mr Thurgood was no longer quite so greyish, but his expression wasn't comforting at all. It was set, and a strange gleam flickered in his dark eyes.

"He can go inside somewheres if he's gotta," Mr Quartine said, with sharp finality. He rubbed his right-hand knuckles along his jaw, scratching his stubble. "When we leave we can muzzle him to get him into the truck. Ain't no problem."

Traveller, maybe understanding they were talking about him, wagged his tail, tentatively. It whapped Steph's shins, and she folded down to the floor in a hurry, scratching the dog behind his ears. He made throaty little sounds of joy and flopped almost into her lap, his nose pushing into her face. Probably thought she wanted to play. Her mama had a pug once—Baxter, who ended up dying of cancer when Steph was four. "He's a good dog," she said. "A real good dog. The *best* dog, aren't you? You are."

Her daddy hated dogs. *Factory shit-sniffers*, he called them, which always made her mama smack him lightly on the shoulder and say, *Language, Bull!*

"Miss Virginia?" Mr Quartine glanced away from Mr Thurgood, who looked sour as hell and spread his hands a little. "You mind stayin here with Steph and Mark while we make sure we're buttoned up?"

"All right." Miz Ginny nodded, slowly. *Virginia* was a pretty name, to match the rest of her. "And thank you for asking."

For some reason, that made Mr Quartine smile, a tight, rueful expression. He looked at Miz Mills like she was the only thing in the world for just that brief moment, and it was almost painful to see, Steph decided. Like you were peeping something you shouldn't. "Old dogs and new tricks."

"Let's get goin." Mr Thurgood headed for the door, with long swinging strides. "I ain't had lunch yet."

God, I never want to eat again. Steph pressed her fingers against her mouth. Traveller, thinking it was a game, licked at them. His nose was cold, and wet, and his big brown eyes were patient and merry.

"I keep losing count," Mark Kasprak muttered, again.

Nobody but Steph heard him.

[11]

MACABRE GAME

I should've thought about a pet store on the way back. Ginny hugged herself, cupping her elbows in her palms and stepping out into a gloomy, rainy late afternoon. The exercise room on the ground floor looked out onto a little bit of landscape and concrete around a winter-drained pool. It also had a brick wall and a locked iron gate a chihuahua couldn't have wriggled through; Traveller's shoulders were far too thick for him to fit.

It didn't stop him trying, and Ginny called him back, whisper-yelling his name. He listened reluctantly, and did another circuit of the area, finally deciding one of the potted bushes was acceptable to pee upon.

The Best Western was a dark cave now, and the parking lot an indistinct smear full of fading reflected snowlight. The shambling things—oh, hell, why *not* call them "zombies," it was a good, precise word—had lost interest after bumping against the foyer door for a little while. Afternoon had turned into a soggy, chilly evening, the temperature rising enough to make the sleet plain old liquid rain again. At least it wasn't freezing; the roads would be sloppy but passable in the morning.

Hopefully.

Ginny stepped back in through the sliding glass door, careful not to get in front of Juju's rifle. "If he was a phone, he'd have a silent switch."

"We can duct-tape his lips," Juju said, and it took her a moment to figure out he was joking, he sounded so level. She elbowed him, and he swallowed a laugh. It was good to hear, Ginny thought.

She was willing to bet nobody was laughing a lot right now.

Even though the zombie-things were nowhere in sight, their entire group was speaking softly, even upstairs. Except Traveller, who trotted back inside and gave himself a hearty shake, splattering rain everywhere and telling them all about the weather. She got a thin white hotel towel over him and scrubbed while he moaned happily, staring up at her like she was the best thing since kibble or an empty bladder.

Juju slid the door closed, locked it, and peered out into the dimness. "Looks clear. Mebbe they don't come out at night."

"We can hope." She got the dog's undercarriage too, wrinkling her nose a bit at the reek of wet canine. At least there would be no shortage of shampoo, dog or otherwise; that didn't go bad. She'd read somewhere you could wash a dog with tomato sauce, too—or was that only when they came across a skunk?

Which made her think about the local flora and fauna. This disaster was probably good for the environment. Not a lot of engines running, humans no longer taking habitat. You could get a headache untangling all the ecological ramifications. Greenpeace was probably overjoyed.

If there were any of them *left* to be overjoyed. And really, they weren't horrible people. Just enthusiastic. You couldn't wish bad things on anyone for *that*. "God," she muttered, pushing an escaped curl back up into her braids and returning to scrubbing Traveller dry.

"You all right?" Juju backed away from the door, one-two, quick graceful steps, placing his damp, Army-issue boots just so. He managed to make carrying a gun look natural instead of awkward, and moved lightly even though those thick-soled green clodhoppers probably weighed a ton apiece.

"I keep thinking about unpleasant things." Ginny whisked the towel away. "Okay, little fellow, let's get you some dinner."

"Man, me too." Juju held out a warm, strong hand, bracing her as she rose. The hound capered around their feet, sensing the magic food-time was near.

"Dinner, or uncomfortable things?"

Juju's half-wry smile stretched into a downright grin. "Both."

"Which ones are you thinking?" Ginny folded the towel. Maybe she should leave it near the door? It would mildew, but that couldn't be helped.

There was so much that couldn't be helped right now. But at least Juju was smiling. Her own mouth corner-tilted in response.

He tugged at the hem of his black-and-yellow sweater, settling it under the rifle strap. "Well, if those critters folla their ears, the dog's gonna bring 'em like flies to...uh, well, like flies to dog doo."

Maybe Ginny would eventually come to find the *don't swear around a lady* thing charming instead of irritating. Today, however, was not that day. She brushed at her own clothing, wishing for a lint roller. Another thing that couldn't be helped, along with the whole virgin-whore dichotomy the patriarchy labored under. When they decided they *could* swear around her, what would happen? "We can muzzle him, Lee said."

"Ayuh." Juju's tone said he didn't think much of the idea. "But a hound don't take kindly to that, specially a bluetick. Your turn."

What a gruesome game. Still, there was a certain amount of comfort in knowing she wasn't the only one being morbid. "I was thinking that with so many people gone, there's less pollution." She draped the towel over an ancient exercise bike so it could air-dry. That was better, she decided. "Coast-to-coast, the man on the TV said, and possibly worldwide. Your turn."

"How many left you think might be bad apples, Miss Ginny?"

"Quite a few, Mr Juju." Yes, she decided, hearing someone else say it out loud was both comfort and a fresh worry. Like tearing a scab free, a momentary relief. "If they weren't before, all this might *make* them that way." Her own jacket, sleet-spotted, wasn't nearly warm enough.

Or maybe her shivers had nothing to do with the temperature.

"Yeah." Juju peered through the door, checking the hall. "Lots of folk don't need a reason, but when they got one, look out."

That was certainly one way to put it. "You're a scholar of human nature, sir."

"I know a thing or two about folk gettin nasty." He swept the door open and nodded her through. His smile had vanished.

So had hers. *I'm pretty sure you do.* Whether he meant the Army or bigots wasn't quite clear. Probably both. Traveller nosed at Ginny's calves before prancing ahead, stopping to look back and dance in place every little bit. Both Lee and Juju seemed to take it for granted that they had to test every hall and doorway now. Was this what living in a war zone was like?

No, a war zone was probably louder. And there might not be many wars now. Small-scale engagements, but humanity would have to rebuild before it started killing itself again, right?

She suspected she was wrong.

"Your turn," Juju said.

She picked the least grim idea parading through her overworked brain. "All the machines have stopped. In all the factories. No more packaged goods." She followed him, meekly enough. Her own boots —the new ones Lee had picked out—were uncomfortably stiff, and squeaked on uncarpeted surfaces. "No more deliveries of anything."

"Bet someone's still makin whiskey, though."

"Well, yeah. If it can ferment, people will drink it." Come to think of it, a bottle of wine—or even something harder—sounded powerfully appealing right now. So did loosening her braids and rubbing at her scalp while drinking. "History's full of that."

Juju made a short huffing sound, half disbelief, half amusement. "Didn't teach me that in school."

"They never do teach the good stuff." Blank faces on either side—the rooms wearing proud, neat little numbers, maintenance doors tucked away blank and featureless. The sheer amount of people necessary to run a hotel—cleaning the rooms, walking the halls, answering the phones, dealing with guests, landscapers...all gone. "It's your turn, Juju."

"Ain't no hospitals. No vaccines." He motioned her to wait before checking around the corner, turning them into another hall.

Or antibiotics. Did anyone alive know how to actually make penicillin? "No more Snickers bars."

"Or Twinkies."

Even the pigeons in New York wouldn't eat Twinkies. She decided not to mention that. "I think we're both hungry."

He nodded, holding up a hand while he checked the next hallway. "I could eat some more of your fried rice."

"Glad you liked it." *I'm going to have to learn to cook over a fire.* They'd been transported back to the Stone Age. How soon would it take for everyone to forget science and rationalism? Or, there was another grim thought, the worst one of all. "What if people die out? Like, humanity?"

Juju shrugged. "Can't say as I'd miss 'em."

Ginny restrained a sigh. He was probably right.

Traveller looped back to prance in front of her, already lobbying for an early dinner. The loss of his former owner didn't seem to upset him at all. Dogs were creatures of the Now, and right now Traveller had a pack to yodel around and a steady supply of kibble and clean water. There was nothing more for him to want, except ear-rubs. And plenty of smelly things to stick his snout in.

"God." She shivered. "What if this thing jumps the species barrier?" *Rats, pigeons—they're just flying rats, really. What if it gets into dogs? Cats? Anything larger?*

"Huh." He considered this, his rifle slung easily and his full lips drawn tight. "Now *that's* a bad thought, Miss Ginny."

She was just getting warmed up. "Can you imagine?"

"Not sure I want to." He sped up a little, using his longer legs to good account. "You win this round."

Ginny didn't mind letting him put distance between them. She couldn't help it, she just *thought* of these things. It was her burden, as her mother would say with a shake of her well-coiffed head and a pained grimace.

At least that hadn't changed; at least nobody else really wanted to hear about the consequences she could all too easily—and vividly—forecast. She was still the outsider here.

"The more things stay the same," she murmured, and Traveller yipped in reply.

Great. So I won. She frowned at another maintenance door, and sped up a little, willing to lag but not to be left behind.

Why don't I feel good about it?

[12]

BRANDON FRENCH

A dripping, slushy grey morning rose grudgingly over the hotel, cold mist exhaling from slop-melting snow, visibility down and damp chill biting deep. Ginny and the kids took turns carrying loads to the vehicles, Lee and Juju alternated between lifting the heavies and standing guard. No sign of the critters in the grey vapor, and Lee was hoping it stayed that way.

Wish in one hand, shit in the other, as his daddy used to say during prison visits. *See which fills up first.*

"Hello!" Floating over the parking lot, a resonant cry lifting above the splish-splashing of fat raindrops. "Hey! Hey there! Hello!"

"What the hell's that?" Lee muttered, straightening from the bed of the truck and reaching for his rifle. His back ached a little—he was too damn old for keeping watch in one of the foyer chairs.

"We got movement," Juju said, softly, already drawing a bead. Under the blue pompom hat, his face turned into a statue's, the thoughtful look of a soldier getting ready to let training take over. "Looks like a single, can't be sure."

Lee's skin roughened into pre-combat gooseflesh. He hopped down and brought his rifle around—funny, how a man could get used to carrying one again. It didn't take long at all. Wouldn't take long to get used to using it on anything that moved again, either.

Juju was right. It was a single, now hurry-wading across the lot. Male, looked like, in a blue jacket. He had a big, high-prowed camping backpack on, and Lee was powerfully tempted to put a slug in him just on principle. Ginny wouldn't take kindly to that, but strange men during an apocalypse were question marks at best. Not to mention, if Lee was being strictly honest with himself, he wasn't sure he wanted anyone else tagging along to take care of.

The melt running off the driveway's cover was a silver curtain, blurring the man's outline. "Do I drop 'em?" Juju had his rifle socked and tracking. "Or give 'em a warning?"

"Just cover me." Lee headed for the edge of the dry patch, squinting against the almost-glare. "Keep a sharp eye for friends, if he's bringing 'em." When he stepped away from the protective canopy, cold little kisses spattering his head and shoulders, his back prickled. Breaking cover, again, but this time his heart didn't want to jump around anywhere it shouldn't.

This, he knew how to do.

The new arrival was a broad-shouldered blondish man, early thirties, breathing heavily as he plowed through the melting slush. New boots with orange laces, Lee saw, and a youngish face shaved close and sharp. His backpack was good rig, expensive and quality. A shiny new carbine hung at his chest. Lee halted a good distance away and raised his hands, working for a mix of "peaceful" and "stop right there."

Blond Man didn't get the clue. "Good God, am I glad to see you! At first I thought you were more of those things, but..." Finally, he translated Lee's body language and waded to a halt. High blush of cold on his stubbled-up cheeks, he'd been outside for a while. Blond hair stiff, darkened and flattened by a lack of showering and the knit cap he was mashing in his broad hands. He had the musclebound look of a gymrat—the kind that lost most of his mass and a great deal of his cockiness in basic training before he regained the latter when it came time to haze the newcomers. "Hi. I'm Brandon, Brandon French. God, it's so good to see another person, I can't even tell you." His accent had the rolling of Kentucky behind it, but a laborious crispness, and the expensive watch, told Lee this was a college boy.

"Pleasure," Lee said, even though it was anything but. He dropped his hands, carefully. "You from Kentucky, Mr French?"

"Yessir." The stranger put his manners on, bloodshot blue eyes gleaming, but kept mashing that cap like it felt good. Stress did funny things to people. "I'm so happy to see someone else. Someone alive, I mean."

"Hm." A noncommittal noise. Lee kept his weight easy, let his right hand dangle. He could clear leather on his sidearm and take the bastard before he could unlimber that carbine, if he needed to. "You been bit?"

The man blinked owlishly at him. Bloodshot blue eyes. Had he been drinking? "What?"

"Bit." *I'm usin English, goddammit.* Lee's fingers tingled. He wanted to clear leather, by God, did he ever. "By one of those things."

"Oh. Christ, no." Brandon shook his head, frantically, and almost dropped his hat. "No, I haven't."

"Lee?" Ginny's voice, behind him. Juju trying to shush her, but not getting anywhere. Stubborn girl. "Lee!"

"Wow, there's more of you? This is great!" Brandon sloshed forward, but Lee stepped in front of him, this time with shoulders set and his expression hardening. "Uh. Okay."

Lee took his time, measuring the man from head to toe. The blue jacket was expensive but already showing signs of wear, especially where the backpack straps rubbed. The boots were fine-looking, too, but not waterproof. A show pony, then. The quality of the rig was an accident, and the carbine looked too damn shiny.

More splashing behind him, drawing closer. Lee all but flinched. *God damn it.*

It was Ginny, out of breath, roses in her cheeks, her chestnut hair curling stubbornly out of the braids wrapped around her pretty head.

Juju trailed behind her, keeping an eye out for movement in the misty distance, looking unhappy as hell. Lee could relate—it was a fool's move, running out into the open.

"I can't believe it!" Ginny skidded to a stop. At least she had the new hiking boots, with orange laces. *Good* ones, the ones he'd picked out for her. "You're—you're alive! I mean, you're *alive*-alive! Oh, my God."

"Yes ma'am." A big, easy grin bloomed on the man's face, smug and grateful at once. "I was pretty much saying the same. I haven't seen anyone for a week. I mean, nobody *living*."

Lee's chest deflated, a bicycle tire with a hidden leak. There it was, the subtle, silent signals of city-rich, flashing between them. It was something in the way they talked, and a million other things, like Ginny's earrings and the expensive diver's watch on Brandon's wrist. The man's faintly orange undertone from tanning in a machine had worked off by actual time spent outside, and whatever was backwoods about him had been laboriously clipped away.

It took time to do that, and money.

"We're lucky," Ginny said. "This is Lee—I mean, Mr Quartine, he's kept us alive. And Mr Thurgood here, too." Ginny clasped her grey-gloved hands, a girlish motion; she wasn't wearing the ones Lee had picked out for her yet. Just the boots. "We haven't seen anyone else for a while, either. I was wondering how many...I mean..." Her quick sideways glance at Lee cut right through him, because she immediately dropped her gaze and rocked back on her heels.

Like he'd shouted, or given her a filthy look.

"Jesus Christ, Miss Ginny." Juju said it, maybe so Lee didn't have to. "Bad apples, remember?"

Brandon stepped back too, maybe to make himself a little less threatening. His heel slid, but he just jabbed down sharply, regaining his balance with quick, trained instinct. Football, given his size. "I don't blame you. It's good to be cautious. I've seen a lot of looting. Well, evidence of looting."

Not to mention he'd probably done a bit. Lee throttled a heavy rasp of irritation.

"It *is* best to be cautious, we've been talking about that." Ginny glanced nervously at Lee again. Why? God *damn* it. "And, well." She indicated Mr French's carbine with a graceful motion of her chin. "Especially with people carrying those around."

"This?" The Kentucky boy looked down at his chest like he'd forgotten he was carrying the thing. "Oh. I don't even have any ammo. It's just so...well, you know, people are kind of nuts."

"So how do you fight off the, the *things*?" Her eyebrows drew together, and Lee was happy to see she wasn't taking *everything* about this newcomer for granted.

"Haven't seen many." Brandon's eyelids flickered. A breath of sugary used-up alcohol came off him; the man had spent last night drinking. It was a wonder he *hadn't* been bit, if he was telling the truth. "Discretion and valor, and all that."

Liar. Discretion and what, though? Lee studied the carbine. Never fired, that much might be true, but he'd bet his VA bennies and his mama's name this man had seen *plenty* of the critters, and killed a few too. Even Ginny looked dubious, but any further questions would have to wait.

"Lee?" Juju, warning. Lee's head jerked up, and he glanced over the newcomer's shoulder. Shambling shadows filled the fog.

"Shit," he breathed, and the cold was all through him, not just from the slush. "Uh, sorry, Ginny. We got company. Move."

THE KIDS HAD FINISHED THE LOADING; JUJU HUSTLED THEM into his black four-by-four, trying to close the doors quietly.

Lee hopped into the truck bed to make sure the load was tied down enough. His heart was in his throat, dry and nasty-tasting, throbbing like a bad infection. "Get on in the truck, Ginny." *Shit, goddammit, shitfuck.* "Please."

"Traveller!" She took off for the open glass door, her boots leaving dainty wet prints on dry concrete. Lee swallowed a cascade of colorful words, snapping a glance at the parking lot. Half a dozen shamble-weaving, head-cocked forms, in varying bits of soggy clothing, making a beeline for the front of the hotel. They were a good distance away at the edge of the lot, but they were moving purposefully, in a slow steady staggering. Looked like they'd been clocking Mr French the gymrat.

When they heard the engines, or the slamming doors, or the damn dog yapping, they would put on a burst of that scary speed, and maybe start that deep grind-growling. Then things were gonna get interesting.

"Lee?" With the kids safely stowed, Juju stepped to the side of the truck, taking cover instinctively as his rifle rose again, picking out a target. A faint sheen of sweat gleamed on his broad dark forehead, and Lee had seen that look on him before, trained calm edging out fear. "What's the word?"

Responsibility, like killin', followed a man. Lee ran down the rest of the list in his head, shuffling priorities. "Get in and start up. They start movin fast, you head for the freeway and we'll catch up."

"Don't wanna leave ya." Juju's chin thrust out a little.

Come to think of it, Lee found out he was sweating, too. "Orders, Thurgood." *We ain't in the Army no more, but dammit, I don't wanna lose nobody here.*

"Bite yo'ass, Lieutenant." Juju's drawl turned it into *Loot-nent,* and for a moment the past rose to strangle Lee. Dust and sweat instead of slush and cold, but the pulse pounding in his wrists and throat was just the same, the taste of metal and the clear copper-smelling certainty of danger, too. It was damn good to have backup, but he didn't want to lose anyone.

Except maybe the new fellow.

Brandon, his pack's high prow bobbing above his head, put his hands on the truck's tailgate, hunching as if he thought the critters were gonna start shooting. He was sweating too, but not like Thurgood. No, this boy's eyes were white-ringed and more than a little wild. "I can help you. Take me with you. Please."

You can stay in the hotel, for Godsake. Lee almost twitched with the urge to put his boot in the man's face. "Think we got it handled. Y'all can go in there and close the door, it locks inside. There's food, water. Place still works."

Ginny reappeared, shouldering the door a little wider. Traveller wriggled in her arms, licking at her face, and for once, the dog was too busy getting his tongue all over something to talk about what a wonderful day he was having. His tail whapped furiously, and Ginny's stray curls bounced. The color in her cheeks suited her, and Lee almost lost his breath again, just seeing her move.

Lee hopped down, shouldering Brandon aside, and slammed the tailgate. The sound cracked across the slushy lot, falling dead against the mist at its edges, and Ginny reached the passenger side. He was there in a flash to open it for her, and the things had definitely heard them. A low rumbling growl drifted over waterlogged snow, and they began to splash.

"I can help you," Brandon repeated, desperate, high-pitched. "I'll do anything. Just, just let me ride in the back, even!"

"Lee, they're movin." Juju socked his rifle to his shoulder. "I got six-seven, all heading this way."

"Start it up, Juju!" Lee's jaw ached, he was fixing to grit his teeth soon. "That's an *order.*"

"Lee?" Ginny had Traveller loaded, and the dog began to yap, excited as all get-out by the prospect of a car ride. "Lee, we're not just going to leave him here, are we?"

Oh, for God's sake. "Get in the back," he told Brandon, curtly. His right hand itched for his sidearm—the quickest way to solve the problem, but what would Ginny think of that? "You cause any goddamn trouble, I'll knock your teeth out."

Ginny wasn't satisfied, of course. Maybe she was even offended. She stared at him, wide-eyed, the flush of exertion fading. "Lee—"

"Get *in*, Ginny!" *Damn* the woman, she was going to get herself hurt.

"Thank you!" Brandon clambered up, awkward with the pack, and floundered into the bed. "Jesus, thanks. You won't regret it, I promise!"

Lee was pretty sure he'd regret it plenty, but there wasn't any time. The critters had dropped and were lolloping sideways through the slush, throwing up chunks of dirty ice and snow. Would they try to jump in the back? He should think about a canopy, dammit. There wasn't any time now, he slammed the driver's side door and almost barked at Ginny to put her seatbelt on.

She was already buckled in, though, and she paled alarmingly as she twisted to look through the back window. "Is it safe for him back there?"

"Can't fit him in here with the dog, and I ain't puttin a stranger in with the kids." The truck roused itself with a walloping, welcome purr; he dropped it into gear. Juju's four-by was already moving, chains biting through slop and digging into ice underneath. They'd have to stop to take 'em off if the roads cleared.

"Oh, God." Ginny put her arm around Traveller, who noticed someone was in the back and began to bark, wiggling excitedly. "Shhh, sweetheart, shush..."

"Let him yell." The truck glided into a sea of slush, and Lee hoped the things weren't smart enough to get in the back. He didn't want Ginny seeing that, nosir.

Although, he thought as he feathered the accelerator and saw the lolloping critters drop to all fours and speed up, it would solve the goddamn problem nicely. And wasn't that a measure of how fucked-up things were, that Lee was considering something like that calmly?

It damn sure was, he decided, and was almost disappointed when the critters fell behind, ghosts in the thickening fog.

$$[\ 13\ ]$$

OBSERVATIONS

THE STREETS WERE AWASH, BUT HEADING NORTH OUT OF Lewiston the freeway wasn't that bad. If it stayed a little warmer some pavement might even be visible tomorrow—and along with concrete, the corpses of cars left behind by owners in God knew what sort of a hurry. Once the mist burned off it was achingly bright, melting snow glittering, the truck crunching through ice and gliding around a twisted mass of steel and white froth that looked like a car accident blocking the right two lanes. Juju had dropped back, the truck in front for a while, and the walkie-talkie on the dashboard was off until the next scheduled check-in.

They had everything about traveling figured out, except the man in the back of Lee's truck.

Ginny twisted in the seat, peering through the cab's faintly misted back window. The defroster was working overtime, but the dog probably put out more condensation than both her *and* Lee. "I can't see him." She wouldn't even be able to tell if he'd fallen out. The first real, live person *not* from the Crossing, and he might die of hypothermia before she could get a chance to talk to him.

"Probably bedded down." Lee's jaw was set, hard, and his hazel eyes had lightened. The infected had been easily outpaced, and the truck wasn't going too fast, but still.

She sighed, settled in the seat, and checked the mirror on her side. "He's going to freeze to death."

"Maybe." It didn't sound like Lee minded. He'd unzipped his shearling coat, and today his button-down flannel and leather vest were hidden under a green Army surplus sweater.

"He's a *person*, Lee." She stroked Traveller's back. After the morning's excitement, the dog was dead asleep, his sides and paws twitching every once in a while as he chased scents in canine dreamland. "Can't we stop and—"

"He ain't no better than a question mark, Ginny." Lee's knuckles were white. "Not even sure he ain't been bit." His tone hadn't changed, soft but inflexible, and he'd apologized for yelling at her to get in the truck.

Funny, she'd been in such a hurry she hadn't even noticed the apology, or thought about the possibility of the new guy being a... carrier? Was that the right word? The...the *things*, the infected, only started moving quickly once they dropped to all fours. While they were upright, they wove like drunkards. That was interesting and disturbing, and she could think about it and possibly come up with an explanation if she wasn't so busy worrying over the poor guy freezing in the back. "Okay." Did it occur to Lee that the new guy was back there with a gun? He probably could have carjacked them.

Or still could. You never knew. Should she mention it? Of course, Lee had probably already thought about it.

She bit her lower lip, gently. Her purse, safely tucked near her damp, uncomfortable new boots, had a fresh journal in its back pocket. She'd made sure the pens worked, too, and neatly dated the title page, though she didn't fill in the *Return To Owner* section. What would be the point?

That was a horrible and quite possibly useless thought. Now would be an excellent time to begin making lists. Systematizing her impressions.

Traveller didn't move, but one of his eyelids cracked a bit when she bent down. Lee's hands relaxed a little, and a little more. Ginny uncapped a blue pen, opened to the first blank page...and stared.

Lined cream-colored paper, clean and innocent. Like snow before tires and feet and zombies splattered everywhere. If things were normal, she'd have driven to work on plowed and salted roads, grousing at the inconvenience. She'd be thinking of grocery shopping, alphabetizing, meetings, whether or not to pick up a pint of half-n-half for her tea.

"Whatcha up to?" Lee's voice jolted her.

How long had she been just sitting here looking at a blank page? She glanced up, saw a jumble of cars pulled over to the shoulder, and looked back down. "I thought it'd be a good idea to make a list." As soon as she said it, the whole thing sounded ridiculous. There were infected *zombies*. What good was a list going to do? None of her skills were even remotely applicable here.

"Of?" At least he sounded interested.

Traveller's tail twitched. Ginny loosened her jaw, forced her hand to relax. "Symptoms. Observations about those things. If we know how they behave, we might be able to figure out what kind of sickness it is. To predict their behavior and keep ourselves safer."

"That's smart." Lee squinted at the road, reached for the walkie-talkie, and thumbed it on. Must be a scheduled check-in soon. "Looks like things ease up in a bit, here."

That would be nice. "Good." She touched the pen to paper, took it away. *Where the fuck did you even* start? "Lee?"

"Hm?" They crept around a tangled four-car pileup. The walkie-talkie crackled, hummed.

Ginny tried not to look at the wreck. She tried not to think about the guy in back. Well, he had a coat, at least. And a hat. She opened her mouth to ask again if they couldn't stop and at least make sure he wasn't a Popsicle. Then she took another look at Lee's profile. "Nothing."

"Be stoppin for lunch soon." Quiet, evenly spaced, like they were on a country drive. Or a road trip. Well, it was *kind* of a road trip. "Tomorrow we'll make good time if the roads ain't freezin overnight."

What a time for the National Weather Service to go on strike. "Yeah. Do you think they will?"

"Can't say."

"How long..." She ran up against the question, had to stop and take a deep breath, try again. "How long do you think it'll take? To get there." Once they got closer, she could navigate on her own. There were the backroads around Alton Falls. If she could just get *close* enough, she could...steal a car? Go on her own?

Was that her plan?

"Depends."

For God's sake. Help me out here. "On what?" Now she was wishing she'd spent more time in the shower this morning. Who could tell when the next chance for hot water would come along?

"How bad the roads are." Lee stretched the fingers on his right hand, put them back on the wheel. Stretched his left. "Weather. If those critters stick to towns or run through the woods. How much fuel we find."

"Well, there's gas everywhere." No shortage, if there were only a few...survivors.

"Ayuh." Something in his tone said he'd thought about that, too. "One mile at a time, Miss Ginny. Don't you worry none."

Well, wasn't that nice of him. "I can't *help* it."

"I know. You been on your own for a while, ain't you." It wasn't a question.

She'd always been painfully aware she wasn't *quite* what her parents wanted. All the love in the world didn't change that constant seashell song, but they'd done their best. She knew she was lucky, and the faint nagging guilt at her own dissatisfaction was another familiar tune. "Long enough." She drew a line across the page, another. It didn't help. "What about you?"

"All my life, feels like." Slushy sleet smacked the windshield. The wipers stacked it up on either side, strata of melt and freeze. "Don't mind it."

"What *do* you mind?"

"Not much."

Except, apparently, the guy in the truck bed. Still, something inside Ginny had eased a little, and a little more.

He was good at that.

Okay. She bent her head, looking at the wavering blue lines, and took a deep breath. *Fever,* she began. *Sniffling, sneezing. Convulsions. Frothing at the mouth.*

It wasn't much, but it was a start.

[14]

PUT YOUR MANNERS ON

He was about frozen stiff when they stopped, but Brandon French didn't care. He was alive, and he'd found other people, that was enough for the moment. He huddled among tarp-covered boxes and shivered in the lashing sleet, cussing every time the hick driving the goddamn truck hit a bump. After a while he decided to cuss in Spanish for a change. Mama would have preferred French, but Brandon liked knowing what the staff was saying about him. Like the janitors at the high school, laughing at the *gringos ricos* behind their backs.

The engine cut off while Brandon was describing just how much he'd like to shoot the stupid hick who didn't even want to take a survivor along. Doors slammed, and he stretched, trying to get some feeling back into his arms and legs.

"We could have given him blanket, at least," a soft, educated voice said. The woman with the long hair, the only one out of all these fucks who didn't look inbred. "It's raining."

"Stay in the truck, Ginny." That was the hick. "Ain't cold enough to do him no real harm."

Says you. Motherfucker. Brandon rocked back and forth. He was numb all over. Fortunately, the gloves were okay, and so were his boots. His ass was wet, though. Jesus *Christ*.

"We gonna check that buildin, Lee?" Another goddamn back-woods drawl, maybe the black man.

What a collection to fall in with. Beggars couldn't be choosers when the world turned into a bad horror movie, though. He was just glad to have found people who weren't growling and trying to chew his goddamn throat out. Brandon stretched again, working his fingers, telling his legs they were supposed to move now.

"Might as well. Ginny, for God's sake—"

The tailgate popped and dropped. "It's all right. Maybe get some blankets?" She hopped up, lithe and light, and crouched. "Hi. How are you doing?"

She was older than he liked, but still in shape under layers and a big coat. Just on the edge of cougardom, though her hair was fantastic. You could get a handful of that curling mass and really pull. Big dark eyes, a nice mouth, and a patrician nose. She was *definitely* a higher class than the rest of them. Brandon tried a smile, his cheeks cracking. "Cold," he managed, his teeth chattering. His hat wasn't doing its job, his ears were probably frostbitten. "We stopping?"

"It's a gas station." She duck-walked forward, offered her hand. "Can you stand up? We'll get you dried off, warmed up. And some-thing to eat. When was the last time you ate?"

"I...I don't remember." It was weird, he actually *didn't*. Just the front door of his parents' house in Lourd Bend, breaking glass, then the sports store in Hadisonville, and the *things*. Shuffling around, or running with that weird sideways boom-boom-quick. "Yesterday? Maybe?"

"Well, we'll fix that." She was a lot lighter, but she managed to get Brandon upright. His feet wouldn't work quite right. If he got fucking frostbite riding in the bed, he'd have to beat the shit out of that hick. Get him good, somehow or another. Brandon knew how to wait. "There you go. It's all right."

"For *Christ's* sake, Ginny." The black man appeared at the tail-gate, his broad stupid face glowing with oil. "Bad apples, remember?"

"I think he's too frozen to be a mass murderer, Juju. And he's not feverish." She slipped, and he almost went over too. It was goddamn icy back here; only the boxes and tubs under bungee-lashed tarps had a chance of staying *dry*. "Ouch. Okay, come on, Brandon. It's Brandon, right?"

"Yes...ma'am." *Goddammit, stop talking.* Now that she said *food* he was starving. They probably had nothing nutritious, but he'd eat fucking cardboard if he had to. The gun against his chest flapped, and he put up a numb hand, blindly.

"Be careful!" the black man barked, and Brandon almost toppled out of the truck. "Damnfool sonofabitch!"

"What the hell?" The hick was there—tall, rangy, a real asshole, his hazel-turning-yellow stare just as ignorant and cunning as every other cousinfucking jackass whose ambitions stopped at polishing windshield wipers in a service station. "Jesus *Christ!*"

The next thing Brandon knew, he was flat on his stomach on icy, slippery pavement, the carbine somehow stripped from his chest on the way down, and both of them were yelling.

"He could have *shot* you, Ginny!" The black man was mouthy, that was for damn sure. Brandon tried to to rise, was shoved uncere-moniously back down. His forehead hit pavement, and he let out a short bark of pain.

"Not likely," the white hick said, disdain thick in every drawled-out syllable. "Ain't even loaded."

"He's just a kid." The woman was trying to calm them both down. "Guys, come on, he's just a *kid!*"

No I'm not. I'm Number 23, and you motherfuckers don't know who you're dealing with. "Fuck off!" he yelled, and tried to surge upright.

And subsided, because the hick had a pistol, pressed right against the back of Brandon's skull. "Easy there, fella. The grownups are talkin."

"What is it?" A teenage girl, peering over the black man's shoulder, a blur in Brandon's peripheral vision. Pasty, thin-haired, and mouthbreathing. Right next to her was a boy, probably her brother—he had the same chinless-wonder look. "Oh, man." The girl shook her head, clicking her tongue like a much-older woman.

"Juju, take Ginny and the kids inside." The hick's hand was on the back of Brandon's neck, mashing his face into dirty snow. His knee was in Brandon's kidney, for fucksake. "Imma have a little chat with this fella."

"Lee—" The almost-cougar grabbed the hick's shoulder, but he shook her off, which might have given Brandon an opening except he was too numb to use it. "Lee, come *on!*"

"Ginny." The black man had her arm, and pulled her away. That was disturbing, but Brandon didn't have time for it right now.

It was a Circle M parking lot awash with slush, of all places, the ancient blue gas pumps leering at the spectacle of Number 23, best tight end on the Milville Dodgers team in high school and the newest addition to the Lourd Bend High School *teaching team*, getting his face rubbed in the dirt by some wiry-ass hick bastard. "Calm down," the hick drawled. "I don't want to shoot you, buddy."

God damn you. "Motherfucker! What the *fuck?*" He couldn't wriggle out of his jacket, but he gave it a try. The hick just sank his knee further into Brandon's back, and he was a lot stronger than he looked. Finally, Brandon sagged into the melting snow. *Swear to God, gonna make you pay for this.*

"That's better." The hick paused. He wasn't even breathing hard. "Now. You ain't got no business with a gun. You could hurt someone."

Brandon could have told this jackshit asshole that 23 French could swing a piece of lumber or a crowbar, and that was good enough when the whole world went horror-movie crazy and your elderly parents got up off their sickbeds and started trying to kill you. Bright, sharp hate rotated in the center of Brandon's head. He'd shattered Daddy's spongy-boned, balding head with a broomstick, but his mother...

He didn't want to think about Mama. Especially not the sound made when her neck cracked or her skull shattered.

"You hear me?" The hick shoved him further into the slushy concrete. "You shoulda stayed at the hotel, buddy. But you didn't, so you gonna learn our rules and abide by 'em. Right?"

It was just like his father all over again. *Army make a man outa you, son.* Brandon didn't *want* the fucking Army, he wanted to wear a black turtleneck and go to a city, or anyplace that didn't reek of cowshit, but Gordon French didn't raise no sissyboy, yessir nosir, and Brandon had only just squeaked his way through two hellish years of National Guard weekends before escaping. Even Daddy had to admit he'd tried.

Christ. There was another bad thought. Still, if the world hadn't gone all to hell with zombie fucks running everywhere he'd be thinking about the situation with that little ponytailed bitch of a sophomore. *We think it's best for you to be on administrative leave, Mr French.*

No such thing as tenure at a fucking hick high school, when you'd moved back to take care of your parents like a good son. His entire life, he'd been doing what his goddamn father wanted, and the bastard couldn't even die before the whole country went insane.

"Right," Brandon moaned, his jaw wet and loose. "Fine. I'm *sorry*, okay? I've been in the back of a goddamn *truck* all day!" Even this asshole had to see the justice of that. His arm was twisted painfully behind him, and the muzzle against the back of his head felt very sharp, and very cold.

"Nobody ast you to come along." But the hick eased up. "You put your manners on, Mr...French, is it?"

"Yessir." Fuck, he hated those goddamn cracker backwoods inbred pieces of shit. Fucking Neanderthals. "All right? You done?"

"For now." At least the hick let him up, and even brushed at his shoulders. Like that did any fucking good, after rolling him in snow and slop. "I'm Quartine."

"How do you spell that?" He'd be surprised if the asshole knew how to spell *anything*, but the fellow rattled it off. Brandon took note. Mispronouncing someone's name was an easy way to fuck with them. "Okay, fine. I'm French. Brandon French."

"Yeah." The man stood, hipshot and easy, his pistol pointed at the ground, finger carefully locked outside the trigger guard. He wasn't as old as Brandon had thought, or as wiry. His shoulders weren't linebacker-sized, but then again, neither were Brandon's, now. That direct glare of his was troubling, and the hick's hair was blurring out of a high-and-tight just like a drill sergeant's that gave Brandon the willies. "Come on. Let's get you dry."

Sure thing, you asshole. Brandon followed, meekly enough.

He was already brainstorming how he was going to make this backwoods bastard pay.

[15]

GET CHANGE BACK

EVENING FOUND THEM IN TAGGART, SLOWING BECAUSE OF THE
dropping temperature in a bruise-dark dusk. The melt had halted
halfway as afternoon wore on, and Lee had the kids in the truck
while Juju and Ginny took Brandon and Traveller into the four-by.
Lee didn't like that, and he didn't like how the man's whine switched
off as soon as he saw Ginny. There was a steadily lengthening list of
things Lee didn't like, and fatigue was wearing his nerves to a frazzle.

Or they were already done worn, as Nonna used to say.

Lewiston had spread tentacles toward the joint Army-Air Force
base and in the opposite direction along the interstate. Taggart was a
knot near the end of one long ropy leg, and it was deserted. Lee
finally settled on a locked-up Schnuck's, deserted but not fully dark.
Some power was getting through. The lot was a sea of melt freezing
into odd shapes as the mercury fell, each glowing, guttering lamp
festooned with small icicles. He got the truck right on up near the
doors, cut the engine, and glared balefully at the place, finally realizing neither of the kids had spoken for the past hour. Steph, huddled
near the window, was round-eyed, and Mark held her ungloved left
hand in both of his palms, like it was precious.

"Thank God," Steph said, as the engine started tick-cooling. She was pale, again, her sharp kittenish face drawn tight. "I have to pee."

"Wait a minute." Lee slipped out, freed his rifle, and slammed the door, maybe a little harder than he had to.

Juju was already parked and out of the four-by, scanning the lot. "Hey."

Lee grunted, tipped his head at the store.

Juju fell into step, covering him. "New boy's an asshole."

Yeah, I figured. "Ginny safe in there?"

"He ain't got a fever, she says. But the dog don't like 'im." Juju scratched under the rim of his knitted cap, the pompom nodding, carefully keeping his own piece pointed well away and down while he got the itch settled.

Any man a dog didn't like was better off where you could see him. "Huh."

"Been talking about books with Miss Ginny. College boy. Just graduated, now a teacher someplace called Lourd Bend."

That was all the way on the other side of Lewisville, and a fair way from the Crossing, too. Lee's mood blackened a little more, but there was work to be done, and he set himself to doing it. Juju shut up, too, unless it was to say *clear, right,* or *left.* Jimmying an employee door wasn't hard, and the produce department hadn't gone ripe because of the chill. The entire place was dim and echoing, but the employee break room was a nice one. There were even windows, letting in what little remained of the dying daylight.

At least Ginny hadn't gotten out of the four-by to stretch her legs. Lee motioned them to come on, scanning the parking lot again. No movement. Their own tire tracks, looping neatly, were the only evidence of human passage. There was a belt of ice-freighted scrub brush at the far end of the lot, next to a long squat brick building holding a nail salon, a dry cleaner's, and a take-and-bake pizza joint. No sound of traffic from the freeway, just that deadly, deep quiet, with their vehicles' engines pinging as they cooled a counterpoint to little crackles as the freeze settled in everywhere else.

"Art history," Brandon French continued, as he got out. Fucker didn't even go 'round to open Ginny's door, just stopped to gap and stretch. "I had to go into education, but that was my first love."

Lee popped the handle on Ginny's side, and Traveller yipped a greeting, wriggling to get past her. She just barely managed to get the leash on him, and gave Lee a quick look of thanks when he took the red nylon strap and hefted the dog down.

"I only took a couple semesters, really." Ginny was *smiling*. Her color had come back, and stray curls floated on the cold breeze. "Oof. I'm glad we're stopping. Juju won't let me drive."

He's kind of particular about his car. "Maybe tomorrow," Lee mumbled. She just looked so damn *happy*. Traveller tugged on the leash, and when Ginny tried to reclaim it Lee shook his head. "Go on in, get warm. They got an upstairs, and power still."

Her grin broadened, and she looked up at him, tucking a flyaway curl back into her braid with quick, graceful, tapering fingers. "I should take Traveller—"

"I got 'im, Ginny." He didn't mean to say it so sharply, but maybe she didn't mind. In any case, she nodded a thank-you and slipped past, heading for the back of the truck.

The hound wasn't overly pleased, but at least with Lee he minded his manners. Brandon walked on into the Schnuck's like he owned the place, not stopping to pick up any gear or even his own damn backpack. Probably thought Juju and the kids were the help, for God's sake. Ginny immediately pitched in with unloading instead of heading inside, and Lee turned away, staring across the lot at the greenbelt. There was plenty to think about, and it was getting to where he didn't like a single bit of it.

Had the branches moved? Lee exhaled softly while Traveller wriggled, the dog pulling at the leash, straining to sniff out another patch of ice to pee on. The clouds, scudding away westward, scraped the sky clean, and stars glimmered through. There was Venus, riding low, and with most of the streetlamps and city lights dead he'd lay odds you could see the Milky Way, if you stayed out late enough.

Murmurs behind him. Juju's footsteps, crunching. Lee kept watching the bushes.

"You all right?" Juju asked.

Now why wouldn't he be? "Thinkin."

"Penny for 'em."

The lot's lamps guttered again, came back even lower. "You'd get change back." Lee settled his rifle strap, tugging at the leash. "Come on, dog." Maybe it was just the wind. In any case, they'd barricade the employee door, and Lee thought he was maybe tired enough to actually sleep tonight.

Go figure, right when he had to keep one open eye on this Brandon fella.

A PRACTICALLY NEW MICROWAVE IN THE EMPLOYEE BREAK room had enough buzz to cook up several cans' worth of beef stew for supper; they ate in the breakroom, the overhead fluorescents buzzing and Ginny laughing as Brandon cracked rich-boy jokes. The two of them talked about people he'd never heard of, and sometimes Steph put a word or two in. Mark just hunched over his paper bowl and shoveled down all he could get. Juju, next to Ginny, patted Trav's head every once in a while, sneaking the dog tidbits of whole-wheat bread soaked in stew-juice; and Lee, set back from the circle a little bit, watched Ginny's delicate wrist, the way she glanced down every so often to make sure the dog was still there, how her chin lifted a little when she was amused. There was no shortage of imaginary people and things in books for them to chew over, and after a while it turned to opera, for Chrissake.

"I'm neutral on it, really," Ginny said, her earrings gleaming. The fluorescents buzzed, dimmed like the lot lights, and came back. "Juju's the expert."

"I know what I like," Juju said, brightening visibly. You could probably run a house or two off his face alone whenever anyone mentioned that screechy-time music.

"Aida?" Brandon stretched his legs out, taking up more than his share of space. His boots rubbed mud and melt into the short nylon carpet. "Othello?"

"More a fan of Gluck, actually." Juju's nostrils flared a little, and Ginny looked quickly down, as if embarrassed. Her smile faded a little, and Brandon stretched his legs out even further, taking up more space than he had a right to.

"*Orpheus et Eurydice*?" Brandon took a giant mouthful of stew. His eyebrows went up a little, as if Juju had said something surprising.

Juju shook his head. His hair, crushed from the pompom cap, was springing back slowly but surely. "*Iphigénie en Aulide.* 1953 recording, Wiener Philharmonic."

"You lost me," Ginny said. "I saw *Die Zauberflote* once, and that was enough."

"That's Mozart." Juju managed to sound scandalized and amused all at once, and his shy smile matched hers perfectly.

"I *know*, I'm not a *barbarian*." She bumped him with her shoulder, and *their* shared grin didn't make Lee want to punch something. "I'm not fond of *him*, either. My mother put me through ten years of piano, I quit as soon as I could."

Juju's eyebrows drew together, and his mouth turned down. He stirred his stew with a plastic spoon, meditatively. "Didn't like it?" Like he didn't believe *anyone* could dislike that Mozart fellow, or the piano.

"It could have been worse." It was the first time Ginny had seemed, well, *relaxed*. "My sister had to take clarinet."

Lee's hands tingled a little. He didn't have any appetite, but ate anyway. When you had a job to do, you needed fuel, no matter what your stomach felt like.

"Didn't make you duet, did they?" Brandon found this funny.

"God." Ginny rolled her eyes. "Don't remind me. We sounded like a Canadian goose and a drunken Victor Borge."

Music lessons. Opera. Lee hunched his shoulders. He supposed *he* qualified as a barbarian. Just a dumb backwoods bunny. The next time those zombie critters came around, though, she'd be damn glad he wasn't stupid enough to sling a carbine on without knowing how to use it. Motherfucker could have shot Ginny if he'd loaded the damn thing.

Now Lee was wishing he'd shot the man on sight. A sigh caught him by surprise, so he dropped his gaze back into his bowl and set himself to eating. That, at least, was something he was fairly sure he knew a little about.

$$[\ 16\ ]$$

YOUR USEFUL

The manager's office was small, but at least it had enough room for a sleeping bag or two. Steph would be up in a bit, Mark would settle on one of the couches in the employee breakroom. Lee and Juju had assumed Brandon would take a shift standing watch. He didn't look too happy about it—what English teacher would? Ginny sighed, unpinned her braids, and unrolled her sleeping bag. A courteous knock on the office door made her jump.

"Brought you a candle, and some matches." It was Lee, his flashlight beam bobbing; they'd turned the breakers off for the night. It was nice to have power, but the risk of drawing more of the infected was more than any of them wanted to take. Traveller bustled in after him, and immediately began a circuit of the office, tail held horizontal and wagging businesslike.

"Thanks." She longed for a hot bath. Some scorching Thai curry. A soap-bubble comedy on her laptop and a world going on in its normal way, maybe passive-aggressive texts from her sister or Mom calling with gossip. She'd even settle for spam emails and ads, because that would mean everything was normal. Natural. Sane.

Lee nodded, his eyes turned piercing-light for a moment. "You all right?" His stubble had gold tips, and slid him over the line into borderline-raffish but handsome nonetheless. At least, handsome enough. Or was he just familiar?

"I guess." *Jesus, who could be all right, in this situation?* She tried for a smile; it felt tight and unnatural, her cheeks straining. She'd have to sleep in two pairs of sweatpants—a floor was cold no matter how good your sleeping bag was, or how thick the rolled foam pad Lee had picked up was. "As okay as it's going to get."

"Listen." He glanced over the office, once, a roving sweep to make sure none of the *things* were in the corners, maybe. "There's a lock on the door."

"Oh. Do you think..." The question died in her throat, and she looked down at the plaid sleeping bag. It was probably better not to know.

Lee told her anyway. "We don't know anything about this man, Ginny."

"He's a *teacher*." As if that mattered, but she couldn't help feeling...what? Scandalized, again? She reached for her pillow, pushing Traveller's snout aside. "Don't drool on that, you."

"So he says." Lee's hair was almost long enough to lie down in patches—when you kept it that short, the edges blurred quickly. A little bit of softness suited him. "He could be anything."

"But..." Ginny let Traveller mouth her fingers. He was after her pillowcase, but had to settle for her hand. "God. You're right."

"Odds are he ain't no big deal." He sank down, knees bending, balancing lightly; the pistol riding his hip sat easily even when he shifted. Up on the wall, a whiteboard full of strange numbers and "targets" in multicolored marker frowned at their unprofessionalism. "But I ain't having you hurt."

There it was again. She gazed at the desk. A triangular nameplate announced its owner was Burt Lafontaine, Store Manager. The computer was dead and dark, a failed monolith. Steph would be up soon, to unroll her own foam pad and sleeping bag. "What about Mark?" In other words, a teenage boy was at risk, too, if Lee suspected Mr French of being...not what he appeared.

"Juju and me got our eyes peeled." Lee's expression didn't change, but the faint edge to the sentence held all the meaning in the world.

"Okay. And I know you're looking out for Mr Thurgood." She settled on her own heels and bit her lip, wished she hadn't because his gaze focused on her mouth. "Who's looking out for *you?*"

He ducked his head a little. Traces of melt clung to his boots—he'd been outside after dinner, with the dog. "Juju, I guess."

Oh. "Lee..." Well, maybe it was enough.

"Hm?" He waited, crouching easily. Like he had all the time in the world.

"Nothing." Now she felt ridiculous. Her braids fell down her back, as if she was in elementary again. God, she'd hated long hair then, and got a pixie cut right before high school. *That* about drove Mom up the wall. *That's boy hair,* she'd said. *You shouldn't have.*

Was her mother all right? Had Flo gone into labor? Did they have enough to eat? Was there still power in New York? There was a whole lot of space upstate, but their part of Saratoga wasn't rural by any stretch of the imagination.

"All right." Lee paused. "Know what?"

"What?" Worrying about her family right before bed was getting to be a habit, and one that robbed her of what little sleep she could manage. She wanted to drive through the night, keep going, maybe find a few energy drinks and just keep *moving.* At least when they were traveling she didn't feel so...useless.

Faint reflected glow from the flashlight scoured hollows in Lee's face, turned him into a chiaroscuro. "First time in my life anyone ast me that."

Huh? "Asked you...?"

"Ast me who's lookin out for me." One side of his mouth curled up, lazily. *That* did good things for him, too. He'd taken off his bulky green sweater, so under his well-worn shearling, the leather vest over his flannel button-down looked natural instead of motorcycle-gang. It added to his stubble to make him way less military, and way more... what? He still watched her mouth, and Ginny was very aware of her breath slipping out, mint toothpaste tingling pleasantly—what were the odds she'd ever visit a dentist again?

Now there was an alternately cheerful and horrifying thought. Dinner sat uneasily in her stomach, a congealed lump. "I don't want anything to happen to you, either."

"I'm right useful, huh?" But his expression—mouth softening, eyes no longer yellow-direct but darker and soft as well, head slightly tilted—robbed the words of any sting.

Still, it bothered her. She set her knees down, pushed Traveller's nose away from her pillow again. "Not just useful."

"Oh, it ain't bad." His smile broadened. "I don't mind it, not when it's you."

Huh? Ginny tried to parse that. It was a little difficult, because her pulse had decided to skyrocket. He smelled like male and citrus, with a deep peppery tang that was all...*him*. Funny, she'd missed it, riding with Juju. How soon did you get used to the impossible? Humans adapted, it was their great advantage.

"You hear me?" Lee leaned forward, slightly into her personal space, and that made it even harder to think. "I like being your useful."

What the hell does that mean? Ginny swallowed, hard, and tried to focus, to express what she meant very clearly. "I don't want to use anyone," she managed. "Lee..."

That set him back, physically, onto his boot heels. "Not what I meant." Lee unfolded, and Ginny found herself picking up and hugging her familiar pillow, with Traveller nosing at her elbow, insisting that it was bedtime and he wanted his snuggles, thank you very much. "Just lock the door when Steph gets up here, Ginny."

Was he angry? She couldn't tell, and before she got her wits about her, he was gone. The door closed with a small click, and she looked down at Traveller. Dogs were creatures of routine, Juju said, and humans were too. Canine habits were simple, Traveller didn't seem to care *how* complex the situation was, as long as he had kibble and a warm place to nest.

"God," she whispered, and the hound's ears perked. He stared hopefully at her, scooching as close as he could get for ear-rubs. "I think I like him, I really do."

Unfortunately, the rest of that thought wasn't nearly as nice. *What if it's not him I like, but the fact that he's capable?*

There was no answer. Ginny swore under her breath, and resigned herself to a restless night on a cold floor, even if Lee swore the pad underneath would help.

Oddly enough, though, as soon as she settled Steph, locked the door, and laid down hugging Traveller, she was out like a light.

It was a good thing, too, because the next morning started *way* too early.

"Miz Mills?" Steph, whispering, and a chill-damp hand at Ginny's shoulder, shaking her. "Miz Ginny, wake up."

Traveller yawned and Ginny lunged into consciousness, sweat collecting in every hollow and her heart banging against her ribs. It was damn close to pitch black, only faint paltry moonglow filtering through the office windows. Steph's face was a pale smudge atop a dark shadow, her hair hanging lank on either side.

Ginny rubbed at her eyes. "What?"

"Shhh." Steph clutched at her, and the faint trembling in the girl's hands was unsettling. "I heard somethin. At the door."

Oh, God. "It's locked," she mumbled, trying to shake the cobwebs out of her head. "Was it—"

"Then I went to the window." Steph's fingers bit with hysterical strength, sinking into Ginny's upper arm. "They're *here.*"

That brought Ginny up in a rush, shaking her legs—and her sweatpants—free of the bag. It was cold outside that warm nest; goosebumps rose all over her, and the sour taste in her mouth was early morning and fear. Her sweats had ridden up, ankle cuffs gathered below her knees like she'd gone wading. Traveller nosed at her left leg, a cold, forlorn touch. "Who's here?"

"*Them*," Steph whispered. Pink tank top straps slipped down, and her boxers were on backwards. Her shoulders, sharp and glowing like shells, hunched miserably. "The zombies."

Traveller nosed at Ginny's heels as she shuffled for the window, almost smacking her hip on the desk with its now-useless computer. Paperwork on a cork board fluttered, and the manager's marked-up whiteboard watched two frightened women, one young, one older. The moon hid briefly behind moving clouds, but there was enough of its glow—and reflected light from unmelted snow and glare-ice—to see dark shapes in the parking lot.

A whole crowd of them. Easily twenty, or more.

"OhGod," Ginny whispered, her breath making a circle on the glass. Steph shivered next to her, and she was suddenly very sure that if she said the wrong thing, or even *moved* the wrong way, the girl was going to start screaming. "Shhh," she said, finally, and put her arm around Steph's shoulders. The girl's skin was frigid, and her teeth chattered—Ginny would have to find her better pyjamas. "How long have you been watching them?"

"I d-don't know."

"Okay." *Think fast, Ginny.* "If they'd broken in downstairs we'd hear gunshots. They're on watch down there." She winced as she said it. *Don't worry, the menfolk are watching.* Christ, how civilization faded in the face of disaster. "We'd *hear* it. So they haven't, and in any case, the door's locked."

"I heard it," Steph insisted. Her eyes, wild and white-ringed, glared up at Ginny. "Something rattled the door."

"I believe you." *Lock it*, Lee had said. Was it Brandon? Mark? Or Lee, checking to make sure she had? Maybe that was it. "It could have been the building settling, or the wind."

"I don't think so." Steph shivered again. "But okay."

Ginny watched the slumping, shuffling, chewing crowd. A cold, moon-silvered parking lot full of slush, human shapes gathered in a clot, some of them terribly *wrong*. They took up half the expanse, pressing close to the building, and the ones near the crowd's middle swayed gently like a wheat-field under a breeze. Near the edges, they milled about, a vaguely counterclockwise motion as they bumbled. Hats moved gently, blood-stiffened hair pasted to a sprinkling of bare heads, and it was a mercy Ginny's dinner was fully digested, because otherwise she might have lost it looking at those twitching, jerking, oddly fluid movements. They bumbled against the truck and Juju's 4x4, hands patting spiderlike along metal and glass.

Steph made a soft, hopeless sound, and Ginny landed back in herself with a jolt. "Come on," she said, drawing the girl away from the window. "They can't get in. We'd have heard if they did."

The teenager resisted, leaned towards the chill, slick glass. Traveller's wet nose printed itself on Ginny's bare calf again, and he whined, deep in his throat. Maybe he could smell Steph's fear.

"Don't you start too," Ginny told him, firmly. "I'm *not* taking you downstairs to pee at this hour, for God's sake."

That made Steph giggle, a soft, lonely sound, and the girl relaxed all at once. Ginny pushed the desk aside as far as she could, and they dragged the girl's foam pad and sleeping bag next to hers. The dog wouldn't rest until he had himself snuggled *between* them, and ended up with all four paws in the air, snoring mightily.

Ginny listened for a long time, staring at the ceiling and thinking about the silent, eerie crowd outside, straining her ears.

She was pretty sure Steph did, too.

[17]

EXTRAORDINARY SITUATION

Morning came bright and cheerful, warming up yet again. Water trickled from edges, and cold fog lifted from hillocks and humps of freeze in the parking lot. At least it didn't look like another storm was moving in. "Maybe the Fudders lot, north on the interstate," Juju said, swirling thick sweet coffee inside his black and gold *Viper Tires* travel mug. "Find all sorts of canopies there, somethin's bound to fit. Get you a nice one."

One I couldn't afford otherwise, you mean. Lee made a brief noise of assent, taking a scorching gulp of his own percolator juice. It tasted a little like Nonna's, only without the chicory. For a moment, he wondered what his grandparents would have made of all this. Big Q wouldn't have been surprised, just balefully determined to shoot any critter that got close, and maybe Nonna would have talked Ginny out of this damn trip.

He tried to imagine Ginny at their dinner table, forced to listen Big Q's pronouncements about the state of the world, seeing Nonna jumping up every few moments to fetch something else for the meal. Ginny, of course, would get up with her nine times out of ten, and be waved back to her seat—Nonna would save her own grilling of the

Yankee girl for when they were washing the dishes. And of course Ginny would help her with them, being so polite. That would go a long way with Lee's grandma.

The whole thing was nice to think about, even if it did needle his chest a bit.

"Get some chickens." Mark Kasprak grinned, scratching at the back of his neck. His hair was bound and determined not to take any of this lying down, now that he'd slept through an entire night. "Put a coop on the back of the truck."

Steph rolled her blue eyes; she looked a lot better now that she'd had some rest. Her changecolor hair had thickened up and darkened without washing, and she was busy trying to braid a hank of it on the right side of her head to go with the hank on the left. "I ain't cleaning that shi—" She glanced at Ginny, who was eyeing the glass front door. "That *stuff* up."

Lee was betting she'd try to cross both braids over her head like Ginny often did. How on earth did girls get things like that to stay? That would be something worth figuring out, he decided. A man's fingers would be too blunt, but he could certainly wield a hairbrush.

"Run a hose under the floor. Wash it all right out." Mark was having fun poking at Steph, and she enjoyed shoveling it right back. It was kind of heartening to see.

Ginny poured hot water into her tea mug and rose, gracefully. She plucked at Lee's elbow. "We need to talk." Her curls hadn't worked free of the French braid down her back yet, and she looked a lot smaller without her bulky jacket on. Camping suited her, though, except for the circles under her eyes.

She wasn't sleeping well. At least he didn't have to wonder why. He wasn't getting much rest himself, what with standing watch. As soon as he lay down, one uncomfortable thought after another danced through his head, and he'd lost the soldier's habit of dropping off anyhow. It would come back, he just needed to adjust. He'd managed a few hours last night, listening to Juju breathe while French was at the front of the store on watch.

Lee nodded, steadying his own mug and wondering what the hell. Maybe she wanted to say something about last night. *I like bein your useful.* How stupid was that? He'd spent his entire time on watch blushing about it, and the fact that it was true didn't make it any less embarrassing. "Finish eatin and get packed up," he told the kids. "Wanna be out of here in an hour."

"Yessir," they chorused, and Steph giggled when Mark elbowed her.

Ginny drew him aside, into the mouth of the cereal aisle. Bright boxes marched on either side, promising sugar, fiber, fun, all sorts of things. How long before all the cardboard started to mold? It wasn't that damp yet, but during a howler winter, even the tightest building would develop a few holes.

Especially when abandoned, without anyone breathing inside to hold it together. "Somethin wrong, Miss Virginia?"

"Did you see them?" She'd turned pale, her face tilted up to his like a flower. "Last night?"

His stomach turned over. He didn't drop his coffee, but his fingers loosened and it slopped inside his familiar white and blue NRA mug with the decal wearing off under repeated washing. "See what?"

"There were a bunch of *them* outside the store. The parking lot was full." She swallowed, dryly, and now that the kids couldn't see the worry was printed all over her, ten feet tall and lit up with neon. "They were watching."

Shit. "What time was this?" His back prickled, something close to gooseflesh walking up and down his spine.

"I don't know—maybe four in the morning? A little after?" Ginny studied his face. "Steph heard something and woke up, looked out the window."

"Huh." He'd shaken Brandon awake for watch at four AM, and the parking lot had been an empty wasteland of whipped, frozen melt then. So, afterward. Four-thirty? Five? Why hadn't the college boy said anything about it? "They movin around?"

"Some, at the edges. Some were going around the cars. Others were just standing there, watching the store." She sucked in her top lip, bit it for a moment, and her paleness was alarming. She'd been sitting on this almost all morning, dammit. "If they figure out how to break the doors—"

"Let's not borrow trouble." He had the idea trouble was going to show up, whether borrowed or bought. "We'll be gone tonight."

"But what if they can sense us somehow?" The *I-want* line between her eyebrows was back, and working itself in deeper.

Christ, she was too goddamn smart. He should call that little line the *I-worry* instead. "We keep movin."

"What about when we don't have a store or a building to hide in?" The line didn't go away. Oh, Nonna would have liked her, *I-want* line, Yankee accent, and all. *No moss grows on that girl,* she would have said, her apple-cheeked face crinkling up with amusement.

Or maybe Lee was just thinking what he'd *want* Nonna to say. At least she wasn't asking who'd been on watch. "Then there wouldn't have been enough sick people for a crowd of critters," he said, slowly, giving himself time to think and space between each word to slow her down too. "We keep watch. Sleep in the cars." Getting a canopy for the truck, and maybe something for that Brandon fellow to drive, would be a good idea anyway.

"Great. My back's already killing me." But the worry eased, her face smoothing out, and Lee found out his heart was doing something funny. Swelling inside him, like. It felt good to ease her.

Real good. "Maybe we'll find a hotel tonight." He decided not to tell her any of *his* troubling thoughts. There wasn't any point. "Real sheets and all."

Her shy smile warmed him clear through. Pretty fingers cupped around her tea, steam lifting to touch her face like he wanted to as she inhaled its warmth. Her collarbone looked too fragile to hold her shoulders. "Sounds good." But that worry-line returned and Lee waited, examining her face.

"Well?" he said, finally.

"I hesitate to..." She glanced over his shoulder. Mr French was pontificating about something, sounded like. Boy did *not* know when to shut up, and Lee didn't like the notion of being trapped in a vehicle with him. "Steph said what she heard wasn't out there. It was inside. The doorknob rattling." Ginny's eyes had darkened, and her shoulders curved inward. "Maybe just the building settling, I don't know."

Those eyes of hers said different. They said she was used to men not believing her about other men, and plenty of other things as well.

So *that's* why she didn't ask who was on watch. She already suspected. Lee thought this over, and the idea of shooting the college boy and leaving him for the next wave of snow to cover—or the critters to snack on—was powerfully tempting. "We can tell the French fellow to travel his own way," he said, finally. "Wouldn't mind that at all." And if it took a bullet or two to make it stick, well, that was the way of the world. He supposed he should feel bad about how soon he was thinking of fragging a civilian, but this was what you'd call an *extraordinary situation.*

In enemy territory with your squad to look out for, you got used to that equation—and its solutions, no matter how grim—right quick.

"Shouldn't we stick together, though? We're all, you know. Human." She paused. "Or uninfected, at least." Her expression changed again. "I mean...oh, *hell.*"

"I know what you mean." His face felt funny. He realized he was smiling, and her wry grin in response was a beauty. "I ain't gonna have him with us if he makes you or Steph uncomfortable." There. That was reasonable enough. "Ain't worth it." *Shut up, Lee. Makin a fool out of yourself.* He watched her take another sip of tea, giving herself time to think. Behind him, something clattered—Kasprak, clowning around. Steph's laugh in response, and a clatter of mugs. Juju, telling them to quit monkeyin and get to packin.

"We should stick together," Ginny said, finally. "The more of us, the better, when those things show up."

He didn't necessarily agree, but she sounded sure. And really, if he put one in French's leg and left the motherfucker behind during a scramble it could buy time for the rest of them to get away. "Aight," he said. "But I'm watchin him."

That made her her troubled frown retreat again, worry draining like a bathtub. "Me too." Her earrings glittered, and her eyelashes were a dark fringe, veiling her gaze for a moment. "And maybe it wasn't that, you know? I just...I have a bad feeling." Ready for him to disagree, maybe.

"No shortage of that goin around." Lee decided he wasn't doing too badly. Hell, she might even call him *comforting* now. "Don't you worry, Ginny."

"Can't stop." She was smiling again, and the weight had slipped off those slim shoulders. "But it helps to hear you tell me not to"

Then, wonder of wonders, she stepped forward. He didn't realize what she was fixing to do until she'd gone on tiptoe, her tea and his own coffee splashing a little as her free hand curled around the edge of his leather vest and pulled him down. Her lips touched his cheek— he hadn't had a chance to scrape yet that morning.

Lee froze, hunched uncomfortably, and the simmer-scent of a healthy woman rose from her hair and skin, filling his nose. When she let go of his vest, he didn't straighten, just stared at her like he'd been hit on the head.

And Ginny, of all things, *winked* at him, before swinging around and heading away to help with the packing and loading.

God*damn*.

[18]

KNOWING BE BETTER

She'd seen the ads for this place—**FUDDER'S RV**—on a big revolving sign, the billboard next to it easily viewed from the freeway with a giant, gaudy plywood rendition of Uncle Sam next to a redneck conservative Comment of the Month, one the rotund owner with his shades and white Brimley-esque mustache apparently thought was a crushing response to any "damlibruls" unlucky enough to live in this part of the Greatest States. Ginny had always found it unsettling and funny in equal measure, especially with the full-color ads in the Thursday free newspaper circulars shouting NO MONEY DOWN and WE'LL FINANCE U! The TV spots were even more hilarious, with the owner doing his best Crazy Dave impersonation filtered through a drawl so thick it was a wonder he could stuff all the words into a sixty-second ad.

Now, it was downright creepy. The billboard, unlit, was missing two Fs and a couple Es, and the plywood Uncle Sam was a glaring, beetle-browed, stories-high clown with a misshapen nose. New RVs stood at attention in serried ranks, some with soaped prices on their windshields, all dripping with cold water. The service building with its huge hangar doors and heavy jacks was dark and deserted; so was the cavernous showroom despite its acres of glass. Juju and Mark went off to look for a canopy that would fit Lee's truck.

Lee was going to take a look at the RVs and see if there was one he thought would sleep them all. It was a better idea than snoozing in the truck bed, even with a canopy, but the thought of everyone packed into one vehicle, day in and day out, gave Ginny the shivers.

At least Lee didn't require her to pay attention to him before he felt like he existed. Brandon, on the other hand, was full of the *look-at-me's*. "Don't you think?" His voice bounced off the showroom walls, rocketed between huge, glossy vehicles arranged on smooth concrete ovals fringed with thick blue carpet. All the offices were closed, their gold nameplates neat and set at perfect angles. *Sales. Financing. Marketing. Customer Service.* "I mean, everyone says Wordsworth's overrated, but I like him."

You would. Ginny made a soft noncommittal noise. Two bigscreen televisions sprouted from the walls on metal arms in the wine-carpeted customer lounge, much nicer than the employee breakroom with its bulletin board full of yellowing paper notices and reminders to CHIN UP AND GRIN UP and CLOSE THAT SALE!

Then there was Jefferson B. Fudder's palatial, carpeted office, the desk placed so he could look out over his domain with his fingers laced over his proud, satisfied belly. Where was he now, that big ol' good ol' boy, with his cowboy hats and his hate of anything resembling education and fairness?

Ginny suspected she didn't want to know, and shivered each time she glanced at *that* particular door, thank you very much.

"Of course, getting a kid to read Wordsworth is like getting a dog to quote Kierkegaard." Brandon grinned, spreading his beefy arms. Football, he said. It figured. "But I try! I had this student, she was bright for her age, she just wouldn't do the work. Nose ring, dyed hair, the whole nine."

Lee, eyeing a pegboard full of neatly labeled ignition keys, had already tuned the man out. Steph, her thin fine hair in two spindly braids and her coat zipped to her chin, gave Ginny an agonized look.

I agree, kid. Ginny sighed, spread her hands as Brandon went on telling his story, and headed for the customer lounge, where weak bars of sunlight struggled past slat blinds. At least in there she couldn't hear him. The cabinets were full of the usual—granola bars, powdered creamer, shelf-stable little tubs of half-n-half, cleaning supplies. Working retail in college had given her an appreciation for the spaces behind smooth corporate facades. Behind cabinet doors and employee entrances was where all the real work—and the real dramas—took place.

When she came out through the swinging glass door again, carrying a stack of bulk-bought granola boxes, it was quiet. Steph stood near the door, peering into the glare of the parking lot. Patches of grey pavement had begun to surface through the vanishing snow, rising like humpbacks.

"I found granola," Ginny said, quietly. "You want some?"

Steph peered back at her, one of her thin braids swinging. "Mr Quartine said to stay in here. Took some keys and Mr French and went lookin at RVs."

"Good." Ginny tried not to sound sneakingly grateful they didn't have to listen to Brandon anymore. He seemed nice enough, but he just *had* to fill up the airwaves. Then, of course, there was the question of whether it had been him rattling the doorknob last night. "There's chocolate chips in some of these."

"Yum." A tremulous smile, but the girl turned back to the glass door and stared across the lot. The part down the back of her head was very pale, hair pulled tightly away on either side. Braids suited her. "My mama always wanted a big old RV. Vacations, she said. *Like we ever gonna go anywhere,* my daddy would say." Her voice dropped and broadened, a pretty fair imitation—Ginny could almost *see* her father. Probably a big, blunt man, with surprisingly gentle hands.

Like Lee's. Callused, scraped, grimed with engine muck, but capable of...what? Softness? Was that the right word?

"Then Mama would say we never went anywhere because he was cheap, and he would just..." Steph sniffed, wiped at her nose. "He'd make this noise like a cough, sort of. Then they wouldn't talk to each other."

Oh, God. What could she say? Ginny settled for stepping next to her, and leaning slightly to her right. Her shoulder, under her thick coat, touched Steph's. "My parents did that too."

"Did they fight?" Steph's interest was palpable. She probably thought it exotic that someone as old as Ginny had parents, too.

God, had Ginny ever been that young? She could barely remember. "They didn't yell." But her mother's silences could be Arctic, and when her father decided he wasn't going to discuss something anymore, he just stayed at work. "Sometimes I wished they would."

"Yeah, well, mine yelled. I used to think I could run away just to get some peace an' quiet." Steph sniffed again. "Now I wish they was still yelling. Steada makin that awful grindin noise."

"Yeah." Ginny swallowed, hard. Was Mom staggering barefoot, circling in the cold? Had Dad started to cough, or run a fever? What about Flo?

Would knowing be better than the awful uncertainty? Whatever Ginny would have said was lost when a flicker of motion blurred in her peripheral vision. Steph gasped, stiffening, and grabbed Ginny's arm.

It was a once-hefty, hatless man in the frayed remains of a business suit and overcoat, his jaw working as he dropped to all fours. No, not a man.

One of the infected. Maybe he had even once been Jeff Fudder, because a mustache caked with filth and dried blood crawled over the lower half of his face. His pants were in tatters and a fringe of hair around a bald spot stuck up in patches, glopped with mud and wet and blood. His skin had greyed out, and despite the queer caving-in of the ribs on his right side, he scuttled blur-quick across an empty lane between two lines of RVs.

Just as he did, though, Mark and Juju strolled into view from another empty lane, the teenager with his hand cupped near his mouth, laughing at something the older man had said. The infected thing stopped, clearly visible from this angle, but hidden from the guys. It turned its head, a queer creaking lizardlike motion. Its skinny fingers worked spasmodically, and its chewing of empty air intensified.

"Fuck," Ginny breathed, and Steph, gone paper-white, let out a thin unsteady shocked sound. The stack of boxes fell out of Ginny's nerveless hands, and when they hit the floor she jumped at the sound. "Oh, God. God."

"What do we do?" Steph whispered. "Miss Ginny, what do we *do*?"

Oh, God, Ginny realized. *I don't have a damn clue.*

[19]

SEE WHO DIES

THERE WERE NERVOUS TALKERS, SMOOTH TALKERS, AND STUPID talkers. Then there were the combinations, and the most irritating of all: the people who were simply, merely, and totally in love with their own damn voices. Lee, looking over the RVs, wasn't sure if he should categorize French just yet, but he was leaning towards putting him in the love-your-own-voice group. The blond, manicured sonofabitch nattered on about teaching and about how he wasn't surprised about the zombies because most people were asleep all the time anyway, and surely the government would have everything under control soon.

"So what do you do?" Brandon asked after a while, and Lee had a longing vision of getting out his duct tape. Or a staple-gun, and fixing the idiot's lips up permanent-like.

Either would be satisfying. "This an' that," he said, finally, since the man seemed to be waiting on an answer. There really was no point in getting a *huge* RV, but one that could sleep six was pretty goddamn big by definition. Then there was the problem of fuel. The more he thought about it—

"Oh, unemployed? That's okay." Like he was conferring a big

favor. Brandon toed the tire of a nearby road-schooner, then did it again. His hair, dark and unwashed, was still combed neatly, and that expensively useless diver's watch on his thick wrist glittered. "I mean, sometimes you can't help it, right?"

Jesus Christ. Lee set his jaw, glancing up and down the row of RV noses. There was an intersection about twenty feet ahead, and maybe he could send the bastard off one way and take the other. That idea had a certain appeal, too. Maybe French would get lost, and they could leave quiet-like.

Wouldn't Ginny shake her head at that. Lee's smile faded; he cocked his own head, straining to hear.

"*No!*" A high, wild cry. "*Goddammit, look out!*"

Lee's heart dropped and his hand did too, closing around his gun. He cleared leather, locked his finger outside the trigger guard, and pushed past French, who was still babbling about the economy.

"*Over here!*" It was Ginny, and she was yelling. "*No, over here, you sonofabitch!*"

The girl had a mouth on her, and Lee might have been amused except his skin had shrunk two sizes and the world was too goddamn bright, tunnel vision threatening to close him down and render him useless. Training took over, keeping him to one side, wishing he had Juju behind him instead of the teacher asshole, who had finally figured out something was wrong. Lee picked up the pace, his boots hitting hard, each step jolting hips and shoulders, pounding up his neck and threatening to shatter his teeth.

When he burst out of the walkway, gun low and ready, the thing was already committed to its jump. It was a mustachioed man in a business suit and a string tie, or at least, it had been at one time or another. Now it was just a critter, making that deep grinding noise in its chest as it landed and staggered for Ginny. She danced nimbly aside, those orange-laced boots too clumsy for her grace. Juju had a knee taken, but she was right in his line of fire, and from the way his mouth moved, he was swearing and trying to get a clear shot. Mark Kasprak sprawled on the pavement, sickly pale, one side of his old anorak torn open and all of it sopping wet from being rolled in melt. The soles of his new boots, already gray from dirt and slush, scrabbled.

"Come on!" Ginny yelled, and the thing darted for her again. She dodged, and it ran into an RV with a sick crunching sound mixed with that deep, terrible grinding. She was keeping it away from Mark, but Juju ran the risk of hitting her if he pulled the trigger. "Come on, you cheap lemon-selling bastard!"

Lemon bastard? Everything inside Lee stilled. He brought the gun up, smoothly, tracking the thing as it staggered. The sun dimmed, clouds racing across a cold, pale sky, and every inch of the terrain stood out hard and clear. Ginny backed up, a ballerina's light shuffle, Lee's finger tightened, *almost there, just keep moving, darlin, just keep moving the way you've been...*

Then Brandon French, all however-many pounds of proud football-playing idjit, ran smack into Lee, almost knocking him over. The shot went wide, digging a furrow in the pavement and zinging off, ricocheting down a lane of RVs. Glass shattered, and the thing stopped, confused for a crucial moment.

Fury boiled up Lee's throat. He tracked again, exhaling smoothly, and the second shot was a good solid hit. Ginny screamed, and for a ludicrous, terrifying moment he thought he'd hit *her.*

The critter's head evaporated, and Juju's gun barked too. Lee glanced out from cover; his guts turned over again before changing to ice, the clear cold freeze of an adrenaline rush and the old familiar feeling of *well, this is interesting, let's see who dies.*

There was another critter, this one also in the remains of a polyester business suit. Its potbelly sagged, a slice of pale black-furred skin poking obscenely from the ruins of blue-checked polyester, its wine-red tie flapping, and its wingtips—probably once polished to a fare-thee-well—scraping through slush. Juju's shot had sank into its chest, but wasn't slowing it none. It was bearing down on Ginny's back, and the door to the showroom was opening too slowly, Steph Meacham's ghostly face behind it a picture of horror.

Lee's lungs filled. Ginny stopped, her sides heaving, staring at the mess of the critter in front of her. She was back in Juju's line of fire, again, because the second zombie critter had staggered sideways a few critical steps.

"*Get down!*" Juju yelled, the words stretching through syrup because everything had slowed.

This wasn't the range or the training field. It wasn't the desert or the jungle, heat and sweat and grit and blood. Still, it felt just the same, except for the sickening chance of something happening to—

Lee exhaled and squeezed the trigger. The gun barked again. Ginny let out a soft, hurt little sound, flinching to her left.

The critter behind her folded down with a splashing thump, dark blood and spongy brain flying. The hole in its left temple seeped a thin trickle of blackish blood, a good clean hit, and the other side of its head splattered wide. Lee's aim was only off by a quarter of an inch.

Ginny whirled, sharply. Stared at him, at the thing spilled on the ground.

He lowered the gun, and his gaze locked with Ginny's. Big, dark, clear, clean eyes, and for a moment, she could see right down into the bottom of him. He was a pond, silt at the bottom stirred by something cold and scaled and awful, and she was a girl on the shore, peering into the depths.

Ginny folded, her knees hitting concrete with a thump he felt all the way across the space between them. The hideous sinking thought that he'd hit *her* tiptoed through his head on padded, painful little feet. But no, she just turned on her knees to look at the critter that had almost leapt on her back and bent over, retching.

Time resumed its regular march. Lee swept the area again, stuffed his gun back into its small dark home, and turned on his heel. Brandon French was standing beside him, uselessly, mouth hanging open instead of flapping for once.

Lee punched him. It was a good solid hit, and blood flew.

[20]

THAT'S REALLY UNFORTUNATE

WEAK SUNLIGHT FELL THROUGH THE SMALL WINDOW IN THE employee break room, casting watery squares and rectangles on cream-colored linoleum. Her heart was still pounding and Ginny's teeth kept wanting to chatter, but she folded her arms and enunciated clearly. "That wasn't a very reasonable response to the situation."

"The shootin, or the punchin?" Juju shook his head, mashing his pompom hat in both hands. He wasn't greyish anymore, and some of the wildness had left his dark eyes. His rifle's snout poked up over his shoulder, and at least he wasn't keeping his right hand near his pistol. "What kind of idiot runs up on a man with a gun?"

"I said I was sorry." Brandon clapped a Ziploc bag of compressed snow to his face; his bloodshot left eye was already puffing shut. "Jesus fucking Christ, what is *wrong* with you people?"

"Watch your mouth," Lee said, quietly, but with a great deal of force. He stood near the door, his arms folded and his shearling buttoned; Ginny got the idea it wasn't because *he* was cold. No, Lee's chin had dropped, and his gaze had grown piercing and almost-yellow once more. He glared at Brandon like he was a hairsbreadth away from punching him again, and Ginny cleared her throat, nervously.

Mark had his arm around Steph. He was damp all over, and paper-pale. He also needed a new coat. The thing had gotten its fingers in and yanked, ripping the side-seam of his anorak. "I didn't even see it," he muttered. "God damn, I didn't even see it."

"You watch your mouth too." Lee tipped back on his heels a little, leaning on the wall. That was deceptive, the tension his stance told her he was close to exploding.

And *that* was a scary thought. Ginny took a deep breath, searching for the right words. "Let's all calm down, all right?" *At least, let's all be a little calmer than we were ten minutes ago.* "That was surprising, but it worked out, everyone's okay."

"No thanks to *him*." Juju was not going to be graceful about this. He didn't even point at Brandon, but he didn't have to. The disdain was palpable.

"Mr Thurgood." Ginny suppressed the urge to pinch the bridge of her nose, or start screaming. Neither would help. Besides, her hands were shaking. "We weren't all in the Army, okay? We're not *all* going to know exactly what to do when...when dead people are chasing us." *Good Lord, I never thought I would ever use* that *particular sentence.*

"Zombies," Steph corrected, playing with the ends of one of her thin braids. "Might as well call 'em what they are."

Oh, for God's sake. "Okay. Zombies." Ginny's fingers sank into her upper arms, hard. At least nobody could see her trembling. "Can we at least all agree that when the infected are chasing us, naturally we're going to make mistakes?"

"Mistakes can kill." Juju, unmollified, looked to Lee for backup. He unrolled his hat, and lifted it with the expression of a man who had his opponent wriggling in the crushing grip of logic. "Ain't that right?"

Not helping, sir. Not helping at all. She didn't want to give Lee a chance to get started again. "But it *didn't* this time. It worked out just fine, so let's just all take a deep breath and *chill the fuck out*, all right?"

A sullen silence filled the room. At least Lee didn't tell *her* to watch her mouth.

Small mercies. "Good," Ginny said. "Great. Okay, let's keep our eyes on the prize here." Christ, the clichés posted on the walls were infecting her. Her knees were suspiciously noodle-floppy and she really, really wanted to lock herself in a restroom stall for a little while. The physiological responses to fear were fine to read about, but uncomfortable as fuck in real life. "Lee?" *Come on, cowboy. Help me out.* "Do you think we should, um, steal an RV?"

That got Lee's gaze off Brandon and onto her, which was only a halfway relief. His cheeks were reddened from the chill, and his knuckles were white, fingers digging into his upper arms too. If he was copying her, it was probably unconscious. He studied her for a long, tense moment, his mouth a straight line, and Ginny was about to repeat herself when he finally spoke.

"Not sure it's stealin, at this point."

I'm not either, but that's not what I'm asking. "We can debate the morality of it later. For right now, do you think we should?" *Help me, for God's sake.* Giving everyone a task and a reason to stick together was the best thing, right? The idea that it might be beyond her capability to keep everyone calm enough to work together was almost as frightening as seeing that second...infected.

Zombie. God.

Lee's knuckles lost their bloodless look. His shoulders didn't quite sag, but they relaxed a little, and a muscle in his cheek flickered before he spoke. "Ayuh," he said, at last. "A smallish one, for the gas mileage."

"Okay." *Fantastic. Awesome. Making progress.* "That's decided, then."

"We found a canopy," Mark piped up. Steph's hands stopped scrubbing at each other, and the girl at last looked like she believed everyone had survived the last half-hour. "Get that on your truck, too, sir."

"We'll do that first." Lee's expression didn't alter, but he dropped his hands. "French?"

"What?" Brandon hunched his shoulders.

"You're comin with me, Juju, and Kasprak. We're gonna get that canopy on my truck, then we'll get the RV. I got one in mind."

Well, wasn't that a relief. "Great," Ginny said. "What can Steph and I do?"

"*You* stay in here, and out of trouble." The way he said it, he expected her to salute and bark aye, sir, or some variant thereof.

No you don't, Mr Caveman. "Maybe we should stick together—"

"Safer for you in here." Lee's chin set, and Ginny realized he wasn't looking at her anymore. He was staring at the employee fridge, an ancient Amana number that probably contained a colony or two of semi-sentient penicillin inside by now.

Oh, you sexist pig. "Fine." Ginny's teeth ached, she longed to grind them. At least she wasn't shivering anymore; irritation was dispelling the cold, loose sensation of *oh God I could have died.* The second zombie—where had it come from? Jesus, she hadn't even *heard* it. "Then get going, will you? It's already past noon."

That earned her a sideways, yellow-eyed glare. Was he angry at *her* for keeping the damn thing occupied long enough for him to shoot it? That would be just like a man. She glared back, and he said nothing else, just nodded, turned like he was in a military parade, and stalked away. Juju hurried to follow, and Mark patting Steph's shoulder awkwardly before following suit, and Brandon huffed out a sigh and trailed in their wake, clasping the plastic bag to his face.

"Great," Ginny muttered at their retreating backs. "Just *great.*"

Steph, perhaps wisely, said nothing.

CLASS C MOTORHOME, THE BROCHURE SAID. GINNY PROPPED her damp boots on the dash and began reading while the giant, wallowing thing banked cautiously out of the parking lot, following Lee's truck with its shiny new camper. They'd even found one that matched the red-and-white Chevy. Fashionable indeed.

The brochure was full of breathless excitement. *Sleeps up to 6!* Cherry veneers, a new-car smell threatening to give her a headache, and absolutely abysmal mileage. Brandon, ensconced in the throne-like driver's seat, wasn't talking, for once. Mark, buckled into a bucket seat behind the driver, whistled every once in a while when the gigantic craft bounced a little.

"This is a nice one," the kid said, again. Ginny glanced at the rearview—Juju and Steph were in the 4x4, and Traveller was with Lee in the truck. They were quite a convoy, moving down a road awash with slush and dotted with abandoned vehicles, not to mention the occasional crash. "We're on a road trip for sure, now."

Brandon grunted, a noise of grudging assent. His face was bruising up really well, his hair darkened and rising in messy unwashed chunks. The snow-filled Ziploc had vanished, and she was sure he hadn't bothered to put it in a garbage can. No, he'd probably thrown it somewhere. He wouldn't take any ibuprofen, either.

Ginny suppressed a sigh. At least there weren't many crackups to navigate around on the freeway. There hadn't been one they couldn't squeak past on one side or the other yet, but she was already worried about coming across the first. "All we need are snacks and caffeine, and loud music while we cruise."

"Ain't never been on a road trip." Mark fidgeted in his seat. At least he wasn't playing with its recliner capability anymore. Lee had thought to get extra coats, and Mark's side-shredded anorak was left behind at the RV lot. This one was a black, high-grade shell over a couple Thinsulate layers, and it fit him a lot better. "Lee says we goin all the way to New York."

Ginny nodded, flipping past a few more pages full of glossy photos—RVs speeding along mountain roads, airbrushed nuclear families enjoying the camping, a rope swing over a jewel-blue lake clustered with summer greenery. Probably alive with poison ivy, swarming with mosquitoes, and polluted as fuck. "Yeah." *Wait a second.* "You mean you came along without even knowing where we were headed?"

"It's a zombie 'pocalypse, Miss Ginny." Just like he'd say *it's raining,* or *grass is green.* "Get together and go, that's what you *do,* right?"

Good God. "I guess." The instinct to band together and ask no questions when you were terrified was probably the second-most powerful force in the universe, right after the attraction between the buttered side of toast and an unmopped kitchen floor. Besides, almost every zombie movie had a road-trip portion. It was a given to anyone soaking in American culture.

"New York, huh?" Brandon's knuckles were white on the steering wheel, and the bruises on his face were gathering all sorts of Technicolor. Lee's truck pulled further ahead, taillights a steady ruby glow. *Keep your lights on,* he'd said. *Safer.* "What's there?"

"My parents." Ginny stared at the brochure. Underneath it was the user's manual. It made sense to be prepared. The only other option was listing more observations about the infected and their behavior, and if she did, Ginny had the notion she'd lose everything she ever thought of eating, right out the window of this brand-new road barge. She probably shouldn't have her feet on the dash, but that was a small consideration, right?

A thunderstruck silence filled the vehicle. "Your...parents?" Brandon glanced at her. "And what else?"

"My sister. She's pregnant." *Overdue, by now.* One problem at a time, Ginny reminded herself, and turned another color-saturated, shining brochure page. Her scalp itched. A hot shower sounded heavenly. And while she was dreaming, some decent tea, a night's sleep in her own bed, and a pony would be nice too. Another sigh caught itself halfway out of her mouth, and she bent her head a little further, her vision blurring.

Good God. Was she going to *cry?* That would just cap today off nicely, wouldn't it. She sniffed as quietly as she could, trying to clear her nose.

Slush swooshed away under the tires. "Uh, so..." Brandon goosed the gas, returning his attention to the road with a start as Lee's truck crept far to the left, threading around a clot of dead vehicles, bumper-to-bumper, leading to another discarded checkpoint. "We're traveling across multiple zombie-infested states for a family reunion?"

"I was going to go, with or without Lee." Did she even have to explain? A bubble of liquid heat bloomed in her chest; Ginny forced the irritation down. The blurring in her eyes retreated, promising more trouble later. "He insisted on coming with me, and on our way out of town we found Juju, and the kids."

Brandon gave her another odd look. His face looked like it hurt, a small cut right on his cheekbone with the tissue around it swelling. "Just like that?"

"Just like that." *Keep your eyes on the road,* she wanted to say, but that wasn't even close to helpful, was it. Her stock of patience and diplomacy was falling like a storm barometer.

"Sounds fishy." Brandon clutched at the wheel afresh, the RV swaying as its left-hand side leaned towards the grassy slope of the meridian. Ginny had the idea he hadn't driven one of these before, despite his insistence. *All over the US,* he'd told Lee. *Of course, ours was bigger.*

"Oh?" Ginny closed the brochure and opened the owner's manual. Maybe he'd get the clue and stop talking if she studied it intently enough.

No, she really didn't expect that. It would be too much to ask for.

Brandon sank to her expectations. "I mean, you know, that hick just doesn't seem like the normally helpful type."

"Hey." Mark Kasprak eyed the bulkhead behind the driver's seat, his eyebrows up so high they were almost melding with his hairline. "Don't you talk about Mr Quartine that way."

"The adults are talking, kiddo." Brandon shot Ginny a glance meant to be conspiratorial, but she busied herself with reading the table of contents. The manual was a goddamn phone book. How much of it was in different languages? Her high-school Spanish was no doubt abysmal by now.

"Mark's right," she informed him, quietly. "Lee's saved my life more than once now. Saved *all* of us. If you don't like him, that's really unfortunate." *He's closest thing to a leader we've got.* Ginny had some hard thinking to do, but it wouldn't get done with this guy trying divide-and-conquer.

"I get that he's King Shit of Turd Hill. If you want to stick around and get punched, okay." Brandon scowled, his chin jutting forward. His coat was still damp from landing on the ground, and probably his jeans, too. "If he hits me, he'll hit you sooner or later."

I can't afford to break a tooth, Ginny told herself, loosening her jaw with a sigh. "Will you just concentrate on driving? I thought you said you'd handled one of these before."

It was a low blow, but at least it shut him up. Ginny bent back over the manual. Next time, *she* would drive, and maybe this guy could be stuck in the truck with Lee.

That thought gave her a great deal of grim amusement. When she glanced back at Mark, he was still studying what he could see of driver's seat, and his expression was thoughtful and worried all at once.

Me too, kid. Ginny suppressed yet another sigh. *Me too.*

[21]

ENOUGH TO BLEED

AN EARLY WINTER EVENING FOUND THEM AT A LOW BRICK REST
stop near the county line, its restrooms labeled BUCKS and DOES.
Everyone seemed glad of the stop, Ginny and Steph hardly waiting to
check the ladies' before they pushed Juju out and shut the door. Lee
wrinkled his nose at the gents', and so did Juju, but they'd pissed in
worse, and Mark didn't complain. Brandon didn't use the indoor
facilities, taking himself around a corner instead, and Lee found
himself glad.

Relieving your bladder was best done when there weren't
assholes around giving a play-by-play.

There was a small white sedan parked at the other end of the vast
lot. It looked abandoned, but it didn't hold any orange grease pencil
on its windows. The tires were nice and plump too, even if bald. If its
driver was now a critter, maybe it had wandered into the woods. *Stay
together*, Lee told them after everyone had finished their bathroom
break, glowering, and nobody dared do anything but nod.

Traveller bounded through slop and mud on a slope leading
down to what was probably a meadow in summer but was a shallow,
ice-locked pond now. The dog sprayed slushmelt everywhere, his

nose full of adventure. "Might as well camp here tonight," Juju said, his shoulder almost touching Lee's as they watched the dog speed in a circle. For once, the hound was too busy even to warble, but that was a mercy of short duration.

Lee decided he'd never be as happy over anything as the damn dog was about sticking his snout into random corners. "Might as well," he agreed. His jaw ached from gritting his teeth, and his neck itched. A metallic sourness of post-combat letdown filled the back of his throat. A shot of something eye-watering alcoholic would go down easy right about now, or any sort of hard work to let the sweat carry it out through his skin. Instead, he was all balled up, no place for the shakes or the leftover aggression to go.

If Juju felt the same, he didn't show it. "What you gonna do about that French feller?"

Christ, who nominated me the guy who had to do anything? But he knew. He'd done it his own damnself. Shit flowed downhill, and he was the one with the bucket. "Thinkin about it."

"Mark!" Ginny called, behind them. "Come help with this, will you?"

Lee's heart thumped. All day, driving, the same thing played over and over in his head. Ginny, dancing away from the critter, like playing bulldog in the schoolyard. She probably hadn't even thought twice before running out to distract it from Juju and Mark, making enough noise to bring an entire herd of the bastards around. *Jesus Christ.*

And Lee'd just hauled off and socked the fancypants bastard, too. He'd do it again, but that didn't mean it had been the best choice in the situation,. Ginny probably didn't think much of him for it.

Oh, hell.

"Not likely to be many of the critters around here tonight," Juju said. Maybe he was working for diplomacy. "Lee..."

Whatever he was about to say was gonna be a problem for Lee to solve, he could just tell. "What?"

"She saved my life." Juju sounded like he was having a difficult time with the idea. His lips were tight, and his pompom cap was pulled almost all the way down to his eyebrows. "The damn thing was quiet, we'd'a walked right out in front of it."

"More sand than sense." It was bravery, and that was a beautiful thing until it got a civilian killed. You learned to clap a lid on foolishness, that's what training was *for*, but she was woefully underprepared. The thought of what *almost* happened kept dancing through Lee's head, and there was nothing to chase it with but worry, worry, and yet more worry.

"Still..." Juju decided to let it go, stuffing his hands in his jacket pockets. "All right. What we gonna do about him, Lee?"

Now it was *we*. "I know what I'd *like* to do."

"Yeah, well." Juju toed the fraying concrete at the edge of the parking lot. There was a crick down the hill to the left, not quite frozen yet, and its thin music would have been mighty soothing if everything about this goddamn situation hadn't been so goddamn dangerous. "You just say the word, sir."

"I ain't in service no more, Juju." *If it needs doin, I'd do it myself, anyway.*

"Shame. Seems like that's a good way to get through this."

And that, really, was the core of it. Survival was a goddamn merciless business. Ginny was a *civilian*. The kids knew when to shut their mouths and get along, but that French fellow was deadweight. Getting rid of him would be optimal.

But how would Ginny like that?

It shouldn't have mattered how she'd like it. But there it was. He half-turned, looking over his shoulder.

Ginny pushed a few chestnut curls out of her face, standing at the hind end of Lee's beaten-up old truck. French was loitering there, not helping with the unloading, his mouth going a mile a minute. Ginny nodded, politely smiling at something he said, and Lee's stomach curdled.

God *damn* it. "Juju."

"Huh?"

"Watch the dog?"

"All right." Juju followed his gaze, and his eyes widened. He stuck his hands deep in his pockets and rocked back on his heels. "Sonofabitch got no sense at all."

"Neither does the damn dog." Lee's hand fell away from his gun. It was just too tempting.

He ambled across the lot, taking his time. There was no comfortable way to do this.

"French!" he barked, as soon as the fellow was in range. "Shut your mouth and help the kids. Ginny. This way." He grabbed her arm, and they were off.

On the far side of the brick visitor's center, a snowy hill stretched down to the shallow meandering crick, the melt freeing patches of grass leaching into dead winter yellow. Ginny, her elbow caught in his left hand, dug her heels in. Lee stopped, realizing he'd all but bodily dragged her here, and that she'd been talking to him.

"Lee," she repeated, perplexed, her arm stretched awkwardly between them. "What? What's wrong?"

You really have no idea? "We're havin a talk, you and me." He could haul her a fair bit further, if he had to, decided against it.

But only just. His hand wasn't tight on her arm, but it was inescapable, or so he hoped.

"Oh?" Her eyebrows rose, a blush of chill on her pretty cheeks. "So I gather, from you dragging me over hill and dale. What the hell?"

"Listen to me." He grabbed her other arm, too, for good measure. Just to keep her still while he got his thoughts in order, her jacket sleeves slick and cold under his palms. "Jesus Christ, woman, *listen to me.*"

"You're shouting," she observed, calmly enough, dark eyes

widening and that stubborn lift to her chin coming back. "I don't like being yelled at."

A tiny little voice inside his head that sounded oddly like his Nonna's was trying to tell him to calm down, but Lee was not having any of it. "Fine. Then I'll say it slow, and quiet-like. *You could have died.*"

Those big dark eyes, calm and quiet. She gazed up at him, blinking owlish. "I know."

"No, you *don't* know. Nobody thinks they gonna die, Ginny." That one simple truth, hammered home the first time he was under live fire, copper in his mouth and Peanut next to him cussing up a storm—oh, dear God, he was in bad shape if he was thinking about *that*. Lee shook his head, trying to get the words in some kind of reasonable order. "You are still actin like the world is the way it was, and it *ain't*. You gonna get yourself hurt or God forbid kilt, and I ain't gonna have it. I just *ain't*."

"It worked out, Lee." Softly, soothing. She reached up, either trying to pry his hands away or calm him down, settled for grasping his wrists. "I know it was probably upsetting, but—"

"You *ain't* listening, goddammit." His fingers tensed up so hard they were creaking and he was tempted to shake her, just to drive the point home. "You coulda gotten *bit*. You coulda got—"

"I *didn't*." Like it was logical, like it was reasonable, like it mattered that this single time she'd been lucky. "You were right there, and if you hadn't been Juju would have—"

"Juju couldn't get no clear shot, goddammit." He suppressed a wince at swearing in front of her. "You have got to listen to me, Ginny. You *stay under cover*."

Clearly it made no sense to her. "But they didn't see—"

"I don't *care*." His yell rocked her backward, and he knew he was puttin' his feet wrong, but he couldn't stop himself. "You ain't trained, you can't handle yourself, and you see one of them critters coming for anyone, you do *not get in the way*. You *stay put* and you wait for me to fix it!"

"You weren't around to fix it!" she flared. "And it was *fine*! Everything's fine, it worked out, so why are you yelling?"

You weren't around to fix it. Jesus Christ, he couldn't keep his eyes on her every second of the day. Nevermind that he wanted to. It would ease his mind powerfully, that was the truth.

Everything he'd planned on saying jammed up in his throat. *Because you could have gotten hurt. You could have died.*

Ginny leaned back, and his arms straightened. He didn't *want* them to, he wanted to pull her in, get her close. Fold around her, and pretend that cold scaled thing in the bottom of him wasn't thrashing around. But she kept going, until he had to let go, either that or bruise her. His hands dropped to his sides, and God help him, but they were working like he had a throat he wanted to squeeze.

It wasn't far wrong. He did. Just not hers.

"It worked out *this time*." His lips were numb. "It ain't gonna work out every time, Ginny. This ain't no *game*. It ain't no Sunday drive." What would get through to her? "Them things are gonna kill, and we got nothin on our side but ammo." *And baseball bats, but I ain't too sure about those.* She didn't even know how to use the lady Glock they'd picked up for her in the sporting goods store. There wasn't a lot of time for shootin' practice while they were moving, and the risk of drawing more critters put a dent in lessons as well.

And her expression whenever he mentioned practicing, like it was a bad smell.

"We're also smarter than they are," Ginny pointed out. Soft, crisp, and reasonable, like they were standing in the Crossing library with the counter and manners between them on a Sunday afternoon. "I'm not going to stand and do nothing when someone needs help, Lee."

"Yes, you are." There it was, plain and simple. "You are going to keep yourself out of trouble when I can't, or I'll—"

"You'll *what*? Are you threatening me?" Her chin came up again, her arms folded, and there was that *look*. Stubborn enough to drive a man's fist through a wall, and so beautiful it stole all his breath and every bit of good sense he had left too. "You want to think really, really carefully about how you end that sentence, Mr Quartine."

A dry rock lodged itself in his throat. This was why a man didn't open his mouth, it only led to trouble. *Juju can handle himself, I don't worry none about him*, he wanted to say. Even the kids were familiar with hunting, so they were better equipped than she was, for Godsake, and Lee wouldn't cry if the French fellow got himself bit or worse. But Ginny was Yankee, she was *city*, she didn't have the sense or the training to keep out of the way in combat and he didn't have the time to teach her thoroughly.

The silence, full of dripping water and the thin melody of the crick, rasped across his frayed nerves. Their voices would carry down the hill to the lot, dammit. He searched for something, anything to say that would drive the point home, that could shatter that goddamn rock in his throat and make her *understand*.

"Now," she said finally, a high flush working up her throat to her cheeks, "I get you're upset. This is an upsetting situation." Precise and educated, every Yankee word a tiny bullet striking home. "But you will not *ever* drag me around like luggage again, or yell at me, or threaten me. I'll take my chances alone before I put up with that behavior. Is that clear, Mr Quartine?"

God *damn* the woman. Lee stood, frozen. If he moved, if he even *twitched*, he was pretty sure he'd do something he'd regret.

She waited, time ticking out in drip-drop increments. Finally, she nodded as if he'd agreed. "Good. I think this discussion's been productive, at least. I'm going to go back and help with setting up for the night." Her small hands were whiteknuckle, and her shoulders trembled. The words weren't quite as steady as they could have been, either, and Lee could have kicked himself up one side and down the other.

He watched her walk away, her head down and her steps a little uncertain. The new boots were holding up nicely, and dear Sonny Jesus but the way a woman's hips moved was not even remotely fair to a poor sucker like Lee Quartine. Now she was probably afraid of him, too. He was a goddamn idiot.

Lee shut his eyes, listening to the water, and found out his palms hurt, four little jabs in each. He'd driven his fingernails in.

Hard. Hard enough to bleed.

$$[\; 22 \;]$$

A FUCKIN' UNICORN

Juju settled himself a little more comfortably in the driver's seat, cold air slipping through the window, open half an inch to keep the windshield clear. The driver's cabin was dark, faint moonlight outside bouncing off small, thin scrims of snow. It hovered just above freezing. They'd make good time tomorrow.

Even with the accordion door pulled closed behind him, he could hear the familiar song of a barracks at night. Mark was already out, to judge by the snoring, and Steph's faint whistles as she breathed out through a partially-blocked nose provided counterpoint. Ginny's breathing was regular and deep, and Lee was on the floor in his sleeping bag, quiet as a meditating snake.

You sleep in the truck, Lee'd informed French shortly, glowering so hard the frat-boy bastard hadn't dared make a noise. At least the canopy meant French wouldn't get snowed on, and they all had quality sleeping bags. Juju would have put the asshole in a tent to teach him a lesson. Either that, or told him to get lost. Why Lee was letting him stay was beyond Juju.

No, he decided, it wasn't. It was because of Ginny and her *we've got to stick together.* Christ. Apparently she was thinking this was a buddy movie or some shit. All the same, she'd busted out of the RV showroom yelling, distracting the first critter and drawing the second one out too. *You couldn't see it,* she'd said. *I had to do something.*

At least she wasn't a coward. But misguided bravery was worse than none at all. What would Tip say about this?

Well, right on schedule, the worst thought in the world showed up when he was on watch. Cool tickling fingers went down Juju's back. He shifted in the seat again, reaching for his inside pocket. The flask was there, but as soon as his fingertips touched the warm metal he decided *that* was a bad idea, too. Lee was just about mixed-up enough to bust his chops for drinking on watch, and he'd be right, too.

Still, it was awful tempting.

The rest stop was deserted except for a small white Toyota two-door parked all the way at one end. Obviously abandoned, it still bothered both Juju *and* Lee. Maybe it had been left there before the Pocalypse hit. There was no orange Highway Patrol grease-pencil on its windows, though. A car meant a person, and a person possibly meant one of the walking...dead.

Zombies, the kids called 'em. Maybe the remaining living had overslept through Gabriel's trump, and only the dead hadn't hit their snooze buttons.

His watch ticked on, second by second. The lot was empty except for the glimmer of that white Toyota. Juju kept reaching for the flask, fingertips running over a sharp engraved edge, deciding not to draw it out. Finally, unable to help himself, he began to imagine what Tip would say about all this.

You just stick with Lee, and you'll be all right.

That was comforting. It was what Juju had a mind to do anyway. Staying in the Crossing or traveling didn't make a damn bit of difference now. It might even be good to get out of the state, Christ knew he hated it, but *every* fucking place was the same when your skin wasn't whipped-cream.

And what about that French feller?

You watch him. Boy'll get snake-mean, sooner rather than later.

Which wasn't *exactly* what Tip would say. He'd more likely point out that a fucker like Brandon French would shoot you in the back if he thought he could get away with it, and let both Lee and Juju come to their own conclusions.

There was the trouble. You couldn't be *absolutely* certain of what a dead buddy would say. You could guess, sure, but you'd never know if you were right. People changed, and they could surprise you. Like Lee, falling all over himself for a Yankee girl. Or Tip himself, keeping to his word over and over again. When you found a cracker who did what he said he would, it was like seeing a fuckin' unicorn.

Juju stiffened and leaned forward, the blood draining from his cheeks. He *felt* it go, everything withdrawing from extremities and retreating to his core, fingers going cold, toes too, balls drawing up and and his scalp stitch-twitching as his hair tried to stand. Something moved in the darkness near the brick building, BUCKS on one side, DOES on the other, a breezeway around a closed-off portion in the middle for the Kiwanis to hand out coffee or the Parks Service to sell maps, the two vending machines standing dead and dark. He exhaled, his hand falling away from the flask yet again.

The thing—zombie, dead thing, critter, whatever you wanted to call it—darted from one pool of shadow to another. If not for slices of pale skin showing through ripped clothing, Juju might've missed it, because the damn thing froze for long periods of time before lunging with that eerie, gut-clenching speed. Then it would hunch again, and Juju squinted, toying with the idea of turning the headlights just to get a clear look.

Bad idea, Juju. Might be more than one.

The shape was small, and something about the way it moved said *female*. It made another one of those spooky, darting movements, and Juju realized what the fuck it was doing. Once the shapes he saw made sense, he stared, transfixed.

There was something every rest stop or restaurant parking lot had, something that followed humans over the globe, digging in accumulated detritus. Where there was food, the rats always followed.

Winter would be lean without people throwing away pizza boxes and chicken bones. Although there were bound to be plenty of corpses around, maybe the rats wouldn't go for them if they were ambulatory?

The thing halted again, and Juju held his breath, black flowers blooming over his vision and every inch of him cold as if he was outside. He forced himself to exhale again, wishing he could roll the window all the way up. To do that, he'd have to turn the key, and the parking lights would come on. No need to tell every potential attacker where there were more snacks inside a vehicle casing, no sir.

He was ready for it, but still, Juju flinched when the thing jerked forward, its bony paws closing around a bundle of struggling fur. Its arms bent, and its moon-pale face dropped. A faint crunching noise reached Juju, or maybe it was just his ears expecting and informing his brain like the good Boy Scouts they were. His stomach turned over, and bile scorched his throat. *Holy shit.*

The thing finished its meal, crouching in the lee of the brick wall. Its head came up and it sniffed, blackish stuff smeared over those flour-white cheeks, before it dropped to all fours and loped around the corner of the building, a quick insectile movement.

He was holding his breath again, Juju realized. And sweating.

For the rest of his time on watch, he didn't feel sleepy at all.

[23]

HUNT EAT SLEEP

THE CREATURE THAT HAD ONCE BEEN PENNY ELAINE EDWARDS, *running out of money on a cross-country trip, hunched and scuttled down the hill, splashing through the thin thread of running water at its bottom with an animal's instinct to break its trail. The white Toyota at the rest stop had been hers, and once or twice in the last week the creature had approached it warily, some ghost of a memory lingering in the soup of hunt-eat-sleep-hunt filling a collection of frayed nerves and twitching muscles. There was something locked in the Toyota's trunk, reeking of food, but instinctive nervousness—and the complexity of the task of opening—dissuaded the creature each time.*

It chewed as it ran, loading its stomach uncomfortably, and slowed, working halfway up another hill. The world was a grey smear in daytime, but in the darkness its filmed and useless eyes tracked any movement with uncanny accuracy. The rustle of twigs or fall of a thin droplet from naked tree branches was a clarion, echoes rippling in every direction, tiny details leaping out as sound pushed at air. The habit of using predator's forward-facing vision to track was cut deeply into its smoothing, cheese-eaten brain, so the eyes rolled uselessly to follow what it could hear.

A confusing, complex tangle of scents thickened, became a clot, and the creature with its flayed hands plunged into a dark, stinking hole. Wriggling past a narrow throat-entrance, it tumbled into darkness, and a small grinding noise welcomed it. It hunched, its hands grabbing and grasping, and when its fingers met the border of another feverish body they stopped and became gentle pats instead of claws.

Stomach-bloat squeezed, a sudden cramping, and the larger, female creature regurgitated a torrent of fur, flesh, and squirming naked tails still twitching with nerve-death, all greased with digestive fluid. The smaller moving thing—once Jonathan Edwards, on a road trip with his mother and wondering why they had to pack and leave in the middle of the night again—buried its face in the mess, slurping and chewing.

The bigger creature settled at the entrance, gnawing at a still-warm bundle of fur. After a short while, it dozed, its jaws still grinding at tiny bones. The smaller one, gorged to bursting, crept to its side and snuggled in, its mouth still working absently too.

They dozed, their ratcheting chest-deep growling taking on the quality of a purr. Jonathan had forgotten leaving behind his teddy bear Mr Stumpf, his mother's frantic insistence on flight, and the cigarette burns, healed and fresh, crawling over his arms and legs. He'd forgotten his daddy's bleary red eyes and horrifying hot breath, too. Little Jon's feverish little claws had torn his mother's shirt, his teeth working into her flesh spreading infection, and now Penny had also forgotten whatever had driven her into the Toyota and over the state line, the trunk full of thudding awful heaviness and a growling noise.

They had both forgotten fever, and landlords, fathers, and father-cigarettes with their hateful, hurtful red eyes. Now the world was simple.

Hunt to eat. Eat to sleep. Hunt again.

And again.

[24]

ACTUALLY IN KENTUCKY

Rolling hills rose on either side, patched with snow behind the thin strip of leafless trees on either side of the interstate. "God," Ginny said, despairingly, tucking a curl behind her ear and returning both aching hands to the wheel. "I'm actually in Kentucky." She leaned forward, peering out the wide, spatter-dotted windshield, and Steph laughed.

"What's wrong with Kentucky?" Mark wanted to know. "It don't look no different."

The RV was a whale, and it wallowed like one. Ginny's shoulders were tight as bridge cables, but it was better than watching Brandon drive, and at least this beast was an automatic.

Brandon was in the truck with Lee, and she was *extremely* glad she wasn't trapped in a small space with both of them. It was much better with Mark and Steph, even though they were healthy young animals confined for far too long. The kids, trading off the shotgun seat every hour with Traveller scrambling into the lap of whoever had that coveted real estate, were wide-eyed with wonder. Steph had taken trips out of state before, but Mark admitted he'd never even been over the county line.

"Nothing's really wrong with Kentucky," Ginny amended hurriedly. "I just...haven't been here before." *And never expected to visit during a zombie apocalypse.*

Scabrous dark patches dotted the countryside, winter's first snow fading as the melt deepened. The nights hovered around freezing, mornings slick until the temperature ticked upward a crucial few degrees. The RV was a lot better than camping, Ginny had to admit, but pumping gas in and waste out were hardly her favorite chores. Her mother would have been horrified; Mom's idea of travel involved a decent hotel as a bare minimum; if there wasn't a Four Seasons, she wasn't interested.

House-sitting while Mom and Dad went to the time-share in Mexico wasn't ever going to happen again, Ginny thought. Add that to the long, long list of things extinct as the dinosaurs.

Steph snorted. "Probably expect everyone to be toothless."

It was a little uncomfortable to hear it said aloud. Ginny aimed for a neutral tone and feathered the accelerator as the road rose. "Or to be riding thoroughbreds. I'm not sure this is bluegrass country yet, though. Too rocky."

Juju's black 4x4 was in the lead, its taillights weak rubies in the thin sunshine. He was cheerful, but Brandon was starting to get to *him*, too. Behind the RV was Lee's truck, a comforting red-and-white bulk peeking at her from the mirrors every time she glanced. They had the walkie-talkies, switching off front and rear every few hours to give the lead driver a rest. Each time they did, Ginny turned on the radio and let it scan both FM and AM.

Nothing. Nada. Zip. Zilch. There wasn't even static.

"That's the fourth time you've sighed," Mark said, helpfully. He scrubbed at his hair, trying to make the unruly patches lie down.

"Fifth." Steph piped up, from the seat behind. "It's my turn for shotgun, Mark."

"You can't wait until we stop?" Ginny suppressed the urge to rub at her temple or pinch the bridge of her nose to ward off a rising headache. *God, please let us stop at a hotel tonight. I want a door I can close, and a mattress that isn't made of foam.* "Fine, just...be *careful,* for God's sake."

Traveller scrambled, his tail blurring, intent on herding Steph into the seat. She'd taken to sneaking him tiny bits of Slim Jim, which led to more bathroom stops, but all the gentle scolding in the world wouldn't stop her dosing the dog with oversaturated pepperoni. *He likes it,* she'd say, her chin settling defiantly, and sneak him yet another.

He would be round as a pig soon, Ginny was sure. And the inevitable result of all that preserved grease hitting his stomach was going to be hideous. Maybe she could talk Juju into taking him for the next stretch. Steph settled into the passenger seat with a satisfied sigh and set about getting the dog settled.

Juju slowed, ahead. Ginny rubbed first at one eye, then the other. Another rest stop coming up. Juju hit his blinker, Ginny followed suit, and they crept along a slow-yourself-down stretch. She was faintly uneasy at disobeying the RV arrow-signs. It didn't matter, the world had ended and traffic wasn't a consideration, but still.

It irked her to break a law, even an inapplicable one.

This particular rest area was a lot more ramshackle than the last, and the parking lot was a broad expanse of weedy, cracked pavement without lines. Ginny hit the brakes a little harder than she meant to, and the RV rocked, protesting a little. "Oh, wow," Steph said, softly.

"What?" Mark was suddenly *there,* leaning over Ginny's shoulder to peer out the windshield. "Holy cow!"

"Get *back in your seat!*" Ginny snapped, and realized it was the same tone her mother used when either of her daughters did something potentially unsanitary and *definitely* unsafe. "And put your belt on!"

The lot wasn't empty. A gigantic black and white truck with man-high tires and an RV just as shiny and new as their own sat right in front of the restrooms. Ginny could see at least two wide-bottomed men in camouflage pants and jackets standing at the rear of that monstrous truck. They wore matching camo baseball hats, too, and both had very businesslike, very ugly-looking rifles.

Ginny let the RV slow to an idle. Juju had stopped, the 4x4 pulling slightly to the right. Lee's truck swung out and he goosed his accelerator, bringing his vehicle between the RV and the parked ones. Ginny's heart leapt into her throat and stayed there.

Oh, fuck. I have no idea what to do.

The RV's engine purred along, wheels slowing. Ginny glanced at the far end of the lot. The exit was there, partially blocked by a the wreck of a pearl-grey Subaru. Something about it bothered her, turned her stomach to mush and filled her chest with uneven, unsteady thumping.

The old song—should she stay, or should she go? It wasn't just her. It was the kids in the car too. *Bad apples, Ginny, remember?*

She twisted the steering wheel. "Is your seatbelt on, Mark?"

"We're not stopping?" He sounded much younger, the end of the question spiraling up into something perilously like a squeak.

"*Is your seatbelt on?*" She sounded like Lee, she realized, except without the drawl.

"Yes ma'am." Mark's voice cracked in the middle of the second word.

Steph clutched at Traveller, who whined uneasily. Ginny eased down on the gas, and the RV wallowed for the exit. The two armed men watched, neither of them moving, their rifles pointed loosely at the ground. Ginny's palms were soaked, and her breath came high and fast. The world tried to shrink, and Steph let out a soft, strange sound as the RV straightened itself, drew forward—and the burned-out hulk of the battered Subaru, blocking the right half of the exit, came fully into view.

It was still smoking, and the only way past it was to scrape a concrete divider on the opposite side.

Ginny pressed down on the accelerator, and the men, their mouths dropping open, brought their guns up.

• • •

It happened so *FAST*. Afterward, Ginny wasn't quite sure of the exact timeframe, but she knew one thing: they shot at the RV, bullets pinging and popping over concrete, stitching a line *awfully* close to the right-side wheels. Steph cried out, and Mark swore with breathtaking creativity Ginny might have raised an eyebrow at if the world hadn't narrowed to a pinhole and her foot stamped on the gas.

The tires barked, the engine gulped, and the RV lurched drunkenly as physics fought with all the different forces, came up with an answer, tossed it back, redid everything, and shoved the entire collection of *V8!* and *LUXURY OUTDOOR LIVING!* for the exit. The smoke from the torched grey Subaru thickened as they drew closer, and Mark whooped in a breath and yelled another string of colorful language. Traveller barked, Steph clutching the dog with hysterical strength, and Ginny's brain struggled with gauging the room on the left side of the wreck. Glass glittered sharp on concrete, cheap diamonds, and she measured the distance again.

Oh, that's not good, not good...

It was too late. She was committed now, and the RV had finally found its balance, potential energy transferred to kinetic, the tires chirping again and the engine making a deep-throated sound as gas flooded its factory-clean chambers.

Juju and Lee were both behind her. If she wrecked this giant piece of overpriced sleeps-six shit, they'd be oh God trapped, oh, *God*, the guns barked, safety glass shattered, and Steph outright howled, more from surprise than hurt. Or at least, so Ginny hoped as she hunched over the gigantic wheel, Steph folding over Traveller who thought this was all some sort of wonderful game, not even dimly understanding that *deep shit* had landed and the humans might not be able to fish themselves out, let alone him.

Metal crunched, the big blundering vehicle shouldering the wrecked Subaru aside with a deep, nasty sound, and Ginny heard someone whisper-chanting, "Please don't pop a tire, please don't pop a tire, God please God please don't pop a tire—" She barely realized it was her own voice and the speedometer's needle jerked, rising steadily. Wind whistled through broken windows, cold and bracing, and she didn't dare look at the mirrors—were Juju and Lee still behind her? Oh, *God.*

The interstate ribboned in front of her, another tangle of suspiciously placed wrecked vehicles at the end of of the ramp, but she squeezed past *those* as well, more metal crunching. *And it's practically new,* she moaned internally. *Sorry, sorry, sorry...*

Traveller wriggled and yelped in Steph's clutching arms, and the RV lunged past the last obstacle. Mark kept cussing, hysteria rising under the words, and Ginny, her constricted lungs sucking frantically at enough air to keep her conscious, kept mashing the accelerator.

And hoping.

[25]

MOMMA HAS TO EAT

"Well *damn* it." Ritchie slung his rifle and narrowed his baby blues, scratching at the back of one hand as soon as he had both free. He was shorter than his brother, but far more powerfully built. His love for processed sugar in all its forms no doubt helped. Couldn't even hit a damn tire, Jack."

His brother, scruffy blond almost-beard gleaming at the tips, considered the fleeing shapes for a long moment, finally taking his finger from the trigger. "They were already turning." He enunciated each word crisply. Their cream-colored six-sleeper, parked a safe distance from the truck, rocked a little on its springs. Webs of dull grey duct tape reinforcing the windows were holding up just fine, thank goodness, especially with the sheets and blankets taped on the inside too. "I told you firing that wreck there was a bad idea."

"We can move it. Better than havin to talk 'em up. I hate that." Ritchie glanced nervously at the RV, digging in his jacket pocket for a smooshed Ding Dong and realizing he'd already eaten it It was his turn to go inside next, and if they'd managed to bag a few, it would've been sooner rather than later. "You think..." He shifted, shaking out his hand and rubbing his right boot-toe low on his left calf, a holdover from childhood.

"I do, Rich. Leave that up to me." A deep, guttural cough shook Jack's entire body from surprisingly spindly knees to hard little beer gut and camo *America's Great* baseball cap. Red splotched his cheeks and his nose was full. Still, his own blue eyes were piercing-sharp, and narrowed. "You weren't going to suggest we do something about Momma, now, were you?"

"No! Unless it's feed her." Rich stepped back in a hurry. "You're the boss, Jackie."

"Damn right." Pickings got slim in town, that's why they rolled out here. The most nerve-wracking bit was driving the big ol' six-sleeper with Momma taped and tied; once she'd almost wriggled free on the interstate, and the last thing you wanted while you were piloting a big old bus was something mean careening around the inside. Plus, there was that grinding noise she made, deep in her chest. Like a purr, except not nearly as nice.

Jack would never admit he actually liked kittens. Not *cats*—those fuckers pissed ammonia on everything and swiped at you with their claws. They were only fit for drowning, but kittens were another ball of wax, as Momma used to say. He almost wished they didn't grow up, the same way he wished Ritchie hadn't. Things would be so much simpler if his baby brother was still a kid, instead of two pounds of idiot in a pound-and-a-half sack.

"You okay?" Ritchie gave him another one of those irritating side-long looks. He'd been doing that a lot, lately, ever since Jack began coughing and blowing his nose. The entire world had gone wackadoo, Momma was Not Herself, as they said, and there was nothing on the radio.

Nothing at all.

"Just fine." Jack finally slung his own rifle. They'd managed pretty consistently so far. Last time his brother had made trouble, refusing to shoot that one blonde cheerleader girl, and this time Ritchie's bright idea of burning the Subaru blocking the exit had turned out half-baked. He wasn't looking forward to dousing the wreck and winching it further into place, no sir.

Something would have to be done soon. Momma had to eat, after all.

Jack coughed again. His head hurt, and even though it was chilly enough to turn their breath into clouds sweat greased him all over. It was only a cold, he'd told Ritchie, not the bad flu that had done for Momma and every other blessed soul in Crampton, Kansas.

It was a good thing Ritchie was stupid enough to believe him.

...to be continued

SEASON THREE: POCALYPSE ROAD

[1]

I KILLED THE CAR

A BRAND NEW, BULLET-SPATTERED BROWN-AND-WHITE RV rollicked down the unplowed, snow-choked freeway, swaying danger-ously as it slalomed past abandoned cars clotted near exits and onramps. A black 4x4 and a white-and-red Chevy truck followed in its wake, anxious herd dogs hanging back only because cutting in to slow their charge might founder it. Melting slush splashed from miraculously unharmed tires, and after a good fifteen miles of wild motion, the RV's brake lights came on and stayed lit, ruby eyes in the glare of an early winter afternoon. Smoke and steam boiled from its front end, streaming along its brown-striped sides.

That much momentum was difficult to halt, but the RV was barely going at an idle when it kissed the shattered edge of a jack-knifed semi reclining across a heavy concrete divider. It jolted to a stop, and the hazard lights began to stutter. The sun slid behind a scrim of grey cloud and the other two vehicles came to a cautious halt as well, both with plenty of room in front, their noses pointed unerringly for the clear lane heading east and slightly north.

"God *damn* it." Broad-shouldered Juju Thurgood slammed the

black 4x4's door, all but vibrating with fury inside his fatigue jacket. Underneath, yellow stripes on his black sweater glowed. "Look at this! Just *look* at this bullshit!" The four-by's spare, held on its metal arm, was Swiss-cheese riddled. Juju flung his arms out, his pink-palmed hands knotted. "Fucking crackers!"

"You hit?" Lee Quartine barked, his window all the way down and a high blush on his stubbled cheeks from cold or adrenaline—or both. He jammed the truck's gear-lever into park and stamped on the emergency brake, barely pausing before wrestling his door open and unfolding all six-feet-odd of his lanky frame out into the cold. "Juju, you fuckin *hit?*"

That settled Thurgood something wonderful. "No. Ain't hit." He glared, hazel eyes wide and wild but full of sense, and the pompom on his blue knit cap bobbed as he shook his head. "You?"

"Watch the road." Being under fire again felt almost normal. Lee glanced back into the Chevy's cab, and the bruised blond man huddled in the passenger seat glared at him, too. *Idiot.* Big bear-shouldered Brandon French was worse than useless, but Lee had other concerns at the moment. "French, grab that first-aid kit under the seat." He set off for the RV, steam and smoke boiling from its front end. Ginny had kept it floored for a good bit, slewing around abandoned cars whenever they appeared, showing a fair bit of fancy driving. She was probably in a state, and Lee's shoulders were about to crawl up near his ears. He wasn't breathing quite right, and he'd been swearing under his breath for at least five miles. That was probably why he felt like he couldn't get a good lungful in. Probably why he was sweating, too, under every layer meant to conserve body heat.

What had tipped Ginny off and made her hit the gas away from the trap? Probably the still-smoking wreck blocking the rest stop exit. The murderous assholes had put it too far up the curve, it was plainly visible if you were in anything higher than a sedan. Lee hadn't been sure she'd make it once they started shootin'; Brandon French was fucking useless, whimper-yelling in the passenger seat without even the sense to return fire even if he'd had his damn empty carbine.

Miraculously, none of the tires on the assorted vehicles had blown. They were goddamn luckier than they had any right to be, every single mother's child of them, especially if no bullets had tumbled into flesh instead of engine or car-body.

Lee skipped the regular door halfway down the RV's long, bullet-dotted side, stalking for the front. Passenger windows were broken into glittering chunks, some of the screens on the back ones punched clean off by flying lead, and his guts seized up.

A bluetick coonhound was barking furiously. Lee grabbed for the passenger door's handle. It was locked, and the slumped form in the seat was Steph Meacham, her fine dark-to-blonde changecolor hair free of its usual scrunchie and blowing every-which-way. "Steph." He didn't even *sound* like himself, it was a dry croak. "Stephanie Meacham, you sit on up and unlock this, now."

It just proved he was a real bastard, he knew. Because what Lee was thinking was, *fine, let one of the kids get hit. Just not Ginny. Just let her be all right.*

Steph twitched. She uncurled, slowly, and her big, haunted blue eyes peered over the windowsill at Lee. Strands of her hair moved on the cold breeze. "Mr Quartine?" she whispered, a smattering of freckles glaring across her nose since she was transparent-pale. "Is it... is it over?"

"Seems to be." *They could be comin after us in that big old truck. If so, we've got a few minutes, but I don't like our chances.* Still, it was one thing to trap the unwary, and another thing to go after fore-warned and possibly armed prey. Juju's swearing drifted past, borne on a cold wind. The man was probably all but kicking his tires. "But we've got to move. You hit? Anyone in there hit?" *Please, God. I don't care what you have to do.*

Just let her be all right.

"M-M-Miz G-Ginny..." Steph straightened further, turning in the seat, and Lee's heart hit the bottom of his guts with a splash.

Christ. No. Please, no.

"I'm all right," he heard, from deeper in the RV. Hoarse, husky, and sweeter than all the angels singing to God whenever the Big Fellow had a desire for some music. "Mark? Mark, say something?"

There was another mutter from inside—Mark Kasprak, proving he was still among the living. Lee hopped up on the running board, peering into the now-mangled RV. Driven off the lot less than three days ago, dammit.

Ginny Mills, deathly pale, still clutched at the steering wheel. She stared at Lee like she didn't recognize him, her pupils wide and black, chestnut curls escaping her French braid. Her lips, slightly parted, were bloodless, and her black jacket almost swallowed her whole. Her chin trembled a little before she gulped in a shallow breath and her gaze snapped forward, and he realized she was practically standing on the brake and probably the emergency as well. The engine bumped and thumped, and more steam boiled free.

Big blond useless Brandon banged on the door midway down the RV. Steph jumped, her pupils swelling, eating at her irises. Lee almost swore, swallowed it, and reached in to get the door unlocked. Traveller, yelping and yowling, was careening all over the inside.

Dogs didn't take to upsets in their routine well. It had been nothing *but* upset for a while, despite Ginny's insistence on regular bathroom stops and mealtimes.

"Steph." Gently, firmly, Lee pitched the words low and soothing. "Let's get this door open and that seatbelt off. Come on, now."

Bad enough they had to deal with the chewing, once-human critters. Now they had to be wary of other survivors, too. The only wonder was that it'd taken people this long to start being assholes again—or that it had taken Lee and his group this long to come across said assholes.

"O-Okay." Steph fumbled at her belt catch; Mark Kasprak peered around her, his eyes huge and the rest of him cheese-pale, his dark hair standing up like it wanted to make its own break for freedom.

"What *happened?*" The boy's Adam's-apple quivered. He looked scared enough to pass out or piss himself, and Lee hoped he wouldn't do either.

We can chowder-to-cashew it later, kid. Lee settled on the most pressing question. "You hit?"

"I...I don't think so." Mark swallowed hard, again, and swayed, almost falling onto the center console. "No, I don't...What *was* that?"

"Someone who didn't want to play nice." Lee hopped down and wrenched the door open. Steph spilled out, clearly in one piece, and Traveller scrabbled right after her, hit the ankle-deep slush, and began prance-dancing in a circle, yip-barking. "*Shit.*"

"Language," Steph said faintly, and swayed. Lee propped her against the vehicle-side and was about to climb back in, but next came Mark, his hands trembling. Lee grabbed his elbow and helped him down. Back up on the running board again, almost cracking his head a good one on the top of the doorway, he pitched forward and got his feet in. The dog was running loose, but right now Lee Quartine didn't give a single damn about anything other than the woman in the driver's seat.

"Ginny. *Ginny.*"

Slowly, dreamily, Ginny put the RV in park, eased of the emergency brake. Twisted the key, and the engine died with a thankful wheeze. Then, she stilled, staring out through the cracked windshield. It was a wonder the vehicle had kept going as long as it did, there were bullet holes stitched along the side. More than likely at least one had found its way into the engine, and that was enough to make Lee sweat.

Lucky, again. Goddamn lucky. Unless she was hit, and just didn't know it. "*Ginny.*" He grabbed her shoulder. "Darlin, come on. We've got to move."

That got her attention. "Move?" Her lips were downright chalky, and she didn't even shiver at the chill coming through her own rolled-down window. Both were bad signs. "Oh. I...sorry, the car won't...it's not running well."

No shit. "You did real good, darlin. But they may be comin up the road. Grab your bag, let's go."

"Okay." She nodded. Blue veins stood out against her paleness.

She was almost transparent, like Steph. "Okay." She didn't move. Her hands clutched the steering wheel, her arms tense. Soft grey sunlight fell across her wrists, sparkling on those thin gold bangles caught below the cuff of her jacket. Tiny gold hoops in her ears, too.

Even in the middle of all this, she was so damn *city*. Soft and classy and civilized, and whatever the bastards with their big truck and sealed-up RV at the rest stop wanted, it wasn't anything nice at all if they were gonna shoot to get it. A hot complex burst of something too sharp to be relief and too crooked to be clean fury filled Lee's chest, and he had to exhale sharply to shove it back down and clap a lid on. "Ginny." He jostled her shoulder again, as gently as possible. "Come on. We've got to move."

"All right." Still, she didn't let go of the wheel; she probably thought she was moving already. Shock. If she hadn't headed for the rest stop exit, God alone knows what would have happened. There were no casualties only because she was smart, and had made the right decision under pressure.

Now ain't the time for that, Lee. "Ginny." It had to be right tone— firm, but not commanding. Gentle enough not to spook her, but sharp enough to get her attention. "Undo your seatbelt."

When she still didn't move, he hit the catch. It unrolled over her chest, and that made her look up at him.

Those big dark eyes, pupils too far dilated, were now swimming with hot water. Which made him feel twice as unsteady, his head full of colorless fumes. Just looking for a spark.

Christ. "Come on." He had to work her fingers free of the wheel. "You got anything in here you can't leave?" Most of their luggage was in the back of the truck, but she needed something to focus on.

"J-just my purse." She blinked at him, and a single tear tracked down her left cheek. Slushmelt, dripping from every surface, made a thin staticky noise while she paused. "I'm sorry. I...I think I killed the car."

"You did good, darlin." More than good, she'd done *fantastic*, especially for a civilian. He found her leather purse, its contents thankfully not scattered hither and yon, and scooped it up. "Come on. Let's get out of here."

[2]

PLUMBDAMN INSANE

"Why would they do that?" Skinny Steph Meacham hugged herself, pushing back into her seat with her legs like she thought she was driving and wanted to slow down. At least she was behind the front passenger seat and not Juju's. "Why?"

"Some people are assholes." Mark, his arm over her shoulders, glanced guiltily at Juju. It was pretty lucky a bullet hadn't made it into the four-by's engine; they'd been shooting mostly at the RV to bottle up their victims. It was a plain miracle Miz Ginny had been able to ram past the wreck blocking the exit, too.

For a librarian, that was some damn fine driving.

"That they are." Juju didn't quite have the shakes, but it was close. Nobody ever *liked* getting shot at, but it was worse when you were almost helpless, crouching in the driver's seat and praying nothing would give out while training fought with the body's idiot responses, adrenaline soaking every tissue it could reach and your balls crawling northward to find a more congenial home. Worst was trying to look everywhere at once, because tunnel vision snuck up on you. "But it don't matter why they shot at us, kids. What matters is we got away."

"Yeah." Mark, his skinny shoulders hunched, squeezed Steph again. The boy was plain gone over young Miss Meacham, and his awkward attempts at comfort probably did more to help his ownself than her. Still, it was kind of nice to see. "Everyone's okay. Lee said Miss Ginny was fine."

Traveller hunched on Steph's other side, his slobbery wet nose pressed to the back window Juju refused to have rolled down for him. The last thing they needed was the idiot hound deciding to take a header onto the highway. The dog didn't like being separated from Ginny, but he put up with it. And Juju was damn glad that French fellow wasn't in his four-by too. The blond college boy would *not* shut up, he needed Maalox for the mouth. *I don't want him in with the kids*, Lee had said, glowering, and that gave Juju a whole lot to think about.

All of it was unpleasant.

To cap it all, the season was just beginning. This melt, forgiving and sloppy as it was, wouldn't last forever, and they were heading northeast. Right through mountains, and toward winter's icy heart. Lee kept poring over atlases when they stopped, the old worry-line between his eyebrows and his expression the same as it had been in the jungle once or twice, when he was chewing on how to get his team out of yet another blood-drenched manure pile the brass had landed them in. You didn't have to worry *too* much when you were one of Little Lee's folk, long as you kept your head down and did your damn job.

But the man was not thinking straight, taking them towards the North Pole in winter during the gat-damn Pocalypse. That library gal had him all turned around. And even if she *had* done Juju a good turn or two, he was about wishing Lee had never laid eyes on her.

Tires shushed through slush; Lee's taillights ahead glowing as the truck sped up a little. In a half-hour they'd have another check-in with the walkie talkies. This stretch of freeway was deserted, and it was a nice change. Juju forced his fingers to stop clutching the wheel. His knuckles creaked but his legs were steady enough, especially since he was sitting down. Steph sniffled a little, and Mark said something in her ear, soft and soothing. The two of them were a pair of turtledoves, all right.

Christ, he wished Billy Tipton was here. He'd have a thing or two to say about Brandon French. The two of them could even suss out how to solve the damn problem for Lee. What the Lieutenant didn't know wouldn't hurt, right? You did for your own, and if he and Billy Tipton had any "own" to speak of, it was Lee Quartine.

Except Tip was dead, his head beaten in with his own flea-market lamp, and the fact that he'd been trying to chew his good buddy Juju's throat out at the time didn't change the fact of murder.

Just like nothing would change the fact that the survivors of the goddamn Pocalypse were just as likely to bite you as the walking dead. Shit was deep and getting deeper, with no shovel in sight.

The sky was getting uglier and uglier. The walkie-talkie on the dashboard crackled with formless static. French was no doubt filling up the Chevy's cab with noise, and Lee was probably wearing that faint grimace he got when brass dogs was barkin' and the shit was rollin' downhill. Traveller whined a little, and Steph patted the dog's head, smoothing behind his left ear. Mark closed his eyes, his Adam's-apple moving as he swallowed, over and over again.

There was nothing that would make this pill any easier going down.

"Mr Thurgood?" Steph's voice was a pale copy of its usual self. "Sir?"

"Huh?" A few spatters hit the windshield. It wasn't quite sleet *or* snow, a sloppy in-between mix. The Chevy slowed, brake lights brightening, and a green sign proclaiming they were ten miles from Evansboro hunched against the cold. At least they'd made it over Ole Miss.

"I got a question." Soft, and tentative.

Well, obviously. Juju swallowed a sudden hot bite of irritation. Post-combat jitters made a soldier likely to bark, if not bite, but neither of the kids deserved a toothing. "Uh-huh?"

Steph cleared her throat, nervously, then jumped right in. "You think anyone else we come across is gonna shoot at us?"

Christ, you mean you think there's a chance they won't? "I ain't sure," he hedged. Scaring the young 'uns wasn't any use, either. "But if they do, we gotta be ready."

"It's like in the movies." Mark squeezed Steph tighter, and Juju forced himself to look away from the rearview and at the road in front of them. "First people die, then the survivors go crazy."

The freeway dipped and rose gently as the slush receded from bare patches that would be ice come morning, and there was a four-car smashup looming on the horizon. Looked like it had been one of those damn checkpoints. Wouldn't that have been a shit duty, waving cars past or checking them for sick 'uns? "I ain't fixin to go crazy anytime soon, kid." Juju watched as Lee's truck swung wide, creeping around bleached bones of twisted metal.

Snow still lingered in the hollows and shadows, turning the wrecks—looked like one car had rammed another, then both had piled into a third, and the fourth who knew, maybe it had happened along later—into one of those farfetched modern art pieces. The checkpoint shack looked like something had beaten it with a hammer, frozen canvas flopping stiffly as the breeze rose. Its supports were all twisted, and he decided not to look too closely at the shapes inside.

At least those shapes weren't moving.

"Well, I mean, nobody ever *wants* to go crazy." Kasprak said it like he'd thought the matter over some.

A half-snort of laughter caught in the back of Juju's throat. He coughed, and almost spat on the windshield. "Wellnow, Mark, let me tell you somethin. Most people were plumbdamn insane before this Pocalypse. This just lets 'em all the way loose, steada worrying about what the neighbors gonna think."

Neither of them had anything to say to *that*, and it was just as well. Juju had some hard thinkin' to do and wanted some quiet to get through it. He squinted at the sky again, and turned the wipers on.

Looked like it was deciding to snow instead of sleet.

[3]

GOOD BREEDING

Evansboro was a good-sized town, clinging to the edges of "city." Its building-bones hunched dark and dispirited under a pall of falling snow, just like Ginny huddled in the middle of the Chevy's bench seat. Her hands hurt, because they kept balling up, trying to drive her fingernails into her palms. Her head hurt, too. Her shoulders, her teeth, her legs, all aching. Why? She'd only driven through a hail of bullets and several miles down a freeway before running a new RV into a jacknifed semi hunching over a concrete divider, the truck's other half squatting on a red Dodge SUV that stood with all its doors open at the tail end of a clot of smashed glass and twisted metal from the opposite direction.

It had *felt* like she was going fifty, but the airbags hadn't even deployed. She hadn't been going very fast at all.

Lee made a soft sound, not quite a whistle, one of his driving-noises. The wipers went, back and forth, clumping up wet snow along the edges of the windshield. Brandon, big, blond, and bulky on her other side, stared out the window. A faint ghost of cologne still clung to his jacket. It wasn't like Lee's peppery aftershave; Brandon's held an edge of sweat and expensive chemicals. Both of them had five o'clock shadows, though.

At least they had something in common.

She suspected it wasn't enough to get them to work together, and she couldn't figure out how to make them. A great exhaustion at the pointlessness settled over her whenever she thought about trying, too. It wasn't worth it. Was anything?

That made twice in the recent past she'd been shot at. First by the Army in Cotton Crossing as they chased one of the...the things, the shuffling, chewing infected.

The zombies.

Then, shot at again...God, why? Why would anyone who survived the past few weeks want to shoot anyone else? At least, anyone presumably healthy enough to drive?

Trying to guess why people acted the way they did was useless too, at least at this juncture. Ginny shut her eyes. Every time she did, though, she heard the little popping noises of bullets hitting thin metal and fiberglass, and felt the RV jerk under her hands. Her eyelids flew open again, and she shuddered, her shoulder bumping Brandon's.

"Hey." Brandon's large gloved mitts swallowed her right hand. The bruised left side of his face looked like it hurt. "Loosen up a little, huh?"

I can't. "Sorry," she managed. Her throat was raw-dry. Tea sounded good. Water sounded better. A hot bath and crawling into a bed, any bed, as long as the room was dark and quiet, sounded best of all. God, what she wouldn't give to be in her own house right now.

Except the power was out all over Cotton Crossing, and on the other side of the wall separating her half of the duplex from her neighbors', there were the bodies. An entire family, gone. An entire *town* gone. *Coast to coast*, the man on public television had said.

The mind boggled. Except her problem was it *didn't* boggle, she could imagine it all too vividly. "Sorry," she mumbled again, forgetting she'd already apologized. The truck bumped over ridges of snow melted, compacted, refrozen, and melted again. Chains bit deep and Lee exhaled again, concentrating on keeping them on the road.

"Don't be." Brandon considered her hand for a second, then stripped his right glove off, pulling on the fingertips with his teeth. With that done, he got her glove off as well, which meant she had to spread her fingers. They kept wanting to curl back up, but he patiently undid them each time. After a little while he got her left glove off too, and his own. His skin was warm, and he stretched her fingers out, rubbed between them. "My mom had arthritis," he said, finally, blue eyes half-lidded. "I used to help her, massage her fingers and stuff. We weren't supposed to, but she said it felt good." His head dropped forward. With his chin down and the longer top of his blond hair falling across his forehead, he looked very young. The puffing and bruising from Lee's punch would take a while to go down. "Dad said she just wanted a young man to hold her hand."

A faint, ghostly smile touched Ginny's lips. "They sound nice." Unlike the twisted, jumbled car wrecks Lee was piloting them through. They were everywhere.

"Yeah." Brandon spread her left-hand fingers, gently manipulated her thumb. "They were. Until..."

"Until." Another shudder went through her, less intense. Her teeth didn't hurt quite so much—she hadn't even realized how hard she was clenching her jaw. Dental care was likely to be nonexistent for the foreseeable future. "My mom called. Before all this. I couldn't get to the phone." She swallowed, heard a dry click from her own throat. "I wish I had."

"Where exactly are your parents?" For once, Brandon's tone was quiet, without any bluster. He didn't look at her, gazing at her fingers as if they were the most interesting thing in the world. "I mean, I know you said New York, but what part of the city?"

"Oh." She shut her eyes again, and this time the pock-pock of bullets and the metallic taste of terror didn't replay in her head. Instead, she felt him working on her hands, rubbing gently, stretching her fingers with careful pressure. The darkness behind her lids was calmer, now. "No, they're upstate. Near Saratoga Springs."

"Oh. I thought you meant the city itself." A short pause. He rubbed at the pad under her thumb. Maybe his hands weren't scorching, maybe it was that she was cold all over. "That's a long way from here."

"I would have gone by myself, but Lee said no." She darted a quick glance at Lee. He leaned forward a little, hazel eyes a few shades paler than usual, peering through the windshield; his own capable hands gentle on the wheel. He might as well have been alone in here, for all the attention he was paying to either of them. His profile was set, and he wasn't pale or upset-looking at all. It was like getting shot at was normal, for him.

She was grateful for his calm, but at the same time...it was disturbing.

Everything about this was disturbing. She'd thought she was holding up well, but now...

"Well, of course he did." Brandon didn't bother looking at Lee. Instead, he kept watching Ginny's hands. His fingers had cooled down, or hers had warmed up. "A gentleman doesn't let a lady go off through a zombie-infested wilderness all on her own."

Her face felt strange. Funny and tight, her cheeks bunching up a little. She realized she was trying to smile, but it didn't feel like her expression at all, wooden and false. "Is that Southern charm?"

"Nah. It's just good breeding." A crooked smile, and Brandon glanced at her. Outside his window, the light was failing, dusk creeping between wrecks and rising buildings. "Better?"

She nodded, stretching her fingers. They didn't want to immediately curl up again. It was a relief, and her shoulders were not quite as tense. "Thanks. I just..."

"You saved everyone's life." It was a little awkward, him holding her wrist like that while he shook out her glove. He pulled it back on for her, snugging between the fingers with a quick combing motion. "That was some real stunt driving."

"It was accidental." There. It was out. It was said. If anyone complimented her on saving them, she would have to start screaming. "I couldn't think of what else to do. We're lucky the RV could get over on the shoulder. If it couldn't—"

"You did right," Lee said, a little too loudly. His eyes had lightened again, a yellowish glare. Maybe he wasn't as calm as he looked. "No good to second-guess it."

Ginny nodded. But oh, she didn't believe it. A few tendrils of her hair had escaped the morning's braid, falling into her face, and she fought the urge to bend over, rest her head on the dashboard, and cover her ears. Shutting the rest of the world out sounded *wonderfully* enticing.

Brandon got her other glove on. "He's right." He patted her hand, a quick one-two tap. "There you go. Better, right?"

"Yeah." Her shoulders relaxed a little, then a little more. "Thanks, Brandon."

"Anytime, Ginny." His grin was lopsided, probably because one side of his face hurt. His left eye was almost puffed shut, and the bruise was glaring. Lee certainly hadn't held back.

Lee hit the turn signal, and they drifted slowly into the sloppy, icy wasteland of a Marriott parking lot. The hotel, a large white bulk, towered over them, its ranks of windows gazing blankly out at a world that had spun all the way off its axis. "Miss Virginia." Harshly. "You gonna stay in the truck while we sweep the place?"

Was he angry at her? Or just worried? Here she was, all shaky, while he had to drive *and* find them a place for the night. Jeez. "Of course."

"Good," he said, and the silence inside the cab thickened like the snow.

[4]

GETTING ALONG

"Mr Thurgood?" Steph, her arms full, peered over the top of a brown paper bag. Wispy, neatly pinned braids crossed the back of her head in imitation of Ginny's—they were too short to make a crown—and it suited her. The pink in her cheeks from up and down staircases did too. "Where you want this?"

Juju pointed at the room he and Lee would be sleeping in, its door propped open. A lantern glowed, set carefully on the pink and green carpet, lighting up the brass numbers on every door. "Right over there. Thanks." He glanced down the hall, and irritation rasped down his back. "What in God's name is that idjit doin?"

Brandon French stood near the stairs, his big shoulders set and his thumbs in his jean pockets, studying the wall like there was art hung on it or something. The door bumped, and Steph swung her flashlight on her hurried way back to push it wide for Mark, laden with a box of ammo French should have been helping to carry. The boy tripped on his way through, another lantern set on the landing below casting crazy shadows on the ceiling as he teetered on the edge of collapse. Steph grabbed at the other side of the box, trying to hold the stairwell door with one hip at the same time, and Juju strode down the hall, his boots mashing carpet thicker than the stuff in his living room at home.

If he still *had* a home. Tip's body was upstairs in a bedroom over the state line, and Juju was left to deal with this pile of shit. No reason to stay in the Crossing with Tip gone and Lee haring off, but he hadn't signed up for *this*.

Well, there was what you signed up for, and what you got, and Juju's sainted grandmother had known the difference. What was more, she taught it to her Jujube-boy, and Christ knew she was the only one who'd cared enough when he was below six feet tall.

Son of a bitch. He got his hands under the edge of the box, and Mark let out a whooshing breath. The boy looked about ready to faint, bright crimson dotting his cheeks. His acne was clearing up wonderfully, though. The end of the world agreed with him. "Careful," Mark gasped. "It's heavy."

"It sure is." Steph flattened herself against the wall, trying to get out of the way and hold the heavy fire door at the same time. "Why we gotta carry this up every night anyway?"

"So we have it if the critters come walkin on up to our bedrooms," Juju said, shortly, and heavy cardboard dug into his forearms. Mark's feet tangled again—the kid couldn't see where he was going, plus the door kept trying to close on him and Steph, scooting both of them into the hall —and Juju stepped sideways as the box shifted, trying to get *under* it.

"Makes sen—oops!" Steph's hip banged the door again, and the box tipped dangerously. One corner poked Juju hard in the shoulder, and he pitched back and to the side, trying to get under the damn weight again. If you could just get the right angle, all sorts of things could be carried.

Unfortunately, though, the movement dumped him right into Brandon French's back. Later, Juju would think maybe he hadn't quite tried to stop himself, and maybe it was satisfying to hear the man hit the wall.

"Sonofabitch!" Juju barked. Bad language in front of the kids; his conscience pinched, there was no help for it. They probably heard worse at school anyway.

No more school for them. Well, unless you counted God's own academy of Real Life. Juju figured they were all in college now, and the grading was a regular old bitchkitty.

Mark bolstered the other side of the damn box, and between the two of them they got the sagging cardboard wrestled into the room and onto the closest bed's rose-colored duvet. The heavy corrugated fiber was damp, and the entire thing needed repacking in something sturdier if they could find it.

Now wasn't that a metaphor for current events.

Steph trailed in their wake, stray wisps of hair working free of her braids, all but wringing her small, fine-boned hands. Juju shook his head while he straightened, rubbing at his lower back like an old woman, and turned to find Brandon French filling up the door, shoulders wide and the same sullen look on his bruised face Juju had seen on a thousand other crackers.

"What the fuck did you say to me?" Brandon barked. The last of the dying winter evening sent a few faint gleams through the room's French door, and yet another Coleman on the nightstand glowed comfortingly.

"I didn't say nothin." Juju shook out his hands, loose and ready, tiny hairs on his nape tingling as they tried to rise. "What you doin just standin around? Even the kids is workin." He didn't add *you asshole* to the end of the last sentence only through sheer force of will. Sweat collected on the curve of his lower back and the first jolt of the day's adrenaline was coming back, sour metal filling his mouth and his heart settling into a gallop.

Mark, bent over trying to catch his breath with his hands on the box, looked very young, peering at Brandon and hunching his skinny shoulders even further. No help there, and Steph, bless her heart, wasn't any either. Juju braced himself.

"I was *thinking*," Brandon retorted. "Someone around here has to." A ratlike gleam filled his good blue eye, and the one puffed shut held a matching spark. "*You* help them, boy."

There it was, that hateful little syllable. *Boy*. Juju's hands ached, and the thought—*got me a rifle, and this motherfucker needs a lesson*—was quite natural. His hand dropped to his sidearm instead, and Steph gasped.

"You gonna shoot me?" Brandon's smile wasn't nice at all, shadows filling the dips and hollows of his sneer. "You gonna, huh, *Juju?*" Drawing out each syllable. *Juuuuuujuuuuuu.* "That what you gonna do, *boy?*"

Oh, I'd sure like to. "Ain't worth the bullet, *Brandon*."

Steph's hands flew to her mouth, two tiny birds looking for shelter. Mark, his cheeks now ugly brick-red instead of crimson with effort, stared at the box on the double bed, its corners mashed and its bulk making the mattress sag. They weren't gonna be any damn help, but Juju was past the point of caring.

Or so he told himself.

"You better 'pologize." Brandon's face suffused with plum-colored hate. "For runnin into me."

Oh, hell no. "Soon's you 'pologize to the kids for leavin them to hassle everything up alone." A little voice that bore a suspicious likeness to his grandmother's was trying to tell Juju to calm down, to drop his gaze, to get along.

Well, the world wasn't what it had been, and Juju was *sick* of gettin along.

"I'm sorry," Steph Meacham squeaked, through shaking fingers. Her blue eyes were the size of saucers, and her slim hands worked at each other, an unconscious washing motion. "I bumped him into you, Mr French."

A ringing silence fell, the quiet after a stinging slap. Mark Kasprak stiffened, visible in Juju's peripheral vision, and he wondered which way the boy was gonna jump. It was all Juju could do not to clear leather and solve the fucking problem of this shitheel once and for all.

Brandon measured Juju one last time. He raised his right hand, stiffly, and pointed—a jabbing, accusatory little motion. "Imma get you, *boy*."

"When you think you man enough, cracker." It wasn't the wisest thing in the world, and if the world hadn't gone to shit in a shuttle Juju probably wouldn't have said it.

But here they were. Home was behind them, and without backup, the Kentucky college boy maybe wasn't as powerful as he thought he was. Maybe Lee would come down on the bastard so Juju didn't have to, and if he didn't, probably all Juju had to do was mention Miz Ginny.

It wasn't right to play dirty, and it wasn't fair, but when you were dealing with the massive bloat of a white-man ego, you did your belt and your suspenders, too. Lee was good folk, but you could never be sure a paleface would do what he ought.

Even if you called him your brother.

Brandon pitched forward, like he was going to come on into the room, getting ready for a tango. Then he glanced at Steph, and Kasprak. Whatever he saw there didn't make him brave enough, Juju guessed, because the idiot turned on his heel and strode away down the darkened hall, smacking the wall once or twice for good measure. Brandon's blundering passage was that of every balked bigot since time began, and Juju let out a long breath, his hands still itching. It wouldn't take much to step out into the hall and draw a bead.

Not much at all.

"You shouldn't have said that," Kasprak said, heavily, finally straightening. The brick-color was draining from his cheeks leaving them cottage-cheesy. He rubbed his hands over his hair, ruffling it up like a cartoon halo. "Oh, man."

"Shut up, Mark." Steph Meacham rounded on him, her arms swinging angrily. "How could you just stand there with him talkin to Mr Thurgood like that?"

The kid blinked owlishly, his jaw dropping a little. He yanked on the cuffs of his expensive new coat, pulling the sleeves down. "What?"

"Never mind. Mr Thurgood?" Anxious, wide-eyed, the girl took two nervous steps and ended up next to Juju. "You okay? He's awful mean. Imma tell Miz Mills."

Go runnin to the teacher. Juju shook his head. You couldn't tell which way a damnyankee librul would jump when the chips hit the fan, either. "Ain't gonna do a bit of good. Just be careful." Might as well give all the warnings, now. "Don't you be alone around that man, Steph. You hear me?"

"Hey." Mark, a faint objection. "That's...what d'ya mean, don't be alone around him?"

"You either, Kasprak." Juju headed for the door, shaking his head. *And I sure as hell won't be alone with that bastard unless I have a full clip and one in the chamber.* "Let's finish the haulin."

[5]

SAFE SECOND

DINNER WAS A SOBER AFFAIR. KASPRAK DIDN'T LAUGH, TOO BUSY
hunching his broadening shoulders and casting worried looks at
Steph. The girl was quiet, her blue eyes moon-huge, and Juju had
retreated into familiar post-combat taciturnity. Even Brandon was
morose, though he made a show of collecting the paper bowls for the
garbage bag after everyone was done.

At least the college boy had helped Ginny feel a little better, even
if Lee could have cheerfully chopped both his big manicured hands
right off. Taking off a woman's gloves—did he learn that at school, or
was it one of the secret things rich boys were told? It seemed indecent, but maybe that was only because Lee wouldn't have thought of
it and besides, needed both his own paws for driving.

If only he'd thought of it, though. Lee had been too damn busy
sitting there in a cold sweat thinking of what *could* have happened to
her instead of figuring out she'd need a bit of...comfort. Something.
Anything other than to sit there ignored until the rich boy took it into
his head to touch between her pretty fingers and tell stories about his
mama.

The hotel was cavernous and silent, one half of the glass front door shattered and the check-in desk a bullet-riddled ruin. There wasn't anyone in the place; near as Lee could figure, someone looking for loot had come through. Why they chose a hotel rather than stores or gas stations in whatever place the rich of this town settled was beyond him, but it took all types to make the world go round, as his sainted Nonna said more than once with varying degrees of disapproval each time.

Nobody asked why he didn't have them staying in houses instead of looking for hotels or grocery stores. Juju would know, of course, but the rest of them probably didn't think about it, just followed his lead. Maybe Ginny would figure out it was to cut down on potential contact with the critters, she was smart enough.

It wasn't anything he wanted her thinking on. People tended to crawl home to die; there was less chance of them hanging out in a hotel. The last thing Lee's squad needed was the surprise appearance of a shambling almost-corpse, chewing and making that awful grinding noise.

Ginny didn't eat much. Her pretty face looked downright haunted, and she didn't make any sort of trouble over staying in the truck while Lee and Juju swept the hotel. Nor did she try to draw Steph out, or comfort Mark. She barely patted Traveller's head, but the dog was just fine with that as long as he could lean against her shin and beg for a treat or two. He ate more of her preservative-laced cold cuts and cheese than she did, and that was worrisome.

No power was worrisome too, but they had the Colemans, and there was no shortage of fuel. Yet. After a while, he was going to have to start thinking about fire just like a caveman.

Food, fire, protection. At least they weren't fighting off the critters in the dark with sticks.

Yet.

Lee decided the third floor was best for all of them, and after dinner everyone set to carrying up the rest of the baggage and supplies for the night while Juju muttered about barricading the shattered front door or the stairwell exits. The kids skipped the usual malarkey, and Brandon did his fair share for once. Which was great, it was wonderful, it was fantastic—but Lee was not happy. At all.

He finally got a chance, though, when Ginny took Traveller out near the hotel pool. The chain link fence surrounding it wouldn't be a problem to a bored or halfway determined hound, but with the snow coming down and Ginny standing in the doorway, he didn't think it too likely Trav would wriggle out even if his nose did catch a hint of something fine. The day's excitement had tired everyone out, even the dog.

Lee stood just behind Ginny, looking down at the top of her head wrapped in a pair of braids she'd done before dinner, hands moving quick and deft. A pretty crown for a pretty girl. Her shoulders slumped, and she leaned against the side of the door like it was too much trouble to stay upright.

Shit. He glanced at the pool. Nobody was going to swim in *there* for a while. Already the chlorinated water was frozen, since the pump and heaters were out of commission. Traveller watered the side of a stack of white plastic deckchairs. Might as well have been a tree, for all the dog cared.

Lee's hands itched. Finally, he lifted the left one, and closed it around Ginny's shoulder. Gently. There was a trembling going through her, humming high voltage.

Was she crying? Oh, *hell.* Lee made sure his rifle was well out of the way and tugged on her shoulder. She turned, willingly, and he didn't have to do anything. She buried her face in his chest, and she wasn't crying, really. Just...shaking. Her faint sniffle could be from the weather, the temperature was dropping right quick now that darkness had crawled out of its hole.

"It's all right," he said, keeping an eye on the dog's tail, wagging businesslike as Traveller stuck his nose under a blue plastic cover shrouding another stack of deckchairs. "It's all right, Ginny."

"It's not." Plaintive, muffled against his coat and his rifle strap. "It's *not* all right. Someone could *die*, Lee."

So she'd finally realized as much. He'd been waiting for that particular point to hit home, *really* home, for her. Now that it had, he wasn't sure he liked the result. The unsteady looking-for-a-spark feeling inside his chest and skull meant he wasn't quite calm, and she needed him steady.

They all did, but Ginny *especially*. Or maybe he just wanted to be that way, for her. What would be the most soothing? He settled for bare fact. "I ain't gonna let that happen." *Well, unless it's Mr French. Motherfucker can vanish, that would suit me fine.* That would be the wrong thing to say, though.

Ginny shook her head, slightly. "You might not be able to do anything about it." Her trembling paused, resumed, a little less intense. Her chin was against his rifle strap, and he hoped the tough webbing wasn't rasping at her skin.

Been doing all right so far. That wasn't the point, though. "Well, guess I'll just do what I can." He hunched a little, and rested his chin lightly on her braided hair. "You did a good job today, Ginny. Now listen. You listenin to me?"

"Y-yes." One pale, sighing little word.

"Right this second, there ain't nothin to worry about. We're safe, we have food, and even the dog is fine." He paused, glancing at the whirling snow, the dog's businesslike tail-wagging. "And look at that, another safe second." Another pause. "Another one there, too."

"Is that what you do?" Thankfully, the words didn't break or tremble. She was calming down. Maybe he was doing all right. "Just... second by second?"

"It gets easier with practice." His stubble scraped at the edge of her braid. Soft, silken hair, even unwashed. If she relaxed a little, *he* could. Or at least, the fumes in his head could settle a bit. He didn't much like the idea that he could explode if even a hint of heat hit. "Getting shot at shakes you up, takes a while to come down."

"I feel like a coward," she whispered, like it was a secret.

Do you now? "Darlin, that is the *last* thing I'd call you."

That seemed to be the right thing to say, because she relaxed all at once, leaning into him. "What's the first?"

"I'll tell you later." Lee shifted a little, leaning back on his heels. Not because he wanted to pull away, but because a few parts of him were *very* aware of both an adrenaline hangover *and* a soft, slim, very pretty woman right up close. She still smelled clean, though none of them were particularly fresh. Just the slightly spicy odor of a healthy female, one he wanted to curl up around and simply breathe in for a good long while. "Right now, look. Another safe second."

Her shoulders dropped. "And another one." A little more confident. "That helps."

"Soon enough you'll be able to get whole minutes going." *You never get the hang of weeks, though. Leastways, I never have.* Maybe she would, if he could keep steady enough.

Her sigh took them both by surprise, a deep, hitching exhale. "Sounds like a useful skill."

He expected a betraying little movement to tell him she was done being held, but none came. She shifted to rest her cheek against his rifle strap, and her breathing evened out. The wonderful simmering scent of her hair brushed his face, loosening every string inside him. Traveller shook slush out of his coat and trotted for them, yip-yowling his commentary on the damp, his dinner, and everything else in the blessed world.

Lee couldn't help himself. He pressed his lips onto the top of her head, gently. Maybe she'd think it was still his chin. His arms tightened, and he hugged her the way he'd wanted to for long, long time. Ginny's arms slipped around him, and, wonder of wonders, she hugged back.

They stood like that, in the door of a darkened hotel, until Traveller shouldered past them to get inside and shook, ridding himself of slushwater. That meant Lee had to close things up, and Ginny busied herself drying Traveller off with harsh white hotel towels, scrubbing at the hound's undercarriage and murmuring *who's a good boy*. Her cheeks were flushed, and when she glanced up at Lee, she smiled, tentatively.

His face felt strange, because he was grinning like a fool, too.

[6]

THE DECENT THING

"It ain't right." Steph's chin set, her sharp-pretty face pale as milk as she stood in the doorway. "He threatened Mr Thurgood, and Mark just stood there." It was hard to tell which disturbed her the most. She clasped her hands; her knuckles turned white and you could almost hear the joints creak. Faint pink nail polish, carefully applied but now chipped and cracked, gleamed a little.

Current events were hard on the manicure.

"Threatened him?" Ginny pushed a stray curl away, tucking it behind her ear as she patted at her cheeks with a towel. A tealight candle on the bathroom counter gave enough golden glow to see by, falling into the mirror and multiplying. It smelled of bleach and dampness in here, the first from the stacked towels and the second from the hotel standing empty. It was amazing how soon rooms became stale without someone breathing in them.

At least this place had been nice before the disaster. The maroon carpet was thick enough to lose a dime or two in, the beds were likely to be comfortable, and if she couldn't sleep alone at least she'd be warm. She'd almost gotten used to Steph's slightly whistling breath at night.

"Said he was gonna *get* him." Steph's expression hovered between worry and relief, switching back and forth as thoughts raced through. It was amazing, Ginny thought, how open someone's face could be, especially a young someone. "And he wasn't talkin about no Christmas present."

At least the pipes weren't frozen here; Ginny set the towel aside, twisted the faucet off, and wrung out the washcloth halfway, again. Traveller's ears perked; two sharp raps on the room door made Steph jump.

It was only Lee, his hair ruffled and his hands washed, on his usual nightly visit to "get them settled." Ginny drew him into the room, the sopping washcloth in her hand and her headache intensifying. It was probably normal to stress-cry after a day that included being shot at, but at least Steph hadn't noticed one of the adult losing their cool; a cold cloth to the face worked wonders when a girl needed to camouflage.

He didn't need a neon sign to tell something had happened. Lee took a long look at her, hazel eyes back to dark but piercing, and his hair was beginning to fall stubbornly over his forehead. "Ginny? Somethin wrong?"

"You mean, something *else*?" She tried for a smile, but her face simply wouldn't cooperate. The urge to lean forward, rest her forehead on his shoulder, and close her eyes once more was almost overwhelming. A girl could get used to that faint, slightly lemony smell on a man. "Tell him," she said, and retreated to the bathroom again, smoothing icy-wet terrycloth over her face. It felt good, and she listened as Steph haltingly described Brandon's latest bad behavior.

Christ. Getting shot at in the morning and having to deal with this bullshit at night. Why did things have to be so goddamn *difficult*?

Then she felt like an idiot for even thinking such a thing in the middle of a disaster zone full of the walking dead. Were there places the…the sickness hadn't reached? Enclaves that hadn't been infected?

Her head ached too badly to pursue that line of thought. They didn't say *coast to coast* on public television for a few scattered sniffles. Was the entire continent...but she didn't want to think about that, either. She had to leave the bathroom's safety; Steph was finishing her story.

Lee listened quietly, his arms folded and his head cocked, and his eyes had lightened once more. "Pointed at him," he repeated, slowly and distinctly. Almost like a lawyer, repeating what he already knew, giving his interlocutor time to think of more. Seen in profile, with his hair mussed and his cheeks scuffy, he was no longer the slightly oddball library patron. Instead...well, he was something else. "And said *Imma get you.*"

"Yeah." Steph hugged herself. She'd taken her pins and rubber bands out; her changecolor hair was now full of soft waves. *If I'd a known it was so simple I'd a worn it like this all the time,* she'd said when Ginny showed her how to pin the braids across the back of her head. "Mr Thurgood said it wouldn't do any good to tell, but...I'm worried, Mr Quartine. Real worried." Did the girl know, could she guess, how obvious it was she was braced for an adult not to believe her?

God, Ginny remembered that feeling from her own teenage years. She also remembered Brandon's warm fingers on hers, working out tension, soothing. How could he do that, then turn around and threaten Juju afterward?

Bigots could be nice, they could even be kind. It didn't change the ugly parts. Brandon didn't pull his weight, that much was obvious too. To be absolutely, strictly honest, Ginny didn't *like* him. He was a blowhard and yes, a racist. And just what had he been doing, testing doorknobs in the middle of the night while the zombies roamed outside? It *had* to have been him rattling at the door.

There was being fair to someone you didn't particularly get along with, and then there was this. Juju would call it a bad apple, and Ginny agreed. Maybe that morning she would have tried to gloss over this, make it all right, convene a meeting to talk it out. Bend over backward to be scrupulously, blindly just.

Not now. "You did the right thing," Ginny heard herself say. "This is something we needed to know about."

Perhaps she sounded strange, because they both looked at her. Steph's hands halted their scrubbing at each other, and her shoulders relaxed a little, then a little more. Her bare toes, painted pink like her fingernails, looked cold.

Lee, on the other hand, hunched slightly, new weight resting on him. "Ayuh," he said, finally. "It is."

"Mr Thurgood told both of us not to be alone around him," Steph added. A good little student, reciting for extra credit.

"Did he now." Lee nodded thoughtfully. Gold gleamed along his stubble. His jacket, unzipped, showed a blue sweater, the kind with leather patches at the elbows and two buttons at the neck. He was probably wearing that old, worn leather vest underneath it. No rifle, but a handgun, right on his belt. "That's good advice. Go on and get ready for bed, Steph. Ginny, you mind steppin outside with me?"

Gee, I'll have to ask my chaperone. "There's no need for discussion; I think Mr French should go his own way." That, Ginny decided, was putting it mildly. Maybe that was all she'd have to say and by morning the problem would be solved.

Was it just the tiniest bit lazy or cowardly of her to hope so? Frankly, with the headache, she didn't care. She didn't even care about Lee's gun in plain sight, and that was a new, worrisome development. So many troubling things were getting to be usual.

"No stickin together?" Lee ducked his head a little, maybe surprised she didn't want to discuss the damn issue.

"Not if he's going to threaten one of us." Another funny thing, how she could delineate *one of us* from *not one of us*, and who was on which side of the line. One of those things you learned in a disaster, maybe.

Or maybe she was simply tired of all the bullshit.

It was downright disconcerting when Lee's eyes lightened up and he looked so intensely at something. That gaze could burn holes in concrete, especially when his eyebrows came together a little and his jaw hardened. "I thought you'd need convincin."

Steph closed the bathroom door, which meant the only light was from the pair of emergency candles in heavy glass holders on the room's flimsy table, pulled away from the window and its long, buff-colored drapes.

Ginny restrained the urge to pinch at the bridge of her nose *or* start swearing. Or possibly both. The very idea was wonderfully therapeutic. "I'm not stupid, Lee."

"Indeed you are not." He rubbed a his cheek, fingertips scraping on that six o'clock shadow, before recrossing his arms firmly. He looked deceptively lean, but standing this close she was very aware of his wide shoulders and the amount of leashed strength in that rangy frame. "But I was gonna ask about movin him on his way tonight or in the morning."

"Oh." God, wouldn't today ever *end?* All she wanted was to crawl into the tightly made bed, close her eyes, and pretend that something, *anything* about this was okay. Or normal. Or sane.

"At night's when the critters seem more active," Lee continued. "Maybe lettin him go in the morning and gettin some distance would be best."

"You're right." Still...what if Brandon tried something tonight? Her headache intensified, something she hadn't thought possible until that very moment. Even her *hair* hurt. "Maybe you lock your door too, and don't go downstairs to, you know, keep watch? If you do, someone's alone. That's not good." Besides, the stairwell doors were blocked, in defiance of the fire codes.

Not that there would be an inspector around anytime soon.

"Don't like it either way." His eyes narrowed, and it occurred to her that he probably had his own headache. Nobody asked him how he was doing, or visibly worried over his state of mind. They piled decisions on him, all day, and he didn't seem to mind much...but still.

Ginny touched the back of his left wrist, damp fingertips on his warm skin. "I'm sorry."

"For what?" Honestly baffled, he peered at her. Traveller sat down and leaned against his leg, gazing at her too; Lee didn't push the dog away. Instead, he shifted his weight slightly, answering the pressure, letting Traveller know he was welcome.

Such a little thing, to tell you everything you needed to know about Lee Quartine. Just like this latest incident told you everything you needed to know about Brandon. Ginny balled up the washcloth. It would be satisfying to pitch it across the room, but not very mature. "If I hadn't invited him along, none of this would have happened."

"You did the decent thing, Ginny." Quiet and level, meaning every word.

Of course, Lee Quartine didn't say things he didn't mean. One more thing to like about him, when you could get him to talk.

"Maybe I shouldn't have." Good Lord. Had that really come out of her mouth? A zombie apocalypse was really bad for your ethics.

"Nah. That bit's my job, darlin. Get some rest." He paused at the door. "Make sure you use the deadbolt, now."

"Yes, sir." She didn't salute, but it was close, and his brief, tight smile was a reward. She *did* lock the deadbolt, and wondered if he waited outside the door to make sure.

Probably. He was like that.

Steph peered out of the bathroom, a gleam of suppressed cheer in her blue eyes. "He *really* likes you, Miss Ginny."

"Maybe he's just a gentleman." *Good breeding*, Brandon had said. The English teacher would probably be a lot happier on his own, or he'd find other survivors. People like him always landed on their feet, right? "I don't think we'll be traveling with Mr French for much longer."

The girl let out a long, soft breath. "Ain't *that* a relief." She shook out her small, fine hands, every trace of anxiety washed away.

It must be nice to be able to turn off the worry-tap like that. "Yes." Ginny's head hurt too badly to feel anything but the deep desire to crawl into bed. "Brush your teeth, sweetie."

"Yes ma'am."

Ginny thought she'd have no trouble passing out. Instead, she lay in the dark, watching the shadows from the candle in the bathroom and listening to Steph's deep breathing from the other bed. Traveller twitched as he dreamed his doggie dreams near her knees, sprawled with supreme unconcern. Shadows danced, the eerie silence closing around their tiny island of sanity was large, and for the first time in a very long time, Ginny Mills felt very, very small.

[7]
CUTTING DEADWEIGHT

THE PREVIOUS NIGHT'S SNOW AND SPATTERS OF SLEET HADN'T amounted to much; the clouds had decided to warm up a little instead of dumping their cargos, so morning was full of the slithering of melt and larger patches of wet but clear concrete in the parking lot. Good traveling weather, though he didn't like the way the wind tasted when it veered northward. At least Lee got a cup of coffee and a reasonable breakfast before the disagreeableness started in the hotel's busted foyer.

"I don't *believe* this." Brandon puffed up in front of the elevators, the bruise up his face garish-colored and his blue eyes blazing, and for a moment Lee thought the college boy was going to cause even more problems. "You can't make me leave." It didn't look like French had slept much, between the tangle of his unwashed hair to the bags under his unwounded eye. His coat still showed marks from his ridiculous backpack, and the scruffy-unshaven made him look a little older than he was.

Older. Not more mature. It was a damn good thing he'd told the college boy to bunk alone last night, even if Juju's baked beans had been doing their work with a vengeance.

"Ain't no need for fuss, Mr French." Lee stood, loose and easy, his right hand close to his hip just in case. "You can find yourself a car and be on your way." There wasn't any shortage of vehicles lying around, that was for damn sure.

"But why?" Injured innocence shone from the man's swell-distorted face. He glanced past Lee—the others, in a tight knot around a Coleman lantern in the cavernous dark foyer and occupied with their own breakfasts, were uneasily quiet except for Traveller, who was begging hard for the remains of whatever Juju had in his bowl. Mark kept glancing over, perplexity written across his beaky face. Steph huddled on the other side of Ginny, finishing the steady consumption of a whole box of strawberry-frosted toaster pastries. Girl had a sweet tooth. "What's going on?"

For Christ's sake. How much clearer did Lee have to be? "You're not travelin with us anymore. That's all."

"Well, where the hell do you expect me to *go?*" The English teacher—if that's what he really was—started getting loud, maybe thinking volume would change Lee's mind or somehow overwhelm him.

Lee forced himself not to shrug. He'd been yelled at by the best, and this chickenshit was nowhere in that league. "Ain't my problem."

Brandon glanced past him again, and it became obvious why a few moments later. Ginny, twin braids hanging down her back and her coat unzipped, halted next to Lee, her hands wrapped around her travel mug. A paper slip fluttered—the teabag-tag, a fancy heavy one, hanging outside the screw-on top. *Earl Grey.* Smelled like perfume, but she seemed to like it. Maybe it was a girl thing? They liked frilly stuff, strange smells, different tastes.

Mysteries, every damn one of them. At least this jumped-up jackass was something Lee knew how to handle.

"Ginny?" Brandon turned the charm on, smiling like a man whose credit card was no longer working. Spreading his hands a little, tilting his head. "He's saying I can't travel with you anymore. What's going on?"

Her eyebrows rose. "Do you really not know?" Dead level, her mouth set, she might have been back in the library, dealing with someone who Had Ideas, as Lee's Nonna would have said. She lifted her mug, took a decorous sip.

Lee was glad she'd never unleashed that look on him. Very little stung like a woman measuring you and visibly finding you short.

"You're a liability." Lee stepped forward—not much, just a bit, to keep himself on the front line. "There ain't no need for anything other than goin your way."

"I don't *believe* this," the man repeated. His face probably hurt, the way he was working it. Like a rubber mask, trying to squinch itself into the right expression. "For what? Seriously, what is wrong with you people?"

"Please." Ginny, soft but inflexible. "Just go, Brandon. We're done."

"Ginny. Come on. Please. What did I do?" French looked honestly perplexed. Still, Lee would bet cash he at least suspected, and was hoping to gut his way out of it.

If Ginny was traveling alone, how much would she have put up with from this fellow? He didn't want to think about that.

"Do you really think you could threaten one of us and still ride with us all day?" Ginny's mouth turned down at the corners. "Really?"

"Threaten? Threaten who?" But the man's expression changed by a critical few degrees.

Lee wished Ginny wasn't standing so close, and further wished she'd just let him handle this. There was no use *talking* about it. The longer French had to work himself up, the worse he'd get.

"You've been nasty and dismissive to Mr Thurgood all along." Soft but relentless, Ginny's look hadn't changed at all. "And yesterday, you threatened him. That's unacceptable, Brandon."

"What? No way." Hands up now, lines of grime under his fingernails. It was hard to keep clean in the apocalypse, but it didn't look like he was trying too hard, either. Brandon shook his head, his hair flopping. "He threatened *me*, Ginny. He called me a cracker."

Hard to tell which upset him more. "And called the sky blue, too." Lee's fingertips touched the butt of his sidearm. If Ginny would step back a bit, he'd feel a lot better. "It's settled. You ain't comin with us. Best bet would probably be to stay here a couple nights until you get yourself a car, and move on." *Since you already know it's safe here.*

Brandon straightened, dropping his hands. Behind him, the dead elevators gleamed, their blank faces watching without much interest. "Like hell." *Now* it was beginning to sink in, apparently. "Ginny, you're not gonna let him do this, right? You can see what's happening, can't you?"

"Oh, yes." Ginny lifted her mug and took another dainty sip. Her gaze never left his. "Very clearly."

Whatever Brandon was expecting, it clearly wasn't that. His mouth actually fell open slightly, and as much as Lee disliked the man, he could relate. Lord, how on earth did she sound so...Lee searched for a word. Like she wouldn't spit on him to put him out, but polite at the same time. They probably taught her that at college, or her mama passed it down.

Lord, Ginny's mama must be a firecracker.

Brandon recovered quickly, though. He shifted back to injured, righteous pride like putting on an old pair of socks. "He's gonna do this to you, too, Ginny. I told you."

"I'll take my chances." Then, deliberately, Ginny turned her slim, pretty back, and walked away. Lee had to force himself not to turn and look.

That deflated Mr French. His shoulders sagged, and for a moment Lee almost felt sorry for the fucker.

But not quite. "Juju? We about packed up?"

"Yessir," Juju called from the breakfast circle. Ginny rejoined them, and both the kids, probably reading something on her face, hurried into motion. The garbage bag was tied off—*don't leave a campsite dirty* was a good rule. It wouldn't take long to get moving.

Especially since they were cutting deadweight loose. Lee backed up a step, two. "Mark, you and Steph get loaded. Ginny, you wanta ride with me?" Oh, it probably wasn't kind of him to rub it in, but Lee didn't care at the moment. Now he was the one holding Brandon French's gaze.

A deadly ratlike gleam lit itself far back in those blue eyes, and all of a sudden Lee felt strangely comfortable again. Women were a mystery, but a bastard too big for his educated britches was something any Quartine could handle.

"Sure. Come on, Traveller." Ginny clicked her tongue and the dog scurried after her, nails clicking on hard flooring. The kids followed her out the door. Juju lingered, picking up the Coleman lantern, waiting.

Watchful.

Ginny's shadow danced in the doorway. She paused, making sure the parking lot was clear, and beckoned the kids out.

Which freed Lee up to deal with this in his own way, if it was necessary.

"That's how it is?" Brandon had turned the volume down. Now would come the nasty. "Just toss me out, on his say-so?" He had more to say, Lee could see it boiling behind bloodshot blue eyes and a prettyboy mouth. Before the world went to hell, he probably got everything he wanted. Must be quite a shock, to have something *not* go his way. "On the say-so of a goddamn ni—"

"Shut up." It felt good to say, Lee decided, and even better to have the bark cut right through Brandon's nastiness. That was one thing about the Army, it taught you how to stop a jackass—if he was wearing a lower stripe-count, that was. "Nobody here wants to hear a damn word you have to say."

"Sonofa*bitch*—" And then, as expected, Brandon took a swing.

Lee leaned aside, barely having to move his feet. The boy was no brawler, despite his size. Lee dropped his hip, got a fist going, and socked French one in the gut about half-strength; that dumped the younger man onto the hard, cold fake stone. No carpet in front of the elevators, no sir, the entire lobby was floored with something that was supposed to be marble but didn't quite have the heft or look of real quality.

"Lee?" Juju, taut and ready, hurrying forward. Lee held up a hand, and considered kicking the collapsed, moaning mess of said-he-was-a-teacher.

Looked like he'd learned a lesson, all right.

"...*get* you," Brandon wheezed, curled up like a worm with a hook in its belly.

Yeah, Lee wanted to say. *Sure you will.* You killed a rattler when you could, and with things the way they were now, well, what was to stop him from solving a problem permanent-like?

In the end, though, he simply stepped back, turned on his heel, and left the man there.

Later, he wondered. But all he felt at that particular moment was relief.

[8]

MANDY AND CARLINE

Lunch was at another rest area, a bowl of dense pines surrounded by ugly clearcut slopes fading under a white blanket. Ginny, pale but composed, flinched when Juju slammed the driver's door; it was a miracle none of the four-by's windows were broken. The spare tire was a goner until they could find another one to hook on there, but auto dealerships weren't marked in the atlas. It was extremely lucky neither of their remaining vehicles were leaking anything vital, either.

They could stop for another RV, but Lee hadn't suggested it. It would probably take some convincing to get Ginny behind the wheel again.

Without Brandon, the stop took less than twenty minutes, and plenty of that was leg-stretching time with Traveller amid a snow flurry, thick white feathers melting almost in midair before the temperature plunged. The sky turned depthless later that afternoon, and it began snowing in earnest as they bumped along unplowed and melt-freed roads. At first the flakes vanished when they touched bare concrete, but soon enough they spread tiny lacework over every surface, clotting quickly. By four o'clock it was already dusky, daylight struggling through iron-colored clouds and snow turning to harder, ice-ridged pellets.

Finally, during a check-in at the edge of a small town—the sign said *Simonson, pop 7498*, and it looked like an even smaller dead end than Cotton Crossing—Juju suggested waiting out whatever this was. There was a brand new blue-and-yellow Bargain Zone box store on the outskirts, with acres of parking lot, but Lee was uneasy seeing the number of cars in the parking lot. Plenty of them were drawn into a circle in defiance of neatly painted lines, all blurring under fresh snow.

"Are you sure..." Ginny didn't finish the sentence. He glanced at her over Traveller's perked ears. The dog sat between them, staring out the windshield like the snow had a message for him.

Maybe it did.

"Juju and me'll check it first." He gave the lot another going-over. No footprints, but with the melt, there wouldn't be a bunch of tracks. The cars had to have been in place before it first snowed. "Don't worry. We're old hands."

"I know." Still, her hands clutched at each other again, those pretty grey gloves developing a hole near her left thumb. "I just..."

He waited, but she simply shook her head. She hadn't put her braids up, and though he liked her dark curls coming free, it was a little...disturbing...to see her disheveled. Welcome, yes, and powerfully attractive, but at the same time, almost uncomfortable. Especially when added to her uncharacteristic quiet. She wasn't a talker like Brandon, by any means, but he missed her occasional observations.

Should he reach over the dog and take her hand? It was uncomfortably close to French's talking her out of the shakes. And there was getting them all inside, out of the weather, to consider.

But he couldn't get out of the truck and leave her like this. He set the parking brake, and the walkie-talkie crackled.

"What's the plan?" Juju's voice came through loud and clear. He hadn't said a word about French threatening him, *or* about leaving the motherfucker behind.

There was, really, nothing to say. Lee reached for the talkie. "On the ground in five. Gear up."

"Ten-four."

Lee slid his sidearm free, checked it. Familiar, habitual movements he could perform in his sleep. He pushed the gun back home, lifting his hip off the seat, and glanced at her. "Don't worry," he said, again.

"I'll try." Two pale, faint little words. Traveller, quivering in place like the good hound he was, shifted a little to settle his hind end more firmly against Ginny's hip. Scooching over to get as close to her as he could.

Lee could relate. "Safe seconds, remember? Just keep counting them off while I'm gone."

"I...I don't feel safe at all," she whispered, staring at the front of the store. She was too pale. "Can I go with you?"

I'd like that, really I would. But she was safer in here, so Lee shook his head slightly. "Trav needs someone to keep him company."

"Blame it on the dog."

"Big Q always said that was the secret to a good marriage." That, and letting a woman have whatever she needs. His grandfather never said the latter when Nonna was around, but it rubbed through in little ways. The man had been done gone over his wife, and Lee supposed his own daddy had been the same over Lee's mama.

That was an unpleasant thought, though, one he shelved with a mental effort so reflexive he barely remembered when it had started. Enough that it went quietly.

Ginny tried to smile. "You ever been married?"

"No ma'am." It almost hurt him to see the effort she was making. Trying to put him at ease? It was just like her.

"Me either." She settled herself, turning back to the windshield, chin rising a little, defiant. "Okay, go on. I'm hungry."

· · ·

No sign of critters, and the windowless employee breakroom was neat as a pin. There was enough room in there, if they pushed an ancient couch up against the wall, for everyone to spread out their foam pads and sleeping bags. Steph and Mark went off in search of something for dessert, Ginny to look for first-aid supplies—you could never have too much, in her opinion, and she was the one with medical training—and Juju was on a mission for a certain beloved kind of baked beans again.

Maybe, Lee thought, he should let Juju bunk somewhere else for the night.

Lee, flashlight beam bobbing, moved aimlessly through the store, looking at the shelves and thinking. One problem was solved, but a few others were raising their ugly heads. They'd been almost unbelievably lucky so far, and you couldn't count on that. It was vanishingly unlikely that Ginny's parents were still alive, and his little group weren't making good time through the slippery roads, especially with the weather deciding to turn all at once. Going north into snowstorms was a fool's move.

He was racking his brains to think of a better destination that wasn't in Grandon's letter when the fine hairs all over him stood up and he froze between one step and the next, listening intently. What had he heard? Something familiar, but out of place.

Thunk. The sound of a swinging door sealing itself, to his left. But nobody was over there—or at least, nobody from *his* group.

"Lee?" Ginny, from the end of an aisle behind him. Maybe she'd found all she needed. "Is that—"

"Shhh." His hand blurred for his gun just as the girl came around the corner and dropped her own weatherproof flashlight. The beam swung crazily, narrowly avoiding blinding him, and she dug frantically at her belt.

Sixteen tops, with a fine-carved face and dark eyes, the black girl peered wildly from under a hunter-orange knit cap. Her blue coat was a little too big for her but she had a well-worn .45, and she finished lifting it as Ginny appeared from behind the aisle-end and a glossy stack of plastic sacks on display.

Lee eyed the girl, she eyed him right back, and Ginny outright gasped.

"Who the hell are you?" the girl demanded, quickest off the mark.

Oh, good Lord. The business end of a pistol always looked *very* big, and very dark, when it was pointed at you. "Easy there, miss." Lee took his hand away from his own gun, and spread his arms a little. "Ginny, stay back."

The girl, thin braids holding small blue beads doing their best to escape her hat, narrowed those velvety dark eyes. She had a fine stance; someone had taught her how to shoot. "Who the *hell* are you?"

"Oh, my God." Ginny peered the rest of the way around an endcap stacked high with chips—potato and corn, and glass bottles of salsa or queso dip. "Oh. Hello." The words shook a little. "You're alive."

The girl's gaze flicked past Lee to Ginny. If she was relieved at seeing a woman, it didn't show. "What?" At least she had some trigger discipline.

"Please." Lee cleared his throat. "Put the gun down, miss."

"Like *hell*." The young lady didn't think much of this notion. "Who the hell *are* you?"

"He's Lee," Ginny said, helpfully. "I'm Ginny, Ginny Mills. We don't mean you any harm."

"Yeah, well..." The girl studied them both, and Lee waited for her to make up her mind. No need to shoot, but accidents happened. And he didn't want to be in the path of one, or God forbid, have a stray shot hit Ginny. Calm and easy was called for here.

Another small sound—*thunk-chock*. It was an employee door, Lee realized, swinging wide and closing—he and Juju had gotten in through the employee entrance on the west side, sheltered from the wind, but any grocery store had holes in the back, as well. Quick footsteps followed, squeaking slightly. Another female voice, very young. "Mandy! Mandy, there's people—oh." Another teenage girl, a redhead with milky skin and sleepy pale eyes, halted behind the dark-haired one. "Hi." A red jacket to match that carrot-top, and her jeans were almost wet to the knee.

"Hi." Ginny stepped out, slowly, her hands held high. "I'm Ginny. You are?"

"I'm Carline. That's Mandy." The redhead stepped close and jostled the other girl, and Lee's back prickled with sweat. You didn't bump someone who had a bead, for Chrissake. "She's, uh, a little wired."

Lee decided to keep his mouth shut. Ginny was going to be way more soothing than *him*, and he had to focus on breathing. If that girl put her finger on the trigger, things were going to get unhappy right quick.

"We all are," Ginny soothed. "We've been shot at, and then there's the..." She took a deep breath. "The zombies."

"Any of y'all sick?" Mandy demanded. The gun shook a little; her boots were damp and very new. "At all?"

"No. No fever, no convulsions, not even a sniffle." Ginny spread her hands a little more, and sonny Jesus save him from a heart attack, stepped in *front* of Lee. She moved towards the girls, hands still up, her braids dangling down her back. "We're all healthy. We're just here for food, and we'll leave if you want us to."

That was music to the dark-haired girl's ears, apparently. "Promise?"

"Mandy. Stop it." The redhead elbowed her again. Christ, if that gun went off—

"Jesus." Mandy lowered the .45. Her dark eyes were huge, and Lee thought it pretty likely she was the decision-maker in this little couple. "Okay, just...you know, a guy shows up, and we're alone, and..."

The redhead—Carline—snorted a half-giggle. "Don't *tell* them that, idiot!"

"Lee?" Juju called. "*Lee?*"

"It's all right," Ginny called back. "Stay where you are, please." Her tone dropped, became businesslike. "That's Mr Thurgood, he travels with us. There's Mark and Steph too, they're about your age."

Carline brightened. "Oh. Y'all travelin? Where you goin?"

"New York."

"What's there?" Mandy holstered the shootin' iron, very slowly. She didn't have to look to do it. A very capable little miss, right here.

"My parents." Ginny relaxed a little, lowering her hands. Was she smiling? It sounded like it. Lee's palms were damp, and he was pretty sure his balls had crawled northward to escape carpetbaggers.

Lucky again. But he was gonna have to have a talk with her about stepping in front of guns.

The girls stared at Ginny like they couldn't quite believe what they'd heard. Lee let out a long, soft breath. "Ginny," he managed, through a throat gone dusty-dry. "Maybe we should, uh, let these ladies get back to whatever they was doin."

"Huh." Carline studied him. "We'll let you stay here. For a bit, at least."

"Unless you're a rapist," Mandy chimed in, bending for her flashlight. It was a good thing it had a heavy rubberized cover, or the damn thing would have cracked. "Then I'll shoot you."

"Yes, well, if he was I'd shoot him myself," Ginny said, calmly. "But for right now, maybe we could try to get along without guns?"

At that, both girls began to laugh. It was a screechy, not-quite-sane sound, but nice and comforting nonetheless.

That was how they met Mandy and Carline.

[9]

EARLY ENOUGH FOR RULES

STERNO CANS SIZZLED BUSILY UNDER RICKETY GRILLWORK. HOT dogs, frozen solid in the depths of the grocery store's coolers a short while ago, were now sweating grease and charring a little. The buns hadn't gone bad—preservative-laced bread was doing better than the organics, that was for sure. Ginny longed for some Thai food, or Chinese. Egg flower soup would have gone down *really* easily. With a salad. A big, deep-green salad with bright red tomatoes. Bagged kale was probably still good, but the tomatoes in the produce section were all liquified by now.

She poked at the hot dogs and suppressed a sigh.

"Carline's mama worked here." Mandy accepted hot cocoa from Steph with a smile, obviously much easier now that she saw someone her own age in this new group.

"Night manager," Carline chimed in. "So she had keys. When everyone got sick and started zombifying, we figured it was safer here."

Mark was eyeing these new arrivals with no little trepidation. "What about your parents?"

The black girl turned somber and stared into her cup, her chiseled lips pursing. "Well, once they get sick, they don't seem to care 'bout no family ties."

"We had to beat her mama off with a two-by-four." Carline shuddered, only a little theatrically.

"Wasn't much of a change," Mandy muttered, and took a large gulp of cocoa. It was probably too hot, but she didn't grimace.

Steph nodded, pouring hot water into another mug with Swiss Miss mix. A high pretty flush stood out on her cheeks. "We had to run over my daddy. Well, Mark did. And my mama...well."

"Gruesome." Carline was a little ray of sunshine. It was both disturbing and heartening to see the girls feeling each other out, subtle social cues flashing between them lightning-quick. "I had to use a lacrosse stick on mine. She was always on me to practice."

Mandy swallowed, her shoulders hunched. There was more to that story, anyone could tell just by looking.

"Maybe exchanging the details could wait until after dinner, ladies." Ginny glanced at Mark. "Hand me the platter, will you?"

Lee and Juju hurried in through the unlocked front door, stamping fresh snow loose. They were getting really good at finding employee doors and getting glass ones open without making them unusable afterward. Finding a place to shelter the vehicles was going to be a problem, since the power was out and that meant no engine-block heaters. Or so it appeared to Ginny.

That wasn't something she could solve. It was a relief to find something she *didn't* feel responsible for, frankly.

"Nothin movin outside." Lee set his rifle down, carefully, and stretched his hands over the grill. Juju got the door closed and locked, peering out into a wind-whirling white dusk. Dim light from the blue flames and the Coleman lamps reflected off the end of a few check-stands; there was an entire display of charcoal in paper bags. There was a propane refill station here too; Ginny had, after much thought, opted for the cans of alcohol gel. The risk of carbon monoxide poisoning precluded any large barbecue plans, but Ginny was just tired enough to find the idea funny.

The grilling, that was. Not the poisoning. It was the end of the world, and here they were with a cookout.

Mark's head swiveled, trying to keep track of the new arrivals as he held a red plastic platter. It tipped dangerously as Ginny loaded it with hot dogs, each nestled in a toasted bun. "Careful, kiddo."

"Oh, yeah." He righted the plate, but his gaze wandered again. Impossible to tell which new girl he was more fascinated with. Lee might have been about to bark at him, but Ginny shook her head a little. Let the kids the kids.

Just as she thought it, Carline hopped to her feet and shouldered Mark aside. "You gotta hold it straight. Jeez." She made a little motion with her head, either tossing her hair or dismissing him, it was hard to tell which.

"I'm surprised y'all ain't goin to Georgia." Mandy finished her cocoa with another gulp, put her elbows on her knees. Her cornrow braids, each a neat ridge, ended with blue beads that made tiny cheerful noises whenever her hair swing. Her hunter-orange hat lay neatly in her lap. At least she'd laid the gun aside. It looked like a real cannon, but Lee didn't seem concerned about her carrying it. Not like Brandon's carbine.

She didn't want to think about Brandon. At least they were miles away, and he was presumably an adult. He could shift for himself.

"Why?" Ginny loaded another batch of hot dogs onto the grill. Still half-frozen, they were easier to handle with tongs and she was going to err on the side of burning them, just to make sure. The last thing they needed was food poisoning. "Juju, come eat while it's warm. Steph, sweetie, we need something other than chips, really. Something with fiber."

"Fiiiiiber." Steph giggled, and the other two girls did too. Ginny couldn't help but smile.

Mandy sobered first. "The last thing we heard on the radio was the gov'mint tellin everyone to go there. Atlanta, the CDC." She pushed herself upright, stuffing her hat in her jacket pocket. "We were talkin about goin out that way, maybe."

"Said they was working on a cure." Carline made a slight *tsking* noise. Her cheeks were downright rosy. "I'll take this, you pass out the plates."

Mark hurried to obey, his Adam's-apple moving as he swallowed nervously. Lee pulled his hands back like they'd been singed, and straightened. "Atlanta, huh?" His gaze rested on Ginny, thoughtful and distant.

Go ahead, if you want to. She busied herself with laying some more buns down to toast, too. Sterno was nontoxic, right? The flames were small enough dioxide poisoning wasn't a huge risk. She'd carefully thought that out before approaching the problem of cooking tonight. Her fingers were numb; her headache had retreated but her neck was still tense.

"That's what they said." Mandy did a smart about-face, unearthing her big rubberized flashlight from inside her coat. "Imma go find something healthy, Miz Mills."

"It's Ginny. And you don't have to—"

"Take someone with you," Lee piped up. "Safer."

"Ain't nothin in here, sir." She slipped between two checkstands and was gone in a wink, flicking her flashlight into life.

"Stubborn," Carline called after her, then dropped her tone. "But she's used to going off alone. 'Nough to drive you crazy."

Lee looked about ready to pick up his rifle and follow the girl, but Ginny shook her head again. "Don't." Softly, so it wouldn't carry. "Better for me to go, or Steph. Or just let her be."

Puzzlement wrinkled his forehead, but smoothed as soon as it dawned on him. Ginny waited for him to get angry, but his expression settled between remote and rueful. "Aight." He scratched at his cheek, stubbling up fast. "Glad we cut that feller loose." It was obvious who he meant.

"Me too." She didn't ask what had happened once she and the kids had left the foyer that morning. There was no point—she couldn't see Brandon agreeing gracefully, or Lee caring at that point. "This'll be done in a little bit."

Civilization was a thin veneer indeed. How long before it cracked like an egg?

"Just let 'er go, I guess." Lee tucked his gloves in a pocket. "Tomorrow's early enough for rules." *If they're coming along*, was the unspoken corollary. He reached for the tongs, but she whisked them away. "Why don't you go sit down? Have Steph bring you some cocoa. You look peaked."

"I'm fine." She watched Steph load a plate for Juju, who settled on an upended milk crate, sideways so he could keep an eye on the door. "This batch is all yours."

"What about you?"

"Cook eats last. You know that." She was turning into her mother. *Cook sits down last,* Mom would say, with the unspoken corollary that she got up at least fifteen times during the meal to fetch things, fuss at something, or refill a glass.

Lee's smile crinkled the corners of his eyes. "Next time I'm on KP."

"No thanks."

"You don't think I can?"

She glanced up, hurriedly, to check his expression. The smile remained, and she almost sighed with relief. Then she felt like an idiot, but that quick jab of social discomfort was damn near instantaneous. "I want to feel useful."

"You're right useful."

Somehow I don't think my skillset is particularly applicable. "Maybe you guys should go to Atlanta. If they—"

"No." He didn't even let her finish.

"Lee." She poked at a charring hot dog, turning it over.

"I told you, I ain't havin you hurt."

She kept fiddling with the grill. The buns looked toasted enough, so she pulled them off, and he held another platter for them. "It's just a suggestion, Lee."

"Ma'am?" Carline was at her elbow. "You need some help?"

A salad and a long vacation is what I need. Some white wine would go down really easily, too. Or maybe a shot of something stronger. "I'm all right. What have you guys been eating?"

"Oh, whatever we've a mind to." Carline's teeth gleamed. Some people were just natural optimists, and she looked like one. "Be good to have something regular-like, though. I thought I'd never get sick of Pringles, but there's only so much a body can eat."

"I'll bet." Ginny found herself smiling, again. Pringles sounded good, too. No fiber in *those*, though.

Lee regarded her steadily, and got quiet.

Again.

$$[\ 10\ ]$$

BATTER UP

ONE MOMENT HE WAS OFF WATCH, ROLLING INTO HIS SLEEPING bag in the manager's office; the next, Lee was awake, his heart in his throat, Mark Kasprak's fingers sinking into his shoulder with hysterical strength. "Lee," the kid whisper-yelled, his breath touching Lee's cheek. "Mistah Lee, wake *up*."

Lee's fingers loosened on the knife's hilt; he slid it back into the sheath under his pillow and sat up, nearly cracking foreheads with Kasprak. Cold air touched his bare arms—sleeping in his jeans and a T-shirt wasn't the most uncomfortable thing in the world, but it wasn't quite pillows and bacon, either. "What?" he barked, and the sudden change in Juju's breathing was as loud as a shout.

"They're at the door." The words whistled, probably because Mark's throat was constricted with terror. "They're *pushing*."

Jesus Christ. Lee thrashed free of the sleeping bag, and his boots were right where they should be. He got his sock feet jammed in and everything tied in a trice, snagged his sidearm, and was on his feet heading for the office door while Juju cussed in an undertone. "How many? How many, Mark?"

"I...I dunno, a *lot*—"

Lee grabbed the kid's arm. "Get to the girls." The ladies were all in the employee breakroom, new additions to the group meaning there was no longer space for everyone in there. "Bang on that door, you wake em up, and you *get inside and lock it again,* you hear me? Juju, incoming!"

"On it, Loot." Thank God, the man was steady.

"Go." Iron in his mouth, Lee pushed Mark out the door and to the left. The breakroom here wasn't nearly as comfortable as the last place, but they could brace the door and hold out for a while, depending on the situation. Lee turned hard right, and the darkness was a wet bandage against his eyes. No flashlight, but he'd counted the ancient, linoleum-slick stairs after dinner and on his way back from watch, a habit burned into him from night-time drills. Another hard right at the bottom, another door that could be braced if shit went even further sideways, and he pounded down a short hall past the two customer restrooms. Smacking his shoulder against the wall at the end of the hall, sweeping what he could see with night vision and his sidearm—should have grabbed his own goddamn rifle, but Juju would bring it.

This was better for close work, anyway. Muzzle flash and the noise were a factor here too.

Juju clattered up. "Behind you," he said, clear but low, and from there it was old work, clear and move, clear and move, pounding heart and adrenaline a coppery slick on the back of his tongue, skin tight with cold and danger.

It felt familiar, if not comfortable. Like this was where he belonged.

They were at the front door, a clot of shambling critters pressing against the glass. Stiffened, sausage-clumsy fingers worked wormlike across the clear surface, and Lee was faintly glad it was dark because *fuck* if he had to see that wall of rancid flesh in daylight...well, it was enough to unsettle a man's stomach. A faint scratching and waxy squeak-noises from their bloated fingertips on the dry slick glass echoed in eerie snowbound silence—it was still coming down out there, big fluffy flakes whirling and reflecting what little light there was.

Automatic doors could be opened from inside, it was in the fire codes. The critters were working against the hinges and their uncoordinated surging added to slipping feet meant it wasn't time to worry just yet.

Just as he decided that, though, two of the critters leaned at the same time, and their weight wrung a slight groan from the metal frame. It was like those sales after Thanksgiving, everyone crowded at a box store entrance, not caring what the discount was as long as there *was* one.

The noise maddened the creatures. They heaved forward as one, straining, and the metal frame made another groan. How many were there? Ten? A dozen? More?

"Oh, shit," Juju whispered, hunching for cover; neither of them had ever sheltered behind a cash register before. First time for everything.

"How long you think that door'll last?" Lee whispered back.

"Not long enough." Juju raised his rifle, slowly, a man caught in a bad dream.

He was right. Once the frame gave the glass was a goner, then there'd be hungry critters inside the store. However many there were, it wasn't likely to be a good time. There wasn't much around to brace the *front* doors with; he should have thought of that. But the things had *never* acted like this before.

They heaved again. Juju socked the rifle to his shoulder. "Lee?"

"No." Lee decided. His brain was working fast enough, or so he hoped. "Not yet."

Juju hoped so, too, but was apparently not quite convinced. His eyes gleamed in the faint snowlight. "We just gonna *wait?*"

"Bottle 'em there." He holstered his sidearm and took his own rifle. "Go get a bat or two. We can choke 'em in the door."

"What if they's more behind 'em?"

That was the last thing he wanted Juju worrying about. God and sonny Jesus knew Lee was worried enough about it for both of them. "I got ammo, I'll be just fine. Go on, now." Lee lifted his own rifle, his breathing settling.

Juju's boots squeaked as he took off. The door's metal frame groaned again, and a long silvery crack grew up the middle of the left-hand glass panel, blooming into tree-branches at the top. Looked like either they'd figured out how to heave together—probably quicker than healthy people could—or any noise made them frantic and they scrabbled for the source. What fixed their attention on the door? He had questions for Kasprak.

Just as soon as he survived this.

Now they began that grinding, growling noise, and he realized they'd been silent before. More cracks bloomed on the big sheet-panes. Didn't look like safety glass. A lawsuit waiting to happen if someone walked through, but really, who could have expected shambling not-quite-dead critters? Were they still alive? Ginny's voice floated through his head—*metabolically expensive*.

Thank God she was behind a locked door.

Except she wasn't, because he heard voices behind him, just as the glass decided its duty was done and shivered into long shards.

Female voices. Looked like nobody had enough sense to stay put while he and Juju dealt with this.

"*Batter up!*" one of the girls yelled, and Lee swore.

CARLINE'S CHEERLEADER YODEL GOT THE CRITTER'S ATTENTION, and the redhead in a too-big blue Gap sweatshirt laid about her with more enthusiasm than skill. Mandy, in a tank top, flannel over-shirt, and a pair of brand new but untied Nikes, moved in with a Louisville slugger, swinging from the hip and splattering spongy skulls with long efficient swipes. Mark lost his dinner next to a checkstand and waded back into the fray, grimly determined, and

Steph's night-time braids bounced as she darted in and out, smacking heads. Ginny, deathly pale in sock feet, her hair a wild cloud of curls, clutched at a bat, looking for an opportunity that never came.

The kids had this handled. It was, Lee thought, pretty goddamn terrifying. He couldn't get a clear shot with the young 'uns clustering the door. Juju had a big old Fenix lantern picked up somewhere, and he'd thought to grab it so the kids could see what they were hitting. Or maybe he'd brought it down thinking to headlight the critters. Either way, its dancing glare splashed over writhing limbs and flickering bats. The broken door kept the things coming through one at a time, working slowly through the mass of others trying to widen the breach, and Lee cast around for something to block the hole. All Lee could see that might possibly serve was the display of charcoal and firewood, so he kept looking. Bargain Zone had a hardware section, but no lumber.

"*Get* it!" Carline yelled, but Mandy was ahead of her, crushing the last one's head. The smell might have been bad except for the refrigerator cold. Grey matter and blackish blood flew; Steph let out a short disgusted sound as splatter painted the large, wafer-thin, rubbery mat meant to catch slush and pebbles before they could be tracked in. The bone chips weren't ivory, or maybe it was the light.

The corpses looked *wrong*.

"Thirteen," Mark said, in a high unsteady voice. "Baker's dozen." He whacked a questing, skeletal, rotting hand away from Steph's ankle with a short, popping strike.

"Don't get it on you!" Ginny wasn't hysterical, but it sounded a near thing. "It could be communicable—"

"Motha*fuckas*." Carline didn't care about hygiene at the moment. The redhead had a mouth on her, that was for damn sure. "Not in *my* house!"

"Swing-batta-batta," Mandy chanted, stepping back and surveying their work. Her beaded braids clicked against each other. Calm, efficient, methodical, and barely sixteen, she smacked heads with a minimum of fuss and a maximum of force. Lee got the idea this wasn't her first time.

He could almost hear his grandfather's snort and almost-constant refrain of *Kids these days*. Lee let out a breath he hadn't even been aware of holding. "That it?"

"Looks like." Carline peered at the hole in the door, now almost fully plugged by critter bodies, and swung her dripping bat with a pro's thoughtless, testing motion. "I knew they'd eventually figure out a door. Didn't I tell ya?"

"Mh." Mandy agreed with a short sound, all her attention on the pile of carcasses, watching for motion.

Mark retched again, his head hanging, the drenched business end of his bat smearing linoleum, and scrubbed the back of his free hand across his slack mouth.

"Water." Ginny held her own weapon gingerly. She hadn't even had a chance to use it, and from the awkward way she kept it at arm's length, it was a good thing. "Soap. And hand sanitizer."

"Jesus, kids." Juju shook his head. He'd only gotten a couple taps in, when one looked likely to slip-scramble to the left over the mound of spongy flesh. "I think they're dead."

"Make sure they *know* it." Carline brought her bat down smartly on a female in a flopping red and blue muumuu, its chest still vibrating with a final growl. "Hey, shine the light. Mandy?"

"Can't see." Mandy now peered through the jagged hole in the door. The dead were stacked like cordwood, caught trying to wriggle over each other to get in. They could rig something around the bodies to block the hole, keep the worst of the cold out too.

Lee shook his head. He'd seen carnage before, but this was... something else. The critters just kept *coming*, even though the ones in front got their heads bashed in and fell, blocking the aperture. They came right on *over* their compadres, mindless and chewing. "Mark? Mark, you with me?"

The boy shook his spiky dark head, staring at the floor. "Thirteen," he muttered. "Lucky number. Baker's dozen."

"Kasprak." Lee approached him cautiously. The girls ringed the dead bodies, their bats ready, and Carline let out a harsh little giggle.

"Huh?" Mark looked up. His eyes were wide and haunted, his mouth loose. "Mr Lee?"

For some reason, that made Carline laugh even harder, and Mandy too. Steph caught on a second after they did, and it was goddamn chilling all the way around to hear young women laughing like that. A chorus of sweet high voices, spilling out into the deadening snowfall.

Lee had a question he needed answered. "What set them off?"

"I dunno. I did a circuit of the store like Mr Thurgood tole me. On the hour." Mark shook his head, like whipping away water or a bad thought. His mouth worked a little, turning loose, but he swallowed, buttoned up, and went on. "One round, nothin there but snow. Next time, they were all standing under the roof there, in the dry bit. All in a group, standing there and sorta swaying-like. Then they started movin, and one of em—that one, I think—sort of like he was drunk, kind of bounced off the door."

"Herd behavior," Ginny muttered. "I'll go find some soap."

"I'll go with," Steph piped up.

"Then they all started pushing..." Mark shook his head again, a galvanic shudder running all the way down his bony body. His boots moved uneasily. He almost retched again, his Adam's-apple bobbing, and his chin lifted. He glared at Lee, and it was official, the boy was growing up the way a green grunt did all at once if he survived his first kill.

"You didn't catch their attention?" Lee ached for the kid, really. Could he even remember the moments after his first? It would take some doing, digging in that mental vault. He only remembered the prickling relief when he went numb. "Bang on the door? Anything?"

"Nosir." Mark blinked, sense coming back home to roost behind his dark gaze. "You think I would?"

Lee exhaled, rubbing at his forehead. "Just wonderin why they suddenly wanted in."

"Maybe it's the weather." Juju stared at the bodies. He wasn't wild-eyed, but it was close, and his hair, getting longer, was a short-curled halo. The lantern bobbed, casting crazy shadows over the tangled bodies, dappling the snow and pavement outside. Lee was feeling pretty goddamn wild-eyed himself.

"I know I'd want to get inside." Carline swung her bat, a tiny twitching movement. Critter-blood splattered. "It's cold."

"You're in your sock feet," Mandy pointed out, helpfully. "Get some shoes on. There's plywood in the back."

Good time to let me know. Lee's relief was hot, sharp, and entirely out of proportion. Nobody was dead, nobody was bitten. Well, except the assholes stacked in the door. "Is there?"

"Yeah, they had it for when the parking lot iced over and stuff." Mandy let out a long, shaky breath, the first sign of nerves she'd shown.

"I'm not stupid," Mark said suddenly. The cuff of his new flannel shirt flapped a little, probably splattered with gore now. "I wouldn't do anything like that."

Juju glanced at the kid. "I know." It was his job to smooth out troubled nerves, while Lee made the decisions. Habit was a bastard, it kept grinding its way in even when you set it down and left it alone for years. Had he *or* Juju really left the Army behind?

It sure as shit didn't feel like it nowadays.

"I know too, Mark." The words were heavy on Lee's tongue. He hoped he sounded something other than exhausted and jangled. "Miss Mandy, you wanna show me the plywood? Best we close this up soon."

That brought up another problem, and Juju arrived there first. "I ain't touchin those, Lee. Sorry, but I ain't."

"It's all right." Lee tried not to sigh. "We'll brace the door. They plugging it up anyway." *And tomorrow we can get the hell out of here. If the snow ain't too deep.*

He was beginning to think maybe they'd survived when one of the bodies twitched. Carline jumped, let out a soft, ugly little cry, and brought her bat down again. A sponge-boned skull spattered into pieces.

Kids these days, Lee thought grimly. Anyone left alive was gonna grow up right quick. Or die.

With that cheerful thought to keep him company, Lee turned to the next problem in front of him.

[11]

SWEETHEART HONEYPOT

UP IN THE EMPLOYEE BREAKROOM, WITH AN ELECTRIC LANTERN glowing in the corner, the two girls got their beds re-settled.

"What do you think?" Carline Goldisch bit her soft bottom lip, worrying. Her front two teeth were slightly crooked, and she had a habit of running her tongue over them when concentrating. It was the first thing Mandy had noticed about her, the first thing that made her neck go hot and her hands not know what to do with themselves. "Should we go with 'em?"

"They seem okay," Mandy Hopper said, slowly. She settled her sleeping bag—the foam pads were a good idea, and the travelers had extra. It was good they didn't mind sharing. "But New York? We should go to Atlanta, if we're gonna go anywhere."

"Maybe. But what if..." Carline scooted her own bag closer, pushing the pad snugly into the corner. She liked sleeping sandwiched between the wall and Mandy. It made her feel safer, she said. Her hair lay on her shoulders, its coppery gleam dulled a little but the texture a whole lot easier to work with since she'd tried the cornstarch method Mandy used on her own head. "We can't stay here. Not all winter."

"Oh, we could." Mandy smoothed her pillow. The teacher lady had told them to wash up first, and was putting the rest of them through a cold-water scrubbing downstairs. *We don't know how contagious this is,* she'd said, which made for some bad thoughts. "But what about after? *That* worries me."

"If we go with, you think they'll be mean?" Carline hopped onto the foam pad, punched her pillow twice, and wormed into her bag. "About us?"

That was one thing the End Times had saved them from—whispers at school, the shoves and nasty comments in the lunchroom, and Carline's fundamentalist mama with her suspicious glares, hornrim glasses, and double-scrubbing every dish Mandy touched in their trailer. As if she was better than Mandy's mama and daddy, who even if they yelled and made her cut the yard had their own house on Sellwyn Avenue, neat and trim and tidy.

Or they had, until the bad stuff started happening. Now there were no parents, no school, no mean kids to pull on your braids or ask you what rhymed with *lesbo*. And, best of all, no church on Sundays, where people shouted and jumped like they was having a good time, then went home and did awful things once the front door closed behind them.

Still, if this was indeed Revelations, Mandy had no problem with it so far, except for the lack of curly fries. "Dunno. Maybe the Rapture missed 'em like it missed us."

"Rapture says the godly vanish." Carline moved her hips, turned this way and that. It took her a while to settle, just like a dog.

"Can't think of anyone in town good enough to sit with Jesus, Car." Mandy preferred to wait until Carline was done before stretching out herself, so she didn't get a stray elbow in the ribs. "Not even on the doorstep."

"Yeah, well." Carline finally stretched and yawned, pink mouth and little white teeth like a kitten. "Come on, lay down. I'm cold."

"Shoulda put yo' shoes on." Mandy set their bats—rinsed in the meat department's giant sinks, their wooden grain darkened now—

down in their accustomed places. *Gonna be up early*, Mr Quartine had said. *You're welcome to come along.* He was in for a surprise if he expected to be able to move with it snowing like it was. Still, he might have a trick or two up his sleeve, and he treated that Mr Thurgood and Mandy herself just like the rest of them. *That* was a good sign.

Any adult with a low bullshit factor was a treasure, in Mandy's humble opinion, and that cracker looked about as low-bullshit as they came despite his gym-teacher hair and military bark-and-bite. She kept expecting him to tell someone to take a couple laps 'round the gym or drop and give him ten, like nasty bullet-headed Mr Connors who always wore grey sweats.

That asshole was probably dead, and the thought pleased Mandy immensely.

She unlaced her sneakers a little more, slid them off, and wriggled into her own plaid sleeping bag from the camping department of this very same store. Spent a few moments arranging herself suitably. Carline nestled close, and Mandy shut her eyes, breathing deeply. Beads dug into the back of her head until she moved with a quick habitual shake, and Carline waited for a few moments before pressing her lips to Mandy's cheek.

"They'll be up soon," Carline whispered, a hot breath against her ear. "You think we have time...?"

"Girl, you're insane." But Mandy couldn't help but grin, her eyes closed tight. "We should zip our bags together if we go with 'em. Then we could whenever we wanted."

"Just have to be quiet." Carline sounded like she liked the idea.

Heat bloomed in Mandy's belly, spread up to touch her heart. "Like at home."

"You ever glad this happened?"

No point in lying. "Kind of."

"Me too." Carline's tongue flicked along the curve of Mandy's earlobe. "You think we're goin to hell?"

A zing went down Mandy's spine. "Course not." Didn't the girl know? *We're already there.* "Close your eyes, sweetheart."

"I like the way you say that." Carline kissed her braids. "Honeypot."

"Sugar britches."

That cracked them up good, and by the time Steph came up the stairs with her flashlight bobbing, the teacher lady right behind her, they were both fast asleep, unconcerned, Carline breathing into Mandy's nape.

[12]

NO USE IN SHOULDAS

"That's not what I'm saying," Ginny repeated, pulling her jacket lapels closer and searching for the zipper. "It's all the same."

"It ain't." Lee rubbed at his forehead as if he was developing a headache to match hers. He was in a thicker coat today, too, and even Juju had swapped out his fatigue jacket for something more substantial. "Help me out here, Ginny."

I wish I could. "I don't want to drive another RV. But that's *not* what I'm saying, Lee." At least a foot and a half of snow lapped at the walls, drifting over the roads. The melt might as well not have happened. At the same time, staying in this place another night, with all the dead bodies stacked in the door, possibly frozen together—dear God, but *no.*

Worst of all was the fact that sometime during Juju's watch near dawn, most of the flesh from the back ends of the dead zombies had been stripped away. There were even gnaw marks on the discolored, queerly spongy bones.

It reminded her of cadaver classes in med school. Some profs let you cover the faces, but most didn't. You had to get used to it. The thought that all that muscle mass—glutes, hamstrings, quadriceps, gastrocnemius and soleus, lo and behold she remembered her A & P —was probably very attractive to wandering cannibal zombies wasn't helping her retain her cool, as Steph might say.

Speaking of Steph, the girl had given Mark the cold shoulder all morning, and watching him follow her around like a spike-haired puppy was slightly funny and disconcerting at the same time. From his expression, the kid had no idea what was wrong. Neither did Ginny, but she suspected he wasn't going to win any points by trying to horn in on a developing female troika. Carline and Mandy were a tight unit, but they graciously folded their collective social wings over Steph while observing just enough distance to make it clear she was on probation.

High school really never ended, even now.

Lee kept going, obviously in problem-solving mode. Just like a man, not listening. "We can make it to the freeway. We'll get to Louisville, bound to be supplies and a place to hole up there if it gets worse—"

"Lee. Really." She folded her arms. "How much *worse* can it get?"

"Ginny..." He stopped, probably having run out of solutions. He'd come up with a few more if she let him get started again.

Maybe she could get through to him during the pause. "It'll take *days* to get to my parents at this rate," she continued. "Normally, it takes about eighteen hours nonstop, if you've got enough caffeine and know the roads. I should have left before the snow, I should have left when Mom called me, I should have—"

"Ain't no use in *shouldas*, Ginny." He was going to get started on solutions again, she could just tell. "What we got in front of us is more than enough."

Well, she couldn't argue with that. Her temples ached, and she fought the urge to massage them. "Look, all I'm saying is, if there's even a *chance* there's some kind of government presence in Atlanta, you should take the kids there."

"I *ain't leavin you.*" He said it very quietly, but he leaned forward a bit, shoulders swelling and his dark eyebrows drawing together. "I thought that was clear enough for even your stubborn Yankee head."

It didn't help her temper that he said *Yankee* like it was a dirty word. Ginny zipped her coat up and tried again, searching for a tone much calmer than she felt. "There are bigger issues here, Lee. Look at them. They're *kids*. And the only reason Juju's along is because of you. You have a responsibility to them that you don't have to me."

"The *hell* I don't. What part of this do you not understand? I'm a-goin with you, to see to your folk. They probably ain't even alive, Ginny, unless they're fast and lucky."

For a moment, she couldn't believe he'd actually said it. From the look on his lean, freshly shaven face, he couldn't either.

Ginny was abruptly conscious that the kids were staring. Juju wasn't only because he'd taken Traveller out after breakfast. The tea she'd managed to sip this morning sloshed uneasily in her gurgling stomach. "They may not be," she agreed, quietly. "I've thought of that." Except it was different, hearing someone say it out loud. "And I have to make sure. I'm asking you to help me find a vehicle that can get me there, that's all." Then she'd be out of his hair, and on her own.

"Why are you alla sudden like this?" At least he quit looming over her, his shoulders slumping instead of tense under the navy Thinsulate coat. It was a relief.

Maybe because last night showed me something. "Because it has to be said, Lee. I can't risk the kids' lives, and yours, and Juju's. I *have* to get to my parents, and Flo, even if..." Her throat refused to work for a moment. "Even if something's happened to them. I am *not* asking anyone else to come along. In fact, I'd actively discourage it, because—"

"What the *fuck* are you talking about?" Lee's eyes had done their funny thing again, turning yellowish and intense. She'd heard of people whose irises changed colors under stress. There was a medical term for it, surely. Good luck remembering it now.

"I'm talking about my conscience." *And the sound of baseball bats hitting skulls, and washing the splatter in freezing water with not enough soap.* They were here because Ginny was fixated on getting *home*. Well, Carline and Mandy weren't here because of it, but if Ginny's group hadn't shown up, would the zombies have attacked the way they did? Somehow, the creatures could tell where food was, it was the only thing that made sense. "It wasn't right of me to allow you to come along—"

"Allow me?" Now he was dangerously quiet, both eyebrows lifting. Ginny could see, now, how someone might find him...imposing.

"Yes, Lee. I do have a say in who I travel with." God. She'd been mentally practicing this interaction ever since she laid down early this morning to try to sleep again, and it was *not* going in any direction she'd prepared for. Her eyes were grainy, the tea she could choke down was *not* helping her sore throat, her headache was back and mounting. "I am an *adult*. Just because it's the goddamn Apocalypse doesn't mean you can order me around, or control where I go or what I do."

"Likewise."

What was that supposed to mean? She wasn't telling him what to do, really. "You have a responsibility, Lee."

"Who nominated me, huh?" His hands moved a little, like he wanted to fold his arms, but he put them back down. "You? You won't last a day out there, Ginny."

"Thank you for your confidence." She tried not to sound sarcastic, and failed utterly. It didn't help that he was probably right, but if she was careful she could avoid the zombies, right? She could sleep in whatever car she...stole, that was the only word for it. And pee in a bottle or something.

I can't believe I'm even considering this. Ginny took a deep breath, bracing herself to try again.

Help—or at least, a distraction—arrived from an unexpected quarter. "What the hell's going on?" Juju stopped between them and the kids, hands on his lean hips and the pompom on his blue hat nodding slightly. His cheeks were raw with the cold, and Traveller, silent for once, trotted worriedly behind him, tail sinking as the dog got closer and scented tension. The kids were in a tight knot, Carline's arm over Mandy's shoulders, Steph hugging herself, Mark's big-knuckled hands—he hadn't grown into them yet, though his shoulders were acquiring a respectable size—working at each other as if he still had zombie blood on them. "You two havin a fight?"

"Not a fight," Ginny hurried to explain. Her scalp itched; whoever had said the body would clean itself without modern detergents was a liar. God, what she wouldn't give for a hot shower. "I'm telling him he should go to Atlanta with you and the kids, Juju. He's being stubborn."

"And what would you be doin if we go Atlanta way, Ginny?" Juju shook his head. "He ain't the stubborn one here. It ain't *certain* there's anything in Georgia worth goin for, and I'd like as not go North. South ain't never been good for me."

Well, that was one way to put it. Ginny paused, absorbing this. "If there's even a chance that the CDC there has a facility—look, we might be immune." At least Juju would listen to reason, instead of running over the top of her with suggestions and pronouncements and *this is what we're gonna do.* "And if so, they'll need us to help engineer some kind of cure."

"Oh, *hell* no," Juju said. "Heard that shit before, ma'am. Ever hear of Tuskegee? *Fuck* that noise, and I ain't apologizin for my language, ma'am. *I* ain't goin to no Atlanta, and I'll thank you not to bring it up."

"Oh." Ginny blinked. Her arms loosened, her hands falling to her sides. "I didn't know you felt that way, Juju. I'm so sorry." God, now she felt like an ass. She hadn't even *considered* that side of it.

"Yeah, well." He nodded, briskly, and Traveller reached her side, stropping against her left shin, circling worriedly. "Don't pay it no more mind. Wanna help me pack up beds? Like to get goin soon."

"Yes, of course." She glanced nervously at Lee, who said nothing, just glowered at her, at Juju, and the whole world. *Now* she'd pissed him off. "I guess I'm wrong. I'm sorry."

Lee shrugged, turned on his heel, and stalked off for the cereal aisle. Maybe he needed some time to cool down.

Great. Ginny rubbed at her temples and hurried after Juju. Traveller, sensing the tension had blown over, began to yip-yowl his usual excited commentary when he knew his pack was Getting Ready to Go.

[13]

ENOUGH TO SHINE YOUR SHOES

"You mad at me?" Mark hefted the box of canned food onto the tailgate and scratched under the brim of his knit cap, rubbing hard enough to reach brains—if he'd had any.

Steph shook her head, settling the box where it should be. Like playing that old game on the school library's ancient computers, where you had to fit funny falling shapes into each other until they vanished. Even as short as she was, there was a real danger of forgetting she was under a canopy and giving herself a concussion. "Nah." *Mad* wasn't really the word, so it wasn't really a lie, was it?

They'd shoveled paths to the truck and the 4x4, and white undulating hills stretched in every direction. Zombie tracks circled the entire building, but they'd stopped coming around to the side entrance before the snow ceased, so *those* furrows were mercifully blurred.

She couldn't decide which was worse—zombie tracks, or the vast swathes of unbroken white. No tire tracks, no footsteps, nothing. Like the whole earth had closed up for the winter.

"Then what is it?" He was persistent, she'd give him that. "You been avoidin me."

"I can't avoid you, Mark. There ain't enough space." She settled another box, made sure it was fastened, and crouched on the tailgate, leaning back to get her rear down and her legs off the shelf, so to speak. Hopping down was a jolt each time, but when Mark moved to help she pushed off before she was ready, hit hard, and almost went sprawling.

"You could let me help." He reached for her arm again. "What the fuck, Steph?"

She leaned away and almost snapped *watch your mouth*, like she was an adult and he wasn't. But Lord, didn't she feel like it, sometimes.

The front of the Bargain Zone was all blue and yellow, but the side was just plain concrete and anonymous metal doors. Mr Lee and Miz Ginny were deep in conversation again near Mr Juju's black four-by-four, Lee leaning in and looming over the library lady, Miz Ginny's arms folded and her expression plainly shouting she didn't like it. She was patient, and Mr Lee wasn't mean. Still, Steph found herself copying the older woman's body language when Mark stepped close—folded arms, chin up, *don't touch me* closing around her like old-timey knight's armor. "Don't talk that way to me," she managed. "It ain't proper."

"Oh, proper." Mark nodded. His dark eyes managed to look both velvety and burning at the same time, like briquettes before they grew a coat of white and Daddy said you could lay the steaks down. "Okay. You got yourself new friends now, and don't need trailer trash like me around?"

Oh, for God's sake. Now his *pride* was involved. "Why would you say somethin like that?" Steph cast a quick look around. Thin, cloud-filtered sunlight bounced off the snow; you needed to wade through it, and driving was likely to be a piece. Still, she didn't like the idea of staying here either, and if Mr Lee thought they could make it to a better location, she was all for it. "Fine. We might as well talk about it now."

"I'm all ears."

She refrained from pointing out he was all *nose* instead. That was, in her mama's words, not helpful at all. "Why didn't you say nothin when that man was mean to Mr Thurgood, huh?"

"What?" Baffled, he stared at her. His red-rimmed nostrils flared a little whenever he was mad, but when he was puzzled his mouth loosened a little and his forehead wrinkled.

Steph set herself to try to explain, nice and calm, like how Miz Ginny would. "You just *stood* there."

"Is that...what?" He studied her face. The cold pinkened him in some spots, reddened him in others, and curled his shoulders up. He was bulking out a little. Traveling agreed with him.

Or maybe being in a car all day and eating crap was making everyone rounder.

The words she'd been sitting on tumbled out, jostling each other. "Why didn't you say nothin? Why didn't you, I don't know, stand up to him? You can't just...he was so mean to Mr Thurgood. You heard it, you were right there."

"Mr Juju can handle himself." Mark dropped his gloved hands and stepped back a little, cocking his head like the dog when he wasn't quite sure what he'd heard.

Oh, for God's sake. It was like talking to a wall. "That ain't the point."

"What, I should've punched him? Like Carty?"

"No." *Yes. Maybe.* "But you didn't do *nothin*, Mark."

"What was I s'posed to do?"

Something. Anything. "Nothin, I guess." She backed up two steps, and turned on her heel. These boots were killer; Mama would never have bought her a pair this good. The Meachams didn't go camping enough, and shoes were *expensive*. You could tell these were quality from the way they cradled her feet and gripped through packed-down snow.

All sorts of stuff was standing on shelves now, waiting for someone to come along and pick it up. There weren't any shortages, and nobody needed money anymore. Unless there were places the sickness didn't reach? It was enough to make a body wonder. How long would the supplies last? How many survivors were there? There had to be some math that would tell her, right? Maybe Miss Ginny would know. A percentage, maybe.

Steph had a suspicion that percentage wasn't likely to be high, or even medium.

"Steph." Mark grabbed her shoulder, his fingers sinking in through her coat. It didn't quite hurt, but it wasn't gentle, either. "Dammit, come on. I'm sorry, okay? Next time I'll—"

"Ain't gonna be a next time, Mark." Because she wasn't gonna sit around waitin, that was for damn sure. If Carline and Mandy could survive on their own just fine, and bash in zombie skulls, what was there to stop Steph from takin' matters into her own hands? And Miz Ginny, too, standing up to Mr Lee like it was no big thing. Steph suspected Miss Ginny could have handled even Daddy in one of his his bull-roarin rip-snorts, too.

"What the hell you talkin about?" Mark's voice bounced off the concrete wall but fell dead into the snow.

Carline appeared with an armful of rolled-up sleeping bags, the employee door swinging almost-closed behind her, hitting the wedge they put to keep it from latching. The redheaded girl glanced up, and almost dropped the bags in their bulky waterproof sleeves. "Steph?" She had a high, light, pretty voice, and her hair was coppery in the morning light. "You okay?"

There were a lot of things that could mean, from *is he hassling you* to *do you need rescuin?*

"Fine." Steph waved, to make it official, and pasted a smile on. Carline didn't smile back, just stood there with her arms full, watchful, a slight blush on her smooth porcelain cheeks. Even her eyebrows glittered a little, and the same old familiar popped-balloon feeling filled Steph's chest. It wasn't nice or right or proper to feel bad now that there was a prettier girl around, but there it was. "We're just talkin."

"No, you're just tellin me I ain't good enough to shine your shoes." The fringe of dark hair across Mark's forehead, pushed down by his hat, almost hid his eyes. Especially since he dropped his chin and stared at the ground. "I thought you was different, Steph."

Good *Lord* and Sonny Jesus, as Mama would say when exasperated. "If that's what you wanna turn this into, fine. Go ahead." She pushed past him, her shoulder striking his since he didn't move, and her eyes blurred a little. Stupid of him to get all *boy*, when all she was doing was trying to *talk* to him. He'd started it, anyway, acting like she should be all grateful or something, and for what? Just because he'd punched Carty didn't mean his shit didn't stink.

Carline let her take two of the sleeping bags. "Thanks," the redhead said, gazing past Steph, steadily. Her blue eyes, lighter than Steph's and fringed with thick coppery lashes, were prettier, too. "You sure you okay?"

"Fine. He just gets that way sometimes." *Chip on his shoulder*, Mama would call it.

It was Mark who had banged Mama on the head with the cast-iron, too. And held Steph in her bed afterward, not trying anything mean or crazy. Just...held her.

Maybe she shouldn't have said anything. But it bothered her. How could he be so good some ways, and then just stand there when Mr French...said what he said, did what he did?

"Boys do." Carline made a little motion, like tossing her hair over her shoulder. "Where do these go?"

There was work to do. She could worry about Mark later. "In the truck. I'll show you."

[14]

TWO CONVERSATIONS

Gettin' through the snow wasn't the problem. The four-by was a little lower than the truck, which meant Lee plowed ahead and they stopped to clear the grilles every so often, but that was to be expected. The freeway was even relatively clear, and the snow was wet and clumping, falling in on itself as the temperature crept above freezing in the afternoon. They made it to the outskirts of Louisville just as clouds began threatening from the north—if the weather would make up its mind, Lee could settle his own.

No, the problem was completely different, and it wasn't one he had any goddamn answer for.

With Ginny in the four-by with Juju and the girls, Lee was left with Mark and Traveller. Neither were ideal companions, between the boy's morose silence and the dog's slobber. At least with Ginny in the car Lee could have tried to undo some of the damage. He hadn't meant to snap at her, but dear Lord, what was the woman *thinking*?

You have a responsibility, she kept sayin'. Well, he was out of the Army, and his responsibility was what he damn well *wanted* it to be. That was what mustering out meant, and he'd been looking forward to it all his life. Now that he had it, she just wanted to what? Send him off with a pat on the head? While she took herself off through hostile territory infested with God-knew-what, into the teeth of winter?

"Women," Lee muttered, squinting at the melting snow. It was getting easier to goose the truck through, though this long shallow curve heading into the city had just enough of a slope to be troublesome.

Amazingly, that broke Mark's silence. "Amen."

Now just what do you know about 'em, son? That was probably the wrong thing to say. Lee hadn't missed Steph sidling away from the boy. Well, girls got clannish, and she was probably liking talkin' to her own kind after so long without. "Somethin on your mind, Mark?"

"Nosir." It only took another thirty seconds before it burst out, since Mark had been sitting and stewing all damn morning. "How do you deal with 'em, sir?"

"Deal with who now?" Lee had a sinking sensation he knew. He turned the defroster up a notch, even though the windshield was perfectly clear.

"Women, sir." Mark cracked his left knuckles, a nervous movement and one Lee hoped wasn't going to be a habit. That noise was annoying as fuck. "Girls."

"Never had much luck, myself. They a different species." A pretty one, though. One that could make even a closed-up oyster feel like singing.

Or drive Job himself mad with the galloping conundrums.

"Aliens." Mark pulled his cap off, running his fingers through dark hair. It stood up like it was full of shortening. Now that he'd said something about the burr in his saddle, he couldn't sit still. "You think they like you, then alla sudden wham they turn round and you ain't even good enough to shine their shoes. Daddy was right about 'em. He said they're all...well, you know."

"Hold up now." *I don't think I'd trust anything Kasprak Senior said about anythin other than beer, kid.* "No call for that kind of talk, young 'un."

"Yessir." Mark shot him an uncertain glance. "But Miz Ginny this mornin—"

Trust a kid to put an elbow right into a sensitive spot. "She wasn't tellin me I ain't fit. She got an idear in her head, that's all." Lee found out he believed it as soon as it left his mouth. "Thing about women is, they get those idears, and a man goes along if he knows what's good for him." Well, that wasn't the *whole* truth. Lee eased off the accelerator, and the hill leveled out a little bit. The chains bit packed snow, and he steered into the slide that wanted to happen. It straightened out right quick, and at least he could do *that* without screwing up. "Unless he can't. Then there's some sparks."

Sparks could start a forest fire, if you let 'em. Best just to not give 'em any fuel, that was all.

Mark ket chewin' at the rough spot, just like a hound. "You ever been married, Mr Lee?"

That made two people asking him about it lately. "You know I ain't, kid." Once or twice, he'd thought maybe he might want to...but it never seemed like there was any prospect. He was used to being invisible, and sometimes it was easier to buy what you needed rather than get foolish.

Especially because of Lee Senior. No reason to risk bad blood coming out, even if Big Q and Nonna both told him he wasn't like his daddy. Lee's daddy was held to have a certain mean streak, all the more potent because it was kept bottled until that one rainy night.

Don't you talk to me about that boy, Big Q had said once, when Nonna mentioned taking Lee to visit his daddy. *He done turned mean.*

That was one way of puttin' it.

"Well, you was in the Army. Figured sometimes guys get married, you know, in other ports. And stuff." Was Mark blushing? It certainly *sounded* like it.

"That's the Navy." Lord, how did he get into this conversation? More importantly, how did he get *out*?

"Oh." Mark sat on it for another half-mile, absently petting Traveller's head. The dog sprawled between them snoring peacefully, drool bubbling at the corners of his lips. "Steph's mad at me because I didn't punch Mr French. When he was mean to Mr Thurgood."

Now that was interesting. Lee filed it away for further thought. "I'll bet Ginny'd be mad if she knew I did."

"You did?" Damn the kid, he didn't have to sound so impressed.

Lee squinted against the snow-glare even behind his sunglasses. "He was fixin to hit me."

"But you punched *him?*" Mark's voice cracked on the last word.

"I did." *I'd be lyin if I said it didn't feel good, too.* The only thing that would've felt better was hitting the yellow-ass sonofabitch twice.

"Oh."

Good Lord, now he was a role model, and had to say something wise. "Don't you get the idea punchin's the way to go, son. It ain't." Made more problems than it solved, sometimes.

"But Steph said—"

"I ain't sayin *don't fight.* Man's got to, one way or another." Given current events, there was a lot more coming sooner, Lee figured. He feathered the accelerator, chains digging in to get them over a slight hump. "What I'm sayin is, don't *start* one. Finish it if you gotta, but don't start nothin."

"Okay." Mark nodded thoughtfully, mashing his hat back on, crushing his hair. "So Steph don't like that I didn't punch him, and Miss Ginny wouldn't like that you did."

"I ain't sayin it makes sense." *Because women don't, my grand-daddy told me often enough.* "It's just the way it is."

"But how do you *talk* to them?"

Wasn't *that* an age-old question. "Same way you do to anyone else." With a heavy helping of shutting up when you could, and keepin' it short when you couldn't.

"Aliens," the kid muttered darkly, staring out the windshield like there might be an answer somewhere on the snowbound highway. "What am I gonna do?"

Lee might have offered a suggestion or two, despite the inherent risk of such things where women were involved, but he was saved from an unlikely quarter. A sudden, roiling, ugly stench filled his nostrils and made his eyes water. "Good *God*," he blurted, and his hand darted to roll down his window.

"Jesus!" Mark said at almost exactly the same moment, and reached for his.

Traveller, supremely unbothered by either their conversation or its subject, snored, shifted his hindquarters a little, and farted again.

"Forty years," Juju answered darkly, squinting. The four-by crept in the truck's wake, and the glare off melting snow was dazzling even with sunglasses on. "That's how long."

"What's syphilis?" Carline wanted to know, leaning forward and peering out at the windshield. She wore a faint powdery perfume, pleasant despite the close quarters.

"A sexually transmitted disease." Ginny's *of-course-your-request-is-normal* librarian voice was coming in handy all the time, now. The Merck Manual's thin pages fluttered a little in her lap, the heat turned up since one or two bullets had punched all the way through the car's hard shell. A cold draft every once in a while was a reminder she did *not* need of how far off-course the planet was veering.

"Ain't just *any* disease, it's the mother of 'em all." Juju shook his head, the pompom on his cap bouncing. "Makes you insane, makes parts of you fall off—"

"Which parts?" This was the most interesting discussion Steph had been party to in a while, and it was obvious by the way she leaned forward too, almost breathing in Ginny's hair.

I can't believe I'm having this conversation. "Your nose, for one. There can be lesions on your, ah, your genitals." Ginny kept her tone level. "It can also be passed to babies when the mother gives birth. Congenital, that's the word. It's very nasty."

"And they didn't treat it?" Mandy's disbelief spiraled up into almost-supersonic from the window seat behind Juju. "For *forty years?*"

"Oh, maybe they treated some." Juju's knuckles stood up as he gripped the wheel, the burn scar on his left hand shining. He'd taken his gloves off, *to feel the road*, he said. "But mostly they wanted to know what happened if you didn't. Since it was only black men."

A short, breathless, pained silence filled the four-by-four's cabin, broken only by soft static from the radio as it scanned endlessly, searching for a signal, and the faint whistling of cold air from somewhere.

"That's fu—uh, that's effed up." Carline leaned back, sandwiched between Mandy and Steph. Her left hand, caught in Mandy's right, tensed. "They just *let it happen?*"

"Ain't the first time." Mandy stared out her window, her snub-nosed profile thoughtful and oddly serene. "Been experimenting on brown people since they met 'em, really."

Ginny's head throbbed, and her throat ached. The Merck manual on her lap had started this whole thing, really. Trying to find a disease that fit what they'd seen, however loosely, was difficult. The current subject wasn't helping her concentration, either. She hadn't gone after an education degree, but it looked like she was about to have a teacher's duties thrust upon her anyway.

"You got that right." Juju's frown deepened, if that were possible. "What you want to bet this whole thing ain't some gummint crap that escaped the test tube, huh?"

Ginny nodded, slowly. "It would make sense." *But that doesn't help me treat it.* Were there any doctors left capable of figuring this out? What would happen when the current stock of antibiotics behind pharmacy counters or tucked away in hospitals ran out? Was there an antibiotic that worked against this thing? If there was, why hadn't anyone hit on it—or had they by now, and lacked the means to deploy it? How many medical professionals were left, after all? Once she got started on that mental merry-go-round, it was goodbye to her calm, and hello to steadily mounting anxiety. "I just wish I could figure out what this illness might have mutated from, or where it started."

"Why?" Carline wanted to know.

It's certainly not for my own amusement. "That would give me some idea of how to treat it, the forms it's likely to take, how to deal with the sufferers."

Mandy snorted, a very teenage sound. "Sufferers? They're zombies."

"That's what we call them, yes." *Be patient*, she reminded herself, and took a deep breath. "A lot of times though, with diseases, if you catch it early you can treat it. In this case, once the seizures start..." She almost lost her train of thought, staring down at the page.

"Yeah, my daddy threw himself all over the room when the shakes hit him." Mandy shuddered. "Mama thought he was possessed."

It was Carline's turn to laugh. "Your mama thought everything was possessed."

"So did yours." Both girls cracked up.

Steph smiled uncertainly, a stranger to their in-jokes. "My mama made my daddy go and get a flu shot with her. Funny, they got 'em and...and died anyway."

"My daddy said flu shots were just a way to make money off'n you." Mandy sobered. "He said that about a lot of things."

"Insurance?" Carline piped up. "I remember him talking about that."

"Yeah, and magazines." Mandy's tone was thoughtful.

Steph had to know more about this. "Magazines?"

"Subscriptions, you know. Pay good money for something you end up wiping with."

Steph, of course, took it one logical step further. "Did he think toilet paper was a scam?"

All three girls laughed, like bright birds. The sound was a tonic, but it also made Ginny's head hurt more.

"You okay?" Juju glanced at her, his eyebrows almost meeting over the top edges of his cat's-eye sunglasses. They had heavy tortoiseshell rims, and suited him immensely. "You lookin a little peaked."

"I didn't sleep well." That was the understatement of the year. "And this morning wasn't...pleasant." It was, in fact, a downright mess. Lee was probably furious at her, especially after the second round of not-quite-argument outside.

It was hard to tell, he was so quiet. If he'd simply get mad she could deal with it, but his silence was...uncomfortable.

"Yeah, well." Juju's right hand twitched, like he wanted to reach across the intervening space. He didn't, but the gesture warmed her. "Lot of that goin around."

Carline began telling a long involved joke about toilet paper, two grandmothers, and a traveling salesman. Ginny did her best to concentrate, paging through arcane diseases and contraindications. The vehicle bumped, her head throbbed, and she wished, suddenly and with uncharacteristic viciousness, that she hadn't stopped for coffee on her way out of Cotton Crossing.

[15]

LOOKING UP

"It's okay." Brandon French kept his hands up and tried a nice, easy smile. He hadn't shaved—what was the point? Except now he wished he had, looking good was the secret to success. "I'm human, all right? *Human*."

"You been bit?" The grey-haired woman—she was clearly in control here, from the way she stood in front of her group bunched in the dark hotel foyer and held the shotgun in her capable little paws—eyed him mistrustfully behind her steel-rimmed glasses. "Answer me!"

"No ma'am." Oh, he knew what was necessary now, in this brave new world. More of the smiling and scraping he hated in the *old* one. "No bites, no sniffles, no fever."

Why had he stayed at the hotel? Well, it was at least familiar, and he had the pleasure of pissing in the bed that hick motherfucker had slept in. That particular room was was looking a little worse for wear, but Brandon could use a different one each night. There was no shortage.

There was no shortage of anything, really. Except women. He'd had a chance with Ginny, but she apparently liked hicks, inbreds, and affirmative action better. Who needed a cougar when there was fresh meat around, anyway? This group—not all white, but all female, mostly under twenty and only two of them fat—was much better.

The grey-haired one with the shotgun was round, and her wire-rim glasses glinted. So did the bluing on her shotgun's barrel. Pale, glinting eyes peered from under a shock of silvery hair, and her chin was too soft to give him any real concern. She looked like his mother, actually—though Sylvia French would never have *dreamed* of holding a shotgun, especially with unmanicured, nail-bitten hands.

"Shura?" One of the girls—they looked like they were on a private school field trip, every social clique represented from the thick glasses and frizzy hair to two polished mannequins—moved behind the woman, uncertainly. "Is he okay?"

"Don't know yet." Grey Hair examined Brandon for a few more moments, then lowered her gun. "Provisionally, I suppose. Harper, Cora, you two find us some rooms, top floor. Juana, Maria, get started on dinner. Minnie, Shanice, you're weapons detail tonight. Allison, you'll come with me for reconnaissance."

She must have been a fellow teacher. Maybe even a gym teacher, though she wasn't the rangy dyke type. Maybe a fellow humanities educator? The girls scattered, and Grey Hair made a tiny clicking noise with her tongue as Brandon lowered his hands. "You. How long have you been here?"

"A few days." He decided some groundwork needed to be laid, just in case. "I was traveling with another group, but they were...well, we didn't get along."

Instant suspicion. "Why?"

He indicated his face. The bruising was going down, but it was still mottled. Hopefully she could see it in the uncertain light.

The hotel was no longer quiet. Soft, birdlike voices and the sounds of light, stealthy movement echoed. "I don't like bullies." His stomach hurt too, that hick fuck had sucker-punched him. It was unlikely he'd ever see them again, but if he did, Brandon French was going to get him back.

He already had a few satisfying ideas.

"Huh." The shotgun lowered still further. "I'm Miz Halloran. My girls and I are going to Atlanta."

Miz, she said, not offering a first name. She was a bitch, Brandon decided, but that wouldn't stop him from trying to be nice enough to tag along. One of the girls was a hot little number with long dark hair and sloe eyes, reminding him of that sophomore before she turned all bitchy on him, too.

The zombie apocalypse had saved him from that, at least.

It was an unpleasant thought, so Brandon pushed it away and kept his hands where Grey Hair could see them. "Yeah? What's in Atlanta?"

"The Center for Disease Control was telling everyone to go that way, before everything stopped working." Halloran freed one plump hand long enough to push her glasses up on her nose, a thoughtful, entirely habitual motion. "You didn't hear?"

"No, I was taking care of my parents. They got sick." Just the right tone, he hoped—sincere, grieving, reticent to discuss the gory details. "I, uh...is there something I can do to help you? Anything at all? You need something carried, something put together?" Of course they needed some muscle. Girls always did.

The frizz-haired girl with her Coke-bottom glasses peered at him, trying to hide behind the little round woman. Maybe she was subnormal. Maybe both of them were, but he wasn't about to pass this chance up. Hell, if he cozied up to this Halloran he could be in clover.

"That's nice of you." Halloran smiled, but something about those bluish eyes peering through her own metal-rimmed spectacles made him a little uneasy. Kind of like the other English teacher at Lourde Bend High, the bitch the sophomore had gone trotting to. "I think we've got it handled. We'll be out of your way tomorrow."

"Sure," Brandon said, easily. He knew the hotel layout better than they did, and a lot could happen between now and morning.

"Come on, Allison." Halloran edged away, towards the check-in desk. "Let's look around, huh?"

"Okay." The frizzed girl, her broad poreless face escaping attractiveness by a mile but still glowing with youth, gave Brandon another long, fearful look, but trotted behind the older woman obediently enough.

Yes, Brandon told himself, a lot could happen in a single night. His big mistake had been not realizing that sooner.

Things were looking up.

"I know him," Allison said, her dark eyebrows drawing together. Her hair was a halo of tight curls starred with tiny blue barrettes over her temples; she'd stopped trying to straighten it *and* quit pulling it out. Maybe travel agreed with her. She aimed her flashlight beam at the computer in the manager's office, glancing at the dead eye of its monitor longingly. Without electricity, it was just a paperweight. "I *know* I know him."

Shura Halloran, part-time janitor at Maryhill High School before the world ended, examined the rest of the office. Whoever this fellow had been staying with was smart enough to jimmy a side employee door like Shura and her new brood. That kind of went against the man's explanations, but there were three rooms trashed which sort of bore out his story of looters and bullies. The front glass door was smashed and the reception desk rifled, but someone had made an attempt to put some order into things.

It was a puzzle, and one Shura didn't like. "Maybe he's just got one of those faces," she said, diplomatically enough.

Each of the girls was handling this better than Shura had ever thought possible. Even Harper, rich little white girl that she was, seemed happier in the ruins of civilization than she ever had in the hallowed hallways of Maryhill. Given that Harper's parents were dyed in the wool sonofabitches—even her mother, the lacquered Mrs

Faye Feuillette, what a name to marry into—it made a certain amount of sense.

A whole lot more was making sense these days. Things had become very...well, basic, ever since she'd come across Allison cornered in the Stockton Bargain Zone's dairy department by three men, none of them the walking dead.

The zombies were easy to deal with. It was the humans—or, the ones that *called* themselves humans—she didn't really like. Except her girls.

"No, I know him." Allison frowned at the check-in desk, her lazy eye rolling slightly behind her own glasses. "I'll think of it..." She stopped, her mouth open a little, and stared into space.

Shura waited, patiently. If you let them finish thinking, teenagers came up with the damndest things. Why, just this morning Juana was telling them all about physics during class time, and how space was full of dimples. Shanice hadn't believed her until Juana pulled out a textbook, and there it was in black and white.

Dimples, in space. It boggled the mind.

"French," Allison mumbled. "Mr French."

"Whatnow?" Shura pushed open the office door and played her own flashlight across the front desk, eyeing the damage. Someone had made an attempt to clean up in here, too, which wasn't like any looters she'd ever heard of. It also wasn't like a man that looked that way—big, blond, expensive watch, an ingratiating smile—to tidy anything up after his royal self.

"Brandon French, 34, of Currie Lourd, Kansas. English teacher, Lourd Bend High School. It was in the free paper with the coupons. Second page." Allison trailed behind her, eager to help as always. The girl's memory was a steel trap, once you found the right way to plug it in. "Allegations, it said."

"Allegations of what?"

"I knew I knew him." Allison's pleasure at dredging up helpful information was all but incandescent. "Allegations. Yeah."

Shura turned, careful not to spook the girl. "Hm. Did it say anything else?" If Allison thought she was being laughed at—or, worse, if she thought she'd displeased someone she was anxious to be nice to—she'd clam up for a long while, with that peculiar dead-eyed stare.

"Allegations," the girl said, softly. "Sophomore, it said. Name withheld."

"Interesting." Well, that answered that. Shura smiled. A few of the girls—certainly Minnie, and maybe Cora—would know that soft, unpleasant expression of hers already, and have a bright-penny grin in return. They were good girls, and each of them knew what Shura knew too, about men.

Namely, you couldn't trust a single one of them. Allison hadn't even covered her eyes when Shura shot the three men who had finally caught her after a chase through Bargain Zone's aisles.

Here at the end of the world, there were things that needed to be done, and Shura had found out she didn't mind doing them one bit. Not if it kept her girls safe. "Allison," she said, softly, "go tell the girls we have some business to handle tonight."

Allison nodded. Happy to oblige, she loped off, her flashlight bobbing. Shura's hand dropped, and she rubbed the knifehilt at her right hip with her fingertips, a loving little gesture.

[16]

IMMUNITY FACTOR

Some of the lights were on in Louisville, twinkling as shadows gathered. Whole sections of the city were starred with streetlamps flicking on in the early dusk, and Lee was faced with a choice. On the one hand, it would be mighty nice to have power. On the other, other survivors would be thinking the same thing. Just because they'd struck out twice didn't mean *every* other survivor was going to be troublesome, but it wasn't like playing cards. Each draw from the deck wasn't going to narrow their chances of coming across an asshole or two.

Or more, and worse.

Still, electricity was attractive, and there was a Hyatt downtown with its lights on and a restaurant attached. That meant a working kitchen, and maybe Steph and Ginny could scare up something good.

Which was how Lee ended up looking into the barrel of a shotgun, his hands spread wide and harmless, and his shoulders tighter than bridge cables. "Friendly," he said, again. "We're friendly, ma'am. None of us bitten, none of us wantin any trouble."

"Well, that's good news," the slim, velvet-eyed black woman said, lowering the shotgun a little—but not all the way. Blue cotton peeked out from under her unzipped parka and hand-knitted yellow cardigan. Looked like a scrubs top, and her shoes were comfortable thick-soled cream-colored numbers that all but shouted *nurse*. The rest of her followed it up with *no nonsense, thank you*, and the shotgun put a period on the whole damn paragraph. "How many of y'all?"

The Hyatt's foyer was cavernous despite being brightly lit, a wilderness of pseudo-marble flooring, thin red carpet, and bright brass. Behind Lee, Juju let out a sharp breath. He hadn't cleared leather, but it was probably close.

"Half a dozen." Lee didn't move. He was too busy being relieved Ginny and the kids were safely tucked away, and bracing himself for whatever would happen next. This group must've parked in the underground garage, which was what Lee had been aiming to do once he and Juju checked the place. "We can move on, if you'd like."

"We're a half-dozen too. There's plenty of room here, as long as you're not assholes." A small gold cross winked at the nurse's throat.

"Try not to be." Which was, Lee thought, about all a man could lay claim to. His lower back was unhappy with sitting in the truck all day, and he wanted a bathroom like nobody's business.

"Maybe." But her expression eased a little, the line between her eyebrows easing a little. "I'm Frank. Kasie Frank."

"Lee Quartine, ma'am. This is Mr Thurgood, friend of mine."

Miz Frank gave Juju a thorough visual going-over, and maybe that decided her. "Y'all got any booze?"

"No ma'am." *Though I wouldn't say no to some of Horace's Wild Turkey again.*

"Good." The slim woman had good trigger discipline, and thin golden hoop earrings that reminded him of Ginny's. Even the way she held her chin reminded him; he was probably about doomed to measure every woman in the world by a librarian now. "Give me ten minutes or so to let the rest know we've got company. I'd hate for anyone to get itchy."

"Likewise," Juju muttered.

Kasie Frank smiled, a thin, unamused expression, and Lee backed carefully away. It never did to mess with a woman who knew how to handle a shotgun.

Miz Frank was indeed a nurse. Her little group had obviously nominated its leader for capability, and you could tell she measured up handsome by the way they all glanced at her whenever a question came up. Two men and four women; the fellows were Jorge, a cop, and Mike, a weedy-looking dental technician who wore a magenta scrub top under his flannel shirt, too. Besides Miz Frank, there was Holly, another nurse, and Colleen and Chantal, the former a hostess at some place called Bardi's. Between her, Steph, Mark, and Ginny, the kitchen was humming, and once they'd pushed a few tables together there was plenty of room in the middle of the Hyatt's attached restaurant—red carpet more plush than in the foyer, reddish drapes, and a snap-freezing night outside the smoked-glass windows —for everyone to take a seat and help themselves.

It wasn't the kind of place Lee would've chosen to eat in, but right now it was welcome.

Chantal, a sleek-haired ebon lady of about forty-five, owned a salon. She picked nervously at hot, crispy French fries produced by the cavernous, eerily clean kitchen. "Had one of them run right through our plate glass window. Bit Leanne. She was one of my best nail girls." Her fingertips were crimson, the polish a bit ragged and two of her nails ripped down to the quick. "Poor thing."

"I worked at Evansville General, about a hundred miles north." Kasie Frank, her smooth brown cheeks blanching a bit, accepted a refill of hot cocoa from Carline, who handled the thermal pitcher like a girl used to pouring sweet tea. "One day we had a lot of flu cases, the next we had people coding and going berserk. It was like hell opened up and tossed out everyone behind on their rent."

Traveller was having a fine time of it, cleaning up dropped French fries under the table, nosing at knees, sniffing shoes, and generally making a nuisance of himself. Jorge didn't like dogs, but he put up with it, and each time Traveller passed Miz Frank she put down a hand to scrub at his ears.

That made Lee feel a whole lot better about everything, really.

Juju settled, after loading his plate. His jacket hung on the back of his chair, and though he'd left the rifle in his room, his shoulder holster was full and ready, like Jorge's. "Lee saw the Army shoot up the street in our town, chasing some of the critters."

"Zombies," Mark muttered, but not very loudly, from his seat right next to Steph. The girl didn't scoot away, and Lee thought it likely Mark was very conscious of the fact, by the way his cheeks kept reddening and paling in quick succession.

Skinny redheaded Mike the dental tech—his last name was Mock, the poor fella—lifted his enamel mug of strong coffee in a salute. "*Thank* you. I been calling 'em that for ages now, but these guys don't like it." His battered Timex, probably handed down from a family member, was turned around on his wrist like Lee's own watch.

He was betting Mike had some military in his past, too.

"It's a loaded word." Colleen the hostess busied herself with handing out napkins, black hair pulled back in a tight ponytail. Her earrings—much larger gold hoops—glittered as they swung, and of all the women, she was the only one wearing perfume, grimly determined not to let the end of the world interrupt her style. "There's gotta be a reasonable explanation. *Got* to be."

God bless women. When it came time to rebuild, they were gonna make it worthwhile. Not the skyscrapers or the big machines, no sir. Women were the ones with all those little things that made you realize life wasn't just surviving.

"Ginny was in med school," Juju said, stabbing at a steak that had been frozen a little while ago but was now mouthwatering, and perfectly seared. It looked damn good. "She's been trying to figure it out."

That perked Kasie right up. "Really? Where?" She and Mike both straightened, interest bright in their gazes.

Ginny looked up, dragged out of whatever worry was running

around behind her pretty eyes now. "Stanford, but I washed out." She was pale, and tendrils of her dark hair stuck to her forehead. She all but glowed under the electric lights, a faint dewy sheen on her forehead and cheeks. "I ended up a librarian."

"Kind of the same as nursing, only with less bedpans." Kasie grinned, used to putting people at their ease, and it was nice to see Ginny tentatively smile back. Looked like she was about to make a remark, too, but didn't get the chance.

"We didn't have Army shooting up the streets in Columbus," Jorge cut in, as if about to burst. Looked like the law in his part of the world carried Glocks, and he sat with his knees spread like his balls needed to dry off or somethin'. "But we had a lotta domestics, and those damn checkpoints. Half the force had a bad cold, and then whammo, everyone's dropping and Dispatch overloaded."

"Everyone at church had a cold the week before," Steph piped up, handing the fried chicken platter to Holly. Miss Meacham had moved to Jell-O salad already, her sweet tooth probably doing jumping jacks for joy. "They say that's how it starts."

"Fever, flu symptoms, then the convulsions." Ginny shuddered, her shoulder hitting Lee's. Close quarters were nice as far as he was concerned, it might remind her she didn't have to worry alone. It probably helped everyone to Monday-morning quarterback the end of the world, but it seemed fair to put her off her feed, by the way she kept pushing her food around her plate. Very little of it made its way down the hatch.

Lee didn't like that at all.

"Nothin about it on the radio." Juju laid his fork and knife down, reached for his own coffee mug. The way he and that Mock fella were drinking it, they'd be up all night unless they planned on going round the curve and using it as a soporific. "If I'd'a known—"

"There was no way of knowing." Ms Frank jumped in before anyone else could. "I had me some damn fine doctors trying to figure it out, but they got bit by patients." She glanced across the table at Lee. "How about you, Mr Quartine?"

Huh? Lee blinked. "Don't know many doctors."

"No, what happened to you and your girlfriend?"

"I'm not his—" Ginny began, at the same time Lee started with, "Well, they shot up a diner..."

Steph laughed, elbowing Mandy, who joined in merrily. Mark looked baffled for a moment, but then a grin spread over his beaky face, and he bent over his chow as if to hide it.

Juju snorted, almost choking on his coffee. "Lord, you two."

The cop—Jorge—stared down at his plate. "My wife took my daughter to the hospital." He shook his head, slowly. "Went there to try an find 'em, and that's how I met Kasie."

"I was glad to see someone who wasn't growlin and chewin air." Miz Frank stretched her legs under the table and rounded her shoulders to stretch, catlike, carefully in case the dog was in the way. Cords stood out in her slim neck, warm and carved. "We came across Chantal and Holly a couple days later, they'd teamed up to get out of Hadsburg."

"My husband came after me," Holly said, softly. "For the *last* time," she added.

"My boyfriend just vanished." Chantal sighed. "Don't know if he got sick or what."

"My partner got bit," Juju said. "I had to beat his head in with a lamp."

Good God, was everyone gonna *talk* about it? Lee fought the urge to hunch his shoulders. Let them jabber, if it helped. He was content with holding his peace, and watching Ginny push her food around.

"Yeah." Mike rubbed at his cheek, fingertips rasping on thin stubble. "Mine came home sick from work. I made him chicken soup. That night he got the shakes, then tried to bite me."

Juju opened his mouth, closed it with a snap. Lee's eyebrows wanted to rise, but he busied himself with his plate. No business of his, especially when nobody else seemed to blink an eye. And sometimes, he'd wondered about Juju's...feelings, maybe, for Tip. Still, Juju had gone on rec with the rest of them, right?

Who cared? Not Lee Quartine, he decided. There were too many other fish needing to go in the pan.

"It was my daughter." Colleen smoothed her hair back with her fingertips, touched one earring. "Everyone was sick at the restaurant, they had to close down. I went home, and Erica was in the hallway. Just standing there, chewing." She shuddered, and reached for her bottle of grape soda like she wished it was something stronger.

"My mama tried to kill me." Steph sank back in her chair, her gaze fixed over Chantal's head across from her. "Mark had to hit her with a fryin pan."

"It weren't no big deal," Kasprak mumbled, dropping his chin.

"It was," she insisted. "I'd've died."

An uncomfortable silence fell, but Ginny roused herself. "Immunity," she said. "We should compare notes, and figure out if we have commonalities. To see why we didn't end up catching it."

"Handwashing, probably." Mike applied himself to Steph's fried chicken. "Hey, this is good."

Kasie pushed her chair back, half-rising to reach for one of the unopened Evian bottles in the center of the table. "That's why we're going to Atlanta."

"You too?" Mandy's braids swung, the blue beads clicking. "You heard about the CDC there?"

"Yeah. If anyone can find an immunity factor, it's them." The nurse sounded very certain, and Lee sensed Ginny's stiffening next to him. "Y'all are goin there too?"

"We're heading New York way," Lee said, steadily. Traveller pushed his head between Lee's knees and peered up at him past the edge of the tablecloth. "Leastways, I am, with Ginny. Juju too, far as I know."

"Amen to that." Juju lifted his coffee cup. "I ain't goin south unless I *have* to."

"Don't blame you." Kasie's mouth drew down at the corners as she settled, but whether it was distaste for going south or a pucker from her almost-finished lemonade was unclear. "What's in New York?"

"Excuse me." Ginny rose, carefully. Traveller tensed, his tail thwomping under the table.

"Ginny—" Lee began. *Oh, darlin. Don't.*

"I need the restroom," she said, in a low, unsteady voice. "And no, Lee, nobody needs to go with me. It's *fine.*" She pushed her chair all the way back, turned so quickly her single French braid bounced, and set off for the front of the Hyatt's in-house restaurant where the ladies' room—probably full of taupe and powder—was. Probably even had dishes of mints on the counters. The entire place was class.

"I guess that's a sore subject," Colleen said softly. "Is she okay?"

Lee held Traveller's collar, keeping the dog from trotting after her. "Ain't been sleepin well, I guess." A chill ran down his back, cold fingers tracing little signs on his skin. It wasn't just that, though. She was sitting on something, and he had to get her to spill it so that awful weight would slide off her shoulders and onto his. "She's got people in New York. Worried about 'em."

"Lord, I'm *glad* I haven't heard from my in-laws," Jorge muttered, and a laugh ran around the table on heavy, unsteady feet.

[17]

PROSAIC COMFORT

It was the first time Ginny was truly alone in ages, and she wasn't enjoying it much. She even missed the dog's constant neediness. She caught herself looking down, quick glances to check on the adorable little furry roadblock; each time, she shook her head and told herself it was a good thing he hadn't followed her upstairs. She turned the deadbolt and leaned against the door for a moment, resting her forehead against its wonderful coolness. Carting her luggage and a few bottles of water in while everyone else was at dinner might be impolite, but good God, she was *done*. Her bra was chafing, her headache was monumental, and now that she had access to a hot shower, all other considerations became secondary.

Not that it would matter, soon, if what she suspected was true. Ginny laid out her supplies neatly—alcohol wipes, a digital thermometer and an analog one, the stethoscope and blood pressure cuff filched from the pharmacy of the Bargain Zone where they'd met Carline and Mandy. Soap, shampoo, razor. There weren't going to be any more Gillettes made, not if this thing was worldwide.

The more she tried to think through the implications, the harder her brain resisted. The headache probably bore some responsibility for that, but the rest of it was...well, it was just so *big*. You couldn't stare something huge in the face for long before it took a toll.

It was fine for the abyss to look back into you. What she couldn't take was seeing the implications at the bottom of the void anymore. Instead, Ginny took her vitals, including her temperature twice with each thermometer, logged the numbers in her notebook. Laid her pen down and struggled out of her sweater, unbuttoning the flannel shirt underneath.

Her skin crawled while she stripped down, and the first blast of warm water felt so good she exhaled sharply, almost moaning. Finally washing her hair again was an almost religious experience. Sponge baths just didn't do it, and hair-washing with cold water might be great for the cuticles, but it meant the rest of her froze.

Another thing that would soon be academic, she suspected. The only thing disturbing her enjoyment was the headache, and her nose filling up again. She'd been sniffing all day, the back of her throat raw with postnasal drip. Nobody noticed because the cold made every-one's nose stuffy. It wasn't really bad until the warmth of the hotel freed up all the mucus. Still, she took her time enjoying the shower. Her favorite almond-drop bodywash was just as creamy and fragrant as ever, and shaving again was pure heaven. Good grooming was a way to help yourself feel better; it was an article of faith for a Mills girl.

She could have stayed under the warm stream forever, if she hadn't started coughing. Deep, chesty coughs, full and productive.

Ew. It helped to regard the symptoms clinically, but still, gross. There was no shortage of towels. At least she'd be...comfortable? Was that the word?

It could just be a cold, Ginny told herself. Stress taking its toll on the immune system.

She took her vitals again afterward. Her temp had risen by less than a half-degree, hovering at 101.7F. Pulse slightly elevated, blood pressure a little high, too. At lunch, her temperature had been 99F. She noted it all again, and doubled over as another wave of coughing struck. Finally, gasping for breath and hanging onto the counter, she peered at her indistinct ghost in the condensation-clouded mirror.

What would she look like after the...

"Oh, God," she whispered. "It could be a cold. It *could*."

Could she take the chance? Of course not. Ridiculous, and downright cowardly, to even *think* about it.

Her most comfortable boxers, covered in penguins and with the waistband of popped and snarled elastic, were like freedom itself. Her old Moss Bridges T-shirt, soft and wide-necked, stuck to the dampness on her lower back. Ginny turned the fan timer on, carried the med supplies into the bedroom, and laid them out on the nightstand.

With that done, she eyed all the furniture in the room again, and set to work. A half-hour of tugging, swearing, and coughing, and her room door was well-blocked. Finally, nursing a bruised knee from the dresser—it was admirably heavy, real quality or maybe just weighted down—she stood for a moment contemplating the drapes. Sick people always wanted them closed, but she wanted light in the morning. Besides, who would be peeping now? The "balcony" was six inches of space with welded iron grill masquerading as a balustrade, probably full of cigarette butts, and the only thing below was the parking lot. Five stories below, to be precise.

Ginny turned the bed down. Who cared what was on the sheets at this point? She crawled gratefully into linens that appeared clean, settling on pillows that had cradled many a head before hers. Her phone, plugged in and charging on the nightstand, had no service, but it was a prosaic comfort nonetheless.

She longed to call home. Even a half-hour of Mom's vapors would be welcome. Maybe Flo was rethinking blaming Ginny, that would be nice too. So nice.

It could simply be a cold. Or even, laughably, the flu. If it *wasn't* the zombie sickness, hydration and rest would help. Also, if everyone left and she pulled through, she could easily find a car and be on her way. Dad would be so happy to see her.

If the fever, headache, chills, and coughing were what she suspected, she wouldn't be able to get out and hurt anyone else. She'd blocked the door as well as she was able, and if she made it out to the balcony five stories up had a comfortably non-survivable percentage, at least from what she could recall.

Ginny turned the terrible attempt at blown-glass lamp off. The faint edge of reflected glow from the snowbound lot under sodium lights was comforting. If she kept her eyes mostly closed, she could pretend everything was fine, that she was on a road trip to see her parents, that the hideous growling, chewing things were simply a nightmare from an unfamiliar bed and bad food.

Lying to herself was a bad habit to start, but Ginny, damp all over with fever-sweat and the remains of her shower, didn't care, and fell into a restless doze.

[18]

DEMOCRACY IN ACTION

They didn't set a watch, and though it bothered both Lee and Juju, a solid night's sleep made a world of difference. Lee was out as soon as his head touched the pillow, Traveller making himself at home on the damn bed as well, and not a single bad dream troubled either of them. Later, he'd kick himself up and down for it, but at the time he assumed Ginny was already asleep when he knocked on her door. Missing the usual nightly chat bothered him, and so did finding the Do Not Disturb tag still hung neatly on her door the next morning, and her nowhere in sight.

Well, maybe she was sleeping in. God knew she needed it, he hadn't missed the circles under her eyes. If she was getting some rest, he shouldn't disturb it.

"If you want to," he repeated, "go ahead."

"Well, I dunno." Mandy rubbed at the back of her neck with one slim hand, her beaded hair clicking gently. Her wide dark eyes were troubled. "We don't know 'em, though that lady in charge looks like good people. And they're goin Atlanta way."

Cool air filtered into this service hall from the propped-open door to the concrete well of underground parking. "Maybe they should take all the kids," Juju commented. He'd buzzed his hair back down, and looked far more comfortable now that he was back in order.

"I ain't no kid." Mark Kasprak balanced on both feet, his hat shoved back and his dark hair—clean now—finally behaving, falling over his eyes in a dark swoop. A beaky little rooster, spurs ready. "Neither is Steph."

Juju's wry grin made him look like a teenager himself. "Y'all are what, sixteen?"

"Eighteen," Mark fired back, and he looked every inch. "And we ain't kids after all this, Mr Thurgood."

Lee could have taken issue with that, but it would push the conversation off-track. Miz Frank's group was almost ready to leave, and offered to take anyone who wanted along to Atlanta. It was the best choice, really, and his conscience—such as it was—had taken to pinching him hard whenever he heard the city's name.

God damn Grandon. If the syringes were what Lee *thought* they were...

Lee surfaced from that particular unpleasant thought, aware of several gazes on him. Juju's eyebrows were up, Mark's cheeks were freshly shaved even though he had very little to clearcut on those hills, and Steph's sharp kittenish face was bright as a new penny. She stood close to Mark again, maybe because the boy made a point to defer to Juju. Traveller trotted between their group and the other one, nosing at everything, tail held high and excited, ears perked.

Carline was slightly behind Mandy, pale under her brightly colored cap and glancing at the staging area for the Frank group every once in a while like she thought they were gonna leave without her. It was obvious what *she* wanted.

The way Mandy examined Lee was almost uncomfortable. She looked like she expected him to start yelling, maybe, and he didn't miss the way she was carefully out of arm's reach with her new snow-boots poised to carry her back if necessary.

"Ain't gonna force any of you," he said, finally. Didn't they know that by now? "If y'all wanna to to Atlanta, they's a good group to go with. Miz Frank knows what she's doin, she'll keep you safe."

"You sure?" Mandy glanced at Steph, not waiting for Lee's answer. "You wanna come?"

It was democracy in action, Lee mused. Everyone gettin a vote, if they could just make up their damn minds. He kept his thumbs in his pockets, enjoying the luxury of not having to stand to attention—and making himself smaller, as much as he could.

"We're all from the same town," Steph said, slowly. She leaned toward Mark and he replicated the motion, two plants each thinking the other was the sun. "And Miz Ginny doesn't have anyone else to go with her, you know?"

"Well, we'll save you some room down there." Apparently that was that, Mandy swung around and headed for their gear, stacked neatly at the edge of the Frank group's. The nurse waved, and Chantal dropped a cheeky wink; Mike Mock lifted a case of bottled water with a grunt and Jorge, his broad back alive with muscle, shouldered the door wide on his way out carrying another two cases. The underground garage looked clear, but Holly and Colleen were on shuttle duty with shotguns.

It paid to be careful. Lee whistled for Traveller, who tore himself away from examining a pile of waterproof-bagged sleeping bags and trotted for him, reluctant but obeying. Carline picked up their backpacks, Mandy their two sleeping bags and rolled foam, and the girls joined the other group. Miz Frank nodded, and set them to work right away.

"Is Miz Ginny up?" Steph stuck her hands in her pockets, pulling her gloves out and folding them neatly.

"Ain't seen her." Juju shook his head. Even buzzed, his hair was springing up right cheerful, and there was a gleam in his gaze Lee hadn't seen for a while.

A shadow crossed the girl's sharp face. She put her folded gloves away and rubbed at her hair, probably wishing Ginny was up to help her braid it. "Ain't like her to sleep in."

"We all need the rest." Lee sighed, bending to smooth Traveller's head and scratch behind the hound's ears. "Steph, you wanta go up and see if she answers her door?"

"Yessir." The girl grabbed Mark's hand and tugged him away, both of them breaking into a run before they reached the staff elevator. If the power went out while they were in there it was going to be a pickle, but Lee didn't have the heart to yell. He snagged the hound's collar before he could take off after them, though. Getting a canine out of a dangling tin box sounded like even *more* of a pickle.

"Shoulda told them they had to go," Juju muttered. He waved his hat once, twice, the pompom bobbing punctuation. "Damn kids."

"Think they'd listen?" Lee clipped the leash on, and Traveller, betrayed, stared at him mournfully despite Lee's skritch behind the hound's ear before straightening.

"If *you* said it? Maybe." The younger man patted at his breast pocket, a holdover from Army life. "Makes me wish I still smoked."

"Me too." Cigarettes would probably become currency after a while, just like in any war zone. Lee had a couple other suspicions about what would be tradable after a while, too. "You sure you don't wanna go to Atlanta, Juju?"

"I'm stickin with you, Loot."

It should have made him feel better, but Lee's conscience pinched again. Hard. Each day they spent moving was a spin of a wheel Juju hadn't signed up for.

There was no help for it if the man was determined. "Maybe after Ginny looks in on her folks we'll go thataway." Lee had a healthy respect for Thurgood's stubbornness, having a good share of that particular quality himself.

"Might be better to head Canada way." Juju rolled up his hat, the pompom waving its tentacles. "I hear they're more civilized up there."

"Maybe so." Lee suppressed another sigh, and handed Juju the leash. "Keep this fool inside, willya?" It was no use, he might as well go up and see if Ginny would open her door. It was selfish, she needed the rest...but something bothered him. And if she was gonna change her mind bout New York, now would be the best time to find out.

He knew something was wrong as soon as he cleared the door to the fifth floor. Stairs would keep him in shape, but god *damn* he was missing elevators. There never seemed to be enough air inside the contraptions, but Lord, now he appreciated the convenience.

There were a whole lot of conveniences he would have liked to have back.

Steph, paper-pale, stood on navy carpet outside Ginny's door, sandwiched between the room the teenage girls had shared last night and Lee's own. She turned, her blue eyes huge, and Mark leaned close to the door, finishing up a very loud sentence. "...go get Mr Lee."

"I'm here," Lee said, and the relief crossing their transparent faces gave him a hell of a bad feeling, way down low. "What's all this?"

"She...she..." Steph's eyes welled with trembling tears; her pupils were wide and black. "She says she's...Mr Lee, she says she's..."

"She says she's got it," Mark cut in. His hands worked at each other, scrubbing hard, and the cuffs of his jacket whispered while he did. "She says she got the zombie flu."

The bottom dropped out of Lee's brain and stomach at the same time. "Slow down. She says what now?" He might have blinked across the intervening space, because all of a sudden he was shouldering Kasprak aside and reaching for the prissy silver bar of the doorknob. It rattled, locked.

Of course.

"Go away." Ginny's voice came, muffled and sweet, through the door. She *never* sounded this sharp, not even when she was angry. "Just go *away*." The words trailed off in a barrage of deep, crouplike coughing, and when it faded, he heard something shifting on the other side.

"Can't do that, darlin." He sounded numb, even to himself. *Tell me the damn kids misunderstood. Tell me you're havin allergies or some such.* "Ginny? Talk to me. What's goin on in there?"

"High fever," she gasped. "Flulike...symptoms. Blood pressure elevated, heart rate..."

God damn it. Lee's hands ached. One of them, gripping the doorknob, creaked white-knuckle, the other was a fist, fingernails digging into his palm. "Ginny." Very calmly. "Ginny, darlin, unlock this door, and we'll see about this."

"No." A short, sharp, tortured breath. Sounded like she was breathing through wet cotton, and his own lungs were starved just hearing it. "I've blocked...blocked it. If it's the...the zombie flu, I won't...won't hurt anyone." Another barrage of coughing, and Steph made a small sound behind Lee, a half-moan. "Go away."

There was a terrible finality to the last two words, soft though they were. Virginia Mills had made up her mind about something.

"Ginny. *Ginny.*" He shouted, and rattled the doorknob. No use. He considered putting his shoulder to the work, but if she'd blocked it...

Oh hell no. No, no, no. Fuck no.

Lee heard his own voice from a great distance away, calm and cold. "Get down to Juju and y'all pack up. If I ain't down in an hour, y'all get the hell out of here. Go on, now." Receding footsteps—the kids knew when to shut their mouths and get moving, thank Jesus. Lee found himself at the door to his own room, the card-key slipping a little against sweating fingertips.

Now just what are you doin, son? He could almost smell Big Q's aftershave patted on greying cheeks, and feel the paralyzing weight of his grandfather's Quartine-brand yaller-stare when the old man suspected Lee of some hijinks.

"What I gotta," he mumbled, and took a good look at the wall separating his room from Ginny's. No connecting door, of course. It couldn't be that easy.

Only what I gotta, Poppa. Like usual.

[19]

DARK WELL

Later, he figured he just could have gone through the drywall, except if there was something load-bearing in the way. Finding that out would have been un-fuckin'-comfortable indeed.

Instead, Lee strode to the bed, where his baggage waited in a neat pile. A few moments of digging in his go-backpack unearthed what he wanted—he wrenched the hardpac open, and the three capped glass syringes nestled in foam looked way too small to carry any salvation. He stuck one in his mouth, careful with a horizontal glass tube, and ran for the sliding glass door to the balcony, ripping the curtains aside so hard material tore and something in the metal track above pinged as it broke.

Freezing weather was no match for the ice inside him, a sword from his belly all the way up his spine, filling his head with what needed to happen and how to do it. Getting over the cheap metal railing wasn't hard; the real problem was an outcropping of concrete between his balcony and Ginny's. It was probably designed to stop what he was doing right now, but Lee took a deep breath, clinging to an ice-slick rail with his right hand, and put his foot out. His arms straightened, and the consciousness of hanging off the side of a building with something hard, and chilly, and glass clutched in his teeth hit him.

He didn't have time to think about it. Lurching sideways, letting go of his railing, he hung in space for a long moment before his toes caught on the closest baluster of the railing next door—Ginny's room. His stomach cramped like he was doing the mother of all crunches or was back in basic, dropping and giving a hundred sit-ups under a sadistic drill sergeant. Lee curled around the concrete, almost tearing two fingernails on his right hand as his fingers skittered across the bulge, looking for purchase, looking for something, anything that would push him over to where he needed to be.

His left hand banged on spindly iron, there was a screech of bolts loosening in concrete, and for a sickening moment everything lurched and he knew he was going to fall when the *cheap*ass *son*uvabitch rail pulled loose of its moorings.

Then physics was, for once, kind to him, and Ginny's balcony railing stopped rocking, the bolts almost—but not quite—torn free. Lee clambered carefully over it, not quite sure how he'd turned the corner and not caring, either. He almost went right through the French door too, deciding at the last moment he didn't need broken glass to add to the shitshow. So he set his boots, curled his bruised left hand and bloody right around the handle, and reminded himself not to clench his teeth and get a mouthful of shards and the vile green liquid inside the tube.

Of course, conscientious soul that she was, Ginny had locked the glass balcony door, too. The curtains were open, and Lee caught a blur of paleness on the rosy carpet. Ginny, tossed like a broken doll on the floor, probably about to start convulsing.

God, if you're there...

But God never had been. It was up to him.

Lee's back arched, his feet dug into icy concrete, and he heaved again. And again. His mouth was full, so he couldn't say her name, but it echoed all the way down inside him, a flare dropping into a dark well.

[20]

NOISY DEATH

The convulsions were going to start again, she could *feel* them hovering, trembling in every muscle group. Cold, she was so, so *cold*. A gush of icy fluid crawled over her, skittering insect feet pinch-pricking her skin. The fever had mounted all through the night, she could barely see to scrawl her symptoms, but at least she'd made everyone else safe. Someone pounding at the door, and she heard herself, precise and sharp, telling them she was sick. *Just go away*, she heard herself say. *I've blocked it.*

With that task finished, she retreated from the jumble of furniture near the door. Her legs gave out, and all she could think was that it was a shame she hadn't figured out more about the illness. At least someone would be proud of her for not putting others in harm's way.

Who, though? She couldn't quite remember. Her father? Yes, that was it, he'd be proud of her for...

The world spun away, came back. There was a banging, a clattering, and a fresh, frigid breeze touched her sweat-slick skin. Jolting, jittering, muscles locking, her right wrist trapped and the rest of her body trying to curl up around it, an iron bar across her chest. Something around her right biceps, cruelly tight, a stinging slap inside her right elbow.

An icy spike shoved its way into the crook of her arm, and Ginny moaned weakly.

"Don't you give up on me now." Male, rough and low. "Ginny, sweetheart, darlin, don't you dare give up on me."

Who was it? For a moment she had the name, it trembled on tongue- and brain-tip before vanishing under another gathering convulsion, tired muscles locking.

Get away from me. Was she hallucinating? The fever could be cooking her brain right now. *Get away.*

He kept talking. "Don't you dare, don't you *fucking* dare, sweetheart, I will get you to New York, I will carry you there on my goddamn back if I have to, *don't you dare give up on me.*"

The spike jammed into her arm reached her shoulder. Ginny screamed, hoarsely. It was an involuntary noise, her diaphragm and core muscles locking down and her vocal folds slamming shut. Dimly, she heard...barking? The dog, where was the dog? She hadn't locked him in here with her, had she?

Oh God please, please. She only wanted it to be over. It *hurt.*

"*Goddammit, stop!*" her hallucination yelled. She remembered his name right before she lost it under a wave of sticky, gelatinous agony. "There's shit in front of it, just calm down!"

Ginny choked. Hot, rancid liquid filled her throat. She couldn't *breathe,* was this what it felt like to die? Choking on her own vomit— well, she hadn't had much of an appetite, it would only be thin scorching bile and...

The world blinked away again, came back at high speed, ran over her. A wheel spun, light and dark pie-slices alternating. More yelling.

If this was death, it was *noisy.*

A wintry fist reached through her ribs and squeezed everything caught inside that bony cage, her heart stuttered, and Ginny Mills knew no more.

[21]

TAKE CARE OF MYSELF, THANK YOU

"IT AIN'T THAT. LOOK, SHE AIN'T GOT NO FEVER."

"I ain't convinced, Lee. What in hell are you doin?"

"What I gotta, Juju. As fucking usual."

"So she stacked all that in front of the door, and...dear Lord and sonny Jesus, look at this. Wrote down her temperature."

"Stay outta that. It's her diary."

"Sure you don't want a peek?"

"Juju, for God's sake."

"When's the weddin? Rough findin a preacher round here. Course, if she starts chewin—"

"She ain't gonna. No fever, and she's restin quiet. You want to do something useful, or you gonna keep bein a shithead?"

"Stickin with what I know. You broke the door. How in hell did you...Good Lord. You crazy sumbitch."

"That a compliment?"

"Partly." Metal ground against metal, a French door sliding inside a warped track. "We stayin here for a while, then?"

"You could catch up with 'em, if you left now."

"Not what I asked, Lee."

A long pause. "We'll see when she wakes up."

"Aight then. I'll get the kids settled."

"Juju?"

"Yeah?"

"You're a good man."

"Yeah. Right." Footsteps receding. "'M I s'posed to shoot you if you get sick?"

"Take care of myself, thank you."

"Yeah." Wood crunched, a boot aimed viciously at a chair leg. "Right."

Hinges groaned. Excited barking, and a babble of questions. Cloth moved. "All right, darlin," Lee Quartine said, softly. "Let's get you in a room that ain't busted."

[22]

ALL SORTS OF MESSED UP

It was a long, grey, cold afternoon, and it didn't get any better when they stopped at a Marathon off the freeway. Traveling, Carline Goldisch had decided, was for the birds. Especially when you were having what Mom termed *monthlies* or what the girls at school called, with pitiless amusement, *the rag*.

She was getting tired of looking out a window onto snow, more snow, and busted-up cars, too. Stopping wasn't much better, because then she had to move around and hope nothing escaped around the plug, so to speak. "You got any aspirin?"

"What hurts?" Miz Frank was just as interesting as Miz Mills. The lean black lady leaned against the side of her shiny, red, definitely new Toyota SUV. It even had that new-car smell, which Mandy said was mostly chemicals. It made Carline's nose tingle and her head ache, even with the window down a bit, and even with her tampon worries she was glad they stopped every couple hours.

Women traveled different than men, that was for sure. Mr Quartine didn't want to stop for *nothin*, it took Miz Ginny putting her foot down to get them a bathroom break. He crushed on her so hard it was a wonder the snow didn't melt around him, too.

They were nice, but going to Atlanta was the better bet. At least, Mandy said so, and she was the one with the brains. Why she hung around with a dumbass white girl was anyone's guess, and sometimes Carline was pretty sure it was because there weren't many other options in town.

Options *out* of town didn't seem too plentiful either, right now. Carline sucked in a small breath. "Got cramps." They weren't bad as Mandy's. Nothing in Carline's life was as bad as Mandy's, and sometimes she didn't know how to feel about that. Even though Mandy's parents had a nice house, and they churched regular and sent Mandy to a good school, there were still...problems. Carline's mama wasn't the only one who scrubbed every dish twice, so to speak.

"Oh, Lord, honey. I've got some Midol." Miz Frank bustled for the back of the Toyota. The glass door of the Marathon station—what Dad would've called a "stop-n-rob"—reflected the side of the red car and the blue-and-white pumps, snow-packed pavement and the hind end of Chantal's pink Cadillac. *I didn't sell no Mary Kay to get that,* Chantal said, smiling in her peculiar way, and Carline got the idea you didn't want to ask any questions.

Mandy put an arm over her shoulders, the shell of her brand new, thickly insulated coat rasping against Carline's. "Is it bad?" The tips of her beaded braids made soft sweet music as they moved.

They didn't really have to worry about people seeing them now, but each time they touched in public the thump at the bottom of Carline's stomach hit and she had to work not to glance around like she was guilty.

Which she was. The sinners were the only ones left, and she might have had fun guessing everyone else's secret crimes if her lady bits didn't feel like they were trying to escape by doing the Jackalemon Twist and sending bad thoughts all through her lower back as well.

"I hate it." She hoped she didn't sound whiny.

Mandy nodded, glancing at the road. She wasn't very relaxed, but then, being out in the open was dangerous. "You could take the pill straight through."

"Didn't know I'd need it." That was something good about sinning girl-like—there wasn't any chance of getting knocked up and having to drive over the state line *or* figure out how to scrape together cash. Some places had that morning-after pill, but you needed your parents' say-so to get it, and while Carline was secretly of the opinion hell wasn't gonna be *that* bad, asking your mama and daddy for that particular signature was uncomfortable to contemplate.

You could fake it, like you did with absence-or-tardy notes. But the risk of the pharmacist calling…Well, nobody was gonna be calling Mama and Daddy to confirm anything now.

And *that* was how Carline knew she was a sinner in truth, because she was secretly but undeniably glad.

Oh, she missed Mom, to be sure. She'd about cried her eyes out, and the nightmares showed up like clockwork. Hell would probably be those nightmares all the time and never waking up.

But she didn't miss her daddy's first-of-the-month whiskey tots, or Mom's midnight prayin', or the yellin' near the end of the month when Dad's disability check ran thin, or—really, the list was pretty long.

She laid her head on Mandy's shoulder. "How *you* doin, sweetpants?"

"Better than you, looks like." Mandy's smile, sensed more than seen, was all the sunshine the day needed. "I wonder—"

She didn't get a chance to say what she wondered, because a gunshot cracked close by and Mandy dragged her down, Carline's knees banging on concrete and her shoulder hitting the side of the Toyota. "*Ow!*" she yelled, and immediately felt like a fool. Shouting bounced off the pavement, fell dead in the snow. Two more shots, close together, sounded like they were coming from behind the Marathon.

Where the bathrooms were, and the employee entrance they'd worked open to get inside.

"Into the car," Mandy gasped. "Girl, get your *ass* in the *car!*"

Miz Frank slammed the back of the Toyota shut and came around the end, her shotgun in both hands and her face set and grim. "Get in!" she yelled, and lifted the gun, slow, slow, like she was working through syrup. Carline snapped a glance at the side of the gas station while she floundered on her knees, grabbing for the door-handle.

The zombie staggered into view, wearing a blue polyester vest that flapped over its chewed-up ribs. It was once a skinny teenage kid, and for a weird, dreamlike moment she thought it was Mark Kasprak, somehow come along and dressed up to play a prank on them because he was a boy and they did things like that.

"Get *up!*" Mandy screamed, and Carline's fingers found what they were looking for. She ripped a fingernail as she surged upwards, hauling on the handle, and almost clocked herself in the face with the door too.

"*Shitfuck!*" Carline yelled, and that would have been funny if the zombie hadn't seen them and dropped to all fours, its growl a thin nasty buzz. Snow made a weird squeaky sound under its palms and filth-crusted wingtips; Carline grabbed Mandy's shoulder and the back of her jeans too, all but lifting her bodily into the backseat. She piled in afterward and lunged desperately for the door, dragging it shut and yelling because her foot was caught. Metal banged off her ankle, and she let out a roar that would have surprised exactly nobody who had ever seen her at cheerleading practice.

Carline didn't believe in doing anything halfway, ever. Which was partly why she'd asked Mandy out, her heart in her throat and her entire body aflame with almost-shame. Mandy hadn't laughed at her, or told any of her friends.

Sometimes, late at night, Carline thought of the bubbling happiness that filled her when Mandy smiled and said *sure, sugar,* and thought maybe that was why the zombies had come. Anything that hot-sweet-good had a bite at the end.

Miz Frank had the shotgun settled. "Come on, you sonofabitch," she yelled, and Carline yanked her foot in. The door slammed, and a variety of quiet fell, broken only by heaving breathing, thudding pulses, and Mandy's muttered *oh shit oh shit*, her own particular chorus of disaster.

The shotgun barked. Once, twice. Carline lay, half on Mandy, her ankle throbbing and her hand, too. Jesus, she was just all *sorts* of messed up today.

"Ohshit," Mandy whispered. "Ohshit mama, shoot him again, shoot him...good *Lord*."

Carline's middle hurt, but she still managed to curl up enough to peer out the window.

Miz Frank, the shotgun reversed, clubbed the zombie right in the head. Brains and spongy, discolored skullbone spattered. Carline, her jaw dropping, choked on a warning scream.

More zombies boiled around the corner of the building, dropping to all fours and scrambling for the Toyota. Where were they *coming* from? Glass shattered, and Jorge stepped through the shivering ruins of the Marathon's front door, firing his pistol at the mass. "*Go!*" he yelled, and behind him, Chantal and Holly half-carried Colleen, whose head hung. Colleen's hair swung heavily, splattering drops of bright red. Skinny, nervous Mike Mock followed at high speed, paper-white, a hand clapped to his shoulder where a bright crimson rosette bloomed through his flapping flannel shirt. He'd hadn't worn his coat inside, because Jorge kept the heat blasting in his truck. Mike's red hair stuck up, coppery in the snowy light.

Miz Frank almost ran into the Toyota's side, blundered along it, and finally ripped the driver's door open. She piled in, the shotgun shoved barrel-down into the passenger footwell, and had to jab twice at the door locks to get them to closed with that sweet chucking sound of safety.

Jorge kept firing until there was nothing but dry clicks, backing up and damn near running into Mike. Chantal and Holly almost had Colleen to the Cadillac, and Mike staggered for Jorge's big old Ford monster truck with its *La Vida Loca* decal on the canopy's back window and the funny little plastic statue of Mother Mary glued to the dash. Jorge dropped the old clip out and slammed new ammo in, quick habitual movements. He kept backing up, now taking his time and choosing his shots. The zombies couldn't decide whether to go after Holly, Chantal, and Colleen *or* him, and a couple had reached the Toyota and started slapping at the windows, their bloated, discolored, or skinny hands leaving wet prints as they smacked.

"Ohgod," Carline choked. "Ohgodohgod get us out of here, *get us out of here!*"

Mandy started moving. "Ma'am!" She poked at Miz Frank's shoulder, and the older woman, as if in a dream, fumbled the key towards the ignition. She'd been occupied in fishing it out of her jacket pocket. The shotgun's stock, splattered with oddly dark zombie blood, slid sideways to tap at the passenger door. *Better put your seatbelt on,* Carline's mother said dimly in the recesses of her memory, and the Toyota purred into life.

"Put your belts on, kids," Miz Frank said, softly, and Carline flinched. Her ankle sent up a red-hot distress signal, and she sobbed out a breath.

"Oh no," Mandy moaned. "Oh, God, no."

Mike had made it to Jorge's truck, but he was having trouble getting in. Jorge was holding the zombies off, Colleen was loaded into the Cadillac. The things growled, milling around, indecisive.

Miz Frank glanced at the rearview. Someone was home behind her eyes again, and that someone had a steely glare Carline had never seen on a mom-aged woman before. "Put your belts on!" she snapped, and dropped the SUV into reverse. She paused, then, deliberately, laid on the horn.

Each zombie stopped and turned unerringly for the source of the sound, their heads cocked at strange doglike angles. Kasie Frank hit the gas, soft thudding sounds at the back of the car accompanied by shudders as it plowed through a knot of zombies, and twisted the wheel. Dropped it into drive, and hit the horn again. "Come on, you cheapshot motherfuckers!" she yelled, as Jorge boosted Mike into the passenger side of the truck and clambered up behind him. The pink Cadillac's brake lights flashed, and Miz Frank let out a sobbing breath of relief. "Thank you, God. Come on, Jorge. Come on."

The Ford's door closed—Jorge and Mike were loaded. Miz Frank stamped the gas, chained tires bit packed snow, and Carline was shoved back into Mandy's lap by the acceleration. She didn't mind so much, because Mandy folded over her, and for a few moments, in the darkness behind Carline's eyelids, her breathing muffled by Mandy's coat, things were safe and they had survived.

Again.

[23]

STAY HANDLED

Step. A pause. Another soft footfall. Whoever it was,
they were trying to move quietly, and that brought Lee out of his bag
in a thrashing hurry, yanking the knife under his pillow free and
ending up in a fighting crouch, ready for anything.

Anything, that was, except Ginny, her T-shirt torn half off and
glaring bruises down her soft shoulders, braceleting her pretty wrist.
The wrist was his fault, he'd had to put his boot there while she
thrashed and he tried to get the bandanna around her upper arm
tourniquet-like to jab her with the needle. There was a rough abrasion where he'd yanked the bandanna tight, and vivid red-black
bruising marched down both her long, pretty, pale legs under the
penguin-starred boxer shorts. She'd probably been throwing herself
around the room for a bit, banging against things. Or maybe he'd hurt
her that badly, trying to get the needle in.

Jesus.

Ginny stopped, her pupils huge in the dimness. The drapes were
closed, but the bathroom light was on and the door ajar. She stared
down at him, her hair a soft, wild cloud, and Lee exhaled hard,
lowering the knife. "Uh," he managed, and had to clear his throat.

She'd almost stepped on him, his sleeping bag barring the way to the hall door just in case. If anyone came in, he'd give them a bad time—and he'd wanted to wake up if she moved.

Well, he had, thank Jesus. His heart thundered northwards, attempting to lodge in his throat; he tried to force it down. "Ginny." Raspy as a smoker's morning growl. His voice didn't want to work. "It's all right."

Was she sleepwalking? She just *looked* at him, and Lee was suddenly very aware that he was barefoot in his thermals and she was barely even half dressed. Lord, even after all that, she was...

Well, she was just plain beautiful. That glory of hair, and the bruising only underlined how fine her skin was. The beautiful bow-curves of her hips, the softness of a woman's belly, one of her breasts rising like a moon behind a scrap of cotton T-shirt—he could stare for hours, every circuit in his fool head fusing.

Her fingers twitched, and she peered at him. "Lee?" Like she didn't recognize him. "Am I..."

He straightened, keeping the knife well back. Had she noticed it? "You're all right, sweetheart. Get some rest."

"I just...I need the bathroom." She took a swaying sideways step. "I hurt all over."

Lee winced. "Well, yeah. It got...I'm sorry. I just..." God *damn* it. Couldn't he keep his damn mouth shut?

She headed for the bathroom and closed the door, leaving him in welcome darkness. Lee got the knife stowed and rubbed at his face, trying to wake the fuck up and get himself together. She was bound to have questions.

Water ran. Thank God the pipes weren't frozen. He made his way over to the bed and worked at the pillows, getting them straight, the covers too. She'd probably appreciate that, though she'd barely disturbed them once he'd laid her down.

She turned the light off with a quick habitual flick when she left the bathroom, and stumbled in the dark. His eyes were better adapted; he made it across a few feet of scratchy carpet, guided her around his sleeping bag, and got her to the bed. "There you are. Just lie down. It's all right." *Don't let her ask what I did. Now's not the time.* She was sleep-warm, but not feverish. Her skin didn't feel stove-hot anymore, no damp dewy breath of clinging fever.

When she put a few things together, he'd have to explain Grandon and the syringes. He'd managed to get the empty one hidden before dragging hotel furniture away from her door—how a bitty thing like her had managed *that*, he didn't want to think about. When she got determined, it *stuck*.

Lee liked that about her, even though it was fair to driving him up the wall. He was beginning to believe she was still alive.

"Lee?" She settled on the edge of the bed, tipping her chin up and squinting, trying to get her night vision working. "I was sick. I had a fever."

"You're all right now," he said, numbly. He couldn't bring himself to step away, everything about her was goddamn distracting. That faint perfume of hers was tantalizing, even with the coppery musk of sweat and fear underneath. "No fever, no nothin."

"Oh." She swayed again, and he touched her shoulder gently. She eased down, and he got her settled, pulling the covers up, tucking her in. He was about to leave her there, too, by God he truly was, but she reached out, her slim fingers catching his wrist. The touch was warm, and soft, and likely to drive him out of what little remained of his mind. "Lee? Don't go."

Oh, my dear Lord. How many times had he wanted to hear that? "Uh," he managed. "I'll be right there. On the floor."

"If you want." The words caught, and her fingers tensed. "I just... I was going to die. I knew it."

"Nah. You were sick, is all. Not eatin, and the stress." The lie rolled off his tongue, smooth and natural, like he'd practiced it a million times. "Just a touch of somethin. You got worked up, but it's all right now."

"Please," Ginny persisted. "Please don't go."

What was the word for a reward a man didn't deserve but got

anyway? Lee racked his brain, trying to come up with it. "Uh," was all he could produce. Again. He was a gatdamn idiot.

He was the idiot who had kept her *alive*, though. Surely that was worth something.

Lee tried to stretch out on top of the covers, but she moved over and pulled on him with surprising strength. Once he got under the sheets, she cuddled against him just like in his nicer dreams, and dear Jesus in heaven she fit right-perfect. Her head settled on his shoulder, her arm over his chest, and the slim sweet soft length of her all along his side threatened to short-circuit anything approaching rational thought.

"I'm probably dead," Ginny whispered. "This is a lot quieter."

"You ain't dead," he managed. *I'm not gonna let that happen.*

"Okay." Her breathing deepened, and she dropped into sleep. Must've been tuckered right out. Probably wouldn't remember asking him to lie down in the morning, but Lee couldn't make himself move. Her breath made a soft warm spot through his thermal top, and her hair tickled his chin. His free hand lifted, worked its way out from under blankets and sheets, and touched a soft springing curl, another. Traced the line of her forehead, skated across her cheek. His fingertips found her cracked lips; she'd need some ChapStick. Or whatever girls used now.

How the *hell* was he gonna explain this? Juju hadn't asked many questions, but he was going to. And Ginny was too goddamn smart for her own good. Lee needed a reasonable story, and he couldn't figure one out with her snuggled up against him as if...

"You just got yourself tangled up," he whispered, smoothing her hair. "Combat nerves." Juju would believe that. They'd both seen what unremitting tension could do to the trained and untrained alike. The quiet ones, when they snapped, snapped *hard*.

But what if she asks about...

No. What mattered, Lee decided, was that it had worked. She was alive, Juju and the kids and the damn dog were fine, and if Grandon hadn't been looking to rope Lee into whatever had gone screaming sideways and pulled them all into this shit, it could have turned out very differently. But it hadn't, and it didn't matter if it was luck or Lee finally getting a few good breaks to make up for the bad ones. He had a handle on this, and it would *stay* handled, God willing. Whatever story he told would have to work, because Lee wasn't having it any other way.

The vile-looking crap in the syringe had done its job. He'd figure out the rest after Ginny saw to her folks. Maybe then she'd listen to reason. Certainly wasn't the best plan he'd ever come up with, but Lee was tired too. And, amazingly, even as his arm started to go numb from being trapped under Ginny's head, he smiled, and fell into night's embrace.

[24]

HEIGHTENED CIRCUMSTANCES

Her Moleskine journal was a bit battered. Hell, Ginny *herself* was a bit battered. She was bruised all over, and every muscle ached savagely. It took a few liters of bottled water before her head stopped pounding, and she longed for nothing more than some strong tea, some of Mom's chicken soup, and a stack of latkes a mile high. With extra garlic. So much garlic her breath could kill a cactus at fifty paces.

Instead, she had percolator coffee and protein bars, and everyone looking at her like she was crazy. Steph almost burst into tears, hugging her just short of ribcracking before bounding away to fetch more coffee. Mark, his thumbs in his belt in a completely unconscious imitation of the older men, looked from Ginny to Lee several times, hunching his broadening shoulders like he expected an explosion.

Not from her end, though. She was too damn tired. Getting cleaned up and dressed had absorbed all her limited energy, and her lips were so cracked and chapped she tasted blood when she licked them.

Finally, the kids took Traveller down to the parking garage for his afternoon piddle, which left her with Juju. And Lee's thick, not-quite-cold silence.

She flicked through her journal pages, her eyebrows drawing together. "I had a fever, though. I logged it." *Several times, as a matter of fact.* In increasingly shaky handwriting, along with rising blood pressure and approximations of her pulse. "It rose, and rose, and then...God."

Lee stood by the French door, late-afternoon sun catching highlights in his dark hair. Gold threads and a few honey streaks, and it was beginning to develop a bit of a curl, which suited him even more. Long nose, strong jaw, his mouth a straight line, he said nothing. At least he wasn't wearing that disconcerting, light, intense stare. His gaze was dark, and wholly shuttered.

Juju glanced at him, then at her. "I knew this guy when I was in Iraq." He leaned forward in the bedside chair, elbows braced on his knees. His sleeves were rolled up to show his forearms, fuzzed with dark hair. The pink-cushioned hotel chair squeaked a little. "It got to him. He started sweating, and said there were worms everywhere. Even under his skin. Had to send him out to get his head back together, but get this. He kept yelling about it, and you could see his skin move. Like there was worms underneath." The black man took a deep breath. "We've all been through some shi—ah, stuff. Heavy-duty stuff. And if your nose starts runnin, and you start feelin peaked —you see what I mean? You can get a little weird, especially if you bottle it up."

"Yeah." Ginny's shoulders slumped. *A little weird* was putting it kindly. "How embarrassing."

Because it was. They were not pointing out that she'd gone completely bananas and slowed down their travel, but they were certainly thinking it.

"Nah. You tell a lot about someone by how they go crazy." Juju glanced at Lee again, obviously hoping for some kind of help. He rubbed at the burn scar on his left hand, a thoughtful motion, and his velvety eyes were kind. "I mean, if you really *had* it, blocking off your door like that? Shows some real grit, ma'am. You was lookin out for us, wasn't you. An' anyone else who happened along."

Of course. "Well, yes. I thought I wouldn't be able to get out the door, and the drop to the parking lot..." She hunched even further. "I'm sorry. For making you worry."

"Why? You did the best you could." Juju pushed himself upright. "You'll bounce back. Promise." He held out his hand and she took it, slightly baffled. But he simply shook, carefully, no bone-grinding pressure. "One smart cookie, Miz Ginny."

"Thanks." Her unwilling smile made her lips crack even more, and she stared down at the journal pages. At least she hadn't written anything...oh, *God*, there was a whole page with Lee's name written, again and again. With curlicues. And hearts.

Great. Hopefully he hadn't seen that. Hopefully *none* of them had seen it.

Lee simply stood there, arms crossed, while Juju shut the door gently as if on an invalid. Well, technically, she *was* one. Her legs had a little starch to them, but not much. She braced herself, but Lee still said nothing.

It was probably best to plunge right in. So she did. "You're mad at me."

That made him move a little, restlessly. The hem of his leather vest peeked out from beneath his blue sweater, vanished.

"Go ahead and yell," she continued. "I can tell you want to."

"I ain't." He stepped out of the sunshine and stalked across the room to the bedside and halted, looking down at her. The gun riding his belt sat quietly, and his boots were scraped conscientiously clean. "You ain't never gonna see me mad at *you*. But you listen to me, Ginny. You have *got* to start tellin me what's in that pretty head of yours. Christ, you coulda thought you could fly or some foolishness, and stepped off that balcony."

Startled, she studied his set chin, his dark eyes. He still wasn't wearing that yellow-eyed stare, which was good. "Lee..." Her breath failed her. She waited for the coughing, but none came.

Which was *bizarre*. The postnasal drip, the deep productive coughing, the fever...Had it all been psychosomatic? Surely it couldn't be, even in heightened circumstances.

But she had bruises all over, and dried sweat thick enough to crackle when she'd leaned against the shower wall an hour ago. Her hair had been positively stiff; it took two rounds of shampoo before all of it washed out.

"You got to, Ginny." His hands tensed, not quite fists but definitely not relaxed. A thin scar along the bottom of his jaw flushed. What was the story behind that one, she wondered? It looked like a childhood injury. "So's I can do what you need me to."

Well, he was already upset, she might as well ask. "Why do you say things like that? I mean, you barely even know me, and—"

"I can spend however long you like gettin to know you, Ginny. Be right happy to." He made another restless movement, and she was suddenly extremely aware of her own weakness. Bruised all over, barely able to walk across a room without heavy breathing that would make a horror movie proud, and alone in here.

With him.

Oh, God. She gathered what little intelligence had managed to ride some caffeine into her bloodstream, and folded her hands primly. "What I mean is, this is a...an extreme situation, and it can make you think you feel things you don't." There. It was out, it was said, and she was an idiot for even trying to broach this subject now.

There was never a good time to tell a guy that what he was feeling, although probably intense, might not be...real.

"Like I'm havin a heart attack each time I see you?" Lee's mouth turned up at the corners, and some of the tension left his shoulders. "I got news for you, darlin, that happened the first time I laid eyes on you, and hasn't stopped since."

"Oh." Any shred of caffeinated brainpower drained away.

Because, damn the man, he looked...serious. Well, to be honest, he rarely looked anything *but* solemn, you had to watch closely to get the shadow of amusement or perplexity crossing his face, like cloud-shadows on the Great Plains. Ginny's back seized up as she shifted, and the pillows behind her weren't helping.

He kept going, spacing the words evenly, taking his time. "I know I'm just a backwoods redneck without fancy manners or a divin watch, but I can get you through this, if you let me. You gotta start tellin me what's goin on, so I can do what I gotta."

A diving watch? What? "And what is it, precisely, that you've got to do?" Taking refuge in politeness was pretty much all she could muster.

"Keep you alive, Miss Virginia." He relaxed even further, and that smile widened. He looked flat-out happy, now, the corners of his eyes crinkling. Like he'd just figured something out. If he had, she wished he'd share. "You got some sort of problem with that?"

"No. I don't. Thank you." She sounded unhelpful, even to herself. It was a reflex, deployed over and over ever since she'd broken up with Alec in med school.

After that party. That stupid, awful, frat-boy party. Sometimes she wished she hadn't gone, but then, she would have found out about him later rather than sooner. He'd begun to make hints about marriage as soon as he finished his residency.

Wouldn't *that* have been a nightmare.

"Ginny." Lee half-turned and settled on the edge of the bed, and she was very conscious that the pillow next to her own when she woke up had most *definitely* been used. He considered her journal, lying closed on her lap, but it was her left hand he picked up, gently, rubbing his thumb over her knuckles, smoothing, comforting. "You got to help me out here. Start tellin me those worries before you end up doin somethin I can't fix."

It was ridiculous, but her mouth opened and what she was thinking fell right out. "There's nothing you can't fix, Lee."

"God, I hope you're right." His smile turned into a downright grin. He held her hand like it was fragile, turned it over, touched her palm. There was a red stripe of abrasion there, probably from moving the dresser.

And there was the little matter of the bruise on the inside of her right arm. It looked, for all the world, like a needle had gone in, almost missing a vein.

There had to be another explanation, she told herself firmly.

Ginny let Lee pull her forward. He slid his arms around her, and she rested her forehead against his shoulder, the hard edges of her journal digging into her ribs. It hurt a little, but so did the rest of her.

Her nose wasn't stuffy at all.

That night, the power in Louisville—which meant the hotel— went out, and a cold, heavy sleet rattled on every wall and window.

[25]

ENTIRELY DECIDED

Lee grabbed for it, but Ginny backed up and he had to
stop for fear of toppling her.

"I'll be *fine*." She hefted the heavy plastic tub, RIDGID stenciled
on its side in glaring yellow. Traveller wove underfoot, and she almost
staggered when he stropped her leg. "I promise. Just don't give me
two at a time."

"No ma'am." Steph grinned, thin twin braids crossed at the back
of her head again. She was even trying to copy Ginny's posture, head
up and shoulders back. "I ain't gonna take two either." She hefted her
own tub, its yellow highlights cheerful spots of color in the dim,
echoing stairwell. It was full of ammunition, and there were two final
ones stacked neat and prim on the landing. Mark had a good head on
him, suggesting these tool-haulers rather than the cardboard boxes.

Lee suppressed the urge to follow Ginny and snatch the heavy
box from her trembling hands. "You two get on, then. We'll finish the
haulin."

"Nothin but those left to drag out." Mark stretched, leaning from
side to side, his arms overhead. He was bulking up, no longer swimming in his new coat. Which wasn't as new as it had been, seeing

hard use lifting and carrying. Either he'd shot up a few inches, or he was holding himself taller now. Growing into adulthood all at once, the way some grunts did over the course of basic. "You sure Miz Ginny's okay, Lee?" Even his nose looked different, the rest of his face finally rising to meet it.

She'd better be. He contented himself with a nod. "Just needs some rest."

Juju was in the parking garage with his rifle, one foot bracing the door and his gaze roving. It was dark as sin down there, even with both vehicles running and their headlights on.

"Well, we'll be sittin all day." Mark bent, and grabbed the last two ammo tubs. "I swear, I thought she was a goner. She kept coughin."

Lee grunted. No use in giving the kid anything to feed the hamster inside his head with. He glanced around one final time to make sure everything was dealt with, picked up the lantern, and shouldered through the door, nodding at Juju. Traveller, excited to be on the move again, pranced and yipped. Ginny, determined, muscled her burden onto the tailgate and leaned against the truck, her ribs heaving and her cheeks blanched.

Dammit.

Steph had clambered inside, and snagged the box. "Go sit down," she told Ginny. "For God's sake. You're white as a sheet."

"I think I will." Ginny turned, her hip bumping the tailgate as Mark's elbow almost hit her arm. "Whoops, sorry."

"Heavy," Mark said, and heaved his double up. The truck groaned a little, accepting the weight with only token protest. "You go get on in the Jeep, Steph. I got this."

"Ain't gonna argue." She hopped down lithely into his waiting arms, and Lee thought the boy was smart if he used that moment to attempt a kiss on her cheek. Her laughter was a bright ribbon, and the stairwell door banged shut. Traveller scrambled for Ginny, his nails clicking and scraping, and his yipping shifted as Juju yelled.

"Incoming!"

Shadows milled at the edge of headlight glare. One, two, darting across the cone of light. Lee's entire body turned cold. He pushed Kasprak and Steph to the left, for Juju's four-by. "Go on now. *Go.*"

"Traveller!" Ginny bent, scooped up the dog, and almost went over sideways as the animal wriggled in a dual ecstasy of attention and discomfort.

Lee shoved the ammo boxes further in and slammed the tailgate; buckling them down could wait for the next stop. The sound cracked, echoing among an empty forest of concrete pillars, and maybe it was the bouncing, careening reverberations that made the things halt and crane their dripping heads. Sleet-lashed, following some blind instinct to burrow and confused for a few crucial seconds by the advent of loud, mouthwatering prey, they froze in listening attitudes, eerily, inhumanly still.

It wouldn't last long. The two biggest—one with a big ol' yellow hard hat, of all things, clamped to his noggin by a too-tight throatlatch —dropped to hands and knees with a wet slapping sound. "Juju! Load up!"

Juju was already moving for the four-by's driver-side, maybe a *little* bit quicker than he should have while armed. Ginny, clasping a good seventy pounds of wriggling hound, lurched drunkenly for the truck, and Traveller, protesting afresh, began to growl. Not at her, no —the hound's nose had alerted him to the presence of danger.

Lee slammed the top canopy door and brought his rifle up, tracking the motherfucker with the hard hat. The critter zeroed in on Ginny and crept forward, palms slapping smooth concrete. The cold was all through Lee again, steadying ice. "Get in!" he called, and squeezed off a shot.

The round took Hard-Hat in the chest. Lee didn't want a ricochet, dammit, off the damn hat or any of the pillars. The big critter went down hard, and a low grinding rose, a buzz thrum-bouncing around concrete pillars and empty painted lines.

Shit. Tiny eyegleams lit in the darkness, ringing both vehicles. "*Get the fuck in!*" he yelled, and shot another one.

How long had they been creeping in the dark?

"Clear!" Juju yelled, and his door slammed. Ginny was having trouble with the passenger door on the truck. Traveller almost wriggled free, the dog's growl deepening into an *I mean business* sound.

He wanted to yell at her to get the fuck *in*, but she was doing the best she could. Lee moved up behind her, teeth clenched so he didn't goddamn swear again, his heart pounding along. A smaller critter—female, half her face mottled and dark and one of her feet bare, the other in a thick brogan with red laces—darted forward, and the rifle spoke again.

They were going to break for him *really* damn soon.

He reached past Ginny, got the door, and she elbowed it open, letting out a miserably strained little cry. Lee moved out of her way, wishing he had eyes in the back of his head. Lee swept the rifle in a smooth tracking arc, Ginny clambered up behind him. He crowded close, got his back against hers, and pushed. Traveller yelped, Ginny did too, then Lee inhaled, squeezed off another shot because their weird immobility had broken and they surged forward, lolloping sideways. Juju laid on the four-by's horn and their charge scattered, the critters shaking their heads, maybe freshly blinded by the echoes.

His legs wouldn't move fast enough. The Jeep's engine coughed into life and the horn blare was distracting, so he simply shut both noises out. He never remembered afterward how he got all the way in, slamming the door twice because the first time a critter's fingers shot forward and tried to wrench it open.

"*Go!*" he barked, but Ginny was ahead of him. She'd scooted across the bench seat and had the key in the ignition, twisted it, and thank God she didn't grind the starter. Lee banged the lock down on his side, and almost fell into the footwell when the truck jerked. "Shit!"

"Sorry!" Ginny yelped. The Jeep leapt forward; she got the truck into drive. She revved the engine like she'd been born driving stock cars and popped the emergency brake almost as an afterthought. Lee tipped his head back, only dimly realizing he was laying on the damn dog and half in her lap to boot, and stared up at her.

"Oh God oh God," she kept whispering, her cheeks dead pale and her eyes narrowed. Lee got his arms and legs sorted out as the truck lurched, slewing wildly around a corner. "Sorry, oh, sorry, ouch—"

It was a good thing the parking garage was deserted. Skidding, sliding from side to side, the passenger mirror ripped and dangling as they plowed through a living wall of critters and brushed against the curved wall of the exit. Downhill, bumping and screeching, the paint job was never gonna be the same. She kept right on Juju's bumper, it was damn miraculous she didn't run him over when he went right through the little arm meant to keep you where the pay booth attendant wanted you while you counted out your dollars or showed your room slip.

"Sorry!" Ginny almost yelled. "Oh, God, I'm sorry!"

It was unbelievable, there was nothing to be done, his fate was entirely decided. So Lee Quartine, as usual when shit was sideways and there was nothing for it but to hold on and hope, began to laugh. He got his feet down where they belonged and held onto the dog as they smoked into a chain-biting, slop-melt hard right turn at the entrance, the truck's front bumper less than two feet from the tattered leather cover of Juju's useless spare tire, and hoped they'd at least make it a few blocks.

[26]

ONLY NEED ONE

When they stopped, it was at another gas station about fifteen minutes east of the last, this one already plundered but thankfully—as far as they could tell—zombie-free. The wound was a ragged mess, blood welling from tooth-torn tissues. Mandy peered over Miz Frank's shoulder, trying to hold the flashlight steady and not retch at the same time. Mike, carroty hair plastered to his sweat-drenched forehead, sagged against a display of cheap American flags and red-white-blue pinwheels, bald eagle keychains and I HEART USA mugs. He gasped when the nurse probed at his shoulder with latex-gloved fingers.

"Shit," Miz Frank breathed. "Mike..."

"It's bad, isn't it." He swallowed, hard. "I'm bit. I'm fucking *bit*."

"God *damn* it." Jorge, holding another flashlight, leaned in. "It's my fault. I didn't see the fucker."

"He was quiet. Until he got close." Mike's apologetic grin was more of a rictus. Mandy's stomach kept turning over, a dog not certain of its resting place. Carline was getting her ankle wrapped over by the wreckage of the checkout counter. The bandage around

Colleen's head glared white—she'd been clocked a good one by a flying wire shelf holding Doritos as the zombies blundered through the Marathon station looking for their next meal.

"Compress," Miz Frank muttered, and ripped open a steri-pak of gauze. "Stop the bleeding, and then—"

"Why bother?" Mike shook his head. "I'm *bit*, I'm fucking bit. Leave me a gun and keep going. Jesus."

"You're not dead yet." Miz Frank clapped the gauze on and began making a compression bandage. "Holly? What you got over there?"

"Head wounds are messy," Holly answered. Chantal hugged Colleen, patting her back and rubbing in little circles, her earrings glittering. "No concussion, though. Bandaged up, and I'm wrapping Carline's ankle."

"Good deal." Kasie Frank peered at Mike's face, her lower lip trembling for a moment before it firmed. "It's not far to Atlanta."

"In this weather? With all that crap on the road?" Mr Mock shook his head. Sweat stood out in big clear beads on his forehead, soaked into the collar of his Superman T-shirt. "No, ma'am. Just leave me a gun and a couple cans of beans. I'll get a car and meet you there."

Miz Frank didn't think much of that notion. "Mike..."

"He's right," Holly weighed in, ruthless and practical. "See how that feels, honey."

Carline gingerly worked her foot into her lace-loosened boot, and put both boots flat on the floor. She swayed when she stood up, and her gaze swam to Mandy's. Carline's pupils were so big her eyes looked dark as Mandy's own, and little threads of sweat-curled gingery hair stuck to her forehead. "It's okay," she said. "We ain't gonna leave him here, are we?"

"I'm *bit*," Mike repeated. "It's fast. We know that. Like Hannah."

Hannah? Mandy realized this had happened before to these people, and the sudden knowledge almost wrung her stomach inside out. She held on, grimly, but a whooshing sound started in her ears.

That was bad news. If the noise got any louder she'd probably throw up. So she began to count inside her head, up to five and back down, trying to slow her breathing too. Mama called it meditation, but Mandy thought it was a simple way of chopping the world up into manageable chunks. You couldn't say as much, though. People wouldn't pay for it unless you dressed it up a bit.

"Hannah hid her bite." Miz Frank finished tying the bandage on with quick, efficient jerks, her dusky hands sure and deft. But her face contorted, like she tasted something super-bitter. "We don't know how long—"

"Kasie." The redheaded man pulled away, yanking shreds of blood-caked blue flannel up over the bandage. "It's my own damn fault. I should have been wearing my coat."

"Shit," Jorge muttered, and turned away. His flashlight beam swung crazily, merged with the thin grey afternoon light coming through the cockeyed but unbroken glass door. "Oh, *shit*, man."

The redheaded man winced, touching the bandage with blood-stained, blunt-nailed fingers. "Pack up and get out of here before it gets worse, okay? Please, Kasie."

Carline limped across ancient, worn linoleum, shuffling through little bags of potato chips, scattered Slim Jims, and a drift of cigarette lighters tossed higgledy-piggledy. Most of the Hostess stuff was gone, and plenty of the cigarettes. That had probably been the first round of looting, Mandy bet. *One, two, three.* She lost count, had to start over again.

"Mandy?" Carline reached her. "You okay?"

"Get the kids out of here," Mike said. "I just want my suitcase. And a gun, okay?"

Jorge snorted. "Gonna fight 'em off by your lonesome?"

"I only need one bullet, motherfucker." Mike shifted, and the pinwheels above him glittered. One of them caressed his hair with a blunt plastic blade. "Get loaded up and *go*." *Before I lose my nerve,* his face said, before he gulped, his Adam's-apple bobbing, and his chin firmed.

Miz Frank glanced at Mandy. She looked ashy, and for a moment, Mandy saw an expression that had crossed her own mama's face more than once. Unwillingness, and a dull hatred of the burdens the world kept piling on you. Girls learned that weight early, and black girls even earlier.

"Okay." Carline took the flashlight, and tugged at Mandy's arm. Occupied with counting, Mandy didn't protest. "We're gonna wait outside."

"Yeah, you do that. Keep a sharp lookout." Miz Frank accepted the flashlight, and turned it off with a click. Jorge hung his head, and his shoulders were bowed. It was weird to see a big old dude with a cop haircut stand like he felt the weight, too. Generally, those motherfuckers just shoved it off onto whatever uterus-carrier was nearby. "Go on, now. Jorge—"

"I'll stay with him," Jorge said, almost unwillingly.

"No, you won't." Mike sighed, his bloody hand gripping at the clean white bandage.

Holly, brisk and decisive, made a shooing movement at the girls with both arms. "Come on, ladies. I'll go with them."

"Oh, God." Chantal shook her head, her earrings swinging. "Mike..."

"It's all right." Mr Mock shifted against the display. A mug fell, the jolt of its shattering breaking the numbers inside Mandy's skull. "Go on, now."

Outside, the sky had closed over, and more snow whirled down. Mandy braced Carline, who grimaced each time her injured foot came down. They ended up near the Toyota; Carline sighed when they stopped moving.

When Miz Frank came out of the gas station, neither of the men followed her.

"Kasie?" Holly opened her arms, and Miz Frank stepped into them. Chantal hugged them both and Colleen too, everyone blinking as pellets too thin and hard to be called snow began to fall with tiny rattles.

Mandy turned her face into Carline's neck and stayed there. Her eyes squeezed shut, and she supposed she wasn't right in the head, because she only felt a distant, hollow sense of relief.

They were gonna get on the road again right soon, she reckoned.

[27]

IT GOT LOUD

The mom-and-pop Kwik-Stop, gas station and sundries, was set in the opposite corner of a parking lot from a strip mall, brick buildings hunch-shivering under a swiftly darkening sky. A deserted Laundromat with soaped harvest decorations on its windows, a tobacco shop that probably did all sorts of business before the world ended, an empty storefront with a FOR RENT sign blaring a telephone number that was no doubt dead, and at the very end, blacked-out windows with neon XXX and ADULTS ONLY signs, also dead and dark now.

You could wash your clothes, grab some smokes, get some porn, and fill your gas tank all at the same time. America in a nutshell, only without a gun store. Lee didn't like stopping here, but Ginny had broken her long silence to ask for a bathroom break ten miles ago. The truck bumped up into the parking lot through the closest approximation of a driveway, the mangled mirror on the passenger side tapping as it swung.

Should get some duct tape and fix that fucker. At least she'd stopped apologizing for scratching up his truck.

Pale and composed, looking out the window with her hands

folded just-so, she was a magazine illustration of a woman lost in the scenery. Except there was nothing nice out there, just mangy patches of cracked concrete surfacing through ridged, re-freezing melt and the ribbon of a two-lane highway, a dilapidated garage on the other side of the road. Not even a one-horse town; not even a stoplight.

He opened his mouth to make some sort of remark—maybe ask Ginny if she wanted anything special likely to be in a stop-n-rob gas station, maybe tell her they weren't gonna halt here for the night since it was only a little while longer to Carrolton—when his peripheral vision caught motion and he swung the truck aside, chains biting the freezing, ridged crust of slopmelt. Someone had been in and out of here since the snow. Several someones, and all driving.

He might have been heartened, except the motion was a staggering figure clutching at his belly. It was a middle-aged man in a hunting vest, and he wasn't moving like a critter. One begging, blood-spattered hand outstretched, he tacked drunkenly for the truck, drawn by headlights in the gloom-grey afternoon.

Traveller, awakened by the bumping and the change in speed, scrabbled to sit upright. Ginny's soft, indrawn gasp was lost in the crackling of static from the walkie-talkie on the dash.

"Incoming!" Juju barked through it. "Ten o'clock!"

The critters had dropped to all fours, hunch-galloping after the tubby fortysomething man whose yellow-laced Timberland boots had seen some hard working wear. Their prey's balding head glowed, steam rising from tight-drawn skin. He looked a little like ol' foul-mouthed Cyrus Patchman, and why Lee was thinking about an old logistics officer he'd never done more than say *hello Captain* to once or twice was a mystery.

The mind did funny things when adrenaline started flowing.

"*Help!*" The man waved his free arm wildly, words thin and tinny through the rolled-up windows. "*Help me!*"

"Oh, God," Ginny whispered. "They're going to...oh, God, *Lee...*"

He was already reaching for the talkie. "Back on the road, get back on the road, copy."

"Copy that." Juju didn't sound fazed in the slightest. The Jeep curved, bumping over heaving pavement full of ridged ice, heading for the second driveway. The chains rasped as Lee turned the wheel, intending to fall in line. Juju could take point for a while.

"Lee..." Ginny, breathlessly. "They're going to get him."

"We can't help him." Was he telling her, or himself? The man's gut was bleeding badly, a line of crimson spatters charting his weaving course from the jimmied-open door of the Kwik-Stop. "We just can't."

The man put on a burst of incredible, unbelievable speed, and cut right across the truck's arc. The critters sped up too, maybe sensing their target was about to escape. Had the fellow been hiding inside the store, waiting for someone to come along? Hoping against hope?

More critters boiled from the Kwik-Stop's door. Who knew what desperate battle this fellow had been waging inside? Lee's conscience pinched, but faintly. Even if they could stop, picking up this fellow and trying to stop the bleeding...well, it didn't look good.

Nothing about this looked good except the chances of getting one of his own people bit.

The critters began leaping for the truck and the man skidded to a stop, one arm folded over his gushing midriff and the other outflung. "Please!" he yelled. "*Please!*"

Right in their way. Right in front of the truck.

God *damn* it, what was he hoping for? Lee swore, and the truck kept going, gaining speed as it came out of the curve. "Motherfucker," Lee muttered, losing the swear-battle with himself, and Ginny's legs were stiff, pushing her back into the seat like she thought she was standing on the brake.

Thud. Thudthud. Impacts against the sides of the Chevy, the critters throwing themselves at the metal beast. A wet, livid hand splatted against Ginny's window; she cried out and Traveller was in her lap, barking furiously.

When shit went bad, it never stopped to brace itself before the plunge, and it got *loud*. Lee pushed the accelerator, the chains ground down to the paving, and the truck lurched as something soft got caught under the back left wheel. The grill plowed right into the wounded man, who went down with an approximation of a grateful moan—or a horrified one, and Lee knew, miserably, that he was going to have nightmares about this. They were lining up at the door already, just waiting for him to close his eyes.

Heavy American metal on practically new, chained-up tires barely paused, jolting over flesh, bone, and slippery spraying blood.

Traveller's nose was against the window, his barking reaching a furious pitch. He scrabbled in Ginny's arms, tearing at her coatsleeves with blunt doggy claws.

Lee twisted the wheel again to get them out of the parking lot and onto the highway once more. The walkie-talkie lit up, Juju needing a status update, and Lee reached for it with a dry mouth, sweat all down his back and his skin too tight all over him. He heard himself, calmly, giving the a-ok and telling Juju to look out for a better bathroom stop, since he was in front now.

Ginny hitched in a sobbing breath. There was a dragging under the truck, and he had to give the engine more fuel to shake it free. Was it the man or one of the critters? In any case, it fell off a few moments later, the back wheels lifting and dropping like they'd put a speed bump on the highway, and Ginny, milk-pale, made another small sound, a hitching moan.

Traveller finally calmed, Ginny smoothing his fur and crooning to him, a wordless tranquilizing hum probably doing double duty to soothe herself as well. Lee turned the wipers on, pressed the button for the washer fluid. Nothing was on the windshield, he just...needed to clean it, that was all. He was pretty sure that when they stopped, Ginny wouldn't want to be in the truck with him no more.

But dear God and sonny Jesus in Heaven, what else could he have done?

[28]

REASSURANCE

CARS CLUSTERED NOSE-TO-TAIL BOTH WAYS ON I-71 OVER THE
Ohio River, but Juju and Lee had anticipated as much and the
Roebling was far less choked. Edging past the checkpoints at either
end of the big suspension bridge was par for the course now, but
midway across something very much like panic gripped every inch of
Ginny's body, and she went rigid.

Traveller whined a little, but Lee said nothing, and when the fear
passed, she ached all over worse than she had after the flu.

A thin misting drizzle turned into steel-colored rain on the other
side of Cincinnati, and Ginny suspected everyone else was as glad to
be over the state line as she was. It wasn't Kentucky's fault, really. No
state of the Union *asked* to be full of walking dead. Or mostly dead.
Or *whatever* they were. The more Ginny thought about it, the more
she wished she hadn't been a rationalist by both birth and education.
Some brain-numbing religion to crawl into would be *awful*
comforting right now.

Though whispering *Jesus please* occasionally as the afternoon
wore on didn't seem to be helping Lee any. And every bump in the
road made Ginny flinch again.

Their halt that evening was office building—the sign blared *Kenwood Parke*, a big block of concrete with awnings and tattered landscaping attempting to dress up its edges. The brick structure stared with dark windows across a maze of similar buildings. Juju avoided the residential areas—he was right, nobody would come to this honeycomb of mid-grade offices to loot, and most of the professionals here while the world crumbled probably had the luxury of calling in sick.

There was a suite shared by a psychiatrist and several therapists on the second floor, and when Ginny pointed out they were likely to have snacks and couches, it was settled. Again, Lee said nothing, just nodded, hung his rifle on his shoulder, and began carrying luggage inside after the usual check to make sure it was deserted. The kids chattered nervously, stealing little glances at him every once in a while as they worked, and Juju, standing at the side door they'd managed to pry open, shook his head and told Ginny to *stay in sight with the dog, ma'am.*

The quiet wore on her nerves. God, if only Lee would *say* something. Yell, even. Instead, he'd barely even spoken into the walkie-talkie. The soft pleas for Jesus to do something nameless didn't really count, either.

Traveller slunk around her ankles, trotting away to do his business near a bank of thorny evergreen bushes that must have been trimmed before everyone got sick. He didn't pull at the leash to get one more delicious smell stuffed in his nose, either, but came right back to her, his tail at half-mast and his big brown eyes saddened.

"I know it's almost supper time," she told him. "You really don't have to remind me."

He perked up, tail lifting, and she wished it was as easy to cheer up a human.

A human being who had to drive over a wounded man and several...zombies. *We can't help him.* And Lee's ashen face. How did you talk about something like that? How on God's earth could you reassure someone in the face of *that happy horseshit*, as her neighbor

Harry McCoy used to bellow in his living room when some kind of football game had gone awry on their flatscreen? You could hear him on spring evenings when the windows were open, before summer heat closed everyone in their own little air-conditioned cells.

How often had Ginny wished he would just be quiet? Quiet forever, now. She shuddered, and Traveller trotted obediently at her side, back into the shelter of a deserted building.

Six offices, two with at least a loveseat, three with full-size couches. There was even a tiny kitchenette, and of course the therapists wouldn't have discussed their cases with identifying details, but had any of them sitting at the small lunch table with its two spindly chairs wondered why everyone had come down with the flu? Had someone locked up the deserted office and gone home to find a fever-stricken loved one, or a roommate making that awful grinding noise?

Ginny stood in the kitchenette doorway, imagining, and jumped when Lee bumped into her. Her MagLite clattered on linoleum. She ducked for it, he did too, and Ginny braced herself.

Instead of grabbing the fallen light, she caught his hand.

Lee's skin was cold, for once. Callused, work-roughened, and tense, his fingers trembling. It hadn't stopped him from piloting the truck smoothly, or checking the building with Juju while she and the kids waited. He'd just...what? Compartmentalized? Put everything else aside?

Did he ever rest?

He balanced on his haunches and went still, except for that almost imperceptible tremor.

Ginny's throat dried up. "Lee," she whispered. Juju said something in one of the other rooms, and Mark laughed. Quietly, hushed as if this were a doctor's office.

In a way, it was.

"Say something," she persisted, softly. "Anything. Just to me. Please." Her knees ached, and her back too. She kept hearing the soft *thud-thud* and feeling the jolt as the truck mowed down flesh and bone in its way.

The horrible thought—that running over the man had been a kindness, given what was chasing him—just wouldn't go away.

Lee shook his head. The beam from his flashlight sliced to the side, catching pasteboard cabinets and the shiny edge of a refrigerator, probably growing a culture or two of penicillin inside. They'd joked, at work in the county library, about leftover lunches achieving sentience inside a fridge or two.

Wouldn't it be funny if all of this was, at bottom, just some microwaved something left too long in a Frigidaire?

Yeah. Hysterical. Ginny held on with her free hand too, cupping his and threading her fingers through. Her knees hit the floor, which was all right, because she suspected they'd gone a little jelly-like anyway. She tugged, and he didn't fight her, leaning forward until his balance shifted and his own knees smacked the linoleum. If it hurt, he made no sign. Not even a sharp breath.

Shadows danced. Ginny pulled, a little more sharply. *Why am I doing this?*

It didn't matter. For once, she didn't think about how silly it would look if anyone came down the short internal hallway to the kitchenette. They were unpacking, and Traveller was making low yipping sounds as Steph talked to him. It was a comfort to hear quiet human voices, not close but not too far away.

It was another comfort when she awkwardly shuffled her knees across industrial linoleum and got her arms around Lee. His shaking intensified.

"It's all right," she whispered. He sagged against her, his flashlight trapped between them now and the darkness returning except for the forlorn gleam of her dropped MagLite, pointed into a corner. "There was nothing you could do. Nothing at all."

Maybe he believed her. In any case, he went limp, and the shaking all through him jarred her teeth, her shoulders, her knees. She cradled him as best she could, and pressed her lips to his damp temple, her nose buried in his lengthening hair. A breath of leather, a tang of lemon, and a dark, golden scent that was purely male wrapped around her, and she found herself rocking slightly, thankful he'd set his rifle aside and doubly thankful he wasn't wearing a base-ball cap. That would have been uncomfortable indeed.

"It's all right," she kept whispering. "Shhh, Lee. It's all right. There was nothing we could do." Her lips pressed against his skin, and his shoulders shook. His arms slithered around her, and held tight. "Shhh, Lee. It's okay. Everything's all right."

God, I hope he believes me.

"IF YOU DO, USE PROTECTION." GINNY SPLASHED HER FACE WITH cold water, patted dry with paper towels. At least the restrooms on this floor were well-stocked, and there was the luxury of three pillar candles to fill the ladies' half with a tolerably romantic glow. "Do you need condoms?"

Steph turned pink and choked, her toothbrush hanging from her mouth. "Mrphle *Mlls!*" she squeaked, perilously close to spraying Crest foam on the mirror.

"What?" It was kind of amusing to shock a teenager. "I remember what hormones were like. The last thing you need is to be knocked up in the middle of all this, right?"

Steph spat and rinsed her mouth. "I, uh. Yeah, I guess." She kept running the water, splashing, making sure all the toothpaste went down on its frigid, rippling back. "But...can't you count days since your last period, or something? And if the guy doesn't, you know, if he doesn't, do the *you know*, in your hoo-haw..."

Dear God, I'm about to give a crash course in sex ed. "Good Lord." Ginny eyed her in the mirror. "What did they tell you in school, sweetie?"

It turned out to be the usual hodgepodge of ancient pseudo-science and emphasis on abstinence the evangelical troglodytes had inflicted on any school that needed federal funding, and quite a few of the rest besides. Fifteen minutes later, much better informed,

Steph accepted three foil-wrapped squares Ginny dug out of her purse.

"*Don't* keep them in a pocket, body heat degrades them." Ginny held the girl's gaze, steadily. Her scalp tingled from brushing her hair. Who knew when the next warm shower would be? "And remember, even if you don't catch pregnant you can get a disease, so *use* them. If Mark doesn't want to, then not even a kiss for him. Promise me."

"Yes ma'am." Steph's blue eyes were huge. "Miz Ginny, ma'am?" She crumpled the condom packets in her palm, and Ginny was hard-pressed not to smile. "Does it hurt? I heard it hurts like fire the first time."

"Did it hurt the first time you rode a bicycle?" *Or fell off one?*

Puzzled, the girl bit her lower lip. A glimmer of the beauty she'd have as an adult worked through when she was thoughtful like this. "Huh?"

"It's a skill. You learn how to do it, and it gets better." *I can't believe I'm having this conversation.*

"So you're sleepin' in Mr Lee's room tonight?"

Well, of course it was obvious. "I am."

"Oh, wow." A slow, scandalized grin worked its way across Steph's kittenish face. Candle-glow kissed her cheeks and glimmered in her blue eyes. "Hope you kept yourself some of these."

Oh, for God's sake. "I'm a responsible adult, Steph. You're getting to be one. Remember, not even a kiss if he doesn't want to wear a hat. You've got to look out for yourself, now more than ever."

"Yes ma'am. Miss Ginny?"

"What?" *Please don't let her ask about porn.*

"Thanks. Maybe my mama would have told me this, but...well, anyway. Thanks."

Ginny nodded, hugged the girl, and got out of of the bathroom while she could still keep a straight face. It was short work to haul her sleeping bag and foam pad into the office Lee had put his own luggage in, and even shorter work to settle her suitcase in the corner near his. When Traveller appeared, cold night caught in his fur, Lee couldn't be far behind, since he'd taken the dog out.

Juju came through the door first, though. "—like it," he was saying. "But that ain't no difference." He saw Ginny and halted, tipping forward as Lee crowded behind him. Lee made a short sound, not quite a word, expressing mild frustration. Then he peered over Juju's shoulder, and in the dimness, she couldn't tell if his expression was welcoming or shocked.

Traveller nosed at her hands, examining her pillow. His paws were damp, and she scrubbed behind his ears, dropping her gaze to his. "Did you have a good time?" God, she sounded like one of the old ladies from the Cotton Crossing branch, cooing to their tiny handbag dogs. "Yes, we're sleeping in here, but you are *not* putting your feet on my pillow. Nuh-uh. Nope. Come over here and settle down."

"Uh." Juju stepped aside, clearing the doorway. "Yeah. So, uh, I'm thinkin that's best, Lee." He tried to look anywhere except at Ginny, and if this was a movie, Ginny might have laughed at the screen.

Lee cleared his throat. Now she could see his expression, and it was, in a word, dumbfounded. The urge to smile rose, but she killed it. Normalcy was called for here.

Well, it was in short supply everywhere, but she could try.

Juju apparently took that as agreement, because he motioned Lee inside. "All right, then. Imma turn in." He all but shoved past the motionless man, the pompom on his hat bouncing, and Ginny could swear he was grinning. "Uh, see ya in the mornin."

Ginny gathered herself. "No watch tonight?"

Lee finally moved, slow as a man in a dream. "Uh." He cleared his throat. "Uh, nah. We hid the, uh, the cars."

"Good. You need the rest. I'm in here tonight." Why was he just *standing* there? It was going to be embarrassing if she had to pick another office to overnight in. Rejection wouldn't kill you, certainly, but it was uncomfortable. "Just sleeping," she added, hastily. "Nothing else."

"Ginny..." He sounded breathless.

"I need to feel safe." *So do you.* Was that a good enough explanation? "If you don't like it, I can choose another room and—"

"No." Lee made it through the door, half-turned, swung it closed. It latched, gently, quietly. He stepped to the side, then again, and turned, and she realized he was deliberately not putting his back to the door *or* locking it. Whether it was to make sure she didn't feel trapped, or for some other reason, didn't matter. Cold blushed his stubbled cheeks, and his hands were raw with the chill.

Ginny's heart beat high and thready in her wrists, her ankles, her throat. Traveller nosed at her fingers. She patted the end of her sleeping bag, and the hound hopped onto it, turning around and around like he always did before settling. She'd have to shove her feet underneath him and listen to his groaning before he finally cuddled next to her stomach; this was all part of the nightly ritual. "Good boy," she told him, and tried not to look at Lee. Her cheeks were afire. "Did you brush your teeth?"

There was a long pause. "You askin me, or him?" Lee's voice was rusty. Of course, he hadn't used it for hours.

You're a funny guy, Lee Quartine. Add that to the list of things she liked about him. "You."

"Yes ma'am." He coughed, slightly.

"Good. Get some rest." She slid her unlaced boots off and snuggled into her sleeping bag. True to form, Traveller protested, but when she clicked off the LED reading light she used as a nightlamp, he snuggled in his accustomed spot near her right hip.

Lee moved around with his flashlight, putting things away, finally unrolling his own foam mat and sleeping bag. Once he was settled, she turned on her right side and regarded him, steadily. He lay on his back, his flashlight pointed straight at the ceiling, and his profile was chipped out of some ancient, steady rock, polished just enough to show its bones.

The flashlight clicked off, and he set it aside with a precise little sound. Traveller sighed, and spread out on his side. Ginny closed her eyes.

"Goodnight," she whispered.

"Night." Lee cleared his throat again, softly. "Goodnight, darlin."

A smile spread through every part of Ginny, blooming like a rose. Outside, the cold rain intensified, the river swelled, and stealthy movement slunk between buildings in the winter dusk.

...to be continued

SEASON FOUR: ATLANTA BOUND

SUPPORTIVE

BEFORE THE WORLD ENDED, IT GENERALLY TOOK FOUR TO SIX hours between Cincinnati and Cleveland, depending on traffic. Now it took two days even though Lake Erie hadn't frozen yet, and the snow cleared enough they had to take the chains off both Lee's battered red truck and Juju Thurgood's black 4x4. Empty cars scattered everywhere—everyone had tried to get out of town, and road-clearing had fallen further and further down the emergency services priority list. No few of the abandoned vehicles had a door or two hanging open or windows starred with breakage.

If you were in a car with a sick 'un when the convulsions hit, it probably got confusing. Or if, God forbid, you had a loved one *past* the convulsions and that awful, gripping growl started and what was now a hungry corpse lunged for the closest victim, Lee Quartine figured a body would want to get out of a car right quick if that happened, and not be too choosy about the escape direction, so to speak.

On the first afternoon out of Cincinnati raw grey chill roughened the ironpan sky, billows heavy with precipitation refusing to drop just yet. Crashes clogged the road-arteries, and just outside Columbus was a snarl of deserted checkpoints, most with bullet holes chewed through thin plywood walls—holes they added to when they stopped.

"That's right," Lee murmured, wishing he had a baseball cap to shade his eyes, not to mention cover up how long his hair was getting. He kept his tone soft, level, conversational. Some people needed a bark or two to keep their mind on the task at hand, but not *her*. "Now breathe out, and in the middle, squeeze. Don't pull."

Ginny Mills did her best. The gun barked, the recoil went all the way up her shaking arms and if Lee hadn't been bracing her, the pistol probably would have flown backward and clocked her a good one.

Well, maybe not, but in any case, she couldn't help but clap her eyes shut each time she got off a shot. As a result, the bullets went wide.

Real wide. And each time, she lowered the gun instead of tracking, frowning a little and biting her soft lower lip.

Traveller, in the truck with both windows rolled a third of the way down, yip-howled unhappily. The bluetick coonhound plain hated being put inside and told to stay, but Lee didn't want him pulling on a leash while someone was aiming. Or, God forbid, goin' downrange.

Young Steph Meacham took a bead next, concentrating so hard her feathery eyebrows almost met in the middle. She had a good stance, nice and braced, and hit what she was aiming at more often than not. Once, twice, thrice, a neat little grouping of holes exploded in the side of a plywood shack set in the left lane ahead of them.

Each time a gun went off, Ginny flinched. There was just no way around it. Cold wind riffled stray chestnut curls escaping from her black knit cap. Lee stood behind her, his arms on either side of hers, walking her through the motions of checking the gun. "How many shots you got left?"

"Th-thirteen." Ginny's teeth all but chattered. Lean black Juju Thurgood was coaching Steph, beak-nosed Mark Kasprak leaning in to listen with his big gloved hands dangling. Next time they stopped, it would be Mark shooting and Steph observing, and Kasprak had a good steady hand with a pistol, better with a rifle. They were both coming along right well.

Ginny was a different story.

"You get used to it," Lee said. If there hadn't been firearms involved, he would have downright enjoyed being so close. Bracing her and teaching her to deal with the recoil had its pleasant parts. "Don't worry."

"I *am* worried." She lowered the pistol even further, index finger locked conscientiously outside the trigger guard. "I've got to get this down."

"Well, you're doin all right far as I can tell." Lee couldn't hope for a better student. She took every safety measure to heart and didn't do a damn thing he didn't tell her specifically to. If only more of the asshole kids coming through basic had been half as careful.

Steph squeezed off another shot, putting a hole neatly in the middle of a sign saying TURN OFF YOUR LIGHTS.

"You see that?" Mark crowed, hopping in place. "*Damn*, girl!"

"Mama always said girls're good shots. Said it was hand-eye coordination." Steph blinked owlishly, her face smoothing out. "Your turn now, Miz Ginny."

"I'd rather not." But Ginny gamely lifted the piece again, and Lee stepped back to give her room this time.

"Keep yo arm straight," Juju said.

"I don't *like* guns," Ginny said through gritted teeth for the fiftieth time, and *blam*, muzzle flash. This time she actually hit the checkpoint, about shoulder-height on the plywood. "Oh. *Oh.*"

"Yeah!" Mark cheered, pumping his fist in the air. "Now *that's* what I'm talkin about!"

"You're such a dork," Steph said, but gently. She wasn't keeping her distance from the boy anymore, but something had sure enough changed between them. Puppy love grew just like the puppies did, maybe.

"I'm bein *supportive*," the boy popped back, with a grin. He was filling out his expensive new parka with a vengeance now.

Travel agreed with him.

"Check yo clip, Steph." Juju squinted, glancing down the freeway. They could get past on the shoulder here, but a crash near the checkpoint had involved fire. Twisted metal corpses stood silent sentinel, charred and dripping with melt. "Comin up on fifteen, Lee."

"Yeah." Lee checked his half of their surroundings—a modesty screen of wind-torn bushes, an embankment full of yellowed winter grass and patches of slush crowned with a high fence and the back end of mini-mall. "Ginny, check and clear, now."

"Okay." Her fingers trembled visibly. Still, she popped the clip out and checked the chamber, carefully pointing the business end away from Juju and the kids. A high, pretty flush stood out on her cheeks, and her dark eyes were still and liquid with concentration. "Like that?"

"Just like that." He didn't miss her sigh of relief when she surrendered the gun, or her almost-flinch when he clipped it again and holstered. "You're doin all right, Ginny. Learnin just fine."

"Great." She bit at her lower lip again, and he was powerfully aware that she'd moved her sleeping bag closer to his last night. He kept meaning to stay awake and listen to her breathing, but as soon as the light was off, he was too, just like the damn dog. It was the best sleep of his life, nevermind the cold office floors. If she curled up next to him again he'd probably snore until spring.

At least she'd stopped saying *sorry* each time she pulled the trigger. That was progress.

"Uh..." Steph said, and pointed ahead past the abandoned checkpoint, the wrecks, and another thin dribble of abandoned cars. "Mr Thurgood?"

Juju glanced the way she was looking, and his face hardened, full lips compressing. "Get on in the four-by, kids. Lee?"

He saw it, too. Shuffling down the middle of the highway, blundering between wrecked cars, its head cocked at that queer angle and its eyes filmy-grey, a walking corpse in tattered desert camouflage dragged its boots along. So far, there was just the one.

That was why the practice stops were only fifteen minutes long. The noise inevitably drew shuffling, chewing, dead-eyed critters.

"Pack it up," Lee said. "Next stop's t'other side of the city, we'll find food. And more ammo." Always, *always*, they looked for more ammo.

"I'm not *that* bad a shot." Ginny edged for the truck. Her dark eyes were wide, and Traveller's yodeling took on a sharper edge.

Lee caught another flicker of motion between the back of the mini-mall and a sagging chainlink fence. "Rather have it and not need it, darlin."

"*Darlin*," Mark mouthed, and Steph giggled, elbowing him as she lengthened her coltish stride.

Inside the truck, Ginny held Traveller's collar and soothed him, petting behind his ears while Lee twisted the key. Juju had scouted a way around this checkpoint when they stopped, so now he took it, the four-by's tires crunching on wet shoulder gravel, sinking a bit in freezing mud before hauling along. Lee followed along, nosing the truck carefully through the tangle.

All told, it wasn't a bad morning.

[2]

DARLING

THE RED CHEVY RATTLED, AND GINNY JOLTED INTO wakefulness. She just couldn't seem to get enough sleep, though she passed out each night despite the discomfort of sleeping bags, foam pads, and cold. It was probably just the recovery from her bout with the flu, and thank goodness it hadn't been *the* flu, the one that turned everyone into...well, *zombies* was the word the kids used, and she might as well.

It was certainly a more efficient term than "shuffling, chewing, groan-grinding corpses." If they weren't dead, they were certainly close—higher brain function seemed to be gone. The only thing remained was the imperative to bite, and the hunt for...well, they were no doubt looking for food.

The thought of maybe turning into one of those brainless foot-dragging *things* sent a chill down her back even now. She was lucky. How long until luck ran out? For her, or for someone else in their little group?

"It's all right," Lee said quietly, the same way he did every time she startled out of a nap. He gazed out the windshield, a clean-cut profile. "Just lookin for a place to spend the night."

Her mouth tasted like morning all over again. Hopefully she hadn't been snoring; she wiped at her chin. No drool. That was a blessing. "I hear Ohio hotels are good." She stretched her arms, then her legs, careful not to dislodge Traveller. The dog preferred to nestle between them on the bench seat, but Lee had suggested Ginny sit in the middle so she could lean on a shoulder instead of the window. Easier to sleep that way.

It was a logical idea, and a nice one, too. So far, he was the same steady, quiet man he'd been since Cotton Crossing, even if she was sleeping in the same room with him when their stops permitted. It wasn't like she *expected* him to change...but you never could tell, with guys.

"Might stop in one. Or another grocery store." He didn't quite squint, but his gaze sharpened. His sandy-darkish hair was growing out and curling a little, stubbornly, and it suited him, along with the five o'clock shadow. Back in the Crossing, her private nickname for him had been *Military Felon*, and now she felt a little guilty about it.

It wasn't a nice thing to call someone who had yanked you out of gunfire and beaten off your zombified neighbor, or someone who had climbed outside a fifth-story window and busted a glass door to help you, or someone you'd held in a darkened office kitchen and whispered *there was nothing you could do* to while he shook with dry, suppressed, silent sobs.

If there was an etiquette manual for these situations, she'd missed when they were handing it out.

The sky had turned ugly-grey and infinite, clouds smoothing out. It looked like more snow, and Lee's window, rolled down just a little though the heat was on, breathed a cold metallic tang into the truck's cab. It wasn't cold, but she shivered anyway. "It's going to snow."

"Most likely. Have to chain up again." He glanced at her. "How you feelin?"

That was something else he asked every time. Her mouth was rancid, her neck hurt, and dear God, she wanted a salad. Maybe if they stopped at a grocery store she could try to find some unspoiled produce. Carrots, maybe some apples that hadn't gone mushy. "Fine. Are we stopping to shoot again?"

"Not until tomorrow." The truck slowed, edging past a pileup in the right lane. Lee's hands were raw and reddening; she had to find him some good lotion when they stopped in a place likely to have some.

No more shooting today. Relief filled her chest. "Great."

He smiled, and it did good things for his face as well. People got a lot more attractive when you liked them, there were all sorts of studies proving it. How many scientists had been lost when the sickness swept the world?

Well. She'd lasted a few minutes without a hideous thump in her stomach when she realized one more awful thing about current events. It was a new record.

At least they were getting closer to New York. If this was a normal trip home, she'd generally have a hotel room planned somewhere just before Cleveland so she could handle Buffalo and the tolls afterward while she was relatively fresh. Or she'd have taken the train, and Dad would have picked her up in Albany. Flying home had become ridiculous ever since they added all the security theater.

God. Imagine someone sick on a flight, going into seizures in a pressurized aluminum tube at thirty thousand feet...

Another horrible thought, like clockwork. They wouldn't stop while she was awake, but at least she wasn't remembering her dreams. They were probably real creature features by now. Ginny bent, restless, rummaging in the footwell on the passenger side for her purse and the two books—a relatively recent Merck Manual and an early volume of Foxfire.

One for trying to figure out what this illness was and the other for rebuilding. If they survived.

The closer New York and her family got, the faster she wanted to be going—and the more uncomfortable thoughts rose. Her sister had probably gone into labor by now. Well, women had been giving birth for millennia, Flo should be okay. There were retired doctors all over the gated community her parents had retired to. "Gated" meant "safe," right?

But Mom and Dad were elderly. Hopefully they were riding all this out. If Ginny was immune, if what she'd had was only the regular flu, then hopefully they should be immune too, or at least halfway? And Flo, and her baby? Or maybe only one of her parents had immunity...

She was still bruised all over. High fever, febrile convulsions—if it hadn't been the zombie flu, it was *like* it, even if Juju had stories about soldiers and stress-triggered illnesses. "Lee?"

"Hm?"

There was a bruise on the inside of her right arm that looked for all the world like a needle had gone in. But that was ridiculous. Nobody had injected her with anything, she must have done something to herself when the fever spiked.

She had a hazy memory of Lee breaking into her hotel room and holding her down as the seizures hit again, and the layers of bruises all over her were from throwing herself all over said room. "Nothing," she said, finally, opening the Merck Manual again. Tissue-thin pages carrying a civilization's cargo of medical knowledge, more precious now than ever. "I'm just a little weirded out."

"Be strange if you wasn't, darlin." One half of his mouth curled up and he ducked his head a little, a shy movement from the boy he must have been. He was probably quiet then, too.

Darling. It sounded different when he said it, and it wasn't just his accent.

She tried to imagine bringing him home to meet Mom and Dad. In the normal course of things, would he have talked to her before she finally got an offer and left for a bigger city, a bigger library system? Would she have seen the steadiness in him, the calm, or any of a hundred other things she was now taking for granted, outright relying on?

A goy, Mom would say to her friends, looking to the sky to witness her eldest daughter's latest not-quite-measuring-up. *He's very handy, though.*

Dad would like Lee—he respected competence. Her mother's disdain was somewhat expected, but her father's would be harder to bear, if it happened. Flo, of course, would take one look at him and decide Ginny was going way below the Mills pay grade. It might even make her sister stop blaming her for the great soon-to-be-ex-husband debacle.

None of that would matter if they were alive, and well. She could even put up with her mother's anxiety with good grace. Mom would probably go into a tizzy about how Ginny shouldn't have traveled, fussing and fretting that would even be welcome because her mother never panicked during the emergency, only when things were settled and there was spare time for thinking about it.

Please let them be all right, she thought, again. *Please, please, let them be all right.*

She bent over the book, blinking against a sudden swell of hot water, and a few thin hard flakes of snow hit the windshield with soft pop-slithering kisses.

[3]

IF YOU'RE GONNA

They stopped just off the freeway at a fancy grocery store, all-natural and organic plastered on every shelf. The glass doors in front were boarded up by some punctilious manager, and the parking lot held only two abandoned SUVs standing lonely sentinel at either end. Rattling bits of snow came down, more ice than flake, and Juju didn't like the way the wind smelled of cold iron and heavy moisture on the way.

He also didn't like the way Mark kept sidling after him, the kid's beaky face full of something. Like he was congested with a secret and just had to share.

Nothing good ever came from a white boy followin' you with something on his mind, and that was a fact.

It was beginning to get damn eerie, being in deserted grocery stores. At least this one didn't have a goddamn zombie hiding behind the meat counter. The side door Lee and Juju chose had been jimmied once, inexpertly, but whoever came through had left little trace except in the paper aisle, where someone had cleaned out a whole stand of recycled-paper asswipe.

Why they bothered, Juju had no idea. *Recycled* meant *rough*, and after the Army he had no desire to ever scrape his nethers with substandard tissue ever again. Tip had laughed at him for being serious over TP, but he also used Juju's luxury buttscrub with abandon.

Well, Tip was past the problem of finding something to wipe with. He was past all the problems, forever.

Juju stopped next to a display of biodegradable cleaning supplies, rubbed at his eyes, and continued on. As if good old Clorox wasn't good enough for rich folk. Damn it all.

It was in the soup aisle, both of them looking for dinner, that Mark finally busted. "Mr Thurgood, sir?"

"Spit it out." Juju peered at the shelf in front of him. Tomato bisque, what the hell was that? There wasn't a decent can of Campbell's Chunky in this entire place. "Whatever you been sittin on, Kasprak, just let it loose."

The boy's ungloved hands dangled. He was growing into them, and filling out around the shoulders. "I owe you an apology, Mr Thurgood. And I'm gonna give it." The words came out in a rush, and Mark hunched a little, as if expecting Juju to yell.

Uh. What? "What for, son?" Juju's flashlight flicked over cartons of beef stock, chicken stock, pasture-raised, organic feed. Yes sir, they were definitely in Yankee land now.

"Mr French. When he called you...when he did what he did. I shoulda said somethin. I didn't, and I'm sorry." Mark didn't quite mumble, but he didn't raise his voice either.

Well, now. The world was still a surprising place. "Ain't nothin you could have said," Juju answered, finally. Even though Steph had spoken up. Still, if French had wanted to push it, neither of the kids would have been worth a red snoot. "Get yo'self some food."

Whatever Mark was expecting, it wasn't that. "I shoulda said somethin," he repeated. "Next time I will."

"No need to tell me that." Juju found a couple cans of beef stew that didn't look like they had any weird ingredients like lemongrass or soy. "Just do it, if you're gonna." Maybe there was some bread that hadn't passed, or instant rice? He was missing vegetables, truth be told, and *that* was a sure sign of the Pocalypse too. Spinach, or some carrots—well, maybe the carrots might still be good, even if the produce department was a little fragrant right now. Ginny had hied herself over there with a purposeful look when they separated to look for dinner.

"I just wanted you to know." Mark's bare hands wrung at each other, reddened knuckles glaring. Wasn't enough to just say he was sorry, the kid expected Juju to soothe him, too. Maybe before the wrath of God came down on the whole world Juju would have tried.

"Well, thank you, Mr Kasprak." Juju nodded, selecting a couple more cans. Might as well stock up. "You want some of this?"

"Nosir." Mark's expression cleared. "I like tomato, myself. With some grilled cheese."

Well, there was bisque right there. Why they didn't just call it plain ol' tomato was beyond Juju Thurgood. "Was thinkin of findin some bread." He pointed vaguely down the aisle, in the general direction of the bakery at the back. "If there's any that ain't gone over." Cheese might be still good, maybe they could dig up some of that Velveeta.

That shit *never* went bad.

"I'll go look." With that, the kid was off, his flashlight bobbing. They shouldn't split up further, but Juju didn't say a word. His left hand, hidden, had turned into a fist.

Kasprak's conscience was relieved. That was nice for him. Real nice. All the weight slid right off him and onto Juju. They just didn't seem to get that *"next time"* didn't—and would never—do any fucking good. White people were gonna white people, and even the end of the world didn't change that.

Still, the boy had made the effort. That was pretty much all you could expect, even now in the goddamn ruins of civilization.

Why did they call it that? There was nothing *civilized* about the world. There was technology, sure, but manners and decency were another thing entirely, and rare all down through history as far as Juju could tell.

Real rare.

Juju sighed, shook out his left hand, and didn't look at the burn scar. It twinged, a reminder that he'd only known one goddamn unicorn in his life, and was lucky to have got as much even if that creature was lying dead on a bed in Cotton Crossing with his head stove in. He grabbed a couple cans of the best-looking beef stew, hesitated, and got a carton of fancy tomato soup, too.

Might as well.

[4]

RAPTURE

IN YET ANOTHER GROCERY STORE MANAGER'S OFFICE, THE DESK and ergonomic chair pushed against the wall bearing a whiteboard full of retail hieroglyphics, Steph smoothed her sleeping bag over the foam pad. Her pillow was gonna be cold, and it would smell like the back of Mr Lee's truck. Still, it was better than being in a tent. "Hope tomorrow we get into another hotel," she said, tentatively. "These floors ain't—*aren't* good. They hurt my back."

"You're too young for back pain." Miz Ginny smiled, a gentle expression. Her cheekbones stood out alarmingly, and in the soft candlelight in the manager's office she looked like a religious statue. An icon, her hair freed from its usual braids and flowing in soft rippling waves. She drew a wooden brush through the long flow, wincing a little bit when she came across a slight tangle. "But I hear you. I was wishing up a salad earlier, myself."

"Ew." Steph couldn't help herself, her face wrinkled, and Ginny laughed. It was a thin, tired sound.

"Some day you might appreciate them. I found some carrots and a couple apples, but if we get back to growing lettuce commercially, I might not ever eat anything else." The older woman sighed, laid the brush aside, and began to braid, quick and deft. If she minded having to bunk with Steph instead of with Lee tonight, it didn't show.

Funny how it was decided, girls in one room, boys in another. If Steph was older, she could probably sleep next to Mark and nobody would mind, right? There weren't any parents or schools anymore, nothing to stop her from doing any damn thing she pleased.

The thought should have filled her with excitement, but instead, all she felt was a creeping, tired dread. Steph stared at her pillow, taken from the fancy hotel where they'd left Mr French. Now that was a good thought, the relief of getting rid of *him*.

Good thoughts were few and far between. "I wish my mama was here." The words burst out, surprising her.

Ginny's hands paused, and she nodded. "I was thinking about mine earlier, too."

You've got a mama? Well, of course, everyone did, but it was funny to think of *grownups* having them. Or thinking about them. She'd always assumed grownups only thought about things like taxes, insurance, and vegetables. "You think she's okay?"

"I hope so." Ginny began braiding again. "I talked to her...oh, before this all started." Her mouth drew down, a strangely bitter curve. She didn't usually look like she was sucking on something sour, but she did now. It was kind of a relief to see her with an unpretty expression.

Steph pulled her knees up and hugged them, wiggling her toes inside a double pair of thick woolen socks and her good cushioned boots. You couldn't sleep if your feet were cold, Mama said, and the office here had a skylight, which was gonna let any heat right out. Maybe she should put on yet another pair of socks. "Yeah?"

"Yeah. She was telling me about my sister, and about how they'd closed the bridges into the city—into New York. I should have left then." A deep, probably unconscious sigh finished the sentence.

"There was no way you could have known." It was a grownup

thing to say, but Steph found out she meant it. The worst thing was, she couldn't figure out what *else* to say to make it better. Still, she gave it a try. "It was all just little things. Isolated things, they called 'em. Incidents." A prissy little word, with a hiss in the middle and at its ass-end. "They didn't have the Pocalypse on the news, you know."

"Not as such, no." Ginny's face softened. "You've been talking to Juju. He thinks it's the Reckoning, or whatever—when all the people vanish, right?"

"Rapture." Steph hugged her knees harder and tried not to feel scandalized. How was it possible not to know that? And the older woman was a *librarian*, too. Maybe she didn't church, though. Liberals were always godless, Steph's Mama said, and librarians were probably all close to flag-burning Commies if Daddy could be believed. "When Jesus takes all the good ones home."

"Yes, I've heard that's big in mega-churches. They just don't say *how*."

Was Miz Ginny joking? Steph couldn't tell; she let go of her knees and rubbed at her scalp, her nose wrinkling again as her fingers slipped. Her hair was a little easier to handle now that she wasn't washing it every day, but it felt wrong. Greasy, but dry at the ends. "Well, they's—*they're* supposed to vanish and their clothes'll be left."

"Does it say that in Revelations?" Ginny's eyes turned thought-ful. "I don't remember that bit."

So Miz Ginny had read the Bible? But if she didn't church, how was that possible? "I...dunno." Steph realized she *should* know. Imag-ine, going to church every Sunday and not knowing about something important like that. There were whole sermons about the clothes left behind, not to mention the cars and planes that would go wild when their owners were taken up to heaven. "That's what they say in church."

"Hm."

Now curious, Steph worked her boots off and settled cross-legged on her sleeping bag. "What did they say at yours?" Was Miz Ginny an actual atheist, instead of just unchurched? She seemed too nice, though.

Ginny turned somber, her thoughtful gaze directed past Steph at a corner of the manager's office. "I think the Torah's pretty silent on the matter."

"The whatnow?"

"Torah." The librarian finished her braid and tied it off with an elastic.

Steph blinked. "What's that?"

"Jewish holy book." Now Ginny looked amused, her mouth softening.

"You're *Jewish*?" Oh, wow. Mama wouldn't mind so much, but Daddy said an awful lot of things about "*the Jews*." According to him, they were all rich and nasty, and wanted the United Nations to govern the world or something. They were supposed to all be snooty.

As far as Steph could tell, Miz Ginny was city but she wasn't, you know, *rich*, not like rich people on TV. She wasn't snooty either.

The corners of Miz Ginny's pretty dark eyes crinkled up as she smiled. "Well, my mom is, so I am by default."

Was that how it worked? "And you read the Bible?" Go figure. Jewish. Steph would never have guessed in a million years.

"In high school." A single shrug, like it was no big deal to read the Good Book cover to cover. "I wanted to see what it said."

"Oh." Come to think of it, had Daddy or Mama ever read it? Both of them were big on church, though Bull Meacham often muttered about the youth pastors and their guitar-playin' foolishness. Mama didn't mind that as much, but her people had been Clutters and hard-core Baptists, so she didn't want to let Steph go to any school dances, not even the cotillion.

Now have you told Steph about how we met? Daddy had said, and Mama threw up her hands and taken Steph dress-shopping for "something modest." Lord, how many dresses had Steph tried on that trip?

Steph had also tried to work up the courage to ask Mama how they met, but failed. Daddy solved the mystery one hunting trip, while Steph shivered in early-morning mist. *We was in a bar—a honkytonk, you'd call it if you were our age. Your mama was somethin then, Stephanie Mae. Prettiest girl I ever did see until you was born.*

"Hey." Miss Ginny tucked her brush away. "Sweetie, it's okay. It's all right."

Steph realized her cheeks were wet. She snuffled, her nose full of slimy heat, and her fingers had somehow gotten tangled in each other, knotting hard. They hurt, but she kept tensing up, a fish pulling on a line, maddened as the hook tore through its cheek.

"Oh, honey," Ginny whispered, suddenly on her knees right next to Steph, who kept trying to hunch over around the hole in the world that had just walloped her with no warning.

It was a big hole, and deep, and it was full of Mama's biscuits and hip-bumps in the kitchen, and Daddy's aftershave and his snoring swallowed by his old recliner in the fourth quarter of almost every football game. Then he would wake up, irritable, and wonder who had won the damnthing—said all in one breath, *damnthing.*

Ginny was warm and soft and she held Steph, rubbing the girl's back in little circles just like a mama, but oh, it wasn't the same. Nothing was the same, it was all wrong, and they were in a cold, shitty manager's office in a hoity-toity grocery store, it was the end of the world, and there was nothing familiar or comfortable.

Steph wanted *her* mama, her very own, and each little thing she missed about her parents led inevitably to those few horrible minutes when zombie-Daddy was in front of the truck, and then zombie-Mama in the kitchen, trying to chew her girl's throat out.

Maybe Jesus had just taken the souls of the blessed, and left their bodies behind to chew and chew. Everything had gone wrong, and it wouldn't ever go right again.

There wasn't a damnthing Steph could do, and there wasn't a damnthing any of the grownups could do, either. Everything was gone wrong, the Rapture had probably happened and called Jesus's chickens home, and Steph was left behind, stumbling around in the wreckage like the bad girl she always suspected, deep down, that she was.

It wasn't a surprise, but oh, it hurt.

It hurt a *lot*.

[5]

GOOD NEWS

"I remember this rest stop." Ginny leaned forward. Her window, down slightly, sent a cold breeze riffling through the truck's cab, and her hair was neatly braided and pinned again, no stray curl escaping. "At least, I think I do."

She was getting right sunny the further east they went. Lee touched the brakes and the chains bit in. A moment later, Juju's brake lights flashed.

There was movement around the low concrete rest-stop building, and a large, battered Ford Explorer sat neatly parked, its outline blurred under fast-falling snow. Looked like it had been there since the weather started. Movement at one end of the building was a canary-red coat, and the walkie-talkie crackled.

"Contact. Looks human." Juju swung the four-by wide, pointing it for an easy getaway. "One armed, I repeat, one armed."

The red coat was on a tall, slim woman; the other shape was a stocky dark-haired man with a blue knit cap and a rifle, business end pointing down. The woman waved, excitedly, but the man stood still, watching the two vehicles through the falling snow.

If it was a trap, it was a piss-poor one. There wasn't enough cover, unless there was someone a fair ways away with a sniper rifle. Why bother lying in cold bushes with the damn critters roaming around, unless you were dumb as a post?

Still, caution was best. Lee reached for the talkie. "Stay ready."

"Ten-four."

Lee studied both figures, waiting for the little tickle along his nerves that would tell him *stay* or *go*. Traveller wriggled with delight at the prospect of a stop, making a low moaning noise. Ginny, her fingers tangled in the dog's collar, sucked in a small wounded breath, staring at the broken-down Ford. The woman in the red coat waved again, and the man, deliberately and *very* slowly, lowered the rifle still further, carefully not pointing it their way and letting the strap take its weight. Then he lifted his hands, the universal signal for "peaceful," and beckoned them closer.

"We can go," Ginny whispered. She'd gone pale, again. The circles under her eyes weren't as dark, but she was still drawn tighter than a piano wire. "We can just go, Lee."

So she'd learned. There wasn't any joy in the fact, not now.

The red-coat woman stepped from under the overhang, shading her eyes with one slender coppery hand. Something in the set of her head said *ballerina*, that pretty grace you only got from classes with tutus and special shoes.

Ginny had it, too.

The woman smiled, pearly teeth visible even at this distance. Red lipstick to match that coat, and her hood had fallen back, exposing a wealth of dark curly hair. She waved again, bouncing a little on her forefeet, and the man still kept his hands far away from the trigger.

Lee's mouth was dry. The woman called something excited, and the sound filtered in through Ginny's window.

"Hey! We're friendly! We're not sick! Hey!"

She waved again, and the man's stance remained easy. He knew how to handle that rifle, but that posture said he was hoping he wouldn't have to.

"Lee?" Ginny whispered.

The calmer he was, the calmer she'd be. "When I get out, slide on over to the driver's side." He hit his seatbelt. "Just in case."

"Lee..." Damn it, now she sounded scared. But, like any good recruit, she exhaled shakily and braced herself. "All right."

The longer he waited, too, the more nervous everyone would get. Lee's door opened, and snow kissed his hair as he headed along the side of the truck, peering around the windshield. At least it didn't *feel* like a trap. The red-jacketed woman bounced out into the whirling flakes like she had a personal exception to gravity and was in a good mood as well.

The weather was starting to thicken up, and though he hated to stop early it looked like they were going to have to halt in the next town.

The stocky, olive-skinned man made a despairing sound. *"Phil! Goddammit!"*

But Red Riding Hood kept right on going, curls bouncing, and Lee wondered if the other fellow was feeling the way Lee himself did when Ginny took off.

Red Riding Hood skidded to a stop halfway between the primer-scarred Explorer and Lee's own truck, eyeing him curiously. "We're not sick!" she called, waving her red-gloved hands for emphasis. A color-coded miss, this was. "No bites, we're not sick."

"Neither are we," Lee called back. "Your buddy there, he friendly?"

"Duncan? Friendly enough." She waved her arms some more, an expansive, happy windmilling full of that graceful ballet-motion. "If you're not into murder, rape, or arson, he's a downright hoot. Are you guys?"

Was she asking if they were all men? "Are we what?"

"Into all that?" She bounced again. Looked like she went along at sixty while the rest of the world was doing thirty-five, and he almost pitied the fella with the rifle.

Said fella stepped forward, said rifle well down and his hands still loose. "Phyllis, for God's sake."

"It's the *end* of the *world*, Duncan," she called back. "We can't be picky. Unless they're murderers." She sized Lee up again. "Are you?"

Like she thought killers looked any different than regular folk. Lee felt the soft thudding under chained truck tires again, and his throat would *not* wet up. "No ma'am," he called, hoarsely. "We're headin north and east. Near New York." Juju would be keeping an eye out for other movement in the falling snow, but the walkie-talkie stayed silent. "Got ourselves a mission."

"Well, we can come along," she blurted, "because the damn car won't start."

DARK-HAIRED, STOCKY DUNCAN HARRIS WAS YOUNGER THAN HE first looked, but his brawn and posture shouted *tough*. He reminded Lee of Rooster Cogburn, but without the unsteady explosiveness lurking in Rooster's banty frame. "Just needs a jump, maybe," he said, while Lee peered under the Explorer's hood. "The cold does things to t'engine."

"We could have just stolen a working one," Phyllis Lampke chimed in. She'd wrapped a large, pink, hand-knit scarf around her pretty throat, bits of snow caught in her curls like stage-dressing. "But *no*, Mr Law and Order there wouldn't hear of it."

"That was before we knew how bad it was," Duncan returned, imperturbable. "Been avoiding cities since. Glad you happened along. Hate to have to sleep here again *or* hike out."

"You headin to Atlanta?" Lee eyeballed the engine again. There wasn't any good news in there. The Explorer was well-maintained, but a little problem in current conditions could turn into a huge fucking snarl given very little prompting.

Still, this Harris fellow took care of his vehicle, which was a cautious mark in his favor.

Juju was on watch, scanning the parking lot and the snowy slope behind the concrete restrooms; Mark Kasprak, somber with responsibility, was near the truck and four-by, keeping a sharp eye the other direction. Steph, right next to him, watched Traveller, who ran in merry barking circles, his excitement falling flat against deadening flake-curtains.

"What's in Atlanta?" Phyllis's eyes were large and dark, and her high gloss was almost unreal. Perfect, poreless coppery skin, that dancer's grace, and that cloud of shining, curly dark hair—even her unpolished nails gleamed a little, and her old boots and painted-on jeans partook of that smooth, shining surface.

Some women were just blessed that way. Like Ginny, too—all the seams tucked away and the edges buffed, even when they were disheveled.

"The Center for Disease Control was broadcasting near the end." Ginny kept glancing nervously at Duncan and stayed on Lee's other side. A vote of confidence, sure, but he didn't like how tentative she sounded. "Everyone we've met has been going to Atlanta."

"We didn't hear none of that." Duncan didn't seem to notice Ginny's caution, but he didn't make any sudden moves, either. And he carefully did not look at her *or* Steph, resting his gaze on the engine instead. "Phyl here was heading to New York."

Ginny perked up a little. "Really?"

The pretty girl gave another megawatt smile, her eyes lighting up. "Was gonna break into modeling. Then the world ends, and I'm stranded in *Ohio*." She jerked a thumb in Duncan's general direction. "Then I ran across *this* guy fighting off a bunch of dead people. He thinks it's religious. I'm pretty sure God is auditioning us all for a big role or two."

Duncan grunted. "Yeah, well, she crashed *her* car trying to outrun some of those mother—I mean, uh, some of those wild Army boys in Pittsburgh."

"What happened there?" Lee wanted to know.

"Some of the checkpoint boys figured since it was the end of the world, they were gonna get what they could *while* they could." Duncan shrugged, but his jawline hardened. "Figured they'd shoot me and have Phyl all to themselves."

Phyllis shuddered, only slightly theatrically. "Yeah, well." She glanced away, and Lee got the idea there was more to that story.

So, apparently, did Ginny. "Civilization breaking down," she said, softly. "Hey, you want to get out of the cold?"

"Not much of it to break down," Duncan said, morosely, with the air of a much older man. "Phyl, go on and warm up. If this gentleman'll give us a jump, we'll be all right."

"I'm fine." Phyllis hugged herself. "I just want to get out of this rest stop. I do *not* want to sleep in the car with you again, Duncan. No offense."

"None taken." The man even looked like he meant it. "You snore anyway."

"So do you, you jerk." But Phyllis's laugher was just as bright and pretty as the rest of her, and maybe that was what decided the issue.

"You got some leakin in there," Lee said, almost unwillingly. "A jump'll just put it off until it freezes. We can take you along, get you a better car up the road."

Duncan didn't bite immediately at the offer, but gave Lee a long considering look. "Where are *you* headed?"

So he was no fool. That was good to know. "New York. Ginny's got kin there." Lee dug for a pocket rag to wipe his hands with, even though he hadn't touched anything greasy. You could never tell, with engines. Best to be safe.

"New York after all." Phyl brightened. "I mean, if you wouldn't mind having us along. Duncan's great with that gun, you know. And I can cook. That's what I was doing, food service. Before I started out for the Big Apple and everything went to shit."

Lee glanced at Ginny. She met his gaze, pale and drawn, and something tugged at the inside of his chest. Still, he didn't need her to say a word. "Be right happy to have more hands. Let's get you loaded, I don't think this beast is movin anytime soon. Y'all got luggage?"

[6]

HOME FOREVER

Deep River RV & Motor hunched under curtains of snow, heavy mounds of damp white standing ghostly sentinel. Fortunately, the dealership had its own gas pumps, and a couple of the newer RV models even had solar panels—snowed under and no good in the failing light, but it was a wonderful idea, and it meant the bigger, more luxurious ones had some juice left. Their small windows glowed, they had cramped but actual *bathrooms*, and if the travelers could find a water source that wasn't frozen, a tepid shower could even be arranged.

Best of all? Everyone could have their own separate sleeping-RV for the night.

Or not, as the mood took them.

Steph shook her head, turning from the small stove. "Not like that," she said, firmly. "Do it again."

"Aw, *man*." But Mark, obediently, slammed the door on his way out, then carefully opened it again, stamped his feet to rid them of snow, and re-entered. "I'm *home!*" he yelled.

"Oh, for God's sake, you don't *beller* it!" Steph put her hands on her hips. She looked a little like her mama when she did that, and it was an uncomfortable echo.

Especially when Mark had beaten Mrs Meacham with a cast-iron skillet, the morning's scrambled eggs still clinging to its insides. "I ain't goin out there again." He locked the door and swept his knit cap off, shaking melting snowflakes from his dark hair. A high blush stood out on his newly shaved cheeks, and he bent to work at his bootlaces. "You can't make me."

"Well, fine." Steph's hands dropped, but she wore a small, cat-satisfied smile. "Just remember next time, don't *beller*. Call it out. Just sing it out like you're happy."

"I *am* happy." Half upside down and scowling, he picked at the wet rawhide laces until they gave. "Why are we playin this game? It's dumb."

"It's not *dumb*. I want to see what it's like and you said okay. If you don't wanna, you can sleep in one of the others, there ain't no shortage." Steph folded her arms defensively. She'd let her hair down, full of soft waves from the braids, her cheeks were flushed, and Mark Kasprak about lost his breath for no good reason at all.

So he dropped his head again, staring at his laces. "I told you, I ain't goin out there again." He finally got his boots undone and loosened. Stepping out of heavy leather and standing in sock feet was almost like heaven. Wool socks were good, even if they got a little damp. Still, he couldn't wait to get dry ones on. "So what now?"

Steph shook her head a little, as if she couldn't believe he didn't know. "Now I ask how your day went."

"You were right next to me the whole time!" And Lord, but he could have kicked himself, because her face fell.

"Mark." One soft little word. Maybe she was taking lessons from Miz Ginny, because she sounded just like her. High-class but not uppity, and disappointed as well.

"Okay, fine." If it made her happy, why not? And if they were playing this game, it maybe meant a kiss.

Or something. Anything. Even

"How was your day, honey?" Steph turned back to the tiny stove-top, where fancy tomato bisque from a carton warmed a small tin pot. Right next to it, a tiny frying pan was only big enough for one slice of frozen fancy bread, some cheese slices that hadn't gone bad yet, and some margarine defrosted from brick-hardness were all in the process of becoming a tolerable grilled cheese.

She called me honey. A big, dopey grin spread across Mark's face, and he didn't have to hide it, neither. He'd watched families on TV, so this was no different. It wasn't like his dad stamping in the front door and yelling *you little shit* or just grunting and heading for the fridge. This was kind of, well, *normal.* Despite the zombies. "It was all right. I'm glad to be home."

"I'm glad you're home too." She pushed her chin down a little and eyed him sidelong, with that shy kittenish smile of hers just the same as when he asked her if they were maybe, well, not *dating,* but maybe something like it, and she said *why not dating?*

Mark lost all his air again. His heart blew up like one of those expensive foil balloons, the fancy ones at the Bargain Zone in Lewis-ton. Maybe she was just reciting the lines from the tee-vee shows, but still...it felt good.

Real good.

"Supper's almost ready." She sounded just like a movie star. The girl next door, the one the hero never thought he was good enough for until he did something great.

So far, he hadn't had much of a chance, but he was gonna grab it. In the zombie apocalypse, anyone could be a hero. "I can't wait."

"I put your slippers right there." She pointed with her chin, and Lord have mercy on his soul, but that lit up the balloons inside Mark's chest something fierce.

The tee-vee shows didn't say how good it felt when someone had your slippers out, and maybe this wasn't such a kid's game after all. Maybe, just *maybe,* he'd get a real kiss. With tongue.

Or even something better.

．．．

Juju Thurgood leaned back, and back, and *back* with a long satisfied sigh. The chair—whoever heard of a recliner in an RV, but it was surely comfortable—cradled him just right, and he had a warm bowl of his favorite beans. There was even Wonder Bread for dipping, rescued from a convenience store's deep freeze and carried in the four-by's cab all day to defrost. Extra blankets waited on a brand-new bed, and this RV was too big to go under a bridge but still...there was somethin' about havin' wheels ready to go at any moment that appealed to him.

Sometimes he'd thought of gettin one of them Airstream trailers and a truck to hitch it to, and just...drivin'. Billy Tipton would have laughed at the idea, being of the persuasion that you didn't go camping if you had a perfectly good house unless you were lookin' to bring home some meat. All during their tours that boy had wanted to go home, couldn't shut up about it.

Well, he was home forever, now, lying on his bed with a smashed-in skull. At least Juju didn't have to dream about Billy shuffling through the snow makin' that grindin' noise. Instead, Juju wiggled his bare dry warm toes, luxuriously, and could remember good times with ol' Tip. Or even middling ones.

This RV had a CD player, and Leontyne Price was just warming up to *Semper libere* and that high ol' E-flat. He could play it as loud as he wanted without Tip making a face. Still, he'd turn it down after a little bit, since the things hunted by sound.

Maybe Verdi would draw a higher class of critter.

Juju smiled ruefully, shaking his head, his hair scratching against the chair-back. It wasn't as good as having Billy's steady breathing presence in another room, but after the last few weeks, it was pretty damn all right.

There was even some glass-bottle fancy beer, not too bad, to wash down the beans and bread with. Ginny was frettin' about nutrition, and Juju figgered he needed some Vitamin C or somethin' healthy in a little bit, but not tonight.

No, tonight was for enjoyin' some of the finer things in life. There was a whole Sara Lee cheesecake on the counter of Juju's chosen RV, defrosting. While it certainly wasn't his grandma's chess pie, it didn't have to be.

Yes sir, Juju thought as he settled back in the recliner, he was going to have a fine old time all by himself. There was no better company, and even with the whole world gone to shit, he was content.

PHYLLIS FROWNED AT HER NAILS. THE PAST FEW WEEKS HAD been hell on her manicure schedule, and she was ready for a break. It was pure luxury not to have to listen to Duncan. He was all right, for a guy, but he was boring, and to top it all off, he *snored*. Sleeping in the back of a car might have been fine in high school, but it was *not* fine in subzero temperatures with the chewing, shuffling dead on the loose.

Especially when he insisted on keeping the cooler between them. She'd thought it was chivalry, but maybe he just wasn't interested. Which would be a blessed first for Phyl, indeed, and while it was welcome, she didn't know if she quite liked another change.

The world had been full of them recently, and she'd about hit her capacity to adapt.

There was a stack of silvery pie-shaped pans with handles on the fake-wood counter, the kitchenette barely stamp-sized but still quiet, trim, and blessedly empty except for her own sweet self. She was going to pop some popcorn, do her nails, and luxuriate in electric heat. It would be like a slumber party, except with no other girls to make envious remarks or babble on about *boys*. And if the salt would bloat her, well, she'd get enough exercise to work it off.

A zombie apocalypse was good for *something*.

There wasn't any TV, but she had something even better—a big, thick, handsome hardcover of *Ulysses*, full of long, complex, deceptively roundabout sentences. There was nobody around to laugh at her for reading or sidle up and try to make small talk, interrupting her flow. Nobody to mock her, or tell her it was a big book for a little girl.

A little girl who'd shot two men and saved Duncan Harris, thank you very much. Even if it had taken zombies to get her out of that one-horse town and there were probably no modeling agencies left in New York, Phyllis Anne Lampke was damnwell doing all right.

She kept James Joyce in the very bottom of her luggage and Henry James in her purse, a pair of good-luck charms; tonight she was going to carefully lick her fingers before touching any pages. She was *also* going to read as late as she wanted, and nobody but *nobody* would stop her.

Tomorrow was soon enough to worry.

The end of the world had so far been kind to Duncan Harris.

He stood in the middle of an RV he wouldn't have been able to afford even if he hadn't blown his inheritance in Miami, his eyes closed and electric light pressing against his lids. He was finally, completely, blessedly alone.

Phil wasn't *bad*, and she'd saved his bacon. Still, she talked all the damn time, and she was a goddamn optimist. Dunc needed peace and quiet like others needed air, and the fact that he hadn't had a tot of whiskey since the crash was wearing on his nerves something awful.

It was faint consolation that the thing in the road that icy night had already been, well, dead. He was just goddamn lucky he'd decided to get the hell out of there instead of trying to check on the human-shaped thing he'd run over in a haze of Blue Öyster Cult and Johnnie Walker Red.

The fact that he'd nerved himself up to go back the next day to find the champing, slavering, growling, broken thing in the bracken didn't change him being a murderer, and a common drunk as well.

That thought jolted him into quiet, catlike motion.

He turned off all the switches except the night-light over the RV's unused stove, and brushed his teeth in the tiny sink. There was a trickle of unfrozen water, but deep winter was on its way, and these idiots were going north-ish.

Still, there was nothing else to do, and he might as well go with them in the absence of any other options. And there was lean dark-skinned Juju with his quiet voice and electric smile, too.

Thinking about that would just make him more damn skittish, so Duncan climbed into the bunk over the driver's cabin, burrowing himself in a little hole, and let out a long soft breath. He would have liked a little music; it kept you from thinking.

But the music might also draw some more of those dead, eye-collapsed assholes, so Duncan was stuck with the tapes in his head playing the Cult and scraping his nerves raw all at once. The Reaper was here, and fearing him, despite the song's advice, seemed like a pretty goddamn good idea. Fear kept you sharp, even if it made you long for a tot or two to take the edge off.

Nobody had asked any questions he couldn't answer, and nobody had to know he was a small-change felon with a dishonorable discharge. A washout, a drunk, a coward—only he didn't have to be, now. The entire town of Pomokie, Ohio was wiped off the map, just like he'd wished so often, both out loud and in the quiet secret rooms of his heart.

If this was a movie, the disaster would turn him into a hero. He'd been waiting for something like this all his life, without ever thinking he'd get it.

Now that it had, he wasn't gonna let anything stop him.

Lee knocked the snow off his left boot, put it inside, then knocked the other clean. It was bright in here, though not quite *warm.* Traveller yip-yodeled with glee, prancing down the RV to tell Ginny all about the last few minutes in the snow; Lee swung the door shut, latched it, turned the lock.

Now they could conserve some heat.

No sign of anything movin' out there. Nothin' but a whiteout and a faint mutter from Juju's RV—hopefully the sound would fall dead in the snow, and Lee didn't have the heart to knock on Thurgood's door and tell him to turn that shit down. The weather was too foul for anything to be moving, even the critters. This far from Cleveland the pickings were probably thin, too, and predators went where the food was.

"Look at you." Ginny beamed, bending over to scrub behind Traveller's ears. "There's a boy who needs his dinner, hm? Two of them, in fact. You don't get any rice and tofu, though. You just get kibble. There's a boy."

She'd found blocks of shelf-stable tofu and looked so happy at the prospect Lee didn't dare complain. Soy sauce, frozen vegetables—it smelled good in here. Like cooking, and the breathing of a pretty woman. Lee stood, stooped a little, uncomfortably tall for the interior unless he stayed in the well of the step.

Golden electric light played over Ginny's single loosened braid, honey-highlighted curls working free and framing her thin face. Her jacket was open, and she swept Traveller's bowl off the counter with easy natural grace as she straightened and pointed. Traveller scrabbled for the back of the RV and the bathroom door with a will, sat like a good hound, and got the bowl for his reward, set carefully on a folded-up towel.

Lee closed his eyes. *Just let me stay here. Just for a minute.*

"Still snowing?" she asked, returning to the stove and flicking off a burner.

And Lee, just for a moment, let himself imagine. A good job somewhere, maybe in another garage. He liked engines, right? And Ginny, working in a library. Or even that daydream, him getting a fine enough job that she could stay home and read all day in a trim little house the bank wouldn't own for too much longer, maybe a piece of land with a tiny vacation cabin on it too. A drive on Sundays, maybe lunch in-town, and throwing a ball for Traveller in a fenced backyard.

It would suit him right down to the ground, but it wouldn't be good enough for her. She was used to more, and deserved it, too.

"Hey. Lee." Soft, concerned, and very close. "You all right?"

His eyes flew open. She was right in front of him, and Lee's hands itched while he stripped his sodden gloves off. The interior was new —perfect, polished, expensive, well-made. So was she, her wide dark gaze focused on him. The most beautiful woman in the world, looking at *him*. That attention was pure sunlight, and he was a helpless plant stretching for it.

"Ginny." He was hoarse. His throat was seizing up at strange times. Like whenever she got close, or whenever he thought about what might have happened if the world hadn't gone to hell in a handbasket all around them. He probably would never have worked up the courage to talk to her, for God's sake.

"I'm right here." Wonder of wonders, Ginny's hands came up, and her fingertips scraped his stubble. She cupped his cheeks and examined him, a somber doctor ready to cure all ills. "You look a little upset. You okay?"

Oh, upset wasn't the word. He couldn't tell what *was*, though.

If not for all this, he wouldn't have had a chance with her. It was a fine time to start feelin' guilty over as much.

"Hey," she persisted, leaning in a little, peering at his face. "If you want me to talk, you're going to have to as well, you know. You're going to have to—"

She didn't get another word out. Because Lee Quartine, at the very end of his patience, dropped his wet gloves, took her face in his hands, and kissed her.

Dinner, that evening, was very late.

[7]

SOME MEANNESS

Ginny lay on her side, her arm tucked under her head and her entire body full of heavy pleasantness. She should have been dead asleep, really. She was warm, *really* warm, for once, and it was hard *not* to feel safe with Lee breathing into her tumbled hair.

Maybe that was the problem. It was a blessed change, as the folks in Cotton Crossing would say, and she wanted to savor it before the next terror came along. Or maybe it was that the longer they went on, the less likely Mom and Dad and Flo were all right, and the closer she got to having even that faint hope snatched away.

She made a slight restless movement. Traveller was unhappy at sleeping on the floor, but there just wasn't room for him up here. There was barely room for six-foot-plus of Lee and her own five-foot-mumble-mumble. Close quarters added something, though, right?

A faint edge of glow spread from the nightlight over the small stove, the metal burner covers gleaming. His hand was spread against her belly, calluses a little raspy on her cotton tank top matching the slight prickling of his chest hair against her bare shoulders. *I can sleep down on the couch, if you'd like.* Shyly, ducking his head like he considered it a done deal.

The problem wasn't falling into bed with him. That part was probably pretty inevitable.

No, the problem was at the end of a few more days of travel, depending on how bad the weather got. Once they were over the state line she was in home territory. Then, if Mom and Dad and Flo were all right, she would...what? Stay with them? Would she find an empty house and a note—*Gone to Atlanta?*

Maybe some of the neighbors would band together and caravan south. Maybe they'd left when things began to get bad. If so, she could try to guess their route, try to catch up with them. Flo might even have to give birth in an RV, or an ambulance, or whatever vehicle they could find.

No, it wasn't very likely they would want to travel with her due any day. Overdue, now. And setting off through a wasteland with an elderly couple and a new baby? Even Flo's bossiness probably couldn't handle that particular configuration. Even *Mom's* probably wasn't up to the task.

She could boss me around all day, as long as she's alive. There were, of course, other possibilities. Darker ones.

A sigh surprised her, and she shifted uneasily. Lee didn't wake, but his arm tensed, an instinctive hug. *Let me sleep near the edge, then*, he'd said. *Safer.* He only backed down on that when she pointed out she'd probably need the bathroom in the middle of the night.

Oh, she liked him, she really did. How could you *not*? And how could she still be awake despite some very athletic, head-bumping giggling and soft swearing? He was wiry, but strong.

It was like riding a bicycle—you didn't forget. It helped a lot when the other person was paying attention, too. Best of all was when you could laugh, and a man didn't take it as a comment on *him*. Or his technique.

God. Here she was thinking about carnality when her parents and Flo might be in a dark, freezing house, or afraid, or trying to reach Atlanta through blizzards and hordes of grind-chewing zombies.

Mom hated guns, Dad had one in a safe for home defense, but it could have rusted solid by now for all Ginny knew.

She moved again, unable to stop herself, and Lee's breathing changed. "Hm?" Not quite a word, an inquisitive sound clinging to the edge of waking.

"It's all right," she whispered. "Go back to sleep."

He shifted, his arm under the pillow, and cleared his throat, softly. "You're worryin."

I can't help it. It's congenital. "Just about my parents."

"Nothin we can do until we get there." He hunched his shoulders, stretching—his toes bumped the end of the bed and he winced.

While that was the absolute truth, it wasn't exactly *comforting.* "I just hope they're still alive."

There was a long silence, and she thought perhaps he'd fallen asleep again. Instead, he moved, turning and tugging on her shoulder. A few moments of rearranging ended up with her head on his chest, his own propped on a pillow thumped into submission, and his chin in her hair again. One arm around her, his other hand smoothing curls away from her forehead, and he moved his shoulders again, settling just like Traveller. "Aight." Combing her hair with his fingers, patting at the strands. "Tell me bout it, darlin."

Tell you what? His heartbeat ka-bumped along under her cheek, comforting thunder. "Not much to tell. I'm just...what if they've headed for Atlanta? What if they haven't? What if they're not immune? If immunity is genetic, maybe my sister's all right, but she's overdue if she hasn't hatched yet, and my parents...they're not young. I just...what happens when we get there?"

There were other questions crowding her, but she ran out of breath and Lee spoke, spacing the words out nice and slow. "If they're alive, we figger it out. If they ain't, we do what we can to rest them decent. Either way, Ginny, I'll make sure you're all right."

Oh, God. Hearing it that way was almost worse. "They should be fine. I mean, they're in a gated community. That means safe, right?"

"Mh." A nod she felt, stubble scraping at her hair. He kept

smoothing her temple with his fingertips, occasionally stroking her cheek as well. "Your daddy believe in guns, Ginny?"

"Mom doesn't like them. Dad...well, he's a lawyer. He believes in negotiation." *And golf, and whiskey. Straight As, achievement. Not to mention basketball.* Mom believed in manners, and safety, and marrying well.

"Lawyer, huh?" He sounded amused. At least he wasn't the sort who thought lawyers were an alien life form.

"Corporate law." A lot of staying late at the office and two-martini lunches, good cigars and setting aside plenty for your kids' college, not to mention retirement, and cash in a safe just in case.

"I wondered what your folks did." Lee's fingertips traced her cheek. "And your sister?"

"Flo? Oh, she got a degree in design before she married Sam. Making a good marriage is a Mills family tradition. Only I found Sam on a washing machine with some chippie dental hygienist from Flo's book club. It was embarrassing."

"A washin machine?" Now Lee sounded baffled, but his fingers didn't halt their steady motion.

"Yeah. Here's Flo, six months pregnant, and he's banging Mercy —that was her name—on a *washing machine.*"

"Must've been a sight." He probably found it as funny as she did, because she could *hear* the wry smile in the words.

And honestly, it hadn't been very funny at the time. "Yeah, well, I had to tell Flo. And she was furious."

"At him or at this Mercy?"

Well, either would have been a relief. "At me."

"Whatnow?"

"It's complex. Sibling stuff." It was probably because Ginny was *safe* to be mad at, she wasn't going anywhere. Still...it hurt.

It hurt a lot.

A slow nod. "Never had me a sibling."

"What about your family?" Here she'd been tossing her worries all over him. It was easy to do, he was so *quiet.* He really listened, instead of just nodding and planning his next sentence inside his head. "Your grandparents raised you, right?"

"Ayuh. Big Q and my Nonna." He hesitated, but only slightly, his voice a chest-rumble. "My daddy was in county since I was three."

It was so nice to finally be warm again. "In county?" Was that some sort of exotic way of saying *overseas*?

"Prison, ma'am."

Traveller shifted down on the floor, making soft doggie-dream noises.

"Oh." What was a polite way to ask *what did he do*? Did she want to know? Silence cradled them both. Outside, the noiseless snow smothered every surface. It was probably still coming down out there. "Did you ever get to visit him?"

"Nonna took me. Wasn't much to talk about. Big Q would never go."

"Oh." It couldn't have been comfortable. She rubbed her cheek against his shoulder, imagining solemn young Lee visiting a large grey dreary prison. "What about your mom?"

"Dead when I was three." It was his turn to make a slight, restless movement. "It ain't comfortable."

Time for a subject change, then. "I can move—"

"No, I mean about my mama. Poppa—that's Big Q—always said ain't no kind of man what'll hurt a woman, and my daddy never talked about it. Guess I looked a little too much like her for his taste, too."

That sounded pretty bad. "I'm sorry."

"Ain't no need to be, darlin."

"What happened?" She was going to add *you don't have to tell me, if you don't want to*, but apparently he wanted to.

"Well, my mama was wild." Quiet and flat, a recitation of *just the facts, ma'am*. He played with her hair, lifting a single curl, letting it spring free, catching it again with fingertip gentleness. "Guess Lee Senior thought marryin would settle her down. Didn't. Then there was one night, she left me with Nonna and Big Q and went out to a roadhouse for a good time. Don't know if he caught her in some man's truck or just on the dance floor, but my daddy saw red. He pleaded guilty and they locked him up for it, and a good thing too. Nonna said he'd always had some meanness in him, kept it bottled up until *pow*."

Pow. Ginny shuddered.

"I always wondered if I had that meanness in me." Soft, reflective, Lee sounded thoughtful. "I don't want to tell you this, Ginny."

"Why not?" It wasn't exactly the sort of story you blurted out on first meeting someone, true.

"Ain't exactly nice." The calm, even stroking didn't pause. "Big Q used to sit up of nights, thinkin. Nonna said he was broodin on if he'd done something to turn my daddy mean. Quartines got a streak in 'em, everyone says. Figured I'd join the Army and use it that way."

"Did it work?" What a thing to ask someone you'd just slept with. Ginny almost winced. "I mean, you don't *seem* mean." Not unless there were shuffling corpses to deal with, but that was a *good* kind of mean, right? Like being aggressive or stubborn to protect your fellow employees, or presenting a united family front to a soon-to-be-ex-husband of your younger sister.

"Thank you, ma'am." Warmth shading his voice. "But I figure some meanness gonna get us through this."

He was probably right. Ginny turned her chin, pressed a kiss against his shoulder. A patch of smoothness, though the rest of him was furred with gold-tipped hair. He inhaled, a sharp sipping soft sound, and it made her smile. "Was your grandfather mean?"

"Maybe, when he was young. But then Nonna got hold of him. She didn't stand for no foolishness." Lee nuzzled her hair, his breath a warm spot. "She'd'a liked you, Yankee girl."

Said that way, it was probably a high compliment. "Mh. You call me that again and I'll bite you."

"Do that." Quiet amusement filled the words. "See what it gets you."

Oh, he was dangerous to her pulse, this guy. But Ginny sobered. "Lee?"

"Hm?"

"If my parents...if they're..."

Lee didn't make her say it. "We'll take care of it, Ginny. Whatever it is."

He sounded so certain, and Ginny's eyelids were heavy. Maybe it was his certainty, maybe it was the warmth, but in the end, she fell asleep against his shoulder while he stroked her hair and every once in a while, softly, quietly, touched her cheek again.

[8]

ROUTES

"They closed up Albany." Ginny leaned over Lee's shoulder. "That's what my mom said, anyway."

"Yeah, you couldn't even get a bus out that way." Phyllis, her nails now bright scarlet and her hair a fall of glossy raven curls, peered out the window over the tiny kitchen sink. "We're gonna have to find a snowplow just to move."

"It's melting again," Juju said, but mildly. Braced against the engine hump between the driver's and front passenger's seat, he was bright-eyed and plumb-near cheerful, and his hair was springing up in a halo of tight curls.

"Northern route's probably best," Duncan agreed. "This early in winter the lake'll probably keep it from freezing too bad. In another month or so, you ain't goin nowhere."

"It's about an eight-hour drive normally, with traffic." Ginny's warm, soft pressure against his shoulder was distracting as all get-out, especially since she'd awakened him with coffee this morning.

Coffee, and a soft, toothpaste-scented kiss that about drove him out of his mind.

The kids were out with Traveller, who was almost lost in the snow, bounding stiff-legged and for once not setting up an unholy racket. Lee stared at the atlas's colored lines, thinking.

"I ain't so familiar with the roads around here," he said, finally. "Where the checkpoints likely to be at?" Those plywood sheds meant traffic snarls and possibly more critters. On the other hand, they had three armed men now, though Duncan was a bit of a question mark. Kasprak would probably do in a pinch, and Steph was a fair shot. Phyllis was a bigger question mark, and then there was Ginny. She'd try, sure—but civilians froze under fire.

Froze, or did some damn thing like run the exact wrong direction. You sank to the level of your training when the booms started, instead of rising to the occasion.

"Rochester. Syracuse. Utica." Ginny's finger, unpolished nails still smoothly shaped, tapped each. "On the south route...well, probably less traffic, and smaller towns, but then there's Albany."

"Always a hellhole." Duncan, settled across from Lee, stared at the atlas too. He was rising steadily in Lee's estimation—didn't say much, but what he did was to the point. He and Phyllis didn't seem to be together; maybe he didn't think he had a chance with someone so perfectly finished. "This early, north's better. Unless we get a howler."

Ginny smelled like coffee, warm perfume, and the brunette spice of a pretty woman. It was a powerful mixture. "There's the tolls, too."

"Everywhere they got booths they'll have road-clearers." Duncan scratched his cheek with a blunt finger. He probably stubbled up hard and early, and though he was clean, there was a line of good honest engine grease under each nail. "I can drive one, if I gotta. Clear a lane."

"We can take an RV or two." Lee nodded. Things were shaping up fine. "Juju, your four-by..."

"Ain't leavin her until she kicks the bucket, Loot." Sardonic amusement filled Juju's tone. "You gonna leave yo truck?"

"Might have to." He didn't *want* to, that was for damn sure.

"Another RV." Ginny shuddered. "Sure, why not. We'll need the space if Mom and Dad..."

An uncomfortable silence fell. A few moments later, the door banged open and Traveller burst in on a cloud of cold, snow-metallic breeze. "Get on in," Steph Meacham finished saying and hopped up neat as you please, knocking her boots free of snow with quick graceful taps. "It's all gooshy out there."

"Is it, now." The accessories shop here probably had window-mounting thermometers. That would be a good find to fix on every vehicle, and Lee made a mental note to search some out.

"Shut the damn *door*." Mark crowded behind Steph, almost lifting her bodily off the step while Traveller gave a single happy yip and set to shaking his coat dry and telling them all about his travels in the great white wasteland. "It's cold out there."

"Language," she sassed back, and stepped smartly away, ending up near Phyllis. Her two thin braids bounced against her shoulders. "Imma make some hot cocoa. Anyone want some?"

Lee thought it was likely her teeth were gonna rot right out of her head, but cocoa was warming and packed full of energy. It was gonna warm up in here right quick with so many breathing bodies packed into a smallish space. "Make enough for everyone, and some more coffee too. Anythin movin out there?"

"Nothin except birds. Heard a bunch of them." Mark stripped off his gloves and shook his hood back, scratching luxuriously under his black knit cap. "We stayin here tonight?"

Birds meant a thaw. Lee twisted, and Ginny moved aside so he could look at Juju, who shrugged and spread his pink-palmed hands, the scar on his left showing stretched and shiny. "Gettin warmer if the chickadees is out. Might as well see what happens."

Ginny made a restless movement, turning to peer out another window.

"Cause if we are, they's got some ATVs on a lot kitty-corner." Mark wrung his gloves, an unconscious movement. "We can look around, get some more food."

Only trouble with that was the noise of those little engines. Still, the idea had merit. Towing a trailer with one or two of the little buzzers could be useful.

"Another night?" Ginny shifted from one foot to the other, her hair swaying. "Sure, why not. It's taken this long." Her voice didn't break, but it was probably close, and there was a pinching up under Lee's left ribs.

"More haste, less speed, Miz Ginny." Juju's face turned thoughtful instead of almost-cheerful, but he wasn't mournful yet. It was a good sign. He studied the air over Duncan's head, turning over another idea or two inside his head. "You know, Lee, a trailer with one of them little scooters..."

It was damn good to work with the man, really. Lee grinned. "Be a right useful thing, wouldn't it? 'Cept the extra gas for towin.'"

Juju nodded, digging in his pockets like he did when he was almost done thinking and getting ready to move. "None of these bas— uh, none of these big ol things gonna get good mileage. There ain't no shortage of gas for a while, though."

Not until more survivors started draining the gas stations along the way. *If* they did. Lee looked back at the atlas. He just didn't have enough information, and he hated the feeling. "Be nice to get a weather report."

"They've got them weather stations," Duncan piped up. "I mean, uh, personal ones. Get 'em at a Bargain Zone. Tell you pressure, temperature, predict a bit. Expensive, need batteries, but pretty cool."

"Now *that's* a good idea." Ginny perked up slightly, and her approving smile, bestowed on Duncan, was a warm glow. "Why didn't I think of that?"

Lee shook his head a fraction. He should've thought of it, too. "Wellnow. Mr Harris, you know how to ride one of them ATVs?"

"Yessir." The man straightened, and it was official, he'd been in the service. It was all over him, despite his aggressively unbuzzed hair. "I'll take someone else who knows, and we can get supplies and one-two of them weather stations. Put it on one of these-here RVs or another and we have ourselves some warning."

That sounded like a plan. Lee looked up at Ginny. "Can you wait a night for us to get this all settled? More we plan now, the easier the last bit of the trip'll be."

"Why not? It's taken us this long." But the color was high in her pretty cheeks. She didn't like it at all, that much was clear. There was nothin' to be done about it, though, and she didn't want to make a fuss.

If hurryin' would get them there faster, he'd do it. That pinch under his left ribs got worse, seeing her square her shoulders and nod slightly. A good little soldier, making the best of it.

Good Christ. She was one in a million, was Miss Virginia Mills.

"Just be careful." Phyllis shook her glossy head, making a *tch-tch* sound a grandma would be proud of. "You get flipped over on one of those and lose your teeth, your grille is *jacked*."

"Thanks, Phyl," Duncan muttered, and laughter washed the inside of the RV.

It sounded good. Warm, and hopeful, and Lee smiled, the weight of responsibility easing for a moment.

But only a moment.

[9]

DIZZY

Duncan might have just broken in through the front
door, but lean dark handsome Thurgood was also *smart*. He jimmied
an employee entrance with a lot less fuss and broken glass, and one-
two-three, they were spelunking in a stale-smelling Bargain Zone and
Duncan had a chance to talk to the man without the roaring of ATV
engines.

"Figger we'll look for those weather thingummies first." Thurgood clicked his flashlight on, playing the beam over a bulletin board
full of fluttering, unnecessary paperwork. Nobody was going to be
looking at the OSHA notices and paper schedules on the cork board
ever again. "Camping?"

That was a question Duncan could answer, thank God. "More
likely in the garden section."

"Go figure." The lean black man walked easily, hipshot, and his
free hand dangled near his sidearm. Nice, capable hands, the left
with a shiny burn scar across the palm that must hurt sometimes.
Looked like a bitch of a wound, and Duncan wondered about the
story behind it.

He wondered about other stories, too. Like Thurgood's bond with

Lee. The latter fellow looked done gone over quiet, dark-haired Ginny, which was a relief. But still...there was history there, and you could never tell for sure.

Juju didn't send any of the signals, but then again, Duncan did his best not to. Yet another thing you never could tell, how someone would react when you showed that part of yourself.

Their flashlights bobbed side by side, easy and companionable; they cut across a row of dead checkstands and started looking at aisle signs, staggering their line instinctively. At least Bargain Zones were all laid out the same. Duncan searched for something to say. "You been travelin with them long?"

"We from the same town." Juju swept his flashlight beam to one side, checking out a suspicious gleam. "Before that, Lee and I were in the service together."

So he *was* a military man. It made sense, and that was a minefield. If they found out what Duncan was Before, well. Even Sandy, who he'd thought was his friend, looked at him different after the discharge. "I wondered." Shelves of goods lay pristine and unplundered on every side, just waiting for someone to pick up.

There were onion-mesh bags of bulbs in cardboard displays, ready for getting into the ground and coming up in spring. Hoses, lawnmowers, birdhouses, bags of birdseed. If someone got hungry enough they might even try to eat that. Cook it up like oatmeal.

Duncan wondered if it would work, and also wondered if he'd get that hungry. Ginny said this thing was likely worldwide, and wasn't *that* a piece of news? Trust a librarian to figure that out, and to drop it casual in conversation with Phyl like it was no big deal.

"What 'bout you?" Thurgood finally asked, casting him a curious glance. "Where you from?"

"Pomokie." Duncan's heart lodged in his throat halfway through the word. He coughed, and found what looked like the right aisle. "Look at that. Squirrel food. They *feed* the motherfuckers."

"Like feeding rats." Thurgood shook his finely carved head. His blue cap mashed his hair flat; Duncan wondered what it would be like to touch the tight curls. "Windchimes. You sure they're around here?"

"Right there." Duncan's heart sped up. He hadn't been wrong. There were the stations, from the tiny bare-bones ones to the fancy-dancies with rain gauges and wires.

"Well, would you look at that." Thurgood sounded pleased, now. "Which one's the best, you think?"

Duncan was about to reply, but stopped, his mouth open a little. He tilted his head—they taught you in the military that you had a dominant ear, and his was apparently his left. What the hell was that?

Thurgood gave him a curious look and opened his mouth too, maybe to repeat the question.

Duncan heard it again.

Squish-squish. A splashing, a splatter. A heavy, nasty dragging sound.

Thurgood dropped his flashlight, letting it dangle at the end of its lanyard. He also unlimbered his rifle, slowly, quietly. He motioned at the end of the aisle, and Duncan was glad he'd stayed in the Army long enough to know what the fuck that hand signal meant. Goose-bumps rolled down both sides of his back, and he found out his own hand had gone for his sidearm—better for indoor work. He was endlessly glad he'd snagged a wrist *and* a neck-cord for his own MagLite, seeing both Lee and Thurgood with theirs. His was from the accessories shop at Deep River, a fugly orange piece of shit that was nevertheless saving him from embarrassment.

Don't fuck this up, Harris. His throat was desert-dry, not just needing-whiskey-dry. He edged for the aisle end, and behind him, Thurgood inhaled sharply.

The zombie blundered through wet-ink darkness and crazycast shadows, a scarecrow that had once been a skinny middle-aged man with iron-colored hair. A fraying, melt-soaked uniform hung on him, a badge glinting at chest height.

It's the po-lice, Duncan thought, and a mad braying laugh rose in his throat. Only it wasn't, it was store security rent-a-cop, that refuge of wannabes and serial killers who couldn't hack actual dirty work.

He tasted bile; his gun rose in slow dreamlike motion. The zombie stopped, its head cocking like a dog's. Did they have dominant ears too?

Those grey-filmed eyes barely blinked, beginning to desiccate and collapse inside the sockets. Its jaw champed once, twice. Could it *smell* them? They seemed to hunt by sound, Lee and Thurgood agreed, but Duncan only cared that it took cracking their goddamn skulls to get them to stop comin' after you.

Were there more creeping behind this shitsucking cop wannabe? The dark beyond the motherfucker was a heavy curtain, just the edge of flashlight shadows painting him in short strokes—gleaming badge, yellowing teeth, sunken eyes, heavy steel-toed Red Wings covered in dribbles and drabbles of wet stuff that wasn't slush or rain. A hole in the zombie's side glistened, too, a slow seeping.

Duncan's gun barked, muzzle-flash blinding white. The rent-a-cop's head evaporated, and the body fell in slow motion, a cut-string puppet.

"Nice shot." Thurgood squeezed his shoulder. "Keep yo' ears peeled. If they's more—"

"Yeah." A thin, unhealthy tremor ran through him. There was liquor here. Shelves and shelves of it, just waiting. A tot would set his nerves easy, amen and hallelujah. Duncan wet his lips. His throat was puckered like a lemon-sucker's asshole. "What else we got to get?"

"Batteries. Ammo if we come cross't. Food that ent spoilt." Juju nodded, finishing the list. He still had his rifle ready, carefully pointed away. "You need gear?"

"Could use some good boots." Duncan stared at the corpse's twitching Red Wings. *And a fifth of somethin hard.*

"Aight. Gimme a second." The black man turned away to look over the weather stations, trusting him to keep watch, and a hot spill of shame went all the way from Duncan, scalp to toes.

No, he decided. He wouldn't drink. Not as long as Thurgood was here, with his easy grace and that faint smell of leather and some strange cologne like something crisp and hot and good fresh from a fryer and settin' your mouth to watering.

Duncan played the flashlight beam over the the empty space between aisles, a cardboard bin full of discounted stuffed animals with their beady little eyes glinting, the twitching feet in their Red Wings. His ears rang from the shot, a funny high buzzing threatening to make him dizzy.

His shoulder burned, too, with the leftover pressure of those strong, dark, beautiful fingers. Lord, he wanted a drink.

But he wanted to not fuck this up even more.

[10]

PAINTED DOLLS

"Oh, God," Miz Ginny said, softly, and her shoulders sagged. Steph, crowding close behind her to avoid the swinging door, blinked.

It was a fancy bookstore, one of a chain, and the smell of dusty paper made Steph's nose itch. Miz Ginny clasped her hands and glanced at Mr Lee, who drew himself up like a kid expecting a yelling, a small self-conscious movement.

"Figured you'd want to look around," he said, and scanned the store's interior. Strong, misty grey daylight came in through the glass all along one side of the building, and they all had flashlights.

"Oh, *God*," Miz Ginny said again, like she was hurt, but her face shone. Thin and wan, she was nevertheless pretty, and Steph caught herself trying to figure out the difference between her and flat-out-gorgeous Miz Phyllis. Maybe Miz Ginny was just-plain-pretty because she was older? But there was somethin' else there, too, and try as she might Steph couldn't put a brainfinger on it.

At least it would give her something to think about while they were driving.

"Bet they've got Vogue." Miz Phyllis, in a hushed tone. She

hefted a baseball bat—it was painted pink, for breast-cancer aware-ness. That pink paint was stained near the end, and there were a few scrapes in the wood, too. Pretty *and* functional. "Imma go look."

"I'll go too," Steph volunteered. She had a snub-nosed .38, and the holster weighed on her belt. *Since you's a good shot,* Mr Juju had said, and didn't that warm her all the way through? It was nice to be good at something, to feel like a part of the group instead of a useless scrub at the fringes.

That was one good thing about the end of the world. There was no high school to attend. She was just glad the only person she really liked from school had made it out, too. He was back at the RVs with Traveller, keeping watch for zombies and probably drinking a mess of hot cocoa. Staying where it was warm suited him today, and Steph was happy to get out and move around.

"Be careful," Mr Lee said. "Not likely to be a critter in here, but you never know."

"Yessir." Steph trailed after the model, who walked just like she was on one of them runways. You could probably get into the habit of walking that way, if you practiced enough. Chin up, feet coming down in a straight line, hips moving—it felt funny to imitate, you had to swing your hips something sassy. Hard on the knees, but she would try it, when nobody was looking.

"Craft books," Miz Ginny said, behind them. "And anything medical I can find. What are you looking for?"

Mr Lee was gonna follow her around the whole time, betcha anything. He cleared his throat, softly. "Just along for the ride, darlin."

Darlin. Steph's cheeks turned hot when he said that. Not for any regular reason, but because it sounded, well, *private*-like. Intimate, that was the word.

"He's a goner," Phyllis said, casting a single glance over her red-jacketed shoulder. Her grin was electric, white perfect teeth and full, beautiful lips. "They been like that the whole trip?"

"Not so much." Steph fell into step beside her and watched how the model moved. Head high, chin set, with your hips doing a funny wiggle instead of walking natural. She tried a few steps again, hoping the woman wouldn't notice. "Was—*were* you ever in a magazine?"

"Not so much." Miz Phyllis smiled, a wry flash of perfect white teeth. "A couple catalogs. I was doin beauty pageants when I was younger than y'all, though. Learning all the tricks, like double-stick tape and superglue."

Wow. Pageants, like that show about the little girl who got all dolled up and earned her family money that way. Mama had hated that show like fire. *It's trash*, she'd said over and over, *white trash*, but Steph had sneaked a few episodes. "Superglue? What's that for?"

"Keeps your nails on." Miz Phyllis laughed, a carefree chuckle falling dead against carpeting and shelves. "Among other things. Not gonna be much use now, but still, there's good lessons in that."

This was the most interesting conversation in days. Steph's ears were perked so far they'd probably fall off her head. "Like what?"

"Oh, like holdin your head up no matter what. Like believing. Sounds corny, but it's true. I could tell when I was gonna win, because I *felt* good, you know? Like a badass." She cupped her free hand over her mouth, her velvety eyes sparkling, then flicked her fingers like she was shaking off water and wriggled the bat on her shoulder. "Also, how to swing one of these at a jackass."

Wow. She *cussed*. Did all models do that, or just the grownup ones? "Did you ever have to? Before, I mean?"

"Well, I'll tell you. Lot of men think that because you enjoy dressin up, you must be wantin their hands on you." Miz Phyllis sobered a little, slowing down, and her straight-line walk became a little less confident. "Lot of them thinkin that way now, too, if you catch my meanin."

"I do." It was Mr French Steph thought of, with his mean blue eyes and his sneakin' around rattling at doors. And Carty, too, thinkin' he could put his tongue in her mouth because he was popular, then calling her...what he did. "But Mr Harris ain't like that, is he?"

"Doesn't look like he is. But that's the thing." Miz Phyllis slowed, giving her a sidelong look. "You can't ever be sure, with men. I like Duncan just fine, but I'm *prepared*."

Well, that was just good sense, as far as Steph was concerned. Miz Ginny hadn't said as much, but she would no doubt agree. And what else had Mr Juju meant when he said *don't be alone around him*, after Mr French did that awful, nasty stuff and wanted a fight?

Mark wasn't like that. But still, even he'd been a little childish when Steph wasn't all lovey-dovey with him after Mr French's meanness. Maybe Miz Phyllis was right, and you couldn't ever tell. A funny squirrelly sensation bloomed behind Steph's breastbone, something refusing to sit down and stay.

Phyllis stopped in front of the long magazine racks, playing her flashlight over glossy covers. "Oh, mama, I'm *home*."

Steph almost, almost asked *what about your mama, where is she*, but decided not to. If Miz Phyllis started tellin', Steph might have to talk about bashing her own mama's face with a cast iron skillet full of cooked-on egg, and that wasn't anything she wanted to think about ever again.

Instead, she looked at the covers. Girls with full-lipped pouts and skinny arms, girls half-naked but not cold, girls...well, they were all brushed or something, to look way younger than they were. The paper was shiny, the dresses were pretty, they were painted dolls.

Even the boy magazines were full of shiny, fake things. On the one hand, it was kind of silly with zombies roaming around. On the other, pretending everything was normal and you could get a coffee and look through some slickpaper magazines was a nice thought. Comforting.

Thump. Scritch-squeeeeeak.

Steph jumped and whirled; so did Miz Phyllis, unlimbering her bat with a quick, reflexive, graceful movement.

A zombie in a frayed, slush-soaked green camouflage uniform bumped against the windows. A streak about shoulder-high followed him, and now that Steph looked, she could see the streak wasn't new.

Was he just circling the building, or did other zombies come and drag their shoulders along this glass too, sensing something warm or at least unspoiled inside?

They couldn't stand to see something pretty without ruining it. Just like the still-living.

"Oh, God," Miz Phyllis said, softly. "You okay?"

"I'm fine," Steph heard herself whisper. It was kind of ridiculous to even ask, since the zombie was on the other side of the glass...but still. "You?"

"Yeah." The older woman let out a soft exhale, lowering the bat.

They watched the embroidered stripes on the dead man's arm patch drag along the glass, smearing fluid too dark to be just-plain-melt. The zombie's jaws worked and his eyes had collapsed into their sockets, dried-up like raisins. Livid branching veins crawled over his cheeks and hands and forehead, little blue lines painted with hair-fine brushes. It looked like a bad special effect.

You could get distracted, thinking about how this was like a movie, and get the stares. Steph shook her head, the feeling of unreality swaying inside her skull like her brain was on a tetherball string.

"It can't get in," Miz Phyllis said. "Right? It can't get in."

Mr Lee had studied the front door for a short while and pushed a couple bolts—one at the top and one at the bottom of each swinging wooden half—into their homes, making sure they wouldn't be disturbed. He was good at things like that. "Yeah," Steph said. *I don't sound like I wanna throw up. Huh.* "He bolted the doors. Better go tell 'im, though."

"Yeah." The model exhaled, shakily. "You want to, or should I?"

"It don't matter," Steph realized, dreamily. Her fingers brushed the gun butt at her hip. That would just break the glass and make a big noise; it was a bad idea. "Long as we tell him before we leave."

"Good point." Miz Phyllis didn't sound too steady. "Lord, look at that."

I don't want to, Steph realized. She'd rather look at the magazines, at the darkened coffee counter past the racks—Miz Ginny would probably like some of the teabags from there—or the ceiling. Anything, really, other than the dead man rubbing against the window. "What?"

"His nametag says *Phillips*." A tiny, colorless laugh. Maybe the older woman wasn't as calm as she wanted to look. "Like Phyllis, a little."

"Hey. It does." Steph took a deep breath. "I'll keep an eye on him, if you want to look for magazines."

"Okay." But Miz Phyllis didn't turn around until the zombie's slow, splashing, shuddering steps vanished at the corner where glass window met brick wall.

Neither of them screamin' or losin' their heads over it, just watching a rotting corpse walk around like it was normal. The *new* normal.

Go figure. Steph's arms rash-bumped with prickling goosebumps. They felt the size of oranges. *It ain't like a movie at all, now.*

[11]

POW

"Pow," Mark Kasprak whispered, his breath making a small white cloud. He didn't put his finger on the trigger, though. He just peered through the scope, finding targets and pretending, playing out each shot from the rooftop. It was like a video game, except if he fucked up there were actual consequences.

There weren't any respawns out here.

Not that he'd really played a lot, since Dad drank away most of every paycheck. If Dad had brought home a system in one of his fits of drunken generosity, it would have been smashed within a month. Still, Mark watched enough online videos to know what it was like, and sometimes played at other people's houses. Like Bobby Malone's, or Jed Krasenberger's. They were all right, even if they only wanted to hang with him when nobody else was around.

They were probably zombies now too. Along with Carty Shellack and everyone else. If they'd stayed in Cotton Crossing, how many of his classmates would he have shot or head-bashed? The trouble wasn't that he could imagine it so vividly, especially in Shellack's case.

No, the trouble was he found out he sort of *enjoyed* the notion.

The roof of the RV dealership's main building was a wasteland of melting snow and wind-fluted, slumping ice. Vents and hoods stood silent, watchmen just like he was now. *Watch the RVs, if you've a mind to,* Lee had said before he left. Right casual, like it was no big deal, but Mark thought it over and decided he knew better.

It was a big job, maybe a test. They didn't want to come home to a bunch of walking dead. From here he could see the highway, the turn-off, tracks in the sloppy afternoon melt where the ATVs had taken off and Juju's chained 4x4 had turned a different direction. *Don't get 'er stuck,* Juju said at least four times to Lee, who nodded each time and finally said *if you don't want me to take 'er, I won't.*

But Mr Lee had a mind to give Miz Ginny a surprise, and Mr Juju thought it was a good idea if the melt got going a bit. Which it had, and off Lee and the ladies went across the highway to where a green and white sign proclaimed a chain bookstore.

Mark had enough of books in school. They were dry, heavy things, with letters that turned around while you weren't looking, like his daddy's moods. It was better to study machines, he thought, even halfway simple ones like guns. Compression, ignition, motion—that was better than trying to decode a damn book any day.

It was nice to have some time to himself, he decided, with not even the dog hanging around. Traveller, worn out from a squish-splashing game of fetch, was safely napping in Ginny and Lee's RV. Mark wasn't lonely at all, just...quiet, and it was soothing even if it was cold and there was no power and every plop or drip turned into a shuffling zombie sneaking up on you.

Like in a movie, where one of the stars—not the hero, maybe, but the rookie kid who saves the day—is just playing around, or watching the horizon, and sees the bad guys approaching. How many movie stars were left these days? They were all rich in California, and the rich folk had ways of surviving.

Maybe Mr Lee would move them all out west after Miz Ginny saw to her folks.

Sometimes Mark had thought about finishing high school,

loading his truck—he'd been working and saving for that bastard for a long, long time—and just lighting out. Sleeping in the cab if he had to, picking up whatever work he could, just being...well, free and easy. Later, thinking about it included Steph Meacham, but he'd pretty much figured that was a pipe dream.

A girl wouldn't want to live in a truck.

Sometimes, he thought about making it big somehow in California. The details of just how didn't matter. What mattered was imagining the coming back, Steph working as a waitress still, sweeping her off her feet...and driving past his father's trailer in a brand-new fancy car.

Not stopping. Just drivin' on by.

Thinking of Dad threatened to put his finger on the trigger. Mark took his eye away from the scope and stretched, catlike. It wasn't even that cold up here, except for the wind on his cheeks. His skin had cleared up, even the nest of zits on his right temple where he rested his head on his hand while sleeping. His coat was good, his boots were better, layers and wool socks—everything was better than he could ever remember wearing, or being.

Except for the zombies, of course.

Mark finished stretching and unfolded halfway, handling the rifle just the way Juju had taught him. Just in case, he kept doubled over as he threaded across the roof, checking each vista. It wasn't as easy as the movies made it seem, but that was fine. He expected as much, and it was kind of cool to figure out how to move without showing anything to anyone on the ground.

Nothin' moving on the lot, the RVs everyone had chosen marked by trails of footsteps to their door and Lee's truck sitting in the shelter of the big hangar-garage's overhang. Nothin' moving between the other outbuildings—a smaller showroom for the ATVs, a gift shop, a waste lot behind a chainlink and razor wire fence, its expanse full of hummocks and hillocks of glittering snow. *That* view was actually kind of pretty.

Mark looked down the freeway, not across, and a thin thread of buzzing rose as he began to settle into position.

Looked like Mr Harris and Mr Juju were on their way back. Mark rubbed at his eyes—the snow-glare got to you after a while. He peered again, closing first one eyelid, then the other. Yep, it was them.

He stood for another few breaths, his eyebrows coming together, and finally, dreamily, lifted the rifle. The buzzing got louder.

They was bringing company, too. At least half a dozen zombies lolloped four-legged through the snow, throwing up chunks and clots, an irregular semicircle almost—but not quite—keeping pace with the ratchet-sounding ATVs.

Mark's breath left him in a short huff, as if he'd been punched. He put the rifle to his shoulder and peered through the scope. The guys were ahead of the zombies, but there was another string of the shuffling things silhouetted against the snow, comin' in from the side to cut off the ATVs. They hadn't dropped to all fours yet, but when they did and started movin' quick, things might get ugly.

In the movies, the rookie knew what to do, or at least had an idea. Some sort of plan.

"Fuuuuuuuuck," Mark Kasprak said, a long low word ending on the sharp-cut consonant, and kept his finger alongside the trigger-guard. He was glad the dog was safely locked up.

All he could do was wait for them to get in range.

OBSERVE

"I got me Vogue, and I got me W, and I got me Architectural Digest," Phyllis said. "And a paperback or two. You?"

"Word search." Steph blinked several times, squinting against the sudden glare. "Miz Ginny found me whole *books* of em." The girl also had a couple romances tucked at the bottom of her bag, and a slightly furtive expression.

"Almost as good for your brain as crosswords," Ginny said, pushing the bookstore door closed. "Though it's my dad who likes those. He works the Times one daily." For once, the thought that there weren't going to be any more Times crosswords didn't occur to her right away with a sick thump in her stomach.

Instead, it took a full five seconds before arriving. Progress, maybe.

Lee, scanning the side of the building and the parking lot, ushered them along with a few short chopping motions. "I don't see the critter," he muttered, and his boots crush-crunched heavy snow.

"He didn't see us neither." Steph held her bag to her chest, coltish and deerlike, hopping from one footstep to the next. Phyllis waded, every once in a while kicking a clod of snow to the side with a quick toe-flip that spoke of ballet class.

Ginny was occupied with wrangling her own bags. Walking through knee-high, melting snow was savagely tiring; her quads were never going to be the same. Maybe she shouldn't have gone *quite* so crazy in the medical reference section.

The sound froze them all except Lee, who hunched defensively and almost dropped into a crouch. Ginny stiffened, head high, and Phyllis let out a small, strangled sound, casting around wildly and unlimbering her baseball bat.

"That's a rifle," Lee said, softly. "Let's go."

"Uh—" Steph's mouth fell open as she glanced over her shoulder. "Lee? *Lee!*"

He swung around, and his right hand blurred for the gun at his side. "There you are," he said, conversationally, and Ginny half-turned since he was looking past her, that yellow-eyed glare deadly in its intensity. "Get to the car, ladies. It ain't locked."

The zombie Steph and Phyllis had described—military uniform, face threaded with blue veins—lurched in their wake. Its jaw worked, a rusty sound as dried-out tendons scraped against each other, and Lee pushed past Ginny, his shoulder brushing hers. "Move!" he barked, and she scrambled to obey.

Phyllis got there first and held the back passenger door, waving frantically at Steph, whose boots slid a little as she pitched forward. Ginny shifted her bags, her newly freed hand shot out, and she righted the girl with a quick push. Steph clambered in, almost clipping her head on the doorway, and Phyllis chucked her single bag in as well. She didn't hurry either, but waited for Ginny, who fumbled with the front passenger door and jerked it open just as another rifle shot cracked in the distance and Lee's gun spoke almost at the same moment.

"Get in!" Lee barked, again, and her door slammed. Phyllis pointed, and let out a short screeching cry of warning. "I *know*, get the fuck *in!*"

There were two more zombies coming around the corner of the minimall, both dropping to all fours and shuffling forward with that eerie, darting speed. The human body wasn't really meant to move that way—evolution had closed off that avenue a while ago—but they did their best, and it looked like they didn't mind about pulled muscles or frostbite.

Ginny's door slammed. Her heart was in her mouth, adrenaline laying thin singing copper over its thud-gristle as Phyllis yanked her own door shut. She hit her lock as Lee glided around the front of the vehicle, keeping a bead on the lolloping zombies. "Get in," she whispered. "Oh God, get in."

"Shit," Steph Meacham breathed. "Look. Look over there."

Ginny's head snapped around. More zombies boiled up from the snow at the other end of the parking lot.

Lee wrenched open the driver's door and threw himself inside, handing his rifle to Ginny. "Got it?"

"Yes." She swallowed bitter copper terror, tried to will her heart to stop pounding. "There's more over there."

"Figures." His jaw was set and his eyes blazed. You could imagine him barking orders and wearing fatigues, when he looked like this. "We're gonna lose em on the highway and loop back, aight?"

Why are you asking me? "Sounds good." Her throat wouldn't quite work. "Put your seatbelt on."

"You too." The Jeep roused, and there was a thud against Phyllis's door. The vehicle rocked and the black-haired woman cried out, a half-swallowed yell that ended on something rhyming with *duck*.

"Oh, God," Steph moaned. "They're *chewin.*"

"Course they are." Lee dropped the 4x4 into drive; the chains bit packed, sloppy snow. "Don't you worry, Steph. We got ammo and fuel, we ain't gonna be critter snacks anytime soon."

God, I hope he's right. Ginny studied the creatures as they scuttled for the Jeep. Blue veining marked the periphery of their discolored faces, and the one in a ripped, melt-soaked parka lunged for the side-mirror, chin thrust forward and teeth champing. It didn't seem to realize it could grab at the protrusion with its chapped, dangling hands, which was lucky.

Fine motor function wasn't their strong point. For a dizzying moment, she imagined being locked in that hotel room, throwing herself at the walls or the door as her body rotted around her....and the shudders just wouldn't stop even though she was safe, she *knew* she was.

Good luck convincing her non-zombie body, though.

Spitfoam splattered on the window, shaken free of champing jaws. Ginny flinched; Lee made a soft sound that wasn't quite a word, killing the curse before it could slip out, goosing the accelerator. The Jeep shuddered and flung the zombie like a dog flicking away water, and Ginny was glad Traveller wasn't here barking.

She loved the dog, but really, she had all she could handle at the moment keeping the rifle safely stowed and hoping the window glass held.

"Come on," Lee muttered. "Come *on*."

Another mutter in the back was Steph Meacham repeating *ohGodohGodohGodplease*. Phyllis was deathly silent, and Ginny denied the hot sourness in her throat.

Puking was *not* an option. She clutched her bag of books, and stared at the zombie's collapsed eyeballs, its ice-rimed nose crusted with old, frozen snot, its working jaws and the foam collecting at mouth-corner cracks.

It had once been a feeling, thinking human being. Now it only wanted to bite.

Take notes, she thought, deliriously. *Observe the symptoms. You might not get another chance.*

Her eyes flew shut, she steadied the rifle and clutched at the two bags of books, and Ginny Mills realized that deep down, she was a complete coward.

Really, though, she'd known that all along.

[13]

A MAN'S GOTTA

Inside the biggest, most luxurious RV on the lot, the briefing was well underway. "Shoulda seen it," Juju said, scrubbing at his woolly head with both pink palms. His jacket rustled. "Pow, pow, *pow*, all in a row. Like that wildcat asshole in Syria, remember him? Feathers in his fucking hair for every headshot."

Yeah, he remembered the guy. *Domino*, they called him, because one went down right after another when he was behind the scope. Not a team player, though, the kind of cowboy who was worse than no warm body at all when you were looking to get everyone out alive. "No shit." Lee's hands wanted to shake, so he kept them tight around a travel mug full of hot, sweet, strong coffee. Ginny and the girls were outside with Traveller and Duncan, everyone carrying at least a baseball bat and keeping an eye peeled. *Nobody goes anywhere alone,* Lee had said. *It was a rule before, and it goes double now.* "That's some fine shootin, Kasprak."

The boy—no, he was a young soldier now, there was nothing childlike about this—ducked his spike-haired head a little. "Was afraid I was gonna hit somethin I shouldn't, so I just did like you said, Mr Juju. Breathe out nice and easy, lead em, and don't take it less'n you're sure." His voice dropped on the last sentence, a tolerable Thurgood impression.

Apparently, he'd gone onto the roof of the dealership and picked off the majority of the critters chasing Juju and Duncan on their way back. The leftovers had been easily dispatched; Lee was just thankful he hadn't brought back any more with the Jeep. The one in the parka from the bookstore had vanished into the snow.

Lee was hopin' it had run itself to death, like any rabid critter.

"Well, shitfire and save matches, someone's listenin to me after all." Juju's grin couldn't get any wider, and he lifted his own coffee with a self-satisfied air. "Someone call the tee-vee news and let em know."

All at once Lee's shoulders eased, the little switch in his head clicking back over to *no, ain't no shootin', just relax.* "Gonna get right on that, you sassyass." Post-combat jitters were never any fucking fun. The worst was craving a goddamn cigarette, even though he didn't smoke. "Good job, Mark."

"Thanks, sir." The kid straightened again, self-consciously raking his hair back with stiff bare fingers, and glanced at Juju. "But it's all Mr Thurgood, sir. He's a good teacher."

"That he is." Good of the kid to say it, really. He was shaping up right, was Mark Kasprak, and Lee felt a weary wonder that such a thing could happen in the current situation. "You clean your rifle?"

A jerk of his chin down, a brief nod. "Yessir." Mark's eyes shone with the consciousness of a good job done.

"Clean it again, son, and make sure you got all the ammo you need. You're gonna be on lookout more."

"Thank you, Mr Lee." Mark's broadening shoulders came up high and proud, like Lee had just given him a gift. He also mashed his knit cap in both hands, kneading like a cat with a small toy.

Oh, for Chrissake. Maybe the kid wasn't really a soldier yet; anyone past basic knew that was a shit duty. "Don't thank me, Kasprak. You'll freeze your ass off doin it."

"Yeah, well." Mark shook his head ruefully, and there was a

shadow of his daddy in his semi-mournful expression hiding a twinkle of amusement. Before he started hitting the sauce, old man Kasprak had a helluva sense of humor. If he'd just kept it instead of souring—but *no use in shoulda, coulda, or wouldas*, as Nonna used to say. Life had dealt Kasprak Senior a shit hand or two, and he'd gone bad instead of philosophical over it. "Sometimes a man's gotta."

And what d'you know about that, kid? Lord have mercy. But Lee didn't scowl. There was no need. Instead, he lifted his mug and took a hit, yet another sign that the worst was over. "G'on now." Hot coffee meant good things, relaxation and a chance to breathe. There might have been better ways to get him down from the redline, but coffee was what he had, and there was no use bellyachin'.

"Ayuh." The kid didn't salute on his way out, but it was probably close. He peered through the door carefully before he jumped out, and a thin sound that was Traveller's excited yapping made Lee almost-flinch.

Damn dog. But Duncan was out with the girls, and the man could handle himself. Steph was a fair shot, too, and Phyllis's baseball bat had seen action at least once, if Lee was any judge.

"Lord," Juju said, sliding into the padded bench on the other side of the postage-stamp table. The RV rocked a bit as the door slammed to. "Were we ever that young?"

"Not by a long shot." At least, Lee couldn't remember it, though he knew they had to have been. He could imagine Juju as a young 'un, but all he could remember for himself was feelin' ancient and probably lookin' that way, too. His gloves lay on the table, discarded armor, and there was a faint good smell of boiled caffeine in his nose, warring with a simmering that was too many people and not enough showers gathered in a small place. "You feel okay with him coverin you again?"

"Guess so." Which was high praise, coming from Juju. "If his head don't get big."

"Amen to that." Lee didn't think it very likely, but you never could tell with kids from bad homes. They either buckled down or exploded. Only one of those ways was useful right now, and it wasn't clear yet which Mark would choose.

Juju eyed him, settling his own coffee on the table and cracking his left-hand knuckles. Maybe the scar pained him in this weather. "You look like shit, Loot." Tip had once said something about how Thurgood got that wound, and it about turned Lee sick to his stomach.

Now Lee could talk. "There were some at the mall, too."

"Yeah?" Juju finished with his knuckles and swished his coffee, a familiar thoughtful motion. *Just drink it,* Tip used to bellow, *don't make it into a fuckin hurricane.*

Fuck your mother and drink your own, Juju had been in the habit of replying, the tag line of a very old joke. As old as Iraq itself, maybe. Or just as old as the war that dropped them all in desert shit.

Lord, he missed Billy Tipton. Not as much as Juju was likely to, but enough. "That's why I took the long way home." Losing your buddies never got easier, and there was a whole long list of names Lee could recite if he had a mind to.

That particular rosary lodging in his skull was not a good sign.

"Huh." Juju's frown said he was thinking the same thing Lee was, and was just as unsettled. "They gettin smarter, or just hungrier?"

"Don't know." Lee took another scorching mouthful, forced himself to swallow. "Maybe we shoulda started today." Ginny would have liked that better than the bookstore, indeed.

Still, the way her face had lit up...that was a good thing, and it made him warm all through in a way the coffee couldn't touch.

"Well, that brand-new fancy weather thingummy says it should warm up a little." Juju's full lips tightened. "Harris set it up. Even got a rain gauge."

"Useful." And they'd thought to pick up a few of the less-fancy ones and a mess of batteries, too. Might as well be prepared.

"Yeah. He's okay." It was Thurgood's day for giving out high praise, apparently. "Clipped one at the Bargain Zone."

Shit. "Steady after?" That was the most important question.

"Like a rock. Boy was in the service, he don't get real nervous." Juju's tension eased all at once, with a familiar, gusty sigh. "Got to tell ya, this is lookin up."

Well, for everything that *was*, Lee could think of a few things that weren't quite. That was probably the adrenaline crash talkin', though. "Guess so. Which one of these-here RVs should we take tomorra?"

Juju studied him, sinking into the seat across the dining table. He lay his pompom hat aside and folded his brown hands, like a young, slim preacher regarding one of his flock. "You got that look."

Lee fought the urge to hunch his shoulders protectively. "What look?"

"The look that means there's shit comin downhill."

Well now, if he knew all Juju's tells, the man knew a few of Lee's own. You couldn't escape being known, not when you spent day in and day out getting shot at with a man. Or chased by the walking dead, as it were. "Not really." Lee couldn't drink more coffee, he'd taken off the skin inside his cheeks already with that last gulp, not to mention his tongue. "We're a day, maybe a day and a half out. When we get there, ain't gonna be pretty."

Juju nodded, and swished his coffee some more. "She's tough. She'll make it."

"Oh, yeah." Lee made a wry face. Ginny was too damn brave for his comfort. "But still. She don't need more grief. None o' us do."

"Ain't no way of gettin round it." Velvety dark eyes turned still and somber. "Grief's on the menu, and the only thing doin the cookin too."

"I know." Lord, did he ever. Grey snowlight strengthened in the window, clouds thinning. If the temperature dropped hard overnight it was going to be an icy mess.

"Where we goin after?" Of course Juju would be thinking ahead. It was in his nature.

Lee all but winced internally. "You ain't gonna like it."

"Atlanta." It wasn't a question.

"Got a better idea?" Because really, Lee was fresh out.

Juju's laugh was a little too bitter to be truly amused. "Shit, no. If I did, I'd'a been sayin so before this whole trip started."

"Yeah." There was nothin' more to say, so the two of them sat quietly. Juju's breathing evened out; he was coming down from redline too. Imagine zoomin' across the snow, knowing those critters were after you, hearing the rifle-cracks and hopin' whoever was shootin' had their scope screwed on straight.

It was damn good to have a friend to sit with. You had to take easy time where you found it, and Lee was lucky to have backup who knew what the fuck.

Juju coughed, lightly, cupping his hand over his mouth. "Shit," he said. "Throat's dry."

"Drink yo' coffee." Lee stared out the window, his brow furrowed and a headache gathering behind and between his eyes.

"Fuck yo' mama," Juju muttered.

"And drink yo' own," they both said in tandem, Lee's mouth tugging up in a rueful smile.

Still, he kept looking out the window. Juju coughed again; Lee tried not to notice.

After all, there were two syringes left in the hardpac case Grandon had left him. Neither of them might be necessary.

A man could hope.

HOBBIES

THEY WERE MAKING GOOD TIME. PHYLLIS LEANED FORWARD IN the driver's seat, her eyes narrowed against the glare even behind her large tortoiseshell shades. "This is one big beast," she said again. She didn't quite *mind* driving with the kids, but there wasn't a lot to talk about. Ginny was up front in the red and white truck with Quartine, navigating them through a bright melting midmorning, Duncan was taking a turn in Thurgood's Jeep, and Phyl had never piloted anything this huge and wallowing before.

Fortunately, it was built so even a middle-aged middle manager could grasp the meaning of all the buttons and whistles, and she didn't have to do much other than observe a careful distance from the back of Thurgood's black 4x4.

"Miz Ginny said that too when she was drivin the other one." Of the two kids, the girl was the most interesting. Kitten-faced and thoughtful, she was also bright and needy.

Phyl could relate. Maybe she'd been that transparent once in her life, but not anymore. Getting older was good for something, at least. "What happened to the other one?"

"Got shot up." Mark Kasprak leaned over the back of the shotgun seat, almost breathing in the girl's hair. Puppy love, it looked like, but Phyl itched to smack him and tell him to sit down. "Some guys trying to trap us at a rest stop. They had an RV too."

"And big trucks," Steph added. "Wonder what they wanted."

How sheltered had the girl been that she couldn't guess? On the other hand, no kid should ever have to think about that shit. "Nothing good," Phyl muttered darkly. "Men with guns *never* want anything good."

"Hey." Mark found this objectionable, of course. "*We've* got guns."

"Yeah, and so did Duncan, but that makes you question marks. Not safe bets." Phyllis shook her head and internally poured a little more cold water on her temper. "Maybe you can drive after the next stop, Steph."

Steph ducked her chin, glancing out at the lack of scenery. It looked like a habitual movement, making herself smaller. "Ain't got my license."

"I do." The boy was aching to get his hands on something, anything.

"Maybe." Phyl restrained herself from eye-rolling with a massive effort. It wasn't his fault he was that most irritating of creatures, a teenage male. There was no cure for that condition except time and an application of life lessons, generally with a two-by-four if nothing gentler managed to get through. "So what do you like to do, Steph? You got any hobbies?"

"Not really." Oh, the girl definitely had been taught to hide her light under a bushel. That would change if Phyl had anything to say about it.

"She paints." Mark bounced a little, then swung around and set off down the middle of the RV. Maybe he'd find something to keep him occupied. "Y'all want some hot chocolate or something?"

Phyllis took a tighter hold on her impatience. Her blue-blocker shades were top of the line, she'd never have been able to afford a set before the world went to shit, but she was still squinting fit to ruin her eyes and her neck was tense. "You paint?"

"Watercolors," Steph said, shyly. "Not very good. My daddy got me a paint by numbers set when I was five and I liked it so much he kept bringin em home. Then my mama told him *Bull*—that was his name, Bull Meacham—*Bull*, she said," Steph managed to give the aural impression of an older, wearier woman, *"she don't need the numbers no more,* so he started bringin home paints and stuff. Mama went all the way to Lewiston to get me canvases and brushes sometimes."

"Like ol Miz Clampett and her plates," Mark called from the kitchen section. "You want some coffee, Miz Lampke?" He even mangled her name.

Phyllis took another deep breath. "No thanks, kid."

"You know that show?" Steph stared out her window. Snow, more snow, sometimes an abandoned car under a hood of slipmelting white, dark buildings probably crawling with chewing, growling zombies or people with guns and bad attitudes. "There was this guy. Bob somethin. Anyway, he had a big ol head of hair, and he painted stuff. Happy stuff."

"Bob Ross?" Good Lord, Phyl's *grandma* used to watch that. "Trees and stuff? He was always saying how things were happy. Yeah." An unwilling smile pulled up the corners of Phyllis's mouth; there was no rearview to check, but the dry air hadn't played too much havoc with her skin yet. The cold was murder on complexions. "Yeah, I remember that."

"He ain't paintin no more," Steph said darkly.

Phyl wondered if she should tell the girl Ross had been dead a while, and decided not to. There was only so much bad news any of them could take, these days. "But you remember him, right? I know a lot of people loved that show."

"They're probably dead too," Mark weighed in.

Phyl longed to stamp on the brake, turn around, and give Mr Kasprak some home truths. She counted to five, took a breath, and counted again. Lord, boys irritated her as much as they ever had. It wasn't the kid's fault; being stuck in an RV all day was frustrating for any healthy young animal. Including herself. "Not helpful, kiddo."

"Sorry." At least he sounded a little chastened. Not much, though.

Not enough.

"Are we gettin close?" Steph gave Phyl a funny sideways glance. She could probably tell the older woman was on her last nerve, and her slight grimace said she knew exactly why, too.

"I dunno. Ginny said something about Saratoga. Look for signs." Phyllis forced her fingers to relax, pushed her shoulders down. She longed for a yoga class, a decent cappuccino, and a few hours with a book. "My hobby was always makeup. Kind of like painting, except you've got something living to color in, you know?"

"Painted ladies," Mark said, and laughed. The vehicle shuddered, and there was a splash. "Ow, *shi*—I mean, shoot."

The effort they took not to swear in front of her was oddly charming. Phyllis took her foot off the brake and dispelled a grim smirk. "Rough road ahead, kid. Sit down and put a seatbelt on, willya?"

Steph gave her another sideways glance. The girl was smiling.

And now, so was Phyllis.

[15]

A DIFFERENT VOCATION

"We're getting close." Ginny leaned forward, all but willing the truck to go faster. Her thin wan face was lit up like Christmas and Traveller had caught her excitement. "It's only a couple hours from Oneida. The roads are good, right?"

The hound, sitting right next to her with his ears perked as far as possible, looked at Lee too, obviously expecting him to say something.

Lee feathered the accelerator. "They've been good, ayuh." Caution was called for, even if Harris could pilot a wrecker like nobody's business. Duncan had done some roadwork in his life, looked like.

Lee also suspected some of that roadwork had been of the orange jumpsuit variety, but that was just a feeling. Fellow had been in the service too, and some of the body language was the same. Not all of it, but enough.

Besides, what did it matter? Law trouble didn't matter after the end of the world. Lee had a few uncomfortable suppositions about the sickness going through prisons, though. Men locked in cages just like pets inside houses, and if they were immune...well, it didn't bear thinkin' about, bein' in lockup when the critters came callin'.

"I wonder if Fran's given birth. Mom's going to just be beside herself." Ginny subsided into the seat, but a few moments later was leaning forward again, fiddling with her pretty grey gloves. "She wanted to know, but Fran didn't. If it was a boy or a girl, you know. Fran said it destroyed the mystery, and Mom said she needed to know to buy a layette."

"What's that now?" It sounded fancy.

"The things the baby wears home. You know—onesies, blankets, spit rags, the first few diapers." Ginny caught herself. "What do you call it?"

"Never had any reason to know," he mumbled. Christ in his glory, but she was beautiful when she was this happy. She was beautiful *all* the time, but *especially* when she was happy. And here he was, closer to her than he had any right to be.

Bracing himself for the worst.

"I guess not." She grinned and patted Traveller's head; the truck handled a shallow curve and hit a long stretch of slush.

Every time the chains rasped he all but flinched, dreading having to take them off and deal with Ginny's well-disguised impatience at the delay. "Ginny..."

"Hm?" Her braids glowed. Now he knew what she looked like with her hair down, all that rippling chestnut glory full of golden threads. He even knew what it was like to sink his fingers in, and it was just as soft as he'd imagined.

Everything about her was *better* than he'd imagined.

"We don't know what we're gonna find there." He spaced out the words deliberately, eating up time, slowing her down. "I ain't sayin don't get your hopes up, but..."

"But that's exactly what you're saying," she finished. "And you're right, yes. I'm just excited."

That was one way to put it. She was looking forward to arriving somewhere she thought something good was waitin', and the letdown was gonna be fierce. He'd seen it more than once, when privates were thinking they'd get some rest and a hot meal, finding a cold camp and another serving of shit waiting for them instead.

"I know," he said, helplessly. His knuckles were painfully chapped, rough-reddened skin glaring even in the overcast. Clouds would help keep it warmer at night, but the risk of more water falling from the sky was not to be sneezed at. There was a scrape across the back of his right hand, one he couldn't remember getting. It was a damn shame he was allowed to put those hands on her, even for a moment. "I just don't want you hurt, that's all."

"They might be fine." Those eyes of hers, dark but with a gleam to them. "Right? I mean, it's possible they're...not fine, but really, they *might* be."

"Ayuh." *And Big Rock Candy Mountain might be a real place, too.* Lee turned the wheel a fraction, stopping the slide before it began. No use in saying anything pessimistic.

He wanted to, though. He wanted to prepare her for the likely, if not the inevitable.

Ginny settled in the seat again. Traveller's tail tried to wag, but the dog was sitting on it, so his hind end just scratched itself deeper and deeper. The hound licked his lips and glanced at Lee again, obviously expecting *something*.

Shit. Lee Quartine was talking more than he ever had in his life, but it probably wasn't helping. "If they're all good, Ginny, we got some plannin to do. We'll get 'em into the RV and set out for Atlanta."

"So you have thought about it." Did she have to look so pleased? Her eyes all lit up, studying him like he'd met with expectations for once in his life. Or even surpassed them.

"Course I have, darlin." And wasn't it fine to say *darlin'* out loud, instead of just in his head? "Get close enough to see if'n there's any radio traffic. If not, we head south a bit, then swing west."

"To where? Atlanta?"

"If it looks good there. If it don't, California, I reckon." But only after it thawed, since the Continental Divide was nothing to sneeze at in winter. Then, if ol' Cali was crawling with critters, maybe up the West Coast a bit. Seemed the most reasonable option; less nasty bitey things, plenty of water. "Good weather, lots of stuff layin around to be picked up."

"Crossing the whole continent." She shivered, though the heat was on.

"Won't start until spring, I reckon." And by spring he might have other ideas, or they might have found an enclave of survivors worth settlin' in. Maybe even Atlanta, if they were still functioning and it wasn't a trap or a pipe dream. "If this thing is worldwide, Ginny, we got ourselves a lot of work to do."

"That's true." Now she sagged against the bench seat, a faint frown creasing her forehead. "I've been thinking about that. If it *is* worldwide, like the man on the television said. The implications."

Now *there* was a three-dollar word, and one he didn't like. It was usually used when the brass wanted to hamstring the boots on the ground. "Gonna hafta grow our food. When the gas runs out, there'll be trouble."

"Yeah. They made movies about that part. *Mad Max.* Did you ever see those?"

"Can't say as I did." The last movie he'd seen was *True Grit*, John Wayne and a little girl too brave for her own good.

Wasn't that ironic.

"It's enough to give you nightmares." Ginny stared out the windshield, still strung tight as a guitar string. "You know, I thought I had it. The flu. And it made me think, well, if I wasn't immune, how many survivors are carriers? How many just hadn't caught it through luck?"

Good Lord. She was just too damn smart. He had to tear his gaze away from her pretty profile and watch where the truck was going. "Well, you didn't have it." A lie, a damn lie, and he was storing up trouble.

He just couldn't help himself.

"So immunity is probably a good explanation." But her left hand rubbed at the inside of her right elbow, a quick, unconscious move-ment. Had he hurt her, jamming the needle in? "But I thought about it, and it wasn't comforting."

Don't think about it, he wanted to tell her. That never worked, so he picked something else. "Borrowin trouble, Miss Virginia."

"I specialize in that, I think." A wry smile, lighting her somber-ness. "I have all my life."

"Well, it's my job now. You ever thought about pickin a different vocation?"

Amazingly, she laughed. There was almost nothing as sweet as a pretty woman who liked your jokes. Maybe Big Q felt that little hitch in his chest when Nonna found something funny. Had his grandfa-ther ever felt this...well, unsteady, hoping her gravity could keep him nailed down?

"I'll work on it," she said, and clasped her gloved hands, looking out the windshield like she could see their destination shimmering in the distance. When she found out it was a mirage, well, he wasn't looking forward to that. But he pressed the accelerator again, just a tad.

Every minute shaved off their trip was one less minute she had to work herself up.

[16]

TERRIBLY NORMAL

Fenton Acres, the snow-choked sign on the brick wall said, under a lacework of winter-bare ivy vines. The sky was down-right ugly again, but what concerned Ginny more was the wrought-iron gate.

It was wide open, the small post with the keypad for visitors or those who forgot their clickers wrenched almost-free of its base. Looked like someone had been in a hurry and sideswiped it, and the back of her throat was full of hot acid. "Take the first right," she said, and realized she was leaning so far forward her seatbelt cut into her shoulder.

"All right." Lee reached for the walkie-talkie. "Juju? We're goin in."

"Ten-four." The 4x4 crept behind them. Duncan was taking a turn driving the RV, and after that it would be Ginny's job. Juju had Phyllis in his car, and Ginny might have been amused wondering how they'd get along, but she was too busy trying to calm her heart down and sit still.

The slush had hardened with the temperature dropping, and the melt hadn't reached here. "Maybe I should drive," she said, knowing it would just eat up precious time if they had to stop and change. "I know the roads."

"Doin just fine." Lee's eyes had narrowed again, and the truck drifted up to the first stop sign. "Good thing it's still deep enough for chains."

There was the MacAllisters' sprawling ranch, and the Smiths' high-built Victorian. Both were dark and shuttered, unbroken seas of snow covering driveway, yard, and fence. It could have been just a regular power outage except for the stretches of unplowed white.

Even the houses she didn't know the names for looked wrong, hiding under pale cloaks. The one on Task Street with the cedar almost swallowing its semicircular driveway glowered through broken windows, and her heart plunged before leaping to rabbit in her throat again. "A left at the next one—not the stop sign, before it." *I sound calm.* Giving Lee directions as if this was a normal trip, as if they'd driven from Cotton Crossing on regular roads, passing regular gas stations, talking abut normal things.

Tenth, Eleventh, and Twelfth all passed. Nothing stirred, and the sky was a flat iron pan. It was going to start snowing again. Was anyone watching through the windows? There was the doctor's house, and the lawyer Dad sometimes golfed with—what was his name? She remembered his steel-rimmed spectacles and how his nose always seemed to be sunburned, but not his name.

"You grew up here?" Lee feathered the brake; the truck slid and he immediately eased off.

Was he pitying her? Even though the yards were big, the houses were far too close together for someone who lived on acreage. It wasn't the sort of neighborhood a kid could tear through on their bike, or go exploring and getting dirty. "No, they moved out here when Dad retired. Before that we lived in the city."

"You mean New York?"

"Mh-hmm." Upper West Side probably meant less than nothing

now. Her childhood home had been sold to a nice new lawyer at Dad's firm; Kevin and his partner had been overjoyed.

Nice boys, Mom had said, *but what will they do when one of them gets married?* Neither Flo nor Ginny had the heart to tell her.

Dad had looked slightly pained, that was all. *I'll be at the club, Esther.* Those six familiar words.

"It's up here on the left." No tire tracks. No shoveling. The houses slumped under heavy white blankets, and there was nothing moving. "It's too quiet."

Lee glanced up from the road at regular intervals, taking in the scenery. "Mostly old people livin here?"

"Well, yeah."

"Huh." He said nothing else.

She couldn't tell if that was a good or bad *huh.* He seemed to have several, one for each occasion, each layered with meaning.

Finally, *finally,* their goal came into view. "That's it. There." A familiar stony rectangle built to look like a farmhouse, the apple trees skeletal and naked, the wide front yard an undulating ocean of white. More bare branches lifted in back, the trees Dad groused about in fall, raking even though the landscapers came by weekly.

Ginny let out a small shocked breath.

The huge bay window in the living room was shattered. The garage door was half open, icicles dripping from its edges and reaching for the driveway. The nice, sturdy house leered drunkenly in the failing light. "Oh, God," she whispered. "Lee..."

The blue-painted front door was wide open.

Lee's truck rolled to a halt. He studied the front of the house. It was still deadly silent, not even a quiver of wind among cold branches.

"Coulda been looters," he said, finally. "Couple other places here busted open, too."

Why didn't I think of that? She clutched at the relief, but underneath it was a dark, tight sensation. "Maybe they went somewhere for Fran." Her mouth was dry, her hands numb. Traveller whined softly, sensing tension and maybe, just maybe, a chance to get out and stick his nose into something fragrant.

"Your sister." Lee nodded, but he didn't put the truck into park yet. "She have a place?"

"She moved back in with them while the divorce...God." Ginny fumbled at her seatbelt, her fingers numb and clumsy though the heater was on. "Can I...you don't have to go in, you know. I just have to see if they left a note, or something. Anything."

"No ma'am." He peered through the windshield, craning to look at the second-story windows. Searching for motion, probably. "You ain't gonna let me and Juju sweep it, I bet, so you'll go on in with us."

"Okay." She reached for her purse, thought better of it. What on earth would she need it for?

The walkie-talkie crackled, Juju and Lee repeating cryptic, half-familiar planning. Communication was key, they always said. The RV pulled forward to keep the driveway clear; Juju's 4x4 pushed gently through the box hedge and onto the front lawn. Ginny opened her mouth to say something—but that didn't matter, did it?

Lawncare was not even on the *list* anymore, as Fran would say. Ginny reached for the door handle. Pulled her hand back.

"Easy there," Lee said. "Let me get out first, darlin."

Then do it, goddammit, and stop fucking around. "Okay." She pulled her gloves on once more, pushing Traveller's snout away with gentle fingers. The dog's tail thwapped Lee's arm, but he appeared not to notice, still studying the front of the house. Next would come him checking his gun, and then hopefully they could get out of the damn truck and find out what was inside. There had to be a note. Probably left on the kitchen counter, or on the fridge. Taped to the stainless steel, if she knew Dad.

Mom would hate that. It leaves a mark.

No it doesn't, Dad would say. *Scotch tape never leaves a mark.*

"Please," Ginny whispered, barely aware of the word escaping her. "Oh, *please.*" Her knee hit the baseball bat tucked between the seat and her door, and she decided that was a good idea. Working it free took a few moments.

"Easy, Ginny." Lee finally glanced at her, a tight smile not reaching his eyes. "Place is probably empty, but let's be safe."

Fuck safe. I need to get in there.

But she waited. What else could she do?

THE FOYER WAS DARK, SNOW SPILLING ACROSS SLATE TILES. *Don't drop an egg!* Dad said, the smile lurking around his mouth. "Mom? Dad?" Ginny took a deep, frigid breath; her voice echoed. "Flo? Anyone?"

"Stairs," Lee said. Stairs climbed to the second story, the bedrooms and Dad's study. Past the stairs to the left was the den and the exercise room; she could just see the gleam of stainless steel from the kitchen. Every appliance in the place was silvery. *You can disinfect it,* Mom always said. *Stainless steel means painless clean.*

"Hang on, Ginny." Juju didn't lift his gun. His mouth was set, lips thinned and tense, and even the pompom atop his knitted cap looked businesslike.

"Mom?" she called again. "Flo?"

The living room opened on their right, frozen drapes creaking at the broken bay window. Pitiless snowlight poured past jagged frost-etched glass, and Juju stopped in the archway. "Oh, hell," he said, softly, and Ginny's heart leapt into her throat, the pounding echoing in her skull. "Ginny—"

She pushed past him, clutching the baseball bat in nerveless fingers.

At first, it all seemed terribly normal. Mom had replaced the couch again, this time in blue, and above the gas insert fireplace was her prized Piet Lor painting, bought at the gallery on Fifth Avenue during her fifth month pregnant with Ginny. *I prayed for an easy birth, and you were,* she would always say. *You were my easy child.*

At least she had never told Flo that. If Ginny never quite

measured up, at least she wasn't actively troublesome. It was a thin comfort at best.

Cold's going to be hell on the canvas, Ginny thought, inconsequentially, and looked towards the bay window.

The Tiffany lamps were knocked over, multicolored glass shattered and glowing. Her father's reading chair was pushed aside, just a few degrees askew. The coffee table was swept clear, a star of breakage on the heavy glass top, and the drapes moved, creaking on an icy breeze.

"Daddy," Ginny whispered.

Her father lay on deep navy carpet in front of the bay window.

Daniel Mills looked so *small.* An old, white-haired man with grey lingering at the top of his balding head, his eyes closed and his bluish-frozen face oddly peaceful. Below that tranquility a jagged star of flayed flesh, flash-frozen, showed chips of white cervical bone. His ribs were wrenched wide, too, under a yellow polo shirt. Something had torn at his checked golf trousers to get at muscle on his legs. His slippers were knocked off his feet, and the socks were the red merino ones Ginny had bought him last Father's Day.

Socks? Most-astonishment on his face, the smell of his aftershave. *That's my girl.*

Open the other one, Dad. The socks were a joke, his real present was the fifth of Macallan.

He already drinks too much, Mom weighed in, as she always did.

I'm retired, Esther, Dad replied inside her head, and Ginny's vision blurred. *Scotch and golf are my job now.*

"Ohgod," someone said in a very small voice.

His hands were blue, bent arms drawn up as rigor mortis...

No. Oh no.

"Ginny." Lee was in front of her, suddenly, his chest blotting out the horrible sight. "Ginny, darlin, don't."

Think, Ginny. You've got to think. "Mom." Her mother...maybe Dad had sent her and Flo out and waited here for his eldest daughter? "I need to find..."

"Ginny." Lee had holstered his gun. He reached for her, but Ginny shied away, almost slipping on ice-crunching carpet. Her eyes burned. She turned, caught in the syrup of a hideous, horrible dream, and set off for the kitchen.

"Mom?" she called, her voice high, girlish, breaking. "Flo? *Mom? Mommy?*"

[17]

ICICLE DROPS

I̶T̶ ̶W̶A̶S̶ ̶A̶ ̶B̶E̶A̶U̶T̶I̶F̶U̶L̶ ̶P̶L̶A̶C̶E̶, IT WAS A BEAUTIFUL PLACE, BUILT TO LOOK LIKE AN OLD
farmhouse but clean and modern inside, drenched with the subtle
scent of well-to-do that might have frozen his guts if the first body
hadn't. The kitchen was all stainless steel and stone countertops, the
floor those real slate tiles that no doubt were a bitch to put in and
God help you if you dropped an egg. The blackened husks of potted
herbs stood in a boxy window over the sink, peering out on a wooden
deck festooned with empty birdfeeders.

Looked like charity ran in the family.

They found Ginny's mama in a sort of greenhouse attached to
the kitchen—*the solarium*, Ginny called it later, *her favorite place*.
She'd been thrown through a glass door, and that was when Ginny
crumpled. She reached blindly for the edge of the doorway and might
have cut herself on clear, jagged teeth if Lee hadn't caught her, and
he had to dig his heels in so both of them didn't tumble down the two
wooden steps. The old woman lay on her side, her graying hair a
loose skein with Ginny's curl to it, her peach twinset and skirt torn
and spattered with frozen blood and effluvia. Looked like she'd put
up a helluva fight, too—potted plants were smashed to flinders before

the cold through broken panes came in to kill them, and it looked like the lady had tried to defend herself with a small wrought-iron table.

Plain to see where Ginny got her polish and her guts from.

Somethin' had been gnawing on the missus's body too, and Ginny kept saying *Mom, Mom please, please Mom*, in a broken little voice that hurt him way down deep. The lady's throat was pulled out and her guts splattered, ribs wrenched wide so critters could get at organs. It was damn obvious these two weren't gonna be gettin' up and growlin'.

At least Ginny was spared that. Juju's expression set itself hard, and he looked chalky under his melanin. His lips twitched a little— maybe prayin', or maybe keeping a few cusses locked up in his throat.

Lee had to use a bit more strength than he liked to turn Ginny away from the sunroom, and she struggled when he closed his arms around her. "Don't," he repeated. "Don't look at that, darlin. Don't look."

"*Mommy...*" All the fight went out of her; she crumpled. He rested his chin on her braids, trusting Juju to keep an eye on his six.

"Front door?" Juju said, softly.

"Maybe. Garage door's open too." Lee squeezed her just as tight as he dared. "She got a sister, too. Pregnant."

"I know." Juju's short inhale was now *definitely* a curse caught behind his teeth. "Upstairs?"

"Could be." Lee was hopin' the sister wasn't anywhere in the house, but it was lookin' like none of them were gonna be lucky today.

Figured.

"I'll check it." Thurgood cleared his throat, maybe wanting to add something for Ginny's sake.

"Be careful." Lee knew he should cover Juju, but Ginny was shaking, a silent wild tremor that would break as soon as the shock wore off. You couldn't ever tell what someone would do once they emerged from that deathly daze, and besides, he could no more let go of her now than he could take his own head off.

His arms just wouldn't let him.

"Born that way." Juju edged away down the hall, after one long mistrustful glance across the kitchen. Another archway—utility room, probably, leading to the garage.

And right next to it was a white-painted wooden door. *Huh.*

Lee stood in a cold, dark, expensive kitchen, and held a shivering woman. *Christamighty.* He'd been prepared for somethin' bad, but this...he should never have let her hope. He shouldn't have let her get *near* this place, should have dragged her, kicking and screaming, in another direction. *Any* other direction.

Time ticked by in slow icicle-drops. He kept an ear peeled for the cautious unsound of Juju's progress, but her silence kept distracting him. Finally, she made a muffled, agonized sound against his coat.

"Ginny?" He tightened up again, wishing he could pull her into him, carry her through this. *Distract her.* "Ginny, darlin, this place got a basement?"

She stiffened. Her baseball bat tapped his calf; he tried to keep her but she pulled away and lifted her chin, her cheeks gleaming wetly. So she was one of the ones who liked to cry quiet-like.

Oh, darlin.

She stared at him for a few moments, as if trying to remember who the hell he was and what he was doin' in this familiar house. As if he'd been caught creepin' in.

"Basement?" She wet her lips with a quick flicker, and he was going to hell, because even right now, he wanted to kiss her. It if would make her forget and get her out of here, he would have done it, too. "Uh." Her chin headed for her shoulder, but he caught her again, holding her at arm's length.

"Don't you look back there," he said, quietly. "Basement, Ginny. This place got one?"

"Y-yes." Now she looked the other direction, at the white-painted door. There was a bloody smear about shoulder-high on it, the fluid dried and crusted. "There. The cellar." Then, she tried to turn *again*, and he stopped her.

"Don't."

"That's my mother," she whispered. "Oh, God." Her pupils were swelling, swallowing her irises. "Lee, that's my *mother*."

"I know." He inhaled to say *maybe your sister's hidin'*, not because he thought it likely but because he wanted her to have a shred of something, anything—

"Lee!" Juju's voice bounced off hardwood stairs, slate tile, and every frost-laced surface. "Lee, up here."

He'd found Ginny's sister.

[18]

KADDISH

The thing that used to be Flo was handcuffed to Grandma Ruth's old, heavy iron bedstead in the first guestroom. Stiff hair clung to its livid shoulders, its mouth worked lazily, and a thin threadly growl rose from its flayed chest under a cream-colored, lace-edged camisole. Her distended belly moved strangely, peeking between the cami and pajama pants dotted with tiny cornflowers, skin loosened with slippage and the fluid underneath sloshing.

Like a water balloon.

Flo's eyes, filmy and collapsed, rolled weakly. She twitched, rattling the cuffs. Where had *those* come from? Good God.

"Looks like they decided to treat her here," Juju said, softly. There were long muddy streaks in the rose-carpeted hallway and drag-marks on the walls at shoulder height; some of the creatures had come up. Had Flo driven them off somehow?

Or did they not eat their own until they were dead?

Pictures marched down the hall—graduations, Mom and Dad's wedding and anniversary, Flo's wedding, sepia snapshots of dead relatives, a single picture of Uncle Ezra in Jerusalem before the massive heart attack. None of the carefully framed paper pieces were askew, though the occasional table at the end of the hall had been upended, the crystal vase laying bone-dry with a spill of brown, frost-dried flowers half in its mouth.

Flo stirred again. Her head turned this way and that as she crouched at the bedside, one arm stretched hideously, tethered to the heavy end of the bedstead. The covers were thrown off, a dent in the blue pillow where her living head had rested. The night-table was smashed, the lamp too, and a bracelet of raw, oozing flesh showed above the silver cuff.

Where the thing had been *chewing*.

Lee stared at Flo, a line between his eyebrows. He glanced at Ginny, a swift movement almost lost in her peripheral vision.

Flo.

Her sister's feet were bare, her toes discolored with cold and necrosis. Each nail held carefully applied peach polish, the exact same color as Mom's.

Of course Mom would paint Flo's toes for her. There would be soft laughter, concentration, Flo remarking that maybe the fumes were bad for the baby and Mom saying *it's toulene-free*, and if Ginny had been there she would brush Flo's hair, her fingers working with soft precision. *You always braid it best,* her sister might say, and Ginny would know she was forgiven for past sins, just in time to rack up more.

You always have to ruin everything. Flo yelling, and Ginny's cheeks scarlet with shame as if she'd been slapped. Maybe she shouldn't have said anything, and Ginny couldn't deny a sneaking feeling of vindication for never having liked Samuel and his pretentious bullshit.

Maybe Flo had loved her husband, though. It was, Ginny could admit now, very possible. Maybe Flo had even known about the chippie from the book club, and had closed her eyes to it.

You overlooked things for the people you loved.

And maybe, just maybe, Flo had kept overlooking until Ginny had made it impossible. Once Ginny had told Mom, of course Flo couldn't stay married to Sam. And why hadn't Ginny gone to Flo first?

Because I didn't know what to do! I didn't! I had to ask Mom for advice, right?

Oh, but that was a lie, wasn't it? Hadn't there been a deep, secret, shameful thought wriggling in her subconscious? Flo the younger, Flo the favorite, Flo the troubled, Flo who had "made a good marriage" while Ginny was a disappointment...human memory was fickle, and it was so easy to think you'd done something for the right reasons. Or at least, for better reasons than creeping low-level jealousy?

You always have to ruin everything, Flo yelled, and God, was it true?

Was it? Ginny stared at the thing that had been her sister.

"Juju." Lee finally spoke. "Take her downstairs."

For a long, strange moment Ginny thought he meant Flo, and wondered how. Of course, she was only moving lethargically. It might be easy to get her downstairs, and then what?

And the baby. Ginny shuddered, her gaze riveted to that gently sloshing belly. *What about the baby?*

Lee shifted a little; Juju took Ginny's arm. "Come on, Miss Virginia," he said, softly, and the horrible, sickening knowledge of what had to happen crashed through her.

"No." She pulled her arm away, almost toppling over. The thing cocked its head, listening. "*No.*"

"Ginny—" Juju looked uneasily at Lee.

"*No,* sir." She drew herself up, and the thing that had been Flo moved restlessly again, its growl turning inquisitive as its head moved, chin swinging back and forth. Hunting by sound. Flo's earrings, small gold hoops, glittered feverishly. "Thank you, but no."

"Ginny." Lee, this time, his eyes paled to that peculiar almost-yellow. "You don't want to see this, darlin."

There's a whole list of things I don't want to see. "No, Lee." She searched for the words to make him understand, couldn't find them. She took a deep breath, staring at the tip of Flo's nose. The shape of her lips, the top lip just like Dad's, the full underlip Mom's, both like Ginny's own mouth. Her cheekbones just like Ginny's too. "No. I...I need..."

"You need a moment?"

God *damn* it, she couldn't think with him interrupting her. "No." Another deep breath. It smelled awful in here. Dark clots painted the inside of Flo's cotton-clad thighs, and there was a spreading stain underneath her.

Flo hated to be dirty.

"No," Ginny said, finally. There wasn't enough air in her lungs, but she tried with what she had. "No, Lee. I need your gun."

*N*ICE AND EASY. *T*AKE YOUR STANCE...*THAT'S RIGHT.*

A sobbing breath, way down deep to the bottom of her diaphragm. The thing's belly slip-sloshed as it went back to its lethargic tugging at the handcuffs. Was there something tiny in there, chewing aimlessly as its support system cannibalized other tissues?

Breathe, darlin.

Oh, but it was hard.

Ginny! Her sister's wide smile, teeth missing or braces glittering. Secrets whispered at night, when one Mills girl couldn't sleep and crept into a sister's bedroom. *Ginny, look!* Arms spread wide, pedaling without holding on, or while drifting lazily on warm lakewater. *Look, I'm floating. I'm flying!*

The matching Barbies they received each birthday. Their matching pink bicycles. Flo holding her hand so tight at college dropoff. *You're going to do fine. You're my super-smart big sister.*

Flo yelling. *You never want me to have anything good!* Blotches of red on her sister's cheeks. *He's my husband!*

Ginny, yelling too. *Should I just have said nothing?*

Flo's hands, tight fists, the baby-bump barely visible under her twinset. Soft blue, cashmere, and Mom's pearls glowing against the knitted weave, the two of them facing each other in the upstairs hall of the townhouse Sam and Flo bought the year after they got married, right after Sam made partner at his firm.

Samuel, hop-following Ginny as he hastily buckled himself up. *Virginia? Virginia, wait! It was a mistake!*

Oh, it had been. For all parties concerned. Now Lee's voice whispered in memory, a slow-spaced mutter. *Hard to hit 'em in the head. Aim for the body.*

Not this time. Ginny's boots crushed rose-colored carpet. One step forward, another. The closet was half-open, Flo's clothes hanging in regimented, color-coordinated rows.

No, Lee. You can't do this for me.

The bathroom door was open, too. White tile, towels hanging ready, a frosted window full of dull grey light.

It growled. Its eyes were shrunken raisins, and it didn't even have the strength to sit up. It sprawled amid the splinters of the night-table, shards of the lamp pressing into hip, buttock, calf. The stain underneath it spread, fresh seepage.

Don't get too close, Ginny.

Juju and Lee were out in the hall. Waiting. Everyone else was outside, sitting in a truck, a 4x4, an RV, not knowing what the hell was happening inside the house her mother had picked after rejecting at least twelve others, the house she and Dad were supposed to finish their retirement in.

Well, they had.

Flo's smaller hand in hers while they walked up the broad bright pavement to school, chubby and sweating. *You leave my sister alone,* a younger Ginny yelled on the playground, spreading her arms and afire with injustice. *I need you,* Ginny whispering into a phone after that terrible party and breaking up with Alec, and coming off the plane from dropping out of college to see Flo in the crowd, her arms folded and that worry-line between her eyebrows. *I talked Mom out of coming,* Flo had said, by way of hello.

You're a saint, Ginny had replied.

Hardly. Flo had shaken her head, that impatient hair-toss she'd had all her life. *Let's get something to eat. You're staying with me.*

Great ragged breaths, catching in her throat. A choking, swallowed sob.

"Flo," Ginny whispered. "I love you, Flo."

IT GROWLED, AND ITS TEETH CLICKED TOGETHER, A DEAD-branch snapping. A single gunshot. A steaming splatter.

GINNY'S KNEES HIT PALE, ROSY CARPET. THE SOBS HAD HER IN sharp discolored teeth. They shook her mercilessly. She set the gun down, carefully, and rocked back and forth, arms wrapped around her middle and the words tearing at her throat.

Please. I love you. I love you. Please, oh please God. I love you.

I love you.

[19]
NONE OF US

There weren't any tracks and the whole place was a mausoleum, but the critters always showed up, sooner or later, followin' the livin'. Besides, the ground was frozen too hard for buryin', so the cellar would have to do.

"You go on downstairs," Lee told Phyllis and Steph. "Help her. We'll bring 'em."

Ginny told him where the sheets were—a whole closet full of soft, slippery linens, with small drawstring bags of cedar tucked in the stacks. *Sashay*, she called it, and Lee and Juju's hands smeared crap on fine-grained cloth. *Wrap them up*, Ginny said, distractedly, and Phyllis had taken her shoulders.

Come on, honey. The dark-haired woman, her face set and still, didn't waste time asking questions. *Let's get the downstairs ready.*

Getting the handcuffs could have been a nasty job, but Juju had a bolt cutter in the back of his four-by.

"Oh, Lord." Duncan almost choked when they rolled the sister's body into wrapping. The belly moved slosh-strange, and Lee was hoping nothing in there was still alive. It wasn't right for a corpse to look that way, or a woman's stomach to...to *move* like that, like a water balloon. "Is there...d'ya think..."

"Hope not," Juju replied grimly. "Ain't gonna touch it and find out."

So Lee had to, because you couldn't ask another man to do what you wouldn't, and if there was something in there it had to be dealt with.

The belly gave, resilient, and a gush of something foul oozed between the corpse's loose-trembling legs. Nothing twitched under his palm, no little critter inside wanting to get out. He let out a soft sipping breath of relief, and Duncan turned aside to retch.

Getting the old woman off the cold concrete was a job, but the worst was working the old man in front of the big ol' window free of frozen, blood-drenched carpet. Some of him was probably left there, and Lee had no idea what Ginny would think of that, so he made up his mind to keep her out of the living room on their exit.

Carrying the bodies down the stairs into the basement was another job, but once they were down there...well, it was almost a relief to find a spot in the house that was dusty, furniture standing shrouded and an ancient cellar-hatch stuffed full of insulation under plastic sheeting. The two lanterns gave flickering golden light, and there were other odds and ends down here—an antique bicycle draped with cobwebs, bits of spare lumber, shelves that could have held jars of preserves if Ginny's mama had a mind to make them.

"Here." Mark Kasprak handed Ginny a fresh bottle of water. They had cases stacked in the back of the truck, and he and Steph had hauled a few in.

It hurt to see Ginny attempting to wash frozen or blood-stiffened corpse hair. Phyllis, her pretty face set, rubbed at dead scalps with her manicured fingers, and didn't say a word about the smell, just softly clucked every once in a while like she was at a beauty salon. Steph held a big blue glass basin from the kitchen to catch the flow, dumping it near the hatch where concrete had crumbled enough to show soft, sterile, frozen earth below.

Ginny's lips moved—some kind of prayer, though she had to stop often, tilting her head back and staring at the cobwebbed ceiling and blinking as heavy tears slid down her temples, vanishing into her braided hair. The words were strange, but Juju said she was Jewish, and like every other folk they had their own ways of dealin' with their dead.

Near the end, Ginny tacked unevenly up the stairs, and Lee followed. The snow had started again, and getting to shelter was gonna be work, but there was no hurryin' something like this, ever.

She didn't even glance into the living room, which was a mercy. Instead, she climbed to the second story, and halted at the door of the master bedroom. Her chin dropped, her flashlight bobbing, and she curled in on herself like she'd been sucker-punched.

"Ginny." He grabbed her shoulders, but she shook him away—not violently, just as a sleepwalker might free herself from clinging curtains.

Two twin beds, each with royal-blue covers. The bedroom was bigger than a few places Lee had lived in, and there were vases that had held fresh flowers up here, too. A painting of fruit on a table on one wall, more sepia pictures in nice frames, and even though the house was full of cold outside air, there was a faint, indefinable fragrance still clinging to wood, heavy carpet, lace thingies like doilies but finer than his Nonna crocheted.

She knew what she wanted, evidently. There was an old hand-made wooden hutch taller than Lee against one wall, and she opened the left-hand door. Suit jackets hung inside, and she looked through, her bloody fingers gentle. "Not here," she muttered. "Oh, God."

She opened the second drawer down and found what she was looking for—a scrap of white and blue cloth, tassels on its short ends. Next came the cherrywood dresser, its top holding two lamps with fancy glass dangles that looked older than the house, a small jewelry hutch, and a few silver plates and dishes with bright baubles glittering under flashlight flicker. One of those drawers gave up a pair of blue scraps as well, but without tassels.

"Scissors." She turned away, leaving the drawer open, and her eyes were huge and dark. "In the kitchen, I think."

"What you got there, Ginny?" Softly, trying not to startle her.

"Prayer shawl," she said, distractedly. "You h-have to c-cut a corner...Lee..."

"What is it, darlin?" *Tell me what you need.* He hoped the rest of them were finishing wrapping the bodies up. The sooner they were out of here, the better.

Those big, wounded eyes rested on him. "I...I can't remember."

"What can't you remember?" Christ Jesus, he would do just about anything to get that look off her face, but there was nothing *to* do.

"Some of the Kaddish." She clutched the cloths to her chest, blinking rapidly. Tears trembled on the verge of spilling, both eyes full.

Lee's entire chest ached. He'd'a thought it a heart attack if he didn't know better. "What's that now?"

"It's...my bat mitzvah, we had to study prayers for a year, and I... I'm not sure I remember it right." She sucked in a small, hurt breath, and Lee longed to drag her out of there. Put her in the truck, start it up, and keep driving. All night, if he had to, critters and weather be damned. "The Kaddish."

"Oh." He didn't know any Jewish prayers, but this sounded important. "Wellnow, is there a book, or somethin?"

"I...maybe. Dad wasn't...he..." She almost crumpled again, shoulders curving inward, her arms tightening around the shawls.

Lee took a step toward her. Another, nice and slow. "Is it like Catholic, where you hafta know the words? Latin, or that?"

"N-no." Her mouth worked for a moment, and she swallowed hard. "I don't...I don't *think* so, but..."

"Imma tell you, then." Easy did it here, easy and calm. "We'll do our best, and God'll understand."

"You think so?" A single tear tracked itself down her left cheek, and there was almost nothing he could do about it.

The worst part of anything was bein' helpless. "I know so," he lied. *Give a woman what she needs*, Poppa Q always said, and Lee would, if he could just figure out what that might be. "I *know* so, darlin. Y'all need some scissors?"

"You have to cut the corner," she whispered. "So it's not sacred."

"Aight." *Keep her moving.* Once she settled, the enormity of grief would descend on her like a hawk on a rabbit. "Kitchen, right?"

"Unless Mom's sewing room...no, okay, kitchen. Okay."

She didn't move, so he stepped forward again, turning to put an arm around her shoulders. Pushing her gently for the door. The longer they stayed here, the harder it was gonna get. "We'll find a pair, or I got a pocketknife. Then you can say whatever words you remember."

"We weren't orthodox," she whispered. She didn't quite resist his gentle pressure; she was just slowing down under the weight.

"It don't matter, darlin." *God, get her out of here. Away from this.* She couldn't just walk away from her people without seein' to them decent, though, and he'd promised.

She nodded, put her head down, and started for the door. Halted, and swayed. "Lee?"

"Hm?" His arm fell back to his side.

"Thank you." So soft, he could barely hear it.

Anytime. He wanted to say that, but it sounded awful even inside his head. So he just made a half-coughing noise, ducking his own head. His boots left big black prints on the carpet.

Nothing stayed clean. Especially now.

COME MIDNIGHT IT WAS SNOWING HARD AGAIN, AND IT WAS THE first time Lee Quartine had ever been in a country club. Apparently Ginny's parents had been members of this Saratoga Ash Club, and she suggested it would be defensible and likely deserted, too.

She was right on both counts, but Lee wasn't feeling pleased. Overhead, a wide awning painted to look like canvas stripes kept the swiftly falling white away, and the big oak doors were propped wide. Duncan was on watch, playing his flashlight over curtains of swirling flak, and Traveller's excited cries came from deeper inside, where Mark was throwing a ball for the hound in a cavernous foyer.

"Washin em. Whoever heard of that?" Juju straightened, rubbing at his lower back. "Waste o' water." It was after-combat grousing, adrenaline comin' down and makin' a man cranky, but Lee winced internally just the same.

Phyllis, reaching for a fresh case of water, darted him a venomous glance. "There's plenty just lying around, waiting to be picked up." Her hands were reddened, nail polish chipped—she'd been at a gallon of dry sanitizer while she drove the RV, if the chemical tang of rubbing-alcohol was any indication.

Lee shook his head, hefting a plastic tub of ammo. "We're all tired." His eyes were full of sand, and his own back ached. He wanted to be soothing Ginny, but they needed dinner, a watch schedule, and sleep, in that order. "Tomorrow we'll get more supplies."

"Take a look outside, Loot." Juju spread his arms, a familiar gesture of futility and dull, banked anger. The pompom on his knit hat was crushed by his hood, and his mood was likewise. "It's fu—ah, it's messed up, and now we ain't even got a place to go."

"Atlanta," Lee said, grimly. Might as well. "Good a place as any."

Juju lost the battle with himself and swore. He also almost tossed his flashlight for good measure. It was normal, a product of nerves, and Lee felt like swearing and throwing something himself.

Phyllis, however, had different standards. "You done?" she snapped, and her dark velvety eyes were afire. "Jesus, they were her *parents.*"

"I know, I know." The lean dark man sighed, rubbing at his forehead. His hands were raw too, from weather and work. "I'm sorry, ma'am. I'm worn out."

She studied him for a long moment, and Lee suppressed a sigh. If the two of them were gonna go at each other, he might as well just go inside, get cleaned up, and settle for the night. To hell with dinner, he wanted to close his eyes and escape this for a little while.

Except that wasn't an option, now was it.

But Phyllis evidently decided to err on the side of forgiveness. "Me too." She gave a grudging sigh and blew a stray curl out of her face. "Look, you two can go on in. I can handle this, and Duncan can keep an eye out."

Which was exactly the way to get Juju to settle, really. "No ma'am. I'm just tetchy." He had his manners back on now, and hard, too. "Don't pay me no nevermind."

"Will do." But she smiled, a twinkle in her dark eyes, and was off, carrying a load of sleeping bags. Her hips swished pertly under that red coat, and Lee was glad she wasn't makin' eyes at *him*.

That was more trouble than they needed. Duncan nodded as she passed him, but his gaze didn't follow her. Instead, he peered into falling snow, his flashlight one tiny bar of light swooping restlessly. You wouldn't see one of the critters until they erupted from the curtain. Hopefully, all the damn things were hibernating.

"That girl's trouble," Juju said, darkly, and took his place at the end of the truck, looking for the next load to ferry inside. "Not that you'd notice, now would you."

"I notice." Lee rested the ammo tub on the tailgate, eyeing the snow. "Just don't care."

"Must be nice." Juju glanced over his shoulder at Duncan, a speculative look.

"Don't look like that Harris fellow got his hand in yet." Lee had to suppress a grin. "You might got a chance."

"No thank you, sir. Women're trouble." Juju couldn't find another word.

To be fair, there didn't seem another that applied. "That they are."

"Atlanta, huh?" Which was what the man really wanted to know. "You sure?"

Lee was only surprised it took him this long to ask. "Got yourself somethin else in mind?"

Juju made another sharp, stretching movement. He decided to carry in the lanterns next, and gathered the box they rested in during the day, going up on tiptoe to do it. "Would it do any good if'n I did?"

"Truth be told, Juju, I ain't got no better ideas except movin west if Atlanta goes bust." Lee choked off a sigh at the end fo the sentence. "So if *you* got one, I'm all ears."

"Figured we'd be goin that way soon enough, even if it is south." Juju propped a hip on the tailgate and regarded him. Drops of snowmelt clung to his flattened cap, and his dark eyes were red-rimmed. "Thought you'd talk her into it before we got this far."

Yeah, well, that woulda been best. "Tried."

"What you figger happened?" Another component of post-battle stress; the replay, piecing things together. Juju snatched at his knitted cap, shook it, then rolled it up and stuffed it in his pocket. His hair began to spring back into position, glad to be free.

Lee had been thinking on that, a little. "They opened the door." Neighbor, maybe, or a stranger—probably bitten but before the convulsions. Or the old man didn't look before opening up.

Gated means safe, right? That was where Ginny got her optimism from, he reckoned. Maybe it was just bein' born rich.

"She ain't gonna be all right for a while." Juju kept the lantern box on the tailgate and pulled the last tub of ammo from its resting place too, hefted the former free and turned to carry it inside.

"None of us will," Lee answered, and they went about the business of closing up for the night silently after that.

There was nothing else to say.

[20]

A HUMDINGER

"That's right." Duncan squinted at the snow and the back of Juju's four-by, its brake lights watery rubies piercing a grey day. "You're doin fine."

The teenage girl with her fine, whip-braided hair grinned. "It's easy." Still, her hands were white-knuckled on the RV's giant wheel. The damn thing wallowed, chains on every tire biting wider than tracks made by Juju's 4x4. At least last night's snow was dry and powdery, but it was tortuous going.

Especially with a backseat driver breathing on you. "Because you're goin too *slow*." The boy Kasprak didn't like her behind the wheel, that much was plain. Little dog, all puffed up and barking. Maybe he

"Let her drive, son." Duncan settled deeper in the passenger seat. "Nice and easy on the gas, Miss Meacham."

"You can call me Steph, sir." She bit at her lip and the RV swayed. The girl had her learning permit, but piloting one of these big old buses was a helluva job. Still, she didn't take no for an answer, just sucked it up and stuck her chin out. Reminded Duncan of a girl from high school—Mary Malone, not pretty but striking with high cheekbones and a crop of redgold hair, not one of the big populars but middle-grade. She'd been a good friend to young him, but he'd gone and fucked it up like he always did.

Still, she'd been nice. Married a guy from over the state line, or at least that's what he'd overheard when he came home halfway through his stint to bury Mama. Cheerful, snub-nosed Mary, smart as a whip and kind, too. Worked at the animal shelter all through school.

She was probably growling and trying to bite the throat out of someone right now, though, if she wasn't dead on the floor like Ginny Mills's parents. And thinking about Mary Malone at the animal shelter made him think about all those dogs and cats inside when their owners stopped breathing, or started growling and chewing.

That did his nerves no damn good at all.

Last night—in a goddamn country club, of all places—he'd tossed and turned restlessly in his sleeping bag knowing there was a fully stocked bar so close. When it was his turn to go on watch, he stood in the foyer, watching the truck, 4x4, and the front of the RV tucked under the awning to keep the snow off, and sweated at that very same thought.

"Don't hit the brake now," he said, as they breasted a shallow hill. The clouds promised more precipitation, but not just yet, and the weather station showed the barometric pressure was holding steady. "Just let it slow down on its own."

"Yessir." The girl's knuckles began to pinken up. *Don't you drive that bus right over me,* Juju had said affectionately, and seeing the man smile was its own reward.

That was the only thing that made Duncan feel good about *not* drinking, but it was a humdinger, as his mama would have said.

At least Mama was safely dead before all this bullshit started. She'd gone near the end of his first and last deployment, cancer eating everything in her until the cupboards were bare. That was when the drinkin' started wholesale, though he'd never liked being sober before. Getting home and seeing the cheapass headstone hadn't done him any good.

"Was you in the service?" Mark Kasprak was now leaning over the back of the passenger seat, breathing on Duncan's hair. Boy could just not *wait* for his turn to drive.

What he wanted to do was snap *gitchorass in a seat and stop yammerin', kid.* Instead, Duncan made a gruff noise, somewhere between assent and negation. Let the kid think what he would, and Duncan had made up his mind to keep his temper since it was obvious Thurgood liked both the sprouts.

"Which branch?" the damn kid wanted to know. "Mr Lee thinks you was Army. Mr Juju thinks—"

Steph sighed, a small, aggravated sound. Her eyes were pretty, and her face was kittenish. She'd look like a girl all her life, even when the inevitable wrinkles visited. "He don't want to *talk* about it, Mark. Sit down and put your seatbelt on."

Well, Mark Kasprak didn't want to be told what to do. "We ain't goin fast enough to crash."

"Just in case." Duncan could have stood to hear what Juju thought of anything. Instead, he was stuck on babysitting duty, and this boy was irritatin' when a man had nothing but coffee and Cream of Wheat in his belly. "Hard to practice drivin when you're worried about your passengers."

"Steph don't need to worry about me," Kasprak rapped back.

Lord, it was like looking at a version of his younger self. All that prickliness—but had he ever been so transparent, when he looked at someone he liked? The kid's face all but shouted *puppy love* whenever he got within ten feet of Steph.

"But she does." It was uncomfortable to think he'd ever been that young. Duncan restrained the urge to bark. "Make it easy on her, chief, and sit down for a bit."

The boy pushed his lower lip out, but he settled after that, and Duncan reached for a bottle of water.

It wasn't what he wanted, but it would have to do.

[21]

KINDNESS

The afternoon wore on, as always, staring at the ass end of Lee's truck and listening for the walkie-talkie.

"Ginny?" Juju glanced at his passenger. "You all right?" Then it occurred to him there was no way she'd be *all right*, and being lead driver for a bit in this ugly snow-slop mess required a fair bit of concentration, too. He should've been overjoyed she was quiet, staring blankly out the window...but he wasn't.

At least Traveller was in the truck with Lee and Phyllis. The damn dog's innards were full of SlimJims and kibble, and Juju was tired of smelling the result.

"Hm?" Ginny stirred. Her hair was in a loose braid today, tendrils falling free, and it was...well, a little disturbing to see that slight dishevelment. Her black jacket was only zipped halfway, too, and her gloves lay forgotten in her lap. She wasn't reading the thick black medical manual or anything else, *or* writing in her little notebooks.

No, she just stared out the window. He didn't quite blame her, but it was like having a ghost in the front seat.

"I just wondered..." His damn conscience was pinching, too.

Nobody should have to do what she'd done, especially a fuckin' civilian. "Well, you know, how you was feelin."

A pale, half-smothered laugh escaped her; one bare, cold-reddened hand flew to her mouth to trap it. "Uh." Her hand dropped back into her lap, a wounded bird. "Fine, I suppose. Considering."

Yeah. Considering. There was something dry in his throat, so he coughed a bit to clear it. They were all ass-deep in shit and sinking, why *talk* about it? Still...something impelled him. "Yeah."

Snow crunched and bunched, pushed free of the four-by's grill by sheet of plywood, tilted and braced with 2x4s held by strap tie-downs around the winch. There was another halfass plywood plow on the truck, breaking the crust; the four-by was just picking up the slack and clearing for the RV creeping along behind. They'd find a front-hitch plow somewhere along the way, Lee reckoned, but nobody wanted to stay in Saratoga another day, country club or no country club.

Go figure. First time he'd ever been in one of them damn places, and Juju hadn't even thought to piss in a corner. Might have been satisfying.

The pressure in his throat mounted, until he *had* to say something. "Ginny?"

She made another soft *I'm listening* sound, but he couldn't tell if it was true or not. Christ knew she probably didn't need anyone bothering her, least of all his clumsy ass.

Comforting had never been one of Juju Thurgood's skills, you could say. He left that shit for women and chaplains. "I never thanked you," he found himself saying. "When you an Lee showed up, after Tip...well. You were right kind to me, and I 'preciate it."

"Oh." Now she looked down at her cupped palms instead of out the window. "You were pretty upset."

I was fuckin crazy, thanks. "It weren't no walk in the park." Nobody should have to beat their own buddy's head in with a lamp, either, but at least Juju had been...well, *prepared* wasn't the right word, but being in the service had done him a good turn, he guessed.

The trainin' took over when it was time to do, and you didn't have to think.

It was the thinkin' that knotted you all up.

"Yeah." Ginny's quiet agreement put the entire subject to bed. Or not, but he couldn't figure out anything to add for the life of him.

The four-by wanted to drift; Juju held it steady. He really should retire this piece of machinery and get a big old truck. Half-ton, with a hemi. That would be useful. But he and Tip had worked on the Jeep together, and even with the bullet holes breathing chill-wet air into the cab, it was familiar.

Safe.

Oh, what the hell. Might as well jump in, he wasn't gonna get no peace with himself otherwise. "What you did, back there. For your sister. It was a kindness, Ginny."

Crunch-squeak went the snow. *Hiss-crunch*, when the chains. *Purr* went the engine, and he hit the wipers once to clear spattered droplets.

"Was it?" Ginny spoke to her hands, a few of her unpolished nails broken. The two words were so quiet, Juju almost missed 'em.

"It was." He sounded damn certain, even to himself. "Just like it was a mercy for Tip. He wouldn't have wanted to be no zombie critter." *That's what I tell myself. It's gotta be true.*

If it wasn't, he didn't want to know.

Another long silence. Then Ginny stirred, restlessly. "Flo hated being dirty," she said, finally. "All her life. Even as a kid."

What was it like, Juju wondered, to have that luxury? "Tip didn't mind him no dirt, long as he got to wash his face. There was that one time, in Iraq...you prolly don't want to hear none of that, though."

"I don't mind." Now Ginny was looking at him, studying his profile instead of staring at a snowy wasteland or her own fragile hands. "If you feel like talking, that is."

"Maybe. I dunno." What he felt like was helping her, he guessed, but there didn't seem to be much prospect of that.

Still, he'd beaten his brother's head in, she'd shot her sister. There was a kind of...what was the word? Symmetry. Yeah. That was it.

"Tip was an asshole." Juju settled himself a little more firmly in his bucket seat and glanced at the weather station display taped to the dash. The pressure was holding steady, which was a good thing. In half an hour, Lee would drop back and the four-by would take the lead for a half-hour, snow-pushing along south. "Beg your pardon, ma'am. But he kept his word. That's pretty rare."

"Flo was the favorite." Ginny's throat worked, and she rubbed at her left cheek, a quick, swiping movement. "It sounds horrible to say it out loud."

"Well, ain't no way to hurt 'em now." Dead was dead, and you could say what you pleased. "Might as well be honest."

"That's true." Ginny's fingers interlaced; pulled tight. "Do you think they know? I mean, that we...we were helping them?"

And Lord, that was one thing that kept *him* up at night, when he wasn't exhausted from the day's work. Had there been something of Tip left inside that raving, chewing bastard, screaming to be let out?

Would he be lying if he reassured her? Or was he trying, God help him, to reassure *himself*? "Way I figger," Juju said, slowly, "is that they were hurt, an confused. And it was a mercy to let 'em out. Let 'em free." *O Pharaoh*, his grandmother used to sing. *Let my people go.*

"That's a good way to look at it." Ginny sniffed, hard. Then she sniffed again, and Lord help him, he'd made her cry.

Jesus on a stick. "Didn't mean to—" he began.

"No," she said, quickly. "No, Juju. It's...I just...it occurred to me you understand. You know?" She bent to dig in her purse, probably for tissues. Women always carried tissues.

And everything else.

"Some of it, yeah." Juju nodded, eased off the gas to let the Jeep right itself when the back wheels started to drift a bit. The sky was a flat, iron-colored lid, clapped over a box. "That prayer you got, the one you said over your people."

"The Kaddish?" It *was* tissues, a red and blue travel pack, thin plastic covering battered by rubbing against whatever else a practical, no-nonsense librarian kept in her bag. Ginny wiped at her cheeks, blew her nose. "I might have forgotten some of it."

"Don't think it matters." He hadn't been a church man since his gran went to Jesus. "Wish I'd had me some time to pray over Tip."

"I'm sorry." She blew her nose again, yanked out a fresh tissue, dabbed at her eyes. She even honked snot out gracefully. Maybe they taught that in charm school, or at the goddamn country club. "Juju?"

"Huh?" The Jeep shuddered, and he touched the accelerator to get them over a frozen hump. Snow crunched and splattered aside; he hit the wipers to keep the windshield clear.

"I can say Kaddish for Tip." Shyly, and she didn't look at him, insteady studying the wad of used tissue like it was the most interesting thing in the world. "If you want."

It was right kind of her to offer. Freeway signs, a coating of ice melting off their reflective surfaces, marched slowly beside the road. "You think he'd like it?"

"I guess it's mostly for us, instead of the...the dead." Her breath caught; she blew her nose again. "You can't do anything more for them."

"Guess not." He thought it over. "I'd be right honored. All I got's my grandma's prayers, and I say 'em, but won't do no harm to add none, I reckon."

"Sure. It's basically...you say it and you let God decide how to take it. It's really for those left behind. Funny." She wiped at her nose again. "We weren't orthodox or anything, I'm agnostic, but I guess I absorbed more than I thought."

Well, Juju was pretty agnostic himself, come to think of it. But it couldn't hurt, and if it got her thinkin' on something else, he figured that was a kindness, too.

"Guess I did too." He hit the wipers again. "Only time I ever prayed after leavin home was when I'us gettin shot at."

"No atheists in foxholes," she murmured. "What about Tip?"

"He was raised Catholic." Which reminded him of a lot of things, and surely there was no harm in telling a few of them. "Said he was recoverin. There was this one time, we were gettin our ass—uh, our butts shot off in some podunk sand-town, and Tip started yellin somethin. Latin. He was yellin in Latin at the assho—the, uh, the fellers shooting at us."

Then he was telling the story, Tip yelling any old thing he could think of while they covered and moved, mortars pop-crumping and the taste of metal on Juju's tongue, and later, back at base, when they started calling Tip "the preacher" and it pissed him off so much he snuck in and shut off the hot water for the showers.

The numbers on the weather station began to drop, atmospheric pressure not content to stay still. Weather was massing in the distance, a deeper grey. After a little while, Ginny handed him the tissues.

Juju hadn't even realized he was leaking. So he blew his nose, and Ginny began to tell him about a summer camp, her sister, and an ever-escalating series of practical jokes between two cabins that ended with a laxative baked into chocolate cupcakes.

When the walkie-talkie on the dash crackled with Lee's check-in, they were both laughing helplessly; something in both of them had eased.

And all the tissues were gone.

[22]

EMOTIONAL LITERACY

It was the closest Phyllis had ever gotten to New York, and she couldn't even enjoy it. Plus, even if it was the end of the world, she didn't want dog hair on her coat *or* her wool trousers, and Lee Quartine was not by any stretch of the imagination a *social* creature. If she was in the Jeep with Ginny, at least there would have been something interesting to talk about. Maybe Phyl could even mention *Ulysses* to her. The lady didn't really seem like a Joyce type, but since the internet was down, there were precious few options for discussing literature and a librarian was far from the worst prospect for such a pastime.

Phyllis stared out the window. Snow, snow, abandoned cars, hillocks, hummocks, dark dead buildings, and more snow. They might as well have been back in Ohio.

To be absolutely fair, the dog wasn't bad at all. He stared up at her with big, dopey, mournful eyes, and he'd never yell that she was a dumbass bimbo or mock her for reading something other than a fashion magazine. He liked it when she rubbed the downy top of his canine head, and she was pretty sure he would have leapt through a fiery ring or two if his humans wanted it.

He was also a better conversationalist than the man driving, that was for damn sure.

Just as Phyllis thought that, though, Lee opened his mouth. "Gonna stop in a piece."

"Sounds good." That probably finished up their conversation for another hour or so, and she wished she could dig the book out of her purse. If she did, though, would he expect her to talk about whatever she was reading?

Lee gave her a strange sideways look, chin down and long nose pointed. "Ask you somethin', Miss Phyllis?"

Great. Here it comes. She braced herself, staring out the window. "You can ask." *But I don't have to answer.*

Even though most of the time, she did, because men just didn't stop when you ignored them. They seemed to take it as a challenge.

Lee cleared his throat, a dry scraping sound. "Figgered I'd ask, since you're a girl and all. You, uh...well, Ginny."

"What about her?" She kept smoothing the dog's head, scratching lightly behind his mobile ears. The pattern on his fur was pretty— almost marbled, on the sides. That bitch from the Dalmatians movie might've wanted this hide for a hat. A big tall one, like a Beefeater's headbucket.

Were there any Beefeaters left? The Tower of London was probably full of zombies, too. The British were on their own, just like everyone else. And the Irish? Well, there was no Joyce to do a stream-of-consciousness chapter from a Gaelic zombie's point-of-view. Literature was going to have to live without that particular innovation.

Lee spaced out his words like each one cost him a miser's quarter. "I don't know what to do."

"You're gonna have to be a little more specific there, Mr Lee." Was he actually asking her for relationship advice?

"I just don't know. She ain't gonna be feelin so well."

That was putting it mildly. At least Phyl's own mother and grandmother were safely in the ground before all this went down.

And at least Lee wasn't coming on to her. It was a goddamn miracle. Maybe he was that unicorn, an actual nice guy, after all. "None of us are." Phyllis wiggled her toes inside her boots. Wool socks, nice and cushy, and this was a lot more comfortable than heels. Still, she would have liked to slip into a nice pair, along with her comfortable blue maxidress.

It would mean all this shit was over, that the weather was better, and civilization was still holding. Which was a helluva Christmas list, when she thought about it.

"Well, I guess." Lee coughed uneasily again. "But if there was somethin…you know, anything…I ain't good with girl shi—I mean, stuff."

Go figure, he was actually asking for advice. Whether or not he'd take it was another matter, but Phyl decided she'd give him a hint or two. "Well, I mean, all you gotta do is be there for her."

He squinted at the whited-out highway like it personally offended him. The jury-rigged plow on the front of the truck was holding up pretty well, but if the snow got wetter and heavier it might not. "You wouldn't happen to know no girl details about that, huh?"

"Girl details?" It was Phyl's considered opinion that men spoke a different language, and he was no exception when you could get him to open his mouth.

Lee cogitated for a bit, then spat out the whole point of the conversation. "How you make a woman feel better?"

"Oh, Lord, I dunno." Chalk one up for him, he was trying. "Give her a hug. Do things for her. Let her talk if she wants to, let her get angry if she wants that. This is all basic stuff." Basic emotional literacy, which might as well have been Swahili to most dudes.

Phyl wished again that she was in the 4x4 with Ginny. This was awkward as fuck.

Lee's nose wrinkled a little bit. "Just don't want to do nothin wrong."

"I'm pretty sure you could dump hot soup in her lap and she'd still like you." That was the old joke, wasn't it? Once you liked someone, you were inclined to put the best angle on anything they did.

"Rather not." He grinned, a lopsided, easy expression, and maybe that was what Ginny saw in him. It was clear the guy was gone over her, and he was a real Mister Fixit. All the movies agreed you could do a lot worse in the zombie apocalypse.

"Well, good on you." Phyl restrained the urge to roll her eyes. How did men get past their toddler years without learning empathy, for God's sake? "Just...look, the dog knows what to do, right?" Irritation flooded her shoulders, tightening along her neck.

"He does?" Lee didn't look quite *baffled*, but certainly *questioning*.

"Yeah. They can tell when you're sad. It's science." *Just don't put your nose up her skirt.* She had to stuff that irreverent thought back down her throat in a hurry. Everything was better when you saw the funny side. "Just, you know, follow his lead. If he can tell she's sad, and what to do, so can you."

"I'll do that, then." Now Lee sounded utterly relieved. "Much obliged, Miz Phyllis."

Phyl suppressed a chuckle. Hopefully he wouldn't think she was laughing at *him*. "You're welcome, Mr Quartine." She decided to forgive him, too, mostly because he shut up about it and went back to staring morosely through the windshield, flicking the wipers every so often.

Ten minutes later they began the laborious process of pulling off the freeway to find gas, and Traveller's head was in Phyllis's lap. Cats were best, of course, and men were only borderline okay in exceptional cases.

Dogs? Well, she liked this one, and it was the strangest thing, all of a sudden she didn't mind the hairs working into her wool trousers.

THE SIGNS SAID *ARDONIA*; THEIR LITTLE GROUP DIDN'T GO INTO the town proper but halted just at the periphery where a Marathon station, all its front glass shattered and a path of looting cut straight for the register counter, crouched under a lowering sky. The pipes hadn't frozen all the way yet, thank God.

Just mostly. "Be flushing with bottled water soon," Phyllis grumbled, rinsing her hands in a thin cold trickle from an arthritic faucet. "Lord, I miss plumbing."

"Best invention of civilization," Ginny agreed. Hollow-eyed and hunched, she held the flashlight in one hand and a baseball bat in the other. Phyl's trusty pink warrior was propped next to the door, and Steph, closeted in a stall, cursed under her breath. "Steph? You all right?"

"My tuckus is damn near frozen off," the girl lamented, a young voice bouncing off cold tiles and lino.

"At least you're not on the rag." Phyllis grinned into the mirror. Cold water was doing her skin some good, but when her moisturizer ran out, there was going to be hell to pay. "Right?"

"Ayuh," Steph moaned. "Thank God for that."

"I'll look for more tampons outside," Ginny said, distractedly, tucking a stray curl behind her ear. She didn't look in the mirror or even directly at Phyllis, her gaze skipping nervously along flecks in the linoleum. "And first-aid kits."

"Might as well get some chocolate too." Phyl grabbed a handful of paper towels. Her fingers ached with the cold. "Sooner or later we're gonna need it." Or she could just take the pill all the way through. There was no more hoping a pharmacist wasn't a religious fanatic, not in today's world.

Of course, now the only problem was finding pharmacies and looting enough to keep yourself supplied. And what happened when that ran out, as it inevitably would?

"And some Slim Jims," Steph piped up. "Since we're here."

Phyl rolled her eyes. Planning for a future without birth control was tomorrow's problem, especially when there were none of what her grandmother would have called *prospects* in a hundred-mile radius, or probably more. "Lord, you shouldn't feed that dog any more of those. He reeks."

Steph's giggle bounced around both of them, a playful kitten looking for fun. "He likes 'em."

Ginny didn't say anything. She just stared at the sink, and Phyl's mouth drew down. Poor girl. What was it like, to know your parents had been...eaten? And to think of their bodies rotting in a basement? Phyl tossed the damp paper towels in an overflowing basket.

Nobody was going to be cleaning that up anytime soon. Or anything else. "Ginny?" She touched the woman's elbow. "Honey?"

The librarian blinked, her shoulders coming up like she was bracing herself for the catwalk. "Tampons," she said. "First aid." A few seconds later she was gone, her baseball bat hitting the swinging door with a hollow boom that made Phyl jump and flick her own flashlight on, its beam refracting off the mirror and melding with the faint glow of Steph's.

She would probably never get used to how quiet it was without traffic, or the sense of other people breathing nearby even when you were semi-rural. Joyce's crowded, beloved Dublin might be standing empty now, except for packs of chewing, aimless corpses.

For some reason, that image disturbed her more than the deserted New York skyscrapers, or even Cleveland's suburbs turned into ghost towns.

"We have enough tampons for the next twenty years," Steph finally muttered, and there was a rasp of cheap toilet paper on a spindly cardboard roll.

"When we run out, it's not gonna be pleasant." Phyllis shuddered at the notion, and grabbed for her own bat. "Meet you outside, sweetie." The swinging door hit something soft, and for a moment Phyl thought Ginny had paused just outside.

That was when she heard the growling, and realized they weren't alone.

[23]

PEACE

Shelves of highly processed road food, overpriced toiletries, and various forms of caffeine sat damp and dispirited. The glass cooler doors holding back a tide of overpriced sodas were etched with condensation and frost, except for the one that shattered as Ginny screamed and swung, her bat clipping the head of a shambling, stinking monstrosity.

Phyl was banging on the inside of the swinging restroom door. Ginny backed up, her hip hitting a wire stand full of postcards, and a gun barked outside.

"God *damn* it!" one of the guys yelled outside, the sound carrying under more of that grinding, nasty chest-throbbing. "*Shoot the motherfucker!*"

She hoped they wouldn't. A bullet coming into the store could do all *kinds* of damage.

Everything had slowed down. Ginny hopped sideways, postcards scattering in a paper snowdrift. She brought the bat sideways again, and the sound it made as it crunched onto the zombie's head would have made her lose anything she'd eaten that morning, if she'd bothered.

The zombie wore a flannel shirt over a *Heavy Metal* T-shirt, jeans wet all the way through and hanging off wasted legs, and a belt with a big, glittering brass buckle. A red baseball cap perched on its now-deformed skull. He had to be relatively fresh; the bone wasn't spongy yet and his eyes weren't collapsed, just grey-filmed. Stubble roughened his cheeks, and his mouth hadn't developed the cracks at the corners yet. He dragged his left foot, and it was that slight scraping sound that had warned her as she crouched in the non-food aisle looking at tampon boxes.

She'd almost fallen over, saved only by a wrenching lunge that burned all the way down her left side. Now she was faced with the prospect of beating a newly turned zombie to death.

Oh, God. "Blessed, praised..." Her lips moved, and she realized what she was reciting as her bat thudded home again and broken glass shivered free of more cooler doors. "Honored, exalted, extolled..." Everything around her darkened, a *click* like a stapler's head smacked by an irate coworker echoing inside her head. "Glorified, adored, and lauded be the name..."

I'm saying Kaddish for zombies. The man thudded onto the floor, his feet in high-end, almost brand-new Nikes flopping as nervedeath raced through a corpse.

Phyllis screamed, and the zombie trying to shove through the door to the ladies' was another male, this one heavyset and in a hardhat, its juicy, decomposing hands splattering against the door as it blunder-heaved. "May there be peace," Ginny gasped, jagged pieces of the string of words she'd patiently memorized the year leading up to her bat mitzvah falling higgledy-piggledy from her mouth. She skipped ahead, syllables filling her throat. "*Zichronam liv'rachah!*" Her bat clipped the side of the bright yellow hard-hat, but if she used enough force she could probably snap the cervicals.

More gunshots and yelling outside. She couldn't worry about that right now. Ginny also couldn't worry about Phyllis's screaming *or* the fact that she couldn't look everywhere at once and what if one of them was *behind* her, dear God, all she could do was pull back with the bat while the thing in the yellow hardhat grumble-ground, blindly walking into the door again. It wanted what it could hear behind the obstacle, fixated on the sound of Phyllis switching to a cavalcade of cusswords threatening to scorch the door clean off its hinges.

Ginny gasped in a breath and swung *hard*, aiming not for the bright yellow hat but right under its side. Seasoned, dripping wood met spongy jaw and splattering flesh—this zombie was older, and she was screaming the Kaddish again, her throat raw and a taste of metal along the back of her tongue.

The words were all a jumble, spilling from the year of instruction before the party and the candles and Flo's two years later, and her mother's ill-concealed relief when the lessons stopped. Dad, well, he observed a bit more than Mom did, but Mom was of the opinion that God was a sadist and not fit to be prayed to, though certain social forms had to be observed.

Would God take them both? They wouldn't like being separated.

Ginny swung again, harder this time. A greenstick snap of cervical vertebrae shearing, and the zombie, its main nerve-cable compromised, dropped like a cut puppet. "Hang on!" Ginny yelled at the door. "Just *hold on!*"

The hardhat corpse on the floor convulsed, its feet in sensible brogans leaving black streaks on linoleum. Ginny whirled, her gaze roving. How many more? And outside—good *God*, while they were sitting in the toilet talking about tampons, how many had descended upon the guys?

"Ginny!" Lee, outside, yelling. "*Ginny!*"

She couldn't see over some of the aisles. Phyllis yelled something from the other side of the door, and Ginny swung her bat a little, splattering little nasty drops. Two more shots, close together, and Ginny's heart thundered in her ears, her wrists, her throat, her ankles. All of her was a throbbing, noisy blur, and the corpse on the floor kept twitching like dead branches under a winter wind.

What next? Make a plan, get going, do something. Come on, Ginny.

Her lips moved.

She was still reciting what she could remember of Kaddish in both English and Aramaic between great galloping gulps of frigid, reeking air. If she wasn't kosher and there wasn't a minyan, would God listen? It was a fine time to be wondering about theology.

A scuffling, a high-pitched squeak, and a third zombie in a house-dress and fuzzy pink slippers somehow still clinging to arthritic, rotting feet shuffled out of the candy aisle, high fructose corn syrup and prettily packaged wax falling from shelves with little plopping sounds. Tendons made rusty squeaking sounds as the woman champed, skin splitting along her cheeks as her jaw distended and snapped shut. Muscle glared red and raw; if Ginny had a moment she could remember the exact names for the architecture of the cheeks and chin.

A tight cap of dark, permed curls clung to the woman's head, and her arms lifted as she shuffled forward, probably not dropping to all fours because the aisles were so narrow.

"May the One who creates harmony on high," Ginny recited, and stepped forward.

Crunchsplat.

[24]

SOME DOIN'

It looked like a wandering pack—a half-dozen, maybe a few more—and half of them blundered into the Marathon while the faster ones dropped to all fours and ran for Juju and Duncan, both standing guard near the pumps. It was Duncan's warning yell that brought Lee's head up, and Kasprak, helping him fuel the RV from the overflow valve, turned the color of Swiss cheese when he realized what was going on.

"Get up there," Lee said, and shoved him for the ladder to the top of the RV. "Take yo rifle. Don't take a shot unless you *got* it."

The boy scurried away, gasoline splattering as he dropped the hose. Juju had already cleared leather and was picking his own target; Duncan reached for his belt with the speed of a man who had gone through his drills over and over.

There was *definitely* some Service in that man.

Snow sprayed; Juju took his time as they bore down on him. Duncan squeezed off a shot and one of the critters stumble-staggered, splayed in the snow, and scrabbled back up. Lee got the hose cleared and hooked up his rifle, ticking off the quadrants. Couldn't afford to let any of the bastards sneak up, now.

It was then he saw the others shoving through the holes in the Marathon station's front, glass winking dully as they hopped or heaved through. One had a bright yellow hardhat, bobbing merrily.

Oh, shit. The girls had baseball bats, but—

Then, because things were never content to just be shitty, they had to go for broke, he saw another half-dozen black spots lolloping along the highway. Well, that answered one thing he'd been suspectin'—they *were* being followed. Did the things smell them, or just come along the scrapes in the snow, figuring the trail had to lead to a snack?

It didn't matter, but it would soon.

Juju's pistol barked. The closest critter folded, its head a splatter against bright white snow. Duncan swore with astonishing creativity and bagged the one he'd body-shot before, putting a round right between the fucker's eyes.

Lee settled his rifle against his shoulder, peered through the scope. Yep. Another half-dozen, coming along their trail. How fast *were* the assholes? Did they chase until they got tired or bored?

"Sonofabitch," Juju yelled, and there was a flurry of gunfire. Lee glanced back—oh, yeah, there were some more coming around the side of the building.

This was gonna take some doin', but there was only one thing on his mind.

The girls are in there. "Ginny!" Lee found himself yelling. He slung his rifle and took off across the snow like a pure-dee idiot. *"Ginny!"*

Kasprak's rifle spoke. One of the critters coming around the edge of the building spun and folded, landing in fresh feathery snow windswept over dirty, broken glass. The boy had himself a steady hand, that was for sure, and Lee heard screaming from inside the station. Juju's sidearm barked, a good clean bodyshot on another, and Lee hit the gas station's broken doors at full speed.

It was a good thing they were already jimmied open.

Ginny's mouth was moving; she tugged ineffectually on a corpse wedged against the swingin' door to the ladies'. Lee glanced at the aisles as he passed—all empty, God willin' and sonny Jesus in the crick—before arriving at her side and bending, grabbing one boot. The bones inside jean-clad flesh moved strangely, Ginny firmed her hold on the other foot, and they heaved the critter's barrel torso free just in time for Phyllis to hit the door again and stagger out, wild-eyed, clutching her flashlight and that damn pink bat. Behind her, Steph Meacham peered through the doorway, her flashlight beam bob-wobbling crazily.

Lee spun, his hand blurring for his own sidearm—better for inside work—and a bullet whined crazily against the outside of the building. The window was full of distorted, moving shadows. "Come on!" he yelled, and Ginny gained her feet in a rush. Her cheeks were dead-white except for high spots of crimson high on each, and curls sprang free of her messy braid. Her lips were moving—looked like she was praying.

He wished her luck with that, and snapped a glance at the register counter. It was just the same as it had been during his own bathroom break, the register itself upended and hacked open, cigarette cartons scattered, cans of energy drinks and pornographic magazines lying where they'd landed.

More fire outside. He wasn't worried about Juju and only a little about Duncan, but he hoped like hell that Mark Kasprak wasn't trig-ger-happy. "Group up," he yelled at the girls.

Phyllis gave him a deadly little glance, swinging her pink bat for free play, and pushed forward. "Come on!" the woman yelled, and Ginny was hard on her heels. Steph Meacham stumbled after them, leaving Lee to pick up the rear, exactly where he *didn't* want to be.

They piled out into grey, icy daylight. Phyllis let out a high, short scream like a hawk diving on a rabbit and swung her bat, splattering a cockeyed teenage male zombie with collapsed grey eyes and that hideous blue veining tattooing his face and flayed, dripping hands. She followed through, too, and Lee was getting the idea that Miss

Phyllis Lampke had done quite well by herself before Duncan or anyone else had come along.

Ginny yelled too, the cry shaping itself into a series of words he didn't have time to listen to because the ones coming around the corner of the building were massing. Juju was at work, picking off ones near the end, and it was a goddamn miracle none of Kasprak's shots—also picking off trailing ones—didn't hit anyone living.

Duncan, however, had his thinkin' cap on. He'd holstered up and grabbed a crowbar from its home in the back of Lee's truck, the tailgate down and canopy doors opened so they could stack yet more cases of bottled water inside. The stocky black-haired man grimly waded into the fray, swinging like he was aiming for the bleachers. Dark ichor spattered, and the last critter went down in a heap.

Lee's ribs heaved. *Okay. All right.* "Fuel up!" he yelled at Juju. "Get Kasprak down!"

"Yessir," Juju howled back, and took off.

"Close up the truck, Duncan, you ridin with Juju. Phyl, where you ridin?" He knew, but he wanted her thinking about that instead of some-damn-thing else.

"Driving the RV." She was already heading that direction, swinging the pink bat, scrubbing its end through a handy snowdrift. Her dark curls bounced, and her stride was that of a woman on a mission, praise Jesus and pass the goddamn butter.

"Steph, y'all get on in the RV. Ginny, you in the truck." Now he could hear Traveller yapping, and he was *damn* glad the dog had attended to his business first, while the boys did theirs. "Come on, ladies. Get goin."

"We *are*," Phyllis snapped, like a whipcrack. Ginny stood, clutching her bat, her throat working.

"Where're they all coming from?" Steph whispered. "God, where they all coming from?"

"Who knows?" Some sense came back into Ginny's dark eyes. She pushed Steph for the vehicles. "Go on, sweetie. Lee—"

Kasprak shot again. One of the dots down the road staggered and fell. Juju yelled at him to get the fuck down and help with the gasoline.

Lee grabbed Ginny's arm. His fingers sank into her jacket and he eased up, hoping he wasn't hurting her. "Truck, darlin. Let's go."

[25]

PRETTY AND

"Sonofamotherfuckin*BITCH*," Miz Phyllis said under her breath. She kept the big ol' RV steady, its chains slip-slithering as hard sleet began to finger the wide windshield. "Can't even fuckin piss in peace, the goddamn fucking zombies have to motherfuckin show up and fuckin ruin *everything*." She glared at the road, daring it to get even worse, daring the brake lights in front of her, too.

Steph's mouth was a little open. Sure, Mama could cuss when Daddy wasn't around, and Daddy himself had been able to string F-bombs with the best of 'em, but Miz Phyllis was not just angry, she was flat-out *inspired*, and she'd been goin for twenty minutes now with no sign of letup as dark clouds raced in.

Mark, up in the shotgun seat, blinked almost every time Miz Phyllis said *fuck*. It would have been funny if he hadn't been so pale. He kept his mouth shut, too, which was probably a blessing.

"And New York is fuckin *gone*," Miz Phyllis continued. "Isn't that just the way? Isn't that just the fuckin way it always fuckin goes?"

It didn't sound like she wanted an answer.

Mark twisted in the shotgun seat and glanced back at Steph.

Maybe he wanted her to say something, or he thought her ears would burn and fall off hearing what Gramma Meacham had called "strong language."

At least Steph had stopped shaking. Mostly. And at least the RV had a bathroom; she'd visited it twice. Fear made you have to pee, it looked like. She remembered something about that from middle-school health class, back in the dark ages. Your kidneys got real excited when fun times came around.

Steph's fingers almost creaked, she had them so tightly clenched. A knot of muscle and bone, two small fists that could swing a baseball bat. Some of the splatter had gotten onto her coat. Miz Ginny said they were all likely immune, though.

God, I hope she's right. "Miz Phyllis?" Steph's voice sounded very small, even to her. "Are you okay?"

"Fine," the woman snapped. "Just letting off some steam. How about you, honey?"

Well, she didn't sound mad anymore. Or at least, not *as* mad. Steph decided she might as well ask. "Uh. Does...does stuff like this make you pee a lot?" *Miz Ginny would know.*

"Yeah. Just like doing a pageant."

The more she heard about beauty pageants, the less appealing they were, even if that show with the little girl and her big potty-mouth mother had been funny. "You did a lot of those?"

"Sure did, between catalog work. Gotta practice for the big leagues." Miz Phyllis blew out between her pursed lips. "What a shitty day. What an absolute *shitter* of a day."

Mark stared out the windshield, his arms crossed high over his chest. "They's gettin smarter," he said, darkly.

"Yep." Miz Phyllis nodded. The windshield wipers rolled back and forth, icy pellets gathering at the far ends of their sweep. "Sure seems like it."

Now *there* was a hideous thought. Steph squeezed her eyelids shut, but the dark wasn't comforting. Neither was the realization that it was, well, kind of *easy* to grab your bat and smack someone. The zombies were okay to smack, but really, what was there to stop you from hitting a live person? Not even an a-hole like Mr French—and Lord was she glad he wasn't traveling with them anymore, with his nasty mouth and big shoulders—but just, say, someone who...irritated you?

"But yeah," Miz Phyllis continued. "There's always a million trips to the toilet before the catwalk starts. Getting hyped up makes your body get rid of everything so it can run quicker, I guess. And the girls on laxatives or uppers have all sorts of trouble, not to mention the pukers."

Uppers? Like drugs? Steph's eyes flew open. "Pukers?"

"Bulimics. They'll take over a stall for half an hour before the show starts, if you let 'em. The anorexics just arrange all their makeup and argue over who exercised the most and ate the least." Miz Phyllis freed one hand from the wheel to dig in her jacket pocket. "I wonder what some of them are doing now."

"Probably growling and chewing," Mark muttered.

"Yeah. Along with everyone else." Phyllis sighed. "Hey, Steph? Do me a favor, will you? My purse is down here, can you dig out my lip balm?"

"I can—" Mark began, but Steph was already unclipping her seatbelt.

"No way, kid." Miz Phyllis now sounded amused, a welcome change. "That's my *purse*. Only girls allowed in that clubhouse."

"Oh. Yeah." He subsided, and looked anxiously at Steph as she crept up to the front and picked up the brown leather bag. It had funny round rings for handles, and there was a fancy buckle in the shape of two Cs facing opposite directions on the front. The leather was butter-soft, too, and the inside was ruthlessly neat except for a battered paperback. *Ulysses*, the blue and white cover said. It looked Very Serious, like a book Miz Ginny would know about.

"It's pink," Phyllis said.

"Found it." Steph dug out a small, very expensive-looking plastic ball. The top half screwed off, so she loosened it. The label said *Rose Attar*, in gold foil. "You want the cap all the way off?"

"Sure."

Funny. Miz Phyllis didn't *look* like a reader. She looked like one of the girls in class who got a nerd to do their homework, then flipped their hair and joined the cheerleading squad. Steph studied the woman's balanced profile, her poreless skin. How could someone be so pretty and read something serious at the same time? Or did she carry the book for another reason?

Miz Ginny was pretty, too, but not like Miz Phyllis. Just looking at Ginny was enough to tell you she was Very Serious even if you didn't know she was a librarian. It was just something about her, though right now she was looking darn worn-out.

She had reason, God knew. And that was one of Mama's pet phrases too. *They got reason*, she'd say darkly, when someone did somethin' bad that couldn't be avoided.

"Thanks, sweetie." Phyllis handed the balm back. "You can use some too, if you don't have a cold sore."

"I'm good." Steph capped the balm and put it back in its place. Maybe, if they ever went to another bookstore, she'd look for that Ulysses book, and give it a try.

There was no reason you couldn't be pretty and serious, or pretty and swing a baseball bat hard enough to crunch a zombie's head in. And if you were serious, or could swing a bat, maybe you could learn makeup and be pretty, too.

Steph closed up the purse and went back to her seat. The shakes had gone away, and the unsteady feeling. The world was bigger and scarier than she'd ever dreamed, yeah.

But maybe, just maybe, Steph was too.

DOWN EASY

"Didja see the ones chasin us?" Juju shook his head, his sculpted lips tight. "Man, I don't like that. I don't like it at *all*."

There were a whole lot of things not to like about the whole damn world at this point. Duncan's hands hurt, and his right side did too. He'd gone a little crazy with the crowbar, and his sinuses ached from the change in barometric pressure. "Where did those fuckers come from?" One moment, everything was fine, the next, there were fucking deaders spilling around the corner of the brick gas station like greyhounds let out of the gates.

Just chasing a facsimile of a rabbit, that's all. Galloping along, chewing all the way.

"Dunno. Maybe they heard the cars. Smelled us. Christ." Juju was none too pleased, but even with a line between his eyebrows and a ferocious scowl he was handsome. "Prolly heard us. They don't see too well."

"Yeah, I figgered." If Duncan made fists, the tiny tremors in the middle of his bones wouldn't show. Just as usual—stiffen up, and nobody saw the weakness. Hold yourself tight and strong, so nobody guessed you were fuckin' shittin' peach pits. "Nice shootin there, Thurgood." Was that too much?

"Hey, you did all right yourself, Harris." The scowl eased, a slight smile pulling at Juju's sculpted lips. "Crowbar was a good idea."

Met a few guys who swore by them. A warm glow lit in Duncan's middle. "Just handy," he said, shyly. "Figured it was better for close-up, that's all."

It had started to sleet; at least Lee's truck was doing the majority of snow-moving. The heavier this mess got, the more likely the plywood plows would fail. Of course, they were heading south. If they could just get out of this weather, they could toss the plows and only have to worry about a thousand other hazards.

"Man, I wish I still smoked." Juju bit at his fingertips to loosen his gloves and peeled them off. The engine had warmed, and even though there were trickles of wet chill from outside, the vents were blowing in baked air to beat the band. "Used to be the best goddamn thing about comin back from patrol. Light a stick and all the trouble just poof! Bye."

"Yeah." Duncan couldn't unclench his own fingers enough to get his gloves off, but that was fine. He could look at Juju's clean profile, or at the man's capable brown hands on the wheel. Duncan's skin was alive, both from the fight and from the nearness. "That and a cold beer."

Juju made a short affirmative noise. Even his chapped knuckles were just right, strong and rough, his fingertips surprisingly delicate. "Only if'n it's real cold, though."

"Nothin worse than a warm one." What Duncan really wanted was a fifth of something amber-colored and hard as nails. "Unless that's all you got."

"Shot of whiskey might go down easy, too." Juju grinned, startling white teeth, his cheeks bunching up. The pompom on his hat bobbed a little as the Jeep swayed.

It was like the man was reading his mind. Could he tell? Duncan hated guessing, but it was all he had. "Or more than one."

"Gotta say, I'm right glad to have you and Miz Phyllis along." Juju loosened up on the steering wheel enough to scratch at his cheek. "You right handy."

"Glad to *be* along." *You can't know how glad.* Was he into Phyllis? Trying to find out if Duncan was? The man didn't *seem* to watch her, but you could hide all sorts of things, if you just practiced long enough. "Don't think I've ever seen someone use a sidearm like that. You're a crack shot."

"Long as I ain't no *cracker* shot." Juju started to laugh, and the sound was music. Duncan couldn't help but chuckle too, and finally, finally his fingers stopped wanting to curl up or shake. The big muscles in his legs relaxed too, and he could feel his toes again.

It was getting on to evening, the sky was a flat iron pan dribbling sleet and hurt onto everything below, but as far as Duncan Harris was concerned, the day was looking up.

[27]

WORRYIN LOOK

It was in Allentown that Ginny had her first real sleep since Saratoga, probably a function more of exhaustion than any real relaxation. Lee had decided to keep them well west of both New York and Philadelphia, which meant they spent less time threading through clogged checkpoints but more time scraping at thinning snow with the makeshift plywood plows.

Brief, pale golden sunlight spilled through a French door, and Ginny had to sit for a few moments, clutching thin blankets and two unzipped sleeping bags to her chest, before she remembered where she was. The other half of the bed had obviously been used, but the Motel 6 room was empty except for that wintery sunshine. Her ribs ached, especially on the right, and it was too cold.

For a moment, she was simply waking up from a nightmare. Maybe God had looked down and said, *crap, I spilled something, let me rewind that.* She was on her way to see her parents, to help with the birth of her niece or nephew, soothe Mom's ruffled feathers, hold her nose and drink a whiskey with her father late at night after Mom was in bed.

For a single, precious moment everything was fine, the world put back in its usual track and sleepy relief exploding behind her thundering heart.

Then her long shuddering exhale turned to a puff of white vapor, Traveller leapt into her lap with a wiggle and a thrashing tail, and the bathroom door swung open. Lee stepped out, scrubbing at his hands with a small white motel towel; he halted, seeing her awake. A hot thread of burning wax was probably a candle lit inside said bathroom so she didn't have to carry a flashlight.

It was just the sort of detail he'd take care of. On the one hand, it was comforting. On the other, well, maybe she would have liked a few more moments of thinking the world was normal again.

Or it just might have made the jolt worse when she realized there were no takebacks, no mopping up of the mess, no rewind. Ever. God was asleep and the world was spinning out of control.

Traveller licked at her face in an ecstasy of greeting. *You're up,* he yip-yowled, and his nails dug through sleeping bags, hotel comforter, blanket, and sheet. *You're finally awake! Let's do fun things!*

Lee was freshly shaven, his jeans buttoned and zipped but his belt loose—no holster yet. A clean green Army T-shirt under a new flannel button-down, his old leather vest unbuttoned too. His coat was neatly folded on the dresser across the room, other things laid in their proper places, and the gun itself was on the nightstand, carefully pointed away from the bed.

Lee looked at her, his eyes dark and his hair curling stubbornly. His capable hands dropped, the towel hanging limp.

Ginny cleared her throat. Traveller slid off her lap with a thump, landing belly-up, begging for a good rub along his undercarriage, and she began scratching gently as the dog wriggled with glee. "Hi."

"Hi." Lee studied her, anxiously. "You slept."

"I did." *Try not to sound surprised, Ginny.* She scrubbed the dog's chest with her fingertips. The burnt-iron taste of morning filled her mouth; her throat was dry. "You?"

"Ayuh." A slow nod. Why was he watching her like that? Trying to figure out if she was going to break down and start screaming? "You didn't even move when I went on watch."

"I'm sorry." A quick, reflexive apology. Old habits died hard, even if civilization had slid under with barely a ripple.

"You needed it, darlin." He folded the towel into thirds without looking. "How you feelin?"

Shitty, thanks. "Fine." God, this was awkward. Traveller had stopped yowling, but he was still a-wriggle all over her lap. He licked his chops, long pink tongue flickering. "I guess. You?"

Lee's expression didn't change. "Worried."

Well, that was a reasonable response to the situation. "About?"

"Just our route. Nothin big."

"Except yesterday," she prompted. "That was pretty big."

He finished folding the towel. "Yeah, well. Just have to be careful." Still, his mouth was drawn a little too tightly.

Maybe she was beginning to be able to read him. It didn't take much, just paying attention. "Either they're getting smarter or they're following us." Ginny smoothed Traveller's fur. "Right?"

"Shoulda known you'd think of that." A wry ghost of a smile, and morning light picked out sparse golden highlights in his hair. At least his irises hadn't paled.

"Or maybe they're just getting hungrier, and the stronger ones are surviving." Which was not comforting at all. "But there *were* some following us yesterday."

"Prolly lose em when the snow starts meltin." And that, apparently, was that. "You want some coffee? Tea?"

Caffeine sounded like a wonderful idea. Ginny braced herself. "How about a good morning kiss?"

Small comfort that his face lit up, worry-lines easing and a shy, disbelieving grin pulling up the corners of his mouth, tugging on her heart. Small comfort, too, that he hurried across the room with a long swinging stride, and didn't seem to mind that he'd brushed his teeth and she hadn't. Small comfort that he cupped the back of her head and closed his eyes, that he was gentle, and that he smelled like citrus, leather, and safety.

Tiny comforts, yes. But they still helped, and when the kiss faded he rested his forehead against hers and Ginny had another crazy moment of thinking maybe the world was all right, if not normal. Traveller thrashed, wanting to get between the humans and soak up any attention and stray pets to be had.

Lee folded down and ended up sitting on the bed, pushing the hound's snout aside and peering into her face. "You got that worryin look too."

There was certainly plenty to be worried about, and now that she'd had some sleep she was fresh and ready to begin again, so to speak. "What if we get to Atlanta and nobody's there?"

"Then we find a place to settle for winter, and in spring we start headin west." He sounded certain, at least. It was another relief that he'd obviously thought about that particular contingency. "California's best, I reckon. Specially if it's worldwide."

I'm not sure I want to go back to the West Coast. "Yeah." She rubbed at her bare shoulders, her tank top straps loose. As diets went, this one was a doozy. "I just...how are we even going to do this, Lee?"

"One thing at a time. Same way as everthin else." He laid the towel down and took her left hand with warm fingers. Looked at her palm, running his fingertips over the hollow, calluses rasping. "That day they shot up the diner, you was fixin to head out, weren't you." It wasn't a question.

"You knew that." Her shoulders hunched. It was too cold outside the nest of covers, gooseflesh spilling down her back.

"Wouldn't've done no good." He went right for what worried her most, with unerring accuracy. "You'd'a been too late then, too. They was down a while, Ginny."

That meant Flo had been handcuffed to the bed for...God, she didn't want to think about that. "I don't know," she whispered. "I should have left the last time my mom called. I didn't get to the phone, and I—"

"Sweetheart." He folded her fingers in, carefully leaving her thumb outside. Making a fist, wrapping his own hands around it. "That ain't no way to think. No way of knowin they was gonna be *zombies*, Christ Jesus. Don't eat yo'self up bout it."

Did he understand how helpless she was *not* to? "I should have left right away."

"And got yourself bit, or shot. Sure."

Well, that was reasonable, but still. The idea that maybe it would have been what she deserved didn't bear mentioning. "Maybe I would've been able to—"

"Ain't no way of knowin," he interrupted. "You're alive *now*, Ginny. I aim to keep it that way."

Well, she should be grateful. Instead, she felt like a monster. She hadn't even dreamt of Fran; a good sister would have nightmares, right? Here Ginny was, kissing a man she wouldn't have looked at twice back in Cotton Crossing because he drawled and had laborer's hands. Here was Ginny, a shallow, spoiled, selfish little girl who had let her mother's last call go to voicemail.

And shot her undead, rotting sister in the head. Just yesterday, she'd beaten more of the sick, the infected, to death. How could she be so damn relieved when Lee brought out the comforting platitudes?

"I'm not a very nice person," she murmured, staring at her hand cradled in both of his. *Plus, I'm a coward.* "I'm really not."

"You do what you gotta, Ginny." He squeezed her hand, gently. "Let me do the rest, aight?"

It was seductive to think you could evade responsibility. People did it all the time. It was just awful to find out you, personally, weren't any different. "It's all right." She pasted on a reassuring smile. "I was just thinking about it, that's all. I should get ready, we've got a long way to go today."

"We'll letcha get started then, darlin." He still looked worried, but he let go of her hand, kissed her forehead, and scooped Traveller up, settling him gently on the ground. "Come on, hound."

[28]

UNFULFILLED DREAMS

THE MOTEL 6'S LOBBY WAS DIM AND DANK, BUT ALIVE WITH movement. It was a beautiful morning, even if she was in Pennsylvania; Phyllis stretched to one side, then the other, and accepted a travel mug of hot cocoa from Steph. The girl put three Swiss Miss packets in where one would do, but Phyl had to admit it tasted really good. Not as good as coffee, but the thick black brew the guys made was simply tar in a cup, no substitute for a decent macchiato.

"Flooding," Juju said again, and shook his head mournfully. His hair was growing out, beginning to halo with a vengeance, and it looked good when he wasn't crushing it with that pompom hat. "Goddammit."

"Well, better than snow. Or that sleet." Duncan peered out the wide glass doors, a thoughtful cast to his tight mouth. His cheeks were pretty rosy this morning, and his forehead gleamed damply. He was probably warm—a blue knitted scarf dangled on either side of his chest, a nice wide one. "Looks messy out there. Rained all night."

That was the good news. The parking lot past the shade of a metal awning was full of shining hillocks of soggy snow and widening patches of wet concrete under a migraine attack of morning sunshine.

The less snow, the better—but this soggy stuff would probably break the plywood plows, given half a chance.

"We won't be able to see them as easy," Phyl said, and took a scalding sip of chocolate. Zombies showed up far better against snow.

"Yeah." Ginny, still hollow-eyed but with her hair braided and sturdily pinned down, held a mug of tea in both graceful hands. A thin gold bracelet glittered, peeking from under her coat cuff. "But if they're following the tire tracks...I don't know. There's just not enough data."

"They can hear, but not see." Phyl sighed. Her imagination was working overtime, and each prospect it dug up was worse than the last. "Engine noise?"

"Maybe, or maybe the vibrations. Or like bats." Ginny's shudder made her teabag-tag sway. "Echolocation. But maybe not smell, since they're so...I mean, they're juicy anyway. Mucus production might interfere, unless there's been changes in the nasal receptors."

"Let's just assume they've got super-hearing, for now." Phyllis gave her a small sidelong look, inhaling the cocoa-heat gratefully. "Med school, huh?"

"Yeah." The other woman stared somberly into her tea. Her hair looked heavy, wrapped and pinned down like that. "Some days I wish I'd stayed in."

It sounded like a lot of bodily fluids, harassment, and sleep deprivation to Phyllis. Still, medical knowledge was damn useful now. "My grandma wanted me to be a lawyer."

Ginny's sympathetic glance spoke volumes. "Living out unfulfilled dreams?"

That was one way to put it, though it was more likely Granny wanted safety and a good salary for her little Philly-bear. "You bet. She was *so* pissed when I wanted to model. I told her I could strip to get through law school, too." Phyl shook her head, an unwilling smile cracking the corners of her lips. *That* conversation had been a barrel-of-monkeys fun.

Ginny's laugh was thin, tired, and completely genuine. "I'll bet that went over well."

"Yeah, well. I'm just glad she went before...all this." *Great. Good one, Phyl.* She glanced at the other woman, but Ginny didn't take offense.

"I understand." Ginny tried a sip of her tea and grimaced a little. "Ouch."

"What I wouldn't give for a Starbucks." *I wouldn't even mind sharing a table.*

Ginny sighed, a companionable sound. "A hot shower."

"Central heating." Phyllis decided the other woman needed just a touch of smoky eyeliner, and some nice neutral shadow. The big star would be her mouth, a slightly darker shade of lipstick than Ginny would likely be comfortable with.

It would be nice to get out her makeup kit and give it a try. On Steph, too. They could do it in the RV, make the guys go somewhere else for the night. She wondered if the girls would go for it.

"A salad," Ginny said.

Oh, man, that was a good one. "Sushi."

"A functioning classical music station." The librarian stared into the parking lot. "Uh-oh."

Phyl followed her gaze. There was something stirring across the parking lot, winter-denuded bushes shaking. "Could be an animal."

"Yeah." But Ginny didn't look away, and neither did Phyllis, now. "I just...huh."

Phyl's jaw threatened to drop. Two zombies boiled out of the bushes, one in a strappy bright red dress that swirled around wasted, blue-veined legs. On hands and feet, with that quick scuttering sideways motion, both streaked across the lot, going straight through piles of snow, their palms slapping on bare wet concrete. The second zombie was in wet jeans, bare-chested, wasted breasts flapping against ribs as it scuttled.

"What are they...oh. Oh, my God." Ginny sucked in a small, wounded breath. "No."

They were after, of all things, a cat. An orange and white feline, its tail bottle-brushed up and ears flattened, streaked low and quick from the shelter of a round concrete divider, making for another row of bushes. "Keep going," Phyllis found herself saying. "Oh, Lord, keep going." It was a good thing the dog was nose-down in his food bowl, or he'd probably be barking his idiot head off.

"What is it?" Lee's hand closed around Ginny's shoulder, and the other woman leaned back on her heels a little. Leaning into him. Must be nice. "Shit. Critters."

"They're after—" Ginny stopped, her tea-mug sloshing. "No, not that way." As if the cat could hear and understand.

Another zombie—a balding one in overalls and wet workboots—rose from a screen of bushes on the left side of the lot and lolloped forward, amazingly quick. The one in the red dress put on a burst of speed, but the cat veered away, darting past two cars that had been merely humps of snow last night. One, a nice red Dodge, hung open on the driver's side. The cat scurried underneath it, and the red-dress zombie went down, trying to squirm-wriggle under the vehicle as well, blue-tinged bare-flayed feet kicking.

"Good thing we parked around the side," Lee muttered. "Come on, ladies. Let's not give em any ideas, huh?"

"They're chasing cats." Ginny sounded horrified. "And working together."

"Can't we do something?" Phyl disliked cats on principle—oh, they were okay as other people's pets, but clawing and the peeing was not for her.

Still, the poor thing didn't deserve to be…eaten.

"We got all we can handle." Lee, ruthless, drew Ginny back. "Come on. Get outa the door."

The red-dress zombie kicked again, struggling under the car. The cat shot away from the front end, making for the side of the building, and the other two zombies had thrown themselves down and were trying to wriggle under the Dodge as well.

"Come on." Lee drew Ginny back, and after a few moments, Phyllis followed.

At least the cat had gotten away. But the zombies had been working together, even if they weren't very bright and would probably get stuck under the car.

Phyl didn't like the way this looked.

She didn't like it at *all*.

[29]

LIFTOFF

The roads were clearer, and they kept the stops to a minimum. No more shooting practice, just getting into a gas station or convenience store, using a bathroom, stripping what they could from shelves, and getting out. A big blue and yellow Bargain Zone just over the Maryland border gave them more walkie-talkies; Duncan could fiddle them into talking to the ones they already had. Ginny went through the pharmacy with a list in one of her little note-books, Steph and Mark pillaged the grocery and frozen section, Phyllis gathered spare clothing, wool blankets, and replenished their bottled water stocks.

The front of the store was smashed, a big old half-ton Dodge crumpled against large concrete pylons meant to stop folks from drivin' right on in, and one of the side doors along an ugly, unpainted side of the building had been jimmied too. Whoever had come through had taken some of the water, plenty of paper products, and about cleaned out the sodapop aisle.

It took a few trips to get everything loaded, in a thin driving rain warmer than snow but still miserable. Lee and Juju, standing on guard, were both soaked by the time Duncan came through carrying a load of bottled water and Traveller barked, weaving between ankles and generally making a nuisance of himself.

"In with you," Ginny said, and boosted the dog into the truck. She was about to swing the door closed, her hand on his scruff to keep him from popping back out like a jack-in-the-box, when Juju let out a yell.

"Incoming!"

Lee's head jerked up, his gaze snagging on movement milling at the far end of an empty expanse of parking spaces, deep in a forest of lot-lights marching in regimented rows. This Bargain Zone was set near a dead, darkened mini-mall, and it looked like they were coming from the buffet restaurant at the end.

There was no time to be grimly amused at that little detail; he merely noted it and exhaled sharply, alternatives clicking through his head lightning-fast.

Duncan hefted the case into the back of the truck, pushing it past Steph's ankles as the girl worked her magic on sorting and tying supplies down. "Get in the four-by," he snapped, running the back of his hand under his nose to clear the drips, and she gave him an *I know* look that could have cut right through him.

Juju yelled again, and his rifle barked. "Lee!"

Lee swung around. *Shit.* Those weren't the critters Juju had been warning of; a tight-knit group of five was staggering from the front of the building, probably drawn by the damn dog's yapping. One stumbled and went down hard, curling around Juju's shot to its midriff. "Got em," he said. "Others at our five o'clock, too."

"Shit." Juju drew another bead, exhaled, and fired again. Another critter dropped, its head a splattered mess. The rest of the group didn't seem to notice, but the biggest one shifted to hands-and-feet, and they began lolloping. *"Shit."*

At first, Lee thought Juju's shots were echoing strangely, some trick of acoustics without snow dragging the noises down. Then he realized it wasn't that.

The other shots were coming from *inside* the Bargain Zone.

Ginny slammed the truck's passenger door to trap Traveller, and had the presence of mind to grab her baseball bat, too. She realized where the noises were coming from the same moment he did, and her eyes widened. She broke into a run, heading for the door, and Lee swore again.

Mark and Phyllis were still inside.

IT HAPPENED SO *FAST*.

"Get down!" Mark yelled, and Phyllis threw herself full-length. A bright-white muzzleflash in the crazy, flashlight-stabbed darkness, and the zombie's head splattered. Cold droplets touched Phyllis's hair, and she let out a furious sound interrupted halfway when Mark leaned down, grabbed her arm with surprising strength, and hauled her back upright. Her bat was dripping—she'd taken down the two that almost got him, and now he was returning the favor.

Nice of him; she forgave him every damn bit of irritation he'd ever caused in that one moment.

Jesus, they're everywhere. The growling had warned her—the bastards just couldn't be quiet when there was a meal in sight. It was kind of funny, how the one at the end of the Housewares aisle scuttled forward, then crashed into a display of dishes when Mark shot it. Brittle, heat-tortured clay shattered. Phyl pushed past, her shoulder hitting his, and double-tapped one in a leather motorcycle jacket, half its jaw hanging free but the other half working with that awful metronomic regularity. The teeth were still white, even if the rest of the bone was discolored, and two popped out when she brought the pink bat down the second time, tinkling across linoleum.

"Cleanup on aisle three," she husked.

A short, high-pitched laugh escaped Mark. He gulped in a deep breath afterward, and leaned his slim young weight against her back. "Which way?"

Well, he was thinking, at least, and had the sense to ask. She pointed her bat. "This way, then right near the hardware section. Got to get to the door. Warn the others."

"Yes ma'am." Either he was shaking, or she was. Or both of them, democratically. This place was a giant warehouse, every shadowed aisle holding danger. "I'm ready."

Phyllis's ribs heaved. "Okay. *Go.*" She took off, darting across a long walkway leading past housewares, and he staggered after her, shooting a zombie leaping from an aisle of trashcans and liners. It dropped but kept scrabbling, and another bullet whined down the aisle, exploding a high-end silvery step-can.

"Be *careful!*" Phyllis yelled.

"I am!" he yelled back, right behind her. "*Run!*"

She jagged left, cutting down an aisle full of laundry hampers and the weird chemical scent of holiday sachets, swelling in the damp but still fragrant. *We missed Thanksgiving,* she realized, and was grateful she wasn't wearing heels. Running away from these bastards in wedges would be awful.

A shadow loomed to her right, she swung the bat with a jolt and more weird, goopy non-blood sprayed. Mark shot the thing, too, and there were dancing shadows in front of her now.

"They're in front of us," he yelled, and Phyllis shook her bat as she ran, a deep guttural warcry rising from the pit of her belly.

Splatboomcrunch, her boots skidding in sudden fetid slickness, Mark hauling her aside and shooting in one motion, the flashlight's glow bouncing, they made it to the hardware section and turned hard right, her heels leaving black streaks on the linoleum—probably buffed nightly by a guy named Jerry who had gotten bit by his wife at home, good God, why would her brain not stop serving up hilarious inconsequentials—and there was the door, black shadows against bright yellow sunshine, and she was screaming her fool head off while she ran.

"Keep going!" Mark howled. "Keep going keep going *keep going!*"

She did. She was prepared for liftoff, she had her afterburners on, she didn't even bother to hit the zombie coming from the left because that would slow her down, dear God and sonny Jesus as her Granny used to say—

Sunlight. A burst of cold air. She almost dropped the flashlight, meaning to skip sideways and see if Mark cleared the door...

...when something hit her from behind, and Phyllis went down, *hard*. Her forehead bounced against concrete, her hands unable to stop her fall, and she was unconscious when the zombies spilling from the door swarmed her.

[30]

BLACKBERRY TANGLE

"Nooooo!" Steph almost broke free of Duncan, who dragged her back and grimly shoved her towards the 4x4.

Juju, his cheeks ashen, took careful aim. The critters swarmed like ants—growling, snapping ants—and he was hoping the woman was out cold. He squeezed the trigger and one of them fell crumpled, its head a mess like a punkin with a firecracker shoved inside.

Mark Kasprak staggered, trying to throw off the critter hugging his back. Its head tipped, then it struck snake-quick, nuzzling under his ear. The boy's high, breaking scream was lost in a hideous crunch as his legs tangled and he went down too. They clustered him like a high-school health movie of immune cells attacking an invader.

"*Nooooooo!*" Steph howled again, and Duncan, a fine sheen of sweat on his reddened face, bundled her into the back of the four-by like she was a suitcase. He got her knees in, slammed the door, and snapped a glance over his shoulder at Juju.

"Come on!" Harris bellowed. "Come the fuck *on*, Thurgood!"

Juju backed up, a fast, light shuffle. Lee's rifle cracked, and one of the things that wasn't clustering the fallen went down in a mess of shattered head and flying black blood. The rest didn't look up from their meal, and the ones spilling from the side door went down on all fours and started to worm their way into the scrum.

"Load up!" Lee called.

Juju broke and ran for the four-by. Duncan was already piling in on the driver's side, and Steph's hands were white starfish against the back driver's-side window. Her mouth was open, and he couldn't hear her screaming, but he *did* hear the crunch-slurping, the groan-deep, grinding growls.

Neither Mark nor Phyllis made another noise. And Lord help him, Juju wanted to go back and give them a cleaner end, because thinking of Mark Kasprak shuffling around with chunks of him gone and his eyes collapsing and the flesh drippin' off his hands wasn't right. None of this was *right* but dear Lord and sonny Jesus, not the boy, not the goddamn *boy*.

Lee shot again, downing another one taking more of an interest in ambulatory prey than the downed ones. Juju's Lieutenant was backing up nice and easy, working the rifle, and his face was as white as Juju had ever seen it.

Which was saying something.

The rain intensified, sweeping across the filthy bastards and their meal. *Must've come in through the front door, got that truck there.* It didn't matter now, but he was willing to bet money that was what happened. Juju almost ran into his four-by. Duncan was in the driver's seat, so he had to get *around* the car, and Juju's legs were working through the clotted syrup of nightmares.

Ginny had Lee's truck running. The back was closed up, thank Jesus, and the dog's frantic barks barely made it out of a sliver-lowered window. There were more shuffling, scooching, wetly crunching sounds, and Juju wrenched at the passenger door of the black four-by, threw himself in. "Go! Go, for God's sake, go!"

Lee squeezed off a shot, standing on the passenger-side runnin' board of his truck. The rifle worked again and another bullet cracked air. Some of the critters were losing interest in the downed meat. Why the fuck was Lee still shootin?

Juju peered around Duncan, his ribs heaving, the rest of him occupied stowing the rifle with the ease of long habit. Out of the seething mass of critters, Mark Kasprak's upflung hand was a bird trying to flee a blackberry tangle, and another shot crackled.

Mark's hand jerked, fingers spread wide, before falling.

Steph sob-screamed, her hands still flat on the window. At least she wasn't banging on it, they didn't need broken glass what with the rain coming down.

"Oh, fuck, fuck, *fuck*," Duncan moaned, hitting the gas and coughing. The four-by lurched, cutting a wide arc around the RV, and the walkie-talkie crackled. Lee, checking in, and now Juju knew why he'd kept pulling the trigger.

Shitty way to die, he kept thinking. *Christ Jesus, I hope he got em. I hope he got em both.* Juju heard himself, calmly enough, giving call-sign and relaying their heading. A man didn't rise to the occasion, he sank to the level of his training, and Juju should have taught the kid better. Should have suggested putting a watch on that shattered front door. Should have done something, *anything*.

Too late now. What a shitty, shitty way to die.

Duncan palmed at his wet cheeks and coughed again, taking the turn out of the Bargain Zone parking lot a little too fast. "Son of a bitch," he kept whispering. "Son of a *bitch*."

Steph rested her forehead on the window, and her gulping sobs punctuated the passionless recital, back and forth, of the living on the walkie-talkies.

[31]

JUST GET ME

THE RAIN THICKENED AS THEY DROVE SOUTH UNCHAINED, switching off point every hour. Creeping through clots of abandoned cars at major interchanges, plenty with doors hanging slackjaw-open, they made good time, and when they stopped on the outskirts of Bridgewater for more fuel, Steph was silent and red-eyed. The girl didn't bother looking over her shoulder or jumping when a stray roll of thunder sounded in the distance as they hurried into a closed, pristine mom-and-pop gas station with a sign proclaiming BEER CIGA-RETTES MAGAZINES and an ice machine hanging open near the front door.

Ginny was doing enough jumping for the both of them. Lee had sat for a long time, silent and staring out the passenger window, his rifle clasped loosely, not even pushing Traveller's nose away when the dog tried vainly to comfort him.

Steph, her hair a wild mess since she kept scrubbing her hands through, tugging at the braids, and the humidity was skyrocketing, refused to go into the bathroom stall alone. She just shook her head and stared mutely, pleadingly at Ginny.

"All right." Ginny leaned against the door with her gaze averted, her flashlight beam bouncing off tiles and casting crazy reflections on ceiling tiles already swelling with dampness.

It took so little time for everything to begin to rot. Buildings. People. Ginny's head ached, and she didn't dare meet her reflection's wild, wounded gaze.

Steph sniffled and blew her nose while she peed. Ginny couldn't decide if it was time-sharing or multitasking, and closed her eyes for a moment. The darkness behind her lids was worse than seeing the flyspotted mirror and the spreading yellow stain on the ceiling tiles, so she opened them again.

The old Ginny wouldn't have wanted anyone in the bathroom while she took her turn at the commode. The old Ginny would have been still been screaming, or would have tried to keep Lee from doing...what he'd done. The old Ginny would have flat-out refused to sit on the toilet seat, forcing herself to hover.

That woman, however, was long gone. Maybe she'd died back in that hotel room when Ginny thought she had the zombie flu, or maybe she'd vanished gently, eroding bit by bit. It didn't matter.

At least the pipes hadn't frozen down here; what a difference a few hundred miles could make. She washed her hands with the harsh pink soap clinging to the bottom of the dispenser, and didn't tell Steph to wash *hers*. What was the point? The icy faucet-trickle made her fingers ache, and she dabbed some of it onto her forehead.

She was sweating inside her jacket. Fever, or just stress? If there wasn't anything in Atlanta but zombies, what on earth were they going to do?

None of us are going to survive this. It's impossible. We'll be picked off one by one. She shivered, avoiding her own gaze in the cheap mirror, and motioned Steph out.

When they came out of the bathroom, a glitter-eyed, stiff-walking Duncan went in. Lee and Juju were conferring near the glass front door, Juju leaning forward and pushing his index finger into his opposite palm, Lee shaking his head slightly, his eyes narrowed.

"Let's look at the candy aisle," Ginny said, and Steph made no demur, just put her head down and followed. "Maybe they have Pop Tarts."

Steph just shook her head, a little. She ran her hands through her hair again, scratching at her scalp, turning thin fine hair into a nest. He coat, unzipped, flapped loosely. One of her boots was untied, the laces making little whipping sounds as she moved.

Oh, honey. Ginny's heart squeezed down on itself. How much more of this could the girl take? How much more could *any* of them take? "Let's look, anyway."

"He told me to go on out." Steph stopped in the middle of the aisle, her gaze fixed on her toes. Rainy sunshine filtered through the windows, glass painted with soapy color—a turkey, an ear of corn, a certain percentage off cigarettes. "Said I was good at organizin the truck."

Ginny's throat filled up. "You certainly are." She realized, staring at the painted window, that they'd missed Thanksgiving while traveling. It was a colonialist holiday, sure...but oh, God.

"Why'd he have to stay inside?" Steph finally turned, looked directly at Ginny, and her reddened eyes glowed with tears. "Why? Why they have to get him and Miz Phyllis, too? She was nice."

"Yes. She was." There was nothing else to say. It was all a crapshoot, all of adulthood was and this just made it official. How did you tell a teenage girl that when she'd just seen two people...well, *eaten*, right in front of her? "They both were."

Steph stared like Ginny was speaking classical Greek. "Why it ha'to be *him*, huh?" Her accent thickened, and both her eyes overflowed. She wiped angrily at her already raw cheeks, and stamped her foot. The laces whipped again. "Why?"

"It doesn't make sense." *God, please, I wish I knew what to say.* Ginny bent her knees, and began to work on Steph's untied boot. It only took a moment to double-knot. "None of this does. I know."

"But why *him*? He wa'nt mean. He punched Carty, yeah, but he...he didn't even *try* anything funny after my mama...my mama..."

Steph ran out of words. Her mouth worked for a moment, and Ginny straightened, reached for her shoulder.

She meant to hug Steph, but the girl shied violently away, her hand hitting a box of Reese's and scattering orange-wrapped ersatz peanut butter onto the floor.

"Why din't they get *me*?" Steph tipped her chin back and yelled at the ceiling. "I wish they'd just *get* me!"

"Honey. No." Ginny stepped forward, tried again to catch and hug her. "No, you don't."

Steph flung her arms out. This time, it was M&Ms from one side of the aisle and a bag of circus peanuts from the other, fleeing sudden violence. They plopped onto the floor, tiny dispirited packages. "The hell I don't!"

Oh, honey. Ginny searched for something to say. "That's a normal response, Steph—"

"What about this is gatdamn normal?" the girl wailed, and her hands were fists now, swinging in short, angry arcs. "I wish they'd take me! I wish they'd come right now and take me!"

"Jesus Christ, girl." Duncan appeared at the other end of the aisle, his face damp and his eyes reddened. His hair was a mess, too; looked like he'd ducked under the faucet. "I heard you all the way in the bathroom. You want us to have visitors, huh?"

Steph yelped and spun, and Ginny winced.

"Keep it down," Juju whisper-yelled from the door. "For God's sake."

"I ain't *gonna!*" Steph's fists dropped to her sides, and her cheeks gleamed slick-wet. "I ain't gonna keep it down, I hope they come and eat every last one o'us! I hope we all *die!*"

"Yes, well, this *is* a democracy." Ginny put her palms on her hips, searching for the right words. None sprang to mind. "And your vote has been registered. Come on, kiddo. Let's get something to snack on."

"That's best." Lee stepped into the aisle behind Ginny, and his tone was businesslike. Calm. "We ain't stoppin until Atlanta less'n it's to get fuel."

Great. Ginny suppressed a sigh. *Did they suffer? Phyllis went down pretty hard.* She hoped they were both unconscious, and God knew Lee was probably feeling awful right now, too. But they *had* to get going. "Okay? Come on, sweetie. I know it's hard, I really—"

"Shut up! Just shut up!" Steph turned in a full circle, and Duncan, behind her, folded his arms. He looked over Ginny's shoulder at Lee, and God how Ginny hated that little eyebrow-quirk. *Women,* his expression said, plainly.

"I'd like to," Ginny tried again, grimly. "I really would. But we're alive right now, Steph, and we've got to stay that way. We can't let them win." *They're going to anyway.* The sudden certainty turned her insides cold and loose, but there was no way she was going back into that bathroom.

"They done already won." But Steph's birdlike shoulders deflated. She hunched, small and very young, and her chapped nose glistened as well as her cheeks. "Why'd he hafta do that, Ginny? Why?"

Why the fuck are you asking me? "Sometimes things just happen." Oh, she could lie, maybe, but Ginny was too tired. Her throat was full of a suspicious, heavy weight, and if she slowed down to think about any of this she was going to start sobbing, too, and that was the last thing Steph needed. So she drove her fingernails, two of them broken, into her bare palms, glad she wasn't wearing gloves for once. "None of it *should,* but it does."

"We've gotta go." Juju, near the door, had no patience for philosophical debate. He stood, tense and jaw-clenched, and there was a terrible emptiness to his dark gaze. "Come on, my back teeth're floatin."

"You don't even care." All the fire had gone out of Steph. "None of you do."

"That's not so." Soothing, quiet, careful, Ginny shook out her right hand. Held it out, open and cupped. *Please, Steph. Come on.* "You know that's not true."

"It is so." The girl pushed past her, and ran her shoulder into Lee. He didn't stagger, but he did let her squeeze past, and she stalked for the glass door, her wet boots making little slippery sounds. Ginny followed, her stomach a knot, but at least Steph didn't do anything silly like run.

Instead, the girl stalked to Juju's 4x4, opened the back door, and flung herself mutinously inside. Ginny let out a long, soft breath.

"Does she gotta ride with us?" Duncan rasped, and Ginny almost rounded on him before she realized his nerves were probably frayed down to nothing too. Dull, pointless anger filled the pit of her belly, roiling uneasily.

"Ayuh, she does." Juju headed for the bathroom. "Unless you want the dog, and he's been eatin Slim Jims again, I just betcha."

"Let's get Traveller settled," Lee said. "Come on, Ginny. Move it up, boys."

Ginny blinked furiously, denying her own tears, and had to swallow several times. The window paintings stared vacantly at the almost deserted parking lot, the gas island, and the highway beyond.

"Just a minute," she said, when Lee made a *come on* motion. She scanned the shelves until she found what she wanted, and cleaned out the entire stock of strawberry Pop-Tarts. Sooner or later Steph would want them again.

Or someone else would take them from the wreckage when their little group's luck ran out the rest of the way.

Ginny caught a single dry, barking sob behind her teeth. Her mother was right. God was a monster not fit to be worshipped, and they were on their own.

[32]
BEST ROUTE

Lee's guts were a mass of snakes. He shouldn't have let
Phyllis and Mark stay inside that damn store alone. He should have
been with them, for God's sake. It was too late, and he was sick all the
way through. He gripped the wheel hard, and the back of his neck
was tight as bridge cables. The road wasn't a problem, it was clear
sailing for a while.

No, the problems lay elsewhere. "So, uh. I figger we should talk."

"Hm?" Ginny, pale but composed, spun the radio dial, searching
through soft static. If there was anyone home in Atlanta, maybe
they'd hear something on a frequency soon. Traveller was snoring
softly, all right with his world. Would the damn dog look for Phyllis
or Mark at the next stop? Or would he just assume the pack had
shrunk because the humans wanted it that way, and put it out of his
mind?

Finally, Ginny stole a glance at him. "She's just upset. Who
wouldn't be?"

She thought he was going to say somethin' about Steph. "It ain't
that." Lee wished it was, though the Lord knew Juju had taken the
news well. *Just figured you had your reasons, Loot.* The man hadn't

even asked if Lee would have used one of the nasty-green syringes on *him* if he'd come down with the sweats and convulsions.

The longer Lee sat on the goddamn secret, the worse it was gonna get. There was no good time to explain this, but he was tired of keepin' it locked up.

He was tired of everything except Ginny, Christ knew.

"What?" She spun the dial a little more, hunting. He wanted to tell her to give it a goddamn rest for a few minutes, but that wasn't any sort of decent thing to say. They all coped in different ways, dammit, and...Jesus.

He still felt the recoil against his shoulder, and Mark's hand raised like he was saying *hallelujah* in a church pew. The bitter, utterly familiar taste filled Lee's mouth, the taste of doing what had to be done, since nobody else would.

Since nobody else *could.*

And now he was gonna confess. Lay it all out, because he couldn't carry it no more. Not this one thing. "They's somethin under the seat," he said, finally. "Bend on down, see if you can fish it out."

"Your gun-box?"

He wished that was the only danger. "No ma'am. Plastic. Hard black plastic, shoebox-size."

"Oh. Okay." She bent and dug, Traveller's snores halting as he dimly realized something was occurring without his supervision. The dog was gonna slide right off the bench seat, for Godsake, he stretched out like he owned the entire damn cab. "This?"

There it was, the hardpac with its cargo of secrets. He could tell her just to slide it back on under the seat, that it was some kind of gear she shouldn't be touching and he just wanted to warn her.

That might've been the best route, but he didn't like it. Not one bit.

Not now. He kept his gaze on the road. Ditches were full and lakes swirled over gutters, full of plant and other trash. At least the highway was built to stay clear. "Yeah. That. You gonna listen to me?"

"Of course." She didn't roll her eyes, but it was probably close. "What's in it?"

I'm trying to tell you. Combat nerves, ramping him up with no letdown in sight. Lee exhaled softly, his knuckles creaking. "Just... hear me out, okay?"

"I said I would." She settled the box in her lap, touching one of her braids with her fingertips to make sure it wasn't going anywhere. Traveller shifted again, his ear pricking, then settled too. God, Lee envied the hound's calm. Some sleep would do all of them a power of good right now.

Or if not sleep, just rest. A few hours without some-damn-thing-else going wrong, or likely to go wrong. All he could see was Mark's hand, spread wide.

He'd put a round in the boy's head, and in Phyllis's too. They wouldn't stand up and shuffle around chewin'. That was all he could do for them, but it wasn't enough.

"About a week before everything went bad," he began, "a fellow came to see me. His name was Grandon. Was my CO back in the service."

Her right hand twitched a little as if she wanted to raise it, a good little student with a question. "CO?"

"Commanding officer."

"Oh, of course." All her attention on him, now. It felt good, but at the same time...Christ.

Well, he was in it now. There was no way out. Never had been, even if he'd stolen a little sweetness. "Anyway, he came and left that. I put it in my closet and didn't think about it, because...I don't know. I was out, and I wanted to be that way. Army was good to me, but also gave me bad dreams. You know?"

"I gather it does that a lot." She folded her hands on the hardpac's top. Pretty hands, those thin gold bracelets glowing, her unpainted nails now a little ragged. They were all getting frayed. "So what's in here, Lee?"

Oh, man. He kept his eyes on the road. "Open it up. There's a catch there...yeah."

A long silence filled the truck cab. Static brushed softly through the speakers, and the walkie-talkie was dead until the next check-in. He knew what she was seeing—two sturdy, old-fashioned syringes full of that violently green goo.

And the empty cradle for one more.

He told her what it was, quietly, while the rain intensified and the wipers beat their steady time. Abandoned cars began to clot the road again, and Ginny said nothing while he stumbled over words, trailed off, started once more.

He hated talking. It only led to trouble, and this time was no exception.

[33]

NOT IMMUNE

"Say something," Lee said, almost pleading.

What on earth was there to say? Ginny closed the case, carefully. You could pinch your fingers in one of these, the top was heavy and reinforced.

Of course, you couldn't have the syringes cracking. A safe little cargo, nestled in stuff like florist's foam, but harder. And what syringes, glass and somewhat old-fashioned, their needle-guards barely keeping huge, wicked sharps contained.

It was the missing one she kept looking at. Or more precisely, where the missing one had rested. "Not immune," she finally murmured, glancing out the window. Another clot of abandoned cars, pulled neatly over to the weedy shoulder, one a charred, dripping skeleton.

"What?" Lee leaned sideways a little, cocking his head. His hair was mussed, damp, and dark with a few days' worth of nothing but sponge-baths. He looked...anxious.

He'd better be. God, it was barely three p.m., winter darkness beginning to gather, and she had a feeling this day wasn't ever going to end. First Phyllis and Mark, then Steph, and now... "I'm not immune," she repeated, a little more loudly. "Why didn't you tell me?"

"Uh." He kept trying to glance at her, then correcting the truck's drift on wet pavement. Humps of icy white, melting rapidly under the rain, showed where the snow had dipped south, losing its fury as it worked past DC.

The White House was probably standing empty now. Or maybe the people there who had created this monster and turned it loose had green syringes of their own, and were resting comfortably in bombproof bunkers while all the death and blood and pain roiled in the rest of the goddamn country.

It wouldn't surprise her one bit.

Lee cleared his throat, his Adam's-apple working. "I, uh. There didn't seem to be a...well..."

"You should have told me." The words were dry and terrible, she couldn't get them past the wad in her throat. A hot heavy stone, full jagged edges, tearing at her voice. "We could have—"

"What? What you think we coulda done?" Sounded like he had a rock in his windpipe, too. A big one.

"We could have *saved* people." It was the only thing she could think to say. All the words she'd ever known, all the ones in all the books in the world, hardly seemed applicable.

"Only three of em, Ginny."

Well, that was some pitiless logic. He excelled at it, and Ginny supposed she was lucky he did. "He—this Colonel Grant—said to go to Atlanta?"

"Grandon. Yeah." Two short, bitten-down little words.

Then that's what you should have done. Ginny had the uncomfortable sensation of her brain actually moving inside her skull, vapor-locking so hard it twitched. That was ridiculous, she knew that organ didn't feel pain. And yet. "You should have told me."

Lee's knuckles were white. His irises had lightened too, that peculiar yellowish stare of his. "You was wantin to get to your folk, and I thought—"

"No. You didn't think, Lee." She sounded like Mom, she realized, and her stomach flipped uneasily. "We could have gone straight to Atlanta, with this."

"And left your folk to—"

"Yes." But she wouldn't have. It was impossible to tell, she hadn't had the chance. "Or you could have gone yourself. This is *important*. You could have saved people."

"I did." His chin set, stubbornly. "Leastways, the only one I felt like savin."

Her heart lodged afresh in her throat, her pulse a thin high galloping. "What if Juju got sick? Or one of the kids? What if they got sick and I didn't clue in soon enough because I assumed *I* was immune and they would be too? What about that?" Her voice rose, she couldn't help it. "What about people maybe waiting on this to concoct a cure? You *didn't* think, Lee. How could you? You told me...*Juju* told me—wait." The funny sensation inside her head was simply her brain trying to process and overheating, maybe. Just like a laptop, and just as useless at the moment. Electronics were just giant bricks now. How long before people forgot the secret to making them work? "Did *he* know?"

"Not until about twenty minutes ago."

Oh. That's swell. That's really awesome. "So." Ginny was not taking this calmly, she decided. No, not calm at all."You lied to him too."

"I just didn't say nothin, that's all." Lee actually flinched, shoulders coming up; the truck stayed steady on the road. "He knows I got my reasons."

"I'm sure he does." It was her mother's *you have overstepped* tone escaping Ginny's mouth, and oh, God, wasn't that a pain in her chest as well? A week before things went bad, he said? Plenty of time to get to Atlanta, and maybe, just maybe, she could have gotten to Mom and Dad and Flo, and at least been *with* them at the...

At the end.

Ginny covered her face with her hands. She bent over the shoebox-case, almost to her knees. A thick, slick, muffled sound caught in her throat—maybe a scream?

"Ginny. *Ginny.*"

She leaned away from his reaching hand. "Don't," she said into her cold palms smelling of harsh pink soap. *"Don't."*

The walkie-talkie on the dashboard woke with a feedback squeal. Ginny swallowed convulsively. If he touched her, she was going to scream. Probably scare the hell out of the dog, too.

It was Juju on the walkie-talkie. There was, of course, yet another problem.

[34]

NICE NEWS

Cold rain drummed on the top of the 4x4. Duncan bent in the backseat, coughing. His cheeks were scarlet from the effort, and when Ginny produced the thermometer, he shook his head. "Oh, hell no."

"We've got to know," she said, and there was a set to her chin that reminded him of Phyllis facing down those assholes outside Pittsburgh with just that pink baseball bat and her wits.

Goddammit, Phyl. "I'm fine," he said, and hawked up some phlegm. "Just a little overheated. It's a sweatbox in here."

"Sore throat? Headache?" She was all business, the librarian, raindrops clinging to her piled, dark braids. Steph, mute and mutinous, was behind them in the truck with Lee since it had been time for a change in lead anyway, and Duncan thought maybe Ginny was mad at the man for something.

Not his business, really. His throat was sore and it hurt to swallow his own spit, and he couldn't stop coughing.

The engine idled softly. Juju kept glancing nervously into the rearview. Ginny simply looked at him, those large dark eyes cowpatient, and Duncan gave in. "Throat's been dry since Allentown, but I figured I just wanted some whiskey. Headache, well, yeah." Everything about this was likely to give a man a headache. "You think I got it? The zombie flu?"

"Not sure." She held up the thermometer. "This will help me tell. We probably won't know until you start to convulse."

"Great." He shook his head, but she was persistent, and he finally accepted the metal and plastic, tucking it under his tongue like a good boy.

Wasn't it just his fucking luck?

"Ginny..." Juju shut up when she glanced at the rearview. When a woman looked like that, silence was probably the best policy.

Probably? No, *definitely*.

"He told me, Juju." She had a whole medic's kit in a black faux-leather Bargain Zone handbag—blood pressure cuff, swabs, thermometers, and a bunch of other stuff, including orange prescription bottles. Quite the little pharmacy. Always prepared, like Phyl with that damn Chanel bag of hers. "Drive. We need to get to Atlanta."

"You think there's anyone there?" Juju's worried frown mirrored hers, and he dropped the Jeep into gear. He tapped his brakes twice, and the truck's headlights behind them flickered once.

"Even if there isn't, there's probably facilities. I'll do what I can." She glanced at Duncan, unrolling the blood pressure cuff. "Don't worry, Duncan. I didn't leave med school because I was bad at it."

"Why didja, then?" Juju's mouth set itself, but he popped the emergency brake and touched the gas. Rain drummed tiny wet fingers on the roof.

"Because my boyfriend planned to roofie me and charge attendance to his frat brothers while they did what frat boys do, and I found out." She said it all in one breath, and her expression didn't change. "Let's get your coat off, Duncan. At least on one side. We're going to take your blood pressure."

Juju's mouth fell open. Duncan decided he'd better not mess with this particular librarian, *ever*, and unzipped his own jacket. The walkie-talkie burbled, and he looked out the window. Rain fell in a curtain, an iron-grey line of cloud sweeping overhead and dumping its cargo.

They were a hundred miles from Roanoke. And from what he gathered on the walkie-talkie, there was finally something on the radio.

He was pretty sure it wouldn't do him personally any good, but it was nice news nonetheless.

[35]

TRANSMISSION

"THIS IS DR EMILIANA TORRES OF THE ATLANTA CDC, *broadcasting on both AM and FM frequencies...If you can hear us, we're still functioning, and this is the route you should take to avoid those infected with the LV-426 virus...if you can reach Charlotte, head for the Belmont Army Reserve. Helicopters will circle the facility daily at noon. They will land when and if it's safe, and uninfected civilians will be transported to the Atlanta base. We have food, electricity, and medical care...Again, if you are uninfected, we recommend you head for the Belmont Army Reserve Base near Charlotte. This is the route we recommend in order to avoid the infected..."*

[36]

DAMN KID

They stopped again for gas just past Roanoke; someone had been at work on the freeway with wreckers but left the job unfinished. Still, they made good time, even as a winter night swallowed them and the rain intensified. Windshield wipers thump-swooshed back and forth, and the rain tried to have sleet at its heart and only barely failed.

Duncan slept fitfully, leaning against the window, and Ginny stared out hers, occasionally flicking on a small LED and checking the contents of her medical bag again, as if she'd find something new in there.

Juju drove, thin-lipped, focusing on the cones of headlight glare. His eyes were grainy, and it was a good thing they were switching off point frequently. Lee was monosyllabic during check-ins, and when they stopped for any short while his gaze followed Ginny hungrily, watchful.

She ignored him.

That was a problem, but the two of them were goddamn adults. Juju was more worried about Duncan's shallowing-out breathing. It came on fast, and the man hadn't been bit, had he?

Not bit, Ginny said. Immunity's not a factor, I guess.

Well, she was takin the news real calm-like. There were two of those syringes left, Lee said, but would the man spend one on Duncan? He was, after all, a stranger—a new boot in the platoon, so to speak, and you didn't get close to a new boot until they'd survived long enough to make it worthwhile. Even if he had done his share of wallopin' critter heads.

But that wasn't what was grinding inside Juju Thurgood's skull, circling the way a thought did on watch when you had nothing to do but stand and stare.

No, it was Mark Kasprak Juju was thinkin' on, and it wasn't comfortable. Damn kid, gettin himself killed like that. Hell of a way to go, and even though Lee had done him a mercy at the end.

And Lee *knew* the kid. That was probably tearing him up, but the Loot wouldn't say a damn thing. He kept his bleedin' on the inside.

The kid should be sittin in the passenger seat right now, or in the RV they'd had to leave behind *again*. Couldn't keep a damn one of the big road-hogs to save their life. Woulda been nice to sleep in one, but he agreed with Lee that pushing through the rain was better than risking a crowd of the undead motherfuckas if they stopped to rest somewhere.

Or even if they didn't, because each time Juju rubbed his eyes and looked at the damn road, there were little flickers of motion outside the headlight glow.

Flat shines, like eyes, way down low. Not animal eyes, glowing weird the way they did. Something else.

The highway ribboned, dipping and rising, and the countryside might've been pretty if it wasn't swarming with the things. Of course, it could just be nerves.

Night patrol did that to you. Made you jumpy. So did adrenaline. The radio burbled softly, a recording on repeat. No use getting your hopes up, they could arrive and find out it was just idiot noise running because those responsible for it were dead or chew-shuffling and unable to switch it off.

Duncan moved, and Ginny made a soft soothing noise. "It's all right," she said. "Not far now."

The rain kept going. At least it wasn't snow.

"Damn kid," Juju muttered, under the sound of Dr Torres, whoever she was, repeating the route. "Damn kid."

"I can drive," Ginny said, leaning forward. "Juju?"

"Not yet," he said, and set his jaw. There was another tangle of wrecked cars coming up, and he didn't like the sensation that there were things hiding in the shattered metal and glinting glass, watching them go past.

[37]

WHIRLYBIRD

Smudged, haggard false dawn rose through curtains of
rain northwest of Charlotte, creeping across the top of hills and
between cars shoved to the shoulder, tiptoeing down long stretches of
blank, wet freeway. The radio was on, muttering softly; Dr Torres
had been replaced by a granite-throated fellow whose drawl sounded
perilously close to Lee's own, repeating the same things over and
over. Had to be another recording, and it was a good sign.

Unfortunately, he didn't give a shit. Duncan surfaced from thin,
restless dozing and stared glassy-eyed at Juju. "Uh," he croaked. His
nose wasn't full, so he could smell the faint burnt metal scent of rank
sicksweat. He was greased with it, oily with the aroma of his body
trying to fight something off and failing miserably.

Had he been dreaming? Something about Phyl and those assholes
outside Pittsburgh.

Poor Phyl. Duncan rubbed at his eyes with clumsy fingers. Poor
everyone, putting up with all this bullshit.

"Don't tell me you gotta pee." Juju's lean brown face split into a
sweet, somewhat gentle smile. "We ain't stoppin for nothin now, so you
gonna hafta put yo dick in a bottle." He paused, probably waiting for a

smile or answering witticism, while Duncan worked his jaws and tried to swallow. That made Juju sober, pursing his lips. "We got some of them espresso-in-a-can business if'n you want coffee, but nothin hot."

Duncan's throat was on fire. Something cold sounded really good. His head hurt, too, his temples pounding and sending glass spikes down his neck. His lower back cramped, his legs felt like he hadn't used them in six months, and god *damn* he wanted them to just tip him out of the car onto cool, hard concrete.

Just let him rest. It had been a long damn road, and he was fuckin' tired.

"He's awake?" Ginny was in the driver's seat, thin strands working free of her braided coronet. She edged the Jeep over to the left, avoiding a pile of smashed metal and scattered glass that didn't look quite right. It wasn't a smashup; it looked like a wrecker had been at work. "We could change over, then."

"Nah, keep goin." Juju finally smiled, his dark eyes lighting up. "Me and my man here just gonna chill until we at base. Right, Duncan? You want some water?"

Duncan nodded, carefully, so his fool head didn't fall clean off. Christ, his throat hurt. The rain sounded juicy, delicious. *My man.* Did Juju suspect?

Maybe. Maybe Duncan had been talking in his sleep. Everyone found out everything, sooner or later. You couldn't get away from anything, even during the apocalypse.

"Christ Jesus, he's burning up." Juju's hand was cool as water falling from heaven against Duncan's forehead. He cracked a bottle of generic distilled water and held it to Duncan's lips, and if he had to die, Duncan supposed, it would be nice to do it while leaning on this man, seeing the curling shadow of his stubble along the angle of his beautiful jaw, hearing him speak nice and low, coaxing-like.

"Just hold on, Duncan." Ginny leaned forward, and the 4x4 rocked, speeding up. "Shit."

"Keep it even, woman." Juju was antsy with someone else driving his baby. A man who loved his car was a good one, or so Duncan thought.

Of course, he'd loved plenty of cars, but nobody would ever call Duncan Harris *good*. He tried to laugh, but all that came out was a harsh caw, spilling cool water down his chin. Swallowing hurt, even the water didn't give him any reprieve.

"I just...I can't be sure, but..." Ginny gasped, leaning forward and peering out the windshield. Peering *up*. "It is."

"Ginny, he can't even drink." Juju put his fingers back on Duncan's forehead. "This ain't good."

"Don't sip from his bottle, Juju. Is his throat worse?"

Duncan nodded. Even that hurt. Even his fucking *hair* hurt.

"He says yes," Juju translated.

"Of *course*. Why didn't I..." Ginny's eyes narrowed, clearly visible in the rearview. She'd've made a crackerjack doctor, he decided. That ex-boyfriend of hers sounded like a real turd. "Could be strep. Shit. Dig in the medbag. There's penicillin tabs—is he allergic to penicillin?"

Juju's look was full of inquiry. Duncan managed a shrug. Christ, he didn't care, as long as this stopped.

"Don't look like it." Juju dug in the fake-leather bag. "What's up there, Ginny?"

"A helicopter," she said, in an awed whisper, craning her neck. "Big, and black."

For a moment the words made no sense. Then a cold wire of relief coiled shamefully up Duncan's spine. Helicopter meant people.

"Get on the walkie—" Juju leaned forward, and Duncan sagged bonelessly without his propping. "Christ, maybe I *should* drive."

"Settle down." The librarian had made up her mind. She stared at the road ahead like it personally insulted her, and the wipers cleared the windshield in not-quite-tandem arcs. "We can't change drivers without stopping. Give him five hundred migs of penicillin, that should do for his weight...Duncan, I know it's not pleasant, but you'll have to chew it if you can't swallow."

Great. He shrugged again, now hoping they wouldn't stop the car so Juju could stay right where he was. Ginny reached for the walkie-talkie, pressed the button, and made a face when it squawked. "Lee? Lee, there's a helicopter."

"I see it," came the reply, its throat rough as Duncan's own with static. "Keep goin. How's the patient?"

Ginny's gaze didn't leave the road. "Awake. We need to get there soon."

"Aight. Keep goin, we switch point in thirty, ten-four?"

"Ten-four," she muttered, grimly, and put the talkie back in its jury-rigged holster on the dash. "*Keep going,* he says. As if I wanted to stop."

"Stay focused, woman." Juju found what he was looking for in her bag. "Don't get us in no accident. Amoxicillin? That work?"

"Yes, that will do." Her knuckles pinkened as she eased up a bit on the wheel, and the slice of her he could see in the rearview was wide-eyed. "Five hundred milligrams. I should have thought to get some liquid."

Juju made a short *it-don't-matter* sound. "We got what we got. I'll crush em fo you, Duncan?"

He let his chin tip down in an approximation of a nod again. Oh, God, it was good to hear. Someone was taking care of him, and if there was a whirlybird in sight it meant civilization, the chain of command, and all those things he hated. Authority. Orders. Damned if you do, damned if you don't, and maybe, if he was really lucky, a hospital.

"Yessir," Juju said, softly. "Just gonna crush these up fo you, my man, and get em washed down."

Anything you want, my man, Duncan wanted to say. His throat was too swollen, barely a pinhole to force bitter medication through. *Anything at all.*

[38]

CHECKPOINT GOLF

Sour-faced sharp-shaven men in fatigues? Yep. A tangle of barbwire, concrete placers, and guns in towers? Yep. Floodlights that probably lit up this place to Kingdom Come at night? Oh, yeah. It was Checkpoint Golf, the sign said, and hallelujah, it had *electricity*.

Lee should have felt grateful. He should have felt goddamn relieved. He should have been jumping for shit-bustin' joy.

But Ginny's chin set, stubbornly, and she had her arms folded nice and tight, blinking against fine misting rain turning to gold when the sun peeked through. "Then I won't go in either," she repeated. "He *doesn't have it*. His fever's steady at 102 and he's not convulsing."

"Orders are no infected," the gate CO repeated, matching her tit for tat. His nametag said *Cho*; he was ramrod-straight, smooth-cheeked, bristle-haired, and the kind of jackass Lee would have had longing thoughts of dunking in a hot barrel just to teach him a little bend. "Sorry, ma'am." His expression suggested he wasn't sorry at all, and the way his gaze kept drifting over Ginny's head at the road behind them spoke volumes.

Bulldozers were chugging along that strip, working between big concrete placers meant to channel approaching hostiles. Looked like it had been a busy night out here; critter-corpses crunched and stank while the boots on guard duty held their rifles at jumpy-yeah-shoot-it-and-be-sure angles.

"They come out at night, right?" Lee jerked his head at the mess behind them. At least the morning work details had cleared a path to the gate. And at least the assholes weren't yelling at them to put their hands behind their heads and lie down on the swimming pavement.

It had been a near thing.

"You better believe it." Cho didn't like being reminded. "Look, ma'am, if you're not coming in, you'd better clear the gates. We'll take the uninfected in and—"

"Fine." Ginny turned on her heel and set off for Juju's four-by. *I ain't goin up there,* Juju had said. *White boys with guns, Loot. Sorry.*

He was right. Lee kept his hands visible and his movements slow. Besides, someone had to stay with Duncan. They should have just propped him up and toweled him off to get him through the gate. Steph sat in the truck, huge-eyed, hugging Traveller, and the dog wriggled with glee at the prospect of more humans to sniff.

"Listen." Lee tried again. "You got yourself a Colonel Grandon there? Or General? He's a general now."

"General Grandon?" Cho's backup, a pimple-faced kid with notches on his rifle butt, swallowed hard when Cho swung around to give him a look. Drops of mist hung in Cho's short, stiff black ruff, not nearly as gemlike as the ones on Ginny's braids.

Lee dug for his wallet—nice and slow, his other hand up. Everyone in the damn towers was likely to be twitchy as fuck, too. "Here's my ID. Go get Grandon on the line. We'll wait."

"I can't call the general just because—" Cho huffed, but Lee fixed him with a stare.

"Son," he said, quietly, "I have driven up to New York and back, I got me two ladies, two fellow soldiers, and a dog through enemy territory, we lost al'ost everyone else, and I ain't gonna have no pissant stop me from seein General Grandon like he ordered me to before this bullshit even *started*. So you get on that phone, and you tell him Lieutenant Lee Quartine's here with a delivery."

It wasn't quite a lie, and Lee didn't feel a goddamn bit of guilt over it. He was savin' that guilt for other things, like the look on Ginny's face as if she expected him to go on through the gates and leave her with a sick man.

Christ. You could lose everythin' in an instant with a woman, maybe. Big Q had never warned him about that.

He about-faced and walked away, not in double-time but not slowly either, leaving Cho holding his ID. If the motherfucker didn't call Grandon, well, Lee was gonna hafta get creative.

Fortunately, Cho's understudy was already humping for a box containing a field phone. Ten minutes later Cho came scurryin out, waving Lee's ID like it was the holy grail, and finally, the tension in Lee's shoulders came down a notch.

It was about damn time.

[39]

VITALS

Electric lights glowed, and the entire building was wonderfully warm. There were clean blankets, clean floors, doors that didn't have to be barricaded, hospital beds, and the hum of conversation. And, best of all, the flat smell of boiled coffee added to antiseptic and detergent that, taken together, shouted *medical care.*

Ginny scrubbed at her forehead with the heel of her hand. "I should have thought strep sooner," she said, numbly. Her skin crawled, her scalp twitched, and she longed to take the pins out of her hair. Instead, she dropped her hands and smoothed the pea-green wool blanket over Duncan's broad chest again. "He's going to be all right?"

He looked smaller, propped up on crisp pillows. An IV drip went about its placid work right next to the bed, and Duncan's stubble glittered under fluorescent light. His chest rose and fell, deeply, regularly, and the bruises on his hands and forearms glared.

They were all walking collections of hematomas. Escaping the walking dead gave you all sorts of aches and pains, and now each one on Ginny's own body was waking up and demanding to be heard.

"Yep. Little hydration, little penicillin—you got the right dosage, too—and he'll be right as rain." Doctor Nguyen smiled, her broad brown cheeks bunching up with a pair of fetching dimples, and patted at one of her scrubs' pockets. Her hair was pulled ruthlessly back and a thin chain showed at her throat, holding a gold ring. Which meant she was married and probably surgical, since taking rings off to wash your hands was a good way to lose them. "Now will you let us take a look at you?"

"I'm fine. Just tired." She didn't think telling them *well, you know, that guy who was hustled off in the helicopter gave me a shot and I got better* was a good move.

Not yet. Probably not ever.

And that was food for thought, wasn't it? The way they had suddenly turned into VIPs once Lee had a chance to talk to the gate-guard alone. After the black-haired guy had come out waving Lee's ID, they'd been ushered in through the gates, given an escort of green and black Humvees, rushed to an improvised hospital settled in a repurposed office building, and hustled inside posthaste.

Except for Lee and Juju, who were taken to the roof; the same black helicopter she'd seen circling over Charlotte—or its twin—had shown up in a hurry.

Considering what Lee was carrying, no wonder. Ginny should have been furious, Instead, she was simply...drained. They'd made it after all.

Now what?

"You probably want a shower, and some food." Dr Nguyen was chirpy-cheerful as anyone on a full ration of sleep could be. "Or some coffee, first? It's horrible because it's the Army, but at least it's caffeine."

Her teabags were in the back of the truck, but trudging into the fitful rain to fetch them was an unappetizing idea at best. The light in here was too bright, her eyes were smarting. "Um. I suppose a shower. Oh, the girl who came in with me—"

"She's being checked out, too. Let's get you looked at, all right?

Most people coming in are malnourished and in shock, they just don't know it."

Which was not precisely news, but hearing other people were coming in was a blessing. "How many have come in? Are they still?"

"There were a lot at first." Dr Nguyen made little shooing *come on* motions, and Ginny let herself be herded. "Now it's a trickle. We had a group of six a couple days ago—a lady named Halloran and another named Frank, a bunch of girls."

"Frank?" It was a pretty common name, but she could hope. "Kasie Frank? A black lady—African-American? A nurse?"

"She's a nurse, yeah—sounds like you know her?" Nguyen led her into the hall, sweeping the door mostly closed. "I don't know her first name. Halloran had a broken arm and a couple of the girls were pretty beat up, I guess they went through Greensboro. Which was exactly the wrong way to go."

Does that mean we came in the right way? It didn't seem possible that there was *any* right way in this situation. "There weren't any guys with them?" *Mike, or Jorge?* Oh, God. Now she was greedy for another set of survivors. Carline and Mandy—were they all right? Chantal? Colleen?

It seemed like a lifetime ago. What were the odds that anyone else had survived? Probably like winning the lottery. They'd all been dumped into one of those wire cages and spun, plucked at random, and deposited here.

"Nope." The doctor's ponytail bounced along just as efficiently as she did. "Come on. We'll just take your vitals, then you can have a shower and a rest. We can use someone with medical training around here. It's been combat trauma for days now, with the nightly swarm."

"That sounds...unappetizing." She peered through the door, one last peek. Duncan's jaw was slack, he was out hard under the woolen blanket. "I should check on Steph first."

"Yes, but we're going to take your vitals." Polite, firm, and utterly immovable, Doctor Nguyen folded her arms. "You can't help anyone unless you help yourself, Ms Mills."

Ginny nodded. "Okay." It felt both welcome and slightly obscene to have lights glowing overhead, to hear movement in the hallways that wasn't dangerous. To feel warm air touching her face, and the safety of human numbers again. "I just...it's been a long trip."

"I'll bet. I heard something about New York?" The doctor set off at a brisk pace, her pink, eminently sensible sneakers making faint sounds on freshly mopped linoleum.

They had enough people to *mop*, here. Her skin began crawling in earnest. "Yeah." Ginny unzipped her jacket. She was sweating, she realized. It felt *too* warm in here. "We started out in Cotton Crossing. Small town. You wouldn't have heard of it."

"You can tell me while we take your stats. This way, honey." She scooped up Ginny's elbow; steady hands, which was a good thing, because Ginny wasn't sure she wouldn't start reeling. Her head was suspiciously light. "You can relax, you're all right now."

God, I hope that's true. Ginny swallowed, hard, and let herself be pulled along.

Later, under a spray of blessed hot water in a shower that more resembled a high-end gymnasium's locker room than an Army base, she finished rinsing shampoo and grime out of her hair, stared at the white tiled wall, and Kaddish rose in her throat. She recited it, start to finish, first in Aramaic, then in English.

She could remember every word, now that it was too late to matter.

God was a monster, yes.

But maybe he would understand.

[40]

THE WHOLE POINT

Rain hit the window of a bare boxlike room, drops
coming together and rolling down. The tiny bits of water didn't really
separate after that, they just went on their way as one instead of two.
Or three, four, five, making a stream. Her English teacher Miz
Uglanov would ask for a list of synonyms.

Coming together. Joining. Balling up? No, that one was wrong.
Steph huddled on the bed, hugging her damp, jean-clad knees. There
were "barracks" here—people sleeping on rows of cots, breathing
each others' breath and whatever else, and that might have been nice
except they were *strangers*, and she'd spent so long looking at the
same faces the new ones made her uneasy.

Besides, the lady doctor Nguyen said there was an adjustment
period. She said other things, like *shock* and *trauma*, but Steph just
watched her mouth move for most of it and nodded every once in a
while, when someone seemed to expect it.

That seemed safest.

Lee and Juju went off to do whatever it was got everyone so
excited at the gate, Mr Duncan was wheeled away on a gurney,
Ginny went with him, and Steph was weighed, blood pressured,

and temperature-taken before being left here with the dog and the rain and her own goddamn thoughts. Traveller sprawled across Steph's feet, snoring mightily. Nobody made any fuss about him strolling along on his leash, thank Jesus, and it wasn't time for his supper yet.

The clock wired to the wall said so, and it was probably right. All of a sudden the world had started working again.

She supposed she should pray. Take a shower in the funny locker room down the hall. Her suitcase had been placed just inside this room's door, but if she opened it up for clothes or shampoo she'd think of Mark saying *y'all can make anything fit in there, man*, and the tears would start on slow leak again.

Not sobbing—she was done cried out, as Mama would say. Just…a trickle from each eye, sliding down chapped cheeks. It was better to just sit, hugging her knees, keep her eyes shut tight, and hold on.

Traveller's paws twitched. He made funny little woofing noises deep in his throat, his lips twitching too. Was he dreaming about Mark, who would always scratch right above his tail and say *there's a good ol' hound?* Maybe he was dreaming Miz Phyllis, who said she didn't want hair on her but still bent down to pet his head with careful fingertips whenever he got close?

Or was he dreamin' about the zombies? Hounds followed their noses, and God knew the zombies were smelly enough.

Rain sounded good on a window when you were warm and safe inside. They had *electricity* here, a whole National Guard base up and running. Lights came on when you flipped the switch. There were people talking in the halls, not caring if noise would draw zombie attention. Thick concrete walls topped with razor wire cuddled all the buildings like a nest holding eggs, and people were strolling out in the daylight. Sure, there were a lot of them carrying rifles, but if any of the zombies got past the gate, the rifles were a *good* thing.

Her breath stank; Steph knew as much because her mouth was rancid even though her nose was full of hot, runny snot. Everything on her stank. It stank like *shit*. She probably smelled as bad as a zombie now.

She could get out of the building, probably. Go down to the gate. They were supposed to stop people comin' *in*, they wouldn't mind one going *out*. She could walk until she found one of the zombies. She could even take her baseball bat, right? The pistol Lee gave her was in his truck, left in a lot with an empty guard shack because nobody here would want to steal it when there were so many others around.

Getting out would be easy, compared to everything else. It really would be.

What would be the point? Well, the whole point was...

"It shoulda been me," she whispered to her dirty jeans, her boots full of dried mud getting on the clean taut blanket, her flannel shirt— *Mark's* red flannel shirt, and it was a good thing her nose was full because she couldn't smell him on it, either.

Steph sniffed, long and deep, packing her nose even harder. Would her head explode from all the snot? Just like a zombie's when you shot it. *Sploosh*.

"Steph?" Tentative, her name lifting at the end. "There you are."

Go away. She hugged her legs harder, pressed her cheek against one knee. There was probably zombie splatter on her jeans too. Maybe she'd even take sick from it, but Miz Ginny said they were immune.

Immune was a big ol' shithead of a word, Steph thought. Like insurance, which Daddy always complained about, it didn't cover everything. It covered hardly nothin' at all.

Traveller stopped dreaming. He shifted on the bed. Of course, he'd want the woman in the door to come over and pet him. Steph wasn't in a petting mood.

Soft sound of footsteps, clothing moving. You got used to quiet just like you got used to the noise of traffic, to the motion of a car. To the sound of a boy sleeping next to you, his arm over your waist and his face in your hair. Keeping the sleeping bag between you so you didn't, well, do anything embarrassing while he was cuddled up. Letting him kiss you, tongue shyly flicking. Making him come back in and yell *I'm home* because you wanted to see what it was like.

Telling him he'd done wrong and then being bitchy when he tried hard to make it up. That, too.

Now there was nothing, just a pack of fucking zombies swarming over a body that used to be someone important, and there wasn't any getting used to *that*. No sir.

Never.

"Steph." A pressure on the mattress beside her. Someone sitting down.

"Leave me alone," Steph moaned into her knees.

"No, sweetie. Not right now." Ginny's arm came over her shoulders. She was just the same—soft like Mama, hugging awkwardly, caring radiating off her like heat from the funny bolted-on things under the windows. "Not right now," she repeated, and the pressure on Steph's shoulders pulled her off-center.

Steph slumped into her softness. *It's not fair. I want him back.* The leaking was back, and she wanted to be *alone*, right?

No. Yes.

She didn't know what the fuck she wanted, really. But Ginny just sat there, holding her, and Traveller lay back down with a satisfied *hrmph* from both ends that would have been funny if Mark was still alive.

But he wasn't. He was gone. Steph was safe and warm, and the leaking turned into soft, hitching sobs while Ginny hugged her and rocked a little, humming quietly.

It was *that* sound that broke her down, because it was just like Mama when you threw up or got kicked during recess or so mad about something you cried. A soft, female song that said *oh honey* and *let it out* and that most important of things, ever.

I love you.

She'd never even told him that.

Later, Ginny would tell her that of course Mark knew. Later,

Ginny would tell her it was natural, and part of the grieving process, and she knew how it felt. Later, Ginny would hug her over and over again, and the best times were when Ginny stroked her back and hummed that wandering melody.

At that moment, though, Steph Meacham just cried, the awful pressure of holding it together draining away and safe haven reached at last.

[41]

HERO

Parts of Atlanta were burned to the ground, but there were fortified cores of activity. Inside the tallest building of the biggest one, the upper windows were huge, but if it bothered General Grandon to sit at a desk with his back to one it didn't show.

"I expected to die out there in bumfuck Missouri." The general sighed, heavily. His left arm was in a cast under a hastily slit sleeve; half his hair, fully grey now, was singed off and his left eye was under a patch and a pad of fresh white gauze. His fatigues, the left sleeve of the top split to allow the cast, were ironed, and his remaining eye was bloodshot but bright as ever. "They were already burning bridges."

Lee didn't care. If this was a debriefing, it was one he wanted no part of, especially with his eyes full of hot sand and his entire body crawling with fatigue, sweat, and dirt. "So you dumped it on me." He kept his hat on, his jacket zipped, and his arms folded, though habit had already made him twitch preparatory to a salute or two on the way in.

Training, grinding in deep. A man in the habit of marching could walk right off a cliff before he knew it. Or step right through that frail shield of plate glass and plummet.

Wouldn't take much, just a few steps. It would take even less to punch a man, dazing him, and shoot the glass, then send the feller in a rolling chair right on through.

That's not a good thought, Lee.

Grandon spread his right hand, and the fingers of his left twitched under the cast. He pressed a button, and the computer to his left woke, a glaring blue screen reflecting on window-glass. "Well...I figured if anyone would get to Atlanta, you would."

Son of a bitch. Lee said nothing else. Juju, standing on his left, was studying the old man, full lips pulled tight and the faintest flicker of *do you believe this shit* around his dark eyes.

It was good to have a united front, even if both of them looked like bandits instead of soldiers. A gust of rain smacked along the window, a dribble of sky-saliva. Raining on the just and the unjust, like his Nonna used to say, except she never added that it all flowed downhill and drowned anyone foolish enough to believe *justice* was an actual thing.

The general studied Lee, letting the quiet stretch out. Finally, though, a faintly nervous half-chuckle covered the last fraction of strained silence. "They've been working on a separate serum. Only got twenty-five percent survivability, though. This one was damn near ninety, and it took a fucking miracle to get it offbase. I figured you'd get it through, if only to spite me." The habitual bluff, cajoling tone, CO to grunt, delivered from a nice dry mountaintop.

"When'd'ja send the cleanup crew?" Juju almost spat the question, and Grandon actually blinked his good eye.

So they were surprising the old man. Good.

"Yeah." Lee added the weight of his own stare to Juju's. It was hard work to get used to electricity again, and the humming of a well-organized base. His nerves were scrubbed damn raw, to match the rest of him. "Was just wonderin that myself."

"Lee—" Now the old man was going to go all *awshucks* and *buddy*, and Lee's patience threatened to snap outright. Even the little voice inside his head that sounded suspiciously like Ginny telling him to calm down had shut up, watching to see what he'd do.

"It's *Quartine*, sir." *You keep my name outta your mouth.* Lee looked past Grandon, through the soaked window. Not a lot of birds out, despite all the free meat on the counter. It was a damn open-air buffet for carrion, just like any war zone. "When *did* you send the cleanup crew out to my place? Couldn't have been long after we left."

"When I finally got to Atlanta." Grandon had paled. "They had orders just to round up, though, not to sweep."

Son of a bitch. As if Lee didn't know exactly how a simple roundup could turn into a morass when the adrenaline started squeezing. Lee imagined how Grandon felt when the cleanup reported Lee's place deserted, and with the snow erasing their quarry's tracks...well, Lee had cursed the weather up one side and down the other, but now it looked like it had done him a favor.

And not just him, but everyone else as well. He didn't think Ginny would take the news well, though.

All he wanted was to get back to Charlotte and find her, maybe try again to explain. It wouldn't do no good, of course. Life only gave you something good to kick you in the teeth and take it away, but at least if he was in her general vicinity, he could...what?

Hope sprang eternal, wasn't that the phrase? She was kind, his Virginia Mills, and he wasn't above usin' that.

Not if he had to. He could even talk himself into thinking it was to keep her safe.

A knock at the office door tensed Lee's shoulders. Juju almost twitched, too—both of them were still on patrol-nerves, and that wasn't good. Nobody had taken their weapons, either.

Lee couldn't suss out just what that meant at the moment, and he was too damn tired to try.

"General." The newcomer was a tall black woman in magenta scrubs and a crisp laundered lab coat, her afro sculpted high and proud. Her ebony skin glowed and her shoes were wicked point-toe numbers, albeit with sensible heels. "Ah. Make it quick, I'm busy."

Her nametag said *Torres*, and she was hoarse, probably from the broadcasts. Lee looked away, towards the window. Hell of a view.

"Dr Torres." Grandon smiled, and indicated the open hardpac on his cluttered desk. "This is our courier, and he's brought the LV-478 serum."

The woman halted, her hands dropping, and gave the hardpac a long, considering look. Then, amazingly, she strode across the worn-down carpeting, those sensible heels jabbing, and flung her arms around Juju. "Thank you," she said, and smooched him a good one right on one stubbled cheek. "Thank you, thank you, thank you."

Well, since he was closest to the door, it wasn't a bad guess on her part. "Um," Juju said. "Um, ma'am..."

Lee had to work to keep the smile down.

"This will save *lives*," the good doctor persisted, holding Juju's shoulders like she was gonna shake him. "So much of the data was destroyed, now we can reverse-engineer—wait. Where's the third syringe?"

"Was just gonna ask that myself," Grandon added, straightening with a wince. He hadn't lowered himself into the chair behind the acres of paper-cluttered desk—maybe because he knew the temptation of the old man right next to the window and on a set of wheels might have been a tad overwhelming for someone like Lee just in from the field.

Lee said nothing. Juju clammed up too, and swallowed, visibly.

"Well, even if the antidote serum's missing, we can engineer from the vaccine." Torres planted another good ol' smacking kiss on Juju's cheek, and, not content, also kissed his other one. "Thank God. Thank God and praise Jesus."

"Amen," Juju muttered.

Wait a goddamn second. "Antidote serum?" Lee wanted to know.

"It's a tri-pac." The doctor barely glanced at him, giving a quick little irritated shake of her sculpted head. "Live virus, dead vaccine load, and antidote." She stepped away from Juju. A few long swinging strides brought her to the desk—looked like the good doctor was not one to let any moss grow on a situation. "I'll get this into the lab. Thank God. General, we should have some good news soon."

Jesus Christ. The words sank in, and Lee's entire body was cold, sweat gathering under his arms again. A roaring rose in his ears, and only habit kept him straight upright instead of staggering like a head-tapped billygoat.

"Yes ma'am. Happy to oblige." Grandon at least waited until she was out of the room before loosing a stream of deep, gritty chuckles. "Well, Thurgood. Lookit that. You're a hero now."

"See if I can't get me a few drinks." Juju glanced nervously at Lee, who kept himself stock-still.

Live virus. Lee's hands were slabs of dead meat, and his knees felt pretty goddamn shaky. What if he'd injected Ginny with *that* mess, instead of with...dear Jesus save him.

Well, that was yet another reason she'd want nothing to do with him, if she knew about it. He'd used up all his luck. The only surprise was that it had lasted as long as it did.

"Well, I'm sure we can find something better." The old man bent a little, like it hurt, and fanned a few file folders on the desktop. The screen to his left had a saver of green lines in loops, and its reflection on the rainy glass was an evil eye. "I could use a few more good men. I could use *both* of you, matter of fact, and—"

Lee cleared his throat. "No." He meant to say it quietly, but it came out with far more bite than usual. "I'll be goin on back to Charlotte, sir, thank you."

Grandon glanced at Juju, but the lean brown man looked studiously over the general's shoulder at the whiteboard full of missions and reminders.

"Come on, Lee." The old chummy tone, the *nobody can do this but you.* And Grandon would know, banged-up and wounded, he could ask for more from the poor schmucks taking orders. Grandon led from the front, and let his soldiers feel he wouldn't ask something from them he wouldn't do his own blessed self. It had taken a while for Lee to figure out the truth.

Oh, if this was the old days, he could make Lee dig his own damn grave, and with a smile, too. *Nobody but you, Lee. Why, it's your job to do what others can't.*

Oh, maybe that was so. But it wasn't good enough for Nonna and Poppa Q's boy anymore. He cleared his throat. "It's Quartine. Sir."

Grandon's shoulders slumped a few fractions. Burden of command, maybe, knowing you'd fucked up something too far to fix. That was a trap too, even though Lee knew that ache.

Christ, did he ever. Especially now.

Grandon let the silence stretch a little more, but this time Lee was determined to outwait him. And Juju said nothing. It was goddamn good to know the man had his back. At the same time, it was a torment to wonder if Juju knew Lee had *his*.

It wasn't somethin' you could ask. Not right-out, like.

Finally, though, the old man decided to cut his losses. "All right. I'll get the bird to drop you back in Charlotte. No shortage of work there." The phone on Grandon's desk shrilled, but he ignored it, watching Lee with his good eye. There was a red rim to it, and some of the blood vessels on his hawk nose had blossomed. The bottle bit back, especially when you depended on it for tranquilizing. "You change your mind, son, there's always a place for you in my command."

That's what I'm afraid of. "Thank you, sir." Lee did his best to sound polite. "Be on our way now."

He about-faced, and Juju did too. But neither of them quite marched to the door. Lee held it open, Juju passed through, and Grandon decided on one last throw.

"Quartine?"

Lee paused. Don't. Don't do it, motherfucker. I'm on the damn edge, it won't trouble me none to go over.

"I meant it, you know." The chair squeaked as Grandon's bulk shifted, the man leaning forward in his wheeled chair. "If I'd had a son—"

Lee swept the door closed, cutting off the sentence, and stepped into the outer office, glancing at the general's beefy, bespectacled Latinx adjutant hunched over a laptop.

Let its last half die in there, ruthlessly used by that fucking old man. Let Grandon use the other sad sacks taking his orders now. Let them fucking find out they were expendable the hard way.

Lee had learned his lesson. Late, but better than never.

"Hey." Juju tapped the adjutant on the shoulder. "We gotta get back to Charlotte, bro."

[42]

A GOOD APPLE

They returned to Charlotte bright and early the next morning, both of them rested because there was no need to stand guard in barracks. Juju was out as soon as his head touched a thin Army pillow, and woke up only when Lee in the bunk below him started to stir. There were showers in Atlanta, hot ones, even though they had to roll back into their clothes afterward if they wanted to make the chopper flight. There were washers and dryers going, computers, fluorescent hallways, the whole nine.

But it was in Charlotte that they got their fucking *coffee*. Better, they could sit themselves down in an echoing cafeteria and actually drink it in peace.

It was like heaven, and the only fly in the ointment was Lee looking mournful as fuck. The man only grunted at anything Juju said, and even the cafeteria—long, scrubbed, brightly lit, real tomatoes, how in the hell did they have *real* tomatoes when the world had gone to shit—didn't cheer him up.

Even the bacon didn't do it, and Juju would have been truly concerned if he hadn't been able to weasel out what the damn problem was.

Ginny had, apparently, not taken the news of Lee's cargo well. "And she ain't gonna change her mind," was all Lee would say, before applying himself to his food with all the gusto of a man with deadened taste buds *and* guts.

Which meant, none at all.

Juju settled himself and his sidearm; plastic armrests always hit in the wrong place. Everyone around here was packing, and it was probably a damn good thing. If the critters got in or someone came down with the damn flu, the firepower would be an asset.

Well, Juju could hope. Everyone with a piece looked like they knew how to use it, at least. "She ain't stupid, Lee. She'll come around."

"Stubborn." Lee poked at a mountain of scrambled eggs—real ones mixed in with protein powder. Someone around here had chickens, which pleased Juju on some deep, wordless level.

As long as someone had managed to save chickens, it made the rest of the shit look somehow less fuckered. Juju crunched through another heavenly slice of bacon, trying to suss out what Lee needed to hear. "Well, *I* ain't gonna tell her you could've given her some-damn-thing else by mistake if you won't. Fuckin Grandon."

"Yeah." Lee's expression said there was more to that story than Juju wanted to know, and it was probably a blessing the lieutenant didn't want to share. It was altogether likely that whatever ol' Strap-yo-Balls had told Lee when he gave him the package hadn't included a warning that it contained somethin' *live*.

For a few seconds, back in Grandon's office, Juju had been sure Lee was gonna volunteer them both to serve under Grandon again, and Juju was going to have to do something drastic. It was a relief to be away from the old man, and Lord Jesus, he hoped it would stick.

Juju straightened a little. "Speak of the devil," he muttered.

Ginny was at the big silver coffee tankers, probably in search of hot water for her endless cups of tea. Her hair was braided up real nice, and she wore jeans and a big bulky green sweater, gold hoops glittering in her ears. Looked like she'd been at some laundry, and that was yet another cheerful thought. Juju could stand some clean threads himself.

Lee craned his neck to look, and the open hunger crossing the man's face was almost comical. Juju restrained the urge to elbow him. "Ain't you gonna go over an *talk* to her?"

Lee shook his head. He'd shaved, but he hadn't gone after his hair with clippers. It was another sign that he wasn't ready to put his name on the dotted line for Grandon again.

Juju made a short plosive sound of irritation. "Oh, for *fuck's* sake. If you won't, I will."

But it was academic, as Ginny herself might say, because she spotted them all the way across the caf's midmorning bustle and made what wasn't quite a beeline, but was certainly her way, over to them. She'd cleaned her boots, too.

Women. Juju shook his head a little, and applied himself to the rest of his bacon.

"You're back." The dark circles around her eyes weren't any bigger, at least. "They're saying we might get snow here, too, by the end of the week. Steph's walking Traveller, they have a park, don't worry, it's safe. And Duncan's resting. Some saline and antibiotics should fix him right up."

That was good to hear. Juju cleared his throat. "Ah. Yeah. That's good, real good."

"Seat taken?" She indicated the one next to him, and damn if she wasn't ignoring Lee's presence.

Oh, for Chrissake. "Take this one." Juju pushed himself up. "Imma go check on Duncan. Where he at?"

She gave him directions that included, *go two doors, then turn left, then check in with Dr Nguyen at the desk,* precise and clear. Then she fixed him with an amused look. "He really likes you, Juju."

Oh, Lord. Juju played dumb. "Huh?"

"He's a good apple. And he *really* likes you." She shouldered him aside and put her tray down. "But you probably knew that."

"Yeah, well." Juju's cheeks warmed. Lee didn't even look up, morosely contemplating his pile of eggs and smaller pile of bacon that hopefully wouldn't go to waste. "Lee's been a goddamn raincloud all morning. You two figger it out, I ain't dealin with it."

"Duly noted." She sank down next to Lee, who hunched his shoulders like he expected the firin' squad, and Juju got while the gettin' was good.

He took care of his tray, got a fresh cup of coffee, and decided to stop in a bathroom somewhere along the way to Duncan's room.

It never hurt to freshen up a bit.

[43]

IMAGINE THAT

Ginny's back ached, and her left hip. Steph hadn't wanted to be alone, so Ginny had spent the night on a twin bed with the girl, Traveller ending up wedged between them paws-aloft and belly-exposed. Still, she'd passed out pretty hard—an actual bed and central heating did wonders for everyone. And at least Steph hadn't tossed or turned.

The girl wasn't cheerful this morning—who the hell *would* be, after all that? But at least she seemed...well, maybe she'd be okay. With some help, and a whole lot of therapy.

If there were any therapists left in the area, they were probably doing a land-office business.

She stole a few glances at Lee. He hunched over his heavy brown plastic tray, eating mechanically. His cheeks were freshly shaved and he had his yellow stare on, thankfully not directed at her but at some arbitrary point across the cafeteria's noise. He was still in yesterday's clothes, too.

It was strange to be in a crowd again, even a small one that rattled inside the cafeteria's empty space without quite filling it. Everyone here walked purposefully; the people who weren't armed were in the minority. There was talk of "patrols" and "clear zones" and "night raids."

Upturn the hive and the ants scurried to rebuild. Her dire prognostications of the end of civilization were bleakly amusing now; of course humanity was going to reorganize, one way or another. The trouble was, she decided, a sense of proportion underwent radical changes during a zombie apocalypse.

Lee finally pushed his plate away, still mostly loaded. He took a long hit off his coffee—a thick, acrid military brew he probably loved. Ginny played with the paper Lipton tag. It wasn't much, but it was tea.

Hot water. An actual breakfast. She'd about eaten herself sick on hothouse tomatoes a few hours ago, and could go for more. Probably would, when lunchtime rolled around.

Only a few inches of space separated her shoulder from Lee's. He still said nothing. Just sat there on an uncomfortable plastic chair, everything bottled up, tucked away.

She studied his profile. The circles around his eyes were so dark they almost looked painted on, and he was thinner than he had been in the Crossing. Worry stamped itself around his eyes, at the corners of his mouth.

He'd probably bleed to death internally before saying a peep. And he was always telling *her* to talk.

Ginny almost flinched when someone dropped a tray with a clatter; her tea sloshed but avoided spillage by a thin margin. She decided she had to say something, since he wouldn't. "Dr Nguyen says they need people to organize things." Neither of them would lack for work, and medical training was a high-value commodity now. *You'll get an entire residency in a month*, the doctor said, sighing and rubbing at her temples. *I could use another pair of steady hands.*

Lee took a gulp of coffee. From the look on his face, it was entirely too hot, but he swallowed anyway. The corners of his eyes glittered—a reflex reaction to a swallow-scorch, of course. That's probably what he'd say if asked.

"Organizin." He needed clean clothes, a few solid meals, and some good sleep. "You're, uh, good at that." He darted her a quick, shy, sideways glance, as if she was too bright to look at.

"So are you." Hopefully it didn't sound like she was damning him with faint praise.

Lee raised his coffee, visibly remembered it was still boiling, and set it down with a click. "You still mad?"

Ginny set her tea-mug—thick white industrial china, warm and solid—down, too. Then, before she could lose her nerve, she grabbed his right hand with both of hers.

He should have said something, true. But there were good reasons for what he *had* done. And Ginny had been so determined to get to her parents—once she knew Atlanta was even an option, she should have insisted they all go, posthaste.

The old Ginny would still be furious at him. Who was she now?

Nobody was going to make good choices in an apocalypse, or on a secret mission to carry what might have been a cure while there was no way of knowing if the destination was overrun by hordes of chewing, groaning, shuffling corpses.

"A little," she admitted, and rubbed his scarred knuckles with her fingertips. He hadn't even taken a change of clothes along, just hopped in the helicopter, determined to do his duty. He was handy, certainly, but he needed someone looking out for him. "We'll talk about it later." She squeezed his hand, very gently.

He squeezed back. Scars on his knuckles flexed. He had quite a collection there, and some of them probably had stories to tell.

There was enough time later for that, too.

Ginny scooted her chair closer, wincing at the venomous screech its legs made against mopped linoleum, and laid her head on his shoulder. It felt nice, and she closed her eyes. "I've got your suitcase from the truck," she said. "You probably want clean clothes. There's laundry here, imagine that."

"Yeah." A hoarse, hollow word. "Imagine that." Holding himself tense, braced. Ready for another disaster. The next few words tumbled out, the trickle over the top of a dam. "Ginny, darlin, I'm sorry."

"Me too." She decided against trying to move her chair closer still, and settled her head more firmly. "We'll get you settled once you're finished with breakfast. Just, for a minute, could you...could we just sit here?"

He moved a little—a nod, she could tell even with her eyes closed. Then his other hand closed over hers, and all the tension spilled out of her with a sigh. His shoulder softened, and he leaned into her. The murmur of several people eating, drinking coffee, chatting, swirled around their tiny isle.

"Long as you want, darlin," Lee finally said. "Be right happy to."

Ginny swallowed tears, and let out another sigh.

"Good," she said.

finis

ACKNOWLEDGMENTS

And it's a wrap on the fourth and final season of Roadtrip Z, my friends. The next serial will be out soon, so I thought I'd take a moment to thank the people that made this one such an amazing ride.

Thanks are due to Mel Sanders, who was always ready to sigh over Lee's competence, and Skyla Dawn Cameron, who never blinks when I wave my arms and say, "Just make it pretty?" A huge shout-out to Miriam Kriss, as well, who believes in me even when I don't believe in myself.

Last (but certainly greatest), a huge and resounding thank you for the patrons and subscribers who kept this serial going for four staggering, shambling, zombie-infested seasons.

You guys are the best. Come in, get a beverage, and lean close. Because I like to thank you in the way we both like best: by telling you yet another story...

ABOUT THE AUTHOR

Lilith Saintcrow lives in Vancouver, WA, with her two children, two dogs, two cats, and assorted other strays, including a library for wayward texts.

www.lilithsaintcrow.com